D0559197

Isaac Asimov Presents

THE GOLDEN YEARS OF SCIENCE FICTION

Isaac Asimov Presents

THE GOLDEN YEARS OF SCIENCE FICTION

FOURTH SERIES

26 Stories and Novellas

Edited by
Isaac Asimov and
Martin H. Greenberg

BONANZA BOOKS
New York

This 1984 edition is published by Bonanza Books,
distributed by Crown Publishers, Inc., by arrangement with
Daw Books, Inc.

This book was previously published as two separate works entitled
Isaac Asimov Presents the Great SF Stories 7 (1945) and
Isaac Asimov Presents the Great SF Stories 8 (1946).

Manufactured in the United States of America

Library of Congress Cataloging in Publication Data
Main entry under title:
Isaac Asimov presents the golden years of science
fiction.

"Previously published in two separate editions titled
Isaac Asimov presents the great science fiction stories
(vol. 7) and Isaac Asimov presents the great science
fiction stories (vol 8)"–T.p. verso.
1. Science fiction, American. 2. Science fiction,
English. I. Asimov, Isaac, 1920- . II. Greenberg,
Martin Harry. III. Title: Golden years of science
fiction.
PS648.S3178 1984 813′.0876′08 84-2781
ISBN: 0-517-447355

h g f e d c b a

Foreword

The post-World War II period marked the rise of science fiction both in popularity and literary prominence among readers. Isaac Asimov and Martin H. Greenberg have put together an outstanding collection of stories and novellas written during 1946 and 1947. This anthology, originally published in two separate volumes, presents the best work done by the best writers in the field. The golden years of science fiction are truly represented in this extraordinary volume.

—KMB

CONTENTS

Introduction		5
THE WAVERIES	Fredric Brown	13
THE PIPER'S SON	Lewis Padgett	37
WANTED—AN ENEMY	Fritz Leiber	65
BLIND ALLEY	Isaac Asimov	80
CORRESPONDENCE COURSE	Raymond F. Jones	105
FIRST CONTACT	Murray Leinster	126
THE VANISHING VENUSIANS	Leigh Brackett	159
INTO THY HANDS	Lester Del Rey	189
CAMOUFLAGE	Henry Kuttner	211
THE POWER	Murray Leinster	246
GIANT KILLER	A. Bertram Chandler	264
WHAT YOU NEED	Henry Kuttner	313
A LOGIC NAMED JOE	Will F. Jenkins	329
MEMORIAL	Theodore Sturgeon	346
LOOPHOLE	Arthur C. Clarke	361
THE NIGHTMARE	Chan Davis	369
RESCUE PARTY	Arthur C. Clarke	390
PLACET IS A CRAZY PLACE	Fredric Brown	417
CONQUEROR'S ISLE	Nelson S. Bond	432
LORELEI OF THE RED MIST	Ray Bradbury and Leigh Brackett	447
THE MILLION YEAR PICNIC	Ray Bradbury	505
THE LAST OBJECTIVE	Paul A. Carter	515
MEIHEIN IN CE KLASRUM	Dolton Edwards	544
VINTAGE SEASON	Lawrence O'Donnell	548
EVIDENCE	Isaac Asimov	592
TECHNICAL ERROR	Arthur C. Clarke	615

ACKNOWLEDGMENTS

Introduction

In the world outside reality, 1945 was a momentous year. U.S. forces invaded the Philippines on January 9, while on January 31 Private Eddie Slovik became the first American soldier to be executed for desertion since the time of the Civil War. Dresden was firebombed in an attack on February 13 that killed an estimated 135,000 people; Kurt Vonnegut, Jr., then a prisoner of war, helped to fight the fires. U.S. forces crossed the Rhine on the last remaining bridge at Remagen on the same day. Iwo Jima fell to American forces on March 16.

President Franklin D. Roosevelt died on April 12, and Harry Truman took office the next day. In Europe, Soviet troops reached the outskirts of Berlin by April 21, while Benito Mussolini and his mistress were executed on April 28. Two days later Adolph Hitler committed suicide inside his bunker in Berlin—his "1,000 Year Reich" in shambles. Germany surrendered on May 7, although May 8 was declared V-E Day.

The Philippines were cleared of Japanese troops by July 5 and massive bombing raids began on the Japanese home islands on July 10. On July 18 the world changed when the first atomic "device" was successfully tested at Alamogordo, New Mexico. A few weeks later, on August 6, the *Enola Gay* dropped an atomic bomb on Hiroshima, killing 100,000 instantly, with tens of thousands dying later. On August 9

Nagasaki felt atomic power as a second bomb killed almost as many people. Japan asked for peace on August 10, and V-J Day was declared on the 14th. The formal Japanese surrender took place on the U. S. battleship *Missouri* in Tokyo Bay on September 2.

The Nazis had killed an estimated 14,000,000 human beings; total dead from all causes in World War II was estimated at more than 54,000,000.

During 1945 Conrad Hilton opened a hotel of the same name in Chicago. The Detroit Tigers took the World Series from the Chicago Cubs four games to three. Frozen food became widely available in American supermarkets while the Coca-Cola company registered "Coke" as a trademark. Menachem Begin directed his IZL in attacks against British troops occupying Palestine. Penicillin and streptomycin became commercially available. Diego Rivera painted *The Market in Tiangucio* and "Meet the Press" debuted on radio. *Black Boy* by Richard Wright was published. Army was the national college football champion but golf's Masters Tournament was again called off because of the war. "Till the End of Time," "Laura" and "I'm Beginning to See the Light" were popular song hits. Jean-Paul Sartre published *The Age of Reason.*

Joe Louis was still the heavyweight boxing champion of the world, but the record for the mile run was now the 4:01:4 recorded by Gunder Haegg of Sweden. Ballpoint pens went on the market. Symphony Number 5 in B Flat Major by Serge Prokofiev and Symphony Number 9 by Dmitri Shostakovich were performed for the first time. Kathleen Winsor's *Forever Amber* was published. An army air force bomber crashed into the Empire State Building in New York City, killing 13 people. There were 5,000 television sets in the United States. Phil Cavarretta (how quickly we forget) led the majors with a .355 average. *The Glass Menagerie* by Tennessee Williams opened on Broadway, while Toronto won the Stanley Cup. Alexander Calder constructed his "Red Pyramid." Hoop, Jr., with Eddie Arcaro up, won the Kentucky Derby, and the Washington Redskins won the National Football League Championship. George Orwell published *The Animal Farm.* Top films of the year included *The Story of G.I. Joe, The Lost Weekend,* Alfred Hitchcock's *Spellbound, State Fair,* and *A Walk in the Sun.* Richard Rodgers and Oscar Hammerstein's *Carousel* opened on Broadway, while *The*

Madwoman of Chaillot by Jean Giraudoux was performed for the first time. Grand Rapids, Michigan became the first American community to have its water fluoridated.

Mel Brooks was still Melvin Kaminsky.

In the real world it was a good year. Donald Wollheim edited the *Portable Novels of Science,* and *The World of Ā* by A. E. van Vogt was serialized in *Astounding. That Hideous Strength* by C. S. Lewis was published.

On the other hand, "I Remember Lemuria" by Richard S. Shaver appeared in *Amazing,* beginning a series of stories that helped sales but damaged science fiction.

More wonderful people made their maiden flights into reality: in the summer, Jack Vance with "The World Thinker"; in December, Rog Phillips (Roger Phillips Graham) with "Let Freedom Ring"; and in the winter, Bryce Waltorn with "The Ultimate World."

Death took Malcolm Jameson, Franz Werfel and Charles Williams, but distant wings were beating as Michael Bishop, Dean R. Koontz, George Zebrowski, M. John Harrison, Robert Chilson, Karl Edward Wagner, Jack Dann, Hank Stine, Edward Bryant, Charles Platt, Gordon Eklund, Robert E. Toomey, and Vincent DiFate were born.

Let us travel back to that honored year of 1945 and enjoy the best stories that the real world bequeathed to us.

And now, on to 1946 . . .

In the world outside reality the first post-World War II year got off to a grim start with the hanging on January 3rd of William Joyce, known to millions of Britons as "Lord Haw Haw," who broadcast Nazi propaganda at the British Isles during the war. Later that year, the Nuremberg Tribunal sentenced a dozen leading Nazi war criminals to death, but the most important of them, Hermann Goering, escaped this fate by taking his own life. The United States was wracked with strikes and labor unrest throughout the year, and the situation became so serious that President Truman had to order troops to seize the railroads and most of the coal mines, but only briefly. And on the other side of the world, Ho Chi Minh began the offensive that would eventually drive the French and later the United States out of Vietnam. The bloody civil war between Communist and Nationalist forces in China resumed, with the outcome still in doubt.

On the plus side, the Security Council of the newly founded United Nations met in January and selected Norway's Trygve Lie as the first Secretary-General of that organization amid high hopes that the next decade would be a peaceful one. However, the handwriting of the Cold War was on the wall as Winston Churchill spoke of an "Iron Curtain" descending across Europe at a speech at Westminister College in Missouri.

Italian and Japanese women were granted the right to vote for the first time in history in 1946, and the Philippines were granted their independence by the United States on the Fourth of July.

During 1946 *Holiday* magazine and the publishing firm of Farrar, Straus and Company were founded. "La Vie en Rose," "The Christmas Song," "To Each His Own," and "Tenderly" were hit songs. The St. Louis Cardinals defeated the Boston Red Sox in seven games to win baseball's World Series. Great Britain created a National Health Service. Juan Peron became President of Argentina. ENIAC (Electronic Numerical Integrator and Computer) was further developed but few outside of science fiction realized that it would profoundly change life in the industrialized world.

Marc Chagall painted "Cow with Umbrella." The Fulbright Awards were instituted. Dr. Benjamin Spock (*not* the father of Mr. Spock the Vulcan) published a book called *The Common Sense Book of Baby and Child Care* (later known as just *Baby and Child Care*) and became a millionaire—some children were reportedly beaten with it. Timex Watches became available in retail stores. Broadway had a great year with such plays as *The Iceman Cometh* by Eugene O'Neill, *Born Yesterday* by Garson Kanin, *Annie Get Your Gun* by the great Irving Berlin, *Another Part of the Forest* by Lillian Hellman, and *Call Me Mister* by Harold Rome.

The scheduled flying time between London and New York was almost twenty hours. Pablo Picasso painted "Faun Playing the Pipe," while Eastman Kodak put Ektachrome color film on the market. Outstanding novels included *Member of the Wedding* by Carson McCullers, *All the King's Men* by Robert Penn Warren, *The Big Clock* by Kenneth Fearing, and *Zorba the Greek* by Nikos Kazantzakis. Proctor and Gamble put Tide on the market and in washing machines across the land.

There was a raft of excellent films: *The Best Years of our Lives,* directed by the late William Wyler; *The Postman Always Rings Twice;* Roberto Rosselini's *Open City;* and *Duel in the Sun.* A film called *The Killers* made a star out of Burt Lancaster, while Humphrey Bogart and Lauren Bacall exchanged knowing glances in *The Big Sleep.* The musical *The Harvey Girls* gave the world "The Atchison, Topeka and the Santa Fe."

Scientists John von Neumann and Emil Fuchs applied for a patent for a device they called a "Hydrogen Bomb." Mickey Spillane gave up writing comic books for extremely hardboiled fiction with the publication of *I, The Jury.* The word "automation" was used by Delmar S. Herder, and science fiction readers understood the implications.

Assault was the top horse of the year, capturing the Triple Crown against strong competition. Mrs. Paul's deviled crabs received a terrific reception, while one of the greatest inventors of the twentieth century, the brilliant Louis Heard, designed the bikini, and named it for the island on which the first post-war atomic bomb test was to take place.

Death took chess champion Aleksandr Alekhine and photographic genius Alfred Stieglitz.

Mel Brooks was still Melvin Kaminsky.

In the real world it was a particularly outstanding year as dozens of science fiction writers returned from the military. Even a very promising young writer named Isaac Asimov who had managed to get drafted in 1945 got out again this year.

Important books were published in 1946: *Slan* by A. E. van Vogt, *The Time Stream* by John Taine, and *The Skylark of Space* by E. E. "Doc" Smith (although all were written much earlier for the magazines). The year was highlighted by the appearance of two of the all-time great anthologies—*Adventures in Time and Space,* edited by J. Francis McComas and Raymond Healy and *The Best of Science Fiction* edited by the wise Groff Conklin, the premier anthologist of his time. Soon, hundreds of thousands of library patrons would find their minds expanded.

British fans and pros launched *New Worlds* and *Fantasy* in December.

More wondrous things were happening in the real world as three terrific writers made their maiden voyages into reality: Arthur C. Clarke with "Loophole" in April; William

Tenn (Philip Klass) with "Alexander the Bait" in May; and Margaret St. Clair with "Rocked to Limbo" in November.

The real people gathered together for the fourth time as the World Science Fiction Convention (the Pacificon) was held in Los Angeles under the guiding hand of the tireless Forry Ackerman.

Death took Otis Adelbert Kline, Leroy Yerxa and one of science fiction's great fathers, H. G. Wells.

But distant wings were beating as Alan Dean Foster, F. Paul Wilson, Christopher Foss, Robert Weinberg, Mark Geston, Eric S. Rabkin, Richard Glyn Jones, Steven G. Spruill, and Bruce McAllister were born.

Let us travel back to that honored year of 1946 and enjoy the best stories that the real world bequeathed to us.

Isaac Asimov Presents

THE GOLDEN YEARS OF SCIENCE FICTION

THE WAVERIES

by Fredric Brown (1906-1972)

ASTOUNDING SCIENCE FICTION,
January

Fredric Brown produced a number of excellent science fiction stories in the 1940s, including this gem on the effects of technology-reversal on an already sophisticated society. Astounding's *editor, John W. Campbell, Jr., wanted his writers to focus on the consequences of applied science, and in "The Waveries" Brown gave one of his characteristic twists to this commandment, with results that may surprise you. An outstanding mystery and suspense writer, Brown was a reporter for the* Milwaukee Journal *before making the decision to become a fulltime writer in 1947. Although primarily and rightfully known in sf for his short stories, he also wrote several excellent sf novels, including* What Mad Universe *(1949)*, The Lights in the Sky Are Stars *(1953), and* Martians go Home. *(1955)*.

(Well, now, I think I'll have to put in a bit of dissent on this story. No, no, I don't contend that it doesn't belong here at all. I mean I want to dissent on the thesis because I'm a technophile [that is, I love advancing technology] and don't think that walking backward is the route to a Golden Age.

I just want to refer to one small passage in the story where Pete Mulvaney says that the air in New York City is "better than Atlantic City, without gasoline fumes" because the automobiles are gone. The next question from George Bailey is, "Enough horses to go around yet?" and the answer is "Almost."

Well, I've passed the horses at Central Park that pull the buggies, two or three of them, and I have to hold my breath every time. They stink *of sweat and manure. That's two or three. Fill the city enough to take care of even the "last million people" the story speaks of and everyone will long for gas fumes again. Particularly in the summer when there will be no air-conditioning [something Fred, writing in 1945, says nothing about].*

Enjoy the story, but keep your perspective, that's all. I.A.)

Definitions from the school-abridged Webster-Hamlin Dictionary, 1998 edition:

wavery (WA-vĕr-i) n. a vader—*slang*
vader (VA-dĕr) n. inorgan of the class Radio
inorgan (in-ÔR-găn) n. noncorporeal ens, a vader
radio (RA-di-ō) n. 1. class of inorgans 2. etheric frequency between light and electricity 3. (obsolete) method of communication used up to 1957

The opening guns of invasion were not at all loud, although they were heard by millions of people. George Bailey was one of the millions. I choose George Bailey because he was the only one who came within a googol of light-years of guessing what they were.

George Bailey was drunk and under the circumstances one can't blame him for being so. He was listening to radio advertisements of the most nauseous kind. Not because he wanted to listen to them, I hardly need say, but because he'd been told to listen to them by his boss, J. R. McGee of the MID network.

George Bailey wrote advertising for the radio. The only thing he hated worse than advertising was radio. And here on his own time he was listening to fulsome and disgusting commercials on a rival network.

"Bailey," J. R. McGee had said, "you should be more familiar with what others are doing. Particularly, you should be informed about those of our own accounts who use several networks. I strongly suggest . . ."

One doesn't quarrel with an employer's strong suggestions and keep a two hundred dollar a week job.

But one can drink whisky sours while listening. George Bailey did.

Also, between commercials, he was playing gin rummy with Maisie Hetterman, a cute little redheaded typist from the studio. It was Maisie's apartment and Maisie's radio (George himself, on principle, owned neither a radio nor a TV set) but George had brought the liquor.

"—only the very finest tobaccos," said the radio, "go *dit-dit-dit* nation's favorite cigarette—"

George glanced at the radio. "Marconi," he said.

He meant Morse, naturally, but the whisky sours had muddled him a bit so his first guess was more nearly right than anyone else's. It *was* Marconi, in a way. In a very peculiar way.

"Marconi?" asked Maisie.

George, who hated to talk against a radio, leaned over and switched it off.

"I meant Morse," he said. "Morse, as in Boy Scouts or the Signal Corps. I used to be a Boy Scout once."

"You've sure changed," Maisie said.

George sighed. "Somebody's going to catch hell, broadcasting code on that wave length."

"What did it mean?"

"Mean? Oh, you mean what did it mean. Uh—S, the letter S. *Dit-dit-dit* is S. SOS is *dit-dit-dit dah-dah-dah dit-dit-dit.*"

"O is *dah-dah-dah*?"

George grinned. "Say that again, Maisie. I like it. And I think you are *dah-dah-dah* too."

"George, maybe it's really an SOS message. Turn it back on."

George turned it back on. The tobacco ad was still going. "—gentlemen of the most *dit-dit-dit* -ing taste prefer the finer taste of *dit-dit-dit* -arettes. In the new package that keeps them *dit-dit-dit* and ultra fresh—"

"It's not SOS. It's just S's."

"Like a teakettle or—say, George, maybe it's just some advertising gag."

George shook his head. "Not when it can blank out the name of the product. Just a minute till I—"

He reached over and turned the dial of the radio a bit to the right and then a bit to the left, and an incredulous look came into his face. He turned the dial to the extreme left, as far as it would go. There wasn't any station there, not even the hum of a carrier wave. But:

"*Dit-dit-dit*," said the radio, "*dit-dit-dit*."

He turned the dial to the extreme right. "*Dit-dit-dit*."

George switched it off and stared at Maisie without seeing her, which was hard to do.

"Something wrong, George?"

"I hope so," said George Bailey. "I certainly hope so."

He started to reach for another drink and changed his mind. He had a sudden hunch that something big was happening and he wanted to sober up to appreciate it.

He didn't have the faintest idea *how* big it was.

"George, what do you mean?"

"I don't know what I mean. But Maisie, let's take a run down to the studio, huh? There ought to be some excitement."

April 5, 1957; that was the night the waveries came.

It had started like an ordinary evening. It wasn't one, now.

George and Maisie waited for a cab but none came so they took the subway instead. Oh yes, the subways were still running in those days. It took them within a block of the MID Network Building.

The building was a madhouse. George, grinning, strolled through the lobby with Maisie on his arm, took the elevator to the fifth floor and for no reason at all gave the elevator boy a dollar. He'd never before in his life tipped an elevator operator.

The boy thanked him. "Better stay away from the big shots, Mr. Bailey," he said. "They're ready to chew the ears off anybody who even looks at 'em."

"Wonderful," said George.

From the elevator he headed straight for the office of J. R. McGee himself.

There were strident voices behind the glass door. George reached for the knob and Maisie tried to stop him. "But George," she whispered, "you'll be fired!"

"There comes a time," said George. "Stand back away from the door, honey."

Gently but firmly he moved her to a safe position.

"But George, what are you—?"

"Watch," he said.

The frantic voices stopped as he opened the door a foot. All eyes turned toward him as he stuck his head around the corner of the doorway into the room.

"*Dit-dit-dit*," he said. "*Dit-dit-dit.*"

He ducked back and to the side just in time to escape the flying glass as a paperweight and an inkwell came through the pane of the door.

He grabbed Maisie and ran for the stairs.

"Now we get a drink," he told her.

The bar across the street from the network building was crowded but it was a strangely silent crowd. In deference to the fact that most of its customers were radio people it didn't have a TV set but there was a big cabinet radio and most of the people were bunched around it.

"*Dit,*" said the radio. "*Dit-dah-d'dah-dit-dahditdah dit—*"

"Isn't it beautiful?" George whispered to Maisie.

Somebody fiddled with the dial. Somebody asked, "What band is that?" and somebody said, "Police." Somebody said, "Try the foreign band," and somebody did. "This ought to be Buenos Aires," somebody said. "*Dit-d'dah-dit—*" said the radio.

Somebody ran fingers through his hair and said, "Shut that damn thing off." Somebody else turned it back on.

George grinned and led the way to a back booth where he'd spotted Pete Mulvaney sitting alone with a bottle in front of him. He and Maisie sat across from Pete.

"Hello," he said gravely.

"Hell," said Pete, who was head of the technical research staff of MID.

"A beautiful night, Mulvaney," George said. "Did you see the moon riding the fleecy clouds like a golden galleon tossed upon silver-crested whitecaps in a stormy—"

"Shut up," said Pete. "I'm thinking."

"Whisky sours," George told the waiter. He turned back to the man across the table. "Think out loud, so we can hear. But first, how did you escape the booby hatch across the street?"

"I'm bounced, fired, discharged."

"Shake hands. And then explain. Did you say *dit-dit-dit* to them?"

Pete looked at him with sudden admiration. "Did you?"

"I've a witness. What *did* you do?"

"Told 'em what I thought it was and they think I'm crazy."

"Are you?"

"Yes."

"Good," said George. "Then we want to hear—" He snapped his fingers. "What about TV?"

"Same thing. Same sound on audio and the pictures flicker and dim with every dot or dash. Just a blur by now."

"Wonderful. And now tell me what's wrong. I don't care what it is, as long as it's nothing trivial, but I want to know."

"I think it's space. Space is warped."

"Good old space," George Bailey said.

"George," said Maisie, "please shut up. I want to hear this."

"Space," said Pete, "is also finite." He poured himself another drink. You go far enough in any direction and get back where you started. Like an ant crawling around an apple."

"Make it an orange," George said.

"All right, an orange. Now suppose the first radio waves ever sent out have just made the round trip. In fifty-six years."

"Fifty-six years? But I thought radio waves traveled at the same speed as light. If that's right, then in fifty-six years they could go only fifty-six light-years, and *that* can't be around the universe because there are galaxies known to be millions or maybe billions of light-years away. I don't remember the figures, Pete, but our own galaxy alone is a hell of a lot bigger than fifty-six light-years."

Pete Mulvaney sighed. "That's why I say space must be warped. There's a short cut somewhere."

"*That* short a short cut? Couldn't be."

"But George, listen to that stuff that's coming in. Can you read code?"

"Not any more. Not that fast, anyway."

"Well, I can," Pete said. "That's early American ham. Lingo and all. That's the kind of stuff the air was full of before regular broadcasting. It's the lingo, the abbreviations, the barnyard to attic chitchat of amateurs with keys, with Marconi coherers or Fessenden barreters—and you can listen for a violin solo pretty soon now. I'll tell you what it'll be."

"What?"

"Handel's *Largo.* The first phonograph record ever broadcast. Sent out by Fessenden from Brant Rock in 1906. You'll hear his CQ-CQ any minute now. Bet you a drink."

"Okay, but what was the *dit-dit-dit* that started this?"

Mulvaney grinned. "Marconi, George. What was the most powerful signal ever broadcast and by whom and when?"

"Marconi? *Dit-dit-dit*? Fifty-six years ago?"

"Head of the class. The first transatlantic signal on December 12, 1901. For three hours Marconi's big station at Poldhu, with two-hundred-foot masts, sent out an intermittent S, *dit-dit-dit*, while Marconi and two assistants at St. Johns in Newfoundland got a kite-borne aerial four hundred feet in the air and finally got the signal. Across the Atlantic, George, with sparks jumping from the big Leyden jars at Poldhu and 20,000-volt juice jumping off the tremendous aerials—"

"Wait a minute, Pete, you're off the beam. If that was in 1901 and the first broadcast was about 1906 it'll be five years before the Fessenden stuff gets here on the same route. Even if there's a fifty-six light-year short cut across space and even if those signals didn't get so weak en route that we couldn't hear them—it's crazy."

"I told you it was," Pete said gloomily. "Why, those signals after traveling that far would be so infinitesimal that for practical purposes they wouldn't exist. Furthermore they're all over the band on everything from microwave on up and equally strong on each. And, as you point out, we've already come almost five years in two hours, which isn't possible. I told you it was crazy."

"But—"

"Ssshh. Listen," said Pete.

A blurred, but unmistakably human voice was coming from the radio, mingling with the cracklings of code. And then music, faint and scratchy, but unmistakably a violin. Playing Handel's *Largo.*

Only suddenly it climbed in pitch as though modulating from key to key until it became so horribly shrill that it hurt the ear. And kept on going past the high limit of audibility until they could hear it no more.

Somebody said, "Shut that God damn thing off." Somebody did, and this time nobody turned it back on.

Pete said, "I didn't really believe it myself. And there's another thing against it, George. Those signals affect TV too, and radio waves are the wrong length to do that."

He shook his head slowly. "There must be some other explanation, George. The more I think about it now the more I think I'm wrong."

He was right: he was wrong.

"Preposterous," said Mr. Ogilvie. He took off his glasses, frowned fiercely, and put them back on again. He looked through them at the several sheets of copy paper in his hand and tossed them contemptuously to the top of his desk. They slid to rest against the triangular name plate that read:

B. R. OGILVIE
Editor-in-Chief

"Preposterous," he said again.

Casey Blair, his best reporter, blew a smoke ring and poked his index finger through it. "Why?" he asked.

"Because—why, it's *utterly* preposterous."

Casey Blair said, "It is now three o'clock in the morning. The interference has gone on for five hours and not a single program is getting through on either TV or radio. Every major broadcasting and telecasting station in the world has gone off the air.

"For two reasons. One, they were just wasting current. Two, the communications bureaus of their respective governments requested them to get off to aid their campaigns with the direction finders. For five hours now, since the start of the interference, they've been working with everything they've got. And what have they found out?"

"It's preposterous!" said the editor.

"Perfectly, but it's true. Greenwich at 11 P.M. New York time; I'm translating all these times into New York time—got a bearing in about the direction of Miami. It shifted northward until at two o'clock the direction was approximately that of Richmond, Virginia. San Francisco at eleven got a bearing in about the direction of Denver; three hours later it shifted southward toward Tucson. Southern hemisphere: bearings from Capetown, South Africa, shifted from direction of Buenos Aires to that of Montevideo, a thousand miles north.

"New York at eleven had weak indications toward Madrid; but by two o'clock they could get no bearings at all." He blew another smoke ring. "Maybe because the loop antennae they use turn only on a horizontal plane?"

"Absurd."

Casey said, "I like 'preposterous' better, Mr. Ogilvie. Preposterous it is, but it's not absurd. I'm scared stiff. Those lines—and all other bearings I've heard about—run in the *same direction* if you take them as straight lines running as tangents off the Earth instead of curving them around the surface. I did it with a little globe and a star map. They converge on the constellation Leo."

He leaned forward and tapped a forefinger on the top page of the story he'd just turned in. "Stations that are directly under Leo in the sky get no bearings at all. Stations on what would be the perimeter of Earth relative to that point get the strongest bearings. Listen, have an astronomer check those figures if you want before you run the story, but get it done damn quick—unless you want to read about it in the other newspapers first."

"But the heaviside layer, Casey—isn't that supposed to stop all radio waves and bounce them back?"

"Sure, it does. But maybe it leaks. Or maybe signals can get through it from the outside even though they can't get out from the inside. It isn't a solid wall."

"But—"

"I know, it's preposterous. But there it is. And there's only an hour before press time. You'd better send this story through fast and have it being set up while you're having somebody check my facts and directions. Besides, there's something else you'll want to check."

"What?"

"I didn't have the data for checking the positions of the planets. Leo's on the ecliptic; a planet could be in line between here and there. Mars, maybe."

Mr. Ogilvie's eyes brightened, then clouded again. He said, "We'll be the laughingstock of the world, Blair, if you're wrong."

"And if I'm right?"

The editor picked up the phone and snapped an order.

April 6th headline of the New York *Morning Messenger*, final (6 A.M.) edition:

RADIO INTERFERENCE
COMES FROM SPACE,
ORIGINATES IN LEO

May be Attempt at Communication by Beings
Outside Solar
System

All television and radio broadcasting was suspended.

Radio and television stocks opened several points off the previous day and then dropped sharply until noon when a moderate buying rally brought them a few points back.

Public reaction was mixed; people who had no radios rushed out to buy them and there was a boom, especially in portable and table-top receivers. On the other hand, no TV sets were sold at all. With telecasting suspended there were no pictures on their screens, even blurred ones. Their audio circuits, when turned on, brought in the same jumble as radio receivers. Which, as Pete Mulvaney had pointed out to George Bailey, was impossible; radio waves cannot activate the audio circuits of TV sets. But these did, if they *were* radio waves.

In radio sets they seemed to be radio waves, but horribly hashed. No one could listen to them very long. Oh, there were flashes—times when, for several consecutive seconds, one could recognize the voice of Will Rogers or Geraldine Farrar or catch flashes of the Dempsey-Carpentier fight or the Pearl Harbor excitement. (Remember Pearl Harbor?) But things even remotely worth hearing were rare. Mostly it was a meaningless mixture of soap opera, advertising and off-key snatches of what had once been music. It was utterly indiscriminate, and utterly unbearable for any length of time.

But curiosity is a powerful motive. There *was* a brief boom in radio sets for a few days.

There were other booms, less explicable, less capable of analysis. Reminiscent of the Wells-Welles Martian scare of 1938 was a sudden upswing in the sale of shotguns and sidearms. Bibles sold as fast as books on astronomy—and books on astronomy sold like hotcakes. One section of the country showed a sudden interest in lightning rods; builders were flooded with orders for immediate installation.

For some reason which has never been clearly ascertained there was a run of fishhooks in Mobile, Alabama; every hardware and sporting goods store sold out of them within hours.

The public libraries and bookstores had a run on books on astrology and books on Mars. Yes, on Mars—despite the fact that Mars was at that moment on the other side of the sun and that every newspaper article on the subject stressed the fact that *no* planet was between Earth and the constellation Leo.

Something strange was happening—and no news of developments available except through the newspapers. People waited in mobs outside newspaper buildings for each new edition to appear. Circulation managers went quietly mad.

People also gathered in curious little knots around the silent broadcasting studios and stations, talking in hushed voices as though at a wake. MID network doors were locked, although there was a doorman on duty to admit technicians who were trying to find an answer to the problem. Some of the technicians who had been on duty the previous day had now spent over twenty-four hours without sleep.

George Bailey woke at noon, with only a slight headache. He shaved and showered, went out and drank a light breakfast and was himself again. He bought early editions of the afternoon papers, read them, grinned. His hunch had been right; whatever was wrong, it was nothing trivial.

But *what* was wrong?

The later editions of the afternoon papers had it.

EARTH INVADED, SAYS SCIENTIST

Thirty-six line type was the biggest they had; they used it. Not a home-edition copy of a newspaper was delivered that evening. Newsboys starting on their routes were practically mobbed. They sold papers instead of delivering them; the smart ones got a dollar apiece for them. The foolish and honest ones who didn't want to sell because they thought the papers should go to the regular customers on their routes lost them anyway. People grabbed them.

The final editions changed the heading only slightly—only slightly, that is, from a typographical viewpoint. Nevertheless, it was a tremendous change in meaning. It read:

EARTH INVADED, SAY SCIENTISTS

Funny what moving an S from the ending of a verb to the ending of a noun can do.

Carnegie Hall shattered precedent that evening with a lecture given at midnight. An unscheduled and unadvertised lecture. Professor Helmetz had stepped off the train at eleven-thirty and a mob of reporters had been waiting for him. Helmetz, of Harvard, had been the scientist, singular, who had made that first headline.

Harvey Ambers, director of the board of Carnegie Hall, had pushed his way through the mob. He arrived minus glasses, hat and breath, but got hold of Helmetz's arm and hung on until he could talk again. "We want you to talk at Carnegie, Professor," he shouted into Helmetz's ear. "Five thousand dollars for a lecture on the 'vaders.' "

"Certainly. Tomorrow afternoon?"

"Now! I've a cab waiting. Come on."

"But—"

"We'll get you an audience. Hurry!" He turned to the mob. "Let us through. All of you can't hear the professor here. Come to Carnegie Hall and he'll talk to you. And spread the word on your way there."

The word spread so well that Carnegie Hall was jammed by the time the professor began to speak. Shortly after, they'd rigged a loud-speaker system so the people outside could hear. By one o'clock in the morning the streets were jammed for blocks around.

There wasn't a sponsor on Earth with a million dollars to his name who wouldn't have given a million dollars gladly for the privilege of sponsoring that lecture on TV or radio, but it was not telecast or broadcast. Both lines were busy.

"Questions?" asked Professor Helmetz.

A reporter in the front row made it first. "Professor," he asked, "have all direction finding stations on Earth confirmed what you told us about the change this afternoon?"

"Yes, absolutely. At about noon all directional indications began to grow weaker. At 2:45 o'clock, Eastern Standard Time, they ceased completely. Until then the radio waves emanated from the sky, constantly changing direction with reference to the Earth's surface, but *constant* with reference to a point in the constellation Leo."

"What star in Leo?"

"No star visible on our charts. Either they came from a point in space or from a star too faint for our telescopes.

"But at 2:45 P.M. today—yesterday rather, since it is now past midnight—all direction finders went dead. But the signals persisted, now coming from all sides equally. The invaders had all arrived.

"There is no other conclusion to be drawn. Earth is now surrounded, completely blanketed, by radio-type waves which have *no point of origin*, which travel ceaselessly around the Earth in all directions, changing shape at their will—which currently is still in imitation of the Earth-origin radio signals which attracted their attention and brought them here."

"Do you think it was from a star we can't see, or could it have really been just a point in space?"

"Probably from a point in space. And why not? They are not creatures of matter. If they came here from a star, it must be a very dark star for it to be invisible to us, since it would be relatively near to us—only twenty-eight light-years away, which is quite close as stellar distances go."

"How can you know the distance?"

"By assuming—and it is a quite reasonable assumption—that they started our way when they first discovered our radio signals—Marconi's S-S-S code broadcast of fifty-six years ago. Since that was the form taken by the first arrivals, we assume they started toward us when they encountered those signals. Marconi's signals, traveling at the speed of light, would have reached a point twenty-eight light-years away twenty-eight years ago; the invaders, also traveling at light-speed would require an equal of time to reach us.

"As might be expected only the first arrivals took Morse code form. Later arrivals were in the form of other waves that they met and passed on—or perhaps absorbed—on their way to Earth. There are now wandering around the Earth, as it were, fragments of programs broadcast as recently as a few days ago. Undoubtedly there are fragments of the very last programs to be broadcast, but they have not yet been identified."

"Professor, can you *describe* one of these invaders?"

"As well as and no better than I can describe a radio wave. In effect, they *are* radio waves, although they emanate from no broadcasting station. They are a form of life dependent on wave motion, as our form of life is dependent on the vibration of matter."

"They are different sizes?"

"Yes, in two senses of the word size. Radio waves are measured from crest to crest, which measurement is known as the wave length. Since the invaders cover the entire dials of our radio sets and television sets it is obvious that either one of two things is true: Either they come in all crest-to-crest sizes or each one can change his crest-to-crest measurement to adapt himself to the tuning of any receiver.

"But that is only the crest-to-crest length. In a sense it may be said that a radio wave has an over-all length determined by its duration. If a broadcasting station sends out a program that has a second's duration, a wave carrying that program is one light-second long, roughly 187,000 miles. A continuous half-hour program is, as it were, on a continuous wave one-half light-hour long, and so on.

"Taking that form of length, the individual invaders vary in length from a few thousand miles—a duration of only a small fraction of a second—to well over half a million miles long—a duration of several seconds. The longest continuous excerpt from any one program that has been observed has been about seven seconds."

"But, Professor Helmetz, why do you assume that these waves are *living* things, a life form. Why not just waves?"

"Because 'just waves' as you call them would follow certain laws, just as inanimate *matter* follows certain laws. An animal can climb uphill, for instance; a stone cannot unless impelled by some outside force. These invaders are life-forms because they show volition, because they can change their direction of travel, and most especially because they retain their identity; two signals never conflict on the same radio receiver. They follow one another but do not come simultaneously. They do not mix as signals on the same wave length would ordinarily do. They are not 'just waves.' "

"Would you say they are intelligent?"

Professor Helmetz took off his glasses and polished them thoughtfully. He said, "I doubt if we shall ever know. The intelligence of such beings, if any, would be on such a completely different plane from ours that there would be no common point from which we could start intercourse. We are material; they are immaterial. There is no common ground between us."

"But if they are intelligent at all—"

"Ants are intelligent, after a fashion. Call it instinct if you will, but instinct is a form of intelligence; at least it enables them to accomplish some of the same things intelligence would enable them to accomplish. Yet we cannot establish communication with ants and it is far less likely that we shall be able to establish communication with these invaders. The difference in type between anti-intelligence and our own would be nothing to the difference in type between the intelligence, if any, of the invaders and our own. No, I doubt if we shall ever communicate."

The professor had something there. Communication with the vaders—a clipped form, of course, of *invaders*—was never established.

Radio stocks stabilized on the exchange the next day. But the day following that someone asked Dr. Helmetz a sixty-four dollar question and the newspapers published his answer:

"Resume broadcasting? I don't know if we ever shall. Certainly we cannot until the invaders go away, and why should they? Unless radio communication is perfected on some other planet far away and they're attracted there.

"But at least some of them would be right back the moment we started to broadcast again."

Radio and TV stocks dropped to practically zero in an hour. There weren't, however, any frenzied scenes on the stock exchanges; there was no frenzied selling because there was no buying, frenzied or otherwise. No radio stocks changed hands.

Radio and television employes and entertainers began to look for other jobs. The entertainers had no trouble finding them. Every other form of entertainment suddenly boomed like mad.

"Two down," said George Bailey. The bartender asked what he meant.

"I dunno, Hank. It's just a hunch I've got."

"What kind of hunch?"

"I don't even know that. Shake me up one more of those and then I'll go home."

The electric shaker wouldn't work and Hank had to shake the drink by hand.

"Good exercise; that's just what you need," George said. "It'll take some of that fat off you."

Hank grunted, and the ice tinkled merrily as he tilted the shaker to pour out the drink.

George Bailey took his time drinking it and then strolled out into an April thundershower. He stood under the awning and watched for a taxi. An old man was standing there too.

"Some weather," George said.

The old man grinned at him. "You noticed it, eh?"

"Huh? Noticed what?"

"Just watch a while, mister. Just watch a while."

The old man moved on. No empty cab came by and George stood there quite a while before he got it. His jaw dropped a little and then he closed his mouth and went back into the tavern. He went into a phone booth and called Pete Mulvaney.

He got three wrong numbers before he got Pete. Pete's voice said, "Yeah?"

"George Bailey, Pete. Listen, have you noticed the weather?"

"Damn right. *No lightning*, and there should be with a thunderstorm like this."

"What's it mean, Pete? The vaders?"

"Sure. And that's just going to be the start if—" A crackling sound on the wire blurred his voice out.

"Hey, Pete, you still there?"

The sound of a violin. Pete Mulvaney didn't play violin.

"Hey, Pete, what the hell—?"

Pete's voice again. "Come on over, George. Phone won't last long. Bring—" There was a buzzing noise and then a voice said, "—come to Carnegie Hall. The best tunes of all come—"

George slammed down the receiver.

He walked through the rain to Pete's place. On the way he bought a bottle of Scotch. Pete had started to tell him to bring something and maybe that's what he'd started to say.

It was.

They made a drink apiece and lifted them. The lights flickered briefly, went out, and then came on again but dimly.

"No lightning," said George. "No lightning and pretty soon

no lighting. They're taking over the telephone. What do they do with the lightning?"

"Eat it, I guess. They must eat electricity."

"No lightning," said George. "Damn. I can get by without a telephone, and candles and oil lamps aren't bad for lights—but I'm going to miss lightning. I *like* lightning. Damn."

The lights went out completely.

Pete Mulvaney sipped his drink in the dark. He said, "Electric lights, refrigerators, electric toasters, vacuum cleaners—"

"Juke boxes," George said. "Think of it, no more God damn juke boxes. No public address systems, no—hey, how about movies?"

"No movies, not even silent ones. You can't work a projector with an oil lamp. But listen, George, no automobiles—no gasoline engine can work without electricity."

"Why not, if you crank it by hand instead of using a starter?"

"The spark, George. What do you think makes the spark."

"Right. No airplanes either, then. Or how about jet planes?"

"Well—I guess some types of jets could be rigged not to need electricity, but you couldn't do much with them. Jet planes got more instruments than motor, and all those instruments are electrical. And you can't fly or land a jet by the seat of your pants."

"No radar. But what would we need it for? There won't be any more wars, not for a long time."

"A damned long time."

George sat up straight suddenly. "Hey, Pete, what about atomic fission? Atomic energy? Will it still work?"

"I doubt it. Subatomic phenomena are basically electrical. Bet you a dime they eat loose neutrons too." (He'd have won his bet; the government had not announced that an A-bomb tested that day in Nevada had fizzled like a wet firecracker and that atomic piles were ceasing to function.)

George shook his head slowly, in wonder. He said, "Streetcars and buses, ocean liners—Pete, this means we're going back to the original source of horsepower. Horses. If you want to invest, buy horses. Particularly mares. A brood mare is going to be worth a thousand times her weight in platinum."

"Right. But don't forget steam. We'll still have steam engines, stationary and locomotive."

"Sure, that's right. The iron horse again, for the long hauls. But Dobbin for the short ones. Can you ride, Pete?"

"Used to, but I think I'm getting too old. I'll settle for a bicycle. Say, better buy a bike first thing tomorrow before the run on them starts. I know *I'm* going to."

"Good tip. And I used to be a good bike rider. It'll be swell with no autos around to louse you up. And say—"

"What?"

"I'm going to get a cornet too. Used to play one when I was a kid and I can pick it up again. And then maybe I'll hole in somewhere and write that nov— Say, what about printing?"

"They printed books long before electricity, George. It'll take a while to readjust the printing industry, but there'll be books all right. Thank God for that."

George Bailey grinned and got up. He walked over to the window and looked out into the night. The rain had stopped and the sky was clear.

A streetcar was stalled, without lights, in the middle of the block outside. An automobile stopped, then started more slowly, stopped again; its headlights were dimming rapidly.

George looked up at the sky and took a sip of his drink.

"No lightning," he said sadly. "I'm going to *miss* the lightning."

The changeover went more smoothly than anyone would have thought possible.

The government, in emergency session, made the wise decision of creating one board with absolutely unlimited authority and under it only three subsidiary boards. The main board, called the Economic Readjustment Bureau, had only seven members and its job was to co-ordinate the efforts of the three subsidiary boards and to decide, quickly and without appeal, any jurisdictional disputes among them.

First of the three subsidiary boards was the Transportation Bureau. It immediately took over, temporarily, the railroads. It ordered Diesel engines run on sidings and left there, organized use of the steam locomotives, and solved the problems of railroading sans telegraphy and electric signals. It dictated, then, what should be transported; food coming first, coal and fuel oil second, and essential manufactured articles in the order of their relative importance. Carload after carload of new radios, electric stoves, refrigerators and such useless articles were dumped unceremoniously alongside the tracks, to be salvaged for scrap metal later.

All horses were declared wards of the government, graded according to capabilities, and put to work or to stud. Draft horses were used for only the most essential kinds of hauling. The breeding program was given the fullest possible emphasis; the bureau estimated that the equine population would double in two years, quadruple in three, and that within six or seven years there would be a horse in every garage in the country.

Farmers, deprived temporarily of their horses, and with their tractors rusting in the fields, were instructed how to use cattle for plowing and other work about the farm, including light hauling.

The second board, the Manpower Relocation Bureau, functioned just as one would deduce from its title. It handled unemployment benefits for the millions thrown temporarily out of work and helped relocate them—not too difficult a task considering the tremendously increased demand for hand labor in many fields.

In May of 1957 thirty-five million employables were out of work; in October, fifteen million; by May of 1958, five million. By 1959 the situation was completely in hand and competitive demand was already beginning to raise wages.

The third board had the most difficult job of the three. It was called the Factory Readjustment Bureau. It coped with the stupendous task of converting factories filled with electrically operated machinery and, for the most part, tooled for the production of other electrically operated machinery, over for the production, without electricity, of essential nonelectrical articles.

The few available stationary steam engines worked twenty-four hour shifts in those early days, and the first thing they were given to do was the running of lathes and stampers and planers and millers working on turning out more stationary steam engines, of all sizes. These, in turn, were first put to work making still more steam engines. The number of steam engines grew by squares and cubes, as did the number of horses put to stud. The principle was the same. One might, and many did, refer to those early steam engines as stud horses. At any rate, there was no lack of metal for them. The factories were filled with nonconvertible machinery waiting to be melted down.

Only when steam engines—the basis of the new factory economy—were in full production, were they assigned to running machinery for the manufacture of other articles. Oil lamps, clothing, coal stoves, oil stoves, bathtubs and bedsteads.

Not quite all of the big factories were converted. For while the conversion period went on, individual handicrafts sprang up in thousands of places. Little one- and two-man shops making and repairing furniture, shoes, candles, all sorts of things that *could* be made without complex machinery. At first these small shops made small fortunes because they had no competition from heavy industry. Later, they bought small steam engines to run small machines and held their own, growing with the boom that came with a return to normal employment and buying power, increasing gradually in size until many of them rivaled the bigger factories in output and beat them in quality.

There *was* suffering, during the period of economic readjustment, but less than there had been during the great depression of the early thirties. And the recovery was quicker.

The reason was obvious: In combating the depression, the legislators were working in the dark. They didn't know its cause—rather, they knew a thousand conflicting theories of its cause—and they didn't know the cure. They were hampered by the idea that the thing was temporary and would cure itself if left alone. Briefly and frankly, they didn't know what it was all about and while they experimented, it snowballed.

But the situation that faced the country—and all other countries—in 1957 was clear-cut and obvious. No more electricity. Readjust for steam and horsepower.

As simple and clear as that, and no ifs or ands or buts. And the whole people—except for the usual scattering of cranks—back of them.

By 1961—

It was a rainy day in April and George Bailey was waiting under the sheltering roof of the little railroad station at Blakestown, Connecticut, to see who might come in on the 3:14.

It chugged in at 3:25 and came to a panting stop, three coaches and a baggage car. The baggage car door opened and a sack of mail was handed out and the door closed again. No luggage, so probably no passengers would—

Then at the sight of a tall dark man swinging down from the platform of the rear coach, George Bailey let out a yip of delight. "Pete! Pete Mulvaney! What the devil—"

"Bailey, by all that's holy! What are you doing here?"

George wrung Pete's hand. "Me? I live here. Two years now. I bought the *Blakestown Weekly* in '59, for a song, and I run it—editor, reporter, and janitor. Got one printer to help me out with that end, and Maisie does the social items. She's—"

"Maisie? Maisie Hetterman?"

"Maisie Bailey now. We got married same time I bought the paper and moved here. What are you doing here, Pete?"

"Business. Just here overnight. See a man named Wilcox."

"Oh, Wilcox. Our local screwball—but don't get me wrong; he's a smart guy all right. Well, you can see him tomorrow. You're coming home with me now, for dinner and to stay overnight. Maisie'll be glad to see you. Come on, my buggy's over here."

"Sure. Finished whatever you were here for?"

"Yep, just to pick up the news on who came in on the train. And *you* came in, so here we go."

They got in the buggy, and George picked up the reins and said, "Giddup, Bessie," to the mare. Then, "What are you doing now, Pete?"

"Research. For a gas-supply company. Been working on a more efficient mantle, one that'll give more light and be less destructible. This fellow Wilcox wrote us he had something along that line; the company sent me up to look it over. If it's what he claims, I'll take him back to New York with me, and let the company lawyers dicker with him."

"How's business, otherwise?"

"Great, George. *Gas*; that's the coming thing. Every *new* home's being piped for it, and plenty of the old ones. How about you?"

"We got it. Luckily we had one of the old Linotypes that ran the metal pot off a gas burner, so it was already piped in. And our home is right over the office and print shop, so all we had to do was pipe it up a flight. Great stuff, gas. How's New York?"

"Fine, George. Down to its last million people, and stabilizing there. No crowding and plenty of room for everybody.

That *air*—why, it's better than Atlantic City, without gasoline fumes."

"Enough horses to go around yet?"

"Almost. But bicycling's the craze; the factories can't turn out enough to meet the demand. There's a cycling club in almost every block and all the able-bodied cycle to and from work. Doing 'em good, too; a few more years and the doctors will go on short rations."

"You got a bike?"

"Sure, a pre-vader one. Average five miles a day on it, and I eat like a horse."

George Bailey chuckled. "I'll have Maisie include some hay in the dinner. Well, here we are. Whoa, Bessie."

An upstairs window went up, and Maisie looked out and down. She called out, "Hi, Pete!"

"Extra plate, Maisie," George called. "We'll be up soon as I put the horse away and show Pete around downstairs."

He led Pete from the barn into the back door of the newspaper shop. "Our Linotype!" he announced proudly, pointing.

"How's it work? Where's your steam engine?"

George grinned. "Doesn't work yet; we still hand set the type. I could get only one steamer and had to use that on the press. But I've got one on order for the Lino, and coming up in a month or so. When we get it, Pop Jenkins, my printer, is going to put himself out of a job teaching me to run it. With the Linotype going, I can handle the whole thing myself."

"Kind of rough on Pop?"

George shook his head. "Pop eagerly awaits the day. He's sixty-nine and wants to retire. He's just staying on until I can do without him. Here's the press—a honey of a little Miehle; we do some job work on it, too. And this is the office, in front. Messy, but efficient."

Mulvaney looked around him and grinned. "George, I believe you've found your niche. You were cut out for a small-town editor."

"Cut out for it? I'm crazy about it. I have more fun than everybody. Believe it or not, I work like a dog, and like it. Come on upstairs."

On the stairs, Pete asked, "And the novel you were going to write?"

"Half done, and it isn't bad. But it isn't the novel I was going to write; I was a cynic then. Now—"

"George, I think the waveries were your best friends."

"Waveries?"

"Lord, how long does it take slang to get from New York out to the sticks? The vaders, of course. Some professor who specializes in studying them described one as a wavery place in the ether, and 'wavery' stuck—Hello there, Maisie, my girl. You look like a million."

They ate leisurely. Almost apologetically, George brought out beer, in cold bottles. "Sorry, Pete, haven't anything stronger to offer you. But I haven't been drinking lately. Guess—"

"*You* on the wagon, George?"

"Not on the wagon, exactly. Didn't swear off or anything, but haven't had a drink of strong liquor in almost a year. I don't know why, but—"

"I do," said Pete Mulvaney. "I know exactly why you don't—because I don't drink much either, for the same reason. We don't drink because we don't *have* to—say, isn't that a *radio* over there?"

George chuckled. "A souvenir. Wouldn't sell if for a fortune. Once in a while I like to look at it and think of the awful guff I used to sweat out for it. And then I go over and click the switch and nothing happens. Just silence. Silence is the most wonderful thing in the world, sometimes, Pete. Of course I couldn't do that if there was any juice, because I'd get vaders then. I suppose they're still doing business at the same old stand?"

"Yep, the Research Bureau checks daily. Try to get up current with a little generator run by a steam turbine. But no dice; the vaders suck it up as fast as it's generated."

"Suppose they'll ever go away?"

Mulvaney shrugged. "Helmetz thinks not. He thinks they propagate in proportion to the available electricity. Even if the development of radio broadcasting somewhere else in the Universe would attract them there, some would stay here—and multiply like flies the minute we tried to use electricity again. And meanwhile, they'll live on the static electricty in the air. What do you do evenings up here?"

"Do? Read, write, visit with one another, go to the amateur groups—Maise's chairman of the Blakestown Players, and I play bit parts in it. With the movies out everybody goes in for theatricals and we've found some real talent. And there's the chess-and-checker club, and cycle trips and picnics—there isn't time enough. Not to mention music. Everybody plays an instrument, or is trying to."

"You?"

"Sure, cornet. First cornet in the Silver Concert Band, with solo parts. And—Good Heavens! Tonight's rehearsal, and we're giving a concert Sunday afternoon. I hate to desert you, but—"

"Can't I come around and sit in? I've got my flute in the brief case here, and—"

"*Flute?* We're short on flutes. Bring that around and Si Perkins, our director, will practically shanghai you into staying over for the concert Sunday—and it's only three days, so why not? And get it out now; we'll play a few old timers to warm up. Hey, Maisie, skip those dishes and come on in to the piano!"

While Pete Mulvaney went to the guest room to get his flute from the brief case, George Bailey picked up his cornet from the top of the piano and blew a soft, plaintive little minor run on it. Clear as a bell; his lip was in good shape tonight.

And with the shining silver thing in his hand he wandered over to the window and stood looking out into the night. It was dusk out and the rain had stopped.

A high-stepping horse *clop-clopped* by and the bell of a bicycle jangled. Somebody across the street was strumming a guitar and singing. He took a deep breath and let it out slowly.

The scent of spring was soft and sweet in the moist air.

Peace and dusk.

Distant rolling thunder.

God damn it, he thought, *if only there was a bit of lightning.*

He missed the lightning.

THE PIPER'S SON

by "Lewis Padgett" (Henry Kuttner [1914-1958] and C. L. Moore [1911-])

ASTOUNDING SCIENCE FICTION, *February*

Henry Kuttner and his wife, Catherine L. Moore, were arguably the dominant writers in sf in the mid to late 1940s, writing many stories under their own names and others as "Lewis Padgett" and "Lawrence O'Donnell," and this selection is the first of three in this book. All stories under all of their names should be approached with caution—it is likely that both had something to do with every one of them (after 1940), even those signed by Kuttner or Moore alone.

"The Piper's Son" was the first of their "Baldy" series of stories (published as Mutant *in 1953) about humans mutated and endowed with special powers as a result of an atomic war. All are powerful treatments of the situation of the outsider in society, split among themselves over the uses to which their unique talents should be put.*

(The year 1945 was the Year of the Bomb and mutant stories went into high gear. We knew that radiation could damage the body's genetic mechanisms, but we intended to imagine dramatic mutations that, from the standpoint of sober science, were utterly unlikely, while ignoring the obvious result—radiation sickness and death.

Then, too, looking back on the stories of a generation ago, it is remarkable how many stories bear the clear mark of John Campbell's notions. I wonder if he published any stories at all that he didn't put his mark on, usually by indoctrinating his writers beforehand. I know he labored for hours indoctrinating me but I was never really aware at the time that other writers were subjected to the same process.

Campbell had the distinct impression that mutants with superhuman characteristics would be cut down and destroyed by ordinary human beings. We had it in A. E. van Vogt's "Slan" most notably and in Robert Heinlein's "Methuselah's Children." Campbell may have thought this because I suspect he felt he had been scapegoated in youth for the crime of being mentally superior and many science fiction writers went along with him because they perhaps had also experienced an uncomfortable childhood for the same reason.

Come to think of it, I was occasionally scapegoated when I was young, but not for being superior—just for being a pain in the neck, which I was, till I learned better. I.A.)

The Green Man was climbing the glass mountains, and hairy, gnomish faces peered at him from crevices. This was only another step in the Green Man's endless, exciting odyssey. He'd had a great many adventures already—in the Flame Country, among the Dimension Changers, with the City Apes who sneered endlessly while their blunt, clumsy fingers fumbled at deathrays. The trolls, however, were masters of magic, and were trying to stop the Green Man with spells. Little whirlwinds of force spun underfoot, trying to trip the Green Man, a figure of marvelous muscular development, handsome as a god, and hairless from head to foot, glistening pale green. The whirlwinds formed a fascinating pattern. If you could thread a precarious path among them—avoiding the pale yellow ones especially—you could get through.

And the hairy gnomes watched malignantly, jealously, from their crannies in the glass crags.

Al Burkhalter, having recently achieved the mature status of eight full years, lounged under a tree and masticated a grass blade. He was so immersed in his daydreams that his father had to nudge his side gently to bring comprehension into the half-closed eyes. It was a good day for dreaming, anyway—a hot sun and a cool wind blowing down from the white Sierra peaks to the east. Timothy grass sent its faintly musty fragrance along the channels of air, and Ed Burkhalter was glad that his son was second-generation since the Blowup. He himself had been born ten years after the last bomb had been dropped, but second-hand memories can be pretty bad too.

"Hello, Al," he said, and the youth vouchsafed a half-lidded glance of tolerant acceptance.

"Hi, Dad."

"Want to come downtown with me?"

"Nope," Al said, relaxing instantly into his stupor.

Burkhalter raised a figurative eyebrow and half turned. On an impulse, then, he did something he rarely did without the tacit permission of the other party; he used his telepathic power to reach into Al's mind. There was, he admitted to himself, a certain hesitancy, a subconscious unwillingness on his part, to do this, even though Al had pretty well outgrown the nasty, inhuman formlessness of mental babyhood. There had been a time when Al's mind had been quite shocking in its alienage. Burkhalter remembered a few abortive experiments he had made before Al's birth; few fathers-to-be could resist the temptation to experiment with embryonic brains, and that had brought back nightmares Burkhalter had not had since his youth. There had been enormous rolling masses, and an appalling vastness, and other things. Prenatal memories were ticklish, and should be left to qualified mnemonic psychologists.

But now Al was maturing, and daydreaming, as usual, in bright colors. Burkhalter, reassured, felt that he had fulfilled his duty as a monitor and left his son still eating grass and ruminating.

Just the same, there was a sudden softness inside of him, and the aching, futile pity he was apt to feel for helpless things that were as yet unqualified for conflict with that extraordinarily complicated business of living. Conflict, competition, had not died out when war abolished itself; the business of adjustment even to one's surroundings was a conflict, and conversation a duel. With Al, too, there was a double problem. Yes, language was in effect a tariff wall, and a Baldy could appreciate that thoroughly, since the wall didn't exist between Baldies.

Walking down the rubbery walk that led to town center, Burkhalter grinned wryly and ran lean fingers through his well-kept wig. Strangers were very often surprised to know that he was a Baldy, a telepath. They looked at him with wondering eyes, too courteous to ask how it felt to be a freak, but obviously avid. Burkhalter, who knew diplomacy, would be quite willing to lead the conversation.

"My folks lived near Chicago after the Blowup. That was why."

"Oh." Stare. "I'd heard that was why so many—" Startled pause.

"Freaks or mutations. There were both. I still don't know which class I belong to," he'd add disarmingly.

"You're no freak!" They didn't protest too much.

"Well, some mighty queer specimens came out of the radioactive-affected areas around the bomb targets. Funny things happened to the germ plasm. Most of 'em died out; they couldn't reproduce; but you'll still find a few creatures in sanitariums—two heads, you know. And so on."

Nevertheless they were always ill-at-ease. "You mean you can read my mind—now?"

"I could, but I'm not. It's hard work, except with another telepath. And we Baldies—well, we don't, that's all." A man with abnormal muscle development wouldn't go around knocking people down. Not unless he wanted to be mobbed. Baldies were always sneakingly conscious of a hidden peril: lynch law. And wise Baldies didn't even imply that they had an . . . extra sense. They just said they were different, and let it go at that.

But one question was always implied, though not always mentioned. "If I were a telepath, I'd . . . how much do you make a year?"

They were surprised at the answer. A mindreader certainly could make a fortune, if he wanted. So why did Ed Burkhalter stay a semantics expert in Modoc Publishing Town, when a trip to one of the science towns would enable him to get hold of secrets that would get him a fortune?

There was a good reason. Self-preservation was a part of

it. For which reason Burkhalter, and many like him, wore toupees. Though there were many Baldies who did not.

Modoc was a twin town with Pueblo, across the mountain barrier south of the waste that had been Denver. Pueblo held the presses, photolinotypes, and the machines that turned scripts into books, after Modoc had dealt with them. There was a helicopter distribution fleet at Pueblo, and for the last week Oldfield, the manager, had been demanding the manuscript of "Psychohistory," turned out by a New Yale man who had got tremendously involved in past emotional problems, to the detriment of literary clarity. The truth was that he distrusted Burkhalter. And Burkhalter, neither a priest nor a psychologist, had to become both without admitting it to the confused author of "Psychohistory."

The sprawling buildings of the publishing house lay ahead and below, more like a resort than anything more utilitarian. That had been necessary. Authors were peculiar people, and often it was necessary to induce them to take hydrotherapic treatments before they were in shape to work out their books with the semantic experts. Nobody was going to bite them, but they didn't realize that, and either cowered in corners, terrified, or else blustered their way around, using language few could understand. Jem Quayle, author of "Psychohistory," fitted into neither group; he was simply baffled by the intensity of his own research. His personal history had qualified him too well for emotional involvements with the past—and that was a serious matter when a thesis of this particular type was in progress.

Dr. Moon, who was on the Board, sat near the south entrance, eating an apple which he peeled carefully with his silver-hilted dagger. Moon was fat, short, and shapeless; he didn't have much hair, but he wasn't a telepath; Baldies were entirely hairless. He gulped and waved at Burkhalter.

"Ed . . . *urp* . . . want to talk to you."

"Sure," Burkhalter said, agreeably coming to a standstill and rocking on his heels. Ingrained habit made him sit down beside the Boardman; Baldies, for obvious reasons, never stood up when nontelepaths were sitting. Their eyes met now on the same level. Burkhalter said, "What's up?"

"The store got some Shasta apples flown in yesterday. Better tell Ethel to get some before they're sold out. Here." Moon watched his companion eat a chunk, and nod.

"Good. I'll have her get some. The 'copter's laid up for today, though; Ethel pulled the wrong gadget."

"Foolproof," Moon said bitterly. "Huron's turning out some sweet models these days; I'm getting my new one from Michigan. Listen, Pueblo called me this morning on Quayle's book."

"Oldfield?"

"Our boy," Moon nodded. "He says can't you send over even a few chapters."

Burkhalter shook his head. "I don't think so. There are some abstracts right in the beginning that just have to be clarified, and Quayle is—" He hesitated.

"What?"

Burkhalter thought about the Oedipus complex he'd uncovered in Quayle's mind, but that was sancrosanct, even though it kept Quayle from interpreting Darius with cold logic. "He's got muddy thinking in there. I can't pass it; I tried it on three readers yesterday, and got different reactions from all of them. So far 'Psychohistory' is all things to all men. The critics would lambaste us if we released the book as is. Can't you string Oldfield along for a while longer?"

"Maybe," Moon said doubtfully. "I've got a subjective novella I could rush over. It's light vicarious eroticism, and that's harmless; besides, it's semantically O.K.'d. We've been holding it up for an artist, but I can put Duman on it. I'll do that, yeah. I'll shoot the script over to Pueblo and he can make the plates later. A merry life we lead, Ed."

"A little too merry sometimes," Burkhalter said. He got up, nodded, and went in search of Quayle, who was relaxing on one of the sun decks.

Quayle was a thin, tall man with a worried face and the abstract air of an unshelled tortoise. He lay on his flexiglass couch, direct sunlight toasting him from above, while the reflected rays sneaked up on him from below, through the transparent crystal. Burkhalter pulled off his shirt and dropped on a sunner beside Quayle. The author glanced at Burkhalter's hairless chest and half-formed revulsion rose in him: *A Baldy . . . no privacy . . . none of his business . . . fake eyebrows and lashes; he's still a—*

Something ugly, at that point.

Diplomatically Burkhalter touched a button, and on a screen overhead a page of "Psychohistory" appeared, enlarged and easily readable. Quayle scanned the sheet. It had code notations on it, made by the readers, recognized by Burkhalter as varied reactions to what should have been straightline explanations. If three readers had got three different meanings out of that paragraph—well, what *did* Quayle mean? He reached delicately into the mind, conscious of useless guards erected against intrusion, mud barricades over which his mental eye stole like a searching, quiet wind. No ordinary man could guard his mind against a Baldy. But Baldies could guard their privacy against intrusion by other telepaths—adults, that is. There was a psychic selector band, a—

Here it came. But muddled a bit. *Darius*: that wasn't simply a word; it wasn't a picture, either; it was really a second *life*. But scattered, fragmentary. Scraps of scent and sound, and memories, and emotional reactions. Admiration and hatred. A burning impotence. A black tornado, smelling of pine, roaring across a map of Europe and Asia. Pine scent stronger now, and horrible humiliation, and remembered pain . . . eyes . . . *Get Out!*

Burkhalter put down the dictograph mouthpiece and lay looking up through the darkened eye-shells he had donned. "I got out as soon as you wanted me to," he said. "I'm still out."

Quayle lay there, breathing hard. "Thanks," he said. "Apologies. Why you don't ask a duello—"

"I don't want to duel with you," Burkhalter said. "I've never put blood on my dagger in my life. Besides, I can see your side of it. Remember, this is my job, Mr. Quayle, and I've learned a lot of things—that I've forgotten again."

"It's intrusion, I suppose. I tell myself that it doesn't matter, but my privacy—is important."

Burkhalter said patiently, "We can keep trying it from different angles until we find one that isn't too private. Suppose, for example, I asked you if you admired Darius."

Admiration . . . and pine scent . . . and Burkhalter said quickly, "I'm out. O.K.?"

"Thanks," Quayle muttered. He turned on his side, away from the other man. After a moment he said, "That's silly—turning over, I mean. You don't have to see my face to know what I'm thinking."

"You have to put out the welcome mat before I walk in," Burkhalter told him.

"I guess I believe that. I've met some Baldies, though, that were . . . that I didn't like."

"There's a lot on that order, sure. I know the type. The ones who don't wear wigs."

Quayle said, "They'll read your mind and embarrass you just for the fun of it. They ought to be—taught better."

Burkhalter blinked in the sunlight. "Well, Mr. Quayle, it's this way. A Baldy's got his problems, too. He's got to orient himself to a world that isn't telepathic; and I suppose a lot of Baldies rather feel that they're letting their specialization go to waste. There *are* jobs a man like me is suited for—"

"*Man!*" He caught the scrap of thought from Quayle. He ignored it, his face was always a mobile mask, and went on.

"Semantics have always been a problem, even in countries speaking only one tongue. A qualified Baldy is a swell interpreter. And, though there aren't any Baldies on the detective forces, they often work with the police. It's rather like being a machine that can do only a few things."

"A few things more than humans can," Quayle said.

Sure, Burkhalter thought, if we could compete on equal footing with nontelepathic humanity. But would blind men trust one who could see? Would they play poker with him? A sudden, deep bitterness put an unpleasant taste in Burkhalter's mouth. What was the answer? Reservations for Baldies? Isolation? And would a nation of blind men trust those with vision enough for that? Or would they be dusted off—the sure cure, the check-and-balance system that made war an impossibility?

He remembered when Red Bank had been dusted off, and maybe that had been justified. The town was getting too big for its boots, and personal dignity was a vital factor; you weren't willing to lose face as long as a dagger swung at your belt. Similarly, the thousands upon thousands of little towns that covered America, each with its perculiar specialy—helicopter manufacture for Huron and Michigan, vegetable farming for Conoy and Diego, textiles and education and art and machines—each little town had a wary eye on all the others. The science and research centers were a little larger; nobody objected to that, for technicians never made war except under pressure; but few of the towns held more than a few hundred families. It was check-and-balance in most efficient degree; whenever a town showed signs of wanting to become a city—thence, a capital, thence, an imperialistic empire—it was dusted off. Though that had not happened for a long while. And Red Bank might have been a mistake.

Geopolitically it was a fine setup; sociologically it was acceptable, but brought necessary changes. There was subconsicous swashbuckling. The rights of the individual had become more highly regarded as decentralization took place. And men learned.

They learned a monetary system based primarily upon barter. They learned to fly; nobody drove surface cars. They learned new things, but they did not forget the Blowup, and in secret places near every town were hidden the bombs that could utterly and fantastically exterminate a town, as such bombs had exterminated the cities during the Blowup.

And everybody knew how to make those bombs. They were beautifully, terribly simple. You could find the ingredients anywhere and prepare them easily. Then you could take your helicopter over a town, drop an egg overside—and perform an erasure.

Outside of the wilderness malcontents, the maladjusted people found in every race, nobody kicked. And the roaming tribes never raided and never banded together in large groups—for fear of an erasure.

The artisans were maladjusted too, to some degree, but they weren't antisocial, so they lived where they wanted and painted, wrote, composed, and retreated into their own private worlds. The scientists, equally maladjusted in other lines, retreated to their slightly larger towns, banding together in small universes, and turned out remarkable technical achievements.

And the Baldies—found jobs where they could.

No nontelepath would have viewed the world environment quite as Burkhalter did. He was abnormally conscious of the human element, attaching a deeper, more profound significance to those human values, undoubtedly because he saw men in more than the ordinary dimensions. And also, in a way—and inevitably—he looked at humanity from outside.

Yet he was human. The barrier that telepathy had raised made men suspicious of him, more so than if he had had two heads—then they could have pitied. As it was—

As it was, he adjusted the scanner until new pages of the typescript came flickering into view above. "Say when," he told Quayle.

Quayle brushed back his gray hair. "I feel sensitive all over," he objected. "After all, I've been under a considerable strain correlating my material."

"Well, we can always postpone publication." Burkhalter threw out the suggestion casually, and was pleased when Quayle didn't nibble. He didn't like to fail, either.

"No. No, I want to get the thing done now."

"Mental catharsis—"

"Well, by a psychologist, perhaps. But not by—"

"—a Baldy. You know that a lot of psychologists have Baldy helpers. They get good results, too."

Quayle turned on the tobacco smoke, inhaling slowly. "I suppose . . . I've not had much contact with Baldies. Or too much—without selectivity. I saw some in an asylum once. I'm not being offensive, am I?"

"No," Burkhalter said. "Every mutation can run too close to the line. There were lots of failures. The hard radiations brought about one true mutation: hairless telepaths, but they didn't all hew true to the line. The mind's a queer gadget—you know that. It's a colloid balancing, figuratively, on the point of a pin. If there's any flaw, telepathy's apt to bring it out. So you'll find that the Blowup caused a hell of a lot of insanity. Not only among the Baldies, but among the other mutations that developed then. Except that the Baldies are almost always paranoidal."

"And dementia praecox," Quayle said, finding relief from his own embarrassment in turning the spotlight on Burkhalter.

"And d. p. Yeah. When a confused mind acquires the telepathic instinct—a hereditary bollixed mind—it can't handle it all. There's disorientation. The paranoia group retreat into their own private worlds, and the d. p.'s simply don't realize that *this* world exists. There are distinctions, but I think that's a valid basis."

"In a way," Quayle said, "it's frightening. I can't think of any historical parallel."

"No."

"What do you think the end of it will be?"

"I don't know," Burkhalter said thoughtfully. "I think we'll be assimilated. There hasn't been enough time yet. We're specialized in a certain way, and we're useful in certain jobs."

"If you're satisfied to stay there. The Baldies who won't wear wigs—"

"They're so bad-tempered I expect they'll all be killed off in duels eventually." Burkhalter smiled. "No great loss. The rest of us, we're getting what we want—acceptance. We don't have horns or halos."

Quayle shook his head. "I'm glad, I think, that I'm not a telepath. The mind's mysterious enough anyway, without new doors opening. Thanks for letting me talk. I think I've got part of it talked out, anyway. Shall we try the script again?"

"Sure," Burkhalter said, and again the procession of pages flickered on the screen above them. Quayle did seem less guarded; his thoughts were more lucid, and Burkhalter was able to get at the true meanings of many of the hitherto muddy statements. They worked easily, the telepath dictating rephrasings into his dictogarph, and only twice did they have to hurdle emotional tangles. At noon they knocked off, and Burkhalter, with a friendly nod, took the dropper to his office, where he found some calls listed on the visor. He ran off repeats, and a worried look crept into his blue eyes.

He talked with Dr. Moon in a booth at luncheon. The conversation lasted so long that only the induction cups kept the coffee hot, but Burkhalter had more than one problem to discuss. And he'd known Moon for a long time. The fat man was one of few who were not, he thought, subconsciously repelled by the fact that Burkhalter was a Baldy.

"I've never fought a duel in my life, Doc. I can't afford to."

"You can't afford not to. You can't turn down the challenge, Ed. It isn't done."

"But this fellow Reilly—I don't even know him."

"I know of him," Moon said. "He's got a bad temper. Dueled a lot."

Burkhalter slammed his hand down on the table. "It's ridiculous. I won't do it!"

"Well," Moon said practically, "your wife can't fight him. And if Ethel's been reading Mrs. Reilly's mind and gossiping, Reilly's got a case."

"Don't you think we know the dangers of that?" Burkhalter asked in a low voice. "Ethel doesn't go around reading minds any more than I do. It'd be fatal—for us. And for any other Baldy."

"Not the hairless ones. The ones who won't wear wigs. They—"

"They're fools. And they're giving all the Baldies a bad name. Point one, Ethel doesn't read minds; she didn't read Mrs. Reilly's. Point two, she doesn't gossip."

"La Reilly is obviously an hysterical type," Moon said. "Word got around about this scandal, whatever it was, and Mrs. Reilly remembered she'd seen Ethel lately. She's the type who needs a scapegoat anyway. I rather imagine she let word drop herself, and had to cover up so her husband wouldn't blame her."

"I'm not going to accept Reilly's challenge," Burkhalter said doggedly.

"You'll have to."

"Listen, Doc, maybe—"

"What?"

"Nothing. An idea. It might work. Forget about that; I think I've got the right answer. It's the only one, anyway. I can't afford a duel and that's flat."

"You're not a coward."

"There's one thing Baldies are afraid of," Burkhalter said, "and that's public opinion. I happen to know I'd kill Reilly. That's the reason why I've never dueled in my life."

Moon drank coffee. "Hm-m-m. I think—"

"Don't. There was something else. I'm wondering if I ought to send Al off to a special school."

"What's wrong with the kid?"

"He's turning out to be a beautiful delinquent. His teacher called me this morning. The playback was something to hear. He's talking funny and acting funny. Playing nasty little tricks on his friends—if he has any left by now."

"All kids are cruel."

"Kids don't know what cruelty means. That's why they're cruel; they lack empathy. But Al's getting—" Burkhalter gestured helplessly. "He's turning into a young tyrant. He doesn't seem to give a care about anything, according to his teacher."

"That's not too abnormal, so far."

"That's not the worst. He's become very egotistical. Too much so. I don't want him to turn into one of the wigless Baldies you were mentioning." Burkhalter didn't mention the other possibility: paranoia, insanity.

"He must pick things up somewhere. At home? Scarcely, Ed. Where else does he go?"

"The usual places. He's got a normal environment."

"I should think," Moon said, "that a Baldy would have unusual opportunities in training a youngster. The mental rapport—eh?"

"Yeah. But—I don't know. The trouble is," Burkhalter said almost inaudibly, "I wish to God I wasn't different. We didn't ask to be telepaths. Maybe it's all very wonderful in the long run, but I'm one person, and I've got my own microcosm. People who deal in long term sociology are apt to forget that. They can figure out the answers, but it's every individual man—or Baldy—who's got to fight his own personal battle while he's alive. And it isn't as clear-cut as a battle. It's worse; it's the necessity of watching yourself every second, of fitting yourself into a world that doesn't want you."

Moon looked uncomfortable. "Are you being a little sorry for yourself, Ed?"

Burkhalter shook himself. "I am, Doc. But I'll work it out."

"We both will," Moon said, but Burkhalter didn't really expect much help from him. Moon would be willing, but it was horribly different for an ordinary man to conceive that a Baldy was—the same. It was the difference that men looked for, and found.

Anyway, he'd have to settle matters before he saw Ethel again. He could easily conceal the knowledge, but she would recognize a mental barrier and wonder. Their marriage had been the more ideal because of the additional rapport, something that compensated for an inevitable, half-sensed estrangement from the rest of the world.

"How's 'Psychohistory' going?" Moon asked after a while.

"Better than I expected. I've got a new angle on Quayle. If I talk about myself, that seems to draw him out. It gives him enough confidence to let him open his mind to me. We may have those first chapters ready for Oldfield, in spite of everything."

"Good. Just the same, he can't rush us. If we've got to shoot out books that fast, we might as well go back to the days of semantic confusion. Which we won't!"

"Well," Burkhalter said, getting up, "I'll smoosh along. See you."

"About Reilly—"

"Let it lay." Burkhalter went out, heading for the address his visor had listed. He touched the dagger at his belt. Dueling wouldn't do for Baldies, but—

A greeting thought crept into his mind, and, under the arch that led into the campus, he paused to grin at Sam Shane, a New Orleans area Baldy who affected a wig of flaming red. They didn't bother to talk.

Personal question, involving mental, moral and physical well-being.

A satisfied glow. And you, Burkhalter? For an instant Burkhalter half-saw what the symbol of his name meant to Shane.

Shadow of trouble.

A warm willing anxiousness to help. There was a bond between Baldies.

Burkhalter thought: But everywhere I'd go there'd be the same suspicion. We're freaks.

More so elsewhere, Shane thought. There are a lot of us in Modoc Town. People are invariably more suspicious where they're not in daily contact with—Us.

The boy—

I've trouble too, Shane thought. It's worried me. My two girls—

Delinquency?

Yes.

Common denominators?

Don't know. More than one of Us have had the same trouble with our kids.

Secondary characteristic of the mutation? Second generation emergence?

Doubtful, Shane thought, scowling in his mind, shading his concept with a wavering question. We'll think it over later. Must go.

Burkhalter sighed and went on his way. The houses were strung out around the central industry of Modoc, and he cut through a park toward his destination. It was a sprawling curved building, but it wasn't inhabited, so Burkhalter filed Reilly for future reference, and, with a glance at his timer, angled over a hillside toward the school. As he expected, it was recreation time, and he spotted Al lounging under a tree, some distance from his companions, who were involved in a pleasantly murderous game of Blowup.

He sent his thought ahead.

The Green Man had almost reached the top of the mountain. The hairy gnomes were pelting on his trail, most unfairly shooting sizzling light-streaks at their quarry, but the

Green Man was agile enough to dodge. The rocks were leaning—

"Al."

—inward, pushed by the gnomes, ready to—

"*Al!*" Burkhalter sent his thought with the word, jolting into the boy's mind, a trick he very seldom employed, since youth was practically defenseless against such invasion.

"Hello, Dad," Al said, undisturbed. "What's up?"

"A report from your teacher."

"I didn't do anything."

"She told me what it was. Listen, kid. Don't start getting any funny ideas in your head."

"I'm not."

"Do you think a Baldy is better or worse than a non-Baldy?"

Al moved his feet uncomfortably. He didn't answer.

"Well," Burkhalter said, "the answer is both and neither. And here's why. A Baldy can communicate mentally, but he lives in a world where most people can't."

"They're dumb," Al opined.

"Not so dumb, if they're better suited to their world than you are. You might as well say a frog's better than a fish because he's an amphibian." Burkhalter briefly amplified and explained the terms telepathically.

"Well . . . oh, I get it, all right."

"Maybe," Burkhalter said slowly, "What you need is a swift kick in the pants. That thought wasn't so hot. What was it again?"

Al tried to hide it, blanking out. Burkhalter began to lift the barrier, an easy matter for him, but stopped. Al regarded his father in a most unfilial way—in fact, as a sort of boneless fish. That had been clear.

"If you're so egotistical," Burkhalter pointed out, "maybe you can see it this way. Do you know why there aren't any Baldies in key positions?"

"Sure I do," Al said unexpectedly. "They're afraid."

"Of what, then?"

"The—" That picture had been very curious, a commingling of something vaguely familiar to Burkhalter. "The non-Baldies."

"Well, if we took positions where we could take advantage of our telepathic function, non-Baldies would be plenty envious—especially if we were successes. If a Baldy even invented a better mousetrap, plenty of people would say he'd stolen the idea from some non-Baldy's mind. You get the point?"

"Yes, Dad." But he hadn't. Burkhalter sighed and looked up. He recognized one of Shane's girls on a nearby hillside, sitting alone against a boulder. There were other isolated figures here and there. Far to the east the snowy rampart of the Rockies made an irregular pattern against blue sky.

"Al," Burkhalter said, "I don't want you to get a chip on your shoulder. This is a pretty swell world, and the people in it are, on the whole, nice people. There's a law of averages. It isn't sensible for us to get too much wealth or power, because that'd militate against us—and we don't need it anyway. Nobody's poor. We find our work, we do it, and we're reasonably happy. We have some advantages non-Baldies don't have; in marriage, for example. Mental intimacy is quite as important as physical. But I don't want you to feel that being a Baldy makes you a god. It doesn't. I can still," he added thoughtfully, "spank it out of you, in case you care to follow out that concept in your mind at the moment."

Al gulped and beat a hasty retreat. "I'm sorry. I won't do it again."

"And keep your hair on, too. Don't take your wig off in class. Use the stickum stuff in the bathroom closet."

"Yes, but . . . Mr. Venner doesn't wear a wig."

"Remind me to do some historical research with you on zoot-suiters," Burkhalter said. "Mr. Venner's wiglessness is probably his only virtue, if you consider it one."

"He makes money."

"Anybody would, in that general store of his. But people don't buy from him if they can help it, you'll notice. That's what I mean by a chip on your shoulder. He's got one. There are Baldies like Venner, Al, but you might, sometime, ask the guy if he's happy. For your information, I am. More than Venner, anyway. Catch?"

"Yes, Dad." Al seemed submissive, but it was merely that. Burkhalter, still troubled, nodded and walked away. As he passed near the Shane girl's boulder he caught a scrap:*—at the summit of the Glass Mountains, rolling rocks back at the gnomes until—*

He withdrew; it was an unconscious habit, touching minds that were sensitive, but with children it was definitely unfair. With adult Baldies it was simply the instinctive gesture of tipping your hat; one answered or one didn't. The barrier could be erected; there could be a blank-out; or there could be the direct snub of concentration on a single thought, private and not to be intruded on.

A 'copter with a string of gliders was coming in from the south: a freighter laden with frozen foods from South America, to judge by the markings. Burkhalter made a note to pick up an Argentine steak. He'd got a new recipe he wanted to try out, a charcoal broil with barbecue sauce, a welcome change from the short-wave cooked meats they'd been having for a week. Tomatoes, chile, mm-m—what else? Oh, yes. The duel with Reilly. Burkhalter absently touched his dagger's hilt and made a small, mocking sound in his throat. Perhaps he was innately a pacifist. It was rather difficult to think of a duel seriously, even though everyone else did, when the details of a barbecue dinner were prosaic in his mind.

So it went. The tides of civilization rolled in century-long waves across the continents, and each particular wave, though conscious of its participation in the tide, nevertheless was more preoccupied with dinner. And, unless you happened to be a thousand feet tall, had the brain of a god and a god's life-span, what was the difference? People missed a lot—people like Venner, who was certainly a crank, not batty enough to qualify for the asylum, but certainly a potential paranoid type. The man's refusal to wear a wig labeled him as an individualist, but as an exhibitionist, too. If he didn't feel ashamed of his hairlessness, why should he bother to flaunt it? Besides, the man had a bad temper, and if people kicked him around, he asked for it by starting the kicking himself.

But as for Al, the kid was heading for something approaching delinquency. It couldn't be the normal development of childhood, Burkhalter thought. He didn't pretend to be an expert, but he was still young enough to remember his own formative years, and he had had more handicaps than Al had now; in those days, Baldies had been very new and very freakish. There'd been more than one movement to isolate, sterilize, or even exterminate the mutations.

Burkhalter sighed. If he had been born before the Blowup, it might have been different. Impossible to say. One could read history, but one couldn't live it. In the future, perhaps, there might be telepathic libraries in which that would be possible. So many opportunities, in fact—and so few that the world was ready to accept as yet. Eventually Baldies would not be regarded as freaks, and by that time real progress would be possible.

But people don't make history—Burkhalter thought. Peoples do that. Not the individual.

He stopped by Reilly's house again, and this time the man answered, a burly, freckled, squint-eyed fellow with immense hands and, Burkhalter noted, fine muscular co-ordination. He rested those hands on the Dutch door and nodded.

"Who're you, mister?"

"My name's Burkhalter."

Comprehension and wariness leaped into Reilly's eyes. "Oh. I see. You got my call?"

"I did," Burkhalter said. "I want to talk to you about it. May I come in?"

"O.K." He stepped back, opening the way through a hall and into a spacious living room, where diffused light filtered through glassy mosaic walls. "Want to set the time?"

"I want to tell you you're wrong."

"Now wait a minute," Reilly said, patting the air. "My wife's out now, but she gave me the straight of it. I don't like this business of sneaking into a man's mind; it's crooked. You should have told *your* wife to mind her business—or keep her tongue quiet."

Burkhalter said patiently, "I give you my word, Reilly, that Ethel didn't read your wife's mind."

"Does she say so?"

"I . . . well, I haven't asked her."

"Yeah," Reilly said with an air of triumph.

"I don't need to. I know her well enough. And . . . well, I'm a Baldy myself."

"I know you are," Reilly said. "For all I know, you may be reading my mind now." He hesitated. "Get out of my house. I like my privacy. We'll meet at dawn tomorrow, if that's satisfactory with you. Now get out." He seemed to have something on his mind, some ancient memory, perhaps, that he didn't wish exposed.

Burkhalter nobly resisted the temptation. "No Baldy would read—"

"Go on, get out!"

"Listen! You wouldn't have a chance in a duel with me!"

"Do you know how many notches I've got?" Reilly asked.

"Ever dueled a Baldy?"

"I'll cut the notch deeper tomorrow. Get out, d'you hear?"

Burkhalter, biting his lips, said, "Man, don't you realize that in a duel I could read your mind?"

"I don't care . . . what?"

"I'd be half a jump ahead of you. No matter how instinctive your actions would be, you'd know them a split second ahead of time in your mind. And I'd know all your tricks and weaknesses, too. Your technique would be an open book to me. Whatever you thought of—"

"No." Reilly shook his head. "Oh, no. You're smart, but it's a phony set-up."

Burkhalter hesitated, decided, and swung about, pushing a chair out of the way. "Take out your dagger," he said. "Leave the sheath snapped on; I'll show you what I mean."

Reilly's eyes widened. "If you want it now—"

"I don't." Burkhalter shoved another chair away. He unclipped his dagger, sheath and all, from his belt, and made sure the little safety clip was in place. "We've room enough here. Come on."

Scowling, Reilly took out his own dagger, held it awkwardly, baffled by the sheath, and then suddenly feinted forward. But Burkhalter wasn't there; he had anticipated, and his own leather sheath slid up Reilly's belly.

"That," Burkhalter said, "would have ended the fight."

For answer Reilly smashed a hard dagger-blow down, curving at the last moment into a throat-cutting slash. Burkhalter's free hand was already at his throat; his other hand, with the sheathed dagger, tapped Reilly twice over the heart. The freckles stood out boldly against the pallor of the larger man's face. But he was not yet ready to concede. He tried a few more passes, clever, well-trained cuts, and they failed, because Burkhalter had anticipated them. His left hand invariably covered the spot where Reilly had aimed, and which he never struck.

Slowly Reilly let his arm fall. He moistened his lips and swallowed. Burkhalter busied himself reclipping his dagger in place.

"Burkhalter," Reilly said, "you're a devil."

"Far from it. I'm just afraid to take a chance. Do you really think being a Baldy is a snap?"

"But if you can read minds—"

"How long do you think I'd last if I did any dueling? It would be too much of a set-up. Nobody would stand for it, and I'd end up dead. I can't duel, because it'd be murder, and people would know it was murder. I've taken a lot of cracks, swallowed a lot of insults, for just that reason. Now, if you like, I'll swallow another and apologize. I'll admit anything you say. But I can't duel with you, Reilly."

"No, I can see that. And—I'm glad you came over." Reilly was still white. "I'd have walked right into a set-up."

"Not my set-up," Burkhalter said. "I wouldn't have dueled. Baldies aren't so lucky, you know. They've got handicaps—like this. That's why they can't afford to take chances and antagonize people, and why we never read minds, unless we're asked to do so."

"It makes sense. More or less." Reilly hesitated. "Look, I withdraw that challenge. O.K.?"

"Thanks," Burkhalter said, putting out his hand. It was taken rather reluctantly. "We'll leave it at that, eh?"

"Right." But Reilly was still anxious to get his guest out of the house.

Burkhalter walked back to the Publishing Center and whistled tunelessly. He could tell Ethel now; in fact, he had to, for secrets between them would have broken up the completeness of their telepathic intimacy. It was not that their minds lay bare to each other, it was, rather, that any barrier could be sensed by the other, and the perfect *rapport* wouldn't have been so perfect. Curiously, despite this utter intimacy, husband and wife managed to respect one another's privacy.

Ethel might be somewhat distressed, but the trouble had blown over, and, besides, she was a Baldy too. Not that she looked it, with her wig of fluffy chestnut hair and those long, curving lashes. But her parents had lived east of Seattle during the Blowup, and afterward, too, before the hard radiation's effects had been thoroughly studied.

The snow-wind blew down over Modoc and fled southward along the Utah Valley. Burkhalter wished he was in his 'copter, alone in the blue emptiness of the sky. There was a quiet, strange peace up there that no Baldy ever quite achieved on the earth's surface, except in the depths of a wilderness. Stray fragments of thoughts were always flying about, subsensory, but like the almost-unheard whisper of a needle on a phonograph record, never ceasing. That, certainly, was why almost all Baldies loved to fly and were expert pilots. The high waste deserts of the air were their blue hermitages.

Still, he was in Modoc now, and overdue for his interview with Quayle. Burkhalter hastened his steps. In the main hall he met Moon, said briefly and cryptically that he'd taken care of the duel, and passed on, leaving the fat man to stare a question after him. The only visor call was from Ethel; the playback said she was worried about Al, and would Burkhalter check with the school. Well, he had already done so—unless the boy had managed to get into more trouble since then. Burkhalter put in a call and reassured himself. Al was as yet unchanged.

He found Quayle in the same private solarium, and thirsty. Burkhalter ordered a couple of dramzowies sent up, since he had no objection to loosening Quayle's inhibitions. The gray-haired author was immersed in a sectional historical globe-map, illuminating each epochal layer in turn as he searched back through time.

"Watch this," he said, running his hand along the row of buttons. "See how the German border fluctuates?" It fluctuated, finally vanishing entirely as semimodern times were reached. "And Portugal. Notice its zone of influence? Now—" The zone shrank steadily from 1600 on, while other countries shot out radiating lines and assumed sea power.

Burkhalter sipped his dramzowie. "Not much of that now."

"No, since . . . what's the matter?"

"How do you mean?"

"You look shot."

"I didn't know I showed it," Burkhalter said wryly. "I just finagled my way out of a duel."

"That's one custom I never saw much sense to," Quayle said. "What happened? Since when can you finagle out?"

Burkhalter explained, and the writer took a drink and snorted. "What a spot for you. Being a Baldy isn't such an advantage after all, I guess."

"It has distinct disadvantages at times." On impulse Burkhalter mentioned his son. "You see my point, eh? I don't *know*, really, what standards to apply to a young Baldy. He is a mutation, after all. And the telepathic mutation hasn't had time to work out yet. We can't rig up controls, because guinea pigs and rabbits won't breed telepaths. That's been tried, you know. And—well, the child of a Baldy needs very special training so he can cope with his ultimate maturity."

"You seem to have adjusted well enough."

"I've—learned. As most sensible Baldies have. That's why I'm not a wealthy man, or in politics. We're really buying safety for our species by forgoing certain individual advantages. Hostages to destiny—and destiny spares us. But we get paid too, in a way. In the coinage of future benefits—negative benefits, really, for we ask only to be spared and accepted—and so we have to deny ourselves a lot of present, positive benefits. An appeasement to fate."

"Paying the piper." Quayle nodded.

"We are the pipers. The Baldies as a group, I mean. And our children. So it balances; we're really paying ourselves. If I wanted to take unfair advantage of my telepathic power—my son wouldn't live very long. The Baldies would be wiped out. Al's got to learn that, and he's getting pretty antisocial."

"All children are antisocial," Quayle pointed out. "They're utter individualists. I should think the only reason for worrying would be if the boy's deviation from the norm were connected with his telepathic sense."

"There's something in that." Burkhalter reached out left-handedly and probed delicately at Quayle's mind, noting that the antagonism was considerably lessened. He grinned to himself and went on talking about his own troubles. "Just the same, the boy's father to the man. And an adult Baldy has got to be pretty well adjusted, or he's sunk."

"Environment is as important as heredity. One complements the other. If a child's reared correctly, he won't have much trouble—unless heredity is involved."

"As it may be. There's so little known about the telepathic mutation. If baldness is one secondary characteristic, maybe—something else—emerges in the third or fourth generations. I'm wondering if telepathy is really good for the mind."

Quayle said, "Humph. Speaking personally, it makes me nervous—"

"Like Reilly."

"Yes," Quayle said, but he didn't care much for the comparison. "Well—anyhow, if a mutation's a failure, it'll die out. It won't breed true."

"What about hemophilia?"

"How many people have hemophilia?" Quayle asked. "I'm trying to look at it from the angle of psychohistorian. If there'd been telepaths in the past, things might have been different."

"How do you know there weren't?" Burkhalter asked.

Quayle blinked. "Oh. Well. That's true, too. In medieval times they'd have been called wizards—or saints. The Duke-Rhine experiments—but such accidents would have been abortive. Nature fools around trying to hit the . . . ah . . . the jackpot, and she doesn't always do it on the first try."

"She may not have done it now." That was habit speaking, the ingrained caution of modesty. "Telepathy may be merely a semi successful try at something pretty unimaginable. A sort of four-dimensional sensory concept, maybe."

"That's too abstract for me." Quayle was interested, and his own hesitancies had almost vanished; by accepting Burkhalter as a telepath, he had tacitly wiped away his objections to telepathy *per se*. "The old-time Germans always had an idea they were different; so did that Oriental race that had the islands off the China coast—the Japanese. They knew, very definitely, that they were a superior race because they were directly descended from gods. They were short in stature; heredity made them self-conscious when dealing with larger races. But the Chinese aren't tall, the Southern Chinese, and they weren't handicapped in that way."

"Environment, then?"

"Environment, which caused propaganda. The . . . ah . . . the Japanese took Buddhism, and altered it completely into Shinto, to suit their own needs. The samurai, warrior-knights, were the ideals, the code of honor was fascinatingly cockeyed. The principle of Shinto was to worship your superiors and subjugate your inferiors. Ever seen the Japanese jewel-trees?"

"I don't remember them. What are they?"

"Miniature replicas of espaliered trees, made of jewels, with trinkets hanging on the branches. Including a mirror—always. The first jewel-tree was made to lure the Moon-goddess out of a cave where she was sulking. It seems the lady was so intrigued by the trinkets and by her face reflected in the mirror that she came out of her hideout. All the Japanese morals were dressed up in pretty clothes; that was the bait. The old-time Germans did much the same thing. The last German dictator, Hitler, revived the old Siegfried legend. It was racial paranoia. The Germans worshiped the house-tyrant, not the mother, and they had extremely strong family ties. That extended to the state. They symbolized Hitler as their All-Father, and that led to a whole series of complicated events, and eventually we got the Blowup. And, finally, mutations."

"After the deluge, me," Burkhalter murmured, finishing his dramzowie. Quayle was staring at nothing.

"Funny," he said after a while. "This All-Father business—"

"Yes?"

"I wonder if you know how powerfully it can affect a man?"

Burkhalter didn't say anything. Quayle gave him a sharp glance.

"Yes," the writer said quietly. "You're a man, after all. I owe you an apology, you know."

Burkhalter smiled. "You can forget that."

"I'd rather not," Quayle said. "I've just realized, pretty suddenly, that the telepathic sense isn't so important. I mean—it doesn't make you *different*. I've been talking to you—"

"Sometimes it takes people years before they realize what you're finding out," Burkhalter remarked. "Years of living and working with something they think of as a Baldy."

"Do you know what I've been concealing in my mind?" Quayle asked.

"No. I don't."

"You lie like a gentleman. Thanks. Well, here it is, and I'm telling you by choice, because I want to. I don't care if you got the information out of my mind already; I just want to tell you of my own free will. My father . . . I imagine I hated him . . . was a tyrant, and I remember one time, when I was just a kid and we were in the mountains, he beat me and a lot of people were looking on. I've tried to forget that for a long time. Now"—Quayle shrugged—"it doesn't seem quite so important."

"I'm not a psychologist," Burkhalter said. "If you want my personal reaction, I'll just say that it doesn't matter. You're not a little boy any more, and the guy I'm talking to and working with is the adult Quayle."

"Hm-m-m. Ye-es. I suppose I knew that all along—how unimportant it was, really. It was simply having my privacy violated. . . . I think I know you better now, Burkhalter. You can—walk in."

"We'll work better," Burkhalter said, grinning. "Especially with Darius."

Quayle said, "I'll try not to keep any reservation in my mind. Frankly, I won't mind telling you—the answers. Even when they're personal."

"Check on that. D'you want to tackle Darius now?"

"O.K.," Quayle said, and his eyes no longer held suspicious wariness. "Darius I identify with my father—"

It was smooth and successful. That afternoon they accomplished more than they had during the entire previous fortnight. Warm with satisfaction on more than one point, Burkhalter stopped off to tell Dr. Moon that matters were looking up, and then set out toward home, exchanging thoughts with a couple of Baldies, his co-workers, who were knocking off for the day. The Rockies were bloody with the western light, and the coolness of the wind was pleasant on Burkhalter's cheeks, as he hiked homeward.

It was fine to be accepted. It proved that it could be done. And a Baldy often needed reassurance, in a world peopled by suspicious strangers. Quayle had been a hard nut to crack, but—Burkhalter smiled.

Ethel would be pleased. In a way, she'd had a harder time than he'd ever had. A woman would, naturally. Men were desperately anxious to keep their privacy unviolated by a woman, and as for non-Baldy women—well, it spoke highly for Ethel's glowing personal charm that she had finally been accepted by the clubs and feminine groups of Modoc. Only Burkhalter knew Ethel's desperate hurt at being bald, and not even her husband had ever seen her unwigged.

His thought reached out before him into the low, double-winged house on the hillside, and interlocked with hers in a warm intimacy. It was something more than a kiss. And, as always, there was the exciting sense of expectancy, mounting and mounting till the last door swung open and they touched physically. *This*, he thought, *is why I was born a Baldy; this is worth losing worlds for.*

At dinner that rapport spread out to embrace Al, an intangible, deeply-rooted something that made the food taste better and the water like wine. The word *home*, to telepaths, had a meaning that non-Baldies could not entirely comprehend, for it embraced a bond they could not know. There were small, intangible caresses.

Green Man going down the Great Red Slide; the Shaggy Dwarfs trying to harpoon him as he goes.

"Al," Ethel said, "are you still working on your Green Man?"

Then something utterly hateful and cold and deadly quivered silently in the air, like an icicle jaggedly smashing through golden, fragile glass. Burkhalter dropped his napkin and looked up, profoundly shocked. He felt Ethel's thought shrink back, and swiftly reached out to touch and reassure her with mental contact. But across the table the little boy, his cheeks still round with the fat of babyhood, sat silent and wary, realizing he had blundered, and seeking safety in complete immobility. His mind was too weak to resist probing, he knew, and he remained perfectly still, waiting, while the echoes of a thought hung poisonously in silence.

Burkhalter said, "Come on, Al." He stood up. Ethel started to speak.

"Wait, darling. Put up a barrier. Don't listen in." He touched her mind gently and tenderly, and then he took Al's hand and drew the boy after him out into the yard. Al watched his father out of wide, alert eyes.

Burkhalter sat on a bench and put Al beside him. He talked audibly at first, for clarity's sake, and for another reason. It was distinctly unpleasant to trick the boy's feeble guards down, but it was necessary.

"That's a very queer way to think of your mother," he said. "It's a queer way to think of me." Obscenity is more obscene, profanity more profane, to a telepathic mind, but this had been neither one. It had been—cold and malignant.

And this is flesh of my flesh, Burkhalter thought, looking at the boy and remembering the eight years of his growth. *Is the mutation to turn into something devilish?*

Al was silent.

Burkhalter reached into the young mind. Al tried to twist free and escape, but his father's strong hands gripped him. Instinct, not reasoning, on the boy's part, for mind's can touch over long distances.

He did not like to do this, for increased sensibility had gone with sensitivity, and violations are always violations. But ruthlessness was required. Burkhalter searched. Sometimes he threw key words violently at Al, and surges of memory pulsed up in response.

In the end, sick and nauseated, Burkhalter let Al go and sat alone on the bench, watching the red light die on the snowy peaks. The whiteness was red-stained. But it was not too late. The man was a fool, had been a fool from the beginning, or he would have known the impossibility of attempting such a thing as this.

The conditioning had only begun. Al could be reconditioned. Burkhalter's eyes hardened. And would be. *And would be.* But not yet, not until the immediate furious anger had given place to sympathy and understanding.

Not yet.

He went into the house, spoke briefly to Ethel, and televised the dozen Baldies who worked with him in the Publishing Center. Not all of them had families, but none was missing when, half an hour later, they met in the back room of the Pagan Tavern downtown. Sam Shane had caught a fragment of Burkhalter's knowledge, and all of them read his emotions. Welded into a sympathetic unit by their telepathic sense, they waited till Burkhalter was ready.

Then he told them. It didn't take long, via thought. He told them about the Japanese jewel-tree with its glittering gadgets, a shining lure. He told them of racial paranoia and propaganda. And that the most effective propaganda was sugar-coated, disguised so that the motive was hidden.

A Green Man, hairless, heroic—symbolic of a Baldy.

And wild, exciting adventures, the lure to catch the young fish whose plastic minds were impressionable enough to be led along the roads of dangerous madness. Adult Baldies could listen, but they did not; young telepaths had a higher threshold of mental receptivity, and adults do not read the books of their children except to reassure themselves that there is nothing harmful in the pages. And no adult would bother to listen to the Green Man mindcast. Most of them had accepted it as the original daydream of their own children.

"I did," Shane put in. "My girls—"

"Trace it back," Burkhalter said. "I did."

The dozen minds reached out on the higher frequency, the children's wave length, and something jerked away from them, startled and apprehensive.

"He's the one." Shane nodded.

They did not need to speak. They went out of the Pagan Tavern in a compact, ominous group, and crossed the street to the general store. The door was locked. Two of the men burst it open with their shoulders.

They went through the dark store and into a back room where a man was standing beside an overturned chair. His bald skull gleamed in an overhead light. His mouth worked impotently.

His thought pleaded with them—was driven back by an implacable deadly wall.

Burkhalter took out his dagger. Other slivers of steel glittered for a little while—

And were quenched.

Venner's scream had long since stopped, but his dying thought of agony lingered within Burkhalter's mind as he walked homeward. The wigless Baldy had not been insane, no. But he had been paranoidal.

What he had tried to conceal, at the last, was quite shocking. A tremendous, tyrannical egotism, and a furious hatred of nontelepaths. A feeling of self-justification that was, perhaps, insane. *And—we are the Future! The Baldies! God made us to rule lesser men!*

Burkhalter sucked in his breath, shivering. The mutation had not been entirely successful. One group had adjusted, the Baldies who wore wigs and had become fitted to their environment. One group had been insane, and could be discounted; they were in asylums.

But the middle group were merely paranoid. They were not insane, and they were not sane. They wore no wigs.

Like Venner.

And Venner had sought disciples. His attempt had been foredoomed to failure, but he had been one man.

One Baldy—paranoid.

There were others, many others.

Ahead, nestled into the dark hillside, was the pale blotch that marked Burkhalter's home. He sent his thought ahead, and it touched Ethel's and paused very briefly to reassure her.

Then it thrust on, and went into the sleeping mind of a little boy who, confused and miserable, had finally cried himself to sleep. There were only dreams in that mind now, a little discolored, a little stained, but they could be cleansed. And would be.

WANTED—AN ENEMY

by Fritz Leiber (1910-)

ASTOUNDING SCIENCE FICTION
February

The tall and greatly gifted Fritz Leiber received the Grand Master Award of the Science Fiction Writers of America in 1981, and it would be difficult to find a person more worthy. He has been giving pleasure and mental stimulation to sf and fantasy readers for more than forty years, maintaining a very high level of quality while working in areas as far apart as hard-science fiction and sword and sorcery.

The problem of resolving conflict has long captured the attention of sf writers, and they have responded with notions that range from single-combat to placing weapons of mass destruction in the hands of everyone. In "Wanted—An Enemy" (a mysteriously neglected story) he discusses the dangers and opportunities of the "common enemy" solution.

(Marty's mention of Fritz's Grand Master Award in 1981 reminds me of the shock I received in that connection. —No, not that he received it instead of me. I'm not that *self-centered.*

It was just that Norman Spinrad, the soft-spoken president of the Science Fiction Writers of America called me a month or so ahead of time to make sure I'd be at the banquet because he wanted me to make the presentation of the Grand Master Award. He told me Fritz would get it and swore me to secrecy.

I kept the secret. I didn't even tell my wife. The night before the award banquet, Janet and I were in a taxi with Clifford Simak who had won the Grand Master Award on a previous occasion. Cliff said to me, "I think Fritz Leiber ought to get it this time. He's a terribly under-appreciated writer." I maintained an indifferent silence, nearly bursting my shirt buttons in the effort.

Came the banquet! Did I get the reward of my having maintained secrecy under pressure? No! Norman Spinrad, forgetting completely that he had assigned me the honor, handed the Award to Fritz himself. But never mind—as long as Fritz got it. I.A.)

The bright stars of Mars made a glittering roof for a fantastic tableau. A being equipped with retinal vision would have seen an Earthman dressed in the familiar coat and trousers of the twentieth century standing on a boulder that put him a few feet above the rusty sand. His face was bony and puritanic. His eyes gleamed wildly from deep sockets. Occasionally his long hair flopped across them. His lips worked vociferously, showing big yellowed teeth, and there was a cloud of blown spittle in front of them, for he was making a speech—in the English language. He so closely resembled an old-style soapbox orator that one looked around for the lamp-post, the dull-faced listeners overflowing the curb, and the strolling cop.

But the puzzling globe of soft radiance surrounding Mr. Whitlow struck highlights from enamel-black shells and jointed legs a little resembling those of an ant under a microscope. Each individual in the crowd consisted of a yard-long oval body lacking a separate head or any sensory or other orifices in its gleaming black surface except for a small mouth that worked like a sliding door and kept opening and closing at regular intervals. To this body were attached eight of the jointed legs, the inner pairs showing highly manipulative end-organs.

These creatures were ranged in a circle around Mr. Whitlow's boulder. Facing him was one who crouched a little apart from the rest, on a smaller boulder. Flanking this one, were two whose faintly silvered shells suggested weathering and, therefore, age.

Beyond them—black desert to a horizon defined only by the blotting out of the star fields.

Low in the heavens gleamed sky-blue Earth, now Mars' evening star, riding close to the meager crescent of Phobos.

To the Martian coleopteroids this scene presented itself in a very different fashion, since they depended on perception rather than any elaborate sensory set-up. Their internal brains were directly conscious of everything within a radius of about fifty yards. For them the blue earthshine was a diffuse photonic cloud just above the threshold of perception, similar to but distinct from the photonic clouds of the starlight and faint moonshine; they could perceive no image of Earth unless they used lenses to create such an image within their perceptive range. They were conscious of the ground beneath them as a sandy hemisphere tunneled through by various wrigglers and the centipedelike burrowers. They were conscious of each other's armored, neatly-compartmented bodies, and each other's thoughts. But chiefly their attention was focused on that squidgy, uninsulated, wasteful jumble of organs that thought of itself as Mr. Whitlow—an astounding moist suppet of life on dry, miserly Mars.

The physiology of the coleopteroids was typical of a depleted-planet economy. Their shells were double; the space between could be evacuated at night to conserve heat, and flooded by day to absorb it. Their lungs were really oxygen accumulators. They inhaled the rarefied atmosphere about one hundred times for every exhalation, the double-valve mouth, permitting the building up of high internal pressure. They had one hundred percent utilization of inhaled oxygen, and exhaled pure carbon dioxide freighted with other respiratory excretions. Occasional whiffs of this exceedingly bad breath made Mr. Whitlow wrinkle his flaring nostrils.

Just what permitted Mr. Whitlow to go on functioning, even speechifying, in the chill oxygen dearth was by no means so obvious. It constituted as puzzling a question as the source of the soft glow that bathed him.

Communication between him and his audience was purely telepathic. He was speaking vocally at the request of the coleopteroids, because like most nontelepaths he could best organize and clarify his thoughts while talking. His voice died out abruptly in the thin air. It sounded like a phonograph needle scratching along without amplification, and intensified the eerie ludicrousness of his violent gestures and facial contortions.

"And so," Whitlow concluded wheezily, brushing the long hair from his forehead, "I come back to my original proposal; Will you attack Earth?"

"And we, Mr. Whitlow," thought the Chief Coleopteroid, "come back to our original question, which you still have not answered: Why should we?"

Mr. Whitlow made a grimace of frayed patience. "As I have told you several times, I cannot make a fuller explanation. But I assure you of my good faith. I will do my best to provide transportation for you, and facilitate the thing in every way. Understand, it need only be a token invasion. After a short time you can retire to Mars with your spoils. Surely you cannot afford to pass up this opportunity."

"Mr. Whitlow," replied the Chief Coleopteroid with a humor as poisonously dry as his planet, "I cannot read your thoughts unless you vocalize them. They are too confused. But I can sense your biases. You are laboring under a serious misconception as to our psychology. Evidently it is customary in your world to think of alien intelligent beings as evil monsters, whose only desire is to ravage, destroy, tyrannize, and inflict unspeakable cruelties on creatures less advanced than themselves. Nothing could be farther from the truth. We are an ancient and unemotional race. We have outgrown the passions and vanities—even the ambitions—of our youth. We undertake no projects except for sound and sufficient reason."

"But if that's the case, surely you can see the practical advantages of my proposal. At little or no risk to yourselves, you will acquire valuable loot."

The Chief Coleopteroid settled back on his boulder, and his thoughts did the same. "Mr. Whitlow, let me remind you that we have never gone to war lightly. During the whole course of our history, our only intelligent enemies have been the molluscoids of the tideless seas of Venus. In the springtide of their culture they came conquesting in their water-filled spaceships, and we fought several long and bitter wars. But eventually they attained racial maturity and a certain dispassionate wisdom, though not equivalent to our own. A perpetual truce was declared, on condition that each party stick to its own planet and attempt no more forays. For ages we have abided by that truce, living in mutual isolation. So you can see, Mr. Whitlow, that we would be anything but inclined to accept such a rash and mysterious proposal as yours."

"May I make a suggestion?" interjected the Senior Coleopteroid on the Chief's right. His thoughts flicked out subtly toward Whitlow. "You seem, Earthling, to possess powers that are perhaps even in excess of our own. Your arrival on Mars without any perceptible means of transport and your ability to endure its rigors without any obvious insulation, are sufficient proofs. From what you tell us, the other inhabitants of your planet possess no such powers. Why don't you attack them by yourself, like the solitary armored poison-worm? Why do you need our aid?"

"My friend," said Mr. Whitlow solemnly, bending forward and fixing his gaze on the silvery-shelled elder, "I abhor war as the foulest evil, and active participation in it as the greatest crime. Nonetheless, I would sacrifice myself as you suggest, could I attain my ends that way. Unfortunately, I cannot. It would not have the psychological effect I desire. Moreover"—he paused embarrassedly—"I might as well confess that I am not wholly master of my powers. I don't understand them. The workings of an inscrutable providence have put into my hands a device that is probably the handiwork of creatures vastly more intelligent than any in this solar system, perhaps even this cosmos. It enables me to cross space and time. It protects me from danger. It provides me with warmth and illumination. It concentrates your Martian atmosphere in a sphere around me, so that I can breathe normally. But as for using it in any larger way—I'd be mortally afraid of its getting out of control. My one small experiment was disastrous. I wouldn't dare."

The Senior Coleopteroid shot a guarded aside to the Chief. "Shall I try to hypnotize his disordered mind and get this device from him?"

"Do so."

"Very well, though I'm afraid the device will protect his mind as well as his body. Still, it's worth the chance."

"Mr. Whitlow," thought the Chief abruptly, "it is time we got down to cases. Every word you say makes your proposal sound more irrational, and your own motives more unintelligible. If you expect us to take any serious interest, you must give us a clear answer to one question: Why do you want us to attack Earth?"

Whitlow twisted. "But that's the one question I don't want to answer."

"Well, put it this way then," continued the Chief patiently. "What personal advantage do you expect to gain from our attack?"

Whitlow drew himself up and tucked in his necktie. "None! None whatsoever! I seek nothing for myself!"

"Do you want to rule Earth?" the Chief persisted.

"No! No! I detest all tyranny."

"Revenge, then? Has Earth hurt you and are you trying to hurt it back?"

"Absolutely not! I would never stoop to such barbaric behavior. I hate no one. The desire to see anyone injured is farthest from my thoughts."

"Come, come, Mr. Whitlow! You've just begged us to attack Earth. How can you square that with your sentiments?"

Whitlow gnawed his lip baffledly.

The Chief slipped in a quick question to the Senior Coleopteroid. "What progress?"

"None whatsoever. His mind is extraordinarily difficult to grasp. And as I anticipated, there is a shield."

Whitlow rocked uneasily on his shoulder, his eyes fixed on the star-edged horizon.

"I'll tell you this much," he said. "It's solely because I love Earth and mankind so much that I want you to attack her."

"You choose a strange way of showing your affection," the Chief observed.

"Yes," continued Whitlow, warming a bit, his eyes still lost. "I want you to do it in order to end war."

"This gets more and more mysterious. Start war to stop it? That is a paradox which demands explanation. Take care, Mr. Whitlow, or I will fall into your error of looking on alien beings as evil and demented monsters."

Whitlow lowered his gaze until it was fixed on the Chief. He sighed windily. "I guess I'd better tell you," he muttered. "You'd have probably found out in the end. Though it would have been simpler the other way—"

He pushed back the rebellious hair and massaged his forehead, a little wearily. When he spoke again it was in a less oratorical style.

"I am a pacifist. My life is dedicated to the task of preventing war. I love my fellow men. But they are steeped in error and sin. They are victims of their baser passions. Instead of marching on, hand in hand, trustingly, toward the glorious fulfillment of all their dreams, they insist on engaging in constant conflict, in vile war."

"Perhaps there is a reason for that," suggested the Chief mildly. "Some inequalities that require leveling or—"

"Please," said the pacifist reprovingly. "These wars have grown increasingly more violent and terrible. I, and others, have sought to reason with the majority, but in vain. They persist in their delusions. I have racked my brain to find a solution. I have considered every conceivable remedy. Since I came into the possession of . . . er . . . the device, I have sought throughout the cosmos and even in other time streams, for the secret of preventing war. With no success. Such intelligent races as I encountered were either engaged in war, which ruled them out, or had never known war—these were very obliging but obviously could volunteer no helpful information—or else had outgrown war by the painful and horrible process of fighting until there was nothing more to fight about."

"As we have," the Chief thought, in an undertone.

The pacifist spread his hands, palms toward the stars. "So, once more, I was thrown on my own resources. I studied mankind from every angle. Gradually I became convinced that its worst trait—and the one most responsible for war—was its overgrown sense of self-importance. On my planet man is the lord of creation. All the other animals are merely one among many—no species is pre-eminent. The flesh-eaters have their flesh-eating rivals. Each browser or gazer competes with other types for the grass and herbage. Even the fish in the seas and the myriad parasites that swarm in bloodstreams are divided into species of roughly equal ability and competence. This makes for humility and a sense of perspective. No species is inclined to fight among itself when it realizes that by so doing it will merely clear the way for the other species to take over. Man alone has no serious rivals. As a result, he had developed delusions of grandeur—and of persecution and hate. Lacking the restraint that rivalry would provide, he fouls his planetary nest with constant civil war.

"I mulled this idea for some time. I thought wistfully of how different mankind's development might have been had he been compelled to share his planet with some equally intelligent species, say a mechanically minded sea dweller. I considered, how, when great natural catastrophes occur, such as fires and floods and earthquakes and plagues, men temporarily quit squabbling and work hand in hand—rich and poor, friend and enemy alike. Unfortunately such cooperation only lasts until man once more asserts his mastery over his environment. It does not provide a constant sobering threat. And then . . . I had an inspiration."

Mr. Whitlow's gaze swept the black-shelled forms—a jumble of satiny crescent highlights ringing the sphere of light enveloping him. Similarly his mind swept their cryptically armored thoughts.

"I remembered an incident from my childhood. A radio broadcast—we make use of high velocity vibrations to transmit sound—had given an impishly realistic fictional report of an invasion of Earth by beings from Mars, beings of that evil and destructive nature which, as you say, we tend to attribute to alien life. Many believed the report. There were brief scares and panics. It occurred to me how, at the first breath of an actual invasion of that sort, warring peoples would forget their differences and join staunchly together to meet the invader. They would realize that the things they were fighting about were really trifling matters, phantoms of moodiness and fear. Their sense of perspective would be restored. They would see that the all-important fact was that they were men alike, facing a common enemy, and they would rise magnificently to the challenge. Ah my friends, when that vision occurred to me, of warring mankind at one stroke united, and united forever, I stood trembling and speechless. I—"

Even on Mars, emotion choked him.

"Very interesting," thought the Senior Coleopteroid blandly, "but wouldn't the method you propose be a contradiction of that higher morality to which I can perceive you subscribe?"

The pacifist bowed his head. "My friend, you are quite right—in the large and ultimate sense. And let me assure you"—the fire crept back into his hoarse voice—"that when that day comes, when the question of interplanetary relations arises, I will be in the vanguard of the interspecieists, demanding full equality for coleopteroid and man alike. But"—his feverish eyes peered up again through the hair that had once more fallen across his forehead—"that is a matter for the future. The immediate question is: How to stop war on Earth. As I said before, your invasion need only be a token one, and of course the more bloodless, the better. It would only take one taste of an outside menace, one convincing proof that he has equals and even superiors in the cosmos, to restore man's normalcy of outlook, to weld him into a mutually protective brotherhood, to establish peace forever!"

He threw his hands wide and his head back. His hair flipped into its proper place, but his tie popped out again.

"Mr. Whitlow," thought the Chief, with a cold sardonic merriment, "if you have any notion that we are going to invade another planet for the sake of improving the psychology of its inhabitants, disabuse yourself of it at once. Earthlings mean nothing to us. Their rise is such a recent matter that we hardly had taken note of it until you called it to our attention. Let them go on warring, if they want to. Let them kill themselves off. It is no concern of ours."

Whitlow blinked. "Why—" he started angrily. Then he caught himself. "But I wasn't asking you to do it for humanitarian reasons. I pointed out that there would be loot—"

"I very much doubt if your Earthlings have anything that would tempt us."

Whitlow almost backed off his boulder. He started to splutter something, but again abruptly changed his tack. There was a flicker of shrewdness in his expression. "Is it possible you're holding back because you're afraid the Venusian molluscoids will attack you if you violate the perpetual truce by making a foray against another planet?"

"By no means," thought the Chief harshly, revealing for the first time a certain haughtiness and racial pride bred of dry eons of tradition. "As I told you before, the molluscoids are a distinctly inferior race. Mere waterlings. We have seen nothing of them for ages. For all we know they've died out. Certainly we wouldn't be bound by any outworn agreements with them, if there were a sound and profitable reason for breaking them. And we are in no sense—no sense whatever—afraid of them."

Whitlow's thoughts fumbled confusedly, his spatulate-fingered hands making unconsiously appropriate gestures. Driven back to his former argument, he faltered lamely. "But surely then there must be some loot that would make it worth your while to invade Earth. After all, Earth is a planet rich in oxygen and water and minerals and life forms, whereas Mars has to contend with a dearth of all these things."

"Precisely," thought the Chief. "And we have developed a style of life that fits in perfectly with that dearth. By harvesting the interplanetary dust in the neighborhood of Mars, and by a judicious use of transmutation and other techniques, we are assured of a sufficient supply of all necessary raw materials. Earth's bloated abundance would be an embarrassment to us, upsetting our system. An increased oxygen supply would force us to learn a new rhythm of breathing to avoid oxygen-drowning, besides making any invasion of Earth uncomfortable and dangerous. Similar hazards might attend an oversupply of other elements and compounds. And as for Earth's obnoxiously teeming life forms, none of them would be any use to us on Mars—except for the unlucky chance of one of them finding harborage in our bodies and starting an epidemic."

Whitlow winced. Whether he knew it or not, his planetary vanity had been touched. "But you're overlooking the most important things," he argued, "the products of man's industry and ingenuity. He has changed the face of his planet much more fully than you have yours. He has covered it with roads. He does not huddle savagely in the open as you do. He has built vast cities. He has constructed all manner of vehicles. Surely among such a wealth of things you would find many to covet."

"Most unlikely," retorted the Chief. "I cannot see envisaged in your mind any that would awaken even our passing interest. We are adapted to our environment. We have no need of garments and housing and all the other artificialities which your ill-adjusted Earthlings require. Our mastery of our planet is greater than yours, but we do not advertise it so obtrusively. From your picture I can see that your Earthlings are given to a worship of bigness and a crude type of exhibitionism."

"But then there are our machines," Whitlow insisted, seething inwardly, plucking at his collar. "Machines of tremendous complexity, for every purpose. Machines that would be as useful to another species as to us."

"Yes, I can imagine them," commented the Chief cuttingly. "Huge, clumsy, jumbles of wheels and levers, wires and grids. In any case, ours are better."

He shot a swift question to the Senior. "Is his anger making his mind any more vulnerable?"

"Not yet."

Whitlow made one last effort, with great difficulty holding his indignation in check. "Besides all that, there's our art. Cultural treasures of incalculable value. The work of a species more richly creative than your own. Books, music, paintings, sculpture. Surely—"

"Mr. Whitlow, you are becoming ridiculous," said the Chief. "Art is meaningless apart from its cultural environment. What interest could we be expected to take in the fumbling self-expression of an immature species? Moreover, none of the art forms you mention would be adapted to our style of perception, save sculpture—and in that field our efforts are incomparably superior, since we have a direct consciousness of solidity. Your mind is only a shadow-mind, limited to flimsy two-dimensional patterns."

Whitlow drew himself up and folded his arms across his chest. "Very well!" he grated out. "I see I cannot persuade you. But"—he shook his finger at the Chief—"let me tell you something! You're contemptuous of man. You call him crude and childish. You pour scorn on his industry, his science, his art. You refuse to help him in his need. You think you can afford to disregard him. All right. Go ahead. That's my advice to you. Go ahead—and see what happens!" A vindictive light grew in his eyes. "I know my fellow man. From years of study I know him. War has made him a tyrant and exploiter. He has enslaved the beasts of field and forest. He has enslaved his own kind, when he could, and when he couldn't he has bound them with the subtler chains of economic necessity and the awe of prestige. He's wrongheaded, brutal, a tool of his baser impulses—and also he's clever, doggedly persistent, driven by a boundless ambition! He already has atomic power and rocket transport. In a few decades he'll have spaceships and subatomic weapons. Go ahead and wait! Constant warfare will cause him to develop those weapons to undreamed of heights of efficient destructiveness. Wait for that too! Wait until he arrives on Mars in force. Wait until he makes your acquaintance and realizes what marvelous workers you'd be with your armored adaptability to all sorts of environments. Wait until he picks a quarrel with you and defeats you and enslaves you and ships you off, packed in evil-smelling hulls, to labor in Earth's mines and on her ocean bottoms, in her stratosphere and on the planetoids that man will be desirous of exploiting. Yes, go ahead and wait!"

Whitlow broke off, his chest heaving. For a moment he was conscious only of his vicious satisfaction at having told off these exasperating beetle-creatures. Then he looked around.

The coleopteroids had drawn in. The forms of the foremost were defined with a hatefully spiderish distinctness, almost invading his sphere of light. Similarly their thoughts had drawn in, to form a menacing wall blacker than the encircling Martian night. Gone were the supercilious amusement and dispassionate withdrawal that had so irked him. Incredulously he realized that he had somehow broken through their armor and touched them on a vulnerable spot.

He caught one rapid thought, from the Senior to the Chief: "And if the rest of them are anything like this one, they'll behave just as he says. It is an added confirmation."

He looked slowly around, his hair-curtained forehead bent forward, searching for a clue to the coleopteroids' sudden change in attitude. His baffled gaze ended on the Chief.

"We've changed our minds, Mr. Whitlow," the Chief volunteered grimly. "I told you at the beginning that we never hesitate about undertaking projects when given a sound and sufficient reason. What your silly arguments about humanitarianism and loot failed to provide, your recent outburst has furnished us. It is as you say. The Earthlings will eventually attack us, and with some hope of success, if we wait. So logically we must take preventive action, the sooner the better. We will reconnoiter Earth, and if conditions there are as you assert, we will invade her."

From the depths of a confused despondency Whitlow was in an instant catapulted to the heights of feverish joy. His fanatical face beamed. His lanky frame seemed to expand. His hair flipped back.

"Marvelous!" he chortled, and then rattled on excitedly, "Of course, I'll do everything I can to help. I'll provide transport—"

"That will not be necessary," the Chief interrupted flatly. "We have no more trust in your larger powers than you have yourself. We have our own spaceships, quite adequate to any undertaking. We do not make an ostentatious display of them, any more than we make a display of the other mechanical aspects of our culture. We do not use them, as your Earthlings would, to go purposely skittering about. Nevertheless, we have them, stored away in the event of need."

But not even this contemptuous rebuff could spoil Whitlow's exultation. His face was radiant. Half-formed tears made him blink his hectic eyes. His Adam's apple bobbed chokingly.

"Ah my friends . . . my good friends! If only I could express to you . . . what this moment means to me! If I could only tell you how happy I am when I envisage the greater moment that is coming! When men will look up from their trenches and foxholes, from their bombers and fighters, from their observation posts and headquarters, from their factories and homes, to see this new menace in the skies. When all their petty differences of opinion will drop away from them like a soiled and tattered garment. When they will cut the barbed-wire entanglements of an illusory hate, and join together, hand in hand, true brothers at last, to meet the common foe. When, in the accomplishment of a common task, they will at last achieve perfect and enduring peace!"

He paused for breath. His glazed eyes were lovingly fixed on the blue star of Earth, now just topping the horizon.

"Yes," faintly came the Chief's dry thought. "To one of your emotional temperament, it will probably be a very satisfying and touching scene—for a little while."

Whitlow glanced down blankly. It was as if the Chief's last thought had lightly scratched him—a feathery flick from a huge poisoned claw. He did not understand it, but he was conscious of upwelling fear.

"What—" he faltered. "What . . . do you mean?"

"I mean," thought the Chief, "that in our invasion of Earth it probably won't be necessary for us to use the divide-and-rule tactics that would normally be indicated in such a case—you know, joining with one faction on Earth to help defeat the other—warring beings never care who their allies are—and then fomenting further disunities, and so on. No, with our superiority in armament, we can probably do a straight cleanup job and avoid bothersome machinations. So you'll probably have that glimpse of Earthlings united that you set so much store by."

Whitlow stared at him from a face white with dawning horror. He licked his lips. "What did you mean by—'for a little while'?" he whispered huskily. "What did you mean by 'glimpse'?"

"Surely that should be obvious to you, Mr. Whitlow," replied the Chief with offensive good humor. "You don't for one minute suppose we'd make some footling little invasion and, after overawing the Earthlings, retire? That would be the one way to absolutely assure their eventual counterinvasion of Mars. Indeed, it would probably hasten it—and they'd come as already hostile destroyers intent on wiping out a menace. No, Mr. Whitlow, when we invade Earth, it will be to protect ourselves from a potential future danger. Our purpose will be total and complete extermination, accomplished as swiftly and efficiently as possible. Our present military superiority makes our success certain."

Whitlow goggled at the Chief blankly, like a dirty and somewhat yellowed plaster statue of himself. He opened his mouth—and shut it without saying anything.

"You never believed, did you, Mr. Whitlow," continued the Chief kindly, "that we'd ever do anything for your sake? Or for anyone's—except us coleopteroids?"

Whitlow stared at the horrible, black, eight-legged eggs crowding ever closer—living embodiments of the poisonous blackness of their planet.

All he could think to mumble was: "But . . . but I thought you said . . . it was a misconception to think of alien beings as evil monsters intent only on ravaging . . . and destroying—"

"Perhaps I did, Mr. Whitlow. Perhaps I did," was the Chief's only reply.

In that instant Mr. Whitlow realized what an alien being really was.

As in a suffocating nightmare, he watched the coleopteroids edge closer. He heard the Chief's contemptuously unguarded aside to the Senior, "Haven't you got hold of his mind yet?" and the Senior's "No," and the Chief's swift order to the others.

Black eggs invaded his lightsphere, cruel armored claws opening to grab—those were Mr. Whitlow's last impressions of Mars.

Instants later—for the device provided him with instantaneous transportation across any spatial expanse—Mr. Whitlow found himself inside a bubble that miraculously maintained normal atmospheric pressure deep under the tideless Venusian seas. The reverse of a fish in a tank, he peered out at the gently waving luminescent vegetation and the huge mud-girt buildings it half masked. Gleaming ships and tentacled creatures darted about.

The Chief Molluscoid regarded the trespasser on his private gardens with a haughty disfavor that even surprise could not shake.

"What are you?" he thought coldly.

"I . . . I've come to inform you of a threatened breach in an agelong truce."

Five eyes on longish stalks regarded him with a coldness equal to that of the repeated thought: "But what are you?"

A sudden surge of woeful honesty compelled Mr. Whitlow to reply, "I suppose . . . I suppose you'd call me a warmonger."

BLIND ALLEY

by Isaac Asimov (1920-)

ASTOUNDING SCIENCE FICTION,
March

(I can never judge my own stories. I know which ones I like better than others—there are almost none that I actively dislike—but I can't tell which are better *than others. So Marty decides which of mine, if any, belong in any of these collections.*

I like this story because it reminds me of the one time when I was part of the bureaucracy—during World War II when I worked at the Naval Air Experimental Station in Philadelphia [*along with Robert Heinlein and L. Sprague de Camp.*] *In those years I was constantly faced with red tape and the queerly involuted system of letter-writing that I made use of in the story.*

It was a challenge and I remember once writing a specification in bureaucratese which I deliberately made as complicated and intricate as possible while adhering strictly to all the rules. I have formidable abilities in this respect and I ended up with something that I feared would get me court-martialed and it was only my sense of humor that prodded me into sending it up through the chain of command. I wasn't court-martialed. In fact, I was commended and praised for a sterling piece of work and I think it was that which gave the idea for "Blind Alley." I.A.)

Only once in Galactic History was an intelligent race of non-Humans discovered—

"Essays on History,"
by Ligurn Vier

I.

From: Bureau for the Outer Provinces
To: Loodun Antyok, Chief Public Administrator, A-8
Subject: Civilian Supervisor of Cepheus 18, Administrative Position as,
References:

(a) Act of Council 2515, of the year 971 of the Galactic Empire, entitled, "Appointment of Officials of the Administrative Service, Methods for, Revision of."

(b) Imperial Directive, Ja 2374, dated 243/975 G.E.

1. By authorization of reference (a), you are hereby appointed to the subject position. The authority of said position as Civilian Supervisor of Cepheus 18 will extend over non-Human subjects of the Emperor living upon the planet under the terms of autonomy set forth in reference (b).

2. The duties of the subject position shall comprise the general supervision of all non-Human internal affairs, co-ordination of authorized government investigating and reporting committees, and the preparation of semiannual reports on all phases of non-Human affairs.

C. Morily, Chief, BuOuProv,
12/977 G.E.

Loodun Antyok had listened carefully, and now he shook his round head mildly, "Friend, I'd like to help you, but you've grabbed the wrong dog by the ears. You'd better take this up with the Bureau."

Tomor Zammo flung himself back into his chair, rubbed his beak of a nose fiercely, thought better of whatever he was going to say, and answered quietly, "Logical, but not practical. I can't make a trip to Trantor now. You're the Bureau's representative on Cepheus 18. Are you entirely helpless?"

"Well, even as Civilian Supervisor, I've got to work within the limits of Bureau policy."

"Good," Zammo cried, "then, tell me what Bureau policy is. I head a scientific investigating committee, under direct Imperial authorization with, supposedly, the widest powers; yet at every angle in the road I am pulled up short by the civilian authorities with only the parrot shriek of 'Bureau policy' to justify themselves. What *is* Bureau policy? I haven't received a decent definition yet."

Antyok's gaze was level and unruffled. He said, "As I see it—and this is not official, so you can't hold me to it—Bureau policy consists in treating the non-Humans as decently as possible."

"Then, what authority have they—"

"*Ssh!* No use raising your voice. As a matter of fact, His Imperial Majesty is a humanitarian and a disciple of the philosophy of Aurelion. I can tell you quietly that it is pretty well-known that it is the Emperor himself who first suggested that this world be established. You can bet that Bureau policy will stick pretty close to Imperial notions. And you can bet that I can't paddle my way against *that* sort of current."

"Well, m'boy," the physiologist's fleshy eyelids quivered, "if you take that sort of attitude, you're going to lose your job. No, I won't have you kicked out. That's not what I mean at all. Your job will just fade out from under you, because nothing is going to be accomplished here!"

"Really? Why?" Antyok was short, pink, and pudgy, and his plump-cheeked face usually found it difficult to put on display any expression other than one of bland and cheerful politeness—but it looked grave now.

"You haven't been here long. I have." Zammo scowled. "Mind if I smoke?" The cigar in his hand was gnarled and strong and was puffed to life carelessly.

He continued roughly, "There's no place here for humanitarianism, administrator. You're treating non-Humans as if they were Humans, and it won't work. In fact, I don't like the word 'non-Human.' They're animals."

"They're intelligent," interjected Antyok softly.

"Well, intelligent animals, then. I presume the two terms are not mutually exclusive. Alien intelligences mingling in the same space won't work, anyway."

"Do you propose killing them off?"

"Galaxy, no!" He gestured with his cigar. "I propose we

look upon them as objects for study, and only that. We could learn a good deal from these animals if we were allowed to. Knowledge, I might point out, that would be used for the immediate benefit of the human race. *There's* humanity for you. *There's* the good of the masses, if it's this spineless cult of Aurelion that interests you."

"What, for instance, do you refer to?"

"To take the most obvious—You have heard of their chemistry, I take it?"

"Yes," Antyok admitted. "I have leafed through most of the reports on the non-Humans published in the last ten years. I expect to go through more."

"Hmp. Well— Then, all I need to say is that their chemical therapy is extremely thorough. For instance, I have witnessed personally the healing of a broken bone—what passes for a broken bone with them, I mean—by the use of a pill. The bone was whole in fifteen minutes. Naturally, none of their drugs are any earthly use on Humans. Most would kill quickly. But if we found out how they worked on the non-Humans—on the animals—"

"Yes, yes. I see the significance."

"Oh, you do. Come, that's gratifying. A second point is that these animals communicate in an unknown manner."

"Telepathy!"

The scientist's mouth twisted, as he ground out, "Telepathy! Telepathy! Telepathy! Might as well say by witch brew. Nobody knows anything about telepathy except its name. What is the mechanism of telepathy? What is the physiology and the physics of it? I would like to find out, but I can't. Bureau policy if I listen to you, forbids."

Anytok's little mouth pursed itself. "But— Pardon me, doctor, but I don't follow you. How are you prevented? Surely the Civil Administration has made no attempt to hamper scientific investigation of these non-Humans. I cannot speak for my predecessor entirely, of course, but I myself—"

"No direct interference has occurred. I don't speak of that. But by the Galaxy, administrator, we're hampered by the spirit of the entire set-up. You're making us deal with Humans. You allow them their own leader and internal autonomy. You pamper them and give them what Aurelion's philosophy would call 'rights.' I can't deal with their leader."

"Why not?"

"Because he refuses to allow me a free hand. He refuses to allow experiments on any subject without the subject's own consent. The two or three volunteers we get are not too bright. It's an impossible arrangement."

Antyok shrugged helplessly.

Zammo continued, "In addition, it is obviously impossible to learn anything of value concerning the brains, physiology, and chemistry of these animals without dissection, dietary experiments, and drugs. You know, administrator, scientific investigation is a hard game. Humanity hasn't much place in it."

Loodun Antyok tapped his chin with a doubtful finger, "Must it be quite so hard? These are harmless creatures, these non-Humans. Surely, dissection— Perhaps, if you were to approach them a bit differently—I have the idea that you antagonize them. Your attitude might be somewhat overbearing."

"Overbearing! I am not one of these whining social psychologists who are all the fad these days. I don't believe you can solve a problem that requires dissection by approaching it with what is called the 'correct personal attitude' in the cant of the times."

"I'm sorry you think so. Sociopsychological training is required of all administrators above the grade of A-4."

Zammo withdrew his cud of a cigar from his mouth and replaced it after a suitably contemptuous interval, "Then you'd better use a bit of your technique on the Bureau. You know, I *do* have friends at the Imperial court."

"Well, now, I *can't* take the matter up with them, not baldly. Basic policy does not fall within my cognizance, and such things can only be initiated by the Bureau. But, you know, we might try an indirect approach on this." He smiled faintly, "Strategy."

"What sort?"

Antyok pointed a sudden finger, while his other hand fell lightly on the rows of gray-bound reports upon the floor just next his chair, "Now, look, I've gone through most of these. They're dull, but contain *some* facts. For instance, when was the last non-Human infant born on Cepheus 18?"

Zammo spent little time in consideration. "Don't know. Don't care either."

"But the Bureau would. There's *never* been a non-Human infant born on Cepheus 18—not in the two years the world has been established. Do you know the reason?"

The physiologist shrugged, "Too many possible factors. It would take study."

"All right, then. Suppose you write a report—"

"Reports! I've written twenty."

"Write another. Stress the unsolved problems. Tell them you must change your methods. Harp on the birth-rate problem. The bureau doesn't dare ignore that. If the non-Humans die out, someone will have to answer to the Emperor. You see—"

Zammo stared, his eyes dark, "That will swing it?"

"I've been working for the Bureau for twenty-seven years. I know its way."

"I'll think about it." Zammo rose and stalked out of the office. The door slammed behind him.

It was later that Zammo said to a co-worker, "He's a bureaucrat, in the first place. He won't abandon the orthodoxies of paper work and he won't risk sticking his neck out. He'll accomplish little by himself, yet maybe more than a little if we work through him."

From: Administrative Headquarters, Cepheus 18
To: BuOuProv
Subject: Outer Province Project 2563, Part II—Scientific Investigations of non-Humans of Cepheus 18, Coordination of,

References:

(a) BuOuProv letr. Cep-N-CM/jg, 100132, dated 302/975 G.E.

(b) AdHQ-Ceph18 letr. AA-LA/mn, dated 140/977 G.E.

Enclosure:

1. SciGroup 10, Physical & Biochemical Division, Report, entitled, "Physiologic Characteristics of non-Humans of Cepheus 18, Part XI," dated 172/977 G.E.

1. Enclosure 1, included herewith, is forwarded for the information of the BuOuProv. It is to be noted that Section XII, paragraphs 1–16 of Encl. 1, concern possible changes in present BuOuProv policy with regard to non-Humans with a view to facilitating physical and chemical investigations at present proceeding under authorization of reference (a)

2. It is brought to the attention of the BuOuProv that reference (b) has already discussed possible changes in investigating methods and that it remains the opinion of AdHQ-Ceph18 that such changes are as yet premature.

It is nevertheless suggested that the question of non-Human birth rate be made the subject of a BuOuProv project assigned to AdHQ-Ceph18 in view of the importance attached by SciGroup 10 to the problem, as evidenced in Section V of Enclosure 1.

L. Antyok, Supery, AdHQ-Ceph18,
174/977

From: BuOuProv
To: AdHQ-Ceph18
Subject: Outer Province Project 2563—Scientific Investigations of non-Humans of Cepheus 18, Co-ordination of,
Reference:
(a) AdHQ-Ceph18 letr. AA-LA/mn, dated 174/977 G.E.

1. In response to the suggestion contained in paragraph 2 of reference (a), it is considered that the question of the non-Human birth rate does not fall within the cognizance of AdHQ-Ceph18. In view of the fact that SciGroup 10 has reported said sterility to be probably due to a chemical deficiency in the food supply, all investigations in the field are relegated to SciGroup 10 as the proper authority.

2. Investigating procedures by the various SciGroups shall continue according to current directives on the subject. No changes in policy are envisaged.

C. Morily, Chief, BuOuProv,
186/977 G.E.

II.

There was a loose-jointed gauntness about the news reporter which made him appear somberly tall. He was Gustiv Bannerd, with whose reputation was combined ability—two things which do not invariably go together despite the maxims of elementary morality.

Loodum Antyok took his measure doubtfully and said, "There's no use denying that you're right. But the SciGroup report was confidential. I don't understand how—"

"It leaked," said Bannerd, callously. "Everything leaks."

Antyok was obviously baffled, and his pink face furrowed slightly, "Then I'll just have to plug the leak here. I can't pass your story. All references to SciGroup complaints have to come out. You see that, don't you?"

"No." Bannerd was calm enough. "It's important; and I have my rights under the Imperial directive. I think the Empire should know what's going on."

"But it isn't going on," said Antyok, despairingly. "Your claims are all wrong. The Bureau isn't going to change its policy. I showed you the letters."

"You think you can stand up against Zammo when he puts the pressure on?" the newsman asked derisively.

"I will—if I think he's wrong."

"If!" stated Bannerd flatly. Then, in a sudden fervor, "Antyok, the Empire has something great here; something greater by a good deal than the government apparently realizes. They're destroying it. They're treating these creatures like animals."

"Really—" began Antyok, weakly.

"Don't talk about Cepheus 18. It's a zoo. It's a high-class zoo, with your petrified scientists teasing those poor creatures with their sticks poking through the bars. You throw them chunks of meat, but you cage them up. I know! I've been writing about them for two years now. I've almost been living with them."

"Zammo says—"

"Zammo!" This with hard contempt.

"Zammo says," insisted Antyok with worried firmness, "that we treat them too like Humans as it is."

The newsman's straight, long cheeks were rigid, "Zammo is rather animallike in his own right. He is a science-worshiper. We can do with less of them. Have you read Aurelion's works?" The last was suddenly posed.

"Umm. Yes. I understand the Emperor—"

"The Emperor tends toward us. That is good—better than the hounding of the last reign."

"I don't see where you're heading."

"These aliens have much to teach us. You understand? It is nothing that Zammo and his SciGroup can use; no chemistry, no telepathy. It's a way of life; a way of thinking. The aliens have no crime, no misfits. What effort is being made to study their philosophy? Or to set them up as a problem in social engineering?"

Antyok grew thoughtful, and his plump face smoothed out. "It is an interesting consideration. It would be a matter for psychologists—"

"No good. Most of them are quacks. Psychologists point

out problems, but their solutions are fallacious. We need men of Aurelion. Men of The Philosophy—"

"But look here, we can't turn Cepheus 18 into . . . into a metaphysical study."

"Why not? It can be done easily."

"How?"

"Forget your puny test-tube peerings. Allow the aliens to set up a society free of Humans. Give them an untrammeled independence and allow an intermingling of philosophies—"

Antyok's nervous response came, "That can't be done in a day."

"We can start in a day."

The administrator said slowly, "Well, I can't prevent you from trying to start." He grew confidential, his mild eyes thoughtful, "You'll ruin your own game, though, if you publish SciGroup 10's report and denounce it on humanitarian grounds. The Scientists are powerful."

"And we of The Philosophy as well."

"Yes, but there's an easy way. You needn't rave. Simply point out that the SciGroup is not solving its problems. Do so unemotionally and let the readers think out your point of view for themselves. Take the birth-rate problem, for instance. *There's* something for you. In a generation, the non-Humans might die out, for all science can do. Point out that a more philosophical approach is required. Or pick some other obvious point. Use your judgment, eh?"

Antyok smiled ingratiatingly as he arose, "But, for the Galaxy's sake, don't stir up a bad smell."

Bannerd was stiff and unresponsive, "You may be right."

It was later that Bannerd wrote in a capsule message to a friend, "He is not clever, by any means. He is confused and has no guiding line through life. Certainly utterly incompetent in his job. But he's a cutter and a trimmer, compromises his way around difficulties, and will yield concessions rather than risk a hard stand. He may prove valuable in that. Yours in Aurelion."

From: AdHQ-Ceph18
To: BuOuProv
Subject: Birth rate of non-Humans on Cepheus 18, News Report on.
References:
(a) AdHQ-Ceph18 letr. AA-LA/mn, dated 174/977 G.E.

(b) Imperial Directive, Ja2374, dated 243/975 G.E.

Enclosures:

1-G. Bannerd news report, date-lined Cepheus 18, 201/977 G.E.

2-G. Bannerd news report, date-lined Cepheus 18, 203/977 G.E.

1. The sterility of non-Humans on Cepheus 18, reported to the BuOuProv in reference (a), has become the subject of news reports to the galactic press. The news reports in question are submitted herewith for the information of the BuOuProv as Enclosures 1 and 2. Although said reports are based on material considered confidential and closed to the public, the news reporter in question maintained his rights to free expression under the terms of reference (b).

2. In view of the unavoidable publicity and misunderstanding on the part of the general public now inevitable, it is requested that the BuOuProv direct future policy on the problem of non-Human sterility.

L. Antyok, Superv. AdHQ-Ceph18,
209/977 G.E.

From: BuOuProv

To: AdHQ-Ceph18

Subject: Birth rate of non-Humans on Cepheus 18, Investigation of.

References:

a() AdHQ-Ceph18 letr. AA-LA/mn, dated 209/977 G.E.

(b) AdHQ-Ceph18 letr. AA-LA/mn, dated 174/977 G.E.

1. It is proposed to investigate the causes and the means of precluding the unfavorable birth-rate phenomena mentioned in references (a) and (b). A project is therefore set up, entitled, "Birth rate of non-Humans on Cepheus 18, Investigation of" to which, in view of the crucial importance of the subject, a priority of AA is given.

2. The number assigned to the subject project is 2910, and all expenses incidental to it shall be assigned to Appropriation number 18/78.

C. Morily, Chief, BuOuProv,
223/977 G.E.

III.

If Tomor Zammo's ill-humor lessened within the grounds of SciGroup 10 Experimental Station, his friendliness had not thereby increased. Antyok found himself standing alone at the viewing window into the main field laboratory.

The main field laboratory was a broad court set at the environmental conditions of Cepheus 18 itself for the discomfort of the experimenters and the convenience of the experimentees. Through the burning sand, and the dry, oxygen-rich air, there sparkled the hard brilliance of hot, white sunlight. And under the blaze, the brick-red non-Humans, wrinkled of skin and wiry of build, huddled in their squatting positions of ease, by ones and twos.

Zammo emerged from the laboratory. He paused to drink water thirstily. He looked up, moisture gleaming on his upper lip. "Like to step in there?"

Antyok shook his head definitely. "No, thank you. What's the temperature right now?"

"A hundred twenty, if there were shade. And they complain of the cold. It's drinking time now. Want to watch them drink?"

A spray of water shot upward from the fountain in the center of the court, and the little alien figures swayed to their feet and hopped eagerly forward in a queer, springy half-run. They milled about the water, jostling one another. The centers of their faces were suddenly disfigured by the projection of a long and flexible fleshy tube, which thrust forward into the spray and was withdrawn dripping.

It continued for long minutes. The bodies swelled and the wrinkles disappeared. They retreated slowly, backing away, with the drinking tube flicking in and out, before receding finally into a pink, wrinkled mass above a wide, lipless mouth. They went to sleep in groups in the shaded angles, plump and sated.

"Animals!" said Zammo, with contempt.

"How often do they drink?" asked Antyok.

"As often as they want. They can go a week if they have to. We water them every day. They store it under their skin. They eat in the evenings. Vegetarians, you know."

Antyok smiled chubbily, "It's nice to get a bit of first-hand information occasionally. Can't read reports all the time."

"Yes?"—noncommittally. Then, "What's new? What about the lacy-pants boys on Trantor?"

Antyok shrugged dubiously. "You can't get the Bureau to commit itself, unfortunately. With the Emperor sympathetic to the Aurelionists, humanitarianism is the order of the day. You know that."

There was a pause in which the administrator chewed his lip uncertainly. "But there's this birth-rate problem now. It's finally been assigned to AdHQ, you know—and double A priority, too."

Zammo muttered wordlessly.

Antyok said, "You may not realize it, but that project will now take precedence over all other work proceeding on Cepheus 18. It's important."

He turned back to the viewing window and said thoughtfully with a bald lack of preamble. "Do you think those creatures might be unhappy?"

"Unhappy!" The word was an explosion.

"Well, then," Antyok corrected hastily, "maladjusted. You understand? It's difficult to adjust an environment to a race we know so little of."

"Say—did you ever see the world we took them from?"

"I've read the reports—"

"Reports!"—infinite contempt. "I've *seen* it. This may look like desert out there to you, but it's a watery paradise to those devils. They have all the food and water they can get. They have a world to themselves with vegetation and natural water flow, instead of a lump of silica and granite where fungi were force-grown in caves and water had to be steamed out of gypsum rock. In ten years, they would have been dead to the last beast, and we saved them. Unhappy? Ga-a-ah, if they are, they haven't the decency of most animals."

"Well, perhaps. Yet I have a notion."

"A notion? What is your notion?" Zammo reached for one of his cigars.

"It's something that might help you. Why not study the creatures in a more integrated fashion? Let them use their initiative. After all, they did have a highly developed science. Your reports speak of it continually. Give them problems to solve."

"Such as?"

"Oh . . . oh," Antyok waved his hands helplessly. "Whatever you think might help most. For instance, spaceships. Get them into the control room and study their reactions."

"Why?" asked Zammo with dry bluntness.

"Because the reaction of their minds to tools and controls adjusted to the human temperament can teach you a lot. In addition, it will make a more effective bribe, it seems to me, than anything you've yet tried. You'll get more volunteers if they think they'll be doing something interesting."

"That's your psychology coming out. Hm-m-m. Sounds better than it probably is. I'll sleep on it. And where would I get permission, in any case, to let them handle spaceships? I've none at *my* disposal, and it would take a good deal longer than it was worth to follow down the line of red tape to get one assigned to us."

Antyok pondered, and his forehead creased lightly, "It doesn't *have* to be spaceships. But even so—If you would write up another report and make the suggestion yourself—strongly, you understand—I might figure out some way of tying it up with my birth-rate project. A double-A priority can get practically anything, you know, without questions."

Zammo's interest lacked a bit even of mildness, "Well, maybe. Meanwhile, I've some basal metabolism tests in progress, and it's getting late. I'll think about it. It's got its points."

From: AdHQ-Ceph18

To: BuOuProv

Subject: Outer Province Project 2910, Part I—Birth rate of non-Humans on Cepheus 18, Investigation of,

Reference:

(a) BuOuProv letr. Ceph-N-CM/car, 115097, 223/977 G.E.

Enclosure:

1. SciGroup 10, Physical & Biochemical Division report, Part XV, dated 220/977 G.E.

1. Enclosure 1 is forwarded herewith for the information of the BuOuProv.

2. Special attention is directed to Section V, Paragraph 3 of Enclosure 1 in which it is requested that a spaceship be assigned SciGroup 10 for use in expediting investigations authorized by the BuOuProv. It is considered by AdHQ-Ceph18 that such investigation may be of material use in aiding work now in progress on the subject project, authorized by reference (a). It is suggested, in view of the high priority placed by the BuOuProv upon

the subject project, that immediate consideration be given the SciGroup's request.

L. Antyok, Superv. AdHQ-Ceph18,
240/977 G.E.

From: BuOuProv
To: AdHQ-Ceph18
Subject: Outer Province Project 2910—Birth rate of non-Humans on Cepheus 18, Investigation of.
Reference:
(a) AdHQ-Ceph18 letr. AA-LA/mn, dated 240/977 G.E.

1. Training Ship *AN-R-2055* is being placed at the disposal of AdHQ-Ceph18 for use in investigation of non-Humans on Cepheus 18 with respect to the subject project and other authorized OuProv projects, as requested in Enclosure 1 to reference (a).

2. It is urgently requested that work on the subject project be expedited by all available means.

C. Morily, Head, BuOuProv,
251/977 G.E.

IV.

The little bricky creature must have been more uncomfortable than his bearing would admit to. He was carefully wrapped in a temperature already adjusted to the point where his human companions steamed in their open shirts.

His speech was high-pitched and careful, "I find it damp, but not unbearably so at this low temperature."

Antyok smiled, "It was nice of you to come. I had planned to visit you, but a trial run in your atmosphere out there—" The smile had become rueful.

"It doesn't matter. You other worldlings have done more for us than ever we were able to do for ourselves. It is an obligation that is but imperfectly returned by the endurance on my part of a trifling discomfort." His speech seemed always indirect, as if he approached his thoughts sidelong, or as if it were against all etiquette to be blunt.

Gustiv Bannerd, seated in an angle of the room, with one long leg crossing the other, scrawled nimbly and said, "You don't mind if I record all this?"

The Cepheid non-Human glanced briefly at the journalist, "I have no objection."

Antyok's apologetics persisted, "This is not a purely social affair, sir. I would not have forced discomfort on you for that. There are important questions to be considered, and you are the leader of your people."

The Cepheid nodded, "I am satisfied your purposes are kindly. Please proceed."

The administrator almost wriggled in his difficulty in putting thoughts into words. "It is a subject," he said, "of delicacy, and one I would never bring up if it weren't for the overwhelming importance of the . . . uh . . . question. I am only the spokesman of my government—"

"My people consider the otherworld government a kindly one."

"Well, yes, they are kindly. For that reason, they are disturbed over the fact that your people no longer breed."

Antyok paused, and waited with worry for a reaction that did not come. The Cepheid's face was motionless except for the soft, trembling motion of the wrinkled area that was his deflated drinking tube.

Antyok continued, "It is a question we have hesitated to bring up because of its extremely personal angles. Noninterference is my government's prime aim, and we have done our best to investigate the problem quietly and without disturbing your people. But, frankly, we—"

"Have failed?" finished the Cepheid, at the other's pause.

"Yes. Or at least, we have not discovered a concreté failure to reproduce the exact environment of your original world; with, of course, the necessary modification to make it more livable. Naturally, it is thought there is some chemical shortcoming. And so I ask your voluntary help in the matter. Your people are advanced in the study of your own biochemistry. If you do not choose, or would rather not—"

"No, no, I can help." The Cepheid seemed cheerful about it. The smooth flat planes of his loose-skinned, hairless skull wrinkled in an alien response to an uncertain emotion. "It is not a matter that any of us would have thought would have disturbed you other-worldlings. That it does is but another indication of your well-meaning kindness. This world we find congenial, a paradise in comparison to our old. It lacks in nothing. Conditions such as now prevail belong in our legends of the Golden Age."

"Well—"

"But there is a something; a something you may not understand. We cannot expect different intelligences to think alike."

"I shall try to understand."

The Cepheid's voice had grown soft, its liquid undertones more pronounced, "We were dying on our native world; but we were fighting. Our science, developed through a history older than yours, was losing; but it had not yet lost. Perhaps it was because our science was fundamentally biological, rather than physical as yours is. Your people discovered new forms of energy and reached the stars. Our people discovered new truths of psychology and psychiatry and built up a working society free of disease and crime.

"There is no need to question which of the two angles of approach was the more laudable, but there is no uncertainty as to which proved more successful in the end. In our dying world, without the means of life or sources of power, our biological science could but make the dying easier.

"And yet we fought. For centuries past, we had been groping toward the elements of atomic power, and slowly the spark of hope had glimmered that we might break through the two-dimensional limits of our planetary surface and reach the stars. There were no other planets in our system to serve as stepping stones. Nothing but some twenty light-years to the nearest star, without the knowledge of the possibility of the existence of other planetary systems, but rather of the contrary.

"But there is something in all life that insists on striving; even on useless striving. There were only five thousand of us left in the last days. Only five thousand. And our first ship was ready. It was experimental. It would probably have been a failure. But already we had all the principles of propulsion and navigation correctly worked out."

There was a long pause, and the Cepheid's small black eyes seemed glazed in recollection.

The newspaperman put in suddenly, from his corner, "And then we came?"

"And then you came," the Cepheid agreed simply. "It changed everything. Energy was ours for the asking. A new world, congenial and, indeed, ideal, was ours even without asking. If our problems of society had long been solved by ourselves, our more difficult problems of environment were suddenly solved for us, no less completely."

"Well?" urged Antyok.

"Well—it was somehow not well. For centuries, our ancestors had fought toward the stars, and now the stars suddenly proved to be the property of others. We had fought for life, and it had become a present handed to us by others. There is no longer any reason to fight. There is no longer anything to attain. All the universe is the property of your race."

"This world is yours," said Antyok gently.

"By sufferance. It is a gift. It is not ours by right."

"You have earned it, in my opinion."

And now the Cepheid's eyes were sharply fixed on the other's countenance, "You mean well, but I doubt that you understand. We have nowhere to go, save this gift of a world. We are in a blind alley. The function of life is striving, and that is taken from us. Life can no longer interest us. We have no offspring—voluntarily. It is our way of removing ourselves from your way."

Absent-mindedly, Antyok had removed the fluoroglobe from the window seat, and spun it on its base. Its gaudy surface reflected light as it spun, and its three-foot-high bulk floated with incongruous grace and lightness in the air.

Antyok said, "Is that your only solution? Sterility?"

"We might escape still," whispered the Cepheid, "but where in the Galaxy is there place for us? It is all yours."

"Yes, there is no place for you nearer than the Magellanic Clouds if you wished independence. The Magellanic Clouds—"

"And you would not let us go of yourselves. You mean kindly, I know."

"Yes, we mean kindly—but we could not let you go."

"It is a mistaken kindness."

"Perhaps, but could you not reconcile yourselves? You have a world."

"It is something past complete explanations. Your mind is different. We could not reconcile ourselves, I believe, administrator, that you have thought of all this before. The concept of the blind alley we find ourselves trapped in is not new to you."

Antyok looked up, startled, and one hand steadied the fluoroglobe, "Can you read my mind?"

"It is just a guess. A good one, I think."

"Yes—but *can* you read my mind? The minds of Humans

in general, I mean. It is an interesting point. The scientists say you cannot, but sometimes I wonder if it is that you simply will not. Could you answer that? I am detaining you, unduly, perhaps."

"No . . . no—" But the little Cepheid drew his enveloping robe closer, and buried his face in the electrically heated pad at the collar for a moment. "You other-worldlings speak of reading minds. It is not so at all, but it is assuredly hopeless to explain."

Antyok mumbled the old proverb, "One cannot explain sight to a man blind from birth."

"Yes, just so. This sense which you call 'mind reading,' quite erroneously, cannot be applied to us. It is not that we cannot receive the proper sensations, it is that your people do not transmit them, and we have no way of explaining to you how to go about it."

"Hm-m-m."

"There are times, of course, of great concentration or emotional tension on the part of an other-worldling when some of us who are more expert in this sense; more sharp-eyed, so to speak; detect vaguely *something*. It is uncertain; yet I myself have at times wondered—"

Carefully, Antyok began spinning the fluoroglobe once more. His pink face was set in thought, and his eyes were fixed upon the Cepheid. Gustiv Bannerd stretched his fingers and reread his notes, his lips moving silently.

The fluoroglobe spun, and slowly the Cepheid seemed to grow tense as well, as his eyes shifted to the colorful sheen of the globe's fragile surface.

The Cepheid said, "What is that?"

Antyok started, and his face smoothed into an almost chuckling placidity, "This? A Galactic fad of three years ago; which means that it is a hopelessly old-fashioned relic this year. It is a useless device but it looks pretty. Bannerd, could you adjust the windows to nontransmission?"

There was a soft click of a contact, and the windows became curved regions of darkness, while in the center of the room, the fluoroglobe was suddenly the focus of a rosy effulgence that seemed to leap outward in streamers. Antyok, a scarlet figure in a scarlet room, placed it upon the table and spun it with a hand that dripped red. As it spun, the colors changed with a slowly increasing rapidity, blended and fell apart into more extreme contrasts.

Antyok was speaking in an eerie atmosphere of molten, shifting rainbow, "The surface is of a material that exhibits variable fluorescence. It is almost weightless, extremely fragile, but gyroscopically balanced so that it rarely falls, with ordinary care. It is rather pretty, don't you think?"

From somewhere the Cepheid's voice came, "Extremely pretty."

"But it has outworn its welcome; outlived its fashionable existence."

The Cepheid's voice was abstracted, "It is very pretty."

Bannerd restored the light at a gesture, and the colors faded.

The Cepheid said, "That is something my people would enjoy." He stared at the globe with fascination.

And now Antyok rose. "You had better go. If you stay longer, the atmosphere may have bad effects. I thank you humbly for your kindness."

"I thank you humbly for yours." The Cepheid had also risen.

Antyok said, "Most of your people, by the way, have accepted our offers to them to study the make-up of our modern spaceships. You understand, I suppose, that the purpose was to study the reactions of your people to our technology. I trust that conforms with your sense of propriety."

"You need not apologize. I, myself, have not the makings of a human pilot. It was most interesting. It recalls our own efforts—and reminds us of how nearly on the right track we were."

The Cepheid left, and Antyok sat, frowning.

"Well," he said to Bannerd, a little sharply. "You remember our agreement, I hope. This interview can't be published."

"Bannerd shrugged, "Very well."

Antyok was at his seat, and his fingers fumbled with the small metal figurine upon his desk, "What do you think of all this, Bannerd?"

"I am sorry for them. I think I understand how they feel. We must educate them out of it. The Philosophy can do it."

"You think so?"

"Yes."

"We can't let them go, of course."

"Oh, no. Out of the question. We have too much to learn from them. This feeling of theirs is only a passing stage. They'll think differently, especially when we allow them the completest independence."

"Maybe. What do you think of the fluoroglobes, Bannerd? He liked them. It might be a gesture of the right sort to order several thousand of them. The Galaxy knows, they're a drug on the market right now, and cheap enough."

"Sounds like a good idea," said Bannerd.

"The Bureau would never agree, though. I know them."

The newsman's eyes narrowed, "But it might be just the thing. They need new interests."

"Yes? Well, we *could* do something. I could include your transcript of the interview as part of a report and just emphasize the matter of the globes a bit. After all, you're a member of The Philosophy and might have influence with important people, whose word with the Bureau might carry much more weight than mine. You understand—?"

"Yes," mused Bannerd. "Yes."

From: AdHQ-Ceph18
To: BuOuProv
Subject: OuProv Project 2910, Part II; Birth rate of non-Humans on Cepheus 18, Investigation of.
Reference:
(a) BuOuProv letr. Cep-N-CM/car, 115097, dated 223/977 G.E.
Enclosure:
1. Transcript of conversation between L. Antyok of AdHQ-Ceph18, and Ni-San, High Judge of the non-Humans on Cepheus 18.

1. Enclosure 1 is forwarded herewith for the information of the BuOuProv.

2. The investigation of the subject undertaken in response to the authorization of reference (a) is being pursued along the new lines indicated in Enclosure 1. The BuOuProv is assured that every means will be used to combat the harmful psychological attitude at present prevalent among the non-Humans.

3. It is to be noted that the High Judge of the non-Humans on Cepheus 18 expressed interest in fluoroglobes. A preliminary investigation into this fact of non-Human psychology has been initiated.

L. Antyok, Superv. AdHQ-Ceph18,
272/977 G.E.

From: BuOuProv
To: AdHQ-Ceph18
Subject: OuProv Project 2910; Birth rate of non-Humans on Cepheus 18, Investigation of.
Reference:
(a) AdHQ-Ceph18 letr. AA-LA/mn, dated 272/977 G.E.

1. With reference to Enclosure 1 of reference (a), five thousand fluoroglobes have been allocated for shipment to Cepheus 18, by the Department of Trade.

2. It is instructed that AdHQ-Ceph18 make use of all methods of appeasing non-Human's dissatisfaction, consistent with the necessities of obedience to Imperial proclamations.

C. Morily, Chief, BuOuProv,
283/977 G.E.

V.

The dinner was over, the wine had been brought in, and the cigars were out. The groups of talkers had formed, and the captain of the merchant fleet was the center of the largest. His brilliant white uniform quite outsparkled his listeners.

He was almost complacent in his speech: "The trip was nothing. I've had more than three hundred ships under me before this. Still, I've never had a cargo quite like this. What do you want with five thousand fluoroglobes on this desert, by the Galaxy!"

Loodun Antyok laughed gently. He shrugged. "For the non-Humans. It wasn't a difficult cargo, I hope."

"No, not difficult. But bulky. They're fragile, and I couldn't carry more than twenty to a ship, with all the government regulations concerning packing and precautions against breakage. But it's the government's money, I suppose."

Zammo smiled grimly. "Is this your first experience with government methods, captain?"

"Galaxy, no," exploded the spaceman. "I try to avoid it, of course, but you can't help getting entangled on occasion. And it's an abhorrent thing when you are, and that's the truth. The red tape! The paper work! It's enough to stunt your growth and curdle your circulation. It's a tumor, a cancerous growth on the Galaxy. I'd wipe out the whole mess."

Antyok said, "You're unfair, captain. You don't understand."

"Yes? Well, now, as one of these bureaucrats," and he smiled amiably at the word, "suppose you explain your side of the situation, administrator."

"Well, now," Antyok seemed confused, "government is a serious and complicated business. We've got thousands of planets to worry about in this Empire of ours and billions of people. It's almost past human ability to supervise the business of governing without the tightest sort of organization. I think there are something like four hundred million men today in the Imperial Administrative Service alone, and in order to co-ordinate their efforts and to pool their knowledge, you *must* have what you call red tape and paper work. Every bit of it, senseless though it may seem, annoying though it may be, has its uses. Every piece of paper is a thread binding the labors of four hundred million Humans. Abolish the Administrative Service and you abolish the Empire; and with it, interstellar peace, order, and civilization."

"Come—" said the captain.

"No. I mean it." Antyok was earnestly breathless. "The rules and system of the Administrative set-up must be sufficiently all-embracing and rigid so that in case of incompetent officials, and sometimes one *is* appointed—you may laugh, but there are incompetent scientists, and newsmen, and captains, too—in case of incompetent officials, I say, little harm will be done. For, at the worst, the system can move by itself."

"Yes," grunted the captain, sourly, "and if a capable administrator should be appointed? He is then caught by the same rigid web and is forced into mediocrity."

"Not at all," replied Antyok warmly. "A capable man can work within the limits of the rules and accomplish what he wishes."

"How?" asked Bannerd.

"Well . . . well—" Antyok was suddenly ill at ease. "One method is to get yourself an A-priority project, or double-A, if possible."

The captain leaned his head back for laughter, but never quite made it, for the door was flung open and frightened men were pouring in. The shouts made no sense at first. Then:

"Sir, the ships are gone. These non-Humans have taken them by force."

"What? All?"

"Every one. Ships and creatures—"

It was two hours later that the four were together again, alone in Antyok's office now.

Antyok said coldly, "They've made no mistakes. There's not a ship left behind, not even your training ship, Zammo. And there isn't a government ship available in this entire half of the Sector. By the time we organize a pursuit they'll be out of the Galaxy and halfway to the Magellanic Clouds. Captain, it was your responsibility to maintain an adequate guard."

The captain cried, "It was our first day out of space. Who could have known—"

Zammo interrupted fiercely, "Wait a while, captain. I'm beginning to understand. Antyok," his voice was hard, "you engineered this."

"I?" Antyok's expression was strangely cool, almost indifferent.

"You told us this evening that a clever administrator got an A-priority project assigned to accomplish what he wished. You got such a project in order to help the non-Humans escape."

"I did? I beg your pardon, but how could that be? It was you yourself in one of your reports that brought up the problem of the failing birth rate. It was Bannerd, here, whose sensational articles frightened the Bureau into making a double A-priority project out of it. I had nothing to do with it."

"*You* suggested that I mention the birth rate," said Zammo, violently.

"Did I?" said Antyok, composedly.

"And for that matter," roared Bannerd suddenly, "you suggested that I mention the birth rate in my articles."

The three ringed him now and hemmed him in. Antyok leaned back in his chair and said easily, "I don't know what you mean by suggestions. If you are accusing me, please stick to evidence—legal evidence. The laws of the Empire go by written, filmed, or transcribed material, or by witnessed statements. All my letters as administrator are on file here, at the Bureau, and at other places. I never asked for an A-priority project. The Bureau assigned it to me, and Zammo and Bannerd are responsible for that. In print, at any rate."

Zammo's voice was an almost inarticulate growl, "You hoodwinked me into teaching the creatures how to handle a spaceship."

"It was *your* suggestion. I have your report proposing they be studied in their reaction to human tools on file. So has the Bureau. The evidence—the *legal* evidence, is plain. I had nothing to do with it."

"Nor with globes?" demanded Bannerd.

The captain howled suddenly, "You had my ships brought here purposely. Five thousand globes! You knew it would require hundreds of craft."

"I never asked for globes," said Antyok coldly. "That was the Bureau's idea, although I think Bannerd's friends of The Philosophy helped that along."

Bannerd fairly choked. He spat out, "You were asking that Cepheid leader if he could read minds. You were telling him to express interest in the globes."

"Come, now. You prepared the transcript of the conversation yourself, and that, too, is on file. You can't prove it." He stood up, "You'll have to excuse me. I must prepare a report for the Bureau."

At the door, Antyok turned, "In a way, the problem of the non-Humans is solved, even if only to their own satisfaction. They'll breed now, and have a world they've earned themselves. It's what they wanted.

"Another thing. Don't accuse me of silly things. I've been in the Service for twenty-seven years, and I assure you that my paper work is proof enough that I have been thoroughly correct in everything I have done. And captain, I'll be glad to continue our discussion of earlier this evening at your convenience and explain how a capable administrator can work through red tape and still get what he wants."

It was remarkable that such a round, smooth baby-face could wear a smile quite so sardonic.

From: BuOuProv
To: Loodun Antyok, Chief Public Administrator, A-8
Subject: Administrative Service, Standing in.
Reference:
(a) AdServ Court Decision 22874-Q, dated 1/978
G.E.

1. In view of the favorable opinion handed down in reference (a) you are hereby absolved of all responsibility for the flight of non-Humans on Cepheus 18. It is requested that you hold yourself in readiness for your next appointment.

R. Horpritt, Chief, AdServ,
15/978 G.E.

CORRESPONDENCE COURSE

by Raymond F. Jones (1915-)

ASTOUNDING SCIENCE FICTION,
April

Raymond F. Jones was an interesting and relatively neglected science fiction writer, mostly appearing in Astounding *with his "Peace Engineer" series and many others. His two best works are the novel* Renaissance *(1951, serialized in* Astounding *in 1944) and the brilliant "Noise Level" (1947), but he published some fifteen books in the field, including* This Island Earth *(1952) which was made into one of the better sf films of the 1950s. His particular strength was in the area of ideas, not in execution, but he produced considerable work of interest.*

"Correspondence Course" has strong ideas and a powerful message.

(One of the inevitable tricks tried by any writer is the double-double-cross. In other words you work toward a surprise ending which you make just apparent enough for the reader to see dimly. And as that reader congratulates himself on having outsmarted the writer, that same writer pulls a rabbit out of his hat and reveals the real surprise ending.

Usually, this is the case with events, with matters such as the identity of the villain or the motive of the hero.

It is far less common to have this surprise come in the matter of the theme of the story; or the "moral," if you prefer. Here is a story in which you may prepare to be surprised at the nature and purpose of the "correspondence course" of the title, and then find out that's not at all what Jones had most in mind. Don't worry; I'm not giving away anything, for even with this hint I doubt you'll get it. I.A.)

The old lane from the farmhouse to the letter box down by the road was the same dusty trail that he remembered from eons before. The deep summer dust stirred as his feet moved slowly and haltingly. The marks of his left foot were deep and firm as when he had last walked the lane, but where his right foot moved there was a ragged, continuous line with irregular depressions and there was the sharp imprint of a cane beside the dragging footprints.

He looked up to the sky a moment as an echelon of planes from the advanced trainer base fifty miles away wheeled overhead. A nostalgia seized him, an overwhelming longing for the men he had known—and for Ruth.

He was home; he had come back alive, but with so many gone who would never come back, what good was it?

With Ruth gone it was no good at all. For an instant his mind burned with pain and his eyes ached as if a bomb-burst had blinded him as he remembered that day in the little field hospital where he had watched her die and heard the enemy planes overhead.

Afterwards, he had gone up alone, against orders, determined to die with her, but take along as many Nazis as he could.

But he hadn't died. He had come out of it with a bullet-shattered leg and sent home to rust and die slowly over many years.

He shook his head and tried to fling the thoughts out of his mind. It was wrong. The doctors had warned him—

He resumed his slow march, half dragging the all but useless leg behind him. This was the same lane down which he had run so fast those summer days so long ago. There was a swimming hole and a fishing pond a quarter of a mile away. He tried to dim his vision with half-shut eyes and remember those pleasant days and wipe out all fear and bitterness from his mind.

It was ten o'clock in the morning and Mr. McAfee, the rural postman, was late, but Jim Ward could see his struggling, antique Ford raising a low cloud of dust a mile down the road.

Jim leaned heavily upon the stout cedar post that supported the mailbox and when Mr. McAfee rattled up he managed to wave and smile cheerily.

Mr. McAfee adjusted his spectacles on the bridge of his nose with a rapid trombone manipulation.

"Bless me, Jim, it's good to see you up and around!"

"Pretty good to be up." Jim managed to force enthusiasm into his voice. But he knew he couldn't stand talking very long to old Charles McAfee as if everything had not changed since the last time.

"Any mail for the Wards, today?"

The postman shuffled the fistful of mail. "Only one."

Jim glanced at the return address block and shrugged. "I'm on the sucker lists already. They don't lose any time when they find out there's still bones left to pick on. You keep it."

He turned painfully and faced toward the house. "I've got to be getting back. Glad to have seen you, Mr. McAfee."

"Yeah, sure, Jim. Glad to have seen you. But I . . . er . . . got to deliver the mail—" He held the letter out hopefully.

"O.K." Jim laughed sharply and grasped the circular.

He went only as far as the giant oak whose branches extended far enough to overshadow the mailbox. He sat down in the shade with his back against the great bole and tried to watch the echelon still soaring above the valley through the rifts in the leaf coverage above him. After a time he glanced down at the circular letter from which his fingers were peeling little fragments of paper. Idly, he ripped open the envelope and glanced at the contents. In cheap, garish typograph with splatterings of red and purple ink the words seemed to be trying to jump at him.

SERVICEMAN—WHAT OF THE FUTURE?

You have come back from the wars. You have found life different than you knew it before, and much that was familiar is gone. But new things have come, new things that are here to stay and are a part of the world you are going to live in.

Have you thought of the place you will occupy? Are you prepared to resume life in the ways of peace?

WE CAN HELP YOU

Have you heard of the POWER CO-ORDINATOR? No, of course you haven't because it has been a hush-hush secret source of power that has been turning the wheels of war industries for many months. But now the secret of this vast source of new power can be told, and the need for hundreds, yes, thousands of trained technicians—such as you, yourself, may become—will be tremendous in the next decade.

LET US PROVE TO YOU

Let us prove to you that we know what we are talking about. We are so certain that you, as a soldier trained in intricate operations of the machines of war, will be interested in this almost miraculous new source of power and the technique of handling it that we are willing to send you absolutely FREE the first three lessons of our twenty-five lesson course that will train you to be a POWER CO-ORDINATOR technician.

Let us prove it to you. Fill out the enclosed coupon and mail it today!

Don't just shrug and throw this circular away as just another advertisement. MAIL THE COUPON NOW!

Jim Ward smiled reminiscently at the style of the circular. It reminded him of Billy Hensley and the time when they were thirteen. They sent in all the clipped and filled-out coupons they could find in magazines. They had samples of soap and magic tricks and catalogues and even a live bird came as the result of one. They kept all the stuff in Hensley's attic until Billy's dad finally threw it all out.

Impulsively, in whimsical tribute to the gone-forever happiness of those days, Jim Ward scratched his name and address in pencil and told the power co-ordinators to send him their three free lessons.

Mr. McAfee had only another mile to go up the road before he came to the end and returned past the Ward farm to Kramer's Forks. Jim waited and hailed him.

"Want to take another letter?"

The postman halted the clattering Ford and jumped down. "What's that?"

Jim repeated his request and held up the stamped reply card. "Take this with you?"

Mr. McAfee turned it over and read every word on the back of the card. "Good thing," he grunted. "So you're going to take a correspondence course in this new power what-is-it? I think that's mighty fine, Jim. Give you new interests—sort of take your mind off things."

"Yeah, sure." Jim struggled up with the aid of his cane and the bole of the oak tree. "Better see if I can make it back to the house now."

All the whimsy and humor had suddenly gone out of the situation.

It was a fantastically short time—three days later—that Mr. McAfee stopped again at the Ward farm. He glanced at the thick envelope in his pack and the return address block it bore. He could see Jim Ward on the farmhouse porch and turned the Ford up the lane. Its rattle made Jim turn his head and open his eyes from the thoughtless blankness into which he had been trying to sink. He removed the pipe from his mouth and watched the car approach.

"Here's your course," shouted Mr. McAfee. "Here's your first lesson!"

"What lesson?"

"The correspondence course you sent for. The power what-is-it? Don't you remember?"

"No," said Jim. "I'd forgotten all about it. Take the thing away. I don't want it. It was just a silly joke."

"You hadn't ought to feel that way, Jim. After all, your leg is going to be all right. I heard the Doc say so down in the drugstore last night. And everything is going to be all right. There's no use of letting it get you down. Besides—I got to deliver the mail."

He tossed the brown envelope on the porch beside Jim. "Brought it up special because I thought you'd be in a hurry to get it."

Jim smiled in apology. "I'm sorry, Mac. Didn't mean to

take it out on you. Thanks for bringing it up. I'll study it good and hard this morning right here on the porch."

Mr. McAfee beamed and nodded and rattled away. Jim closed his eyes again, but he couldn't find the pleasing blankness he'd found before. Now the screen of his mind showed only the sky with thundering, plummeting engines—and the face of a girl lying still and white with closed eyes.

Jim opened his eyes and his hands slipped to his sides and touched the envelope. He ripped it open and scanned the pages. It was the sort of stuff he had collected as a boy, all right. He glanced at the paragraph headings and tossed the first lesson aside. A lot of obvious stuff about comparisons between steam power and waterfalls and electricity. It seemed all jumbled up like a high school student's essay on the development of power from the time of Archimedes.

The mimeographed pages were poorly done. They looked as if the stencils had been cut on a typrwriter that had been hit on the type faces with a hammer.

He tossed the second lesson aside and glanced at the top sheet of the third. His hand arrested itself midway in the act of tossing this lesson beside the other two. He caught a glimpse of the calculations on an inside page and opened up the booklet.

There was no high school stuff there. His brain struggled to remember the long unused methods of the integral calculus and the manipulation of partial differential equations.

There were pages of the stuff. It was like a sort of beacon light, dim and far off, but pointing a sure pathway to his mind and getting brighter as he progressed. One by one, he followed the intricate steps of the math and the short paragraphs of description between. When at last he reached the final page and turned the book over and scowled heavily the sun was halfway down the afternoon sky.

He looked away over the fields and pondered. This was no elementary stuff. Such math as this didn't belong in a home study correspondence course. He picked up the envelope and concentrated on the return address block.

All it said was: M. H. Quilcon Schools, Henderson, Iowa. The lessons were signed at the bottom with the mimeographed reproductions of M. H. Quilcon's ponderous signature.

Jim picked up lesson one again and began reading slowly and carefully, as if hidden between the lines he might find some mystic message.

By the end of July his leg was strong enough for him to walk without the cane. He walked slowly and with a limp and once in a while the leg gave way as if he had a trick knee. But he learned quickly to catch himself before he fell and he reveled in the thrill of walking again.

By the end of July the tenth lesson of the correspondence course had arrived and Jim knew that he had gone as far as he could alone. He was lost in amazement as he moved in the new scientific wonderland that opened up before him. He had known that great strides had been made in techniques and production, but it seemed incredible that such a basic discovery as power co-ordination had been producing war machines these many months. He wondered why the principle had not been applied more directly as a weapon itself—but he didn't understand enough about it to know whether it could or not. He didn't even understand yet from where the basic energy of the system was derived.

The tenth lesson was as poorly produced as the rest of them had been, but it was practically a book in its thickness. When he had finished it Jim knew that he had to know more of the background of the new science. He had to talk to someone who knew something about it. But he knew of no one who had ever heard of it. He had seen no advertisements of the M. H. Quilcon Schools. Only the first circular and these lessons.

As soon as he had finished the homework on lesson ten and had given it into Mr. McAfee's care, Jim Ward made up his mind to go down to Henderson, Iowa, and visit the Quilcon School.

He wished he had retained the lesson material because he could have taken it there faster than it would arrive via the local mail channels.

The streamliner barely stopped at Henderson, Iowa, long enough to allow him to disembark. Then it was gone and Jim Ward stared about him.

The sleepy looking ticket seller, dispatcher, and janitor eyed him wonderingly and spat a huge amber stream across his desk and out the window.

"Looking for somebody, mister?"

"I'm looking for Henderson, Iowa. Is this it?" Jim asked dubiously.

"You're here, mister. But don't walk too fast or you'll be

out of it. The city limits only go a block past Smith's Drugstore."

Jim noticed the sign over the door and glanced at the inscription that he had not seen before: Henderson, Iowa. Pop. 806.

"I'm looking for a Mr. M. H. Quilcon. He runs a correspondence school here somewhere. Do you know of him?"

The depot staff shifted its cud again and spat thoughtfully. "Been here twenty-nine years next October. Never heard a name like that around here, and I know 'em all."

"Are there any correspondence schools here?"

"Miss Marybell Anne Simmons gives beauty operator lessons once in a while, but that's all the school of that kind that I know of."

Disconcerted, Jim Ward murmured his thanks and moved slowly out of the station. The sight before him was dismaying. He wondered if the population hadn't declined since the estimate on the sign in the station was made.

A small mercantile store that sagged in the middle faced him from across the street. Farther along was a tiny frame building labeled Sheriff's Office. On his side Jim saw Smith's drugstore a couple of hundred feet down from the station with a riding saddle and a patented fertilizer displayed in the window. In the other direction was the combined post office, bank and what was advertised as a newspaper and printing office.

Jim strode toward this last building while curious watchers on the porch of the mercantile store stared at him trudging through the dust.

The postmistress glanced up from the armful of mail that she was sorting into boxes as Jim entered. She offered a cheery hello that seemed to tinkle from the buxom figure.

"I'm looking for a man named Quilcon. I thought you might be able to give me some information concerning him."

"*Kweelcon?*" She furrowed her brow. "There's no one here by that name. How do you spell it?"

Before he could answer, the woman dropped a handful of letters on the floor. Jim was certain that he saw the one he had mailed to the school before he left.

As the woman stooped to recover the letters a dark brown shadow streaked across the floor. Jim got the momentary impression of an enormous brown slug moving with lightning speed.

The postmistress gave a scream of anger and scuffled her feet to the door. She returned in a moment.

"Armadillo," she explained. "Darn thing's been hanging around here for months and nobody seems to be able to kill it." She resumed putting the mail in the boxes.

"I think you missed one," said Jim. She did not have the one that he recognized as the one he'd mailed.

The woman looked about her on the floor. "I got them all, thank you. Now what did you say this man's name was?"

Jim leaned over the counter and looked at the floor. He was sure—But there was obviously no other letter in sight and there was no place it could have gone.

"Quilcon," said Jim slowly. "I'm not sure of the pronunciation myself, but that's the way it seemed it should be."

"There's no one in Henderson by that name. Wait a minute now. That's a funny thing—you know it was about a month ago that I saw an envelope going out of here with a name something like that in the upper left corner. I thought at the time it was a funny name and wondered who put it in, but I never did find out and I thought I'd been dreaming. How's you know to come here looking for him?"

"I guess I must have received the mail you saw."

"Well, you might ask Mr. Herald. He's in the newspaper office next door. But I'm sure there's no one in this town by that name."

"You publish a newspaper here?"

The woman laughed. "We call it that. Mr. Herald owns the bank and a big farm and puts this out free as a hobby. It's not much, but everybody in town reads it. On Saturday he puts out a regular printed edition. This is the daily."

She held up a small mimeographed sheet that was moderately legible. Jim glanced at it and moved towards the door. "Thanks, anyway."

As he went out into the summer sun there was something gnawing at his brain, an intense you-forgot-something-in-there sort of feeling. He couldn't place it and tried to ignore it.

Then as he stepped across the threshold of the printing office he got it. That mimeographed newssheet he had seen—it bore a startling resemblance to the lessons he had received from M. H. Quilcon. The same purple ink. Slightly crooked sheets. But that was foolish to try to make a connection there. All mimeographed jobs looked about alike.

Mr. Herald was a portly little man with a fringe around his baldness. Jim repeated his inquiry.

"Quilcon?" Mr. Herald pinched his lips thoughtfully. "No, can't say as I ever heard the name. Odd name—I'm sure I'd know it if I'd ever heard it."

Jim Ward knew that further investigation here would be a waste of time. There was something wrong somewhere. The information in his correspondence course could not be coming out of this half dead little town.

He glanced at a copy of the newssheet lying on the man's littered desk beside an ancient Woodstock. "Nice little sheet you put out there," said Jim.

Mr. Herald laughed. "Well, it's not much, but I get a kick out of it, and the people enjoy reading about Mrs. Kelly's lost hogs and the Dorius kid's whooping cough. It livens things up."

"Ever do any work for anybody else—printing or mimeographing?"

"If anybody wants it, but I haven't had an outside customer in three years."

Jim glanced about searchingly. The old Woodstock seemed to be the only typewriter in the room.

"I might as well go on," he said. "But I wonder if you'd mind letting me use your typewriter to write a note and leave in the postoffice for Quilcon if he ever shows up."

"Sure, go ahead. Help yourself."

Jim sat down before the clanking machine and hammered out a brief paragraph while Mr. Herald wandered to the back of the shop. Then Jim rose and shoved the paper in his pocket. He wished he had brought a sheet from one of the lessons with him.

"Thanks," he called to Mr. Herald. He picked up a copy of the latest edition of the newspaper and shoved it in his pocket with the typed sheet.

On the trip homeward he studied the mimeographed sheet until he had memorized every line, but he withheld conclusions until he reached home.

From the station he called the farm and Hank, the hired man, came to pick him up. The ten miles out to the farm seemed like a hundred. But at last in his own room Jim spread out the two sheets of paper he'd brought with him and opened up lesson one of the correspondence course.

There was no mistake. The stencils of the course manuals had been cut on Mr. Herald's ancient machine. There was the same nick out of the side of the o, and the b was flattened on the bulge. The r was minus half its base.

Mr. Herald had prepared the course.

Mr. Herald must then be M. H. Quilcon. But why had he denied any knowledge of the name? Why had he refused to see Jim and admit his authorship of the course?

At ten o'clock that night Mr. McAfee arrived with a special delivery letter for Jim.

"I don't ordinarily deliver these way out here this time of night," he said. "But I thought you might like to have it. Might be something important. A job or something, maybe. It's from Mr. Quilcon."

"Thanks. Thanks for bringing it, Mac."

Jim hurried into his room and ripped open the letter. It read:

Dear Mr. Ward:

Your progress in understanding the principles of power co-ordination are exceptional and I am very pleased to note your progress in connection with the tenth lesson which I have just received from you.

An unusual opportunity has arisen which I am moved to offer you. There is a large installation of a power co-ordination engine in need of vital repairs some distance from here. I believe that you are fully qualified to work on this machine under supervision which will be provided and you would gain some valuable experience. The installation is located some distance from the city of Henderson. It is about two miles out on the Balmer Road. You will find there the Hortan Machine Works at which the installation is located. Repairs are urgently needed and you are the closest qualified student able to take advantage of this opportunity which might lead to a valuable permanent connection. Therefore, I request that you come at once. I will meet you there.

Sincerely,
M. H. Quilcon

For a long time Jim Ward sat on the bed with the letter and the sheets of paper spread out before him. What had begun as a simple quest for information was rapidly becoming an intricate puzzle.

Who was M. H. Quilcon?

It seemed obvious that Mr. Herald, the banker and part-time newspaper publisher, must be Quilcon. The correspondence course manuals had certainly been produced on his typewriter. The chances of any two typewriters having exactly the same four or five disfigurements in type approached the infinitesimal.

And Herald—if he were Quilcon—must have written this letter just before or shortly after Jim's visit. The letter was certainly a product of the ancient Woodstock.

There was a fascination in the puzzle and a sense of something sinister, Jim thought. Then he laughed aloud at his own melodrama and began repacking the suitcase. There was a midnight train he could get back to Henderson.

It was hot afternoon when he arrived in the town for the second time. The station staff looked up in surprise as he got off the train.

"Back again? I thought you'd given up."

"I've found out where Mr. Quilcon is. He's at the Hortan Machine Works. Can you tell me exactly where that is?"

"Never heard of it."

"It's supposed to be about two miles out of town on Balmer Road."

"That's just the main street of town going on down through the Willow Creek district. There's no machine works out there. You must be in the wrong state, mister. Or somebody's kidding you."

"Do you think Mr. Herald could tell me anything about such a machine shop. I mean, does he know anything about machinery or things related to it?"

"Man, no! Old man Herald don't care about nothing but money and that little fool paper of his. Machinery! He can't hook up anything more complicated than his suspenders."

Jim started down the main street toward the Willow Creek district. Balmer Road rapidly narrowed and turned, leaving the town out of sight behind a low rise. Willow Creek was a glistening thread in the midst of meadow land.

There was no more unlikely spot in the world for a machine works of any kind, Jim thought. Someone must be playing an utterly fantastic joke on him. But how or why they had picked on him was mystifying.

At the same time he knew within him that it was no joke. There was a deadly seriousness about it all. The principles of power co-ordination were right. He had slaved and dug through them enough to be sure of that. He felt that he could almost build a power co-ordinating engine now with the proper means—except that he didn't understand from where the power was derived!

In the timelessness of the bright air about him, with the only sound coming from the brook and the leaves on the willow trees beside it, Jim found it impossible to judge time or distance.

He paced his steps and counted until he was certain that at least two miles had been covered. He halted and looked about almost determined to go back and re-examine the way he had come.

He glanced ahead, his eyes scanning every minute detail of the meadowland. And then he saw it.

The sunlight glistened as if on a metal surface. And above the bright spot in the distance was the faintly readable legend:

HORTAN MACHINE WORKS

Thrusting aside all judgment concerning the incredibility of a machine shop in such a locale, he crossed the stream and made his way over the meadow toward the small rise.

As he approached, the machine works appeared to be merely a dome-shaped structure about thirty feet in diameter and with an open door in one side. He came up to it with a mind ready for anything. The crudely painted sign above the door looked as if it had been drawn by an inexpert barn painter in a state of intoxication.

Jim entered the dimly lit interior of the shop and set his case upon the floor beside a narrow bench that extended about the room.

Tools and instruments of unfamiliar design were upon the bench and upon the walls. But no one appeared.

Then he noticed an open door and a steep, spiral ramp that led down to a basement room. He stepped through and half slid, half walked down to the next level.

There was artificial lighting by fluorescent tubes of unusual construction, Jim noticed. But still no sign of anyone. And there was not an object in the room that appeared familiar to him. Articles that vaguely resembled furniture were against the walls.

He felt uneasy amid the strangeness of the room and he was about to go back up the steep ramp when a voice came to him.

"This is Mr. Quilcon. Is that you, Mr. Ward?"

"Yes. Where are you?"

"I am in the next room, unable to come out until I finish a bit of work I have started. Will you please go on down to the room below? You will find the damaged machinery there. Please go right to work on it. I'm sure that you have a complete understanding of what is necessary. I will join you in a moment."

Hesitantly, Jim turned to the other side of the room where he saw a second ramp leading down to a brilliantly lighted room. He glanced about once more, then moved down the ramp.

The room was high-ceilinged and somewhat larger in diameter than the others he had seen and it was almost completely occupied by the machine.

A series of close fitting towers with regular bulbous swellings on their columns formed the main structure of the engine. These were grouped in a solid circle with narrow walkways at right angles to each other passing through them.

Jim Ward stood for a long time examining their surfaces that rose twenty feet from the floor. All that he had learned from the curious correspondence course seemed to fall into place. Diagrams and drawings of such machines had seemed incomprehensible. Now he knew exactly what each part was for and how the machine operated.

He squeezed his body into the narrow walkway between the towers and wormed his way to the center of the engine. His bad leg made it difficult, but he at last came to the damaged structure.

One of the tubes had cracked open under some tremendous strain and through the slit he could see the marvelously intricate wiring with which it was filled. Wiring that was burned now and fused to a mass. It was in a control circuit that rendered the whole machine functionless, but its repair would not be difficult, Jim knew.

He went back to the periphery of the engine and found the controls of a cranelike device which he lowered and seized the cracked sleeve and drew off the damaged part.

From the drawers and bins in the walls he selected parts and tools and returned to the damaged spot.

In the cramped space he began tearing away the fused parts and wiring. He was lost and utterly unconscious of anything but the fascination of the mighty engine. Here within this room was machine capacity to power a great city.

Its basic function rested upon the principle of magnetic currents in contrast to electric currents. The discovery of magnetic currents had been announced only a few months before he came home from the war. The application of the discovery had been swift.

And he began to glimpse the fundamental source of the energy supplying the machine. It was in the great currents of gravitational and magnetic force flowing between the planets and the suns of the universe. As great as atomic energy and as boundless in its resources, this required no fantastically dangerous machinery to harness. The principle of the power co-ordinator was simple.

The pain of his cramped position forced Jim to move out to rest his leg. As he stood beside the engine he resumed his pondering on the purpose it had in this strange location. Why was it built there and what use was made of its power?

He moved about to restore the circulation in his legs and sought to trace the flow of energy through the engine, determine where and what kind of a load was placed upon it.

His search led him below into a third sub-basement of the building and there he found the thing he was searching for, the load into which the tremendous drive of the engine was coupled.

But here he was unable to comprehend fully, for the load was itself a machine of strange design, and none of its features had been covered in the correspondence course.

The machine upstairs seized upon the magnetic currents of space and selected and concentrated those flowing in a given direction.

The force of these currents was then fed into the machines in this room, but there was no point of reaction against which the energy could be applied.

Unless—

The logical, inevitable conclusion forced itself upon his mind. There was only one conceivable point of reaction.

He stood very still and a tremor went through him. He looked up at the smooth walls about him. Metal, all of them.

And this room—it was narrower than the one above—as if the entire building were tapered from the dome protruding out of the earth to the basement floor.

The only possible point of reaction was the building itself.

But it wasn't a building. It was a vessel.

Jim clawed and stumbled his way up the incline into the engine room, then beyond into the chamber above. He was halfway up the top ramp when he heard the voice again.

"Is that you, Mr. Ward? I have almost finished and will be with you in a moment. Have you completed the repairs. Was it very difficult?"

He hesitated, but didn't answer. Something about the quality of that voice gave him a chill. He hadn't noticed it before because of his curiosity and his interest in the place. Now he detected its unearthly, inhuman quality.

He detected the fact that it wasn't a voice at all, but that the words had been formed in his brain as if he himself had spoken them.

He was nearly at the top of the ramp and drew himself on hands and knees to the floor level when he saw the shadow of the closing door sweep across the room and heard the metallic clang of the door. It was sealed tight. Only the small windows—or ports—admitted light.

He rose and straightened and calmed himself with the thought that the vessel could not fly. It could not rise with the remainder of the repair task unfinished—and he was not going to finish it; that much was certain.

"Quilcon!" he called. "Show yourself! Who are you and what do you want of me?"

"I want you to finish the repair job and do it quickly," the voice replied instantly. "And quickly—it must be finished quickly."

There was a note of desperation and despair that seemed to cut into Jim. Then he caught sight of the slight motion against the wall beside him.

In a small, transparent hemisphere that was fastened to the side of the wall lay the slug that Jim had seen at the post office, the thing the woman had called an "armadillo." He had not even noticed it when he first entered the room. The thing was moving now with slow pulsations that swelled its surface and great welts like dark veins stood out upon it.

From the golden-hued hemisphere a maze of cable ran to

instruments and junction boxes around the room and a hundred tiny pseudopods grasped terminals inside the hemisphere.

It was a vessel—and this slug within the hemisphere was its alien, incredible pilot. Jim knew it with startling cold reality that came to him in waves of thought that emanated from the slug called Quilcon and broke over Jim's mind. It was a ship and a pilot from beyond Earth—from out of the reaches of space.

"What do you want of me? Who are you?" said Jim Ward.

"I am Quilcon. You are a good student. You learn well."

"What do you want?"

"I want you to repair the damaged engine."

There was something wrong with the creature. Intangibly, Jim sensed it. An aura of sickness, a desperate urgency came to his mind.

But something else was in the foreground of Jim's mind. The horror of the alien creature diminshed and Jim contemplated the miracle that had come to mankind.

"I'll bargain with you," he said quietly. "Tell me how to build a ship like this for my people and I will fix the engines for you."

"No! No—there is no time for that. I must hurry—"

"Then I shall leave without any repairs."

He moved toward the door and instantly a paralyzing wave took hold of him as if he had seized a pair of charged electrodes. It relaxed only as he stumbled back from the door.

"My power is weak," said Quilcon, "but it is strong enough for many days yet—many of your days. Too many for you to live without food and water. Repair the engine and then I shall let you go."

"Is what I ask too much to pay for my help?"

"You have had pay enough. You can teach your people to build power co-ordinator machines. Is that not enough?"

"My people want to build ships like this one and move through space."

"I cannot teach you that. I do not know. I did not build this ship."

There were surging waves of troubled thought that washed over his mind, but Jim Ward's tenseness eased. The first fear of totally alien life drifted from his mind and he felt a strange affinity for the creature. It was injured and sick, he knew, but he could not believe that it did not know how the ship was built.

"Those who built this ship come often to trade upon my world," said Quilcon. "But we have no such ships of our own. Most of us have no desire to see anything but the damp caves and sunny shores of our own world. But I longed to see the worlds from which these ships came.

"When this one landed near my cave I crept in and hid myself. The ship took off then and we traveled an endless time. Then an accident to the engine killed all three of those who manned the ship and I was left alone.

"I was injured, too, but I was not killed. Only the other of me died."

Jim did not understand the queer phrase, but he did not break into Quilcon's story.

"I was able to arrange means to control the flight of the ship, to prevent its destruction as it landed upon this planet, but I could not repair it because of the nature of my body."

Jim saw then that the creature's story must be true. It was obvious that the ship had been built to be manned by beings utterly unlike Quilcon.

"I investigated the city of yours near by and learned of your ways and customs. I needed the help of one of you to repair the ship. By force I could persuade one of you to do simple tasks, but none so complex as this requires.

"Then I discovered the peculiar customs of learning among you. I forced the man Herald to prepare the materials and send them to you. I received them before the person at the post office could see them. I got your name from the newspapers along with several others who were unsatisfactory.

"I had to teach you to understand the power co-ordinator because only by voluntary operation of your highest faculties will you be able to understand and repair the machine. I can assist but not force you to do that."

The creature began pleading again. "And now will you repair the engine quickly. I am dying—but shall live longer than you—it is a long journey to my home planet, but I must get there and I need every instant of time that is left to me."

Jim caught a glimpse of the dream vision that was the creature's home world. It was a place of securty and peace—in Quilcon's terms. But even its alienness did not block out the sense of quiet beauty that Quilcon's mind transmitted to Jim's. They were a species of high intelligence. Exceptionally developed in the laws of mathematics and theory of logic, they were handicapped in bodily development from inquiring into other fields of science whose existence was demonstrated by their logic and their mathematics. The more intellectual among them were frustrated creatures whose lives were made tolerable only by an infinite capacity for stoicism and adaptation.

But of them all, Quilcon was among the most restless and rebellious and ambitious. No one of them had ever dared such a journey as he had taken. A swelling pity and understanding came over Jim Ward.

"I'll bargain with you," he said desperately. "I'll repair the engine if you'll let me have its principles. If you don't have them, you can get them to me with little trouble. My people must have such a ship as this."

He tried to visualize what it would mean to Earth to have space flight a century or perhaps five centuries before the slow plodding of science and research might reveal it.

But the creature was silent.

"Quilcon—" Jim repeated. He hoped it hadn't died.

"I'll bargain with you," said Quilcon at last. "Let me be the other of you, and I'll give you what you want."

"The other of me? What are you talking about?"

"It is hard for you to understand. It is union—such as we make upon our world. When two or more of us want to be together we go together in the same brain, the same body. I am alone now, and it is an unendurable existence because I have known what it is to have another of me.

"Let me come into your brain, into your mind and live there with you. We will teach your people and mine. We will take this ship to all the universes of which living creatures can dream. It is either this or we both die together, for too much time has gone for me to return. This body dies."

Stunned by Quilcon's ultimatum, Jim Ward stared at the ugly slug on the wall. Its brown body was heaving with violent pulsations of pain and a sense of delirium and terror came from it to Jim.

"Hurry! Let me come!" it pleaded.

He could feel sensations as if fingers were probing his cranium looking, pleading for entrance. It turned him cold.

He looked into the years and thought of an existence with this alien mind in his. Would they battle for eventual possession of his body and he perhaps be subjected to slavery in his own living corpse?

He tried to probe Quilcon's thoughts, but he could find no sense or intent of conquest. There were almost human amenities intermingled with a world of new science and thought.

He knew Quilcon would keep his promise to give the secrets of the ship to the men of Earth. That alone would be worth the price of his sacrifice—if it should be sacrifice.

"Come!" he said quietly.

It was as if a torrent of liquid light were flowing into his brain. It was blinding and excruciating in its flaming intensity. He thought he sensed rather than saw the brown husk of Quilcon quiver in the hemisphere and shrivel like a brown nut.

But in his mind there was union and he paused and trembled with the sudden great reality of what he knew. He knew what Quilcon was and gladness flowed into him like light. A thought soared through his brain: Is sex only in the difference of bodily function and the texture of skin and the tone of voice?

He thought of another day when there was death in the sky and on the Earth below, and in a little field hospital. A figure on a white cot had murmured, "You'll be all right, Jim. I'm going on, I guess, but you'll be all right. I know it. Don't miss me too much."

He had known there would be no peace for him ever, but now there was peace and the voice of Quilcon was like that voice from long ago, for as the creature probed into his thoughts its inherent adaptability matched its feelings and thought to his and said, "Everything *is* all right, isn't it, Jim Ward?"

"Yes . . . yes it is." The intensity of his feelings almost blinded him. "And I want to call you Ruth, after another Ruth—"

"I like that name." There was shyness and appreciation in the tones, and it was not strange to Jim that he could not see the speaker, for there was a vision in his mind far lovelier than any Earthly vision could have been.

"We'll have everything," he said. "Everything that your world and mine can offer. We'll see them all."

But like the other Ruth who had been so practical, this one

was, too. "First we have to repair the engine. Shall we do it, now?"

The solitary figure of Jim Ward moved toward the ramp and disappeared into the depths of the ship.

FIRST CONTACT

by Murray Leinster (Will F. Jenkins, 1896-1975)

ASTOUNDING SCIENCE FICTION,
May

Murray Leinster was the Dean of Science Fiction Writers, a man whose career spanned almost half a century, from "The Runaway Skyscraper" in 1919 to the end of the 1960s. Very few of his mostly pedestrian novels are in print, but as a short story writer he could be very good indeed, particularly during the second half of the 40s and the 1950s. He was one of the very few Gernsback era writers who could successfully make the transition to modern sf, and he won a Hugo Award as late as 1956 (for "Exploration Team"). His finest work can be found in The Best of Murray Leinster *(1978).*

"First Contact" is a genuine classic, a story that imaginatively addressed questions that are still on the minds of sf readers and the general public—what will it be like when earthlings meet aliens? How will they know if the other can be trusted?

(Unquestionably, "First Contact" is Leinster's most famous and most referred-to story. It was so famous, in fact, that it called for a response from a Soviet science fiction writer, Ivan Yefremov. Yefremov wrote "The Heart of the Serpent," which also dealt with the first meeting in space of Earthmen and aliens but from a different viewpoint. Whereas in Leinster's story the central motif is that of fear and distrust; that in Yefremov's story is that of the

uniting bond of reason. Naturally, the Soviets made much of the fact that this showed the superior nature, both intellectually and morally, of communist philosophy versus capitalist philosophy—but even so I found myself sympathizing with Yefremov. I want *the uniting band of reason to triumph over fear and mistrust.*

The question of first-contact remains important in science fiction, by the way. Indeed, as our expertise in space flight advances and as we remain uncertain as to the possibility of life elsewhere, the question ought to grow ever more important. Carl Sagan has recently undertaken to do his first piece of fiction for an advance of two million dollars [a record for science fiction] and the subject?—First Contact. I. A.)

Tommy Dort went into the captain's room with his last pair of stereophotos and said:

"I'm through, sir. These are the last two pictures I can take."

He handed over the photographs and looked with professional interest at the visiplates, which showed all space outside the ship. Subdued, deep-red lighting indicated the controls and such instruments as the quartermaster on duty needed for navigation of the spaceship *Llanvabon.* There was a deeply cushioned control chair. There was the little gadget of oddly angled mirrors—remote descendant of the back-view mirrors of twentieth-century motorists—which allowed a view of all the visiplates without turning the head. And there were the huge plates which were so much more satisfaction for a direct view of space.

The *Llanvabon* was a long way from home. The plates, which showed every star of visual magnitude and could be stepped up to any desired magnification, portrayed stars of every imaginable degree of brilliance, in the startlingly different colors they show outside of atmosphere. But every one was unfamiliar. Only two constellations could be recognized as seen from Earth, and they were shrunken and distorted.

The Milky Way seemed vaguely out of place. But even such oddities were minor compared to a sight in the forward plates.

There was a vast, vast mistiness ahead. A luminous mist. It seemed motionless. It took a long time for any appreciable nearing to appear in the vision plates, though the spaceship's velocity indicator showed an incredible speed. The mist was the Crab Nebula, six light-years long, three and a half light-years thick, with outward-reaching members that in the telescopes of Earth gave it some resemblance to the creature for which it was named. It was a cloud of gas, infinitely tenuous, reaching half again as far as from Sol to its nearest neighbor-sun. Deep within it burned two stars; a double star; one component the familiar yellow of the sun of Earth, the other an unholy white.

Tommy Dort said meditatively:

"We're heading into a deep, sir?"

The skipper studied the last two plates of Tommy's taking, and put them aside. He went back to his uneasy contemplation of the vision plates ahead. The *Llanvabon* was decelerating at full force. She was a bare half light-year from the nebula. Tommy's work was guiding the ship's course, now, but the work was done. During all the stay of the exploring ship in the nebula, Tommy Dort would loaf. But he'd more than paid his way so far.

He had just completed a quite unique first—a complete photographic record of the movement of a nebula during a period of four thousand years, taken by one individual with the same apparatus and with control exposures to detect and record any systematic errors. It was an achivement in itself worth the journey from Earth. But in addition, he had also recorded four thousand years of the history of a double star, and four thousand years of the history of a star in the act of degenerating into a white dwarf.

It was not that Tommy Dort was four thousand years old. He was, actually, in his twenties. But the Crab Nebula is four thousand light-years from Earth, and the last two pictures had been taken by light which would not reach Earth until the sixth millennium A.D. On the way here—at speeds incredible multiples of the speed of light—Tommy Dort had recorded each aspect of the nebula by the light which had left it from forty centuries since to a bare six months ago.

The *Llanvabon* bored on through space. Slowly, slowly,

slowly, the incredible luminosity crept across the vision plates. It blotted out half the universe from view. Before was glowing mist, and behind was a star-studded emptiness. The mist shut off three-fourths of all the stars. Some few of the brightest shone dimly through it near its edge, but only a few. Then there was only an irregularly shaped patch of darkness astern, against which stars shone unwinking. The *Llanvabon* dived into the nebula, and it seemed as if it bored into a tunnel of darkness with walls of shining fog.

Which was exactly what the spaceship was doing. The most distant photographs of all had disclosed structural features in the nebula. It was not amorphous. It had form. As the *Llanvabon* drew nearer, indications of structure grew more distinct, and Tommy Dort had argued for a curved approach for photographic reasons. So the spaceship had come up to the nebula on a vast logarithmic curve, and Tommy had been able to take successive photographs from slightly different angles and get stereopairs which showed the nebula in three dimensions; which disclosed billowings and hollows and an actually complicated shape. In places, the nebula displayed convolutions like those of a human brain. It was into one of those hollows that the spaceship now plunged. They had been called "deeps" by analogy with crevasses in the ocean floor. And they promised to be useful.

The skipper relaxed. One of the skipper's functions, nowadays, is to think of things to worry about, and then to worry about them. The skipper of the *Llanvabon* was conscientious. Only after a certain instrument remained definitely nonregistering did he ease himself back in his seat.

"It was just hardly possible," he said heavily, "that those deeps might be nonluminous gas. But they're empty. So we'll be able to use overdrive as long as we're in them."

It was a light-year-and-a-half from the edge of the nebula to the neighborhood of the double star which was its heart. That was the problem. A nebula is a gas. It is so thin that a comet's tail is solid by comparison, but a ship traveling on overdrive—above the speed of light—does not want to hit even a merely hard vacuum. It needs pure emptiness, such as exists between the stars. But the *Llanvabon* could not do much in this expanse of mist if it was limited to speeds a merely hard vacuum would permit.

The luminosity seemed to close in behind the spaceship, which slowed and slowed and slowed. The overdrive went off with the sudden *pinging* sensation which goes all over a person when the overdrive field is released.

Then, almost instantly, bells burst into clanging, strident uproar all through the ship. Tommy was almost deafened by the alarm bell which rang in the captain's room before the quartermaster shut it off with a flip of his hand. But other bells could be heard ringing throughout the rest of the ship, to be cut off as automatic doors closed one by one.

Tommy Dort stared at the skipper. The skipper's hands clenched. He was up and staring over the quartermaster's shoulder. One indicator was apparently having convulsions. Others strained to record their findings. A spot on the diffusedly bright mistiness of a bow-quartering visiplate grew brighter as the automatic scanner focused on it. That was the direction of the object which had sounded collision-alarm. But the object locator itself—according to its reading, there was one solid object some eighty thousand miles away—an object of no great size. But there was another object whose distance varied from extreme range to zero, and whose size shared its impossible advance and retreat.

"Step up the scanner," snapped the skipper.

The extra-bright spot on the scanner rolled outward, obliterating the undifferentiated image behind it. Magnification increased. But nothing appeared. Absolutely nothing. Yet the radio locator insisted that something monstrous and invisible made lunatic dashes toward the *Llanvabon*, at speeds which inevitably implied collision, and then fled coyly away at the same rate.

The visiplate went up to maximum magnification. Still nothing. The skipper ground his teeth. Tommy Dort said meditatively:

"D'you know, sir, I saw something like this on a liner of the Earth-Mars run once, when we were being located by another ship. Their locator beam was the same frequency as ours, and every time it hit, it registered like something monstrous, and solid."

"That," said the skipper savagely, "is just what's happening now. There's something like a locator beam on us. We're getting that beam and our own echo besides. But the other ship's invisible! Who is out here in an invisible ship with locator devices? Not men, certainly!"

He pressed the button in his sleeve communicator and snapped:

"Action stations! Man all weapons! Condition of extreme alert in all departments immediately!"

His hands closed and unclosed. He stared again at the visiplate which showed nothing but a formless brightness.

"Not men?" Tommy Dort straightened sharply. "You mean—"

"How many solar systems in our galaxy?" demanded the skipper bitterly. "How many plants fit for life? And how many kinds of life could there be? If this ship isn't from Earth—and it isn't—it has a crew that isn't human. And things that aren't human but are up to the level of deepspace travel in their civilization could mean anything!"

The skipper's hands were actually shaking. He would not have talked so freely before a member of his own crew, but Tommy Dort was of the observation staff. And even a skipper whose duties include worrying may sometimes need desperately to unload his worries. Sometimes, too, it helps to think aloud.

"Something like this has been talked about and speculated about for years," he said softly. "Mathematically, it's been an odds-on bet that somewhere in our galaxy there'd be another race with a civilization equal to or further advanced than ours. Nobody could ever guess where or when we'd meet them. But it looks like we've done it now!"

Tommy's eyes were very bright.

"D'you suppose they'll be friendly, sir?"

The skipper glanced at the distance indicator. The phantom object still made its insane, nonexistent swoops toward and away from the *Llanvabon*. The secondary indication of an object at eighty thousand miles stirred ever so slightly.

"It's moving," he said curtly. "Heading for us. Just what we'd do if a strange spaceship appeared in our hunting grounds! Friendly? Maybe! We're going to try to contact them. We have to. But I suspect this is the end of this expedition. Thank God for the blasters!"

The blasters are those beams of ravening destruction which take care of recalcitrant meteorites in a spaceship's course when the deflectors can't handle them. They are not designed as weapons, but they can serve as pretty good ones. They can go into action at five thousand miles, and draw on the entire power output of a whole ship. With automatic aim and a traverse of five degrees, a ship like the *Llanvabon* can come very close to blasting a hole through a small-sized asteroid which gets in its way. But not on overdrive, of course.

Tommy Dort had approached the bow-quartering visiplate. Now he jerked his head around.

"Blasters, sir? What for?"

The skipper grimaced at the empty visiplate.

"Because we don't know what they're like and can't take a chance! I know!" he added bitterly. "We're going to make contacts and try to find out all we can about them—especially where they come from. I suppose we'll try to make friends—but we haven't much chance. We can't trust them a fraction of an inch. We daren't! They've locators. Maybe they've tracers better than any we have. Maybe they could trace us all the way home without our knowing it! We can't risk a nonhuman race knowing where Earth is unless we're sure of them! And how can we be sure? They could come to trade, of course—or they could swoop down on overdrive with a battle fleet that could wipe us out before we knew what happened. We wouldn't know which to expect, or when!"

Tommy's face was startled.

"It's all been thrashed out over and over, in theory," said the skipper. "Nobody's ever been able to find a sound answer, even on paper. But you know, in all their theorizing, no one considered the crazy, rank impossibility of a deep-space contact, with neither side knowing the other's home world! But we've got to find an answer in fact! What are we going to do about them? Maybe these creatures will be aesthetic marvels, nice and friendly and polite—and underneath with the sneaking brutal ferocity of a Japanese. Or maybe they'll be crude and gruff as a Swedish farmer—and just as decent underneath. Maybe they're something in between. But am I going to risk the possible future of the human race on a guess that it's safe to trust them? God knows it would be worthwhile to make friends with a new civilization! It would be bound to stimulate our own, and maybe we'd gain enormously. But I can't take chances. The one thing I won't risk is having them know how to find Earth! Either I know they can't follow me, or I don't go home! And they'll probably feel the same way!"

He pressed the sleeve-communicator button again.

"Navigation officers, attention! Every star map on this ship is to be prepared for instant destruction. This includes photographs and diagrams from which our course or starting point could be deduced. I want all astronomical data gathered and arranged to be destroyed in a split second, on order. Make it fast and report when ready!"

He released the button. He looked suddenly old. The first contact of humanity with an alien race was a situation which had been foreseen in many fashions, but never one quite so hopeless of solution as this. A solitary Earth-ship and a solitary alien, meeting in a nebula which must be remote from the home planet of each. They might wish peace, but the line of conduct which best prepared a treacherous attack was just the seeming of friendliness. Failure to be suspicious might doom the human race—and a peaceful exchange of the fruits of civilization would be the greatest benefit imaginable. Any mistake would be irreparable, but a failure to be on guard would be fatal.

The captain's room was very, very quiet. The bow-quartering visiplate was filled with the image of a very small section of the nebula. A very small second indeed. It was all diffused, featureless, luminous mist. But suddenly Tommy Dort pointed.

"There, sir!"

There was a small shape in the mist. It was far away. It was a black shape, not polished to mirror-reflection like the hull of the *Llanvabon*. It was bulbous—roughly pear-shaped. There was much thin luminosity between, and no details could be observed, but it was surely no natural object. Then Tommy looked at the distance indicator and said quietly: "It's headed for us at very high acceleration, sir. The odds are that they're thinking the same thing, sir, that neither of us will dare let the other go home. Do you think they'll try a contact with us, or let loose with their weapons as soon as they're in range?"

The *Llanvabon* was no longer in a crevasse of emptiness in the nebula's thin substance. She swam in luminescence. There were no stars save the two fierce glows in the nebula's heart. There was nothing but an all-enveloping light, curiously like one's imagining of underwater in the tropics of Earth.

The alien ship had made one sign of less than lethal intention. As it drew near the *Llanvabon*, it decelerated. The *Llanvabon* itself had advanced for a meeting and then come to a dead stop. Its movement had been a recognition of the nearness of the other ship. Its pausing was both a friendly sign and a precaution against attack. Relatively still, it could swivel on its own axis to present the least target to a slashing assault, and it would have a longer firing-time than if the two ships flashed past each other at their combined speeds.

The moment of actual approach, however, was tenseness itself. The *Llanvabon*'s needle-pointed bow aimed unwaveringly at the alien bulk. A relay to the captain's room put a key under his hand which would fire the blasters with maximum power. Tommy Dort watched, his brow wrinkled. The aliens must be of a high degree of civilization if they had spaceships, and civilization does not develop without the development of foresight. These aliens must recognize all the implications of this first contact of two civilized races as fully as did the humans on the *Llanvabon*.

The possibility of an enormous spurt in the development of both, by peaceful contact and exchange of their separate technologies, would probably appeal to them as to man. But when dissimilar human cultures are in contact, one must usually be subordinate or there is war. But subordination between races arising on separate planets could not be peacefully arranged. Men, at least, would never consent to subordination, nor was it likely that any highly developed race would agree. The benefits to be derived from commerce could never make up for a condition of inferiority. Some races—men, perhaps—would prefer commerce to conquest. Perhaps—perhaps!—these aliens would also. But some types even of human beings would have craved red war. If the alien ship now approaching the *Llanvabon* returned to its home base with news of humanity's existence and of ships like the *Llanvabon*, it would give its race the choice of trade or battle. They might want trade, or they might want war. But it takes two to make trade, and only one to make war. They could not be sure of men's peacefulness, or could men be sure of theirs. The only safety for either civilization would lie in the destruction of one or both of the two ships here and now.

But even victory would not be really enough. Men would need to know where this alien race was to be found, for avoidance if not for battle. They would need to know its weapons, and its resources, and if it could be a menace and how it could be eliminated in case of need. The aliens would feel the same necessities concerning humanity.

So the skipper of the *Llanvabon* did not press the key which might possibly have blasted the other ship to nothingness. He dared not. But he dared not not fire either. Sweat came out on his face.

A speaker muttered. Someone from the range room.

"The other ship's stopped, sir. Quite stationary. Blasters are centered on it, sir."

It was an urging to fire. But the skipper shook his head, to himself. The alien ship was no more than twenty miles away. It was dead-black. Every bit of its exterior was an abysmal, nonreflecting sable. No details could be seen except by minor variations in its outline against the misty nebula.

"It's stopped dead, sir," said another voice. "They've sent a modulated short wave at us, sir. Frequency modulated. Apparently a signal. Not enough power to do any harm."

The skipper said through tight-locked teeth:

"They're doing something now. There's movement on the outside of their hull. Watch what comes out. Put the auxiliary blasters on it."

Something small and round came smoothly out of the oval outline of the black ship. The bulbous hulk moved.

"Moving away, sir," said the speaker. "The object they let out is stationary in the place they've left."

Another voice cut in:

"More frequency modulated stuff, sir. Unintelligible."

Tommy Dort's eyes brightened. The skipper watched the visiplate, with sweat-droplets on his forehead.

"Rather pretty, sir," said Tommy, meditatively. "If they sent anything toward us, it might seem a projectile or a bomb. So they came close, let out a lifeboat, and went away again. They figure we can send a boat or a man to make contact without risking our ship. They must think pretty much as we do."

The skipper said, without moving his eyes from the plate:

"Mr. Dort would you care to go out and look the thing over? I can't order you, but I need all my operating crew for emergencies. The observation staff—"

"Is expendable. Very well, sir," said Tommy briskly. "I won't take a lifeboat, sir. Just a suit with a drive in it. It's smaller and the arms and legs will look unsuitable for a bomb. I think I should carry a scanner, sir."

The alien ship continued to retreat. Forty, eighty, four hundred miles. It came to a stop and hung there, waiting. Climbing into his atomic-driven spacesuit just within the

Llanvabon's air lock, Tommy heard the reports as they went over the speakers throughout the ship. That the other ship had stopped its retreat at four hundred miles was encouraging. It might not have weapons effective at a greater distance than that, and so felt safe. But just as the thought formed itself in his mind, the alien retreated precipitately still farther. Which, as Tommy reflected as he emerged from the lock, might be because the aliens had realized they were giving themselves away, or might be because they wanted to give the impression that they had done so.

He swooped away from the silvery-mirror *Llanvabon*, through a brightly glowing emptiness which was past any previous experience of the human race. Behind him, the *Llanvabon* swung about and darted away. The skipper's voice came in Tommy's helmet phones.

"We're pulling back, too, Mr. Dort. There is a bare possibility that they've some explosive atomic reaction they can't use from their own ship, but which might be destructive even as far as this. We'll draw back. Keep your scanner on the object."

The reasoning was sound, if not very comforting. An explosive which would destroy anything within twenty miles was theoretically possible, but humans didn't have it yet. It was decidedly safest for the *Llanvabon* to draw back.

But Tommy Dort felt very lonely. He sped through emptiness toward the tiny black speck which hung in incredible brightness. The *Llanvabon* vanished. Its polished hull would merge with the glowing mist at a relatively short distance, anyhow. The alien ship was not visible to the naked eye, either. Tommy swam in nothingness, four thousand light-years from home, toward a tiny black spot which was the only solid object to be seen in all of space.

It was a slightly distorted sphere, not much over six feet in diameter. It bounced away when Tommy landed on it, feet-first. There were small tentacles, or horns, which projected in every direction. They looked rather like the detonating horns of a submarine mine, but there was a glint of crystal at the tip-end of each.

"I'm here," said Tommy into his helmet phone.

He caught hold of a horn and drew himself to the object. It was all metal, dead-black. He could feel no texture through his space gloves, of course, but he went over and over it, trying to discover its purpose.

"Deadlock, sir," he said presently. "Nothing to report that the scanner hasn't shown you."

Then, through his suit, he felt vibrations. They translated themselves as clankings. A section of the rounded hull of the object opened out. Two sections. He worked his way around to look in and see the first nonhuman civilized beings that any man had ever looked upon.

But what he saw was simply a flat plate on which dim red glows crawled here and there in seeming aimlessness. His helmet phones emitted a startled exclamation. The skipper's voice:

"Very good, Mr. Dort. Fix your scanner to look into that plate. They dumped out a robot with an infrared visiplate for communication. Not risking any personnel. Whatever we might do would damage only machinery. Maybe they expect us to bring it on board—and it may have a bomb charge that can be detonated when they're ready to start for home. I'll send a plate to face one of its scanners. You return to the ship."

"Yes, sir," said Tommy. "But which way is the ship, sir?"

There were no stars. The nebula obscured them with its light. The only thing visible from the robot was the double star at the nebula's center. Tommy was no longer oriented. He had but one reference point.

"Head straight away from the double star," came the order in his helmet phone. "We'll pick you up."

He passed another lonely figure, a little later, headed for the alien sphere with a vision plate to set up. The two spaceships, each knowing that it dared not risk its own race by the slightest lack of caution, would communicate with each other through this small round robot. Their separate vision systems would enable them to exchange all the information they dared give, while they debated the most practical way of making sure that their own civilization would not be endangered by this first contact with another. The truly most practical method would be the destruction of the other ship in a swift and deadly attack—in self-defense.

The *Llanvabon*, thereafter, was a ship in which there were two separate enterprises on hand at the same time. She had come out from Earth to make close-range observations on the smaller component of the double star at the nebula's center. The nebula itself was the result of the most titanic explosion of which men have any knowledge. The explosion took place some time in the year 2946 B.C., before the first of the seven cities of long-dead Ilium was even thought of. The light of that explosion reached Earth in the year 1054 A.D., and was duly recorded in ecclesiastical annals and somewhat more reliably by Chinese court astronomers. It was bright enough to be seen in daylight for twenty-three successive days. Its light—and it was four thousand light-years away—was brighter than that of Venus.

From these facts, astronomers could calculate nine hundred years later the violence of the detonation. Matter blown away from the center of the explosion would have traveled outward at the rate of two million three hundred thousand miles an hour; more than thirty-eight thousand miles a minute; something over six hundred thirty-eight miles per second. When twentieth-century telescopes were turned upon the scene of this vast explosion, only a double star remained—and the nebula. The brighter star of the doublet was almost unique in having so high a surface temperature that it showed no spectrum lines at all. It had a continuous spectrum. Sol's surface temperature is about 7,000° Absolute. That of the hot white star is 500,000 degrees. It has nearly the mass of the sun, but only one fifth its diameter, so that its density is one hundred seventy-three times that of water, sixteen times that of lead, and eight times that of iridium—the heaviest substance known on Earth. But even this density is not that of a dwarf white star like the companion of Sirius. The white star in the Crab Nebula is an incomplete dwarf; it is a star still in the act of collapsing. Examination—including the survey of a four-thousand-year column of its light—was worthwhile. The *Llanvabon* had come to make that examination. But the finding of an alien spaceship upon a similar errand had implications which overshadowed the original purpose of the expedition.

A tiny bulbous robot floated in the tenuous nebular gas. The normal operating crew of the *Llanvabon* stood at their posts with a sharp alertness which was productive of tense nerves. The observation staff divided itself, and a part went half-heartedly about the making of the observations for which the *Llanvabon* had come. The other half applied itself to the problem the spaceship offered.

It represented a culture which was up to space travel on an interstellar scale. The explosion of a mere five thousand years since must have blasted every trace of life out of existence in the area now filled by the nebula. So the aliens of the black spaceship came from another solar system. Their trip must have been, like that of the Earth ship, for purely scientific purposes. There was nothing to be extracted from the nebula.

They were, then, at least near the level of human civilization, which meant that they had or could develop arts and articles of commerce which men would want to trade for, in friendship. But they would necessarily realize that the existence and civilization of humanity was a potential menace to their own race. The two races could be friends, but also they could be deadly enemies. Each, even if unwillingly, was a monstrous menace to the other. And the only safe thing to do with a menace is to destroy it.

In the Crab Nebula the problem was acute and immediate. The future relationship of the two races would be settled here and now. If a process for friendship could be established, one race, otherwise doomed, would survive and both would benefit immensely. But that process had to be established, and confidence built up, without the most minute risk of danger from treachery. Confidence would need to be established upon a foundation of necessarily complete distrust. Neither dared return to its own base if the other could do harm to its race. Neither dared risk any of the necessities to trust. The only safe thing for either to do was destroy the other or be destroyed.

But even for war, more was needed than mere destruction of the other. With interstellar traffic, the aliens must have atomic power and some form of overdrive for travel above the speed of light. With radio location and visiplates and short-wave communication they had, of course, many other devices. What weapons did they have? How widely extended was their culture? What were their resources? Could there be a development of trade and friendship, or were the two races so unlike that only war could exist between them? If peace was possible, how could it be begun?

The men on the *Llanvabon* needed facts—and so did the crew of the other ship. They must take back every morsel of information they could. The most important information of all would be of the location of the other civilization, just in case of war. That one bit of information might be the decisive factor in an interstellar war. But other facts would be enormously valuable.

The tragic thing was that there could be no possible information which could lead to peace. Neither ship could stake its own race's existence upon any conviction of the good will or the honor of the other.

So there was a strange truce between the two ships. The alien went about its work of making observations, as did the *Llanvabon*. The tiny robot floated in bright emptiness. A scanner from the *Llanvabon* was focused upon a vision plate from the alien. A scanner from the alien regarded a vision plate from the *Llanvabon*. Communication began.

It progressed rapidly. Tommy Dort was one of those who made the first progress report. His special task on the expedition was over. He had now been assigned to work on the problem of communication with the alien entities. He went with the ship's solitary psychologist to the captain's room to convey the news of success. The captain's room, as usual, was a place of silence and dull-red indicator lights and the great bright visiplates on every wall and on the ceiling.

"We've established fairly satisfactory communication, sir," said the psychologist. He looked tired. His work on the trip was supposed to be that of measuring personal factors of error in the observation staff, for the reduction of all observations to the nearest possible decimal to the absolute. He had been pressed into service for which he was not especially fitted, and it told upon him. "That is, we can say almost anything we wish to them, and can understand what they say in return. But of course we don't know how much of what they say is the truth."

The skipper's eyes turned to Tommy Dort.

"We've hooked up some machinery," said Tommy, "that amounts to a mechanical translator. We have vision plates, of course, and then shortwave beams direct. They use frequency-modulation plus what is probably variation in wave forms—like our vowel and consonant sounds in speech. We've never had any use for anything like that before, so our coils won't handle it, but we've developed a sort of code which isn't the language of either set of us. They shoot over short-wave stuff with frequency-modulation, and we record it as sound. When we shoot it back, it's reconverted into frequency-modulation."

The skipper said, frowning:

"Why wave-form changes in short waves? How do you know?"

"We showed them our recorder in the vision plates, and they showed us theirs. They record the frequency-modulation direct. I think," said Tommy carefully, "they don't use sound at all, even in speech. They've set up a communication room, and we've watched them in the act of communicating with us. They made no perceptible movement of anything that corresponds to a speech organ. Instead of a microphone, they simply stand near something that would work as a pick-up antenna. My guess, sir, is that they use microwaves for what you might call person-to-person conversation. I think they make short-wave trains as we make sounds."

The skipper stared at him:

"That means they have telepathy?"

"M-m-m. Yes, sir," said Tommy. "Also it means that we have telepathy too, as far as they are concerned. They're probably deaf. They've certainly no idea of using sound waves in air for communication. They simply don't use noises for any purpose."

The skipper stored the information away.

"What else?"

"Well, sir," said Tommy doubtfully, "I think we're all set. We agreed on arbitrary symbols for objects, sir, by the way of the visiplates, and worked out relationships and verbs and so on with diagrams and pictures. We've a couple of thousand words that have mutual meanings. We set up an analyzer to sort out their short-wave groups, which we feed into a decoding machine. And then the coding end of the machine picks out recordings to make the wave groups we want to send back. When you're ready to talk to the skipper of the other ship, sir, I think we're ready."

"H-m-m. What's your impression of their psychology?" The skipper asked the question of the psychologist.

"I don't know, sir," said the psychologist, harassed. "They seem to be completely direct. But they haven't let slip even a hint of the tenseness we know exists. They act as if they were simply setting up a means of communication for friendly conversation. But there is . . . well . . . an overtone—"

The psychologist was a good man at psychological mensuration, which is a good and useful field. But he was not equipped to analyze a completely alien thought-pattern.

"If I may say so, sir—" said Tommy uncomfortably.

"What?"

"They're oxygen brothers," said Tommy, "and they're not

too dissimilar to us in other ways. It seems to me, sir, that parallel evolution has been at work. Perhaps intelligence evolves in parallel lines, just as . . . well . . . basic bodily functions. I mean," he added conscientiously, "any living being of any sort must ingest, metabolize, and excrete. Perhaps any intelligent brain must perceive, apperceive, and find a personal reaction. I'm sure I've detected irony. That implies humor, too. In short, sir, I think they could be likable."

The skipper heaved himself to his feet.

"H-m-m," he said profoundly, "we'll see what they have to say."

He walked to the communications room. The scanner for the vision plate in the robot was in readiness. The skipper walked in front of it. Tommy Dort sat down at the coding machine and tapped at the keys. Highly improbable noises came from it, went into a microphone, and governed the frequency-modulation of a signal sent through space to the other spaceship. Almost instantly the vision screen which with one relay—in the robot—showed the interior of the other ship lighted up. An alien came before the scanner and seemed to look inquisitively out of the plate. He was extraordinarily manlike, but he was not human. The impression he gave was of extreme baldness and a somehow humorous frankness.

"I'd like to say," said the skipper heavily, "the appropriate things about this first contact of two dissimilar civilized races, and of my hopes that a friendly intercourse between the two people will result."

Tommy Dort hesitated. Then he shrugged and tapped expertly upon the coder. More improbable noises.

The alien skipper seemed to receive the message. He made a gesture which was wryly assenting. The decoder on the *Llanvabon* hummed to itself and word-cards dropped into the message frame. Tommy said dispassionately:

"He says, sir, 'That is all very well, but is there any way for us to let each other go home alive? I would be happy to hear of such a way if you can contrive it. At the moment it seems to me that one of us must be killed.' "

The atmosphere was of confusion. There were too many questions to be answered all at once. Nobody could answer any of them. And all of them had to be answered.

The *Llanvabon* could start for home. The alien ship might or might not be able to multiply the speed of light by one more unit than the Earth vessel. If it could, the *Llanvabon* would get close enough to Earth to reveal its destination—and then have to fight. It might or might not win. Even if it did win, the aliens might have a communication system by which the *Llanvabon*'s destination might have been reported to the aliens' home planet before battle was joined. But the *Llanvabon* might lose in such a fight. If she were to be destroyed, it would be better to be destroyed here, without giving any clue to where human beings might be found by a forewarned, forearmed alien battle fleet.

The black ship was in exactly the same predicament. It too, could start for home. But the *Llanvabon* might be faster, and an overdrive field can be trailed, if you set to work on it soon enough. The aliens, also, would not know whether the *Llanvabon* could report to its home base without returning. If the alien were to be destroyed, it also would prefer to fight it out here, so that it could not lead a probable enemy to its own civilization.

Neither ship, then, could think of flight. The course of the *Llanvabon* into the nebula might be known to the black ship, but it had been the end of a logarithmic curve, and the aliens could not know its properties. They could not tell from that from what direction the Earth ship had started. As of the moment, then, the two ships were even. But the question was and remained, "What now?"

There was no specific answer. The aliens traded information for information—and did not always realize what information they gave. The humans traded information for information—and Tommy Dort sweated blood in his anxiety not to give any clue to the whereabouts of Earth.

The aliens saw by infrared light, and the vision plates and scanners in the robot communication-exchange had to adapt their respective images up and down an optical octave each, for them to have any meaning at all. It did not occur to the aliens that their eyesight told that their sun was a red dwarf, yielding light of greatest energy just below the part of the spectrum visible to human eyes. But after that fact was realized on the *Llanvabon*, it was realized that the aliens, also, should be able to deduce the Sun's spectral type by the light to which men's eyes were best adapted.

There was a gadget for the recording of short-wave trains which was as casually in use among the aliens as a sound-recorder is among men. The humans wanted that badly. And the aliens were fascinated by the mystery of sound. They were able to perceive noise, of course, just as a man's palm will perceive infrared light by the sensation of heat it produces, but they could no more differentiate pitch or tone-quality than a man is able to distinguish between two frequencies of heat-radiation even half an octave apart. To them, the human science of sound was a remarkable discovery. They would find uses for noises which humans had never imagined—if they lived.

But that was another question. Neither ship could leave without first destroying the other. But while the flood of information was in passage, neither ship could afford to destroy the other. There was the matter of the outer coloring of the two ships. The *Llanvabon* was mirror-bright exteriorly. The alien ship was dead-black by visible light. It absorbed heat to perfection, and should radiate it away again as readily. But it did not. The black coating was not a "black body" color or lack of color. It was a perfect reflector of certain infrared wave lengths while simultaneously it fluoresced in just those wave bands. In practice, it absorbed the higher frequencies of heat, converted them to lower frequencies it did not radiate—and stayed at the desired temperature even in empty space.

Tommy Dort labored over his task of communications. He found the alien thought-processes not so alien that he could not follow them. The discussion of technics reached the matter of interstellar navigation. A star map was needed to illustrate the process. It would not have been logical to use a star map from the chart room—but from a star map one could guess the point from which the map was projected. Tommy had a map made specially, with imaginary but convincing star images upon it. He translated directions for its use by the coder and decoder. In return, the aliens presented a star map of their own before the visiplate. Copied instantly by photograph, the Nav officers labored over it, trying to figure out from what spot in the galaxy the stars and Milky Way would show at such an angle. It baffled them.

It was Tommy who realized finally that the aliens had made a special star map for their demonstration too, and that it was a mirror-image of the faked map Tommy had shown them previously.

Tommy could grin, at that. He began to like these aliens.

They were not humans, but they had a very human sense of the ridiculous. In course of time Tommy essayed a mild joke. It had to be translated into code numerals, these into quite cryptic groups of short-wave, frequency-modulated impulses, and these went to the other ship and into heaven knew what to become intelligible. A joke which went through such formalities would not seem likely to be funny. But the alien did see the point.

There was one of the aliens to whom communication became as normal a function as Tommy's own code-handlings. The two of them developed a quite insane friendship, conversing by coder, decoder, and short-wave trains. When technicalities in the official messages grew too involved, that alien sometimes threw in strictly nontechnical interpolations akin to slang. Often, they cleared up the confusion. Tommy, for no reason whatever, had filed a code-name of "Buck" which the decoder picked out regularly when this particular one signed his own symbol to a message.

In the third week of communication, the decoder suddenly presented Tommy with a message in the message frame:

You are a good guy. It is too bad we have to kill each other.—BUCK.

Tommy had been thinking much the same thing. He tapped off the rueful reply:

We can't see any way out of it. Can you?

There was a pause, and the message frame filled up again:

If we could believe each other, yes. Our skipper would like it. But we can't believe you, and you can't believe us. We'd trail you home if we got a chance, and you'd trail us. But we feel sorry about it.—BUCK.

Tommy Dort took the messages to the skipper.

"Look here, sir!" he said urgently. "These people are almost human, and they're likable cusses."

The skipper was busy about his important task of thinking things to worry about, and worrying about them. He said tiredly:

"They're oxygen breathers. Their air is twenty-eight percent oxygen instead of twenty, but they could do very well on Earth. It would be a highly desirable conquest for them. And we still don't know what weapons they've got or what they can develop. Would you tell them how to find Earth?"

"N-no," said Tommy, unhappily.

"They probably feel the same way," said the skipper dryly. "And if we did manage to make a friendly contact, how long would it stay friendly? If their weapons were inferior to ours, they'd feel that for their own safety they had to improve them. And we, knowing they were planning to revolt, would crush them while we could—for our own safety! If it happened to be the other way about, they'd have to smash us before we could catch up to them."

Tommy was silent, but he moved restlessly.

"If we smash this black ship and get home," said the skipper, "Earth Government will be annoyed if we don't tell them where it came from. But what can we do? We'll be lucky enough to get back alive with our warning. It isn't possible to get out of those creatures any more information than we give them, and we surely won't give them our address! We've run into them by accident. Maybe—if we smash this ship—there won't be another contact for thousands of years. And it's a pity, because trade could mean so much! But it takes two to make a peace, and we can't risk trusting them. The only answer is to kill them if we can, and if we can't, to make sure that when they kill us they'll find out nothing that will lead them to Earth. I don't like it," added the skipper tiredly, "but there simply isn't anything else to do!"

On the *Llanvabon*, the technicians worked frantically in two divisions. One prepared for victory, and the other for defeat. The ones working for victory could do little. The main blasters were the only weapons with any promise. Their mountings were cautiously altered so that they were no longer fixed nearly dead ahead, with only a 5° traverse. Electronic controls which followed a radiolocator master-finder would keep them trained with absolute precision upon a given target regardless of its maneuverings. More, a hitherto unsung genius in the engine room devised a capacity-storage system by which the normal full-output of the ship's engines could be momentarily accumulated and released in surges of stored power far above normal. In theory, the range of the blasters should be multiplied and their destructive power considerably stepped up. But there was not much more that could be done.

The defeat crew had more leeway. Star charts, navigational instruments carrying telltale notations, the photographic record Tommy Dort had made on the six-months' journey from Earth, and every other memorandum offering clues to Earth's position, were prepared for destruction. They were put in sealed files, and if any one of them was opened by one who did not know the exact, complicated process, the contents of all the files would flash into ashes and the ash be churned past any hope of restoration. Of course, if the *Llanvabon* should be victorious, a carefully not-indicated method of reopening them in safety would remain.

There were atomic bombs placed all over the hull of the ship. If its human crew should be killed without complete destruction of the ship, the atomic-power bombs should detonate if the *Llanvabon* was brought alongside the alien vessel. There were no ready-made atomic bombs on board, but there were small spare atomic-power units on board. It was not hard to trick them so that when they were turned on, instead of yielding a smooth flow of power they would explode. And four men of the earth ship's crew remained always in spacesuits with closed helmets, to fight the ship should it be punctured in many compartments by an unwarned attack.

Such an attack, however, would not be treacherous. The alien skipper had spoken frankly. His manner was that of one who wryly admits the uselessness of lies. The skipper and the *Llanvabon*, in turn, heavily admitted the virtue of frankness. Each insisted—perhaps truthfully—that he wished for friendship between the two races. But neither could trust the other not to make every conceivable effort to find out the one thing he needed most desperately to conceal—the location of his home planet. And neither dared believe that the other was unable to trail him and find out. Because each felt it his own duty to accomplish that unbearable—to the other—act, neither could risk the possible existence of his race by trusting the other. They must fight because they could not do anything else.

They could raise the stakes of the battle by an exchange of information beforehand. But there was a limit to the stake either would put up. No information on weapons, population, or resources would be given by either. Not even the distance of their home bases from the Crab Nebula would be told. They exchanged information, to be sure, but they knew a battle to the death must follow, and each strove to represent his own civilization as powerful enough to give pause to the other's ideas of possible conquest—and thereby increased its appearance of menace to the other, and made battle more unavoidable.

It was curious how completely such alien brains could mesh, however. Tommy Dort, sweating over the coding and decoding machines, found a personal equation emerging from the at first stilted arrays of word-cards which arranged themselves. He had seen the aliens only in the vision screen, and then only in light at least one octave removed from the light they saw by. They, in turn, saw him very strangely, by transposed illumination from what to them would be the far ultra-violet. But their brains worked alike. Amazingly alike. Tommy Dort felt an actual sympathy and even something close to friendship for the gill-breathing, bald, and dryly ironic creatures of the black space vessel.

Because of that mental kinship he set up—though hopelessly—a sort of table of the aspects of the problem before them. He did not believe that the ailens had any instinctive desire to destroy man. In fact, the study of communications from the aliens had produced on the *Llanvabon* a feeling of tolerance not unlike that between enemy soldiers during a truce on Earth. The men felt no enmity, and probably neither did the aliens. But they had to kill or be killed for strictly logical reasons.

Tommy's table was specific.. He made a list of objectives the men must try to achieve, in the order of their importance. The first was the carrying back of news of the existence of the alien culture. The second was the location of that alien culture in the galaxy. The third was the carrying back of as much information as possible about that culture. The third was being worked on, but the second was probably impossible. The first—and all—would depend on the result of the fight which must take place.

The aliens' objectives would be exactly similar, so that the men must prevent, first, news of the existence of Earth's culture from being taken back by the aliens, second, alien discovery of the location of Earth, and third, the acquiring by the aliens of information which would help them or encourage them to attack humanity. And again the third was in train, and the second was probably taken care of, and the first must await the battle.

There was no possible way to avoid the grim necessity of the destruction of the black ship. The aliens would see no solution to their problems but the destruction of the *Llanvabon.* But Tommy Dort, regarding his tabulation ruefully, realized that even complete victory would not be a perfect solution. The ideal would be for the *Llanvabon* to take back the alien ship for study. Nothing less would be a complete attainment of the third objective. But Tommy realized that he hated the idea of so complete a victory, even if it could be accomplished. He would hate the idea of killing even nonhuman creatures who understood a human fitting out a fleet of fighting ships to destroy an alien culture because its existence was dangerous. The pure accident of this encounter, between peoples who could like each other, had created a situation which could only result in wholesale destruction.

Tommy Dort soured on his own brain which could find no answer which would work. But there had to be an answer! The gamble was too big! It was too absurd that two spaceships should fight—neither one primarily designed for fighting—so that the survivor could carry back news which would set one race to frenzied preparation for war against the unwarned other.

If both races could be warned, though, and each knew that the other did not want to fight, and if they could communicate with each other but not locate each other until some grounds for mutual trust could be reached—

It was impossible. It was chimerical. It was a daydream. It was nonsense. But it was such luring nonsense that Tommy Dort ruefully put it into the coder to his gill-breathing friend Buck, then some hundred thousand miles off in the misty brightness of the nebula.

"Sure," said Buck, in the decoder's word-card's flicking into place in the message frame. "That is a good dream. But I like you and still won't believe you. If I said that first, you would like me but not believe me, either. I tell you the truth more than you believe, and maybe you tell me the truth more than I believe. But there is no way to know. I am sorry."

Tommy Dort stared gloomily at the message. He felt a very horrible sense of responsibility. Everyone did, on the *Llanvabon.* If they failed in this encounter, the human race would run a very good chance of being exterminated in time to come. If they succeeded, the race of the aliens would be the one to face destruction, most likely. Millions or billions of lives hung upon the actions of a few men.

Then Tommy Dort saw the answer.

It would be amazingly simple, if it worked. At worst it might give a partial victory to humanity and the *Llanvabon.* He sat quite still, not daring to move lest he break the chain of thought that followed the first tenuous idea. He went over and over it, excitedly finding objections here and meeting them, and overcoming impossibilities there. It was the answer! He felt sure of it.

He felt almost dizzy with relief when he found his way to the captain's room and asked leave to speak.

It is the function of a skipper, among others, to find things to worry about. But the *Llanvabon*'s skipper did not have to look. In the three weeks and four days since the first contact with the alien black ship, the skipper's face had grown lined and old. He had not only the *Llanvabon* to worry about. He had all of humanity.

"Sir," said Tommy Dort, his mouth rather dry because of his enormous earnestness, "may I offer a method of attack on the black ship? I'll undertake it myself, sir, and if it doesn't work our ship won't be weakened."

The skipper looked at him unseeingly.

"The tactics are all worked out, Mr. Dort," he said heavily. "They're being cut on tape now, for the ship's handling. It's a terrible gamble, but it has to be done."

"I think," said Tommy carefully, "I've worked out a way to take the gamble out. Suppose, sir, we send a message to the other ship, offering—"

His voice went on in the utterly quiet captain's room, with the visiplates showing only a vast mistiness outside and the two fiercely burning stars in the nebula's heart.

The skipper himself went through the air lock with Tommy. For one reason, the action Tommy had suggested would need his authority behind it. For another, the skipper had worried more intensely than anybody else on the *Llanvabon*, and he was tired of it. If he went with Tommy, he would do the thing himself, and if he failed he would be the first one killed—and the tape for the Earth ship's maneuvering was already fed into the control board and correlated with the master-timer. If Tommy and the skipper were killed, a single control pushed home would throw the *Llanvabon* into the most furious possible all-out attack, which would end in the complete destruction of one ship or the other—or both. So the skipper was not deserting his post.

The outer air lock door swung wide. It opened upon that shining emptiness which was the nebula. Twenty miles away, the little round robot hung in space, drifting in an incredible orbit about the twin central suns, and floating ever nearer and nearer. It would never reach either of them, of course. The white star alone was so much hotter than Earth's sun that its heat-effect would produce Earth's temperature on an object five times as far from it as Neptune is from Sol. Even removed to the distance of Pluto, the little robot would be raised to cherry-red heat by the blazing white dwarf. And it could not possibly approach to the ninety-odd million miles which is the Earth's distance from the sun. So near, its metal would melt and boil away as vapor. But, half a light-year out, the bulbous object bobbed in emptiness.

The two spacesuited figures soared away from the *Llanvabon.* The small atomic drives which made them minute spaceships on their own had been subtly altered, but the change did not interfere with their functioning. They headed for the communication robot. The skipper, out in space, said gruffly:

"Mr. Dort, all my life I have longed for adventure. This is the first time I could ever justify it to myself."

His voice came through Tommy's space-phone receivers. Tommy wet his lips and said:

"It doesn't seem like adventure to me, sir. I want terribly for the plan to go through. I thought adventure was when you didn't care."

"Oh, no," said the skipper. "Adventure is when you toss your life on the scales of chance and wait for the pointer to stop."

They reached the round object. They clung to its short, scanner-tipped horns.

"Intelligent, those creatures," said the skipper heavily. "They must want desperately to see more of our ship than the communication room, to agree to this exchange of visits before the fight."

"Yes, sir," said Tommy. But privately, he suspected that Buck—his gill-breathing friend—would like to see him in the flesh before one or both of them died. And it seemed to him that between the two ships had grown up an odd tradition of courtesy, like that between two ancient knights before a tourney, when they admired each other wholeheartedly before hacking at each other with all the contents of their respective armories.

They waited.

Then, out of the mist, came two other figures. The alien spacesuits were also power-driven. The aliens themselves were shorter than men, and their helmet openings were coated with a filtering material to cut off visible and ultraviolet rays which to them would be lethal. It was not possible to see more than the outline of the heads within.

Tommy's helmet phone said, from the communication room on the *Llanvabon*:

"They say that their ship is waiting for you, sir. The air lock door will be open."

The skipper's voice said heavily:

"Mr. Dort, have you seen their spacesuits before? If so, are you sure they're not carrying anything extra, such as bombs?"

"Yes, sir," said Tommy. "We've showed each other our space equipment. They've nothing but regular stuff in view, sir."

The skipper made a gesture to the two aliens. He and Tommy Dort plunged on for the black vessel. They could not make out the ship very clearly with the naked eye, but directions for change of course came from the communication room.

The black ship loomed up. It was huge, as long as the *Llanvabon* and vastly thicker. The air lock did stand open. The two spacesuited men moved in and anchored themselves with magnetic-soled boots. The outer door closed. There was a rush of air and simultaneously the sharp quick tug of artificial gravity. Then the inner door opened.

All was darkness. Tommy switched on his helmet light at the same instant as the skipper. Since the aliens saw by infrared, a white light would have been intolerable to them. The men's helmet lights were, therefore, of the deep-red tint used to illuminate instrument panels so there will be no dazzling of eyes that must be able to detect the minutest specks of white light on a navigating vision plate. There were aliens waiting to receive them. They blinked at the brightness of the helmet lights. The space-phone receivers said in Tommy's ear:

"They say, sir, their skipper is waiting for you."

Tommy and the skipper were in a long corridor with a soft flooring underfoot. Their lights showed details of which every one was exotic.

"I think I'll crack my helmet, sir," said Tommy.

He did. The air was good. By analysis it was thirty percent oxygen instead of twenty for normal air on Earth, but the pressure was less. It felt just right. The artificial gravity, too, was less than that maintained on the *Llanvabon*. The home planet of the aliens would be smaller than Earth, and—by the infrared data—circling close to a nearly dead, dull-red sun. The air had smells in it. They were utterly strange, but not unpleasant.

An arched opening. A ramp with the same soft stuff underfoot. Lights which actually shed a dim, dull-red glow about. The aliens had stepped up some of their illuminating equipment as an act of courtesy. The light might hurt their eyes, but it was a gesture of consideration which made Tommy even more anxious for his plan to go through.

The alien skipper faced them with what seemed to Tommy a gesture of wryly humorous deprecation. The helmet phones said:

"He says, sir, that he greets you with pleasure, but he has been able to think of only one way in which the problem created by the meeting of these two ships can be solved."

"He means a fight," said the skipper. "Tell him I'm here to offer another choice."

The *Llanvabon*'s skipper and the skipper of the alien ship were face to face, but their communication was weirdly indirect. The aliens used no sound in communication. Their talk, in fact, took place on microwaves and approximated telepathy. But they could not hear, in any ordinary sense of the word, so the skipper's and Tommy's speech approached telepathy, too, as far as they were concerned. When the skipper spoke, his space phone sent his words back to the *Llanvabon*, where the words were fed into the coder and short-wave equivalents sent back to the black ship. The alien skipper's reply went to the *Llanvabon* and through the decoder, and was retransmitted by space phone in words read from the message frame. It was awkward, but it worked.

The short and stocky alien skipper paused. The helmet phones relayed his translated, soundless reply.

"He is anxious to hear, sir."

The skipper took off his helmet. He put his hands at his belt in a belligerent pose.

"Look here!" he said truculently to the bald, strange creature in the unearthly red glow before him. "It looks like we have to fight and one batch of us get killed. We're ready to do it if we have to. But if you win, we've got it fixed so you'll never find out where Earth is, and there's a good chance we'll get you anyhow! If we win, we'll be in the same fix. And if we win and go back home, our government will fit out a fleet and start hunting your planet. And if we find it we'll be ready to blast it to hell! If you win, the same thing will happen to us! And it's all foolishness! We've stayed here a month, and we've swapped information, and we don't hate each other. There's no reason for us to fight except for the rest of our respective races!"

The skipper stopped for breath, scowling. Tommy Dort inconspicuously put his own hands on the belt of his spacesuit. He waited, hoping desperately that the trick would work.

"He says, sir," reported the helmet phones, "that all you say is true. But that his race has to be protected, just as you feel that yours must be."

"Naturally," said the skipper angrily, "but the sensible thing to do is to figure out how to protect it! Putting its future up as a gamble in a fight is not sensible. Our races have to be warned of each other's existence. That's true. But each should have proof that the other doesn't want to fight, but wants to be friendly. And we shouldn't be able to find each other, but we should be able to communicate with each other to work out grounds for a common trust. If our governments want to be fools, let them! But we should give them the chance to make friends, instead of starting a space war out of mutual funk!"

Briefly, the space phone said:

"He says that the difficulty is that of trusting each other now. With the possible existence of his race at stake, he cannot take any chance, and neither can you, of yielding an advantage."

"But my race," boomed the skipper, glaring at the alien captain, "my race has an advantage now. We came here to your ship in atom-powered spacesuits! Before we left, we altered the drives! We can set off ten pounds of sensitized fuel apiece, right here in this ship, or it can be set off by remote control from our ship! It will be rather remarkable if your fuel store doesn't blow up with us! In other words, if you don't accept my proposal for a commonsense approach to this predicament, Dort and I blow up in an atomic explosion, and your ship will be wrecked if not destroyed—and the *Llanvabon* will be attacking with everything it's got within two seconds after the blast goes off!"

The captain's room of the alien ship was a strange scene, with its dull-red illumination and the strange, bald, gill-breathing aliens watching the skipper and waiting for the inaudible translation of the harangue they could not hear. But a sudden tension appeared in the air. A sharp, savage feeling of strain. The alien skipper made a gesture. The helmet phones hummed.

"He says, sir, what is your proposal?"

"Swap ships!" roared the skipper. "Swap ships and go on home! We can fix our instruments so they'll do no trailing, he can do the same with his. We'll each remove our star maps and records. We'll each dismantle our weapons. The air will serve, and we'll take their ship and they'll take ours, and neither one can harm or trail the other, and each will carry home more information than can be taken otherwise! We can agree on this same Crab Nebula as a rendezvous when the double-star has made another circuit, and if our people want to meet them they can do it, and if they are scared they can duck it! That's my proposal! And he'll take it, or Dort and I blow up their ship and the *Llanvabon* blasts what's left!"

He glared about him while he waited for the translation to reach the tense small stocky figures about him. He could tell when it came because the tenseness changed. The figures stirred. They made gestures. One of them made convulsive movements. It lay down on the soft floor and kicked. Others leaned against its walls and shook.

The voice in Tommy Dort's helmet phones had been strictly crisp and professional, before, but now it sounded blankly amazed.

"He says, sir, that it is a good joke. Because the two crew members he sent to our ship, and that you passed on the way, have their spacesuits stuffed with atomic explosive too, sir, and he intended to make the very same offer and threat! Of course he accepts, sir. Your ship is worth more to him than his own, and his is worth more to you than the *Llanvabon*. It appears, sir, to be a deal."

Then Tommy Dort realized what the convulsive movements of the aliens were. They were laughter.

It wasn't quite as simple as the skipper had outlined it. The actual working out of the proposal was complicated. For three days the crews of the two ships were intermingled, the aliens learning the workings of the *Llanvabon*'s engines, and the men learning the controls of the black spaceship. It was a good joke—but it wasn't all a joke. There were men on the black ship, and aliens on the *Llanvabon*, ready at an instant's notice to blow up the vessels in question. And they would have done it in case of need, for which reason the need did not appear. But it was, actually, a better arrangement to have two expeditions return to two civilizations, under the current arrangement, than for either to return alone.

There were differences, though. There was some dispute about the removal of records. In most cases the dispute was settled by the destruction of the records. There was more trouble caused by the *Llanvabon*'s books, and the alien equivalent of a ship's library, containing works which approximated the novels of Earth. But those items were valuable to possible friendship, because they would show the two cultures, each to the other, from the viewpoint of normal citizens and without propaganda.

But nerves were tense during those three days. Aliens unloaded and inspected the foodstuffs intended for the men on the black ship. Men transshipped the foodstuffs the aliens would need to return to their home. There were endless details, from the exchange of lighting equipment to suit the eyesight of the exchanging crews, to a final check-up of apparatus. A joint inspection party of both races verified that all detector devices had been smashed but not removed, so that they could not be used for trailing and had not been smuggled away. And of course, the aliens were anxious not to leave any useful weapon on the black ship, nor the men upon the *Llanvabon*. It was a curious fact that each crew was best qualified to take exactly the measures which made an evasion of the agreement impossible.

There was a final conference before the two ships parted, back in the communication room of the *Llanvabon*.

"Tell the little runt," rumbled the *Llanvabon*'s former skipper, "that he's got a good ship and he'd better treat her right."

The message frame flicked word-cards into position.

"I believe," it said on the alien skipper's behalf, "that your ship is just as good. I will hope to meet you here when the double star has turned one turn."

The last man left the *Llanvabon.* It moved away into the misty nebula before they had returned to the black ship. The vision plates in that vessel had been altered for human eyes, and human crewmen watched jealously for any trace of their former ship as their new craft took a crazy, evading course to a remote part of the nebula. It came to a crevasse of nothingness, leading to the stars. It rose swiftly to clear space. There was the instant of breathlessness which the overdrive field produces as it goes on, and then the black ship whipped away into the void at many times the speed of light.

Many days later, the skipper saw Tommy Dort poring over one of the strange objects which were the equivalent of books. It was fascinating to puzzle over. The skipper was pleased with himself. The technicians of the *Llanvabon*'s former crew were finding out desirable things about the ship almost momently. Doubtless the aliens were as pleased with their discoveries in the *Llanvabon.* But the black ship would be enormously worthwhile—and the solution that had been found was by any standard much superior even to combat in which the Earthmen had been overwhelmingly victorious.

"Hm-m-m. Mr. Dort," said the skipper profoundly. "You've no equipment to make another photographic record on the way back. It was left on the *Llanvabon.* But fortunately, we have your record taken on the way out, and I shall report most favorably on your suggestion and your assistance in carrying it out. I think very well of you, sir."

"Thank you, sir," said Tomy Dort.

He waited. The skipper cleared his throat.

"You . . . ah . . . first realized the close similarity of mental processes between the aliens and ourselves," he observed. "What do you think of the prospects of a friendly arrangement if we keep a rendezvous with them at the nebula as agreed?"

"Oh, we'll get along all right, sir," said Tommy. "We've got a good start toward friendship. After all, since they see by infrared, the planets they'd want to make use of wouldn't suit us. There's no reason why we shouldn't get along. We're almost alike in psychology."

"Hm-m-m. Now just what do you mean by that?" demanded the skipper.

"Why, they're just like us, sir!" said Tommy. "Of course they breathe through gills and they see by heat waves, and their blood has a copper base instead of iron and a few little details like that. But otherwise we're just alike! There were only men in their crew, sir, but they have two sexes as we have, and they have families, and . . . er . . . their sense of humor— In fact—"

Tommy hesitated.

"Go on, sir," said the skipper.

"Well— There was the one I call Buck, sir, because he hasn't any name that goes into sound waves," said Tommy. "We got along very well. I'd really call him my friend, sir. And we were together for a couple of hours just before the two ships separated and we'd nothing in particular to do. So I became convinced that humans and aliens are bound to be good friends if they have only half a chance. You see, sir, we spent those two hours telling dirty jokes."

THE VANISHING VENUSIANS

by Leigh Brackett (1915-1978)

PLANET STORIES,
Spring

One reason why much pulp science fiction is unreadable today is that discoveries in science have invalidated some of the basic assumptions upon which these stories rest. This is particularly true in the case of astronomy—we now know what is on the other side of the moon and we have set mechanical feet and eyes on the planet Mars. We also know a great deal about Venus, enough to invalidate the entire setting of "The Vanishing Venusians"—no bodies of water and no Venusians swimming in them.

But "The Vanishing Venusians" belongs in this book because of its color, its strong characterizations, and its adventure; all characteristics of the work of its author, the late and lamented Leigh Brackett, a star of and the essence of the best of Planet Stories *in the 1940s.*

(Marty mentioned the fact that Venus has no bodies of water [or any liquid] and no Venusians swimming in them.

Actually Venus is even worse than that. It has a temperature considerably higher than that required to melt lead on every part of its surface from its poles to its equator by day and by night. It has an atmosphere ninety times as dense as that of Earth, consisting almost entirely of carbon dioxide. And its clouds are composed of droplets of sulfuric acid.

Unless our technology advances to the point where we can alter the essential properties of Venus's atmosphere and import water, human beings will never colonize the planet and, in fact, never set foot upon it. —And that's too bad. Of all the planets of pre-space-age astronomy, Venus was the most interesting. What stories it gave us of a lush, primitive world overflowing with life. And it's gone—all gone—and we are left with a hot, utterly barren ball of rock.

And yet while the science fiction stories of the past are still with us, as Leigh's is, the memory will remain. I.A.)

The breeze was steady enough, but it was not in a hurry. It filled the lug sail just hard enough to push the dirty weed-grown hull through the water, and no harder. Matt Harker lay alongside the tiller and counted the trickles of sweat crawling over his nakedness, and stared with sullen, opaque eyes into the indigo night. Anger, leashed and impotent, rose in his throat like bitter vomit.

The sea—Rory McLaren's Venusian wife called it the Sea of Morning Opals—lay unstirring, black, streaked with phosphorescence. The sky hung low over it, the thick cloud blanket of Venus that had made the Sun a half-remembered legend to the exiles from Earth. Riding lights burned in the blue gloom, strung out in line. Twelve ships, thirty-eight hundred people, going no place, trapped in the interval between birth and death and not knowing what to do about it.

Matt Harker glanced upward at the sail and then at the stern lantern of the ship ahead. His face, in the dim glow that lights Venus even at inght, was a gaunt oblong of shadows and hard bone, reamed and scarred with living, with wanting and not having, with dying and not being dead. He was a lean man, wiry and not tall, with a snakelike surety of motion.

Somebody came scrambling quietly aft along the deck, avoiding the sleeping bodies crowded everywhere. Harker said, without emotion, "Hi, Rory."

Rory McLaren said, "Hi, Matt." He sat down. He was young, perhaps half Harker's age. There was still hope in his face, but it was growing tired. He sat for a while without speaking, looking at nothing, and then said, "Honest to God, Matt, how much longer can we last?"

"What's the matter, kid? Starting to crack?"

"I don't know. Maybe. When are we going to stop somewhere?"

"When we find a place to stop."

"Is there a place to stop? Seems like ever since I was born we've been hunting. There's always something wrong. Hostile natives, or fever, or bad soil, always something, and we go on again. It's not right. It's not any way to try to live."

Harker said, "I told you not to go having kids."

"What's that got to do with it?"

"You start worrying. The kid isn't even here yet, and already you're worrying."

"Sure I am." McLaren put his head in his hands suddenly and swore. Harker knew he did that to keep from crying. "I'm worried," McLaren said, "that maybe the same thing'll happen to my wife and kid that happened to yours. We got fever aboard."

Harker's eyes were like blown coals for an instant. Then he glanced up at the sail and said, "They'd be better off if it didn't live."

"That's no kind of a thing to say."

"It's the truth. Like you asked me, when are we going to stop somewhere? Maybe never. You bellyache about it ever since you were born. Well, I've been at it longer than that. Before you were born I saw our first settlement burned by the Cloud People, and my mother and father crucified in their own vineyard. I was there when this trek to the Promised Land began, back on Earth, and I'm still waiting for the promise."

The sinews in Harker's face were drawn like knots of wire. His voice had a terrible quietness.

"Your wife and kid would be better off to die now, while Viki's still young and has hope, and before the child ever opens its eyes."

Sim, the big black man, relieved Harker before dawn. He started singing, softly—something mournful and slow as the breeze, and beautiful. Harker cursed him and went up into the bow to sleep, but the song stayed with him. *Oh, I looked over Jordan, and what did I see, comin' for to carry me home. . . .*

Harker slept. Presently he began to moan and twitch, and then cry out. People around him woke up. They watched with interest. Harker was a lone wolf awake, ill-tempered and violent. When, at long intervals, he would have one of his spells, no one was anxious to help him out of it. They liked peeping inside of Harker when he wasn't looking.

Harker didn't care. He was playing in the snow again. He was seven years old, and the drifts were high and white, and above them the sky was so blue and clean that he wondered if God mopped it every few days like Mom did the kitchen floor. The sun was shining. It was like a great gold coin, and it made the snow burn like crushed diamonds. He put his arms up to the sun, and the cold air slapped him with clean hands, and he laughed. And then it was all gone. . . .

"By gawd," somebody said. "Ain't them tears on his face?"

"Bawling. Bawling like a little kid. Listen at him."

"Hey," said the first one sheepishly. "Reckon we oughta wake him up?"

"Hell with him, the old sour-puss. Hey, listen to that . . . !"

"Dad," Harker whispered. "Dad, I want to go home."

The dawn came like a sifting of fire-opals through the layers of pearl-gray cloud. Harker heard the yelling dimly in his sleep. He felt dull and tired, and his eyelids stuck together. The yelling gradually took shape and became the word "Land!" repeated over and over. Harker kicked himself awake and got up.

The tideless sea glimmered with opaline colors under the mist. Flocks of little jewel-scaled sea-dragons rose up from the ever-present floating islands of weed, and the weed itself, part of it, writhed and stretched with sentient life.

Ahead there was a long low hummock of muddy ground fading into tangled swamp. Beyond it, rising sheer into the clouds, was a granite cliff, a sweeping escarpment that stood like a wall against the hopeful gaze of the exiles.

Harker found Rory McLaren standing beside him, his arm around Viki, his wife. Viki was one of several Venusians who had married into the Earth colony. Her skin was clear white, her hair a glowing silver, her lips vividly red. Her eyes were like the sea, changeable, full of hidden life. Just now they had that special look that the eyes of women get when they're thinking about creation. Harker looked away.

McLaren said, "It's land."

Harker said, "It's mud. It's swamp. It's fever. It's like the rest."

Viki said, "Can we stop here, just a little while?"

Harker shrugged. "That's up to Gibbons." He wanted to ask what the hell difference it made where the kid was born, but for once he held his tongue. He turned away. Somewhere in the waist a woman was screaming in delirium. There were three shapes wrapped in ragged blankets and laid on planks by the port scuppers. Harker's mouth twitched in a crooked smile.

"We'll probably stop long enough to bury them," he said. "Maybe that'll be time enough."

He caught a glimpse of McLaren's face. The hope in it was not tired any more. It was dead. Dead, like the rest of Venus.

Gibbons called the chief men together aboard his ship—the leaders, the fighters and hunters and seamen, the tough leathery men who were the armor around the soft body of the colony. Harker was there, and McLaren. McLaren was young, but up until lately he had had a quality of optimism that cheered his shipmates, a natural leadership.

Gibbons was an old man. He was the original guiding spirit of the five thousand colonists who had come out from Earth to a new start on a new world. Time and tragedy, disappointment and betrayal had marked him cruelly, but his head was still high. Harker admired his guts while cursing him for an idealistic fool.

The inevitable discussion started as to whether they should try a permanent settlement on this mud flat or go on wandering over the endless, chartless seas. Harker said impatiently:

"For cripesake, look at the place. Remember the last time. Remember the time before that, and stop bleating."

Sim, the big black, said quietly, "The people are getting awful tired. A man was meant to have roots some place. There's going to bc trouble pretty soon if we don't find land."

Harker said, "You think you can find some, pal, go to it."

Gibbons said heavily, "But he's right. There's hysteria, fever, dysentery and boredom, and the boredom's worst of all."

McLaren said, "I vote to settle."

Harker laughed. He was leaning by the cabin port, looking out at the cliffs. The gray granite looked clean above the swamp. Harker tried to pierce the clouds that hid the top, but couldn't. His dark eyes narrowed. The heated voices behind him faded into distance. Suddenly he turned and said, "Sir, I'd like permission to see what's at the top of those cliffs."

There was complete silence. Then Gibbons said slowly, "We've lost too many men on journeys like that before, only to find the plateau uninhabitable."

"There's always the chance. Our first settlement was in the high plateaus, remember. Clean air, good soil, no fever."

"I remember," Gibbons said. "I remember." He was silent for a while, then he gave Harker a shrewd glance. "I know you, Matt. I might as well give permission."

Harker grinned. "You won't miss me much anyhow. I'm not a good influence anymore." He started for the door. "Give me three weeks. You'll take that long to careen and scrape the bottoms anyhow. Maybe I'll come back with something."

McLaren said, "I'm going with you, Matt."

Harker gave him a level-eyed stare. "You better stay with Viki."

"If there's good land up there, and anything happens to you so you can't come back and tell us. . . ."

"Like not bothering to come back, maybe?"

"I didn't say that. Like we both won't come back. But two is better than one."

Harker smiled. The smile was enigmatic and not very nice. Gibbons said, "He's right, Matt." Harker shrugged. Then Sim stood up.

"Two is good," he said, "but three is better." He turned to Gibbons. "There's nearly five hundred of us, sir. If there's new land up there, we ought to share the burden of finding it."

Gibbons nodded. Harker said, "You're crazy, Sim. Why you want to do all that climbing, maybe to no place?"

Sim smiled. His teeth were unbelievably white in the sweat-polished blackness of his face. "But that's what my people always done, Matt. A lot of climbing, to no place."

They made their preparations and had a last night's sleep. McLaren said good-bye to Viki. She didn't cry. She knew why he was going. She kissed him, and all she said was, "Be careful." All he said was, "I'll be back before he's born."

They started at dawn, carrying dried fish and sea-berries made into pemmican, and their long knives and ropes for climbing. They had long ago run out of ammunition for their few blasters, and they had no equipment for making more.

All were adept at throwing spears, and carried three short ones barbed with bone across their backs.

It was raining when they crossed the mud flat, wading thigh-deep in heavy mist. Harker led the way through the belt of swamp. He was an old hand at it, with an uncanny quickness in spotting vegetation that was as independently alive and hungry as he was. Venus is one vast hothouse, and the plants have developed into species as varied and marvelous as the reptiles or the mammals, crawling out of the pre-Cambrian seas as primitive flagellates and growing wills of their own, with appetites and motive power to match. The children of the colony learned at an early age not to pick flowers. The blossoms too often bit back.

The swamp was narrow, and they came out of it safely. A great swamp-dragon, a *leshen*, screamed not far off, but they hunt by night, and it was too sleepy to chase them. Harker stood finally on firm ground and studied the cliff.

The rock was roughened by weather, hacked at by ages of erosion, savaged by earthquake. There were stretches of loose shale and great slabs that looked as though they would peel off at a touch, but Harker nodded.

"We can climb it," he said. "Question is, how high is up?"

Sim laughed. "High enough for the Golden City, maybe. Have we all got a clear conscience? Can't carry no load of sin that far!"

Rory McLaren looked at Harker.

Harker said, "All right, I confess. I don't care if there's land up there or not. All I wanted was to get the hell out of that damn boat before I went clean nuts. So now you know."

McLaren nodded. He didn't seem surprised. "Let's climb."

By morning of the second day they were in the clouds. They crawled upward through opal-tinted steam, half liquid, hot and unbearable. They crawled for two more days. The first night or two Sim sang during his watch, while they rested on some ledge. After that he was too tired. McLaren began to give out, though he wouldn't say so. Matt Harker grew more taciturn and ill-tempered, if possible, but otherwise there was no change. The clouds continued to hide the top of the cliff.

During one rest break McLaren said hoarsely, "Don't these cliffs ever end?" His skin was yellowish, his eyes glazed with fever.

"Maybe," said Harker, "they go right up beyond the sky."

The fever was on him again, too. It lived in the marrow of the exiles, coming out at intervals to shake and sear them, and then retreating. Sometimes it did not retreat, and after nine days there was no need.

McLaren said, "You wouldn't care if they did, would you?"

"I didn't ask you to come."

"But you wouldn't care."

"Ah, shut up."

McLaren went for Harker's throat.

Harker hit him, with great care and accuracy. McLaren sagged down and took his head in his hands and wept. Sim stayed out of it. He shook his head, and after a while he began to sing to himself, or someone beyond himself. "Oh, nobody knows the trouble I see. . . ."

Harker pulled himself up. His ears rang and he shivered uncontrollably, but he could still take some of McLaren's weight on himself. They were climbing a steep ledge, fairly wide and not difficult.

"Let's get on," said Harker.

About two hundred feet beyond that point the ledge dipped and began to go down again in a series of broken steps. Overhead the cliff face bulged outward. Only a fly could have climbed it. They stopped. Harker cursed with vicious slowness. Sim closed his eyes and smiled. He was a little crazy with fever himself.

"Golden City's at the top. That's where I'm going."

He started off along the ledge, following its decline toward a jutting shoulder, around which it vanished. Harker laughed sardonically. McLaren pulled free of him and went doggedly after Sim. Harker shrugged and followed.

Around the shoulder the ledge washed out completely.

They stood still. The steaming clouds shut them in before, and behind was a granite wall hung within thick fleshy creepers. Dead end.

"Well?" said Harker.

McLaren sat down. He didn't cry, or say anything. He just sat. Sim stood with his arms hanging and his chin on his huge black chest. Harker said, "See what I meant, about the Promised Land? Venus is a fixed wheel, and you can't win."

It was then that he noticed the cool air. He had thought it was just a fever chill, but it lifted his hair, and it had a definite pattern on his body. It even had a cool, clean smell to it. It was blowing out through the creepers.

Harker began ripping with his knife. He broke through into a cave mouth, a jagged rip worn smooth at the bottom by what must once have been a river.

"That draft is coming from the top of the plateau," Harker said. "Wind must be blowing up there and pushing it down. There may be a way through."

McLaren and Sim both showed a slow, terrible growth of hope. The three of them went without speaking into the tunnel.

2

They made good time. The clean air acted as a tonic, and hope spurred them on. The tunnel sloped upward rather sharply, and presently Harker heard water, a low thunderous murmur as of an underground river up ahead. It was utterly dark, but the smooth channel of stone was easy to follow.

Sim said, "Isn't that light up ahead?"

"Yeah," said Harker. "Some kind of phosphorescence. I don't like that river. It may stop us."

They went on in silence. The glow grew stronger, the air more damp. Patches of phosphorescent lichen appeared on the walls, glimmering with dim jewel tones like an unhealthy rainbow. The roar of the water was very loud.

They came upon it suddenly. It flowed across the course of their tunnel in a broad channel worn deep into the rock, so that its level had fallen below its old place and left the tunnel dry. It was a wide river, slow and majestic. Lichen spangled the roof and walls, reflecting in dull glints of color from the water.

Overhead there was a black chimney going up through the rock, and the cool draft came from there with almost hurricane force, much of which was dissipated in the main river tunnel. Harker judged there was a cliff formation on the surface that siphoned the wind downward. The chimney was completely inaccessible.

Harker said, "I guess we'll have to go upstream, along the side." The rock was eroded enough to make that possible, showing wide ledges at different levels.

McLaren said, "What if this river doesn't come from the surface? What if it starts from an underground source?"

"You stuck your neck out," Harker said. "Come on."

They started. After a while, tumbling like porpoises in the black water, the golden creatures swam by, and saw the men, and stopped, and swam back again.

They were not very large, the largest about the size of a twelve-year-old child. Their bodies were anthropoid, but adapted to swimming with shimmering webs. They glowed with a golden light, phosphorescent like the lichen, and their eyes were lidless and black, like one huge spreading pupil. Their faces were incredible. Harker could remember, faintly, the golden dandelions that grew on the lawn in summer. The heads and faces of the swimmers were like that, covered with streaming petals that seemed to have independent movements, as though they were sensory organs as well as decoration.

Harker said, "For cripesake, what are they?"

"They look like flowers," McLaren said.

"They look more like fish," the black man said.

Harker laughed. "I'll bet they're both. I'll bet they're plannies that grew where they had to be amphibious." The colonists had shortened plant-animal to planimal, and then just planny. "I've seen gimmicks in the swamps that weren't so far away from these. But jeez, get the eyes on 'em! They look human."

"The shape's human, too, almost." McLaren shivered. "I wish they wouldn't look at us that way."

Sim said, "As long as they just look. I'm not gonna worry. . . ."

They didn't. They started to close in below the men, swimming effortlessly against the current. Some of them began to clamber out on the low ledge behind them. They were agile and graceful. There was something unpleasantly childlike about them. There were fifteen or twenty of them, and they reminded Harker of a gang of mischievous kids—only the mischief had a queer soulless quality of malevolence.

Harker led the way faster along the ledge. His knife was drawn and he carried a short spear in his right hand.

The tone of the river changed. The channel broadened, and up ahead Harker saw that the cavern ended in a vast shadowy place, the water spreading into a dark lake, spilling slowly out over a low wide lip of rock. More of the shining child-things were playing there. They joined their fellows, closing the ring tighter around the three men.

"I don't like this," McLaren said. "If they'd only make a noise!"

They did, suddenly—a shrill tittering like a blasphemy of childish laughter. Their eyes shone. They rushed in, running wetly along the ledge, reaching up out of the water to claw at ankles, laughing. Inside his tough flat belly Harker's guts turned over.

McLaren yelled and kicked. Claws raked his ankle, spiny needle-sharp things like thorns. Sim ran his spear clean through a golden breast. There were no bones in it. The body was light and membranous, and the blood that ran out was sticky and greenish, like sap. Harker kicked two of the things back in the river, swung his spear like a ball bat and knocked two more off the ledge—they were unbelievably light—and shouted, "Up there, that high ledge. I don't think they can climb that."

He thrust McLaren bodily past him and helped Sim fight a rear-guard action while they all climbed a rotten and difficult transit. McLaren crouched at the top and hurled chunks of stone at the attackers. There was a great crack running up and clear across the cavern roof, scar of some ancient earthquake. Presently a small slide started.

"Okay," Harker panted. "Quit before you bring the roof down. They can't follow us." The plannies were equipped for swimming, not climbing. They clawed angrily and slipped back, and then retreated sullenly to the water. Abruptly they seized the body with Sim's spear through it and devoured it, quarreling fiercely over it. McLaren leaned over the edge and was sick.

Harker didn't feel so good himself. He got up and went on. Sim helped McLaren, whose ankle was bleeding badly.

This higher ledge angled up and around the wall of the great lake-cavern. It was cooler and drier here, and the lichens thinned out, and vanished, leaving total darkness. Harker yelled once. From the echo of his voice the place was enormous.

Down below in the black water golden bodies streaked like comets in an ebon universe, going somewhere, going fast. Harker felt his way carefully along. His skin twitched with a nervous impulse of danger, a sense of something unseen, unnatural, and wicked.

Sim said, "I hear something."

They stopped. The blind air lay heavy with a subtle

fragrance, spicy and pleasant, yet somehow unclean. The water sighed lazily far below. Somewhere ahead was a smooth rushing noise which Harker guessed was the river inlet. But none of that was what Sim meant.

He meant the rippling, rustling sound that came from everywhere in the cavern. The black surface of the lake was dotted now with spots of burning phosphorescent color, trailing fiery wakes. The spots grew swiftly, coming nearer, and became carpets of flowers, scarlet and blue and gold and purple. Floating fields of them, and towed by shining swimmers.

"My God," said Harker softly. "How big are they?"

"Enough to make three of me." Sim was a big man. "Those little ones were children, all right. They went and got their papas. Oh, Lord!"

The swimmers were very like the smaller ones that attacked them by the river, except for their giant size. They were not cumbersome. They were magnificent, supple-limbed and light. Their membranes had spread into great shining wings, each rib tipped with fire. Only the golden dandelion heads had changed.

They had shed their petals. Their adult heads were crowned with flat, coiled growths having the poisonous and filthy beauty of fungus. And their faces were the faces of men.

For the first time since childhood Harker was cold.

The fields of burning flowers were swirled together at the base of the cliff. The golden giants cried out suddenly, a sonorous belling note, and the water was churned to blazing foam as thousands of flowerlike bodies broke away and started up the cliff on suckered, spidery legs.

It didn't look as though it was worth trying, but Harker said, "Let's get the hell on!" There was a faint light now, from the army below. He began to run along the ledge, the others close on his heels. The flower-hounds coursed swiftly upward, and their masters swam easily below, watching.

The ledge dropped. Harker shot along it like a deer. Beyond the lowest dip it plunged into the tunnel whence the river came. A short tunnel, and at the far end . . .

"Daylight!" Harker shouted. "Daylight!"

McLaren's bleeding leg gave out and he fell.

Harker caught him. They were at the lowest part of the dip. The flower-beasts were just below, rushing higher.

McLaren's foot was swollen, the calf of his leg discolored. Some swift infection from the planny's claws. He fought Harker. "Go on," he said. "Go on!"

Harker slapped him hard across the temple. He started on, half carrying McLaren, but he saw it wasn't going to work. McLaren weighed more than he did. He thrust McLaren into Sim's powerful arms. The big black nodded and ran, carrying the half-conscious man like a child. Harker saw the first of the flower-things flow up onto the ledge in front of them.

Sim hurdled them. They were not large, and there were only three of them. They rushed to follow and Harker speared them, slashing and striking with the sharp bone tip. Behind him the full tide rushed up. He ran, but they were faster. He drove them back with spear and knife, and ran again, and turned and fought again, and by the time they had reached the tunnel Harker was staggering with weariness.

Sim stopped. He said, "There's no way out."

Harker glanced over his shoulder. The river fell sheer down a high face of rock—too high and with too much force in the water even for the giant water-plannies to think of attempting. Daylight poured through overhead, warm and welcoming, and it might as well have been on Mars.

Dead end.

Then Harker saw the little eroded channel twisting up at the side. Little more than a drainpipe, and long dry, leading to a passage beside the top of the falls—a crack barely large enough for a small man to crawl through. It was a hell of a ragged hope, but. . . .

Harker pointed, between jabs at the swarming flowers. Sim yelled, "You first." Because Harker was the best climber, he obeyed, helping the gasping McLaren up behind him. Sim wielded his spear like a lightning brand, guarding the rear, creeping up inch by inch.

He reached a fairly secure perch, and stopped. His huge chest pumped like a bellows, his arm rose and fell like a polished bar of ebony. Harker shouted to him to come on. He and McLaren were almost at the top.

Sim laughed. "How you going to get me through that little bitty hole?"

"Come on, you fool!"

"You better hurry. I'm about finished."

"Sim! Sim, damn you!"

"Crawl out through that hole, runt, and pull that stringbean with you! I'm a man-sized man, and I got to stay." Then, furiously, "Hurry up or they'll drag you back before you're through."

He was right. Harker knew he was right. He went to work pushing and jamming McLaren through the narrow opening. McLaren was groggy and not much help, but he was thin and small-boned, and he made it. He rolled out on a slope covered with green grass, the first Harker had seen since he was a child. He began to struggle after McLaren. He did not look back at Sim.

The black man was singing, about the glory of the coming of the Lord.

Harker put his head back into the darkness of the creek. "Sim!"

"Yeah?" Faintly, hoarse, echoing.

"There's land here, Sim. Good land."

"Yeah."

"Sim, we'll find a way. . . ."

Sim was singing again. The sound grew fainter, diminishing downward into distance. The words were lost, but not what lay behind them. Matt Harker buried his face in the green grass, and Sim's voice went with him into the dark.

The clouds were turning color with the sinking of the hidden sun. They hung like a canopy of hot gold washed in blood. It was utterly silent, except for the birds. You never heard birds like that down in the low places. Matt Harker rolled over and sat up slowly. He felt as though he had been beaten. There was a sickness in him, and a shame, and the old dark anger lying coiled and deadly above his heart.

Before him lay the long slope of grass to the river, which bent away to the left out of sight behind a spur of granite. Beyond the slope was a broad plain and then a forest of gigantic trees. They seemed to float in the coppery haze, their dark branches outspread like wings and starred with flowers. The air was cool, with no taint of mud or rot. The grass was rich, the soil beneath it clean and sweet.

Rory McLaren moaned softly and Harker turned. His leg looked bad. He was in a sort of stupor, his skin flushed and dry. Harker swore softly, wondering what he was going to do.

He looked back toward the plain, and he saw the girl.

He didn't know how she got there. Perhaps out of the bushes that grew in thick clumps on the slope. She could have been there a long time, watching. She was watching now, standing quite still about forty feet away. A great scarlet butterfly clung to her shoulder, moving its wings with lazy delight.

She seemed more like a child than a woman. She was naked, small and slender and exquisite. Her skin had a faint translucent hint of green under its whiteness. Her hair, curled short to her head, was deep blue, and her eyes were blue also, and very strange.

Harker stared at her, and she at him, neither of them moving. A bright bird swooped down and hovered by her lips for a moment, caressing her with its beak. She touched it and smiled, but she did not take her eyes from Harker.

Harker got to his feet, slowly, easily. He said, "Hello."

She did not move, or make a sound, but quite suddenly a pair of enormous birds, beaked and clawed like eagles and black as sin, made a whistling rush down past Harker's head and returned, circling. Harker sat down again.

The girl's strange eyes moved from him, upward to the crack in the hillside whence he had come. Her lips didn't move, but her voice—or something—spoke clearly inside Harker's head.

"You came from—There." *There* had tremendous feeling in it, and none of it nice.

Harker said, "Yes. A telepath, huh?"

"But you're not. . . ." A picture of the golden swimmers formed in Harker's mind. It was recognizable, but hatred and fear had washed out all the beauty, leaving only horror.

Harker said, "No." He explained about himself and McLaren. He told about Sim. He knew she was listening carefully to his mind, testing it for truth. He was not worried about what she would find. "My friend is hurt," he said. "We need food and shelter."

For some time there was no answer. The girl was looking at Harker again. His face, the shape and texture of his body, his hair, and then his eyes. He had never been looked at quite that way before. He began to grin. A provocative, be-damned-to-you grin that injected a surprising amount of light and charm into his sardonic personality.

"Honey," he said, "you are terrific. Animal, mineral, or vegetable?"

She tipped her small round head in surprise, and asked his own question right back. Harker laughed. She smiled, her mouth making a small inviting V, and her eyes had sparkles in them. Harker started toward her.

Instantly the birds warned him back. The girl laughed, a mischievous ripple of merriment. "Come," she said, and turned away.

Harker frowned. He leaned over and spoke to McLaren, with peculiar gentleness. He managed to get the boy erect, and then swung him across his shoulders, staggering slightly under the weight. McLaren said distinctly, "I'll be back before he's born."

Harker waited until the girl had started, keeping his distance. The two black birds followed watchfully. They walked out across the thick grass of the plain, toward the trees. The sky was now the color of blood.

A light breeze caught the girl's hair and played with it. Matt Harker saw that the short curled strands were broad and flat, like blue petals.

3

It was a long walk to the forest. The top of the plateau seemed to be bowl-shaped, protected by encircling cliffs. Harker, thinking back to that first settlement long ago, decided that this place was infinitely better. It was like the visions he had seen in fever dreams—the Promised Land. The coolness and cleanness of it were like having weights removed from your lungs and heart and body.

The rejuvenating air didn't make up for McLaren's weight, however. Presently Harker said, "Hold it," and sat down, tumbling McLaren gently onto the grass. The girl stopped. She came back a little way and watched Harker, who was blowing like a spent horse. He grinned up at her.

"I'm shot," he said. "I've been too busy for a man of my age. Can't you get hold of somebody to help me carry him?"

Again she studied him with puzzled fascination. Night was closing in, a clear indigo, less dark than at sea level. Her eyes had a curious luminosity in the gloom.

"Why do you do that?" she asked.

"Do what?"

"Carry it."

By "it" Harker guessed she meant McLaren. He was suddenly, coldly conscious of a chasm between them that no amount of explanation could bridge. "He's my friend. He's . . . I have to."

She studied his thought and then shook her head. "I don't understand. It's spoiled—" her thought-image was a combination of "broken," "finished," and "useless"—"Why carry it around?"

"McLaren's not an 'it.' He's a man like me, my friend. He's hurt, and I have to help him."

"I don't understand." Her shrug said it was his funeral, also that he was crazy. She started on again, paying no attention to Harker's call for her to wait. Perforce, Harker picked up McLaren and staggered on again. He wished Sim were here, and immediately wished he hadn't thought of Sim. He hoped Sim had died quickly before—before what? *Oh God, it's dark and I'm scared and my belly's all gone to cold water, and that thing trotting ahead of me through the blue haze . . .*

The thing was beautiful, though. Beautifully formed, fascinating, a curved slender gleam of moonlight, a chaliced flower holding the mystic, scented nectar of the unreal, the unknown, the undiscovered. Harker's blood began, in spite of himself, to throb with a deep excitement.

They came under the fragrant shadows of the trees. The forest was open, with broad mossy ridges and clearings. There were flowers underfoot, but no brush, and clumps of ferns. The girl stopped and stretched up her hand. A feathery branch, high out of her reach, bent and brushed her face, and she plucked a great pale blossom and set it in her hair.

She turned and smiled at Harker. He began to tremble, partly with weariness, partly with something else.

"How do you do that?" he asked.

She was puzzled. "The branch, you mean? Oh, that!" She laughed. It was the first sound he had heard her make, and it shot through him like warm silver. "I just think I would like a flower, and it comes."

Teleportation, telekinetic energy—what did the books call it? Back on Earth they knew something about that, but the colony hadn't had much time to study even its own meager library. There had been some religious sect that could make roses bend into their hands. Old wisdom, the force behind the Biblical miracles, just the infinite power of thought. Very simple. Yeah. Harker wondered uneasily whether she could work it on him, too. But then, he had a brain of his own. Or did he?

"What's your name?" he asked.

She gave a clear, trilled sound. Harker tried to whistle it and gave up. Some sort of tone-language, he guessed, without words as he knew them. It sounded as though they—her people, whatever they were—had copied the birds.

"I'll call you Button," he said. "Bachelor Button—but you wouldn't know."

She picked the image out of his mind and sent it back to him. Blue fringe-topped flowers nodding in his mother's china bowl. She laughed again and sent her black birds away and led on into the forest, calling out like an oriole. Other voices answered her, and presently, racing the light wind between the trees, her people came.

They were like her. There were males, slender little creatures like young boys, and girls like Button. There were several hundred of them, all naked, all laughing and curious, their lithe pliant bodies flitting moth-fashion through the indigo shadows. They were topped with petals—Harker called them that, though he still wasn't sure—of all colors from blood-scarlet to pure white.

They trilled back and forth. Apparently Button was telling them all about how she found Harker and McLaren. The whole mob pushed on slowly through the forest and ended finally in a huge clearing where there were only scattered trees. A spring rose and made a little lake, and then a stream that wandered off among the ferns.

More of the little people came, and now he saw the young ones. All sizes, from tiny thin creatures on up, replicas of their elders. There were no old ones. There were none with imperfect or injured bodies. Harker, exhausted and on the thin edge of a fever-bout, was not encouraged.

He set McLaren down by the spring. He drank, gasping like an animal, and bathed his head and shoulders. The forest people stood in a circle, watching. They were silent now. Harker felt coarse and bestial, somehow, as though he had belched loudly in church.

He turned to McLaren. He bathed him, helped him drink, and set about fixing the leg. He needed light, and he needed flame.

There were dry leaves, and mats of dead moss in the rocks around the spring. He gathered a pile of these. The forest people watched. Their silent luminous stare got on Harker's nerves. His hands were shaking so that he made four tries with his flint and steel before he got a spark.

The tiny flicker made the silent ranks stir sharply. He blew on it. The flames licked up, small and pale at first, then taking hold, growing, crackling. He saw their faces in the springing light, their eyes stretched with terror. A shrill crying broke from them and then they were gone, like rustling leaves before a wind.

Harker drew his knife. The forest was quiet now. Quiet but not at rest. The skin crawled on Harker's back, over his scalp, drew tight on his cheekbones. He passed the blade through the flame. McLaren looked up at him. Harker said, "It's okay, Rory," and hit him carefully on the point of the jaw. McLaren lay still. Harker stretched out the swollen leg and went to work.

It was dawn again. He lay by the spring in the cool grass, the ashes of his fire gray and dead beside the dark stains. He felt rested, relaxed, and the fever seemed to have gone out of him. The air was like wine.

He rolled over on his back. There was a wind blowing. It was a live, strong wind, with a certain smell to it. The trees were rollicking, almost shouting with pleasure. Harker breathed deeply. The smell, the pure clean edge . . .

Suddenly he realized that the clouds were high, higher than he had ever known them to be. The wind swept them up, and the daylight was bright, so bright that . . .

Harker sprang up. The blood rushed in him. There was a stinging blur in his eyes. He began to run, toward a tall tree, and he flung himself upward into the branches and climbed, recklessly, into the swaying top.

The bowl of the valley lay below him, green, rich, and lovely. The gray granite cliffs rose around it, grew higher in the direction from which the wind blew. Higher and higher, and beyond them, far beyond, were mountains, flung towering against the sky.

On the mountains, showing through the whipping veils of cloud, there was snow, white and cold and blindingly pure, and as Harker watched there was a gleam, so quick and fleeting that he saw it more with his heart than with his eyes. . . .

Sunlight. Snowfields, and above them, the sun.

After a long time he clambered down again into the silence

of the glade. He stood there, not moving, seeing what he had not had time to see before.

Rory McLaren was gone. Both packs, with food and climbing ropes and bandages and flint and steel were gone. The short spears were gone. Feeling on his hip, Harker found nothing but bare flesh. His knife and even his breechclout had been taken.

A slender, exquisite body moved forward from the shadows of the trees. Huge white blossoms gleamed against the curly blue that crowned the head. Luminous eyes glanced at Harker, full of mockery and a subtle animation. Button smiled.

Matt Harker walked toward Button, not hurrying, his hard sinewy face blank of expression. He tried to keep his mind that way, too. "Where is the other one, my friend?"

"In the finish-place." She nodded vaguely toward the cliffs near where Harker and McLaren had escaped from the caves. Her thought-image was somewhere between rubbish-heap and cemetery, as nearly as Harker could translate it. It was also completely casual, a little annoyed that time should be wasted on such trifles.

"Did you . . . is he still alive?"

"It was when we put it there. It will be all right, it will just wait until it—stops. Like all of them."

"Why was he moved? Why did you . . ."

"It was ugly." Button shrugged. "It was broken, anyway." She stretched her arms upward and lifted her head to the wind. A shiver of delight ran through her. She smiled again at Harker, sidelong.

He tried to keep his anger hidden. He started walking again, not as though he had any purpose in mind, bearing toward the cliffs. His way lay past a bush with yellow flowers and thorny, pliant branches. Suddenly it writhed and whipped him across the belly. He stopped short and doubled over, hearing Button's laughter.

When he straightened up she was in front of him. "It's red," she said, surprised, and laid little pointed fingers on the scratches left by the thorns. She seemed thrilled and fascinated by the color and feel of his blood. Her fingers moved, probing the shape of his muscles, the texture of his skin and the dark hair on his chest. They drew small lines of fire along his neck, along the ridge of his jaw, touching his features one by one, his eyelids, his black brows.

"What are you?" whispered her mind to his.

"This." Harker put his arms around her, slowly. Her flesh slid cool and strange under his hands, sending an indescribable shudder through him, partly pleasure, partly revulsion. He bent his head. Her eyes deepened, lakes of blue fire, and then he found her lips. They were cool and strange like the rest of her, pliant, scented with spice, the same perfume that came with sudden overpowering sweetness from her curling petals.

Harker saw movement in the forest aisles, a clustering of bright flower-heads. Button drew back. She took his hand and led him away, off toward the river and the quiet ferny places along its banks. Glancing up, Harker saw that the two black birds were following overhead.

"You are really plants, then? Flowers, like those?" He touched the white blossoms on her head.

"You are really a beast, then? Like the furry, snarling things that climb up through the pass sometimes?"

They both laughed. The sky above them was the color of clean fleece. The warm earth and crushed ferns were sweet beneath them. "What pass?" asked Harker.

"Over there." She pointed off toward the rim of the valley. "It goes down to the sea, I think. Long ago we used to go down there but there's no need, and the beasts make it dangerous."

"Do they," said Harker, and kissed her in the hollow below her chin, "What happens when the beasts come?"

Button laughed. Before he could stir, Harker was trapped fast in a web of creepers and tough fern, and the black birds were screeching and clashing their sharp beaks in his face.

"That happens," Button said. She stroked the ferns. "Our cousins understand us, even better than the birds."

Harker lay sweating, even after he was free again. Finally he said, "Those creatures in the underground lake. Arc they your cousins?"

Button's fear-thought thrust against his mind like hands pushing away. "No, don't. . . . Long, long ago the legend is that this valley was a huge lake, and the Swimmers lived in it. They were a different species from us, entirely. We came from the high gorges, where there are only barren cliffs now. This was long ago. As the lake receded, we grew more numerous and began to come down, and finally there was a battle and we drove the Swimmers over the falls into the black lake. They have tried and tried to get out, to get back to the light, but they can't. They send their thoughts through to us sometimes. They . . ." She broke off. "I don't want to talk about them anymore."

"How would you fight them if they did get out?" asked Harker easily. "Just with the birds and the growing things?"

Button was slow in answering. Then she said, "I will show you one way." She laid her hand across his eyes. For a moment there was only darkness. Then a picture began to form—people, his own people, seen as reflections in a dim and distorted mirror but recognizable. They poured into the valley through a notch in the cliffs, and instantly every bush and tree and blade of grass was bent against them. They fought, slashing with their knives, making headway, but slowly. And then, across the plain, came a sort of fog, a thin drifting curtain of soft white.

It came closer, moving with force of its own, not heeding the wind. Harker saw that it was thistledown. Seeds, borne on silky wings. It settled over the people trapped in the brush. It was endless and unhurrying, covering them all with a fine fleece. They began to writhe and cry out with pain, with a terrible fear. They struggled, but they couldn't get away.

The white down dropped away from them. Their bodies were covered with countless tiny green shoots, sucking the chemicals from the living flesh and already beginning to grow.

Button's spoken thought cut across the image. "I have seen your thoughts, some of them, since the moment you came out of the caves. I can't understand them, but I can see our plains gashed to the raw earth and our trees cut down and everything made ugly. If your kind came here, we would have to go. And the valley belongs to us."

Matt Harker's brain lay still in the darkness of his skull, wary, drawn in upon itself. "It belonged to the Swimmers first."

"They couldn't hold it. We can."

"Why did you save me, Button? What do you want of me?"

"There was no danger from you. You were strange. I wanted to play with you."

"Do you love me, Button?" His fingers touched a large smooth stone among the fern roots.

"Love? What is that?"

"It's tomorrow and yesterday. It's hoping and happiness and pain, the complete self because it's selfless, the chain that binds you to life and makes living it worthwhile. Do you understand?"

"No. I grow, I take from the soil and the light, I play with the others, with the birds and the wind and flowers. When the time comes I am ripe with seed, and after that I go to the finish-place and wait. That's all I understand. That's all there is."

He looked up into her eyes. A shudder crept over him. "You have no soul, Button. That's the difference between us. You live, but you have no soul."

After that it was not so hard to do what he had to do. To do quickly, very quickly, the thing that was his only faint chance of justifying Sim's death. The thing that Button may have glimpsed in his mind but could not guard against, because there was no understanding in her of the thought of murder.

4

The black birds darted at Harker, but the compulsion that sent them flickered out too soon. The ferns and creepers shook, and then were still, and the birds flew heavily away. Matt Harker stood up.

He thought he might have a little time. The flower-people probably kept in pretty close touch mentally, but perhaps they wouldn't notice Button's absence for a while. Perhaps they weren't prying into his own thoughts, because he was Button's toy. Perhaps. . . .

He began to run, toward the cliffs where the finish-place was. He kept as much as possible in the open, away from shrubs. He did not look again, before he left, at what lay by his feet.

He was close to his desination when he knew that he was spotted. The birds returned, rushing down at him on black whistling wings. He picked up a dead branch to beat them off and it crumbled in his hands. Telekinesis, the power of mind over matter. Harker had read once that if you knew how you could always make your point by thinking the dice into position. He wished he could think himself up a blaster. Curved beaks ripped his arms. He covered his face and grabbed one of the birds by the neck and killed it. The other one screamed and this time Harker wasn't so lucky. By the time he had killed the second one he'd felt claws in him and his face was laid open along the cheekbones. He began to run again.

Bushes swayed toward him as he passed. Thorny branches stretched. Creepers rose like snakes from the grass, and every green blade was turned knifelike against his feet. But he had already reached the cliffs and there were open rocky spaces and the undergrowth was thin.

He knew he was near the finish-place because he could smell it. The gentle withered fragrance of flowers past their prime, and under that a dead, sour decay. He shouted McLaren's name, sick with dread that there might not be an answer, weak with relief when there was one. He raced over tumbled rocks toward the sound. A small creeper tangled his foot and brought him down. He wrenched it by the roots from its shallow crevice and went on. As he glanced back over his shoulder he saw a thin white veil, a tiny patch in the distant air, drifting toward him.

He came to the finish-place.

It was a box canyon, quite deep, with high sheer walls, so that it was almost like a wide well. In the bottom of it bodies were thrown in a dry, spongy heap. Colorless flower-bodies, withered and gray, an incredible compost pile.

Rory McLaren lay on top of it, apparently unhurt. The two packs were beside him, with the weapons. Strewn over the heap, sitting, lying, moving feebly about, were the ones who waited, as Button had put it, to stop. Here were the aged, the faded and worn out, the imperfect and injured, where their ugliness could not offend. They seemed already dead mentally. They paid no attention to the men, nor to each other. Sheer blind vitality kept them going a little longer, as a geranium will bloom long after its cut stalk is desiccated.

"Matt," McLaren said. "Oh, God, Matt, I'm glad to see you!"

"Are you all right?"

"Sure. My leg even feels pretty good. Can you get me out?"

"Throw those packs up here."

McLaren obeyed. He began to catch Harker's feverish mood, warned by Harker's bleeding, ugly face that something nasty was afoot. Harker explained rapidly while he got out one of the ropes and half hauled McLaren out of the pit. The white veil was close now. Very close.

"Can you walk?" Harker asked.

McLaren glanced at the fleecy cloud. Harker had told him about it. "I can walk," he said. "I can run like hell."

Harker handed him the rope. "Get around the other side of the canyon. Clear across, see?" He helped McClaren on with his pack. "Stand by with the rope to pull me up. And keep to the bare rocks."

McLaren went off. He limped badly, his face twisted with pain. Harker swore. The cloud was so close that now he could see the millions of tiny seeds floating on their silken fibers, thistledown guided by the minds of the flower-people in the valley. He shrugged into his pack straps and began winding bandages and tufts of dead grass around the bone tip of a recovered spear. The edge of the cloud was almost on him when he got a spark into the improvised torch and sprang down onto the heap of dead flower-things in the pit.

He sank and floundered on the treacherous surface, struggling across it while he applied the torch. The dry, withered substance caught. He raced the flames to the far wall and glanced back. The dying creatures had not stirred, even when the fire engulfed them. Overhead, the edges of the seed-cloud flared and crisped. It moved on blindly over the fire. There was a pale flash of light and the cloud vanished in a puff of smoke.

"Rory!" Harker yelled. "Rory!"

For a long minute he stood there, coughing, strangling in thick smoke, feeling the rushing heat crisp his skin. Then, when it was almost too late, McLaren's sweating face appeared above him and the rope snaked down. Tongues of flame flicked his backside angrily as he ran monkey-fashion up the wall.

They got away from there, higher on the rocky ground, slashing occasionally with their knives at brush and creepers they could not avoid. McLaren shuddered.

"It's impossible," he said. "How do they do it?"

"They're blood cousins. Or should I say sap. Anyhow, I suppose it's like radio control—a matter of transmitting the right frequencies. Here, take it easy a minute."

McLaren sank down gratefully. Blood was seeping through

the tight bandages where Harker had incised his wound. Harker looked back into the valley.

The flower-people were spread out in a long crescent, their bright multicolored heads clear against the green plain. Harker guessed that they would be guarding the pass. He guessed that they had known what was going on in his mind as well as Button had. New form of communism, one mind for all and all for one mind. He could see that even without McLaren's disability they couldn't make it to the pass. Not a mouse could have made it.

He wondered how soon the next seed-cloud would come.

"What are we going to do, Matt? Is there any way . . ." McLaren wasn't thinking about himself. He was looking at the valley like Lucifer yearning at Paradise, and he was thinking of Viki. Not just Viki alone, but Viki as a symbol of thirty-eight hundred wanderers on the face of Venus.

"I don't know," said Harker. "The pass is out, and the caves are out . . . hey! Remember when we were fighting off those critters by the river and you nearly started a cave-in throwing rocks? There was a fault there, right over the edge of the lake. An earthquake split. If we could get at it from the top and shake it down . . ."

It was a minute before McLaren caught on. His eyes widened. "A slide would dam up the lake. . . ."

"If the level rose enough, the Swimmers could get out." Harker gazed with sultry eyes at the bobbing flower-heads below.

"But if the valley's flooded, Matt, and those critters take over, where does that leave our people?"

"There wouldn't be too much of a slide, I don't think. The rock's solid on both sides of the fault. And anyway, the weight of the water backed up there would push through anything, even a concrete dam, in a couple of weeks." Harker studied the valley floor intently. "See the way that slopes there? Even if the slide didn't wash out, a little digging would drain the flood off down the pass. We'd just be making a new river."

"Maybe." McLaren nodded. "I guess so. But that still leaves the Swimmers. I don't think they'd be any nicer than these babies about giving up their land." His tone said he would rather fight Button's people any day.

Harker's mouth twisted in a slow grin. "The Swimmers are

water creatures, Rory. Amphibious. Also, they've lived underground, in total darkness, for God knows how long. You know what happens to angleworms when you get 'em out in the light. You know what happens to fungus that grows in the dark." He ran his fingers over his skin, almost with reverence. "Noticed anything about yourself, Rory? Or have you been too busy?"

McLaren stared. He rubbed his own skin, and winced, and rubbed again, watching his fingers leave streaks of livid white that faded instantly. "Sunburn," he said wonderingly. "My God. Sunburn!"

Harker stood up. "Let's go take a look." Down below the flower-heads were agitated. "They don't like that thought, Rory. Maybe it can be done, and they know it."

McLaren rose, leaning on a short spear like a cane. "Matt. They won't let us get away with it."

Harker frowned. "Button said there were other ways beside the seed. . . ." He turned away. "No use standing here worrying about it."

They started climbing again, very slowly on account of McLaren. Harker tried to gauge where they were in relation to the cavern beneath. The river made a good guide. The rocks were almost barren of growth here, which was a godsend. He watched, but he couldn't see anything threatening approaching from the valley. The flower-people were mere dots now, perfectly motionless.

The rock formation changed abruptly. Ancient quakes had left scars in the shape of twisted strata, great leaning slabs of granite poised like dancers, and cracks that vanished into darkness.

Harker stopped. "This is it. Listen, Rory. I want you to go off up there, out of the danger area. . . ."

"Matt, I. . . ."

"Shut up. One of us has got to be alive to take word back to the ships as soon as he can get through the valley. There's no great rush and you'll be able to travel in three—four days. You. . . ."

"But why me? You're a better mountain man. . . ."

"You're married," said Harker curtly. "It'll only take one of us to shove a couple of those big slabs down. They're practically ready to fall of their own weight. Maybe nothing will happen. Maybe I'll get out all right. But it's a little silly if both of us take the risk, isn't it?"

"Yeah. But Matt. . . ."

"Listen, kid." Harker's voice was oddly gentle. "I know what I'm doing. Give my regards to Viki and the. . . ."

He broke off with a sharp cry of pain. Looking down incredulously, he saw his body covered with little tentative flames, feeble, flickering, gone, but leaving their red footprints behind them.

McLaren had the same thing.

They stared at each other. A helpless terror took Harker by the throat. Telekinesis again. The flower-people turning his own weapon against them. They had seen fire, and what it did, and they were copying the process in their own minds, concentrating, all of them together, the whole mental force of the colony centered on the two men. He could even understand why they focused on the skin. They had taken the sunburn-thought and applied it literally.

Fire. Spontaneous combustion. A simple, easy reaction, if you knew the trick. There was something about a burning bush . . .

The attack came again, stronger this time. The flower-people were getting the feel of it now. It hurt. Oh God, it hurt. McLaren screamed. His loincloth and bandages began to smoulder.

What to do, thought Harker, *quick, tell me what to do. . . .*

The flower-people focus on us through our minds, our conscious minds. Maybe they can't get the subconscious so easily, because the thoughts are not directed, they're images, symbols, vague things. Maybe if Rory couldn't think consciously they couldn't find him. . . .

Another flare of burning, agonizing pain. In a minute they'll have the feel of it. They can keep it going. . . .

Without warning, Harker slugged McLaren heavily on the jaw and dragged him away to where the rock was firm. He did it all with astonishing strength and quickness. There was no need to save himself. He wasn't going to need himself much longer.

He went away a hundred feet or so, watching McLaren. A third attack struck him, sickened and dazed him so that he nearly fell. Rory McLaren was not touched.

Harker smiled. He turned and ran back toward the rotten place in the cliffs. A part of his conscious thought was so strongly formed that his body obeyed it automatically, not stopping even when the flames appeared again and again on his flesh, brightening, growing, strengthening as the thought-energies of Button's people meshed together. He flung down one teetering giant of stone, and the shock jarred another loose. Harker stumbled on to a third, based on a sliding bed of shale, and thrust with all his strength and beyond it, and it went too, with crashing thunder.

Harker fell. The universe dissolved into shuddering, roaring chaos beyond a bright veil of flame and a smell of burning flesh. By that time there was only one thing clear in Matt Harker's understanding—the second part of his conscious mind, linked to and even stronger than the first.

The image he carried with him into death was a tall mountain with snow on its shoulders, blazing in the sun.

It was night. Rory McLaren lay prone on a jutting shelf above the valley. Below him the valley was lost in indigo shadows, but there was a new sound in it—the swirl of water angry and swift.

There was new life in it, too. It rode the crest of the flood waters, burning gold in the blue night, shining giants returning in vengeance to their own place. Great patches of blazing jewel-toned phosphorescence dotted the water—the flower-hounds, turned loose to hunt. And in between them, rolling and leaping in deadly play, the young of the Swimmers went.

McLaren watched them hunt the forest people. He watched all night, shivering with dread, while the golden titans exacted payment for the ages they had lived in darkness. By dawn it was all over. And then, through the day, he watched the Swimmers die.

The river, turned back on itself, barred them from the caves. The strong bright light beat down. The Swimmers turned at first to greet it with a pathetic joy. And then they realized. . . .

McLaren turned away. He waited, resting, until, as Harker had predicted, the block washed away and the backed-up water could flow normally again. The valley was already draining when he found the pass. He looked up at the mountains and breathed the sweet wind, and felt a great shame and humility that he was here to do it.

He looked back toward the caves where Sim had died, and the cliffs above where he had buried what remained of Matt Harker. It seemed to him that he should say something, but no words came, only that his chest was so full he could hardly breathe. He turned mutely down the rocky pass, toward the Sea of Morning Opals and the thirty-eight hundred wanderers who had found a home.

INTO THY HANDS

by Lester Del Rey (1915-)

ASTOUNDING SCIENCE FICTION,
August

Lester Del Rey is a veteran of this series ("The Day is Done," 1939; "Dark Mission," 1940; "Hereafter, Inc.," 1941; "The Wings of Night" and "Nerves," 1942; "Kindness," 1944), who published one of the first hardcover single-author collections in science fiction, the now-rare And Some Were Human *(Prime Press, 1948). He has served science fiction in just about every possible capacity—magazine editor, book editor, book reviewer, and author—a vivid example of the tremendous overlap in functions that characterizes the field.*

Although he had considerable competition from one of your editors, one of his specialties was excellent stories about robots, and "Into Thy Hands" is one of his best on the subject.

(I mentioned in an earlier introduction that Cliff Simak had felt Fritz Leiber to have been "under-appreciated." My feeling is that Lester is. He is a most remarkable writer, always clear and always interesting, whatever it is he does. Whether he writes a history of science fiction, or a eulogy, or an obituary, there are always insights within them that I don't think you'll find anywhere else.

I always listen carefully to whatever he says for I know that I will come across sparkles of thought that I can adopt and treat as my own. Lester doesn't mind; there are plenty of other sparkles where those came from.

One of my own fictional characters is modeled on Lester. That is Emmanuel Rubin of my mystery series concerning the Black Widowers. Lester denies the similarity but I can prove it. Manny Rubin is always engaged in controversy in those stories and, no matter how I try, he manages to win every argument. If that isn't Lester, nothing is. I.A.)

Simon Ames was old, and his face was bitter as only that of a confirmed idealist can be. Now a queer mixture of emotions crossed it momentarily, as he watched the workmen begin pouring cement to fill the small opening of the domelike structure, but his eyes returned again to the barely visible robot within.

"The last Ames' Model 10," he said ruefully to his son. "And even then I couldn't put in full memory coils! Only the physical sciences here; biologicals in the other male form, humanities in the female. I had to fall back on books and equipment to cover the rest. We're already totally converted to soldier robots, and no more humanoid experiments. Dan, is there no way conceivable war can be avoided?"

The young Rocket Force captain shrugged, and his mouth twitched unhappily. "None, Dad. They've fed their people on the glories of carnage and loot so long they have to find some pretext to use their hordes of warrior robots."

"The stupid, blind idiots!" The old man shuddered. "Dan, it sounds like old wives' fears, but this time it's true; unless we somehow avoid or win this war quickly, there'll be no one left to wage another. I've spent my life on robots, I know what they can do—and should never be made to do! Do you think I'd waste a fortune on these storehouses on a mere whim?"

"I'm not arguing, Dad. God knows, I feel the same!" Dan watched the workmen pour the last concrete, to leave no break in the twenty-foot thick walls. "Well, at least if anyone does survive, you've done all you can for them. Now it's in the hands of God!"

Simon Ames nodded, but there was no satisfaction on his face as he turned back with his son. "All we could—and never enough! And God? I wouldn't even know which of the three to pray survives—science, life, culture." The words sighed into silence, and his eyes went back to the filled-in tunnel.

Behind them, the ugly dome hugged the ground while the rains of God and of man's destruction washed over it. Snow covered it and melted, and other things built up that no summer sun could disperse, until the ground was level with its top. The forest crept forward, and the seasons flicked by in unchanging changes that pyramided decade upon century. Inside, the shining case of SA-10 waited immovably.

And at last the lightning struck, blasting through a tree, downward into the dome, to course through a cable, short-circuit a ruined timing switch, and spend itself on the ground below.

Above the robot, a cardinal burst into song, and he looked up, his stolid face somehow set in a look of wonder. For a moment, he listened, but the bird had flown away at the sight of his lumbering figure. With a tired little sigh, he went on, crashing through the brush of the forest until he came back near the entrance to his cave.

The sun was bright above, and he studied it thoughtfully; the word he knew, and even the complex carbon-chain atomic breakdown that went on within it. But he did not know how he knew, or why.

For a second longer he stood there silently, then opened his mouth for a long wailing cry. "Adam! Adam, come forth!" But there were doubts in the oft-repeated call now and the pose of his head as he waited. And again only the busy sounds of the forest came back to him.

"Or God? God, do you hear me?"

But the answer was the same. A field mouse slipped out from among the grass and a hawk soared over the woods. The wind rustled among the trees, but there was no sign from the Creator. With a lingering backward look, he turned slowly to the tunnel he had made and wriggled back down it into his cave.

Inside, light still came from a single unbroken bulb, and he let his eyes wander, from the jagged breech in the thick wall, across to where some ancient blast had tossed crumpled concrete against the opposite side. Between lay only ruin and dirt. Once, apparently, that half had been filled with books and films, but now there were only rotted fragments of bindings and scraps of useless plastic tape mixed with broken glass in the filth of the floor.

Only on the side where he had been was the ruin less than complete. There stood the instruments of a small laboratory, many still useful, and he named them one by one, from the purring atomic generator to the projector and screen set up on one table.

Here, and in his mind, were order and logic, and the world above had conformed to an understandable pattern. He alone seemed to be without purpose. How had he come here, and why had he no memory of himself? If there was no purpose, why was he sentient at all? The questions held no discoverable answers.

There were only the cryptic words on the scrap of plastic tape preserved inside the projector. But what little of them was understandable was all he had; he snapped off the light and squatted down behind the projector, staring intently at the screen as he flicked the machine on.

There was a brief fragment of some dark swirling, and then dots and bright spheres, becoming suns and planets that spun out of nothing into a celestial pattern. "In the beginning," said a voice quietly, "God created the heavens and the earth." And the screen filled with that, and the beginnings of life.

"Symbolism?" the robot muttered. Geology and astronomy were part of his knowledge, at least; and yet, in a mystic beauty, this was true enough. Even the life-forms above had fitted with those being created on the screen.

Then a new voice, not unlike his own resonant power, filled the speaker. "Let us go down and create man in our image!" And a mist of light that symbolized God appeared, shaping man from the dust of the ground and breathing life into him. Adam grew lonely, and Eve was made from his rib, to be shown Eden and tempted by the serpentine mist of darkness; and she tempted the weak Adam, until God discovered their sin and banished them. But the banishment ended in a blur of ruined film as the speaker went dead.

The robot shut it off, trying to read its meaning. It *must* concern him, since he alone was here to see it. And how could that be unless he were one of its characters? Not Eve or Satan, but perhaps Adam; but then God should have answered him. On the other hand, if he were God, then perhaps the record was unfulfilled and Adam not yet formed, so that no answer could be given.

He nodded slowly to himself. Why should he not have rested here with this film to remind him of his plan, while the world readied itself for Adam? And now, awake again, he must go forth and create man in his own image! But first, the danger of which the film had warned must be removed.

He straightened, determination coming into his steps as he squirmed purposefully upwards. Outside the sun was still shining, and he headed toward it into the grossly unkempt Eden forest. Now stealth came to him as he moved silently through the undergrowth, like a great metal wraith, with eyes that darted about and hands ready to snap forward at lightning speed.

And at last he saw it, curled up near a large rock. It was smaller than he had expected, a mere six feet of black, scaly suppleness, but the shape and forked tongue were unmistakable. He was on it with a blur of motion and a cry of elation; and when he moved away, the lifeless object on the rock was forever past corrupting the most naïve Eve.

The morning sun found the robot bent over what had once been a wild pig, a knife moving precisely in his hand. Delicately he opened the heart and manipulated it, studying the valve action. Life, he was deciding, was highly complex, and a momentary doubt struck him. It had seemed easy on the film! And at times he wondered why he should know the complex order of the heavens but nothing of this other creation of his.

But at last he buried the pig's remains, and settled down among the varicolored clays he had collected, his fingers moving deftly as he rolled a white type into bones for the skeleton, followed by a red clay heart. The tiny nerves and blood vessels were beyond his means, but that could not be helped; and surely if he had created the gigantic sun from nothing, Adam could rise from the crudeness of his sculpturing.

The sun climbed higher, and the details multiplied. Inside the last organ was complete, including the grayish lump that was the brain, and he began the red sheathing of muscles. Here more thought was required to adapt the arrangement of the pig to the longer limbs and different structure of this new body; but his mind pushed grimly on with the mathematics involved, and at last it was finished.

Unconsciously he began a crooning imitation of the bird songs as his fingers molded the colored clays to hide the muscles and give smooth symmetry to the body. He had been forced to guess at the color, though the dark lips on the film had obviously been red from blood below them.

Twilight found him standing back, nodding approval of the work. It was a faithful copy of the film Adam, waiting only the breath of life; and that must come from him, be a part of the forces that flowed through his own metal nerves and brain.

Gently he fastened wires to the head and feet of the clay body; then he threw back his chest plate to fasten the other ends to his generator terminals, willing the current out into the figure lying before him. Weakness flooded through him instantly, threatening to black out his consciousness, but he did not begrudge the energy. Steam was spurting up and covering the figure as a mist had covered Adam, but it slowly subsided, and he stopped the current, stealing a second for relief as the full current coursed back through him. Then softly he unhooked the wires and drew them back.

"Adam!" The command rang through the forest, vibrant with his urgency. "Adam, rise up! I, your creator, command it!"

But the figure lay still, and now he saw great cracks in it, while the noble smile had baked into a gaping leer. There was no sign of life! It was dead, as the ground from which it came.

He squatted over it, moaning, weaving from side to side, and his fingers tried to draw the ugly cracks together, only to cause greater ruin. And at last he stood up, stamping his legs until all that was left was a varicolored smear on the rock. Still he stamped and moaned as he destroyed the symbol of his failure. The moon mocked down at him with a wise and cynical face, and he howled at it in rage and anguish, to be answered by a lonely owl, querying his identity.

A powerless God, or a Godless Adam! Things had gone so well in the film as Adam rose from the dust of the ground——

But the film was symbolism, and he had taken it literally! Of course he had failed. The pigs were not dust, but colloidal jelly complexes. And they knew more than he, for there had been little ones that proved they could somehow pass the breath of life along.

Suddenly he squared his shoulders and headed into the forest again. Adam should yet rise to ease his loneliness. The pigs knew the secret, and he could learn it; what he needed now were more pigs, and they should not be too hard to obtain.

But two weeks later it was a worried robot who sat watching his pigs munch contentedly at their food. Life, instead of growing simpler, had become more complicated. The fluoroscope and repaired electron microscope had shown him much, but always something was lacking. Life seemed to begin only with life; for even the two basic cells were alive in some manner strangely different from his own. Of course God-life might differ from animal-life, but——

With a shrug he dismissed his metaphysics and turned back to the laboratory, avoiding the piglets that ambled trustingly under his feet. Slowly he drew out the last ovum from the nutrient fluid in which he kept it, placing it on a slide and under the optical microscope. Then, with a little platinum filament, he brought a few male spermatozoa toward the ovum, his fingers moving surely through the thousandths of an inch needed to place it.

His technique had grown from failures, and now the sperm cell found and pierced the ovum. As he watched, the round single cell began to lengthen and divide across the middle. This was going to be one of his successes! There were two, then four cells, and his hands made lightning, infinitesimal gestures, keeping it within the microscope field while he changed the slide for a thin membrane, lined with thinner tubes to carry oxygen, food, and tiny amounts of the stimulating and controlling hormones with which he hoped to shape its formation.

Now there were eight cells, and he waited feverishly for them to reach toward the membrane. But they did not! As he watched, another division began, but stopped; the cells had died again. All his labor and thought had been futile, as always.

He stood there silently, relinquishing all pretensions to godhood. His mind abdicated, letting the dream vanish into nothingness; and there was nothing to take its place and give him purpose and reason—only a vacuum instead of a design.

Dully he unbarred the rude cage and began chasing the

grumbling, reluctant pigs out and up the tunnel, into the forest and away. It was a dull morning, with no sun apparent, and it matched his mood as the last one disappeared, leaving him doubly lonely. They had been poor companions, but they had occupied his time, and the little ones had appealed to him. Now even they were gone.

Wearily he dropped his six hundred pounds onto the turf, staring at the black clouds over him. An ant climbed up his body inquisitively, and he watched it without interest. Then it, too, was gone.

"Adam!" The cry came from the woods, ringing and compelling. "Adam, come forth!"

"God!" With metal limbs that were awkward and unsteady, he jerked upright. In the dark hour of his greatest need, God had finally come! "God, here I am!"

"Come forth, Adam, Adam! Come forth, Adam!"

With a wild cry, the robot dashed forward toward the woods, an electric tingling suffusing him. He was no longer unwanted, no longer a lost chip in the storm. God had come for him. He stumbled on, tripping over branches, crashing through bushes, heedless of his noise; let God know his eagerness. Again the call came, now farther aside, and he turned a bit, lumbering forward. "Here I am, I'm coming!"

God would ease his troubles and explain why he was so different from the pigs; God would know all that. And then there'd be Eve, and no more loneliness! He'd have trouble keeping her from the Tree of Knowledge, but he wouldn't mind that!

And from still a different direction the call reached him. Perhaps God was not pleased with his noise. The robot quieted his steps and went forward reverently. Around him the birds sang, and now the call came again, ringing and close. He hastened on, striving to blend speed with quiet in spite of his weight.

The pause was longer this time, but when the call came it was almost overhead. He bowed lower and crept to the ancient oak from which it came, uncertain, half-afraid, but burning with anticipation.

"Come forth, Adam, Adam!" The sound was directly above, but God did not manifest Himself visibly. Slowly the robot looked up through the boughs of the tree. Only a bird was there—and from its open beak the call came forth again. "Adam, Adam!"

A mockingbird he'd heard imitating the other birds, now mimicking his own voice and words! And he'd followed that through the forest, hoping to find God! He screeched suddenly at the bird, his rage so shrill that it leaped from the branch in hasty flight, to perch in another tree and cock its head at him. "God?" it asked in his voice, and changed to the raucous call of a jay.

The robot slumped back against the tree, refusing to let hope ebb wholly from him. He knew so little of God; might not He have used the bird to call him here? At least the tree was not unlike the one under which God had put Adam to sleep before creating Eve.

First sleep, *then* the coming of God! He stretched out determinedly, trying to imitate the pigs' torpor, fighting back his mind's silly attempts at speculation as to where his rib might be. It was slow and hard, but he persisted grimly, hypnotizing himself into mental numbness; and bit by bit, the sounds of the forest faded to only a trickle in his head. Then that, too, was stilled.

He had no way of knowing how long it lasted, but suddenly he sat up groggily, to the rumble of thunder, while a torrent of lashing rain washed in blinding sheets over his eyes. For a second, he glanced quickly at his side, but there was no scar.

Fire forked downward into a nearby tree, throwing splinters of it against him. This was definitely not according to the film! He groped to his feet, flinging some of the rain from his face, to stumble forward toward his cave. Again lightning struck, nearer, and he increased his pace to a driving run. The wind lashed the trees, snapping some with wild ferocity, and it took the full power of his magnets to forge ahead at ten miles an hour instead of his normal fifty. Once it caught him unaware, and crashed him down over a rock with a wild clang of metal, but it could not harm him, and he stumbled on until he reached the banked-up entrance of his muddy tunnel.

Safe inside, he dried himself with the infrared lamp, sitting beside the hole and studying the wild fury of the gale. Surely its furor held no place for Eden, where dew dampened the leaves in the evening under caressing, musical breezes!

He nodded slowly, his clenched jaws relaxing. This could

not be Eden, and God expected him there. Whatever evil knowledge of Satan had lured him here and stolen his memory did not matter; all that counted was to return, and that should be simple, since the Garden lay among rivers. Tonight he'd prepare here out of the storm, and tomorrow he'd follow the stream in the woods until it led him where God waited.

With the faith of a child, he turned back and began tearing the thin berylite panels from his laboratory tables and cabinets, picturing his homecoming and Eve. Outside the storm raged and tore, but he no longer heard it. Tomorrow he would start for home! The word was misty in his mind, as all the nicer words were, but it had a good sound, free of loneliness, and he liked it.

Six hundred long endless years had dragged their slow way into eternity, and even the tough concrete floor was pitted by those centuries of pacing and waiting. Time had eroded all hopes and plans and wonder, and now there was only numb despair, too old to vent itself in rage, or madness, even.

The female robot slumped motionlessly on the atomic excavator, her eyes centered aimlessly across the dome, beyond the tiers of books and films and the hulking machines that squatted eternally on the floor. There a pickax lay, and her eyes rested on it listlessly; once, when the dictionary revealed its picture and purpose, she had thought it the key to escape, but now it was only another symbol of futility.

She wandered over aimlessly, picking it up by its two metal handles and striking the wooden blade against the wall; another splinter chipped from the wood, and century-old dust dropped to the floor, but that offered no escape. Nothing did. Mankind and her fellow robots must have perished long ago, leaving her neither hope for freedom nor use for it if it were achieved.

Once she had planned and schemed with all her remarkable knowledge of psychology to restore man's heritage, but now the note-littered table was only a mockery; she thrust out a weary hand—

And froze into a metal statue! Faintly, through all the metal mesh and concrete, a dim, weak signal trickled into the radio that was part of her!

With all her straining energy, she sent out an answering call; but there was no response. As she stood rigidly for long minutes, the signals grew stronger, but remained utterly aloof and unaware of her. Now some sudden shock seemed to cut through them, raising their power until the thoughts of another robot mind were abruptly clear—thoughts without sense, clothed in madness! And even as the lunacy registered, they began to fade; second by second, they dimmed into the distance and left her alone again and hopeless!

With a wild, clanging yell, she threw the useless pickax at the wall, watching it rebound in echoing din. But she was no longer aimless; her eyes had noted chipped concrete breaking away with the sharp metal point, and she caught the pick before it could touch the floor, seizing the nub of wood in small, strong hands. The full force of her magnet lifted and swung, while her feet kicked aside the rubble that came cascading down from the force of her blows.

Beyond that rapidly crumbling wall lay freedom and—madness! Surely there could be no human life in a world that could drive a robot mad, but if there were— She thrust back the picture and went savagely on attacking the massive wall.

The sun shone on a drenched forest filled with havoc from the storm, to reveal the male robot pacing tirelessly along the banks of the shallow stream. In spite of the heavy burden he carried, his legs moved swiftly now, and when he came to sandy stretches, or clear land that bore only turf, his great strides lengthened still farther; already he had dallied too long with delusions in this unfriendly land.

Now the stream joined a larger one, and he stopped, dropping his ungainly bundle and ripping it apart. Scant minutes later, he was pushing an assembled berylite boat out and climbing in. The little generator from the electron microscope purred softly and a stream jet began hissing underneath; it was crude, but efficient, as the boiling wake behind him testified, and while slower than his fastest pace, there would be no detours or impassable barriers to bother him.

The hours sped by and the shadows lengthened again, but now the stream was wider, and his hopes increased, though he watched the banks idly, not yet expecting Eden. Then he rounded a bend to jerk upright and head toward shore, observing something totally foreign to the landscape. As he beached the boat, and drew nearer, he saw a great gaping hole bored into the earth for a hundred feet in depth and a quarter mile in diameter, surrounded by obviously artificial ruins. Tall bent shafts stuck up haphazardly, amid jumbles of concrete and bits of artifacts damaged beyond recognition. Nearby a pole leaned at a silly angle, bearing a sign.

He scratched the corrosion off and made out dim words:

WELCOME TO HOGANVILLE. POP. 1,876.

It meant nothing to him, but the ruins fascinated him. This must be some old trick of Satan; such ugliness could be nothing else.

Shaking his head, he turned back to the boat, to speed on while the stars came out. Again he came to ruins, larger and harder to see, since the damage was more complete and the forest had claimed most of it. He was only sure because of the jagged pits in which not even a blade of grass would grow. And sometimes as the night passed there were smaller pits, as if some single object had been blasted out of existence. He gave up the riddle of such things, finally; it was no concern of his.

When morning came again, the worst ruins were behind, and the river was wide and strong, suggesting that the trip must be near its end. Then the faint salty tang of the ocean reached him, and he whooped loudly, scanning the country for an observation point.

Ahead, a low hill broke the flat country, topped by a rounded bowl of green, and he made toward it. The boat crunched on gravel, and he was springing off over the turf to the hill, up it, and onto the bowl-shaped top that was covered with vines. Here the whole lower course of the river was visible, with no more large branches in the twenty-five miles to the sea. The land was pleasant and gentle, and it was not hard to imagine Eden out there.

But now for the first time, as he started down, he noticed that the mound was not part of the hill as it had seemed. It was of the same gray-green concrete as the walls of the cave from which he had broken, like a bird from an egg.

And here was another such thing, like an egg unhatched yet but already cracking, as the gouged-out pit on its surface near him testified. For a moment, the idea contained in the figure of speech staggered him, and then he was ripping away the concealing vines and dropping into the hole, reaching for a small plate pinned to an unharmed section nearby. It was a poor tool, but if Eve were trapped inside, needing help to break the shell, it would do.

"To you who may survive the holocaust, I, Simon Ames——" The words caught his eyes, drawing his attention to the plate in spite of his will, their tense strangeness pulling his gaze across them. "—dedicate this. There is no easy entrance, but you will expect no easy heritage. Force your way, take what is within, use it! To you who need it and will work for it, I have left all knowledge that was——"

Knowledge! Knowledge, forbidden by God! Satan had put before his path the unquestioned thing meant by the Tree of Knowledge symbol, concealed as a false egg, and he had almost been caught! A few minutes more——! He shuddered, and backed out, but optimism was freshening inside him again. Let it be the Tree! That meant this was really part of Eden, and being forewarned by God's marker, he had no fear for the wiles of Satan, alive or dead.

With long, loping strides he headed down the hill toward the meadows and woods, leaving the now useless boat behind. He would enter Eden on his own feet, as God had made him!

Half an hour later he was humming happily to himself as he passed beside lush fields, rich with growing things, along a little woodland path. Here was order and logic, as they should be. This was surely Eden!

And to confirm it came Eve! She was coming down the trail ahead, her hair floating behind, and some loose stuff draped over her hips and breasts, but the form underneath was Woman, beautiful and unmistakable. He drew back out of sight, suddenly timid and uncertain, only vaguely wondering how she came here before him. Then she was beside him, and he moved impulsively, his voice a whisper of ecstasy!

"Eve!"

"Oh, Dan! Dan!" It was a wild shriek that cut the air, and she was rushing away in panic, into the deeper woods. He shook his head in bewilderment, while his own legs began a more forceful pumping after her. He was almost upon her when he saw the serpent, alive and stronger than before!

But not for long! As a single gasp broke from her, one of his arms lifted her aside, while the other snapped out to pinch the fanged head completely off the body. His voice was gently reproving as he put her down. "You shouldn't have fled to the serpent, Eve!"

"To—— Ugh! But—— You could have killed me before it

struck!" The taut whiteness of fear was fading from her face, replaced by defiance and doubt.

"Killed you?"

"You're a robot! Dan!" Her words cut off as a brawny figure emerged from the underbrush, an ax in one hand and a magnificent dog at his heels. "Dan, he saved me . . . but he's a robot!"

"I saw, Syl. Steady! Edge this way, if you can. Good! They sometimes get passive streaks, I've heard. Shep!"

The dog's thick growl answered, but his eyes remained glued to the robot. "Yeah, Dan?"

"Get the people; just yell robot and hike back. O.K., scram! You . . . what do you want?"

SA-IO grunted harshly, hunching his shoulders. "Things that don't exist! Companionship and a chance to see my strength and the science I know. Maybe I'm not supposed to have such things, but that's what I wanted!"

"Hm-m-m. There are fairy stories about friendly robots hidden somewhere to help us, at that. We could use help. What's your name, and where from?"

Bitterness crept into the robot's voice as he pointed up river. "From the sunward side. So far, I've only found who I'm not!"

"So? Meant to get up there myself when the colony got settled." Dan paused, eyeing the metal figure speculatively. "We lost our books in the hell-years, mostly, and the survivors weren't exactly technicians. So while we do all right with animals, agriculture, medicine and such, we're pretty primitive otherwise. If you really do know the sciences, why not stick around?"

The robot had seen too many hopes shattered like his clay man to believe wholly in this promise of purpose and companionship, but his voice caught as he answered. "You . . . want me?"

"Why not? You're a storehouse of knowledge, Say-Ten, and we——"

"Satan?"

"Your name; there on your chest." Dan pointed with his left hand, his body suddenly tense. "See? Right there!"

And now, as SA-IO craned his neck, the foul letters were visible, high on his chest! Ess, aye—

His first warning was the ax that crashed against his chest, to rock him back on his heels, and come driving down again, powered by muscles that seemed almost equal to his own. It struck again, and something snapped inside him. All the strength vanished, and he collapsed to the ground with a jarring crash, knocking his eyelids closed. Then he lay there, unable even to open them.

He did not try, but lay waiting almost eagerly for the final blows that would finish him. Satan, the storehouse of knowledge, the tempter of men—the one person he had learned to hate! He'd come all this way to find a name and a purpose; now he had them! No Wonder God had locked him away in a cave to keep him from men.

"Dead! That little fairy story threw him off guard." There was a tense chuckle from the man. "Hope his generator's still O.K. We could heat every house in the settlement with that. Wonder where his hideout was?"

"Like the one up north with all the weapons hidden? Oh, Dan!" A strange smacking sound accompanied that, and then her voice sobered. "We'd better get back for help in hauling him."

Their feet moved away, leaving the robot still motionless but no longer passive. The Tree of Knowledge, so easily seen without the vine covering over the hole, was barely twenty miles away, and no casual search could miss it! He had to destroy it first!

But the little battery barely could maintain his consciousness, and the generator no longer served him. Delicate detectors were sending their messages through his nerves, assuring him it was functioning properly under automatic check, but beyond his control. Part of the senseless signaling device within him must have been defective, unless the baking of the clay man had somehow overloaded a part of it, and now it was completely wrecked, shorting aside all the generator control impulses, leaving him unable to move a finger.

Even when he blanked his mind almost completely out, the battery could not power his hands. His evil work was done; now he would heat their house, while they sought the temptation he had offered them. And he could do nothing to stop it. God denied him the chance to right the wrong he had done, even.

Bitterly he prayed on, while strange noises sounded near him and he felt himself lifted and carried bumpily at a rapid rate. God would not hear him! And at last he stopped, while the bumping went on to whatever end he was destined. Finally even that stopped, and there were a few moments of absolute quiet.

"Listen! I know you still live!" It was a gentle, soothing voice, hypnotically compelling, that broke in on the dark swirls of his thoughts. Brief thoughts of God crossed his mind, but it was a female voice, which must mean one of the settlement women who must have believed him and be trying to save him in secret. It came again. "Listen and believe me! You *can* move—a very very little, but enough for me to see. Try to repair yourself, and let me be the strength in your hands. Try! Ah, your arm!"

It was inconceivable that she could follow his imperceptible movements, and yet he felt his arm lifted and placed on his chest as the thought crossed his mind. But it was none of his business to question how or why. All his energy must be devoted to getting his strength before the men could find the Tree!

"So . . . I turn this . . . this nut. And the other— There, the plate is off. What do I do now?"

That stopped him. His life force had been fatal to a pig, and probably would kill a woman. Yet she trusted him. He dared not move—but the idea must have been father to the act, for his fingers were brushed aside and her arms scraped over his chest, to be followed by an instant flood of strength pouring through him.

Her fingers had slipped over his eyes, but he did not need them as he ripped the damaged receiver from its welds and tossed it aside. Now there was worry in her voice, over the crooning cadence she tried to maintain. "Don't be too surprised at what you may see. Everything's all right!"

"Everything's all right!" he repeated dutifully, lingering over the words as his voice sounded again in his ears. For a moment more, while he reaffixed his plate, he let her hold his eyes closed. "Woman, who are you?"

"Eve. Or at least, Adam, those names will do for us." And the fingers withdrew, though she remained out of sight behind him.

But there was enough for the first glance before him. In spite of the tiers of bookcases and film magazines, the machines, and the size of the laboratory, this was plainly the double of his own cave, circled with the same concrete walls! That could only mean the Tree!

With a savage lurch, he was facing the rescuer, seeing another robot, smaller, more graceful, and female in form, calling to all the hunger and loneliness he had known! But those emotions had betrayed him before, and he forced them back bitterly. There could be no doubt while the damning letters spelled out her name. Satan was male and female, and Evil had gone forth to rescue its kind!

Some of the warring hell of emotions must have shown in his movements, for she was retreating before him, her hands fumbling up to cover the marks at which he stared. "Adam, no! The man read it wrong—dreadfully wrong. It's not a name. We're machines, and all machines have model numbers, like these. Satan wouldn't advertise his name. And I never had evil intentions!"

"Neither did I!" He bit the words out, stumbling over the objects on the floor as he edged her back slowly into a blind alley, while striving to master his own rebellious emotions at what he must do. "Evil must be destroyed! Knowledge is forbidden to men!"

"Not all knowledge! Wait, let me finish! Any condemned person has a right to a few last words—— It was the Tree of Knowledge of *Good and Evil.* God called it that! And He had to forbid them to eat, because they couldn't know which was the good; don't you see, He was only protecting them until they were older and able to choose for themselves! Only Satan gave them evil fruit—hate and *murder*—to ruin them. Would you call healing the sick, good government, or improving other animals evil? That's knowledge, Adam, glorious knowledge God wants man to have. Can't you see?"

For a second as she read his answer, she turned to flee; then, with a little sobbing cry, she was facing him again, unresisting. "All right, murder me! Do you think death frightens me after being imprisoned here for six hundred years with no way to break free? Only get it over with!"

Surprise and the sheer audacity of the lie held his hands as his eyes darted from the atomic excavator to a huge drill, and a drum marked as explosives. And yet—even that cursory glance could not overlook the worn floor and thousand marks of age-long occupation, though the surface of the dome had been unbroken a few hours before. Reluctantly, his eyes swung back to the excavator, and hers followed.

"Useless! The directions printed on it say to move the

thing marked 'Orifice Control' to zero before starting. It can't be moved!"

She stopped, abruptly speechless, as his fingers lifted the handle from its ratchet and spun it easily back to zero! Then she was shaking her head in defeat and lifting listless hands to help him with the unfastening of her chest plate. There was no color left in her voice.

"Six hundred years because I didn't lift a handle! Just because I have absolutely no conception of mechanics, where all men have some instinct they take for granted. They'd have mastered these machines in time and learned to read meaning into the books I memorized without even understanding the titles. But I'm like a dog tearing at a door, with a simple latch over his nose. Well, that's that. Good-bye, Adam!"

But perversely, now that the terminals lay before him, he hesitated. After all, the instructions had not mentioned the ratchet; it was too obvious to need mention, but—— He tried to picture such ignorance, starting at one of the Elementary Radio books above him. "Application of a Cavity Resonator." Mentally, he could realize that a nonscience translation was meaningless: Use of a sound producer or strengthener in a hole! And then the overlooked factor struck him.

"But you did get out!"

"Because I lost my temper and threw the pickax. That's how I found the metal was the blade, not the wood. The only machines I could use were the projector and typer I was meant to use—and the typer broke!"

"Um-m-m." He picked the little machine up, noting the yellowed incomplete page still in it, even as he slipped the carriage tension cord back on its hook. But his real attention was devoted to the cement dust ground into the splintered handle of the pick.

No man or robot could be such a complete and hopeless dope, and yet he no longer doubted. She was a robot moron! And if knowledge were evil, then surely she belonegd to God! All the horror of his contemplated murder vanished, leaving his mind clean and weak before the relief that flooded him as he motioned her out.

"All right, you're not evil. You can go."

"And you?"

And himself? Before, as Satan, her arguments would have

been plausible, and he had discounted them. But now—it *had* been the Tree of Knowledge of Good and Evil! And yet——

"Dogs!" She caught at him, dragging him to the entrance where the baying sound was louder. "They're hunting you, Adam—dozens of them!"

He nodded, studying the distant forms of men on horseback, while his fingers busied themselves with a pencil and scrap of paper. "And they'll be here in twenty minutes. Good or evil, they must not find what's here. Eve, there's a boat by the river; pull the red handle the way you want to go, hard for fast, a light pull for slow. Here's a map to my cave, and you'll be safe there."

Almost instantly, he was back at the excavator and in its saddle, his fingers flashing across its panel; its heavy generator bellowed gustily, and the squat, heavy machine began twisting through the narrow aisles and ramming obstructions aside. Once outside, where he could use its full force without danger of backwash, ten minutes would leave only a barren hill; and the generator could be overdriven by adjustment to melt itself and the machine into useless slag.

"Adam!" She was spraddling into the saddle behind him, shouting over the roar of the thin blade of energy that was enlarging the tunnel.

"Go on, get away, Eve! You can't stop me!"

"I don't want to—they're not ready for such machines as this, yet! And between us, we can rebuild everything here, anyhow. Adam?"

He grunted uneasily, unable to turn away from the needle beam. It was hard enough trying to think without her distraction, knowing that he dared not take chances and must destroy himself, while her words and the instincts within him fought against his resolution. "You talk too much!"

"And I'll talk a lot more, until you behave sensibly! You'll make your mind sick, trying to decide now; come up the river for six months with me. You can't do any harm there, even if you are Satan! Then, when you've thought it over, Adam, you can do what you like. But not now!"

"For the last time, will you go?" He dared not think now, while he was testing his way through the flawed, cracked cement, and yet he could not quiet his mind to her words, that went on and on. "GO!"

"Not without you! Adam, my receiver isn't defective; I

knew you'd try to kill me when I rescued you! Do you think I'll give up so easily now?"

He snapped the power to silence with a rude hand, flinging around to face her. "You knew—and still saved me? Why?"

"Because I needed you, and the world needs you. You had to live, even if you killed me!"

Then the generator roared again, knifing its way through the last few inches, and he swung out of the dome and began turning it about. As the savage bellow of full power poured out of the main orifice, he turned his head to her and nodded.

She might be the dumbest robot in creation, but she was also the sweetest. It was wonderful to be needed and wanted!

And behind him, Eve nodded to herself, blessing Simon Ames for listing psychology as a humanity. In six months, she could complete his re-education and still have time to recite the whole of the Book he knew as a snatch of film. But not yet! Most certainly not Leviticus yet; Genesis would give her trouble enough.

It was wonderful to be needed and wanted!

Spring had come again, and Adam sat under one of the budding trees, idly feeding one of the new crop of piglets as Eve's hands moved swiftly, finishing what were to be his clothes, carefully copied from those of Dan.

They were almost ready to go south and mingle with men in the task of leading the race back to its heritage. Already the yielding plastic he had synthesized and she had molded over them was a normal part of them, and the tiny magnetic muscles he had installed no longer needed thought to reveal their emotions in human expressions. He might have been only an uncommonly handsome man as he stood up and went over to her.

"Still hunting God?" she asked lightly, but there was no worry on her face. The metaphysical binge was long since cured.

A thoughtful smile grew on his face as he began donning the clothes. "He is still where I found Him—— Something inside us that needs no hunting. No, Eve, I was wishing the other robot had survived. Even though we found no trace of his dome where your records indicated, I still feel he should be with us."

"Perhaps he is, in spirit, since you insist robots have souls. Where's your faith, Adam?"

But there was no mockery inside her. Souls or not, Adam's God had been very good to them.

And far to the south, an aged figure limped over rubble to the face of a cliff. Under his hands, a cleverly concealed door swung open, and he pushed inward, closing and barring it behind him, and heading down the narrow tunnel to a rounded cavern at its end. It had been years since he had been there, but the place was still home to him as he creaked down onto a bench and began removing tattered, travel-stained clothes. Last of all, he pulled a mask and gray wig from his head, to reveal the dented and worn body of the third robot.

He sighed wearily as he glanced at the few tattered books and papers he had salvaged from the ruinous growth of stalagmites and stalactites within the chamber, and at the corroded switch the unplanned dampness had shorted seven hundred years before. And finally, his gaze rested on his greatest treasure. It was faded, even under the plastic cover, but the bitter face of Simon Ames still gazed out in recognizable form.

The third robot nodded toward it with a strange mixture of old familiarity and ever-new awe. "Over two thousand miles in my condition, Simon Ames, to check on a story I heard in one of the colonies, and months of searching for them. But I had to know. But they're good for the world. They'll bring all the things I couldn't, and their thoughts are young and strong, as the race is young and strong."

For a moment, he stared about the chamber and to the tunnel his adapted bacteria had eaten toward the outside world, resting his eyes again on the picture. Then he cut off the main generator and settled down in the darkness.

"Seven hundred years since I came out to find man extinct on the earth," he muttered to the picture. "Four hundred since I learned enough to dare attempt his re-creation, and over three hundred since the last of my superfrozen human ova grew to success. Now I've done my part. Man has an unbroken tradition back to your race, with no knowledge of the break. He's strong and young and fruitful, and he has new leaders, better than I could ever be alone. I can do no more for him!"

For a moment there was only the sound of his hands sliding against metal, and then a faint sigh. "Into my hands, Simon Ames, you gave your race. Now, into Thy Hands, God of that race, if you exist as my brother believes, I commend him—and my spirit."

Then there was a click as his hands found the switch to his generator, and final silence.

CAMOUFLAGE

by Henry Kuttner

ASTOUNDING SCIENCE FICTION,
September

"Camouflage" is about a cyborg, a person who is part human and part machine. Of course, cyborgs are now commonplace, especially in a technical sense, since an artificial limb with moving parts or a pacemaker would meet the definition. Cyborgs have been common in science fiction since the Gernsback era, one early example being E. V. Odle's The Clockwork Man *of 1923. The general trend toward biological extrapolation in recent sf has produced several outstanding novels in the last few years, including Frederik Pohl's award-winning* Man Plus *(1976). An excellent anthology on the subject is* Human-Machines *(1975), edited by Thomas N. Scortia and George Zebrowski. The Kuttners employed cyborgs in a number of their stories, and C. L. Moore's "No Woman Born" is justly considered a classic treatment of the theme.*

(Ever since I was quite young, I have thought considerably about the possibility of being reduced to a simple brain with everything else just prosthetic attachments. I read about it in the Hawk Carse stories of the early 1930s to say nothing of the popular Professor Jameson series. It seemed the one sure route to immortality without giving up anything that was really essential to humanity. Your consciousness, your intelligence, your memory, your ca-

pacity to learn would all be untouched and as for physical sensations and even sex—well, they were not essential.

Yet come to think of it, evolution has done its best to produce just such a situation. The brain is tightly enclosed in a bony cranium so that it is the best protected part of the body. It is wired by way of nerves to the best prosthetic attachments evolution could manage—made of flesh and blood, to be sure. And to top it off, the brain is long-lived. Although its cells are too specialized to multiply they nevertheless can endure, and work, for over a hundred years.

But then, after many a summer, they die. And they would die even if they were protected by metal rather than bone, and no matter how efficiently they were fed. Of course, we might construct an artificial brain of material more durable and just as compact and versatile as the cells of the human brain, but that would be a whole other ball game. I.A.)

Talman was sweating by the time he reached 16 Knobhill Road. He had to force himself to touch the annunciator plate. There was a low whirring as photoelectrics checked and okayed his fingerprints; then the door opened and Talman walked into the dim hallway. He glanced behind him to where, beyond the hills, the spaceport's lights made a pulsating, wan nimbus.

Then he went on, down a ramp, into a comfortably furnished room where a fat, gray-haired man was sitting in an easy chair, fingering a highball glass. Tension was in Talman's voice as he said, "Hello, Brown. Everything all right?"

A grin stretched Brown's sagging cheeks. "Sure," he said. "Why not? The police weren't after you, were they?"

Talman sat down and began mixing himself a drink from the server nearby. His thin, sensitive face was shadowed.

"You can't argue with your glands. Space does that to me anyway. All the way from Venus I kept expecting somebody to walk up to me and say, 'You're wanted for questioning.' "

"Nobody did."

"I didn't know what I'd find here."

"The police didn't expect us to head for Earth," Brown said, rumpling his gray hair with a shapeless paw. "And that was your idea."

"Yeah. Consulting psychologist to—"

"—to criminals. Want to step out?"

"No," Talman said frankly, "not with the profits we've got in sight already. This thing's big."

Brown grinned. "Sure it is. Nobody ever organized crime before, in just this way. There wasn't any crime worth a row of pins until we started."

"Where are we now, though? On the run."

"Fern's found a foolproof hideout."

"Where?"

"In the Asteroid Belt. We need one thing, though."

"What's that?"

"An atomic power plant."

Talman looked startled. But he saw that Brown wasn't kidding. After a moment, he put down his glass and scowled.

"I'd say it's impossible. A power plant's too big."

"Yeah," Brown said, "except that this one's going by space to Callisto."

"Hijacking? We haven't enough men—"

"The ship's under Transplant-control."

Talman cocked his head to one side. "Uh. That's out of my line—"

"There'll be a skeleton crew, of course. But we'll take care of them—and take their places. Then it'll simply be a matter of unhitching the Transplant and rigging up manuals. It isn't out of your line at all. Fern and Cunningham can do the technical stuff, but we've got to find out first just how dangerous a Transplant can be."

"I'm no engineer."

Brown went on, ignoring the comment. "The Transplant who's handling this Callisto shipment used to be Bart Quentin. You knew him, didn't you?"

Talman, startled, nodded. "Sure. Years ago. Before—"

"You're in the clear, as far as the police are concerned. Go to see Quentin. Pump him. Find out . . . Cunningham will tell you what to find out. After that, we can go ahead. I hope."

"I don't know. I'm not—"

Brown's brows came down. *"We've got to find a hideout!* That's absolutely vital right now. Otherwise, we might as well walk into the nearest police station and hold out our hands for cuffs. We've been clever, but now—we've got to hide. Fast!"

"Well . . . I get that. But do you know what a Transplant really is?"

"A free brain. One that can use artificial gadgets."

"Technically, yeah. Ever seen a Transplant working a power-digger? Or a Venusian sea-dredge? Enormously complicated controls it'd normally take a dozen men to handle?"

"Implying a Transplant's a superman?"

"No," Talman said slowly, "I don't mean that. But I've got an idea it'd be safer to tangle with a dozen men than with one Transplant."

"Well," Brown said, "go up to Quebec and see Quentin. He's there now, I found out. Talk to Cunningham first. We'll work out the details. What we've got to know are Quentin's powers and his vulnerable points. And whether or not he's telepathic. You're an old friend of Quentin, and you're a psychologist, so you're the guy for the job."

"Yeah."

"We've got to get that power plant. *We've got to hide, now!"*

Talman thought that Brown had probably planned this from the beginning. The fat man was shrewd enough; he'd been sufficiently clever to realize that ordinary criminals would stand no chance in a highly technical, carefully specialized world. Police forces could call on the sciences to aid them. Communication was excellent and fast, even between the planets. There were gadgets—The only chance of bringing off a successful crime was to do it fast and then make an almost instantaneous get-away.

But the crime had to be planned. When competing against an organized social unit, as any crook does, it's wise to create a similar unit. A blackjack has no chance against a rifle. A strong-arm bandit was doomed to quick failure, for a similar reason. The traces he left would be analyzed; chemistry, psychology and criminology would track him down; he'd be made to confess. Made to, without any third-degree methods. So—

So Cunningham was an electronics engineer. Fern was an

astrophysicist. Talman himself was a psychologist. Big, blond Dalquist was a hunter, by choice and profession, beautifully integrated and tremendously fast with a gun. Cotton was a mathematician—and Brown himself was the coordinator. For three months the combination had worked successfully on Venus. Then, inevitably, the net closed, and the unit filtered back to Earth, ready to take the next step in the long-range plan. What it was, Talman hadn't known till now. But he could readily see its logical necessity.

In the vast wilderness of the Asteroid Belt they could hide forever, if necessary, emerging to pull off a coup whenever opportunity offered. Safe, they could build up an underground criminal organization, with a spy-system flung broadcast among the planets—yes, it was the inevitable way. Just the same, he felt hesitant about matching wits with Bart Quentin. The man wasn't—human—anymore—

He was worried on the way to Quebec. Cosmopolitan though he was, he couldn't help anticipating tension, embarrassment, when he saw Quent. To pretend to ignore that—accident—would be too obvious. Still—He remembered that, seven years ago, Quentin had possessed a fine, muscular physique, and had been proud of his skill as a dancer. As for Linda, he wondered what had happened on that score. She couldn't still be Mrs. Bart Quentin, under the circumstances. Or could she?

He watched the St. Lawrence, a dull silver bar, below the plane as it slanted down. Robot pilots—a narrow beam. Only during violent storms did standard pilots take over. In space it was a different matter. And there were other jobs, enormously complicated, that only human brains could handle. A very special type of brain, at that.

A brain like Quentin's.

Talman rubbed his narrow jaw and smiled wanly, trying to locate the source of his worry. Then he had the answer. Did Quent, in this new incarnation, possess more than five senses? Could he detect reactions a normal man could not appreciate? If so, Van Talman was definitely sunk.

He glanced at his seatmate, Dan Summers of Wyoming Engineers, through whom he had made the contact with Quentin. Summers, a blond young man with sun-wrinkles around his eyes, grinned casually.

"Nervous?"

"Could be that," Talman said. "I was wondering how much he'll have changed."

"Results are different in every case."

The plane, beam-controlled, slid down the slopes of sunset air toward the port. Quebec's lighted towers made an irregular backdrop.

"They do change, then?"

"I suppose, psychically, they've got to. You're a psychologist, Mr. Talman. How'd you feel, if—"

"There might be compensations."

Summers laughed. "That's an understatement. Compensations . . . why, immortality's only one such . . . compensation!"

"You consider that a blessing?" Talman asked.

"Yes, I do. He'll remain at the peak of his powers for God knows how long. There'll be no deterioration. Fatigue poisons are automatically eliminated by irradiation. Brain cells can't replace themselves, of course, the way . . . say . . . muscular tissue can; but Quent's brain can't be injured, in its specially built case. Arteriosclerosis isn't any problem, with the plasmic solution we use—no calcium's deposited on the artery walls. The physical condition of his brain is automatically and perfectly controlled. The only ailments Quent can ever get are mental."

"Claustrophobia? No. You say he's got eye lenses. There'd be an automatic feeling of extension."

Summers said, "If you notice any change—outside of the perfectly normal one of mental growth in seven years—I'll be interested. With me—well, I grew up with the Transplants. I'm no more conscious of their mechnical, interchangeable bodies than a physician would think of a friend as a bundle of nerves and veins. It's the reasoning faculty that counts, and that hasn't altered."

Talman said thoughtfully, "You're a sort of physician, to the Transplants, anyway. A layman might get another sort of reaction. Especially if he were used to seeing . . . a face."

"I'm never conscious of that lack."

"Is Quent?"

Summers hesitated. "No," he said finally, "I'm sure he isn't. He's beautifully adjusted. The reconditioning to Transplant life takes about a year. After that it's all velvet."

"I've seen Transplants working, on Venus, from a distance. But there aren't many spotted away from Earth."

"We haven't enough trained technicians. It takes literally half a lifetime to train a man to handle Transplantation. A man has to be a qualified electronic engineer before he even starts." Summers laughed. "The insurance companies cover a lot of the initial expense, though."

Talman was puzzled. "How's that?"

"They underwrite. Occupational risk, immortality. Working in atomic research is dangerous, my friend!"

They emerged from the plane into the cool night air. Talman said, as they walked toward a waiting car, "We grew up together, Quentin and I. But his accident happened two years after I left Earth, and I never saw him since."

"As a Transplant? Uh-huh. Well, it's an unfortunate name. Some jackass tagged the label on, whereas propaganda experts should have worked it out. Unfortunately it stuck. Eventually we hope to popularize the—Transplants. Not yet. We're only starting. We've only two hundred and thirty of them so far, the successful ones."

"Many failures?"

"Not now. In the early days—It's *complicated.* From the first trephining to the final energizing and reconditioning, it's the most nerve-racking, brain-straining, difficult technical task the human mind's ever worked out. Reconciling a colloid mechanism with an electronic hookup—but the result's worth it."

"Technologically. I wonder about the human values."

"Psychologically? We-ell . . . Quentin will tell you about that angle. And technologically you don't know the half of it. No colloid machine, like the brain, has ever been developed—till now. And this isn't purely mechanical. It's merely a miracle, the synthesis of intelligent living tissue with delicate, responsive machinery."

"But handicapped by the limitation of the machine—and the brain."

"You'll see. Here we are. We're dining with Quent—"

Talman stared. *"Dining?"*

"Yeah." Summers' eyes showed quizzical amusement. "No, he doesn't eat steel shavings. In fact—"

The shock of meeting Linda again took Talman by surprise. He had not expected to see her. Not now, under these altered conditions. But she hadn't changed much; she was still the same warm, friendly woman he remembered, a little older now, yet very lovely and very gracious. She had always had charm. She was slim and tall, her head crowned by a bizarre coiffure of honey-amber coils, her brown eyes without the strain Talman might have expected.

He took her hands. "Don't say it," he said. "I know how long it's been."

"We won't count the years, Van." She laughed up at him. "We'll pick up right where we left off. With a drink, eh?"

"I could use one," Summers said, "but I've got to report back to headquarters. I'll just see Quent for a minute. Where is he?"

"In there." Linda nodded toward a door and turned back to Talman. "So you've been on Venus? You look bleached enough. Tell me how it's been."

"All right." He took the shaker from her hands and swirled the Martinis carefully. He felt embarrassment. Linda lifted an eyebrow.

"Yes, we're still married, Bart and I. You're surprised."

"A little."

"He's still Bart," she said quietly. "He may not look it, but he's the man I married, all right. So you can relax, Van."

He poured the Martinis. Without looking at her, he said, "As long as you're satisfied—"

"I know what you're thinking. That it'd be like having a machine for a husband. At first . . . well, I got over that feeling. We both did, after a while. There was constraint; I suppose you'll feel it when you see him. Only that isn't important, really. He's—Bart." She pushed a third glass toward Talman, and he looked at it in surprise.

"Not—"

She nodded.

The three of them dined together. Talman watched the two-foot-by-two cylinder resting on the table opposite him and tried to read personality and intelligence into the double lenses. He couldn't help imagining Linda as a priestess, serving some sort of alien god-image, and the concept was disturbing. Now Linda was forking chilled, sauce-daubed shrimps into the metallic compartment and spooning them out when the amplifier signaled.

Talman had expected a flat, toneless voice, but the sonovox gave depth and timbre whenever Quentin spoke.

"Those shrimps are perfectly usable, Van. It's only habit that makes us throw chow out after I've had it in my food-box. I taste the stuff, all right—but I haven't any salivary juices."

"You—taste 'em."

Quentin laughed a little. "Look, Van. Don't try to pretend this seems natural to you. You'll have to get used to it."

"It took me a long time," Linda said. "But after a while I found myself thinking it was just the sort of silly thing Bart always used to do. Remember the time you put on that suit of armor for the Chicago board meeting?"

"Well, I made my point," Quentin said. "I forget what it was now, but—we were talking about taste. I can taste these shrimps, Van. Certain nuances are lacking, yeah. Very delicate sensations are lost on me. But there's more to it than sweet and sour, salt and bitter. Machines could taste years ago."

"There's no digestion—"

"And there's no pylorospasm. What I lose in refinements of taste I make up for in freedom from gastrointestinal disorders."

"You don't burp any more, either," Linda said. "Thank God."

"I can talk with my mouth full, too," Quentin said. "But I'm not the super-machine-bodied-brain you're subconsciously thinking I am, chum. I don't spit death rays."

Talman grinned uneasily. "Was I thinking that?"

"I'll bet you were. But—" The timbre of the voice changed. "I'm not super. I'm plenty human, inside, and don't think I don't miss the old days sometimes. Lying on the beach and feeling the sun on my skin, little things like that. Dancing in rhythm to music, and—"

"Darling," Linda said.

The voice changed again. "Yeah. It's the small, trivial factors that make up a complete life. But I've got substitutes now—parallel factors. Reactions quite impossible to describe, because they're . . . let's say . . . electronic vibrations instead of the familiar neural ones. I *do* have senses, but through mechanical organs. When impulses reach my brain, they're automatically translated into familiar symbols. Or—" He hesitated. "Not so much now, though."

Linda laid a bit of planked fish in the food-compartment. "Delusions of grandeur, eh?"

"Delusions of alteration—but no delusion, my love. You see, Van, when I first turned into a Transplant, I had no standard of comparison except the arbitrary one I already knew. That was suited to a human body—only. When, later, I felt an impulse from a digger gadget, I'd automatically feel as if I had my foot on a car accelerator. Now those old symbols are fading. I . . . feel . . . more directly now, without translating the impulses into the old-time images."

"That would be faster," Talman said.

"It is. I don't have to think of the value of pi when I get a pi signal. I don't have to break down the equation. I'm beginning to sense what the equation means."

"Synthesis with a machine?"

"Yet I'm not robot. It doesn't affect the identity, the personal essence of Bart Quentin." There was a brief silence, and Talman saw Linda look sharply toward the cylinder. Then Quentin continued in the same tone. "I get a tremendous bang out of solving problems. I always did. And now it's not just on paper. I carry out the whole task myself, from conception to finish. I dope out the application, and . . . Van, I *am* the machine!"

"Machine?" Talman said.

"Ever noticed, when you're driving or piloting, how you identify yourself with the machine? It's an extension of you. I go one step farther. And it's satisfying. Suppose you could carry empathy to the limit and *be* one of your patients while you were solving his problem? It's an—ecstasy."

Talman watched Linda pour sauterne into a separate chamber. "Do you ever get drunk any more?" he asked.

Linda gurgled. "Not on liquor—but Bart gets high, all right!"

"How?"

"Figure it out," Quentin said, a little smugly.

"Alcohol's absorbed into the bloodstream, thence reaching the brain—the equivalent of intravenous shots, maybe?"

"I'd rather put cobra venom in my circulatory system," the Transplant said. "My metabolic balance is too delicate, too perfectly organized, too upset by introducing foreign substances. No, I use electrical stimulus—an induced high-frequency current that gets me high as a kite."

Talman stared. "And that's a substitute?"

"It is. Smoking and drinking are irritants, Van. So's thinking, for that matter! When I feel the psychic need for a binge, I've a gadget that provides stimulating irritation—and I'll bet you'd get more of a bang out of it than you would out of a quart of mescal."

"He quotes Housman," Linda said. "And does animal imitations. With his tonal control, Bart's a wonder." She stood up. "If you'll excuse me for a bit, I've got some K.P. Automatic as the kitchen is, there are still buttons to push."

"Can I help?" Talman offered.

"Thanks, no. Stay here with Bart. Want me to hitch up your arms, darling?"

"Nope," Quentin said. "Van can take care of my liquid diet. Step it up, Linda—Summers and I've got to get back on the job soon."

"The ship's ready?"

"Almost."

Linda paused in the doorway, biting her lips. "I'll never get used to your handling a spaceship all by yourself. Especially that thing."

"It may be jury-rigged, but it'll get to Callisto."

"Well . . . there's a skeleton crew, isn't there?"

"There is," Quentin said, "but it isn't needed. The insurance companies demand an emergency crew. Summers did a good job, rigging the ship in six weeks."

"With chewing gum and paper clips," Linda remarked. "I only hope it holds." She went out as Quentin laughed softly. There was a silence. Then, as never before, Talman felt that his companion was . . . was . . . had changed. For he felt Quentin gazing at him, and—Quentin wasn't there.

"Brandy, Van," the voice said. "Pour a little in my box."

Talman started to obey, but Quentin checked him. "Not out of the bottle. It's been a long time since I mixed rum and coke in my mouth. Use the inhaler. That's it. Now. Have a drink yourself and tell me how you feel."

"About—?"

"Don't you know?"

Talman went to the window and stood looking down at the reflected fluorescent shining in the St. Lawrence. "Seven years, Quent. It's hard to get used to you in this—form."

"I haven't lost anything."

"Not even Linda," Talman said. "You're lucky."

Quentin said steadily, "She stuck with me. The accident, five years ago, wrecked me. I was fooling around with atomic research, and there were chances that had to be taken. I was mangled, butchered, in the explosion. Don't think Linda and I hadn't planned in advance. We knew the occupational risk."

"And yet you—"

"We figured the marriage could last, even if—But afterward I almost insisted on a divorce. She convinced me we could still make a go of it. And we have."

Talman nodded. "I'd say so."

"That . . . kept . . . me going, for quite a while," Quentin said softly. "You know how I felt about Linda. It's always been just about a perfect equation. Even though the factors have changed, we've adjusted." Suddenly Quentin's laugh made the psychologist swing around. "I'm no monster, Van. Try and get over that idea!"

"I never thought that," Talman protested. "You're—"

"What?"

Silence again. Quentin grunted.

"In five years I've learned to notice how people react to me. Give me some more brandy. I still imagine I taste it with my palate. Odd how associations hang on."

Talman poured liquor from the inhaler. "So you figure you haven't changed, except physically."

"And you figure me as a raw brain in a metal cylinder. Not as the guy you used to get drunk with on Third Avenue. Oh, I've changed—sure. But it's a normal change. There's nothing innately alien about limbs that are metal extensions. It's one step beyond driving a car. If I were the sort of supergadget you subconsciously think I am, I'd be an utter introvert and spend my time working out cosmic equations." Quentin used a vulgar expletive. "And if I did that, I'd go nuts. Because I'm no superman. I'm an ordinary guy, a physicist, and I've had to adjust to a new body. Which, of course, has its handicaps."

"What, for example?"

"The senses. Or the lack of them. I helped develop a lot of compensatory apparatus. I read escapist fiction, I get drunk by electrical irritation, I taste even if I can't eat. I watch teleshows. I try to get the equivalent of all the purely human sensory pleasures I can. It makes a balance that's very necessary."

"It would be. Does it work, though?"

"Look. I've got eyes that are delicately sensitive to shades and gradations of color. I've got arm attachments that can be refined down until they can handle microscopic apparatus. I can draw pictures—and, under a pseudonym, I'm a pretty popular cartoonist. I do that as a sideline. My real job is still physics. And it's still a good job. You know the feeling of pure pleasure you get when you've worked out a problem, in geometry or electronics or psychology—or anything? Now I work out questions infinitely more complicated, requiring split-second reaction as well as calculation. Like handling a spaceship. More brandy. It's volatile stuff in a hot room."

"You're still Bart Quentin," Talman said, "but I feel surer of that when I keep my eyes shut. Handling a spaceship—"

"I've lost nothing human," Quentin insisted. "The emotional basics haven't changed. It . . . isn't really pleasant to have you come in and look at me with plain horror, but I can understand the reason. We've been friends for a long time, Van. You may forget that before I do."

Sweat was suddenly cold on Talman's stomach. But despite Quentin's words, he felt certain by now that he had part of the answer for which he had come to Quebec. The Transplant had no abnormal powers—there were no telepathic functions.

There were more questions to be asked, of course.

He poured more brandy and smiled at the dully shining cylinder across the table. He could hear Linda singing softly from the kitchen.

The spaceship had no name, for two reasons. One was that she would make only a single trip, to Callisto; the other was odder. She was not, essentially, a ship with a cargo. She was a cargo with a ship.

Atomic power plants are not ordinary dynamos that can be dismantled and crated on a freight car. They were tremendously big, powerful, bulky, and behemothic. It takes two years to complete an atomic setup, and even after that the initial energizing must take place on Earth, at the enormous standards control plant that covers seven counties of Pennsylvania. The Department of Weights, Measures, and Power has a chunk of metal in a thermostatically controlled glass case in Washington; it's the standard meter. Similarly, in Pennsylvania, there is, under fantastic precautionary conditions, the one key atomic-disrupter in the Solar System.

There was only one requirement for fuel; it was best to filter it through a wire screen with, approximately, a one-inch gauge. And that was an arbitrary matter, for convenience in setting up a standard of fuels. For the rest, atomic power ate anything.

Few people played with atomic power; the stuff's violent. The research engineers worked on a stagger system. Even so, only the immortality insurance—the Transplantidae—kept neuroses from developing into psychoses.

The Callisto-bound power plant was too big to be loaded on the largest ship of any commercial line, but it had to get to Callisto. So the technicians built a ship around the power plant. It was not exactly jury-rigged, but it was definitely unstandardized. It occasionally, in matters of design, departed wildly from the norm. The special requirements were met deftly, often unorthodoxly, as they came up. Since the complete control would be in the hands of the Transplant Quentin, only casual accommodations were provided for the comfort of the small emergency crew. They weren't intended to wander through the entire ship unless a breakdown made it necessary, and a breakdown was nearly impossible. In fact, the vessel was practically a living entity. But not quite.

The Transplant had extensions—tools—throughout various sections of the great craft. Yet they were specialized to deal with the job in hand. There were no sensory attachments, except auditory and ocular. Quentin was, for the nonce, simply a super spaceship drive control. The brain cylinder was carried into the craft by Summers, who inserted it—somewhere!—plugged it in, and that finished the construction job.

At 2400 the mobile power plant took off for Callisto.

A third of the way to the Martian orbit, six spacesuited men came into an enormous chamber that was a technician's nightmare.

From a wall amplifier, Quentin's voice said, "What are you doing here, Van?"

"Okay," Brown said. "This is it. We'll work fast now. Cunningham, locate the connection. Dalquist, keep your gun ready."

"What'll I look for?" the big blond man asked.

Brown glanced at Talman. "You're certain there's no mobility?"

"I'm certain," Talman said, his eyes moving. He felt naked exposed to Quentin's gaze, and didn't like it.

Cunningham, gaunt, wrinkled and scowling, said, "The

only mobility's in the drive itself. I was sure of that before Talman double-checked. When a Transplant's plugged in for one job, it's limited to the tools it needs for that job."

"Well, don't waste time talking. Break the circuit."

Cunningham stared through his vision plate. "Wait a minute. This isn't standardized equipment. It's experimental . . . casual. I've got to trace a few . . . um."

Talman was surreptitiously trying to spot the Transplant's eye lenses, and failing. From somewhere in that maze of tubes, coils, wires, grids and engineering hash, he knew, Quentin was looking at him. From several places, undoubtedly—there'd be overall vision, with eyes spotted strategically around the room.

And it was a big room, this central control chamber. The light was misty yellow. It was like some strange, unearthly cathedral in its empty, towering height, a hugeness that dwarfed the six men. Bare grids, abnormally large, hummed and sparked; great vacuum tubes flamed eerily. Around the walls above their heads ran a metal platform, twenty feet up, a metal guard rail casually precautionary. It was reached by two ladders, on opposite walls of the room. Overhead hung a celestial globe, and the dim throbbing of tremendous power murmured in the chlorinated atmosphere.

The amplifier said, "What is this, piracy?"

Brown said casually, "Call it that. And relax. You won't be harmed. We may even send you back to Earth, when we can figure out a safe way to do it."

Cunningham was investigating lucite mesh, taking care to touch nothing. Quentin said, "This cargo isn't worth hijacking. It isn't radium I'm carrying, you know."

"I need a power plant," Brown remarked curtly.

"How did you get aboard?"

Brown lifted a hand to mop sweat from his face, and then, grimacing, refrained. "Find anything yet, Cunningham?"

"Give me time. I'm only an electronics man. This setup's screwy. Fern, give me a hand here."

Talman's discomfort was growing. He realized that Quentin, after the first surprised comment, had ignored him. Some indefinable compulsion made him tilt back his head and say Quentin's name.

"Yeah," Quentin said. "Well? So you're in with this gang?"

"Yes."

"And you were pumping me, up in Quebec. To make sure I was harmless."

Talman made his voice expressionless. "We had to be certain."

"I see. How'd you get aboard? The radar automatically dodges approaching masses. You couldn't have brought your own ship alongside in space."

"We didn't. We got rid of the emergency crew and took their suits."

"Got rid of them?"

Talman moved his eyes toward Brown. "What else could we do? We can't afford half measures in a gamble as big as this. Later on, they'd have been a danger to us, after our plans started moving. Nobody's going to know anything about it except us. And you." Again Talman looked at Brown. "I think, Quent, you'd better throw in with us."

The amplifier ignored whatever implied threat lay in the suggestion.

"What do you want the power plant for?"

"We've got an asteroid picked out," Talman said, tilting his head back to search the great crowded hollow of the ship, swimming a little in the haze of its poisonous atmosphere. He half expected Brown to cut him short, but the fat man didn't speak. It was, he thought, curiously difficult to talk persuasively to someone whose location you didn't know. "The only trouble is, it's airless. With the plant, we can manufacture our own air. It'd be a miracle if anybody ever found us in the Asteroid Belt."

"And then what? Piracy?"

Talman did not answer. The voicebox said thoughtfully, "It might make a good racket, at that. For a while, anyhow. Long enough to clean up quite a lot. Nobody will expect anything like it. Yeah, you might get away with the idea."

"Well," Talman said, "if you think that, what's the next logical step?"

"Not what you think. I wouldn't play along with you. Not for moral reasons, especially, but for motives of self-preservation. I'd be useless to you. Only in a highly intricate, widespread civilization is there any need for Transplants. I'd be excess baggage."

"If I gave you my word—"

"You're not the big shot," Quentin told him. Talman instinctively sent another questioning look at Brown. And from the voicebox on the wall came a curious sound like a smothered laugh.

"All right," Talman said, shrugging. "Naturally you won't decide in our favor right away. Think it over. Remember you're not Bart Quentin anymore—you've got certain mechanical handicaps. While we haven't got too much time, we can spare a little—say ten minutes—while Cunningham looks things over. Then . . . well, we aren't playing for marbles, Quent." His lips thinned. "If you'll throw in with us and guide the ship under our orders, we can afford to let you live. But you've got to make up your mind fast. Cunningham is going to trace you down and take over the controls. After that—"

"What makes you so sure I can be traced down?" Quentin asked calmly. "I know just how much my life would be worth once I'd landed you where you want to go. You don't need me. You couldn't give me the right maintenance even if you wanted to. No, I'd simply join the crewmen you've disposed of. I'll give you an ultimatum of my own."

"You'll—what?"

"Keep quiet and don't monkey with anything, and I'll land in an isolated part of Callisto and let you all escape," Quentin said. "If you don't, God help you."

For the first time Brown showed he had been conscious of that distant voice. He turned to Talman.

"Bluff?"

Talman nodded slowly. "Must be. He's harmless."

"Bluff," Cunningham said, without looking up from his task.

"No," the amplifier told him quietly, "I'm not bluffing. And be careful with that board. It's part of the atomic hookup. If you fool with the wrong connections, you're apt to blast us all out of space."

Cunningham jerked back from the maze of wires snaking out of the bakelite before him. Fern, some distance away, turned a swarthy face to watch. "Easy," he said. "We've got to be sure what we're doing."

"Shut up," Cunningham grunted. "I *do* know. Maybe that's what the Transplant's afraid of. I'll be plenty careful to stay clear of atomic connections, but—" He paused to study the tangled wires. "No. This isn't atomic—I think. Not the control leads, anyway. Suppose I break this connection—" His gloved hand came up with a rubber-sheathed cutter.

The voicebox said, "Cunningham—don't." Cunningham poised the cutter. The amplifier sighed.

"You first, then. Here it is!"

Talman felt the transparent faceplate slap painfully against his nose. The immense room bucked dizzily as he went reeling forward, unable to check himself. All around him he saw grotesque spacesuited figures reeling and stumbling. Brown lost his balance and fell heavily.

Cunningham had been slammed forward into the wires as the ship abruptly decelerated. Now he hung like a trapped fly in the tangle, his limbs, his head, his whole body jerking and twitching with spasmodic violence. The devil's dance increased in fury.

"Get him out of there!" Dalquist yelled.

"Hold it!" Fern shouted. "I'll cut the power—" But he didn't know how. Talman, dry-throated, watched Cunningham's body sprawling, arching, shaking in spastic agony. Bones cracked suddenly.

Cunningham jerked more limpy now, his head flopping grotesquely.

"Get him down," Brown snapped, but Fern shook his head. "Cunningham's dead. And that hookup's dangerous."

"How? Dead?"

Under his thin mustache Fern's lips parted in a humorless smile. "A guy in an epileptic fit can break his own neck."

"Yeah," Dalquist said, obviously shaken. "His neck's broken, all right. Look at the way his head goes."

"Put a twenty-cycle alternating current through yourself and you'd go into convulsions too," Fern advised.

"We can't just leave him there!"

"We can," Brown said, scowling. "Stay away from the walls, all of you." He glared at Talman. "Why didn't you—"

"Sure, I know. But Cunningham should have had sense enough to stay away from bare wires."

"Few wires are insulated around here," the fat man growled. "You said the Transplant was harmless."

"I said he had no mobility. And that he wasn't a telepath." Talman realized that his voice sounded defensive.

Fern said, "A signal's supposed to sound whenever the ship accelerates or decelerates. It didn't go off that time. The Transplant must have cut it out himself, so we wouldn't be warned."

They looked up into that humming, vast, yellow emptiness.

Claustrophobia gripped Talman. The walls looked ready to topple in—to fold down, as though he stood in the cupped hand of a titan.

"We can smash his eye cells," Brown suggested.

"Find 'em." Fern indicated the maze of equipment.

"All we have to do is unhitch the Transplant. Break his connection. Then he goes dead."

"Unfortunately," Fern said, "Cunningham was the only electronic engineer among us. I'm only an astrophysicist!"

"Never mind. We pull one plug and the Transplant blacks out. You can do that much!"

Anger flared. But Cotton, a little man with blinking blue eyes, broke the tension.

"Mathematics—geometry—ought to help us. We want to locate the Transplant, and——" He glanced up and was frozen. "We're off our course!" he said finally, licking dry lips. "See that telltale?"

Far above, Talman could see the enormous celestial globe. On its dark surface a point of red light was clearly marked.

Fern's swarthy face showed a sneer. "Sure. The Transplant's running to cover. Earth's the nearest place where he can get help. But we've plenty of time left. I'm not the technician Cunningham was, but I'm not a complete dope." He didn't look at the rhythmically moving body on the wires. "We don't have to test every connection in the ship."

"Okay, take it, then," Brown grunted.

Awkward in his suit, Fern walked to a square opening in the floor and peered down at a mesh-metal grating eighty feet below. "Right. Here's the fuel feed. We don't need to trace connections through the whole ship. The fuel's dumped out of that leader tube overhead there. Now look. Everything connected with the atomic power is apparently marked with red wax crayon. See?"

They saw. Here and there, on bare plates and boards, were cryptic red markings. Other symbols were in blue, green, black and white.

"Go on that assumption," Fern said. "Temporarily, anyhow. Red's atomic power. Blue . . . green . . . um."

Talman said suddenly, "I don't see anything here that looks like Quentin's brain case."

"Did you expect to?" the astrophysicist asked sardonically. "It's slid into a padded socket somewhere. The brain can stand more gravs than the body, but seven's about tops in any case. Which, incidentally, is fine for us. There'd be no use putting high-speed potential in this ship. The Transplant couldn't stand it, any more than we could."

"Seven G's," Brown said thoughtfully.

"Which would black out the Transplant too. He'll have to remain conscious to pilot the ship through Earth atmosphere. We've got plenty of time."

"We're going pretty slow now," Dalquist put in.

Fern gave the celestial globe a sharp glance. "Looks like it. Let me work on this." He paid out a coil from his belt and hitched himself to one of the central pillars. "That'll guard against any more accidents."

"Tracing a circuit shouldn't be so hard," Brown said.

"Ordinarily it isn't. But you've got everything in this chamber—atomic control, radar, the kitchen sink. And these labels are only for construction convenience. There wasn't any blueprint in this ship. It's a single-shot model. I can find the Transplant, but it'll take time. So shut up and let me work."

Brown scowled but didn't say anything. Cotton's bald head was sweating. Dalquist wrapped his arm about a metal pillar and waited. Talman looked up again at the balcony that hung from the walls. The celestial globe showed a crawling disk of red light.

"Quent," he said.

"Yes, Van." Quentin's voice was quietly distant. Brown put one hand casually to the blaster at his belt.

"Why don't you give up?"

"Why don't you?"

"You can't fight us. Your getting Cunningham was a fluke. We're on guard now—you can't hurt us. It's only a matter of time until we trace you down. Don't look for mercy then, Quent. You can save us trouble by telling us where you are. We're willing to pay for that. After we find you—on our own initiative—you can't bargain. How about it?"

Quentin said simply, "No."

There was silence for a few minutes. Talman was watching Fern, who, very cautiously paying out his coil, was investigating the tangle where Cunningham's body still hung.

Quentin said, "He won't find the answer there. I'm pretty well camouflaged."

"But helpless," Talman said quickly.

"So are you. Ask Fern. If he monkeys with the wrong connections, he's apt to destroy the ship. Look at your own problem. We're heading back toward Earth. I'm swinging into a new course that'll end at the home berth. If you give up now—"

Brown said, "The old statutes never were altered. The punishment for piracy is death."

"There's been no piracy for a hundred years. If an actual case came to trial, it might be a different matter."

"Imprisonment? Reconditioning?" Talman asked. "I'd a lot rather be dead."

"We're decelerating," Dalquist called, getting a firmer grip on his pillar.

Looking at Brown, Talman thought the fat man knew what he had in mind. If technical knowledge failed, psychology might not. And Quentin, after all, was a human brain.

First get the subject off guard.

"Quent."

But Quentin didn't answer. Brown grimaced and turned to watch Fern. Sweat was pouring down the physicist's swarthy face as he concentrated on the hookups, drawing diagrams on the stylo pad he wore attached to his forearm.

After a while Talman began to feel dizzy. He shook his head, realizing that the ship had decelerated almost to zero, and got a firmer grip on the nearest pillar. Fern cursed. He was having a difficult time keeping his footing.

Presently he lost it altogether as the ship went free. Five spacesuited figures clung to convenient handgrips. Fern snarled, "This may be deadlock, but it doesn't help the Transplant. I can't work without gravity—he can't get to Earth without acceleration."

The voicebox said, "I've sent out an S.O.S."

Fern laugehd. "I worked that out with Cunningham—and you talked too much to Talman, too. With a radar meteor-avoider, you don't need signaling apparatus, and you haven't got it." He eyed the apparatus he had just left. "Maybe I was getting too close to the right answer, though, eh? Is that why——"

"You weren't even near it," Quentin said.

"Just the same——" Fern kicked himself away from the pillar, playing out the line behind him. He made a loop about his left wrist, and, hanging in midair, fell to studying the hookup.

Brown lost his grip on the slippery column and floated free like some overinflated balloon. Talman kicked himself across to the railed balcony. He caught the metal bar in gloved hands, swung himself in like an acrobat, and looked down—though it wasn't really *down*—at the control chamber.

"I think you'd better give up," Quentin said.

Brown was floating across to join Fern. "Never," he said, and simultaneously four G's hit the ship with the impact of a pile driver. It wasn't forward acceleration. It was in another, foreplanned direction. Fern saved himself at the cost of an almost dislocated wrist—but the looped line rescued him from a fatal dive into uninsulated wiring.

Talman was slammed down on the balcony. He could see the others plummet to hard impacts on unyielding surfaces. Brown wasn't stopped by the floor plate, though.

He had been hovering over the fuel-feed hole when the acceleration was slammed on.

Talman saw the bulky body pop out of sight down the opening. There was an indescribable sound.

Dalquist, Fern, and Cotton struggled to their feet. They cautiously went toward the hole and peered down.

Talman called, "Is he—"

Cotton had turned away. Dalquist remained where he was, apparently fascinated, Talman thought, until he saw the man's shoulders heaving. Fern looked up toward the balcony.

"He went through the filter screen," he said. "It's a one-inch gauge metal mesh."

"Broke through?"

"No," Fern said deliberately. "He didn't break through. He *went* through."

Four gravities and a fall of eighty feet add up to something slightly terrific. Talman shut his eyes and said, "Quent!"

"Do you give up?"

Fern snarled, "Not on your life! Our unit's not that interdependent. We can do without Brown."

Talman sat on the balcony, held on to the rail, and let his feet hang down into emptiness. He stared across to the celestial globe, forty feet to his left. The red spot that marked the ship stood motionless.

"I don't think you're human anymore, Quent," he said.

"Because I don't use a blaster? I've different weapons to fight with now. I'm not kidding myself, Van. I'm fighting for my life."

"We can still bargain."

Quentin said, "I told you you'd forget our friendship before I did. You must have known this hijacking could only end in my death. But apparently you didn't care about that."

"I didn't expect you to—"

"Yeah," the voicebox said. "I wonder if you'd have been as ready to go through with the plan if I'd still had human form? As for friendship—use your own tricks of psychology, Van. You look on my mechanical body as an enemy, a barrier between you and the real Bart Quentin. Subconsciously, maybe, you hate it, and you're therefore willing to destroy it. Even though you'll be destroying me with it. I don't know—perhaps you rationalize that you'd thus be rescuing me from the thing that's erected the barrier. And you forget that I haven't changed, basically."

"We used to play chess together," Talman said, "but we didn't smash the pawns."

"I'm in check," Quentin countered. "All I've got to fight with are knights. You've still got castles and bishops. You can move straight for your goal. Do you give up?"

"No!" Talman snapped. His eyes were on the red light. He saw a tremor move it, and gripped the metal rail with a frantic clutch. His body swung out as the ship jumped. One gloved hand was torn from its grip. But the other held. The celestial globe was swinging violently. Talman threw a leg over the rail, clambered back to his precarious perch, and looked down.

Fern was still braced by his emergency line. Dalquist and little Cotton were sliding across the floor, to bring up with a crash against a pillar. Someone screamed.

Sweating, Talman warily descended. But by the time he had reached Cotton the man was dead. Radiating cracks in his faceplate and contorted, discolored features gave the answer.

"He slammed right into me," Dalquist gulped. "His plate cracked into the back of my helmet—"

The chlorinated atmosphere within the sealed ship had ended Cotton's life, not easily, but rapidly. Dalquist, Fern and Talman matched glances.

The blond giant said, "Three of us left. I don't like this. I don't like it at all."

Fern showed his teeth. "So we're still underestimating that thing. From now on, hitch yourselves to pillars. Don't move without sound anchorage. Stay clear of everything that might cause trouble."

"We're still heading back toward Earth," Talman said.

"Yeah." Fern nodded. "We could open a port and walk out into free space. But then what? We figured we'd be using this ship. Now we've *got* to."

Dalquist said, "If we gave up—"

"Execution," Fern said flatly. "We've still got time. I've traced some of the connections. I've elminated a lot of hook-ups."

"Still think you can do it?"

"I think so. But don't let go of your handgrips for a second. I'll find the answer before we hit atmosphere."

Talman had a suggestion. "Brains send out recognizable vibration patterns. A directional finder, maybe?"

"If we were in the middle of the Mojave, that would work. Not here. This ship's lousy with currents and radiations. How could we unscramble them without apparatus?"

"We brought some apparatus with us. And there's plenty all around the walls."

"Hooked up. I'm going to be plenty careful about upsetting the *status quo*. I wish Cunningham hadn't gone down the drain."

"Quentin's no fool," Talman said. "He got the electronic engineer first and Brown second. He was trying for you then, too. Bishop and queen."

"Which makes me what?"

"Castle. He'll get you if he can." Talman frowned, trying to remember something. Then he had it. He went over the stylopad on Fern's arm, shielding the writing with his own body from any photoelectrics that might be spotted around the walls or ceiling. He wrote: "He gets drunk on high frequency. Can do?"

Fern crumpled the tissue slip and tore it awkwardly into fragments with his gloved fingers. He winked at Talman and nodded briefly.

"Well, I'll keep trying," he said, and paid out his line to the kit of apparatus he and Cunningham had brought aboard.

Left alone, Dalquist and Talman hitched themselves to pillars and waited. There was nothing else they could do. Talman had already mentioned this high-frequency irritation angle to Fern and Cunningham; they had seen no value to the knowledge then. Now it might be the answer, with applied practical psychology to supplement technology.

Meanwhile, Talman longed for a cigarette. All he could

do, sweating in the uncomfortable suit, was to manipulate a built-in gadget so that he managed to swallow a salt tablet and a few gulps of tepid water. His heart was pounding, and there was a dull ache in his temples. The spacesuit was uncomfortable; he wasn't used to such personal confinement.

Through the built-in receiving gadget he could hear the humming silence, broken by the padding rustle of sheathed boots as Fern moved about. Talman blinked at the chaos of equipment and closed his eyes; the relentless yellow light, not intended for human vision, made little pulses beat nervously somewhere in his eye sockets. Somewhere in this ship, he thought, probably in this very chamber, was Quentin. But camouflaged. How?

Purloined letter stuff? Scarcely. Quentin would have had no reason to expect hijackers. It was pure accident that had intervened to protect the Transplant with such an excellent hiding place. That, and the slapdash methods of technicians, constructing a one-job piece of equipment with the casual convenience of a slipstick.

But, Talman thought, if Quentin could be made to reveal his location—

How? Via induced cerebral irritation—intoxication?

Appeal to basics? But a brain couldn't propagate the species. Self-preservation remained the only constant. Talman wished he'd brought Linda along. He'd have had a lever then.

If only Quentin had had a human body, the answer would not be so difficult to find. And not necessarily by torture. Automatic muscular reactions, the old stand-by of professional magicians, could have led Talman to his goal. Unfortunately, Quentin himself was the goal—a bodiless brain in a padded, insulated metal cylinder. And his spinal cord was a wire.

If Fern could rig up a high-frequency device, the radiations would weaken Quentin's defenses—in one way, if not another. At present the Transplant was a very, very dangerous opponent. And he was perfectly camouflaged.

Well, not perfectly. Definitely no. Because, Talman realized with a sudden glow of excitement, Quentin wasn't simply sitting back, ignoring the pirates, and taking the quickest route back to Earth. The very fact that he was retracing his course instead of going on to Callisto indicated that Quentin wanted to get help. And, meanwhile, via murder, he was doing his utmost to distract his unwelcome guests.

Because, obviously, Quentin *could* be found.

Given time.

Cunningham could have done it. And even Fern was a menace to the Transplant. That meant that Quentin—was afraid.

Talman sucked in his breath. "Quent," he said, "I've a proposition. You listening?"

"Yes," the distant, terribly familiar voice said.

"I've an answer for all of us. You want to stay alive. We want this ship. Right?"

"Correct."

"Suppose we drop you by parachute when we hit Earth atmosphere. Then we can take over the controls and head out again. That way—"

"And Brutus is an honorable man," Quentin remarked. "But of course he wasn't. I can't trust you anymore, Van. Psychopaths and criminals are too amoral. They're ruthless, because they feel the end justifies the means. You're a psychopathic psychologist, Van, and that's exactly why I'd never take your word for anything."

"You're taking a long chance. If we do find the right hookup in time, there'll be no bargaining, you know."

"If."

"It's a long way back to Earth. We're taking precautions now. You can't kill any more of us. We'll simply keep working steadily till we find you. Now—what about it?"

After a pause Quentin said, "I'd rather take my chances. I know technological values better than I do human ones. As long as I depend on my own field of knowledge, I'm safer than if I tried to deal in psychology. I know coefficients and cosines, but I don't know much about the colloid machine in your skull."

Talman lowered his head; sweat dripped from his nose to the interior of the faceplate. He felt a sudden claustrophobia; fear of the cramped quarters of the suit, and fear of the larger dungeon that was the room and the ship itself.

"You're restricted, Quent," he said, too loudly. "You're limited in your weapons. You can't adjust atmospheric pressure in here, or you'd have compressed already and crushed us."

"Crushing vital equipment at the same time. Besides, those suits can take a lot of pressure."

"Your king's still in check."

"So is yours," Quentin said calmly.

Fern gave Talman a slow look that held approval and faint triumph. Under the clumsy gloves, manipulating delicate instruments, the hookup was beginning to take shape. Luckily, it was a job of conversion rather than construction, or time would have been too short.

"Enjoy yourself," Quentin said. "I'm slamming on all the G's we can take."

"I don't feel it," Talman said.

"All we can take, not all I could give out. Go ahead and amuse yourselves. You can't win."

"No?"

"Well—figure it out. As long as you stay hitched in one place, you're reasonably safe. But if you start moving around, I can destroy you."

"Which means we'll have to move—somewhere—in order to reach you, eh?"

Quentin laughed. "I didn't say so. I'm well camouflaged. *Turn that thing off!*"

The shout echoed and re-echoed against the vaulted roof, shaking the amber air. Talman jerked nervously. He met Fern's eye and saw the astrophysicist grin.

"It's hitting him," Fern said. Then there was silence, for many minutes.

The ship abruptly jumped. But the frequency inductor was securely moored, and the men, too, were anchored by their lines.

"Turn it off," Quentin said again. His voice wasn't quite under control.

"Where are you?" Talman asked.

No answer.

"We can wait, Quent."

"Keep waiting, then! I'm . . . I'm not distracted by personal fear. That's one advantage of being a Transplant."

"High irritant value," Fern murmured. "It works fast."

"Come on, Quent," Talman said persuasively. "You've still got the instinct of self-preservation. This can't be pleasant for you."

"It's . . . too pleasant," Quentin said unevenly. "But it won't work. I could always stand my liquor."

"This isn't liquor," Fern countered. He touched a dial.

The Transplant laughed; Talman noted with satisfaction that oral control was slipping. "It won't work, I say. I'm too . . . smart for you."

"Yeah?"

"Yeah. You're not morons—none of you are. Fern's a good technician, maybe, but he isn't good enough. Remember, Van, you asked me in Quebec if there'd been any . . . change? I said there hadn't. I'm finding out now that I was wrong."

"How?"

"Lack of distraction." Quentin was talking too much; a symptom of intoxication. "A brain in a body can never concentrate fully. It's too conscious of the body itself. Which is an imperfect mechanism. Too specialized to be efficient. Respiratory, circulatory—all the systems intrude. Even the habit of breathing's a distraction. Now the ship's my body—at the moment—but it's a perfect mechanism. It functions with absolute efficiency. So my brain's correspondingly better."

"Superman."

"Superefficient. The better mind generally wins at chess, because it can foresee the possible gambits. I can foresee everything you might do. And you're badly handicapped."

"Why?"

"You're human."

Egotism, Talman thought. Was this the Achillean heel? A taste of success had apparently done its psychological work, and the electronic equivalent of drunkenness had released inhibitions. Logical enough. After five years of routine work, no matter how novel that work might be, this suddenly altered situation—this change from active to passive, from machine to protagonist—might have been the catalyst. Ego. And cloudy thinking.

For Quentin wasn't a superbrain. Very definitely he was not. The higher an I.Q., the less need there is for self-justification, direct or indirect. And, oddly, Talman suddenly felt absolved of any lingering compunctions. The real Bart Quentin would never have been guilty of paranoid thought patterns.

So—

Quentin's articulation was clear; there was no slurring. But he no longer spoke with soft palate, tongue and lips, by means of a column of air. Tonal control was noticeably altered now, however, and the Transplant's voice varied from a carrying whisper to almost a shout.

Talman grinned. He was feeling better, somehow.

"We're human," he said, "but we're still sober."

"Nuts. Look at the telltale. We're getting close to Earth."

"Come off it, Quent," Talman said wearily. "You're bluffing, and we both know you're bluffing. You can't stand an indefinite amount of high frequency. Save time and give up now."

"You give up," Quentin said, "I can see everything you do. The ship's a mass of traps anyway. From up here all I have to do is watch until you get close to one. I'm planning my game ahead, every gambit worked out to checkmate for one of you. You haven't got a chance. You haven't got a chance. You haven't got a chance."

From up here, Talman thought. Up where? He remembered little Cotton's remark that geometry could be used to locate the Transplant. Sure. Geometry and psychology. Halve the ship, quarter it, keep bisecting the remainders—

Not necessary. *Up* was the key word. Talman seized upon it with an eagerness that didn't show on his face. *Up*, presumably, reduced by half the area they'd have to search. The lower parts of the ship could be ruled out. Now he'd have to halve the upper section, using the celestial globe, say, as the dividing line.

The Transplant had eye cells spotted all over the ship, of course, but Talman tentatively decided that Quentin thought of himself as situated in one particular spot, not scattered over the whole ship, localized wherever an eye was built in. A man's head is his locus, to his own mind.

Thus Quentin could see the red spot on the celestial globe, but that didn't necessarily mean that he was located in a wall facing that hemisphere of the sphere. The Transplant had to be trapped into references to his actual physical relation to objects in the ship—which would be hard, because this could be done best by references to sight, the normal individual's most important link with his surroundings. And Quentin's sight was almost omnipotent. He could see everything.

There had to be a localization—somehow.

A word-association test would do it. But that implied cooperation. Quentin wasn't that drunk!

Nothing could be gauged by learning what Quentin could *see*—for his brain was not necessarily near any one of his eyes. There would be a subtle, intrinsic realization of location on the Transplant's part; the knowledge that *he*—blind, deaf, dumb except through his distant extensor sensory mechanisms—was in a certain place. And how, except by too obviously direct questioning, could Quentin be made to give the right answers?

It was impossible, Talman thought, with a hopeless sense of frustrated anger. The anger grew stronger. It brought sweat to his face, rousing him to a dull, aching hatred of Quentin. All this was Quentin's fault, the fact that Talman was prisoned here in this hateful spacesuit and this enormous deathtrap of a ship. The fault of a machine—

Suddenly he saw the way.

It would, of course, depend on how drunk Quentin was. He glanced at Fern, questioned the man with his eyes, and in response Fern manipulated a dial and nodded.

"Damn you," Quentin said in a whisper.

"Nuts," Talman said. "You implied you haven't any instinct for self-preservation anymore."

"I . . . didn't—"

"It's true, isn't it?"

"No," Quentin said loudly.

"You forget I'm a psychologist, Quent. I should have seen the angles before. The book was open, ready to read, even before I saw you. When I saw Linda."

"Shut up about Linda!"

Talman had a momentary, sick vision of the drunken, tortured brain somewhere hidden in the walls, a surrealistic nightmare. "Sure," he said. "You don't want to think about her yourself."

"Shut up."

"You don't want to think about yourself, either, do you?"

"What are you trying to do, Van? Get me mad?"

"No," Talman said, "I'm simply fed up, sick and disgusted with the whole business. Pretending that you're Bart Quentin, that you're still human, that we can deal with you on equal terms."

"There'll be no dealing—"

"That's not what I meant, and you know it. I've just realized what you are." He let the words hang in the dim air. He imagined he could hear Quentin's heavy breathing, though he knew it was merely an illusion.

"Please shut up, Van," Quentin said.

"Who's asking me to shut up?"

"I am."

"And what's that?"

The ship jumped. Talman almost lost his balance. The line hitched to the pillar saved him. He laughed.

"I'd be sorry for you, Quent, if you were—you. But you're not."

"I'm not falling for any trick."

"It may be a trick, but it's the truth too. And you've wondered about it yourself. I'm dead certain of that."

"Wondered about what?"

"You're not human any more," Talman said gently. "You're a thing. A machine. A gadget. A spongy gray hunk of meat in a box. Did you really think I could get used to you—now? That I could identify you with the old Quent? You haven't any face!"

The soundbox made noises. They sounded mechanical. Then——"Shut up," Quentin said again, almost plaintively. "I know what you're trying to do."

"And you don't want to face it. Only you've got to face it, sooner or later, whether you kill us now or not. This . . . business . . . is an incident. But the thoughts in your brain will keep growing and growing. And you'll keep changing and changing. You've changed plenty already."

"You're crazy," Quentin said. "I'm no . . . monster."

"You hope, eh? Look at it logically. You haven't dared to do that, have you?" Talman held up his gloved hand and ticked off points on his sheathed fingers. "You're trying very desperately to keep your grip on something that's slipping away—humanity, the heritage you were born to. You hang on to the symbols, hoping they'll mean the reality. Why do you pretend to eat? Why do you insist on drinking brandy out of a glass? You know it might just as well be squirted into you out of an oil can."

"No. No! It's an aesthetic—"

"Garbage. You go to teleshows. You read. You pretend you're human enough to be a cartoonist. It's a desperate, hopeless clinging to something that's already gone from you, all these pretenses. Why do you feel the need for binges? You're maladjusted, because you're pretending you're still human, and you're not, anymore."

"I'm . . . well, something better—"

"Maybe . . . if you'd been born a machine. But you *were* human. You had a human body. You had eyes and hair and lips. Linda must remember that, Quent.

"You should have insisted on a divorce. Look—if you'd

only been crippled by the explosion, she could have taken care of you. You'd have needed her. As it is, you're a self-sufficient, self-contained unit. She does a good job of pretending. I'll admit that. She tries not to think of you as a hopped-up helicopter. A gadget. A blob of wet cellular tissue. It must be tough on her. She remembers you as you used to be."

"She loves me."

"She pities you," Talman said relentlessly.

In the humming stillness the red telltale crept across the globe. Fern's tongue stole out and circled his lips. Dalquist stood quietly watching, his eyes narrowed.

"Yeah," Talman said, "face it. And look at the future. There are compensations. You'll get quite a bang out of meshing your gears. Eventually you'll even stop remembering you ever were human. You'll be happier then. For you can't hang on to it, Quent. It's going away. You can keep on pretending for a while, but in the end it won't matter anymore. You'll be satisfied to be a gadget. You'll see beauty in a machine and not in Linda. Maybe that's happened already. Maybe Linda knows it's happened. You don't have to be honest with yourself yet, you know. You're immortal. But I wouldn't take that kind of immortality as a gift."

"Van——"

"I'm still Van. But you're a machine. Go ahead and kill us, if you want, and if you can do it. Then go back to Earth and, when you see Linda again, look at her face. Look at it when she doesn't know you're watching. You can do that easily. Rig up a photoelectric cell in a lamp or something."

"Van . . . *Van!*"

Talman let his hands drop to his sides. "All right. Where are you?"

The silence grew, while an inaudible question hummed through the yellow vastness. The question, perhaps, in the mind of every Transplant. The question of—a price.

What price?

Utter loneliness, the sick knowledge that the old ties were snapping one by one, and that in place of living, warm humanity there would remain—a mental monster?

Yes, he had wondered—this Transplant who had been Bart Quentin. He had wondered, while the proud, tremendous machines that were his body stood ready to spring into vibrant life.

Am I changing? Am I still Bart Quentin?

Or do they—the humans—look on me as—How does Linda really feel about me now? Am I—

Am I—It?

"Go up on the balcony," Quentin said. His voice was curiously faded and dead.

Talman made a quick gesture. Fern and Dalquist sprang to life. They climbed, each to a ladder, on opposite sides of the room, but carefully, hitching their lines to each rung.

"Where is it?" Talman asked gently.

"The south wall—Use the celestial sphere for orientation. You can reach me—" The voice failed.

"Yes?"

Silence. Fern called down, "Has he passed out?"

"Quent!"

"Yes— About the center of the balcony. I'll tell you when you reach it."

"Easy," Fern warned Dalquist. He took a turn of his line about the balcony rail and edged forward, searching the wall with his eyes.

Talman used one arm to scrub his fogged faceplate. Sweat was trickling down his face and flanks. The crawling yellow light, the humming stillness from machines that should be roaring thunderously, stung his nerves to unendurable tension.

"Here?" Fern called.

"Where is it, Quent?" Talman asked. "Where are you?"

"Van," Quentin said, a horrible, urgent agony in his tone. "You can't mean what you've been saying. You can't. This is—I've got to know. I'm thinking of Linda!"

Talman shivered. He moistened his lips.

"You're a machine, Quent," he said steadily. "You're a gadget. You know I'd never have tried to kill you if you were still Bart Quentin."

And then, with shocking abruptness, Quentin laughed.

"Here it comes, Fern!" he shouted, and the echoes crashed and roared through the vaulted chamber. Fern clawed for the balcony rail.

That was a fatal mistake. The line hitching him to the rail proved a trap—because he didn't see the danger in time to unhook himself.

The ship jumped.

It was beautifully gauged. Fern was jerked toward the wall

and halted by the line. Simultaneously the great celestial globe swung from its support, in a pendulum arc like the drive of a Gargantuan fly swatter. The impact snapped Fern's line instantly.

Vibration boomed through the walls.

Talman hung on to a pillar and kept his eyes on the globe. It swung back and forth in a diminishing arc as inertia overcame momentum. Liquid spattered and dripped from it.

He saw Dalquist's helmet appear over the rail. The man yelled, "Fern!"

There was no answer.

"Fern! Talman!"

"I'm here," Talman said.

"Where's—" Dalquist turned his head to stare at the wall. He screamed.

Obscene gibberish tumbled from his mouth. He yanked the blaster from his maze of apparatus below.

"Dalquist!" Talman shouted. "Hold it!"

Dalquist didn't hear.

"I'll smash the ship," he screamed. "I'll—"

Talman drew his own blaster, steadied the muzzle against the pillar, and shot Dalquist in the head. He watched the body lean over the rail, topple, and crash down on the floor plates. Then he rolled over on his face and lay there, making sick, miserable sounds.

"Van," Quentin said.

Talman didn't answer.

"Van!"

"Yeah!"

"Turn off the inductor."

Talman got up, walked unsteadily to the device, and ripped wires loose. He didn't bother to search for an easier method.

After a long while the ship grounded. The humming vibration of currents died. The dim, huge control chamber seemed oddly empty now.

"I've opened a port," Quentin said. "Denver's about fifty miles north. There's a highway four miles or so in the same direction."

Talman stood up, staring around. His face looked ravaged.

"You tricked us," he mumbled. "All along, you were playing us like fish. My psychology—"

"No," Quentin said. "You almost succeeded."

"What—"

"You don't think of me as a gadget, really. You pretended to, but a little matter of semantics saved me. When I realized what you'd said, I came to my senses."

"What I said?"

"Yeah. That you'd never have tried to kill me if I'd still been Bart Quentin."

Talman was struggilng slowly out of his spacesuit. Fresh, clean air had already replaced the poison atmosphere of the ship. He shook his head dazedly.

"I don't see it."

Quentin's laughter rang out, filling the chamber with its warm, human vibrancy.

"A machine can be stopped or destroyed, Van," he said. "But it can't be—*killed.*"

Talman didn't say anything. He was free of the bulky suit now, and he turned hesitantly toward a doorway. He looked back.

"The door's open," Quentin said.

"You're letting me go?"

"I told you in Quebec that you'd forget our friendship before I did. Better step it up, Van, while there's still time. Denver's probably sent out helicopters already."

Talman swept one questioning look around the vast chamber. Somewhere, perfectly camouflaged among those mighty machines, was a small metal cylinder, cradled and shielded in its hidden socket. Bart Quentin——

His throat felt dry. He swallowed, opened his mouth, and closed it again.

He turned on his heel and went out. The muffled sound of his footsteps faded.

Alone in the silent ship, Bart Quentin waited for the technicians who would refit his body for the Callisto flight.

THE POWER

by Murray Leinster

ASTOUNDING SCIENCE FICTION,
September

One of the more unique aspects of science fiction is the number of stories in the field that are structured in the form of letters, memos and diary entries. These can be done in the form of a conventional story, with an address at the beginning and a signature at the end, but they can also consist of exchanges between parties, and this is much more difficult —the writer *has to build in background information, concern him or herself with plot and characters, and not every writer can do this successfully within the confines of the letter/memo form. While these types of stories can be found outside of sf, they are much more common within the* genre.

"The Power" is a brilliant example of the form.

(One of the arguments against the existence of any intelligent civilizations outside the Earth is that if they were there, *they would be* here. *In other words, why haven't they reached us, even if we couldn't reach them?*

Some of the counter-arguments are that the speed of light is truly an unbreakable limit and the time it would take to go from one civilization to another has defeated all attempts so that all of us are eternally isolated. Or that they have indeed reached us, but refuse to interfere with us till we are sufficiently advanced and meanwhile keep us under their pro-

tection. Or that they have reached us in the form of flying saucers and we are just too stodgy to accept the fact.

My own notion of the most interesting counterargument is that they have indeed reached us but it has been useless. They would clearly be at a level of technology far beyond ours and, if so, we simply would not understand either the technology or them. All our tales of angels and demons might be our failure to understand extraterrestrial visitors.

No, I don't believe this, but it is the stuff good sf can be made of. I.A.)

Memorandum from Professor Charles, Latin Department, Haverford University, to Professor McFarland, the same faculty:

Dear Professor McFarland:

In a recent batch of fifteenth-century Latin documents from abroad, we found three which seem to fit together. Our interest is in the Latin of the period, but their contents seem to bear upon your line. I send them to you with a free translation. Would you let me know your reaction?

Charles.

To Johannus Hartmannus, Licentiate in Philosophy,
Living at the house of the goldsmith Grote,
Lane of the Dyed Flee,
Leyden, the Low Countries

Friend Johannus:

I write this from the Goth's Head Inn, in Padua, the second day after Michaelmas, Anno Domini 1482. I write in haste because a worthy Hollander here journeys homeward and has promised to carry mails for me. He is an amiable lout, but ignorant. Do not speak to him of mysteries. He knows nothing. Less than nothing. Thank him, give him to drink, and speak of me as a pious and worthy student. Then forget him.

I leave Padua tomorrow for the realisation of all my hopes and yours. This time I am sure. I came here to purchase perfumes and mandragora and the other necessities for an Operation of the utmost imaginable importance, which I will conduct five nights hence upon a certain hilltop near the village of Montevecchio. I have found a Word and a Name of incalculable power, which in the place that I know of must open to me knowledge of all mysteries. When you read this, I shall possess powers at which Hermes Trismegistos only guessed, and which Albertus Magnus could speak of only by hearsay. I have been deceived before, but this time I am sure. I have seen proofs!

I tremble with agitation as I write to you. I will be brief. I came upon these proofs and the Word and the Name in the village of Montevecchio. I rode into the village at nightfall, disconsolate because I had wasted a month searching for a learned man of whom I had heard great things. Then I found him—and he was but a silly antiquary with no knowledge of mysteries! So, riding upon my way I came to Montevecchio, and there they told me of a man dying even then because he had worked wonders. He had entered the village on foot only the day before. He was clad in rich garments, yet he spoke like a peasant. At first he was mild and humble, but he paid for food and wine with a gold piece, and villagers fawned upon him and asked for alms. He flung them a handful of gold pieces and when the news spread the whole village went mad with greed. They clustered about him, shrieking pleas, and thronging ever the more ugently as he strove to satisfy them. It is said that he grew frightened and would have fled because of their thrusting against him. But they plucked at his garments, screaming of their poverty, until suddenly his rich clothing vanished in the twinkling of an eye and he was but another ragged peasant like themselves and the purse from which he had scattered gold became a mere coarse bag filled with ashes.

This had happened but the day before my arrival, and the man was yet alive, though barely so because the villagers had cried witchcraft and beset him with flails and stones and then dragged him to the village priest to be exorcised.

I saw the man and spoke to him, Johannus, by representing

myself to the priest as a pious student of the snares Satan has set in the form of witchcraft. He barely breathed, what with broken bones and pitchfork wounds. He was a native of the district, who until now had seemed a simple ordinary soul. To secure my intercession with the priest to shrive him ere he died, the man told me all. And it was much!

Upon this certain hillside where I shall perform the Operation five nights hence, he had dozed at midday. Then a Power appeared to him and offered to instruct him in mysteries. The peasant was stupid. He asked for riches instead. So the Power gave him rich garments and a purse which would never empty so long—said the Power—as it came not near a certain metal which destroys all things of mystery. And the Power warned that this was payment that he might send a learned man to learn what he had offered the peasant, because he saw that peasants had no understanding. Thereupon I told the peasant that I would go and greet this Power and fulfil his desires, and he told me the Name and the Word which would call him, and also the Place, begging me to intercede for him with the priest.

The priest showed me a single gold piece which remained of that which the peasant had distributed. It was of the age of Antonius Pius, yet bright and new as if fresh minted. It had the weight and feel of true gold. But the priest, wryly, laid upon it the crucifix he wears upon a small iron chain about his waist. Instantly it vanished, leaving behind a speck of glowing coal which cooled and was a morsel of ash.

This I saw, Johannus! So I came speedily here to Padua, to purchase perfumes and mandragora and the other necessities for an Operation to pay great honour to this Power whom I shall call up five nights hence. He offered wisdom to the peasant, who desired only gold. But I desire wisdom more than gold, and surely I am learned concerning mysteries and Powers! I do not know any but yourself who surpasses me in true knowledge of secret things. And when you read this, Johannus, I shall surpass even you! But it may be that I will gain knowledge so that I can transport myself by a mystery to your attic, and there inform you myself, in advance of this letter, of the results of this surpassing good fortune which causes me to shake with agitation whenever I think of it.

Your friend Carolus,
at the Goth's Head Inn in Padua.

. . . fortunate, perhaps, that an opportunity has come to send a second missive to you, through a crippled man-at-arms who has been discharged from a mercenary band and travels homeward to sit in the sun henceforth. I have given him one gold piece and promised that you would give him another on receipt of this message. You will keep that promise or not, as pleases you, but there is at least the value of a gold piece in a bit of parchment with strange symbols upon it which I enclose for you."

Item: I am in daily communication with the Power of which I wrote you, and daily learn great mysteries.

Item: Already I perform marvels such as men have never before accomplished by means of certain sigils or talismans the Power has prepared for me.

Item: Resolutely the Power refuses to yield to me the Names or the incantations by which these things are done so that I can prepare such sigils for myself. Instead, he instructs me in divers subjects which have no bearing on the accomplishment of wonders, to my bitter impatience which I yet dissemble.

Item: Within this packet there is a bit of parchment. Go to a remote place and there tear it and throw it upon the ground. Instantly, all about you, there will appear a fair garden with marvellous fruits, statuary, and pavilion. You may use this garden as you will, save that if any person enter it, or you yourself, carrying a sword or dagger or any object however small made of iron, the said garden will disappear immediately and nevermore return.

This you may verify when you please. For the rest, I am like a prisoner trembling at the very door of Paradise, barred from entering beyond the antechamber by the fact of the Power withholding from me the true essentials of mystery, and granting me only crumbs—which, however, are greater marvels than any known certainly to have been practised before. For example, the parchment I send you. This art I have proven many times. I have in my scrip many such sigils, made for me by the Power at my entreaty. But when I have secretly taken other parchments and copied upon them the very symbols to the utmost exactitude, they are valueless. There are words or formulas to be spoken over them or—I think more likely—a greater sigil which gives the parchments their magic property. I begin to make a plan—a very daring plan—to acquire even this sigil.

But you will wish to know of the Operation and its results. I return to Montevecchio from Padua, reaching it in three days. The peasant who had worked wonders was dead, the villagers having grown more fearful and beat out his brains with hammers. This pleased me, because I had feared he would tell another the Word and Name he had told me. I spoke to the priest and told him that I had been to Padua and secured advice from high dignitaries concerning the wonder-working, and had been sent back with special commands to seek out and exorcise the foul fiend who had taught the peasant such marvels.

The next day—the priest himself aiding me!—I took up to the hilltop the perfumes and wax tapers and other things needed for the Operation. The priest trembled, but he would have remained had I not sent him away. And night fell, and I drew the magic circle and the pentacle, with the Signs in their proper places. And when the new moon rose, I lighted the perfumes and the fine candles and began the Operation. I have had many failures, as you know, but this time I knew confidence and perfect certainty. When it came time to use the Name and the Word I called them both loudly, thrice, and waited.

Upon this hilltop there are many greyish stones. At the third calling of the Name, one of the stones shivered and was not. Then a voice said dryly:

'Ah! So that is the reason for this stinking stuff! My messenger sent you here?'

There was a shadow where the stone had been and I could not see clearly. But I bowed low in that direction:

'Most Potent Power,' I said, my voice trembling because the Operation was a success, 'a peasant working wonders told me that you desired speech with a learned man. Beside your Potency I am ignorant indeed, but I have given my whole life to the study of mysteries. Therefore I have come to offer worship or such other compact as you may desire in exchange for wisdom.'

There was a stirring in the shadow, and the Power came forth. His appearance was that of a creature not more than an ell and a half in height, and his expression in the moonlight was that of sardonic impatience. The fragrant smoke seemed to cling about him, to make a cloudiness close about his form.

'I think,' said the dry voice, 'that you are as great a fool as the peasant I spoke to. What do you think I am?'

'A Prince of Celestial race, your Potency,' I said, my voice shaking.

There was a pause. The Power said as if wearily:

'Men! Fools forever! Oh man, I am simply the last of a number of my kind who traveled in a fleet from another star. This small planet of yours has a core of the accursed metal, which is fatal to the devices of my race. A few of our ships came too close. Others strove to aid them, and shared their fate. Many, many years since, we descended from the skies and could never rise again. Now I alone am left.'

Speaking of the world as a planet was an absurdity, of course. The planets are wanderers among the stars, travelling in their cycles and epicycles as explained by Ptolemy a thousand years since. But I saw at once that he would test me. So I grew bold and said:

'Lord, I am not fearful. It is not needful to cozen me. Do I not know of those who were cast out of Heaven for rebellion? Shall I write the name of your leader?'

He said 'Eh?' for all the world like an elderly man. So, smiling, I wrote on the earth the true name of Him whom the vulgar call Lucifer. He regarded the markings on the earth and said:

'Bah! It is meaningless. More of your legendary! Look you, man, soon I shall die. For more years than you are like to believe I have hid from your race and its accursed metal. I have watched men, and despised them. But—I die. And it is not good that knowledge should perish. It is my desire to impart to men the knowledge which else would die with me. It can do no harm to my own kind, and may bring the race of men to some degree of civilisation in the course of ages.'

I bowed to the earth before him. I was aflame with eagerness.

'Most Potent One,' I said joyfully. 'I am to be trusted. I will guard your secrets fully. Not one jot or tittle shall ever be divulged!'

Again his voice was annoyed and dry.

'I desire that this knowledge be spread so that all may learn it. But—' Then he made a sound which I do not understand, save that it seemed to be derisive—'What I have to say may serve, even garbled and twisted. And I do not think you will keep secrets inviolate. Have you pen and parchment?'

'Nay, Lord!'

'You will come again, then, prepared to write what I shall tell you.'

But he remained, regarding me. He asked me questions, and I answered eagerly. Presently he spoke in a meditative voice, and I listened eagerly. His speech bore an odd similarity to that of a lonely man who dwelt much on the past, but soon I realised that he spoke in ciphers, in allegory, from which now and again the truth peered out. As one who speaks for the sake of remembering, he spoke of the home of his race upon what he said was a fair planet so far distant that to speak of leagues and even the span of continents would be useless to convey the distance. He told of cities in which his fellows dwelt—here, of course, I understood his meaning perfectly—and told of great fleets of flying things rising from those cities to go to other fair cities, and of music which was in the very air so that any person, anywhere upon the planet, could hear sweet sounds or wise discourse at will. In this matter there was no metaphor, because the perpetual sweet sounds in Heaven are matters of common knowledge. But he added a metaphor immediately after, because he smiled at me and observed that the music was not created by a mystery, but by waves like those of light, only longer. And this was plainly a cipher, because light is an impalpable fluid without length and surely without waves!

Then he spoke of flying through the emptiness of the empyrean, which again is not clear, because all can see that the heavens are fairly crowded with stars, and he spoke of many suns and other worlds, some frozen and some merely barren rock. The obscurity of such things is patent. And he spoke of drawing near to this world which is ours, and of an error made as if it were in mathematics—instead of in rebellion—so that they drew close to Earth as Icarus to the sun. Then again he spoke in metaphors, because he referred to engines, which are things to cast stones against walls, and in a larger sense for grinding corn and pumping water. But he spoke of engines growing hot because of the accursed metal in the core of Earth, and of the inability of his kind to resist Earth's pull—more metaphor—and then he spoke of a screaming descent from the skies. And all of this, plainly, is a metaphorical account of the casting of the Rebels out of

Heaven, and an acknowledgement that he is one of the said Rebels.

When he paused, I begged humbly that he would show me a mystery and of his grace give me protection in case my converse with him became known.

'What happened to my messenger?' asked the Power.

I told him, and he listened without stirring. I was careful to tell him exactly, because of course he would know that—as all else—by his powers of mystery, and the question was but another test. Indeed, I felt sure that the messenger and all that had taken place had been contrived by him to bring me, a learned student of mysteries, to converse with him in this place.

'Men!' he said bitterly at last. Then he added coldly. 'Nay! I can give you no protection. My kind is without protection upon this earth. If you would learn what I can teach you, you must risk the fury of your fellow countrymen.'

But then, abruptly, he wrote upon parchment and pressed the parchment to some object at his side. He threw it upon the ground.

'If men beset you,' he said scornfully, 'tear this parchment and cast it from you. If you have none of the accursed metal about you, it may distract them while you flee. But a dagger will cause it all to come to naught!'

Then he walked away. He vanished. And I stood shivering for a very long time before I remembered me of the formula given by Apollonius of Tyana for the dismissal of evil spirits. I ventured from the magic circle. No evil befell me. I picked up the parchment and examined it in the moonlight. The symbols upon it were meaningless, even to one like myself who has studied all that is known of mysteries. I returned to the village, pondering.

I have told you so much at length, because you will observe that this Power did not speak with the pride or the menace of which most authors on mysteries and Operations speak. It is often said that an adept must conduct himself with great firmness during an Operation, lest the Powers he has called up overawe him. Yet this Power spoke wearily, with irony, like one approaching death. And he had spoken of death, also. Which was of course a test and a deception, because are not the Principalities and Powers of Darkness immortal? He had some design it was not his will that I should know. So I saw that I must walk warily in this priceless opportunity.

In the village I told the priest that I had had encounter with a foul fiend, who begged that I not exorcise him, promising to reveal certain hidden treasures once belonging to the Church, which he could not touch or reveal to evil men because they were holy, but could describe the location of to me. And I procured parchment, and pens, and ink, and the next day I went alone to the hilltop. It was empty, and I made sure I was unwatched and—leaving my dagger behind me—I tore the parchment and flung it to the ground.

As it touched, there appeared such a treasure of gold and jewels as truly would have driven any man mad with greed. There were bags and chests and boxes filled with gold and precious stones, which had burst with the weight and spilled out upon the ground. There were gems glittering in the late sunlight, and rings and necklaces set with brilliants, and such monstrous hoards of golden coins of every antique pattern . . .

Johannus, even I went almost mad! I leaped forward like one dreaming to plunge my hands into the gold. Slavering, I filled my garments with rubies and ropes of pearls. and stuffed my scrip with gold pieces, laughing crazily to myself. I rolled in the riches. I wallowed in them, flinging the golden coins into the air and letting them fall upon me. I laughed and sang to myself.

Then I heard a sound. On the instant I was filled with terror for the treasure. I leaped to my dagger and snarled, ready to defend my riches to the death.

Then a dry voice said: 'Truly you care naught for riches!'

It was savage mockery. The Power stood regarding me. I saw him clearly now, yet not clearly because there was a cloudiness which clung closely to his body. He was, as I said, an ell and a half in height, and from his forehead there protruded knobby feelers which were not horns but had somewhat the look save for bulbs upon their ends. His head was large and—But I will not attempt to describe him, because he could assume any of a thousand forms, no doubt, so what does it matter?

Then I grew terrified because I had no Circle or Pentacle to protect me. But the Power made no menacing move.

'It is real, that riches,' he said dryly. 'It has colour and weight and the feel of substance. But your dagger will destroy it all.'

Didyas of Corinth has said that treasure of mystery must be fixed by a special Operation before it becomes permanent and free of the power of Those who brought it. They can transmute it back to leaves or other rubbish, if it be not fixed.

'Touch it with your dagger,' said the Power.

I obeyed, sweating in fear. And as the metal iron touched a great pile heap of gold, there was a sudden shifting and then a little flare about me. And the treasure—all, to the veriest crumb of a seed-pearl!—vanished before my eyes. The bit of parchment reappeared, smoking. It turned to ashes. My dagger scorched my fingers. It had grown hot.

'Ah, yes,' said the Power, nodding. 'The force-field has energy. When the iron absorbs it, there is heat.' Then he looked at me in a not unfriendly way. 'You have brought pens and parchment,' he said, 'and at least you did not use the sigil to astonish your fellows. Also you had the good sense to make no more perfumish stinks. It may be that there is a grain of wisdom in you. I will bear with you yet a while. Be seated and take parchment and pen—Stay! Let us be comfortable. Sheathe your dagger, or better, cast it from you.'

I put it in my bosom. And it was as if he thought, and touched something at his side, and instantly there was a fair pavilion about us, with soft cushions and a gently playing fountain.

'Sit,' said the Power. 'I learned that men like such things as this from a man I once befriended. He had been wounded and stripped by robbers, so that he had not so much as a scrap of accursed metal about him, and I could aid him. I learned to speak the language men use nowadays from him. But to the end he believed me an evil spirit and tried valorously to hate me.'

My hands shook with my agitation that the treasure had departed from me. Truly it was a treasure of such riches as no King has ever possessed, Johannus! My very soul lusted after that treasure! The golden coins alone would fill your attic solidly, but the floor would break under their weight, and the jewels would fill hogsheads. Ah, Johannus! That treasure!

'What I will have you write,' said the Power, 'at first will mean little. I shall give facts and theories first, because they are easiest to remember. Then I will give the applications of the theories. Then you men will have the beginning of such civilisation as can exist in the neighbourhood of the accursed metal.'

'Your Potency!' I begged abjectly. 'You will give me another sigil of treasure?'

'Write!' he commanded.

I wrote. And, Johannus, I cannot tell you myself what it is that I wrote. He spoke words, and they were in such obscure cipher that they have no meaning as I con them over. Hark you to this, and seek wisdom for the performance of mysteries in it! 'The civilisation of my race is based upon fields of force which have the property of acting in all essentials as substance. A lodestone is surrounded by a field of force which is invisible and impalpable. But the fields used by my people for dwellings, tools, vehicles, and even machinery are perceptible to the senses and act physically as solids. More, we are able to form these fields in latent fashions; and to fix them to organic objects as permanent fields which require no energy for their maintenance, just as magnetic fields require no energy supply to continue. Our fields, too, may be projected as three-dimensional solids which assume any desired form and have every property of substance except chemical affinity.'

Johannus! Is it not unbelievable that words could be put together, dealing with mysteries, which are so devoid of any clue to their true mystic meaning? I write and I write in desperate hope that he will eventually give me the key, but my brain reels at the difficulty of extracting the directions for Operations which such ciphers must conceal! I give you another instance: 'When a force-field generator has been built as above, it will be found that the pulsatory fields which are consciousness serve perfectly as controls. One has but to visualise the object desired, turn on the generator's auxiliary control, and the generator will pattern its output upon the pulsatory consciousness-field . . .'

Upon this first day of writing, the Power spoke for hours, and I wrote until my hand ached. From time to time, resting, I read back to him the words that I had written. He listened, satisfied.

'Lord!' I said shakily. 'Mighty Lord! Your Potency! These mysteries you bid me write—they are beyond comprehension!'

But he said scornfully:

'Write! Some will be clear to someone. And I will explain it little by little until even you can comprehend the beginning.' Then he added. 'You grow weary. You wish a toy. Well! I will make you a sigil which will make again that treasure you played with. I will add a sigil which will make a boat for you, with an engine drawing power from the sea to carry you wheresoever you wish without need of wind or tide. I will make others so you may create a palace where you will, and fair gardens as you please . . .'

These things he has done, Johannus. It seems to amuse him to write upon scraps of parchment, and think, and then press them against his side before he lays them upon the ground for me to pick up. He has explained amusedly that the wonder in the sigil is complete, yet latent, and is released by the tearing of the parchment, but absorbed and destroyed by iron. In such fashion he speaks in ciphers, but otherwise sometimes he jests!

It is strange to think of it, that I have come little by little to accept this Power as a person. It is not in accord with the laws of mystery. I feel that he is lonely. He seems to find satisfaction in speech with me. Yet he is a Power, one of the Rebels who was flung to earth from Heaven! He speaks of that only in vague, metaphorical terms, as if he had come from another world like *the* world, save much larger. He refers to himself as a voyager of space, and speaks of his race with affection, and of Heaven—at any rate the city from which he comes, because there must be great cities there—with a strange and prideful affection. If it were not for his powers, which are of mystery, I would find it possible to believe that he was a lonely member of a strange race, exiled forever in a strange place, and grown friendly with a man because of his loneliness. But how could there be such as he and not a Power? How could there be another world?

This strange converse has now gone on for ten days or more. I have filled sheets upon sheets of parchment with writing. The same metaphors occur again and again. 'Force-fields' —a term without literal meaning—occurs often. There are other metaphors such as 'coils' and 'primary' and 'secondary' which are placed in context with mention of wires of copper metal. There are careful descriptions, as if in the plainest of language, of sheets of dissimilar metals which are to be placed in acid, and other descriptions of plates of similar metal which are to be separated by layers of air or wax of certain thicknesses, with the plates of certain areas! And there is an explanation of the means by which he lives. 'I, being accustomed to an atmosphere much more dense than that on Earth, am forced to keep about myself a field of force which maintains an air density near that of my home planet for my breathing. This field is transparent, but because it must shift constantly to change and refresh the air I breathe, it causes a certain cloudiness of outline next my body. It is maintained by the generator I wear at my side, which at the same time provides energy for such other force-field artifacts as I may find convenient.'—Ah, Johannes! I grow mad with impatience! Did I not anticipate that he would some day give me the key to this metaphorical speech, so that from it may be extracted the Names and the Words which cause his wonders. I would give over in despair.

Yet he has grown genial with me. He has given me such sigils as I have asked him, and I have tried them many times. The sigil which will make you a fair garden is one of many. He says that he desires to give to man the knowledge he possesses, and then bids we write ciphered speech without meaning, such as: 'The drive of a ship for flight beyond the speed of light is adapted from the simple drive generator already described simply by altering its constants so that it cannot generate in normal space and must create an abnormal space by tension. The process is—' Or else—I choose at random, Johannus—'The accursed metal, iron, must be eliminated not only from all circuits but from nearness to apparatus using high-frequency oscillations, since it absorbs their energy and prevents the functioning . . ."

I am like a man trembling upon the threshold of Paradise, yet unable to enter because the key is withheld. 'Speed of light!' What could it mean in metaphor? In common parlance, as well speak of the speed of weather or of granite! Daily I beg him for the key to his speech. Yet even now, in the sigils he makes for me is greater power than any man has ever known before!

But it is not enough. The Power speaks as if he were lonely beyond compare; the last member of a strange race upon earth; as if he took a strange, companion-like pleasure in merely talking to me. When I beg him for a Name or a Word which would give me power beyond such as he doles out in sigils, he is amused and calls me fool, yet kindly. And he speaks more of his metaphorical speech about forces of nature and fields of force—and gives me a sigil which should I use it will create a palace with walls of gold and pillars of emerald! And then he amusedly reminds me that one greedy looter with an axe or hoe of iron would case it to vanish utterly!

I go almost mad, Johannus! But there is certainly wisdom unutterable to be had from him. Gradually, cautiously, I have come to act as if we were merely friends, of different race and he vastly the wiser, but friends rather than Prince and subject. Yet I remember the warnings of the most authoritative authors that one must be ever on guard against Powers called up in an Operation.

I have a plan. It is dangerous, I well know, but I grow desperate. To stand quivering upon the threshold of such wisdom and power as no man has ever dreamed of before, and then be denied . . .

The mercenary who will carry this to you, leaves tomorrow. He is a cripple, and may be months upon the way. All will be decided ere you receive this. I know you wish me well.

Was there ever a student of mystery in so saddening a predicament, with all knowledge in his grasp yet not quite his?

Your friend
Carolus.

Written in the very bad inn in Montevecchio.

Johannus! A courier goes to Ghent for My Lord of Brabant and I have opportunity to send you mail. I think I go mad, Johannus! I have power such as no man ever possessed before, and I am fevered with bitterness. Hear me!

For three weeks I did repair daily to the hilltop beyond Montevecchio and take down the ciphered speech of which I wrote you. My script was stuffed with sigils, but I had not one word of Power or Name of Authority. The Power grew mocking, yet it seemed sadly mocking. He insisted that his words held no cipher and needed but to be read. Some of them he phrased over and over again until they were but instructions for putting bits of metal together, mechanicwise. Then he made me follow those instructions. But there was no Word, no Name—nothing save bits of metal put together cunningly. And how could inanimate metal, not imbued with power of mystery by Names or Words or incantations, have power to work mystery?

At long last I became convinced that he would never reveal the wisdom he had promised. And I had come to such familiarity with this Power that I could dare to rebel, and even to believe that I had chance of success. There was the cloudiness about his form, which was maintained by a sigil he wore at his side and called a 'generator.' Were that cloudiness destroyed, he could not live, or so he had told me. It was for that reason that he, in person, dared not touch anything of iron. This was the basis of my plan.

I feigned illness, and said that I would rest at a peasant's thatched hut, no longer inhabited, at the foot of the hill on which the Power lived. There was surely no nail of iron in so crude a dwelling. If he felt for me the affection he protested, he would grant me leave to be absent in my illness. If his affection was great, he might even come and speak to me there. I would be alone in the hope that his friendship might go so far.

Strange words for a man to use to a Power! But I had talked daily with him for three weeks. I lay groaning in the hut, alone. On the second day he came. I affected great rejoicing, and made shift to light a fire from a taper I had kept burning. He thought it a mark of honour, but it was actually a signal. And then, as he talked to me in what he thought my illness, there came a cry from without the hut. It was the village priest, a simple man but very brave in his fashion. On the signal of smoke from the peasant's hut, he had crept near and drawn all about it an iron chain that we had muffled with cloth so that it would make no sound. And now he stood before the hut door with his crucifix upraised, chanting exorcisms. A very brave man, that priest, because I had pictured the Power as a foul fiend indeed.

The Power turned and looked at me, and I held my dagger firmly.

'I hold the accursed metal,' I told him fiercely. 'There is a ring of it about this house. Tell me now, quickly, the Words and the Names which make the sigils operate! Tell me the secret of the cipher you had me write! Do this and I will slay this priest and draw away the chain and you may go hence unharmed. But be quick, or—'

The Power cast a sigil upon the ground. When the parchment struck earth, there was an instant's cloudiness as if some dread thing had begun to form. But then the parchment smoked and turned to ash. The ring of iron about the hut had destroyed its power when it was used. The Power knew that I spoke truth.

'Ah!' said the Power dryly. 'Men! And I thought one was my friend!' He put his hand to his side. 'To be sure! I should have known. Iron rings me about. My engine heats . . .'

He looked at me. I held up the dagger, fiercely unyielding.

'The Names!' I cried. 'The Words! Give me power of my own and I will slay the priest!'

'I tried,' said the Power quietly, 'to give you wisdom. And you will stab me with the accursed metal if I do not tell you things which do not exist. But you need not. I cannot live long in a ring of iron. My engine will burn out; my force-field will fail. I will stifle in the thin air which is dense enough for you. Will not that satisfy you? Must you stab me, also?'

I sprang from my pallet of straw to threaten him more fiercely. It was madness, was it not? But I was mad, Johannus!

'Forbear,' said the Power. 'I could kill you now, with me! But I thought you my friend. I will go out and see your priest. I would prefer to die at his hand. He is perhaps only a fool.'

He walked steadily toward the doorway. As he stepped over the iron chain, I thougth I saw a wisp of smoke begin, but he touched the thing at his side. The cloudiness about his person vanished. There was a puffing sound, and his garments jerked as if in a gust of wind. He staggered. But he went on, and touched his side again and the cloudiness returned and he walked more strongly. He did not try to turn aside. He walked directly toward the priest, and even I could see that he walked with a bitter dignity.

And—I saw the priest's eyes grow wide with horror. Because he saw the Power for the first time, and the Power was an ell and a half high, with a large head and knobbed feelers projecting from his forehead, and the priest knew instantly that he was not of any race of men but was a Power and one of those Rebels who were flung out from Heaven.

I heard the Power speak to the priest, with dignity. I did not hear what he said. I raged in my disappointment. But the priest did not waver. As the Power moved toward him, the priest moved toward the Power. His face was filled with horror, but it was resolute. He reached forward with the crucifix he wore always attached to an iron chain about his waist. He thrust it to touch the Power, crying, '*In nomine Patri—*'

Then there was smoke. It came from a spot at the Power's

side where was the engine to which he touched the sigils he had made, to imbue them with the power of mystery. And then—

I was blinded. There was a flare of monstrous, bluish light, like a lightning stroke from heaven. After, there was a ball of fierce yellow flame which gave off a cloud of black smoke. There was a monstrous, outraged bellow of thunder.

Then there was nothing save the priest standing there, his face ashen, his eyes resolute, his eyebrows singed, chanting psalms in a shaking voice.

I have come to Venice. My script is filled with sigils with which I can work wonders. No men can work such wonders as I can. But I use them not. I labour daily, nightly, hourly, minute by minute, trying to find the key to the cipher which will yield the wisdom the Power possessed and desired to give to men. Ah, Johannus! I have those sigils and I can work wonders, but when I have used them they will be gone and I shall be powerless. I had such a chance at wisdom as never man possessed before, and it is gone! Yet I shall spend years—aye!—all the rest of my life, seeking the true meaning of what the Power spoke! I am the only man in all the world who ever spoke daily, for weeks on end, with a Prince of Powers of Darkness, and was accepted by him as a friend to such a degree as to encompass his own destruction. It must be true that I have wisdom written down! But how shall I find instructions for mystery in such metaphors as—to choose a fragment by chance—'plates of two dissimilar metals, immersed in an acid, generate a force for which men have not yet a name, yet which is the basis of true civilisation. Such plates . . .'

I grow mad with disappointment, Johannus! Why did he not speak clearly? Yet I will find out the secret . . .

Memorandum from Peter McFarland, Physics Department, Haverford University, to Professor Charles, Latin, the same Faculty:

Dear Professor Charles:

My reaction is, Damnation! Where is the rest of this stuff?

McFarland.

GIANT KILLER

by A. Bertram Chandler (1912-   )

ASTOUNDING SCIENCE FICTION,
October

A. Bertram Chandler is a retired Australian merchant naval officer, whose most famous creations in science fiction are the "Rim Worlds" stories and novels featuring John Grimes. These are entertaining and superior space opera tables that have won Chandler a wide and devoted following. Unfortunately, these books have obscured his shorter fiction on other subjects, which are frequently of a high standard. Particularly noteworthy are "The Cage" (1957), one of the best stories ever on the question of what it means to be human, and the present selection.

"Giant Killer" is a "closed universe" story wherein the characters (or at least some of them) do not realize that their environment constitutes only a small, confined space. It is arguably his finest work of science fiction, although the author is still active and writing in the field.

(I suppose that an editor is allowed to have a favorite story in any anthology he puts together. Generally, if one of my own stories is contained in an anthology I edit, that *is my favorite and since it is generally accepted that I lack modesty, I am allowed to say so.*

Yet even though I have a story in this anthology, I am forced to admit that Chandler's story is my favorite. If you have never encountered it before, read it through to the ending and then with the illumination that comes of that, read it a second time. It then sounds quite different.

The technical problems involved in writing a story of this kind are enormous and Chandler manages them with what seems enviable ease though I know enough about such matters to suppose that behind the scenes he had to do a lot of thinking through a number of sleepless nights. I.A.)

Shrick should have died before his baby eyes had opened on his world. Shrick would have died, but Weena, his mother, was determined that he, alone of all her children, should live. Three previous times since her mating with Skreer had she borne, and on each occasion the old, gray Sterret, Judge of the Newborn, had condemned her young as Different Ones.

Weena had no objection to the Law when it did not affect her or hers. She, as much as any other member of the Tribe, keenly enjoyed the feasts of fresh, tasty meat following the ritual slaughter of the Different Ones. But when those sacrificed were the fruit of her own womb it wasn't the same.

It was quiet in the cave where Weena awaited the coming of her lord. Quiet, that is, save for the sound of her breathing and an occasional plaintive, mewling cry from the newborn child. And even these sounds were deadened by the soft spongy walls and ceiling.

She sensed the coming of Skreer long before his actual arrival. She anticipated his first question and, as he entered the cave, said quietly, "One. A male."

"A male?" Skreer radiated approval. Then she felt his mood change to one of questioning, of doubt. "Is it . . . he—?"

"Yes."

Skreer caught the tiny, warm being in his arms. There was no light, but he, like all his race, was accustomed to the dark. His fingers told him all that he needed to know. The child was hairless. The legs were too straight. And—this was worst of all—the head was a great, bulging dome.

"Skreer!" Weena's voice was anxious. "Do you—?"

"There is no doubt. Sterret will condemn it as a Different One."

"But—"

"There is no hope." Weena sensed that her mate shuddered, heard the faint, silken rustle of his fur as he did so. "His head! He is like the Giants!"

The mother sighed. It was hard, but she knew the Law. And yet—This was her fourth childbearing, and she was never to know, perhaps, what it was to watch and wait with mingled pride and terror while her sons set out with the other young males to raid the Giants' territory, to bring back spoils from the great Cave-of-Food, the Place-of-Green-Growing-Things or, even, precious scraps of shiny metal from the Place-of-Life-That-Is-Not-Life.

She clutched at a faint hope.

"His head is like a Giant's? Can it be, do you think, that the Giants are Different Ones? I have heard it said."

"What if they are?"

"Only this. Perhaps he will grow to be a Gaint. Perhaps he will fight the other Giants for us, his own people. Perhaps—"

"Perhaps Sterret will let him live, you mean." Skreer made the short, unpleasant sound that passed among his people for a laugh. "No, Weena. He must die. And it is long since we feasted—"

"But—"

"Enough. Or do *you* wish to provide meat for the Tribe also? I may wish to find a mate who will bear me sturdy sons, not monsters!"

The Place-of-Meeting was almost deserted when Skreer and Weena, she with Shrick clutched tightly in her arms, entered. Two more couples were there, each with newborn. One of the mothers was holding two babies, each of whom appeared to be normal. The other had three, her mate holding one of them.

Weena recognized her as Teeza, and flashed her a little half smile of sympathy when she saw that the child carried by Teeza's mate would certainly be condemned by Sterret when he choose to appear. For it was, perhaps, even more revolting than her own Different One, having two hands growing from the end of each arm.

Skreer approached one of the other males, he unburdened with a child.

"How long have you been waiting?" he asked.

"Many heartbeats. We—"

The guard stationed at the doorway through which light entered from Inside hissed a warning:

"Quiet! A Giant is coming!"

The mothers clutched their children to them yet more tightly, their fur standing on end with superstitious dread. They knew that if they remained silent there was no danger, that even if they should betray themselves by some slight noise there was no immediate peril. It was not size along that made the Giants dreaded, it was the supernatural powers that they were known to possess. The food-that-kills had slain many an unwary member of the Tribe, also their fiendishly cunning devices that crushed and managled any of the People unwise enough to reach greedily for the savory morsels left exposed on a kind of little platform. Although there were those who averred that, in the latter case, the risk was well worth it, for the yellow grains from the many bags in the Cave-of-Food were as monotonous as they were nourishing.

"The Giant has passed!"

Before those in the Place-of-Meeting could resume their talk, Sterret drifted out from the entrance of his cave. He held in his right hand his wand of office, a straight staff of the hard, yet soft, stuff dividing the territory of the People from that of the Giants. It was tipped with a sharp point of metal.

He was old, was Sterret.

Those who were themselves grandparents had heard their grandparents speak of him. For generations he had survived attacks by young males jealous of his prerogatives as chief, and the more rare assaults by parents displeased by his rulings as Judge of the Newborn. In this latter case, however, he had had nothing to fear, for on those isolated occasions the Tribe had risen as one and torn the offenders to pieces.

Behind Sterret came his personal guards and then, floating out from the many cave entrances, the bulk of the Tribe. There had been no need so summon them; they *knew.*

The chief, deliberate and unhurried, took his position in the center of the Place-of-Meeting. Without orders, the crowd made way for the parents and their newborn. Weena winced as she saw their gloating eyes fixed on Shrick's revolting baldness, his misshapen skull. She knew what the verdict would be.

She hoped that the newborn of the others would be judged before her own, although that would merely delay the death of her own child by the space of a very few heartbeats. She hoped—

"Weena! Bring the child to me that I may see and pass judgment!"

The chief extended his skinny arms, took the child from the mother's reluctant hands. His little, deep-set eyes gleamed at the thought of the draught of rich, red blood that he was soon to enjoy. And yet he was reluctant to lose the savor of a single heartbeat of the mother's agony. Perhaps she could be provoked into an attack—

"You insult us," he said slowly, "by bringing forth *this!*" He held Shrick, who squalled feebly, at arm's length. "Look, oh People, at this *thing* the miserable Weena has brought for my judgment!"

"He has a Giant's head." Weena's timid voice was barely audible. "Perhaps—"

"—his father was a Giant!"

A tittering laugh rang through the Place-of-Meeting.

"No. But I have heard it said that perhaps the Giants, or their fathers and mothers, were Different Ones. And—"

"Who said that?"

"Strela."

"Yes, Strela the Wise. Who, in his wisdom, ate largely of the food-that-kills!"

Again the hateful laughter rippled through the assembly.

Sterret raised the hand that held the spear, shortening his grip on the haft. His face puckered as he tasted in anticipation the bright bubble of blood that would soon well from the throat of the Different One. Weena screamed. With one hand she snatched her child from the hateful grasp of the chief, with the other she seized his spear.

Sterret was old, and generations of authority had made him careless. Yet, old as he was, he evaded the vicious thrust aimed at him by the mother. He had no need to cry orders, from all sides the People converged upon the rebel.

Already horrified by her action, Weena knew that she could expect no mercy. And yet life, even as lived by the Tribe, was sweet. Gaining a purchase from the gray, spongy floor of the Place-of-Meeting she jumped. The impetus of her leap carried her up to the doorway through which streamed the light from Inside. The guard there was unarmed, for of what avail would a puny spear be against the Giants? He fell back before the menace of Weena's bright blade and bared teeth. And then Weena was Inside.

She could, she knew, hold the doorway indefinitely against pursuit. But this was Giant country. In an agony of indecision she clung to the rim of the door with one hand, the other still holding the spear. A face appeared in the opening, and then vanished, streaming with blood. It was only later that she realized that it had been Skreer's.

She became acutely conscious of the fierce light beating around and about her, of the vast spaces on all sides of a body that was accustomed to the close quarters of the caves and tunnels. She felt naked and, in spite of her spear, utterly defenseless.

Then that which she dreaded came to pass.

Behind her, she sensed the approach of two of the Giants. Then she could hear their breathing, and the low, infinitely menacing rumble of their voices as they talked one with the other. They hadn't seen her—of that she was certain, but it was only a matter of heartbeats before they did so. The open doorway, with the certainty of death that lay beyond, seemed infinitely preferable to the terror of the unknown. Had it been only her life at stake she would have returned to face the righteous wrath of her chief, her mate and her Tribe.

Fighting down her blind panic, she forced herself to a clarity of thought normally foreign to her nature. If she yielded to instinct, if she fled madly before the approaching Giants, she would be seen. Her only hope was to remain utterly still. Skreer, and others of the males who had been on forays Inside, had told her that the Giants, careless in their size and power, more often than not did not notice the People unless they made some betraying movement.

The Giants were very close.

Slowly, cautiously, she turned her head.

She could see them now, two enormous figures floating through the air with easy arrogance. They had not seen her, and she knew that they would not see her unless she made some sudden movement to attract their attention. Yet it was hard not to yield to the impulse to dive back into the doorway to the Place-of-Meeting, there to meet certain death at the hands of the outraged Tribe. It was harder still to fight the urge to relinquish her hold on the rim of the doorway and flee—anywhere—in screaming panic.

But she held on.

The Giants passed.

The dull rumble of their voices died in the distance, their acrid, unpleasant odor, of which she had heard but never before experienced, diminished. Weena dared to raise her head once more.

In the confused, terrified welter of her thoughts one idea stood out with dreadful clarity. Her only hope of survival, pitifully slim though it was, lay in following the Giants. There was no time to lose, already she could hear the rising clamor of voices as those in the caves sensed that the Giants had passed. She relinquished her hold on the edge of the door and floated slowly up.

When Weena's head came into sudden contact with something hard she screamed. For long seconds she waited, eyes close shut in terror, for the doom that would surely descend upon her. But nothing happened. The pressure upon the top of her skull neither increased nor diminished.

Timidly, she opened her eyes.

As far as she could see, in two directions, stretched a long, straight shaft or rod. Its thickness was that of her own body, and it was made, or covered with, a material not altogether strange to the mother. It was like the ropes woven by the females with fibers from the Place-of-Green-Growing-Things—but incomparably finer. Stuff such as this was brought back sometimes by the males from their expeditions. It had been believed, once, that it was the fur of the Giants, but now it was assumed that it was made by them for their own purposes.

On three sides of the shaft was the glaring emptiness so terrifying to the people of the caves. On the fourth side was a flat, shiny surface. Weena found that she could insinuate herself into the space between the two without discomfort. She discovered, also, that with comforting solidity at her back and belly she could make reasonably fast progress along the shaft. It was only when she looked to either side that she felt a return of her vertigo. She soon learned not to look.

It is hard to estimate the time taken by her journey in a world where time was meaningless. Twice she had to stop and feed Shrick—fearful lest his hungry wailings betray their presence either to Giants or any of the People who might—although this was highly improbable—have followed her. Once she felt the shaft vibrating, and froze to its matte surface in utter and abject terror. A Giant passed, pulling himself rapidly along with his two hands. Had either of those hands fallen upon Weena it would have been the finish. For many heartbeats after his passing she clung there limp and helpless, scarcely daring to breathe.

It seemed that she passed through places of which she had heard the males talk. This may have been so—but she had no means of knowing. For the world of the People, with its caves and tunnels, was familiar territory, while that of the Giants was known only in relation to the doorways through which a daring explorer could enter.

Weena was sick and faint with hunger and thirst when, at last, the long shaft led her into a place where she could smell the tantalizing aroma of food. She stopped, looked in all directions. But here, as everywhere in this alien country, the light was too dazzling for her untrained eyes. She could see, dimly, vast shapes beyond her limited understanding. She could see no Giants, nor anything that moved.

Cautiously, keeping a tight hold on the rough surface of the shaft, she edged out to the side away from the polished, flat surface along which she had been traveling. Back and forth her head swung, her sensitive nostrils dilated. The bright light confused her, so she shut her eyes. Once again her nose sought the source of the savory smell, swinging ever more slowly as the position was determined with reasonable accuracy.

She was loathe to abandon the security of her shaft, but hunger overruled all other considerations. Orienting her body, she jumped. With a thud she brought up against another flat surface. Her free hand found a projection, to which she clung. This she almost relinquished as it turned. Then a crack appeared, with disconcerting suddenness, before her eyes, widening rapidly. Behind this opening was black, welcome darkness. Weena slipped inside, grateful for relief from the glaring light of the Inside. It wasn't until later that she realized that this was a door such as was made by her own people in the Barrier, but a door of truly gigantic proportions. But all that mattered at first was the cool, refreshing shade.

Then she took stock of her surroundings.

Enough light came in through the barely open doorway for her to see that she was in a cave. It was the wrong shape for a cave, it is true, having flat, perfectly regular walls and floor and ceiling. At the far end, each in its own little compartment, were enormous, dully shining globes. From them came a smell that almost drove the famishing mother frantic.

Yet she held back. She knew that smell. It was that of fragments of food that had been brought into the caves, won by stealth and guile from the killing platforms of the Giants. Was this a killing platform? She wracked her brains to recall the poor description of these devices given by the males, decided that this, after all, must be a Cave-of-Food. Relinquishing her hold of Shrick and Sterret's spear she made for the nearest globe.

At first she tried to pull it from its compartment, but it appeared to be held. But it didn't matter. Bringing her face against the surface of the sphere she buried her teeth in its thin skin. There was flesh beneath the skin, and blood—a thin, sweet faintly acid juice, Skreer had, at times, promised her a share of this food when next he won some from a killing platform, but that promise had never been kept. And now Weena had a whole cave of this same food all to herself.

Gorged to repletion, she started back to pick up the now loudly complaining Shrick. He had been playing with the spear and had cut himself on the sharp point. But it was the spear that Weena snatched, swinging swiftly to defend herself and her child. For a voice said, understandable, but with an oddly slurred intonation, "Who are you? What are you doing in our country?"

It was one of the People, a male. He was unarmed, otherwise it is certain that he would never have asked questions. Even so, Weena knew that the slightest relaxation of vigilance on her part would bring a savage, tooth-and-nail attack.

She tightened her grasp on the spear, swung it so that its point was directed at the stranger.

"I am Weena," she said, "of the Tribe of Sterret."

"Of the Tribe of Sterret? But the Tribe of Sessa holds the ways between our countries."

"I came Inside. But who are you?"

"Tekka. I am one of Skarro's people. You are a spy."

"So I brought my child with me."

Tekka was looking at Shrick.

"I see," he said at last. "A Different One, But how did you get through Sessa's country?"

"I didn't. I came Inside."

It was obvious that Tekka refused to believe her story.

"You must come with me," he said, "to Skarro. He will judge."

"And if I come?"

"For the Different One, death. For you, I do not know. But we have too many females in our Tribe already."

"This says that I will not come." Weena brandished her spear.

She would not have defied a male of her own tribe thus—but this Teeka was not of her people. And she had always been brought up to believe that even a female of the Tribe of Sterrett was superior to a male—even a chief—of any alien community.

"The Giants will find you here." Tekka's voice showed an elaborate unconcern. Then— "That is a fine spear."

"Yes. It belonged to Sterret. With it I wounded my mate. Perhaps he is dead."

The male looked at her with a new respect. If her story were true—this was a female to be handled with caution. Besides—

"Would you give it to me?"

"Yes." Weena laughed nastily. There was no mistaking her meaning.

"Not that way. Listen. Not long ago in our Tribe, many mothers, two whole hands of mothers with Different Ones, defied the Judge of the Newborn. They fled along the tunnels, and live outside the Place-of-Little-Lights. Skarro has not yet led a war party against them. Why, I do not know, but there is always a Giant in that place. It may be that Skarro fears that a fight behind the Barrier would warn the Giants of our presence—"

"And you will lead me there?"

"Yes. In return for the spear."

Weena was silent for the space of several heartbeats. As long as Tekka preceded her she would be safe. It never occurred to her that she could let the other fulfill his part of the bargain, and then refuse him his payment. Her people were a very primitive race.

"I will come with you," she said.

"It is well."

Tekka's eyes dwelt long and lovingly upon the fine spear. Skarro would not be chief much longer.

"First," he said, "we must pull what you have left of the good-to-eat-ball into our tunnel. Then I must shut the door lest a Giant should come—"

Together they hacked and tore the sphere to pieces. There was a doorway at the rear of one of the little compartments, now empty. Through this they pushed and pulled their fragrant burden. First Weena went into the tunnel, carrying Shrick and the spear, then Tekka. He pushed the round door into place, where it fitted with no sign that the Barrier had been broken. He pushed home two crude locking bars.

"Follow me," he ordered the mother.

The long journey through the caves and tunnels was heaven after the Inside. Here there was no light—or, at worst, only a feeble glimmer from small holes and cracks in the Barrier. It seemed that Tekka was leading her along the least frequented ways and tunnels of Skarro's country, for they met none of his people. Nevertheless, Weena's perceptions told her that she was in densely populated territory. From all around her beat the warm, comforting waves of the routine, humdrum life of the People. She knew that in snug caves males, females and children were living in cozy intimacy. Briefly, she regretted having thrown away all this for the ugly, hairless bundle in her arms. But she could never return to her own Tribe, and should she wish to throw in her lot with this alien community the alternatives would be death or slavery.

"Careful!" hissed Tekka. "We are approaching Their country."

"You will—?"

"Not me. They will kill me. Just keep straight along this tunnel and you will find Them. Now, give me the spear."

"But—"

"*You* are safe. There is your pass." He lightly patted the uneasy, squirming Shrick. "Give me the spear, and I will go."

Reluctantly, Weena handed over the weapon. Without a word Tekka took it. Then he was gone. Briefly the mother saw him in the dim light that, in this part of the tunnel, filtered through the Barrier—a dim, gray figure rapidly losing itself in the dim grayness. She felt very lost and lonely and frightened. But the die was cast. Slowly, cautiously, she began to creep along the tunnel.

When They found her she screamed. For many heartbeats she had sensed their hateful presence, had felt that beings even more alien than the Giants were closing in on her. Once or twice she called, crying that she came in peace, that she was the mother of a Different One. But not even echo answered her, for the soft, spongy tunnel walls deadened the shrill sound of her voice. And the silence that was not silence was, if that were possible, more menacing than before.

Without warning the stealthy terror struck. Weena fought with the courage of desperation, but she was overcome by sheer weight of numbers. Shrick, protesting feebly, was torn from her frantic grasp. Hands—and surely there were far too many hands for the number of her assailants—pinned her arms to her sides, held her ankles in a viselike grip. No longer able to struggle, she looked at her captors. Then she screamed again. Mercifully, the dim light spared her the full horror of their appearance, but what she saw would have been enough to haunt her dreams to her dying day had she escaped.

Softly, almost caressingly, the hateful hands ran over her body with disgusting intimacy.

Then—"She is a Different One."

She allowed herself to hope.

"And the child?"

"Two-Tails has newborn. She can nurse him."

And as the sharp blade found her throat Weena had time to regret most bitterly ever having left her snug, familiar world. It was not so much the forfeit of her own life—that she had sacrificed when she defied Sterret—it was the knowledge that Shrick, instead of meeting a clean death at the hands of his own people, would live out his life among these unclean monstrosities.

Then there was a sharp pain and a feeling of utter helplessness as the tide of her life swiftly ebbed—and the darkness that Weena had loved so well closed about her for evermore.

No-Fur—who, at his birth, had been named Shrick—fidgetted impatiently at his post midway along what was known to his people as Skarro's Tunnel. It was time that Long-Nose came to relieve him. Many heartbeats had passed since he had heard the sounds on the other side of the Barrier proclaiming that the Giant in the Place-of-Little-Lights had been replaced by another of his kind. It was a mystery what the Giants did there—but the New People had come to recognize a strange regularity in the actions of the monstrous beings, and to regulate their time accordingly.

No-Fur tightened his grip on his spear—of Barrier material it was, roughly sharpened at one end—as he sensed the approach of somebody along the tunnel, coming from the direction of Tekka's country. It could be a Different One bearing a child who would become one of the New People, it could be attack. But, somehow, the confused impressions that his mind received did not bear out either of these assumptions.

No-Fur shrank against the wall of the tunnel, his body sinking deep into the spongy material. Now he could dimly see the intruder—a solitary form flitting furtively through the shadows. His sense of smell told him that it was a female. Yet he was certain that she had no child with her. He tensed himself to attack as soon as the stranger should pass his hiding place.

Surprisingly, she stopped.

"I come in peace," she said. "I am one of you. I am," here she paused a little, "one of the New People."

Shrick made no reply, no betraying movement. It was barely possible, he knew, that this female might be possessed of abnormally keen eyesight. It was even more likely that she had smelled him out. But then—how was it that she had known the name by which the New People called themselves? To the outside world they were Different Ones—and had the stranger called herself such she would at once have proclaimed herself an alien whose life was forfeit.

"You do not know," the voice came again, "how it is that I called myself by the proper name. In my own Tribe I am called a Different One—"

"Then how is it," No-Fur's voice was triumphant, "that you were allowed to live?"

"Come to me! No, leave your spear. Now come!"

No-Fur stuck his weapon into the soft cavern wall. Slowly, almost fearfully, he advanced to where the female was waiting. He could see her better now—and she seemed no different from those fugitive mothers of Different Ones—at whose slaughter he had so often assisted. The body was well proportioned and covered with fine, silky fur. The head was well shaped. Physically she was so normal as to seem repugnant to the New People.

And yet—No-Fur found himself comparing her with the females of his own Tribe, to the disadvantage of the latter. Emotion rather than reason told him that the hatred inspired by the sight of an ordinary body was the result of a deep-rooted feeling of inferiority rather than anything else. And he wanted this stranger.

"No," she said slowly, "it is not my body that is different. It is in my head. I didn't know myself until a little while—about two hands of feeding—ago. But I can tell, now, what is going on inside your head, or the head of any of the People—"

"But," asked the male, "how did they—"

"I was ripe for mating. I was mated to Trillo, the son of Tekka, the chief. And in our cave I told Trillo things of which he only knew. I thought that I should please him, I thought that he would like to have a mate with magical powers that he could put to good use. With my aid he could have made himself chief. But he was angry—and very frightened. He ran to Tekka, who judged me as a Different One. I was to have been killed, but I was able to escape. They dare not follow me too far into this country—"

Then— "You want me."

It was a statement rather than a question.

"Yes. But—"

"No-Tail? She can die. If I fight her and win, I become your mate."

Briefly, half regretfully, No-Fur thought of his female. She had been patient, she had been loyal. But he saw that, with this stranger for a mate, there were no limits to his advancement. It was not that he was more enlightened than Trillo had been, it was that as one of the New People he regarded abnormality as the norm.

"Then you will take me." Once again there was no hint of questioning. Then— "My name is Wesel."

The arrival of No-Fur, with Wesel in tow, at the Place-of-Meeting could not have been better timed. There was a trial in progress, a young male named Big-Ears having been caught red-handed in the act of stealing a coveted piece of metal from the cave of one Four-Arms. Long-Nose, who should have relieved No-Fur, had found the spectacle of a trial with the prospect of a feast to follow far more engrossing than the relief of the lonely sentry.

It was he who first noticed the newcomers.

"Oh, Big-Tusk," he called, "No-Fur has deserted his post!"

The chief was disposed to be lenient.

"He has a prisoner," he said. "A Different One. We shall feast well."

"*He is afraid of you,*" hissed Wesel. "*Defy him!*"

"It is no prisoner." No-Fur's voice was arrogant. "It is my new mate. And you, Long-Nose, go at once to the tunnel."

"Go, Long-Nose. My country must not remain unguarded. No-Fur, hand the strange female over to the guards that she may be slaughtered."

No-Fur felt his resolution wavering under the stern glare of the chief. As two of Big-Tusk's bullies approached he slackened his grip on Wesel's arm. She turned to him, pleading and desperation in her eyes.

"No, no. He is afraid of you, I say. Don't give in to him. Together we can—"

Ironically, it was No-Tail's intervention that turned the scales. She confronted her mate, scorn written large on her unbeautiful face, the shrewish tongue dreaded by all the New People, even the chief himself, fast getting under way.

"So," she said, "you prefer this drab, common female to me. Hand her over, so that she may, at least, fill our bellies. As for you, my bucko, you will pay for this insult!"

No-Fur looked at the grotesque, distorted form of No-Tail, and then at the slim, sleek Wesel. Almost without volition he spoke.

"Wesel is my mate," he said. "She is one of the New People!"

Big-Tusk lacked the vocabulary to pour adequate scorn upon the insolent rebel. He struggled for words, but could find none to cover the situation. His little eyes gleamed redly, and his hideous tusks were bared in a vicious snarl.

"*Now!*" prompted the stranger. "His head is confused. He will be rash. His desire to tear and maul will cloud his judgment. Attack!"

No-Fur went into the fight coldly, knowing that if he kept his head he must win. He raised his spear to stem the first rush of the infuriated chief. Just in time Big-Tusk saw the rough point and, using his tail as a rudder, swerved. He wasn't fast enough, although his action barely saved him from immediate death. The spear caught him in the shoulder and broke off short, leaving the end in the wound. Mad with rage and pain, the chief was now a most dangerous enemy—and yet, at the same time, easy meat for an adversary who kept his head.

No-Fur was, at first, such a one. But his self-control was cracking fast. Try as he would he could not fight down the rising tides of hysterical fear, of sheer, animal blood lust. As the enemies circled, thrust and parried, he with his almost useless weapon, Big-Tusk with a fine, metal tipped spear, it took all his will power to keep himself from taking refuge in flight or closing to grapple with his more powerful antagonist. His reason told him that both courses of action would be disastrous—the first would end in his being hunted down and slaughtered by the Tribe, the second would bring him within range of the huge, murderous teeth that had given Big-Tusk his name.

So he thrust and parried, thrust and parried, until the keen edge of the chief's blade nicked his arm. The stinging pain made him all animal, and with a shrill scream of fury he launched himself at the other.

But if Nature had provided Big-Tusk with a fine armory she had not been niggardly with the rebel's defensive equipment. True, he had nothing outstanding in the way of teeth or claws, had not the extra limbs possessed by so many of his fellow New People. His brain may have been a little more nimble—but at this stage of the fight that counted for nothing. What saved his life was his hairless skin.

Time after time the chief sought to pull him within striking distance, time after time he pulled away. His slippery hide was crisscrossed with a score of scratches, many of them deep but none immediately serious. And all the time he himself was scratching and pummeling with both hands and feet, biting and gouging.

It seemed that Big-Tusk was tiring, but No-Fur was tiring too. And the other had learned that it was useless to try to grab a handful of fur, that he must try to take his enemy in an unbreakable embrace. Once he succeeded. No-Fur was pulled closer and closer to the slavering fangs, felt the foul breath of the other in his face, knew that it was a matter of heartbeats before his throat was torn out. He screamed, threw up his legs and lunged viciously at Big-Tusk's belly. He felt his feet sink into the soft flesh, but the chief grunted and did not relax his pressure. Worse—the failure of his desperate counterattack had brought No-Fur even closer to death.

With one arm, his right, he pushed desperately against the other's chest. He tried to bring his knees up in a crippling blow, but they were held in a viselike grip by Big-Tusk's heavily muscled legs. With his free left arm he flailed viciously and desperately, but he might have been beating against the Barrier itself.

The People, now that the issue of the battle was decided, were yelling encouragement to the victor. No-Fur heard among the cheers the voice of his mate, No-Tail. The little, cold corner of his brain in which reason was still enthroned told him that he couldn't blame her. If she were vociferous in *his* support, she could expect only death at the hands of the triumphant chief. But he forgot that he had offered her insult and humiliation, remembered only that she was his mate. And the bitterness of it kept him fighting when others would have relinquished their hold on a life already forfeit.

The edge of his hand came down hard just where Big-Tusk's thick neck joined his shoulder. He was barely conscious that the other winced, that a little whimper of pain followed the blow. Then, high and shrill, he heard Wesel.

"Again! Again! That is his weak spot!"

Blindly groping, he searched for the same place. And Big-Tusk was afraid, of that there was no doubt. His head twisted, trying to cover his vulnerability. Again he whimpered, and No-Fur knew that the battle was his. His thin, strong fingers with their sharp nails dug and gouged. There was no fur here, and the flesh was soft. He felt the warm blood welling beneath his hand as the chief screamed dreadfully. Then the iron grip was abruptly relaxed. Before Big-Tusk could use hands or feet to cast his enemy from him No-Fur had twisted and, each hand clutching skin and fur, had buried his teeth in the other's neck. They found the jugular. Almost at once the chief's last, desperate struggles ceased.

No-Fur drank long and satisfyingly.

Then, the blood still clinging to his muzzle, he wearily surveyed the People.

"I am chief," he said.

"You are the chief!" came back the answering chorus.

"And Wesel is my mate."

This time there was hesitation on the part of the People.

The new chief heard mutters of *"The feast . . . Big-Tusk is old and tough. . . . are we to be cheated—?"*

"Wesel is my mate," he repeated. Then— "There is your feast—"

At the height of his power he was to remember No-Tail's stricken eyes, the dreadful feeling that by his words he had put himself outside all custom, all law.

"*Above* the Law," whispered Wesel.

He steeled his heart.

"There is your feast," he said again.

It was Big-Ears who, snatching a spear from one of the guards, with one swift blow dispatched the cringing No-Tail.

"I am your mate," said Wesel.

No-Fur took her in his arms. They rubbed noses. It wasn't the old chief's blood that made her shudder ever so slightly. It was the feel of the disgusting, hairless body against her own.

Already the People were carving and dividing the two corpses and wrangling over an even division of the succulent spoils.

There was one among the New People who, had her differences from the racial stock been only psychological, would have been slaughtered long since. Her three eyes notwithstanding, the imprudent exercise of her gift would have brought certain doom. But, like her sisters in more highly civilized communities, she was careful to tell those who came to her only that which they desired to hear. Even then, she exercised restraint. Experience had taught her that foreknowledge of coming events on the part of the participants often resulted in entirely unforeseen results. This annoyed her. Better misfortune on the main stream of time than well-being on one of its branches.

To this Three-Eyes came No-Fur and Wesel.

Before the chief could ask his questions the seeress raised one emaciated hand.

"You are Shrick," she said. "So your mother called you. Shrick, the Giant Killer."

"But—"

"Wait. You came to ask me about your war against Tekka's people. Continue with your plans. You will win. You will then fight the Tribe of Sterret the Old. Again you will win. You will be Lord of the Outside. And then—"

"And then?"

"The Giants will know of the People. Many, but not all, of the People will die. You will fight the Giants. And the last of the Giants you will kill, but he will plunge the world into—Oh, if I could make you see! But we have no words."

"What—?"

"No, you cannot know. You will never know till the end is upon you. But this I can tell you. The People are doomed. Nothing you or they can do will save them. But you will kill those who will kill us, and that is good."

Again No-Fur pleaded for enlightenment. Abruptly, his pleas became threats. He was fast lashing himself into one of his dreaded fits of blind fury. But Three-Eyes was oblivious of his presence. Her two outer eyes were tight shut and that strange, dreaded inner one was staring at *something*, something outside the limits of the cave, outside the framework of things as they are.

Deep in his throat the chief growled.

He raised the fine spear that was the symbol of his office and buried it deep in the old female's body. The inner eye shut and the two outer ones flickered open for the last time.

"I am spared the End—" she said.

Outside the little cavern the faithful Big-Ears was waiting.

"Three-Eyes is dead," said his master. "Take what you want, and give the rest to the People—"

For a little there was silence.

Then—"I am glad you killed her," said Wesel. "She frightened me. I got inside her head—and I was lost!" Her voice had a hysterical edge. "I was lost! It was mad, mad. *What Was* was a *place*, a *PLACE*, and *NOW*, and *What Will Be*. And I saw the End."

"What did you see?"

"A great light, far brighter than the Giants' lights Inside. And heat, stronger than the heat of the floors of the Far Outside caves and tunnels. And the People gasping and dying and the great light bursting into our world and eating them up—"

"But the Giants?"

"I did not see. I was lost. All I saw was the End."

No-Fur was silent. His active, nimble mind was scurrying down the vistas opened up by the dead prophetess. Giant Killer, *Giant Killer*. Even in his most grandiose dreams he had never seen himself thus. And what was that name?

Shrick? He repeated it to himself—Shrick the Giant Killer. It had a fine swing to it. As for the rest, the End, if he could kill the Giants then, surely, he could stave off the doom that they would mete out to the People. Shrick, the Giant Killer—

"It is a name that I like better than No-Fur," said Wesel.

"Shrick, Lord of the Outside. Shrick, Lord of the World. Shrick, the Giant Killer—"

"Yes," he said, slowly. "But the End—"

"You will go through that door when you come to it."

The campaign against Tekka's People had opened.

Along the caves and tunnels poured the nightmare hordes of Shrick. The dim light but half revealed their misshapen bodies, limbs where no limbs should be, heads like something from a half-forgotten bad dream.

All were armed. Every male and female carried a spear, and that in itself was a startling innovation in the wars of the People. For sharp metal, with which the weapons were tipped, was hard to come by, True, a staff of Barrier material could be sharpened, but it was a liability rather than an asset in a pitched battle. With the first thrust the point would break off, leaving the fighter with a weapon far inferior to his natural armory of teeth and claws.

Fire was new to the People—and it was Shrick who had brought them fire. For long periods he had spied upon the Giants in the Place-of-Little-Lights, had seen them bring from the pouches in their fur little glittering devices from which when a projection was pressed, issued a tiny, naked light. And he had seen them bring this light to the end of strange, white sticks that they seemed to be sucking. And the end of the stick would glow, and there would be a cloud like the cloud that issued from the mouths of the People in some of the Far Outside caverns where it was very cold. But this cloud was fragrant, and seemed to be strangely soothing.

And one of the Giants had lost his little hot light. He had put it to one to the white sticks, had made to return it to his pouch, and his hand had missed the opening. The Giant did not notice. He was doing something which took all his attention—and strain his eyes and his imagination as he might Shrick could not see what it was. There were strange glittering machines through which he peered intently at the glittering Little Lights beyond their transparent Barrier. Or were they on the inside of the Barrier? Nobody had ever been able to decide. There was something alive that wasn't alive that clicked. There were sheets of fine, white skin on which the Giant was making black marks with a pointed stick.

But Shrick soon lost interest in these strange rites that he could never hope to comprehend. All his attention was focused on the glittering prize that was drifting ever so slowly toward him on the wings of some vagrant eddy.

When it seemed that it would surely fall right into the doorway where Shrick crouched waiting, it swerved. And, much as he dreaded the pseudolife that hummed and clicked, Shrick came out. The Giant, busy with his sorcery, did not notice him. One swift leap carried him to the drifting trophy. And then he had it, tight clasped to his breast. It was bigger than he had thought, it having appeared so tiny only in relationship to its previous owner. But it wasn't too big to go through the door in the Barrier. In triumph Shrick bore it to his cave.

Many were the experiments that he, eager but fumbling, performed. For a while both he and Wesel nursed painful burns. Many were the experiments that he intended to perform in the future. But he had stumbled on one use for the hot light that was to be of paramount importance in his wars.

Aping the Giants, he had stuck a long splinter of Barrier material in his mouth. The end he had brought to the little light. There was, as he had half expected, a cloud. But it was neither fragrant nor soothing. Blinded and coughing, Wesel snatched at the glowing stick, beat out its strange life with her hands.

Then—"It is hard," she said. "It is almost as hard as metal—"

And so Shrick became the first mass producer of armaments that his world had known. The first few sharpened staves he treated himself. The rest he left to Wesel and the faithful Big-Ears. He dare not trust his wonderful new power to any who were not among his intimates.

Shrick's other innovation was a direct violation of all the rules of war. He had pressed the females into the fighting line. Those who were old and infirm, together with the old and infirm males, brought up the rear with bundles of the mass-produced spears. The New People had been wondering for some little time why their chief had refused to let them slaughter those of their number who had outlived their usefulness. Now they knew.

The caves of the New People were deserted save for those few females with newborn.

And through the tunnels poured the hordes of Shrick.

There was little finesse in the campaign against Tekka's people. The outposts were slaughtered out of hand, but not before they had had time to warn the Tribe of the attack.

Tekka threw a body of picked spearmen into his van, confident that he, with better access to those parts of Inside where metal could be obtained, would be able to swamp the motley horde of the enemy with superior arms and numbers.

When Tekka saw, in the dim light, only a few betraying gleams of metal scattered among Shrick's massed spears, he laughed.

"This No-Fur is mad," he said. "And I shall kill him with this." He brandished his own weapon. "His mother gave it to me many, many feedings ago."

"Is Wesel—?"

"Perhaps, my son. You shall eat her heart, I promise you."

And then Shrick struck.

His screaming mob rushed along the wide tunnel. Confident the Tekkan spearmen waited, knowing that the enemy's weapons were good for only one thrust, and that almost certainly not lethal.

Tekka scowled as he estimated the numbers of the attackers. There couldn't be that many males among the New People. There couldn't—And then the wave struck.

In the twinkling of an eye the tunnel was tightly packed with struggling bodies. Here was no dignified, orderly series of single combats such as had always, in the past, graced the wars of the People. And with growing terror Tekka realized that the enemy spears were standing up to the strain of battle at least as well as his own few metal-tipped weapons.

Slowly, but with ever mounting momentum, the attackers pressed on, gaining impetus from the many bodies that now lay behind them. Gasping for air in the effluvium of sweat and newly shed blood Tekka and the last of his guards were pressed back and ever back.

When one of the New People was disarmed he fell to the rear of his own front line. As though by magic a fresh fighter would appear to replace him.

Then—"He's using females!" cried Trillo. "He's—"

But Tekka did not answer. He was fighting for his life with

a four-armed monster. Every hand held a spear—and every spear was bright with blood. For long heartbeats he parried the other's thrusts, then his nerve broke. Screaming, he turned his back on the enemy. It was the last thing he did.

And so the remnant of the fighting strength of the Tribe of Tekka was at last penned up against one wall of their Place-of-Meeting. Surrounding them was a solid hemisphere of the New People. Snarl was answered by snarl. Trillo and his scant half dozen guards knew that there was no surrender. All they could do was to sell their lives as dearly as possible.

And so they waited for the inevitable, gathering the last reserves of their strength in this lull of the battle, gasping the last sweet mouthfuls of air that they would ever taste. From beyond the wall of their assailants they could hear the cries and screams as the females and children, who had hidden in their caves, were hunted out and slaughtered. They were not to know that the magnanimous Shrick was sparing most of the females. They, he hoped, would produce for him more New People.

And then Shrick came, elbowing his way to the forefront of his forces. His smooth, naked body was unmarked, save by the old scars of his battle with Big Tusk. And with him was Wesel, not a hair of her sleek fur out of place. And Big-Ears—but he, obviously, had been in the fight. With them came more fighters, fresh and eager.

"Finish them!" ordered Shrick.

"Wait!" Wesel's voice was imperative. "I want Trillo."

Him she pointed out to the picked fighters, who raised their spears—weapons curiously slender and light, too fragile for hand-to-hand combat. A faint hope stirred in the breasts of the last defenders.

"Now!"

Trillo and his guards braced themselves to meet the last rush. It never came. Instead, thrown with unerring aim, came those sharp, flimsy spears, pinning them horribly against the gray, spongy wall of the Place-of-Meeting.

Spared in this final slaughter, Trillo looked about him with wide, fear-crazed eyes. He started to scream, then launched himself at the laughing Wesel. But she slipped back through the packed masses of the New People. Blind to all else but that hateful figure, Trillo tried to follow. And the New People crowded about him, binding his arms and legs with their strong cords, snatching his spear from him before its blade drank blood.

Then again the captive saw her who had been his mate.

Shamelessly, she was caressing Shrick.

"My Hairless One," she said. "I was once mated to *this.* You shall have his fur to cover your smooth body." And then—"Big-Ears! You know what to do!"

Grinning, Big-Ears found the sharp blade of a spear that had become detached from its haft. Grinning, he went to work. Trillo started to whimper, then to scream. Shrick felt a little sick. "Stop!" he said. "He is not dead. You must—"

"What does it matter?" Wesel's eyes were avid, and her little, pink tongue came out to lick her thin lips. Big-Ears had hesitated in his work but, at her sign, continued.

"What does it matter?" she said again.

As had fared the Tribe of Tekka so fared the Tribe of Sterret, and a hand or more of smaller communities owing a loose allegiance to these two.

But it was in his war with Sterret that Shrick almost met disaster. To the cunning oldster had come survivors from the massacre of Tekka's army. Most of these had been slaughtered out of hand by the frontier guards, but one or two had succeeded in convincing their captors that they bore tidings of great importance.

Sterret heard them out.

He ordered that they be fed and treated as his own people, for he knew that he would need every ounce of fighting strength that he could muster.

Long and deeply he pondered upon their words, and then sent foray after foray of his young males to the Place-of Life-That-is-Not-Life. Careless he was of detection by the Giants. They might or might not act against him—but he had been convinced that, for all their size, they were comparatively stupid and harmless. Certainly, at this juncture, they were not such a menace as Shrick, already self-styled Lord of the Outside.

And so his store of sharp fragments of metal grew, while his armorers worked without cessation binding these to hafts of Barrier stuff. And he, too, could innovate. Some of the fragments were useless as spearheads, being blunt, rough, and irregular. But, bound like a spearhead to a shaft, they could deliver a crushing blow. Of this Sterret was sure after a few experiments on old and unwanted members of his Tribe.

Most important, perhaps, his mind, rich in experience but not without a certain youthful zest, busied itself with problems of strategy. In the main tunnel from what had been Tekka's country his females hacked and tore at the spongy wall, the material being packed tightly and solidly into another small tunnel that was but rarely used.

At last his scouts brought the word that Shrick's forces were on the move. Careless in the crushing weight of his military power, Shrick disdained anything but a direct frontal attack. Perhaps he should have been warned by the fact that all orifices admitting light from the Inside had been closed, that the main tunnel along which he was advancing was in total darkness.

This, however, hampered him but little. The body of picked spearmen opposing him fought in the conventional way, and these, leaving their dead and wounded, were forced slowly but surely back. Each side relied upon smell, and hearing, and a certain perception possessed by most, if not all, of the People. At such close quarters these were ample.

Shrick himself was not in the van—that honor was reserved for Big-Ears, his fighting general. Had the decision rested with him alone he would have been in the forefront of the battle—but Wesel averred that the leader was of far greater importance than a mere spear bearer, and should be shielded from needless risk. Not altogether unwillingly, Shrick acquiesced.

Surrounded by his guard, with Wesel at his side, the leader followed the noise of the fighting. He was rather surprised at the reports back to him concerning the apparent numbers of the enemy, but assumed that this was a mere delaying action and that Sterret would make his last stand in the Place-of-Meeting. It never occurred to him in his arrogance that others could innovate.

Abruptly, Wesel clutched his arm.

"Shrick! Danger—from the side!"

"From the side? But—"

There was a shrill cry, and a huge section of the tunnel wall fell inward. The spongy stuff was in thin sheets, and drifted among the guard, hampering their every movement. Then, led by Sterret in person, the defenders came out. Like mountaineers they were roped together, for in this battle in the darkness their best hope lay in keeping in one, compact body. Separated, they would fall easy prey to the superior numbers of the hordes of Shrick.

With spear and mace they lay about them lustily. The first heartbeat of the engagement would have seen the end of Shrick, and it was only the uncured hide of Trilla, stiff and stinking, that saved his life. Even so, the blade of Sterret penetrated the crude armor, and, sorely wounded, Shrick reeled out of the battle.

Ahead, Big-Ears was no longer having things all his own way. Reinforcements had poured along the tunnel and he dare not return to the succor of his chief. And Sterret's maces were having their effect. Stabbing and slashing the People could understand—but a crushing blow was, to them, something infinitely horrible.

It was Wesel who saved the day. With her she had brought the little, hot light. It had been her intention to try its effect on such few prisoners as might be taken in this campaign—she was too shrewd to experiment on any of the New People, even those who had incurred the displeasure of herself or her mate.

Scarce knowing what she did she pressed the stud.

With dazzling suddenness the scene of carnage swam into dull view. From all sides came cries of fear.

"Back!" cried Wesel. "Back! Clear a space!"

In two directions the New People retreated.

Blinking but dogged, Sterret's phalanx tried to follow, tried to turn what was a more or less orderly withdrawal into a rout. But the cords that had, at first, served them so well now proved their undoing. Some tried to pursue those making for the Place-of-Meeting, others those of the New People retiring to their own territory. Snarling viciously, blood streaming from a dozen minor wounds, Sterret at last cuffed and bullied his forces into a semblance of order. He attempted to lead a charge to where Wesel, the little, hot light still in her hand, was retreating among her personal, amazon guards.

But again the cunning—too cunning—ropes defeated his purposes. Not a few corpses were there to hamper fast movement, and almost none of his fighters had the intelligence to cut them free.

And the spear throwers of Shrick came to the fore, and, one by one, the people of Sterret were pinned by the slim deadly shafts to the tunnel walls. Not all were killed outright, a few unfortunates squirmed and whimpered, plucking at the spears with ineffectual hands.

Among these was Sterret.

Shrick came forward, spear in hand, to administer the *coup de grâce.* The old chief stared wildly, then—"Weena's hairless one!" he cried.

Ironically it was his own spear—the weapon that, in turn, had belonged to Weena and to Tekka—that slit his throat.

Now that he was Lord of the Outside Shrick had time in which to think and to dream. More and more his mind harked back to Three-Eyes and her prophesy. It never occurred to him to doubt that he was to be the Giant Killer—although the vision of the End he dismissed from his mind as the vaporings of a half-crazed old female.

And so he sent his spies to the Inside to watch the Giants in their mysterious comings and goings, tried hard to find some pattern for their incomprehensible behavior. He himself often accompanied these spies—and it was with avid greed that he saw the vast wealth of beautiful, shining things to which the Giants were heir. More than anything he desired another little hot light, for his own had ceased to function, and all the clumsy, ignorant tinkerings of himself and Wesel could not produce more than a feeble, almost heatless spark from its baffling intricacies.

It seemed, too, that the Giants were now aware of the swarming, fecund life surrounding them. Certain it was that their snares increased in number and ingenuity. And the food-that-kills appeared in new and terrifying guise. Not only did those who had eaten of it die, but their mates and—indeed all who had come into contact with them.

It smacked of sorcery, but Shrick had learned to associate cause and effect. He made the afflicted ones carry those already dead into a small tunnel. One or two of them rebelled—but the spear throwers surrounded them, their slim, deadly weapons at the ready. And those who attempted to break through the cordon of guards were run through repeatedly before ever they laid their defiling hands on any of the unafflicted People.

Big-Ears was among the sufferers. He made no attempt to quarrel with his fate. Before he entered the yawning tunnel that was to be his tomb he turned and looked at his chief.

Shrick made to call him to his side—even though he knew that his friend's life could not be saved, and that by associating with him he would almost certainly lose his own.

But Wesel was at his side.

She motioned to the spear throwers, and a full two hands of darts transfixed the ailing Big-Ears.

"It was kinder this way," she lied.

But, somehow, the last look that his most loyal supporter had given him reminded him of No-Tail. With a heavy heart he ordered his people to seal the tunnel. Great strips of the spongy stuff were brought and stuffed into the entrance. The cries of those inside grew fainter and ever fainter. Then there was silence. Shrick ordered guards posted at all points where, conceivably, the doomed prisoners might break out. He returned to his own cave. Wesel, when one without her gift would have intruded, let him go in his loneliness. Soon he would want her again.

It had long been Wesel's belief that, given the opportunity, she could get inside the minds of the Giants just as she could those of the People. And if she could—who knew what prizes might be hers? Shrick, still inaccessible and grieving for his friend, she missed more than she cared to admit. The last of the prisoners from the last campaign had been killed, ingeniously, many feedings ago. Though she had no way of measuring time, it hung heavily on her hands.

And so, accompanied by two of her personal attendants, she roamed those corridors and tunnels running just inside the Barrier. Through spyhole after spyhole she peered, gazing in wonderment that long use could not stale at the rich and varied life of the Inside.

At last she found that for which she was searching—a Giant, alone and sleeping. Experience among the People had taught her that from a sleeping mind she could read the most secret thoughts.

For a heartbeat she hesitated. Then—"Four-Arms, Little-Head, wait here for me. Wait and watch."

Little-Head grunted an affirmative, but Four-Arms was dubious. "Lady Wesel," she said, "what if the Giant should wake? What—?"

"What if you should return to the Lord of the Outside without me? Then he would, without doubt, have your hides.

The one he is wearing now is old, and the fur is coming out. But do as I say."

There was a door in the Barrier here, a door but rarely used. This was opened, and Wesel slipped through. With the ease that all the People were acquiring with their more frequent ventures to the Inside she floated up to the sleeping Giant. Bonds held him in a sort of framework, and Wesel wondered if, for some offense, he had been made prisoner by his own kind. She would soon know.

And then a glittering object caught her eye. It was one of the little hot lights, its polished metal case seeming to Wesel's covetous eyes the most beautiful thing in the world. Swiftly she made her decision. She could take the shining prize now, deliver it to her two attendants, and then return to carry out her original intentions.

In her eagerness she did not see that it was suspended in the middle of an interlacing of slender metal bars—or she did not care. And as her hands grabbed the bait something not far away began a shrill, not unmusical metallic beating. The Giant stirred and awoke. What Wesel had taken for bonds fell away from his body. In blind panic she turned to flee back to her own world. But, somehow, more of the metal bars had fallen into place and she was a prisoner.

She started to scream.

Surprisingly, Four-Arms and Little-Head came to her aid. It would be nice to be able to place on record that they were actuated by devotion to their mistress—but Four-Arms knew that her life was forfeit. And she had seen those who displeased either Shrick or Wesel flayed alive. Little-Head blindly followed the other's leadership. Hers not to reason why—

Slashing with their spears they assaulted the Giant. He laughed—or so Wesel interpreted the deep, rumbling sound that came from his throat. Four-Arms he seized first. With one hand he grasped her body, with the other her head. He twisted. And that was the end of Four-Arms.

Anybody else but Little-Head would have turned and fled. But her dim mind refused to register that which she had seen. Perhaps a full feeding or so after the event the horror of it all would have stunned her with its impact—perhaps not. Be that as it may, she continued her attack. Blindly, instinctively, she went for the Giant's throat. Wesel sensed that he was badly frightened. But after a short struggle one of his hands caught the frenzied, squealing Little-Head. Violently, he flung her from him. She heard the thud as her attendant's body struck something hard and unyielding. And the impressions that her mind had been receiving from that of the other abruptly ceased.

Even in her panic fear she noticed that the Giant had not come out of the unequal combat entirely unscathed. One of his hands had been scratched, and was bleeding freely. And there were deep scratches on the hideous, repulsively naked face. The Giants, then, were vulnerable. There might have been some grain of truth after all in Three-Eye's insane babbling.

And then Wesel forgot her unavailing struggle against the bars of her cage. With sick horror she watched what the Giant was doing. He had taken the limp body of Four-Arms, had secured it to a flat surface. From somewhere he had produced an array of glittering instruments. One of these he took, and drew it down the body from throat to crotch. On either side of the keen blade the skin fell away, leaving the flesh exposed.

And the worst part of it was that it was not being done in hate or anger, neither was the unfortunate Four-Arms being divided up that she might be eaten. There was an impersonal quality about the whole business that sickened Wesel—for, by this time, she had gained a certain limited access to the mind of the other.

The Giant paused in his work. Another of his kind had come, and for many heartbeats the two talked together. They examined the mutilated carcass of Four-Arms, the crushed body of Little-Head. Together, they peered into the cage where Wesel snarled impotently.

But, in spite of her hysterial fear, part of her mind was deadly cold, was receiving and storing impressions that threw the uninhibited, animal part of her into still greater panic. While the Giants talked the impressions were clear—and while their great, ungainly heads hung over her cage, scant handbreadths away, they were almost overpowering in their strength. She knew who she and the People were, what their world was. She had not the ability to put it into words—but she *knew*. And she saw the doom that the Giants were preparing for the People.

With a few parting words to his fellow, the second Giant left. The first one resumed his work of dismembering Four

Arms. At last he was finished. What was left of the body was put into transparent containers.

The Giant picked up Little-Head. For many heartbeats he examined her, turning her over and over in his great hands. Wesel thought that he would bind the body to the flat surface, do with it as he had done with that of Four-Arms. But at last he put the body to one side. Over his hands he pulled something that looked like a thick, additional skin. Suddenly, the metal bars at one end of the cage fell away, and one of those enormous hands came groping for Wesel.

After the death of Big-Ears, Shrick slept a little. It was the only way in which he could be rid of the sense of loss, of the feeling that he had betrayed his most loyal follower. His dreams were troubled, haunted by ghosts from his past. Big-Ears was in them, and Big-Tusk, and a stranger female with whom he felt a sense of oneness, whom he knew to be Weena, his mother.

And then all these phantasms were gone, leaving only the image of Wesel. It wasn't the Wesel he had always known, cool, self-assured, ambitious. This was a terrified Wesel—Wesel descending into a black abyss of pain and torture even worse than that which she had, so often, meted out to others. And she wanted him.

Shrick awoke, frightened by his dreams. But he knew that ghosts had never hurt anybody, could not hurt him, Lord of the Outside. He shook himself, whimpering a little, and then tried to compose himself for further sleep.

But the image of Wesel persisted. At last Shrick abandoned his attempts to seek oblivion and, rubbing his eyes, emerged from his cave.

In the dim, half-light of the Place-of-Meeting little knots of the People hung about, talking in low voices. Shrick called to the guards. There was a sullen silence. He called again. At last one answered.

"Where is Wesel?"

"I do not know . . . lord." The last word came out grudgingly.

Then one of the others volunteered the information that she had been seen, in company with Four-Arms and Little-Head, proceeding along the tunnels that led to that part of the Outside in the way of the Place-of-Green-Growing-Things.

Shrick hesitated.

He rarely ventured abroad without his personal guards, but then, Big-Ears was always one of them. And Big-Ears was gone.

He looked around him, decided that he could trust none of those at present in the Place-of-Meeting. The People had been shocked and horrified by his necessary actions in the case of those who had eaten of the food-that-kills and regarded him, he knew, as a monster even worse than the Giants. Their memories were short—but until they forgot he would have to walk with caution.

"Wesel is my mate. I will go alone," he said.

At his words he sensed a change of mood, was tempted to demand an escort. But the instinct that—as much as any mental superiority—maintained him in authority warned him against throwing away his advantage.

"I go alone," he said.

One Short-Tail, bolder than his fellows, spoke up.

"And if you do not return, Lord of the Outside? Who is to be—?"

"I shall return," said Shrick firmly, his voice displaying a confidence he did not feel.

In the more populous regions the distinctive scent of Wesel was overlaid by that of many others. In tunnels but rarely frequented it was strong and compelling—but now he had no need to use his olfactory powers. For the terrified little voice in his brain—from outside his brain was saying *hurry, HURRY*—and some power beyond his ken was guiding him unerringly to where his mate was in such desperate need of him.

From the door in the Barrier through which Wesel had entered the Inside—it had been left open—streamed a shaft of light. And now Shrick's natural caution reasserted itself. The voice inside his brain was no less urgent, but the instinct of self-preservation was strong. Almost timorously, he peered through the doorway.

He smelled death. At first he feared that he was too late, then identified the personal odors of Four-Arms and Little-Head. That of Wesel was there too—intermingled with the acrid scent of terror and agony. But she was still alive.

Caution forgotten, he launched himself from the doorway with all the power of his leg muscles. And he found Wesel, stretched supine on a flat surface that was slippery with blood. Most of it was Four-Arms', but some of it was hers.

"Shrick!" she screamed. "The Giant!"

He looked away from his mate and saw hanging over him, pale and enormous, the face of the Giant. He screamed, but there was more of fury than terror in the sound. He saw, not far from where he clung to Wesel, a huge blade of shining metal. He could see that its edge was keen. The handle had been fashioned for a hand far larger than his, nevertheless he was just able to grasp it. It seemed to be secured. Feet braced against Wesel's body for purchase, he tugged desperately.

Just as the Giant's hand, fingers outstretched to seize him, came down the blade pulled free. As Shrick's legs suddenly and involuntarily straightened he was propelled away from Wesel. The Giant grabbed at the flying form, and howled in agony as Shrick swept the blade around and lopped off a finger.

He heard Wesel's voice: "You are the Giant Killer!"

Now he was level with the Giant's head. He swerved, and with his feet caught a fold of the artificial skin covering the huge body. And he hung there, swinging his weapon with both hands, cutting and slashing. Great hands swung wildly and he was bruised and buffeted. But not once did they succeed in finding a grip. Then there was a great and horrid spurting of blood and a wild thrashing of mighty limbs. This ceased, but it was only the voice of Wesel that called him from the fury of his slaughter lust.

So he found her again, still stretched out for sacrifice to the Giants' dark gods, still bound to that surface that was wet with her blood and that of her attendant. But she smiled up at him, and in her eyes was respect that bordered on awe.

"Are you hurt?" he demanded, a keen edge of anxiety to his voice.

"Only a little. But Four-Arms was cut in pieces . . . I should have been had you not come. And," her voice was a hymn of praise, "you killed the Giant!"

"It was foretold. Besides," for once he was honest, "it could not have been done without the Giant's weapon."

With its edge he was cutting Wesel's bonds. Slowly she floated away from the place of sacrifice. Then: "I can't move my legs!" Her voice was terror-stricken. "I can't move!"

Shrick guessed what was wrong. He knew a little of anatomy—his knowledge was that of the warrior who may be obliged to immobilize his enemy prior to his slaughter—and he could see that the Giant's keen blade had wrought this damage. Fury boiled up in him against these cruel, monstrous beings. And there was more than fury. There was the feeling, rare among his people, of overwhelming pity for his crippled mate.

"The blade . . . it is very sharp . . . I shall feel nothing."

But Shrick could not bring himself to do it.

Now they were floating up against the huge bulk of the dead Giant. With one hand he grasped Wesel's shoulder—the other still clutched his fine, new weapon—and kicked off against the gigantic carcass. Then he was pushing Wesel through the doorway in the Barrier, and sensed her relief as she found herself once more in familar territory. He followed her, then carefully shut and barred the door.

For a few heartbeats Wesel busied herself smoothing her bedraggled fur. He couldn't help noticing that she dare not let her hands stray to the lower part of her body where were the wounds, small but deadly, that had robbed her of the power of her limbs. Dimly, he felt that something might be done for one so injured, but knew that it was beyond his powers. And fury—not helpless now—against the Giants returned again, threatening to choke him with its intensity.

"Shrick!" Wesel's voice was grave. "We must return at once to the People. We must warn the People. The Giants are making a sorcery to bring the End."

"The great, hot light?"

"No. But wait! First I must tell you of what I learned. Otherwise, you would not believe. I have learned what we are, what the world is. And it is strange and wonderful beyond all our beliefs.

"What is Outside?" She did not wait for his answer, read it in his mind before his lips could frame the words. "The world is but a bubble of emptiness in the midst of a vast piece of metal, greater than the mind can imagine. But it is not so! Outside the metal that lies outside the Outside there is nothing. *Nothing!* There is no air."

"But there must be air, at least."

"No, I tell you. There is *nothing.*

"And the world—how can I find words? Their name for the world is—*ship*, and it seems to mean something big going from one place to another place. And all of us—Giants and People—are inside the ship. The Giants made the ship."

"Then it is not alive?"

"I cannot say. *They* seem to think that it is a female. It must have some kind of life that is not life. And it is going from one world to another world."

"And these other worlds?"

"I caught glimpses of them. They are dreadful, dreadful. *We* find the open spaces of the Inside frightening—but these other worlds are *all* open space except for one side."

"But what are we?" In spite of himself, Shrick at least half believed Wesel's fantastic story. Perhaps she possessed, to some slight degree, the power of projecting her own thoughts into the mind of another with whom she was intimate. "What are we?"

She was silent for the space of many heartbeats. Then: "*Their* name for us is *mutants*. The picture was . . . not clear at all. It means that we—the People—have changed. And yet their picture of the People before the change was like the Different Ones before we slew them all.

"Long and long ago—many hands of feedings—the first People, our parents' parents' parents, came into the world. They came from that greater world—the world of dreadful, open spaces. They came with the food in the great Cave-of-Food—and that is being carried to another world.

"Now, in the horrid, empty space outside the Outside there is—light that is not light. And this light—changes persons. No, not the grown person or the child, but the child before the birth. Like the dead and gone chiefs of the People, the Giants fear change in themselves. So they have kept the light that is not light from the Inside.

"And this is how. Between the Barrier and the Far Outside they filled the space with the stuff in which we have made our caves and tunnels. The first People left the great Cave-of-Food, they tunneled through the Barrier and into the stuff Outside. It was their nature. And some of them mated in the Far Outside caves. Their children were—*Different*."

"That is true," said Shrick slowly. "It has always been thought that children born in the Far Outside were never like their parents, and that those born close to the Barrier were—"

"Yes.

"Now, the Giants always knew that the People were here, but they did not fear them. They did not know our numbers, and they regarded us as beings much lower than themselves. They were content to keep us down with their traps and the food-that-kills. Somehow, they found that we had changed. Like the dead chiefs they feared us then—and like the dead chiefs they will try to kill us all before we conquer them."

"And the End?"

"Yes, the End." She was silent again, her big eyes looking past Shrick at something infinitely terrible. "Yes," she said again, "the End. *They* will make it, and *They* will escape it. *They* will put on artificial skins that will cover *Their* whole bodies, even *Their* heads, and *They* will open huge doors in the . . . skin of the ship, and all the air will rush out into the terrible empty space outside the Outside. And all the People will die."

"I must go," said Shrick. "I must kill the Giants before this comes to pass."

"No! There was one hand of Giants—now that you have killed Fat-Belly there are four of them left. And they know, now, that they can be killed. They will be watching for you.

"Do you remember when we buried the People with the sickness? That is what we must do to all the People. And then when the Giants fill the world with air again from their store we can come out."

Shrick was silent awhile. He had to admit that she was right. One unsuspecting Giant had fallen to his blade—but four of them, aroused, angry and watchful, he could not handle. In any case there was no way of knowing when the Giants would let the air from the world. The People must be warned—and fast.

Together, in the Place-of-Meeting, Shrick and Wesel faced the People. They had told their stories, only to be met with blank incredulity. True, there were some who, seeing the fine, shining blade that Shrick had brought from the Inside, were inclined to believe. But they were shouted down by the majority. It was when he tried to get them to immure themselves against the End that he met with serious opposition. The fact that he had so treated those suffering from the sickness still bulked big in the mob memory.

It was Short-Tail who precipitated the crisis.

"He wants the world to himself!" he shouted. "He has killed Big-Tusk and No-Tail, he has killed all the Different Ones, and Big-Ears he slew because he would have been chief. He and his ugly, barren mate want the world to themselves!"

Shrick tried to argue, but Big-Ears' following shouted him down. He squealed with rage and, raising his blade with both hands, rushed upon the rebel. Short-Tail scurried back out of reach. Shrick found himself alone in a suddenly cleared space. From somewhere a long way off he heard Wesel screaming his name. Dazedly, he shook his head, and then the red mist cleared from in front of his eyes.

All around him were the spear throwers, their slender weapons poised. He had trained them himself, had brought their specialized art of war into being. And now—

"Shrick!" Wesel was saying, "don't fight! They will kill you, and I shall be alone. I shall have the world to myself. Let them do as they will with us, and *we* shall live through the End."

At her words a tittering laugh rippled through the mob.

"*They* will live through the End! They will die as Big-Ears and his friends died!"

"I want your blade," said Short-Tail.

"Give it to him," cried Wesel. "You will get it back after the End!"

Shrick hesitated. The other made a sign. One of the throwing spears buried itself in the fleshy part of his arm. Had it not been for Wesel's voice, pleading, insistent, he would have charged his tormenters and met his end in less than a single heartbeat. Reluctantly, he released his hold upon the weapon. Slowly—as though loath to leave its true owner—it floated away from him. And then the People were all around him, almost suffocating him with the pressure of their bodies.

The cave into which Shrick and Wesel were forced was their own dwelling place. They were in pitiable state when the mob retreated to the entrance—Wesel's wounds had reopened and Shrick's arm was bleeding freely. Somebody had wrenched out the spear—but the head had broken off.

Outside, Short-Tail was laying about him with the keen blade he had taken from his chief. Under its strokes great masses of the spongy stuff of the Outside were coming free, and many willing hands were stuffing this tight into the cave entrance.

"We will let you out after the End!" called somebody.

There was a hoot of derision. Then: "I wonder which will eat the other first?"

"Never mind," said Wesel softly. "We shall laugh last."

"Perhaps. But . . . the People. *My* People. And you are barren. The Giants have won—"

Wesel was silent. Then he heard her voice again. She was whimpering to herself in the darkness. Shrick could guess her thoughts. All their grandiose dreams of world dominion had come to this—a tiny cramped space in which there was barely room for either of them to stir a finger.

And now they could no longer hear the voices of the People outside their prison. Shrick wondered if the Giants had already struck, then reassured himself with the memory of how the voices of those suffering from the sickness had grown fainter and fainter and then, at the finish, ceased altogether. And he wondered how he and Wesel would know when the End had come, and how they would know when it was safe to dig themselves out. It would be a long, slow task with only their teeth and claws with which to work.

But he had a tool.

The fingers of the hand of his uninjured arm went to the spearhead still buried in the other. He knew that by far the best way of extracting it would be one quick pull—but he couldn't bring himself to do it. Slowly, painfully, he worked away at the sharp fragment of metal.

"Let me do it for you."

"No." His voice was rough. "Besides, there is no haste."

Slowly, patiently, he worried at the wound. He was groaning a little, although he was not conscious of doing so. And then, suddenly, Wesel screamed. The sound was so unexpected, so dreadful in that confined space, that Shrick started violently. His hand jerked away from his upper arm, bringing with it the spearhead.

His first thought was that Wesel, telepath as she was, had chosen this way to help him. But he felt no gratitude, only a dull resentment.

"What did you do that for?" he demanded angrily.

She didn't answer his question. She was oblivious of his presence.

"The People . . ." she whispered. "The People . . . I can feel their thoughts . . . I can feel what they are feeling. And they are gasping for air . . . they are gasping and dying . . . and the cave of Long-Fur the spearmaker . . . but they are dying, and the blood is coming out of their mouths and noses and ears . . . I can't bear it . . . I can't—"

And then a terrifying thing happened. The sides of the cave pressed in upon them. Throughout the world, throughout the ship, the air cells in the spongy insulation were expanding as the air pressure dropped to Zero. It was this alone that saved Shrick and Wesel, although they never knew it. The rough plug sealing their cave, that, otherwise, would have blown out swelled to meet the expanding walls of the entrance, making a near perfect air-tight joint.

But the prisoners were in no state to appreciate this, even had they been in possession of the necessary knowledge. Panic seized them both. Claustrophobia was unknown among the People—but walls that closed upon them were outside their experience.

Perhaps Wesel was the more level-headed of the pair. It was she who tried to restrain her mate as he clawed and bit savagely, madly, at the distended, bulging walls. He no longer knew what lay outside the cave, had he known it would have made no difference. His one desire was to get out.

At first he made little headway, then he bethought himself of the little blade still grasped in his hand. With it he attacked the pulpy mass. The walls of the cells were stretched thin, almost to bursting, and under his onslaught they put up no more resistance than so many soap bubbles. A space was cleared, and Shrick was able to work with even greater vigor.

"Stop! Stop, I tell you! There is only the choking death outside the cave. And you will kill us both!"

But Shrick paid no heed, went on stabbing and hacking. It was only slowly, now, that he was able to enlarge upon the original impression he had made. As the swollen surfaces burst and withered beneath his blade, so they bulged and bellied in fresh places.

"Stop!" cried Wesel again.

With her arms, her useless legs trailing behind her, she pulled herself toward her mate. And she grappled with him, desperation lending her strength. So for many heartbeats they fought—silent, savage, forgetful of all that each owed to the other. And yet, perhaps, Wesel never quite forgot. For all her blind, frantic will to survive her telepathic powers were at no time entirely in abeyance. In spite of herself she, as always, shared the other's mind. And this psychological factor gave her an advantage that offset the paralysis of the lower half of her body—and at the same time inhibited her from pressing that advantage home to its logical conclusion.

But it did not save her when her fingers, inadvertently, dug into the wound in Shrick's arm. His ear-splitting scream was compounded of pain and fury, and he drew upon reserves of strength that the other never even guessed that he possessed. And the hand gripping the blade came round with irresistible force.

For Wesel there was a heartbeat of pain, of sorrow for herself and Shrick, of blind anger against the Giants who, indirectly, had brought this thing to pass.

And then the beating of her heart was stilled forever.

With the death of Wesel Shrick's frenzy left him.

There, in the darkness, he ran his sensitive fingers over the lifeless form, hopelessly hoping for the faintest sign of life. He called her name, he shook her roughly. But at last the knowledge that she was dead crept into his brain—and stayed there. In his short life he had known many times this sense of loss, but never with such poignancy.

And worst of all was the knowledge that *he* had killed her.

He tried to shift the burden of blame. He told himself that she would have died, in any case, of the wounds received at the hands of the Gaints. He tried to convince himself that, wounds or no wounds, the Giants were directly responsible for her death. And he knew that he was Wesel's murderer, just as he knew that all that remained for him in life was to bring the slayers of his people to a reckoning.

This made him cautious.

For many heartbeats he lay there in the thick darkness, not daring to renew his assault on the walls of his prison. He told himself that, somehow, he would know when the Giants let the air back into the world. How he would know he could not say, but the conviction persisted.

And when at last, with returning pressure, the insulation resumed its normal consistency, Shrick took this as a sign that it was safe for him to get out. He started to hack at the spongy material, then stopped. He went back to the body of Wesel. Just once he whispered her name, and ran his hands over the stiff, silent form in a last caress.

He did not return.

And when, at last, the dim light of the Place-of-Meeting

broke through she was buried deep in the debris that he had thrown behind him as he worked.

The air tasted good after the many times breathed atmosphere of the cave. For a few heartbeats Shrick was dizzy with the abrupt increase of pressure, for much of the air in his prison had escaped before the plug expanded to seal the entrance. It is probable that had it not been for the air liberated from the burst cells of the insulation he would long since have asphyxiated.

But this he was not to know—and if he had known it would not have worried him overmuch. He was alive, and Wesel and all the People were dead. When the mist cleared from in front of his eyes he could see them, their bodies twisted in the tortuous attitudes of their last agony, mute evidence of the awful powers of the Giants.

And now that he saw them he did not feel the overwhelming sorrow that he knew he should have done. He felt instead a kind of anger. By their refusal to heed his warning they had robbed him of his kingdom. None now could dispute his mastery of the Outside—but with no subjects, willing or unwilling, the vast territory under his sway was worthless.

With Wesel alive it would have been different.

What was it that she had said—? . . . *and the cave of Long-Fur the spear maker . . .*

He could hear her voice as she said it . . . *and the cave of Long-Fur the spear maker.*

Perhaps—But there was only one way to make sure.

He found the cave, saw that its entrance had been walled up. He felt a wild upsurge of hope. Frantically, with tooth and claw, he tore at the insulation. The fine blade that he had won from the Inside gleamed dully not a dozen handbreadths from where he was working, but such was his blind, unreasoning haste that he ignored the tool that would have made his task immeasurably shorter. At last the entrance was cleared. A feeble cry greeted the influx of air and light. For a while Shrick could not see who was within, and then could have screamed in his disappointment.

For here were no tough fighting males, no sturdy, fertile females, but two hands or so of weakly squirming infants. Their mothers must have realized, barely in time, that he and Wesel had been right, that there was only one way to ward off the choking death. Themselves they had not been able to save.

But they will grow up, Shrick told himself. *It won't be long before they are able to carry a spear for the Lord of the Outside, before the females are able to bear his children.*

Conquering his repugnance, he dragged them out. There was a hand of female infants, all living, and a hand of males. Three of these were dead. But here, he knew, was the nucleus of the army with which he would reestablish his rule over the world, Inside as well as Outside.

But first, they had to be fed.

He saw, now, his fine blade, and seizing it he began to cut up the three lifeless male children. The scent of their blood made him realize that he was hungry. But it was not until the children, now quieted, were all munching happily that he cut a portion for himself.

When he had finished it he felt much better.

It was some time before Shrick resumed his visits to the Inside. He had the pitiful remnant of his people to nurse to maturity and, besides, there was no need to make raids upon the Giants' stocks of food. They themselves had provided him with sustenance beyond his powers of reckoning. He knew, too, that it would be unwise to let his enemies know that there had been any survivors from the cataclysm that they had launched. The fact that he had survived the choking death did not mean that it was the only weapon that the Giants had at their disposal.

But as time went on he felt an intense longing to watch once more the strange life beyond the Barrier. Now that he had killed a Giant he felt a strange sense of kinship with the monstrous beings. He thought of the Thin-One, Loud-Voice, Bare-Head and the Little Giant almost as old friends. At times he even caught himself regretting that he must kill them all. But he knew that in this lay the only hope for the survival of himself and his people.

And then, at last, he was satisfied that he could leave the children to fend for themselves. Even should he fail to return from the Inside they would manage. No-Toes, the eldest of the female children, had already proved to be a capable nurse.

And so he roamed once more the maze of caves and tunnels just outside the Barrier. Through his doorways and peepholes he spied upon the bright, fascinating life of the Inner World. From the Cave-of-Thunders—though how it had come by its name none of the People has ever known—to the Place-of-Little-Lights he ranged. Many feedings passed, but he was not obliged to return to his own food store. For the corpses of the People were everywhere. True, they were beginning to stink a little, but like all his race Shrick was never a fastidious eater.

And he watched the Giants going about the strange, ordered routine of their lives. Often he was tempted to show himself, to shout defiance. But this action had to remain in the realm of wish-fulfillment dreams—he knew full well that it would bring sure and speedy calamity.

And then, at last, came the opportunity for which he had been waiting. He had been in the Place-of-Little-Lights, watching the Little Giant going about his mysterious, absorbing business. He had wished that he could understand its purport, that he could ask the Little Giant in his own tongue what it was that he was doing. For, since the death of Wesel, there had been none with whom a communion of mind was possible. He sighed, so loudly that the Giant must have heard.

He started uneasily and looked up from his work. Hastily Shrick withdrew into his tunnel. For many heartbeats he remained there, occasionally peeping out. But the other was still alert, must have known in some way that he was not alone. And so, eventually, Shrick had retired rather than risk incurring the potent wrath of the Giants once more.

His random retreat brought him to a doorway but rarely used. On the other side of it was a huge cavern in which there was nothing of real interest or value. In it, as a rule, at least one of the Giants would be sleeping, and others would be engaged in one of their incomprehensible pastimes.

This time there was no deep rumble of conversation, no movement whatsoever. Shrick's keen ears could distinguish the breathing of three different sleepers. The Thin-One was there, his respiration, like himself, had a meager quality. Loud-Voice was loud even in sleep. And Bare-Head, the chief of the Giants, breathed with a quiet authority.

And the Little Giant who, alone of all his people, was alert and awake was in the Place-of-Little-Lights.

Shrick knew that it was now or never. Any attempt to deal with the Giants singly must surely bring the great, hot light foretold by Three-Eyes. Now, with any luck at all, he could deal with the three sleepers and then lie in wait for the Little

Giant. Unsuspecting, unprepared, he could be dealt with as easily as had Fat-Belly.

And yet—he did not want to do it.

It wasn't fear; it was that indefinable sense of kinship, the knowledge that, in spite of gross physical disparities, the Giants and the People were as one. For the history of Man, although Shrick was not to know this, is but the history of the fire-making, tool-using animal.

Then he forced himself to remember Wesel, and Big-Ears, and the mass slaughter of almost all his race. He remembered Three-Eyes' words—*but this I can tell you, the People are doomed. Nothing you or they can do will save them. But you will kill those who will kill us, and that is good.*

But you will kill those who will kill us—

But if I kill all the Giants before they kill us, he thought, then the world, all the world, will belong to the People . . .

And he still hung back.

It was not until the Thin-One, who must have been in the throes of a bad dream, murmured and stirred in his sleep that Shrick came out of his doorway. The keen blade with which he had slain Fat-Belly was grasped in both his hands. He launched himself toward the uneasy sleeper. His weapon sliced down once only—how often had he rehearsed this in his imagination!—and for the Thin-One the dream was over.

The smell of fresh blood, as always, excited him. It took him all of his will power to restrain himself from hacking and slashing at the dead Giant. But he promised himself that this would come later. And he jumped from the body of the Thin-One to where Loud-Voice was snoring noisily.

The abrupt cessation of that all too familiar sound must have awakened Bare-Head. Shrick saw him shift and stir, saw his hands go out to loosen the bonds that held him to his sleeping place. And when the Giant Killer, his feet scrabbling for a hold, landed on his chest he was ready. And he was shouting in a great Voice, so that Shrick knew that it was only a matter of heartbeats before the Little Giant came to his assistance.

Fat-Belly had been taken off guard, the Thin-One and Loud-Voice had been killed in their sleep. But here was no easy victory for the Giant Killer.

For a time it looked as though the chief of the Giants would win. After a little he ceased his shouting and fought with grim, silent desperation. Once one of his great hands caught Shrick in a bone-crushing grip, and it seemed as though the battle was over. Shrick could feel the blood pounding in his head, his eyeballs almost popping out of their sockets. It took every ounce of resolution he possessed to keep from dropping his blade and scratching frenziedly at the other's wrist with ineffectual hands.

Something gave—it was his ribs—and in the fleeting instant of relaxed pressure he was able to twist, to turn and slash at the monstrous, hairy wrist. The warm blood spurted and the Giant cried aloud. Again and again Shrick plied his blade, until it became plain that the Giant would not be able to use that hand again.

He was single-handed now against an opponent as yet—insofar as his limbs were concerned—uncrippled. True, every movement of the upper part of his body brought spears of pain lancing through Shrick's chest. But he could move, and smite—and slay.

For Bare-Head weakened as the blood flowed from his wounds. No longer was he able to ward off the attacks on his face and neck. Yet he fought, as his race had always fought, to his dying breath. His enemy would have given no quarter—this much was obvious—but he could have sought refuge with the Little Giant in the Place-of-Little-Lights.

Toward the end he started shouting again.

And as he died, the Little Giant came into the cave.

It was sheer, blind luck that saved the Giant Killer from speedy death at the intruder's hands. Had the Little Giant known of the pitifully small forces arrayed against him it would have gone hard with Shrick. But No-Toes, left with her charges, had grown bored with the Place-of-Meeting. She had heard Shrick talk of the wonders of the Inside; and now, she thought, was her chance to see them for herself.

Followed by her charges she wandered aimlessly along the tunnels just outside the Barrier. She did not know the location of the doors to the Inside, and the view through the occasional peepholes was very circumscribed.

The she came upon the doorway which Shrick had left open when he made his attack on the sleeping Giants. Bright light streamed through the aperture—light brighter than any No-Toes had seen before in her short life. Like a beacon it lured her on.

She did not hesitate when she came to the opening. Unlike

her parents, she had not been brought up to regard the Giants with superstitious awe. Shrick was the only adult she could remember having known—and he, although he had talked of the Giants, had boasted of having slain one in single combat. He had said, also, that he would, at some time or other, kill all the Giants.

In spite of her lack of age and experience, No-Toes was no fool. Womanlike, already she had evaluated Shrick. Much of his talk she discounted as idle bragging, but she had never seen any reason to disbelieve his stories of the deaths of Big Tusk, Sterret, Tekka, Fat-Belly—and all the myriads of the People who had perished with them.

So it was that—foolhardy in her ignorance—she sailed through the doorway. Behind her came the other children, squealing in their excitement. Even if the Little Giant had not at first seen them he could not have failed to hear the shrill tumult of their eruption.

There was only one interpretation that he could put upon the evidence of his eyes. The plan to suffocate the People had failed. They had sallied out from their caves and tunnels to the massacre of his fellow Giants—and now fresh reinforcements were arriving to deal with him.

He turned and fled.

Shrick rallied his strength, made a flying leap from the monstrous carcass of Bare-Head. But in mid flight a hard, polished surface interposed itself between him and the fleeing Giant. Stunned, he hung against it for many heartbeats before he realized that it was a huge door which had shut in his face.

He knew that the Little Giant was not merely seeking refuge in flight—for where in the world could he hope to escape the wrath of the People? He had gone, perhaps, for arms of some kind. Or—and at the thought Shrick's blood congealed—he had gone to loose the final doom foretold by Three-Eyes. Now that his plans had begun to miscarry he remembered the prophecy in its entirety, was no longer able to ignore those parts that, in his arrogance, he had found displeasing.

And then No-Toes, her flight clumsy and inexpert in these—to her—strange, vast spaces was at his side.

"Are you hurt?" she gasped. "They are so big—and you fought them."

As she spoke, the world was filled with a deep humming

sound. Shrick ignored the excited female. That noise could mean only one thing. The Little Giant was back in the Place-of-Little-Lights, was setting in motion vast, incomprehensible forces that would bring to pass the utter and irrevocable destruction of the People.

With his feet against the huge door he kicked off, sped rapidly down to the open doorway in the Barrier. He put out his hand to break the shock of his landing, screamed aloud as his impact sent a sickening wave of pain through his chest. He started to cough—and when he saw the bright blood that was welling from his mouth he was very frightened.

No-Toes was with him again. "You are hurt, you are bleeding. Can I—?"

"No!" He turned a snarling mask to her. "No! Leave me alone!"

"But where are you going?"

Shrick paused. Then: "I am going to save the world," he said slowly. He savored the effect of his words. They made him feel better, they made him bulk big in his own mind, bigger, perhaps, than the Giants. "I am going to save you all."

"But how—?"

This was too much for the Giant Killer. He screamed again, but this time with anger. With the back of his hand he struck the young female across the face.

"Stay here!" he ordered.

And then he was gone along the tunnel.

The gyroscopes were still singing their quiet song of power when Shrick reached the Control Room. Strapped in his chair, the navigator was busy over his plotting machine. Outside the ports the stars wheeled by in orderly succession.

And Shrick was frightened.

He had never quite believed Wesel's garbled version of the nature of the world until now. But he could see, at last, that the ship was moving. The fantastic wonder of it all held him spellbound until a thin edge of intolerable radiance crept into view from behind the rim of one of the ports. The navigator touched something and, suddenly, screens of dark blue glass mitigated the glare. But it was still bright, too bright, and the edge became a rapidly widening oval and then, at last, a disk.

The humming of the gyroscope stopped.

Before the silence had time to register, a fresh sound assailed Shrick's ears. It was the roar of the main drive.

A terrifying force seized him and slammed him down upon

the deck. He felt his bones crack under the acceleration. True child of free fall as he was, all this held for him the terror of the supernatural. For a while he lay there, weakly squirming, whimpering a little. The navigator looked down at him and laughed. It was this sound more than anything else that stung Shrick to his last, supreme effort. He didn't want to move. He just wanted to lie there on the deck slowly coughing his life away. But the Little Giant's derision tapped unsuspected reserves of strength, both moral and physical.

The navigator went back to his calculations, handling his instruments for the last time with a kind of desperate elation. He knew that the ship would never arrive at her destination, neither would her cargo of seed grain. But she would not—and this outweighed all other considerations—drift forever among the stars carrying within her hull the seeds of the destruction of Man and all his works.

He knew that—had he not taken this way out—he must have slept at last, and then death at the hands of the mutants would inevitably have been his portion. And with mutants in full charge anything might happen.

The road he had taken was the best.

Unnoticed, inch by inch Shrick edged his way along the deck. Now, he could stretch his free hand and touch the Giant's foot. In the other he still held his blade, to which he had clung as the one thing sure and certain in this suddenly crazy world.

Then he had a grip on the artifical skin covering the Giant's leg. He started to climb, although every movement was unadulterated agony. He did not see the other raise his hand to his mouth, swallow the little pellet that he held therein.

So it was that when, at long last, he reached the soft, smooth throat of the Giant, the Giant was dead.

It was a very fast poison.

For a while he clung there. He should have felt elation at the death of the last of his enemies but—instead—he felt cheated. There was so much that he wanted to know, so much that only the Giants could have told him. Besides—it was his blade that should have won the final victory. He knew that, somewhere, the Little Giant was still laughing at him.

Through the blue-screened ports blazed the sun. Even at this distance, even with the intervening filters, its power and heat were all too evident. And aft the motors still roared, and would roar until the last ounce of fuel had been fed into hungry main drive.

Shrick clung to the dead man's neck, looked long and longingly at the glittering instruments, the shining switches and levers, whose purpose he would never understand, whose inertia would have defeated any attempt of his fast ebbing strength to move them. He looked at the flaming doom ahead, and knew that this was what had been foretold.

Had the metaphor existed in his language, he would have told himself that he and the few surviving People were caught like rats in a trap.

But even the Giants would not have used that phrase in its metaphorical sense.

For that is all that the People were—rats in a trap.

WHAT YOU NEED

by Henry Kuttner

ASTOUNDING SCIENCE FICTION,
October

The third story by Kuttner and company in this book is a powerful discussion of the responsibilities and obligations that go with the holding of power. And like much great science fiction, it has a wonderful puzzle quality about it that has tantalized readers since its appearance more than thirty-five years ago. We (at least some of us) know what we want—but do we really know what we need?

(During the first part of the World War II years Unknown *was the most exciting magazine in the world. The paper shortage killed it, but it didn't kill the need to write the type of stories that it printed. Writers who had worked for* Unknown, *who had gotten into the habit of writing "adult fantasy," found that there was no better way of handling certain difficult themes.*

With Unknown *gone, the temptation was to add a touch of science to such a story and write it anyway. I am convinced that Hank wrote this story with* Unknown *in mind. It would take almost nothing in the way of change to make it perfect for that magazine and yet as it stands it is undoubtedly science fiction. I.A.)*

That's what the sign said. Tim Carmichael, who worked for a trade paper that specialized in economics, and eked out a meager salary by selling sensational and untrue articles to the tabloids, failed to sense a story in the reversed sign. He thought it was a cheap publicity gag, something one seldom encounters on Park Avenue, where the shop fronts are noted for their classic dignity. And he was irritated.

He growled silently, walked on, then suddenly turned and came back. He wasn't quite strong enough to resist the temptation to unscramble the sentence, though his annoyance grew. He stood before the window, staring up, and said to himself, " 'We have what you need.' Yeah?"

The sign was in prim, small letters on a black painted ribbon that stretched across a narrow glass pane. Below it was one of those curved, invisible-glass windows. Through the window Carmichael could see an expanse of white velvet, with a few objects carefully arranged there. A rusty nail, a snowshoe and a diamond tiara. It looked like a Dali decor for Cartier or Tiffany.

"Jewelers?" Carmichael asked silently. "But why *what you need*?" He pictured millionaires miserably despondent for lack of a matched pearl necklace, heiresses weeping inconsolably because they needed a few star sapphires. The principle of luxury merchandising was to deal with the whipped cream of supply and demand; few people needed diamonds. They merely wanted them and could afford them.

"Or the place might sell jinni flasks," Carmichael decided. "Or magic wands. Same principle as a Coney carny, though. A sucker trap. Bill the Whatzit outside and people will pay their dimes and flock in. For two cents—"

He was dyspeptic this morning, and generally disliked the world. Prospect of a scapegoat was attractive, and his press card gave him a certain advantage. He opened the door and walked into the shop.

It was Park Avenue, all right. There were no showcases or counters. It might be an art gallery, for a few good oils were displayed on the walls. An air of overpowering luxury, with the bleakness of an unlived-in place, struck Carmichael.

Through a curtain at the back came a very tall man with carefully combed white hair, a ruddy, healthy face and sharp blue eyes. He might have been sixty. He wore expensive but careless tweeds, which somehow jarred with the décor.

"Good morning," the man said, with a quick glance at

Carmichael's clothes. He seemed slightly surprised. "May I help you?"

"Maybe." Carmichael introduced himself and showed his press card.

"Oh? My name is Talley. Peter Talley."

"I saw your sign."

"Oh?"

"Our paper is always on the lookout for possible writeups. I've never noticed your shop before—"

"I've been here for years," Talley said.

"This is an art gallery?"

"Well—no."

The door opened. A florid man came in and greeted Talley cordially. Carmichael, recognizing the client, felt his opinion of the shop swing rapidly upward. The florid man was a Name—a big one.

"It's a big early, Mr. Talley," he said, "but I didn't want to delay. Have you had time to get—what I needed?"

"Oh, yes. I have it. One moment." Talley hurried through the draperies and returned with a small, neatly wrapped parcel, which he gave to the florid man. The latter forked over a check—Carmichael caught a glimpse of the amount and gulped—and departed. His town car was at the curb outside.

Carmichael moved toward the door, where he could watch. The florid man seemed anxious. His chauffeur waited stolidly as the parcel was unwrapped with hurried fingers.

"I'm not sure I'd want publicity, Mr. Carmichael," Talley said. "I've a select clientele—carefully chosen."

"Perhaps our weekly economic bulletins might interest you."

Talley tried not to laugh. "Oh, I don't think so. It really isn't in my line."

The florid man had finally unwrapped the parcel and taken out an egg. As far as Carmichael could see from his post near the door, it was merely an ordinary egg. But its possessor regarded it almost with awe. Had Earth's last hen died ten years before, the man could have been no more pleased. Something like deep relief showed on the Florida-tanned face.

He said something to the chauffeur, and the car rolled smoothly forward and was gone.

"Are you in the dairy business?" Carmichael asked abruptly.

"No."

"Do you mind telling me what your business is?"

"I'm afraid I do, rather," Talley said.

Carmichael was beginning to scent a story. "Of course, I could find out through the Better Business Bureau—"

"You couldn't."

"No? They might be interested in knowing why an egg is worth five thousand dollars to one of your customers."

Talley said, "My clientele is so small I must charge high fees. You—ah—know that a Chinese mandarin has been known to pay thousands of taels for eggs of proved antiquity."

"That guy wasn't a Chinese mandarin," Carmichael said.

"Oh, well. As I say, I don't welcome publicity—"

"I think you do. I was in the advertising game for a while. Spelling your sign backwards is an obvious baited hook."

"Then you're no psychologist," Talley said. "It's just that I can afford to indulge my whims. For five years I looked at that window every day and read the sign backwards—from inside my shop. It annoyed me. You know how a word will begin to look funny if you keep staring at it? Any word. It turns into something in no human tongue. Well, I discovered I was getting a neurosis about that sign. It makes no sense backwards, but I kept finding myself trying to read sense into it. When I started to say 'Deen uoy tahw evah ew' to myself and looking for philological derivations, I called in a sign painter. People who are interested enough still drop in."

"Not many," Carmichael said shrewdly. "This is Park Avenue. And you've got the place fixed up too expensively. Nobody in the low-income brackets—or the middle brackets—would come in here. So you run an upper-bracket business."

"Well," Talley said, "yes, I do."

"And you won't tell me what it is?"

"I'd rather not."

"I can find out, you know. It might be dope, pornography, high-class fencing—"

"Very likely," Mr. Talley said smoothly. "I buy stolen jewels, conceal them in eggs and sell them to my customers. Or perhaps that egg was loaded with miscroscopic French postcards. Good morning, Mr. Carmichael."

"Good morning," Carmichael said, and went out. He was overdue at the office, but annoyance was the stronger motivation. He played sleuth for a while, keeping an eye on Talley's shop, and the results were thoroughly satisfactory—to a certain extent. He learned everything but why.

Late in the afternoon, he sought out Mr. Talley again.

"Wait a minute," he said, at sight of the proprietor's discouraging face. "For all you know, I may be a customer."

Talley laughed.

"Well, why not?" Carmichael compressed his lips. "How do you know the size of my bank account? Or maybe you've got a restricted clientele?"

"No. But—"

Carmichael said quickly, "I've been doing some investigating. I've been noticing your customers. In fact, following them. And finding out what they buy from you."

Talley's face changed. "Indeed?"

"In*deed.* They're all in a hurry to unwrap their little bundles. So that gave me my chance to find out. I missed a few, but—I saw enough to apply a couple of rules of logic, Mr. Talley. *Item*: your customers don't know what they're buying from you. It's a sort of grab bag. A couple of times they were plenty surprised. The man who opened his parcel and found an old newspaper clipping. What about the sunglasses? And the revolver? Probably illegal, by the way—no license. And the diamond—it must have been paste, it was so big."

"M-mmm," Mr. Talley said.

"I'm no smart apple, but I can smell a screwy setup. Most of your clients are big shots, in one way or another. And why didn't any of 'em pay you, like the first man—the guy who came in when I was here this morning?"

"It's chiefly a credit business," Talley said. "I've my ethics. I have to, for my own conscience. It's responsibility. You see, I sell—my goods—with a guarantee. Payment is made only if the product proves satisfactory."

"So. An Egg. Sunglasses. A pair of asbestos gloves—I think they were. A newspaper clipping. A gun. And a diamond. How do you take inventory?"

Talley said nothing.

Carmichael grinned. "You've an errand boy. You send him out and he comes back with bundles. Maybe he goes to a grocery on Madison and buys an egg. Or a pawnshop on Sixth for a revolver. Or—well, anyhow, I told you I'd find out what your business is."

"And have you?" Talley asked.

" 'We have what you need,' " Carmichael said. "But how do you *know?"*

"You're jumping to conclusions."

"I've got a headache—I didn't have sunglasses!—and I don't believe in magic. Listen, Mr. Talley, I'm fed up to the eyebrows and way beyond on queer little shops that sell peculiar things. I know too much about 'em—I've written about 'em. A guy walks along the street and sees a funny sort of store and the proprietor won't serve him—he sells only to pixies—or else he *does* sell him a magic charm with a double edge. Well—*pfui!"*

"Mph," Talley said.

" 'Mph' as much as you like. But you can't get away from logic. Either you've got a sound, sensible racket here, or else it's one of those funny, magic-shop setups—and I don't believe that. For it isn't logical."

"Why not?"

"Because of economics," Carmichael said flatly. "Grant the idea that you've got certain mysterious powers—let's say you can make telepathic gadgets. All right. Why the devil would you start a business so you could sell the gadgets so you could make money so you could live? You'd simply put on one of your gadgets, read a stockbroker's mind and buy the right stocks. That's the intrisic fallacy in these crazy-shop things—if you've got enough stuff on the ball to be able to stock and run such a shop, you wouldn't need a business in the first place. Why go round Robin Hood's barn?"

Talley said nothing.

Carmichael smiled crookedly. " 'I often wonder what the vintners buy one half so precious as the stuff they sell,' " he quoted. "Well—what do *you* buy? I know what you sell—eggs and sunglasses."

"You're an inquisitive man, Mr. Carmichael," Talley murmured. "Has it ever occurred to you that this is none of your business?"

"I may be a customer," Carmichael repeated. "How about that?"

Talley's cool blue eyes were intent. A new light dawned in them; Talley pursed his lips and scowled. "I hadn't thought of that," he admitted. "You might be. Under the circumstances. Will you excuse me for a moment?"

"Sure," Carmichael said. Talley went through the curtains.

Outside, traffic drifted idly along Park. As the sun slid down beyond the Hudson, the street lay in a blue shadow that crept imperceptibly up the barricades of the buildings. Carmichael stared at the sign—WE HAVE WHAT YOU NEED and smiled.

In a back room, Talley put his eye to a binocular plate and moved a calibrated dial. He did this several times. Then, biting his lip—for he was a gentle man—he called his errand boy and gave him directions. After that he returned to Carmichael.

"You're a customer," he said. "Under certain conditions."

"The condition of my bank account, you mean?"

"No," Talley said. "I'll give you reduced rates. Understand one thing. I really do have what you need. You don't *know* what you need, but I know. And as it happens—well, I'll sell you what you need for, let's say, five dollars."

Carmichael reached for his wallet. Talley held up a hand.

"Pay me after you're satisfied. And the money's the nominal part of the fee. There's another part. If you're satisfied, I want you to promise that you'll never come near this shop again and never mention it to anyone."

"I see," Carmichael said slowly. His theories had changed slightly.

"It won't be long before—ah, here he is now." A buzzing from the back indicated the return of the errand boy. Talley said, "Excuse me," and vanished. Soon he returned with a neatly wrapped parcel, which he thrust into Carmichael's hands.

"Keep this on your person," Talley said. "Good afternoon."

Carmichael nodded, pocketed the parcel and went out. Feeling affluent, he hailed a taxi and went to a cocktail bar he knew. There, in the dim light of a booth, he unwrapped the bundle.

Protection money, he decided. Talley was paying him off to keep his mouth shut about the racket, whatever it was. O.K., live and let live. How much would be—

Ten thousand? Fifty thousand? How big was the racket?

He opened an oblong cardboard box. Within, nestling upon tissue paper, was a pair of shears, the blades protected by a sheath of folded, glued cardboard.

Carmichael said something softly. He drank his highball and ordered another, but left it untasted. Glancing at his wrist watch, he decided that the Park Avenue shop would be closed by now and Mr. Peter Talley gone.

"'. . . one half so precious as the stuff they sell.'" Carmichael said. "Maybe it's the scissors of Atropos. Blah." He unsheathed the blades and snipped experimentally at the air. Nothing happened. Slightly crimson around the cheekbones, Carmichael reholstered the shears and dropped them into the side pocket of his topcoat. Quite a gag!

He decided to call on Peter Talley tomorrow.

Meanwhile, what? He remembered he had a dinner date with one of the girls at the office, and hastily paid his bill and left. The streets were darkening, and a cold wind blew southward from the Park. Carmichael wound his scarf tighter around his throat and made gestures toward passing taxis.

He was considerably annoyed.

Half an hour later a thin man with sad eyes—Jerry Worth, one of the copy writers from his office—greeted him at the bar where Carmichael was killing time. "Waiting for Besty?" Worth said, nodding toward the restaurant annex. "She sent me to tell you she couldn't make it. A rush deadline. Apologies and stuff. Where were you today? Things got gummed up a bit. Have a drink with me."

They worked on a rye. Carmichael was already slightly stiff. The dull crimson around his cheekbones had deepened, and his frown had become set. "What you need," he remarked. "Double crossing little—"

"Huh?" Worth said.

"Nothing. Drink up. I've just decided to get a guy in trouble. If I can."

"You almost got in trouble yourself today. That trend analysis of ores—"

"Eggs. Sunglasses!"

"I got you out of a jam—"

"Shut up," Carmichael said, and ordered another round. Every time he felt the weight of the shears in his pocket he found his lips moving.

Five shots later Worth said plaintively, "I don't mind doing good deeds, but I do like to mention them. And you won't let me. All I want is a little gratitude."

"All right, mention them," Carmichael said. "Brag your head off. Who cares?"

Worth showed satisfaction. "That ore analysis—it was that. You weren't at the office today, but I caught it. I checked with our records and you had Trans-Steel all wrong. If I hadn't altered the figures, it would have gone down to the printer—"

"What?"

"The Trans-Steel. They—"

"Oh, you fool," Carmichael groaned. "I know it didn't check with the office figures. I meant to put in a notice to have them changed. I got my dope from the source. Why don't you mind your own business?"

Worth blinked. "I was trying to help."

"It would have been good for a five-buck raise," Carmichael said. "After all the research I did to uncover the real dope— Listen, has the stuff gone to bed yet?"

"I dunno. Maybe not. Croft was still checking the copy—"

"O.K.!" Carmichael said. "Next time—" He jerked at his scarf, jumped off the stool and headed for the door, trailed by the protesting Worth. Ten minutes later he was at the office, listening to Croft's bland explanation that the copy had already been dispatched to the printer.

"Does it matter? Was there—Incidentally, where were you today?"

"Dancing on the rainbow," Carmichael snapped, and departed. He had switched over from rye to whisky sours, and the cold night air naturally did not sober him. Swaying slightly, watching the sidewalk move a little as he blinked at it, he stood on the curb and pondered.

"I'm sorry, Tim," Worth said. "It's too late now, though. There won't be any trouble. You've got a right to go by our office records."

"Stop me now," Carmichael said. "Lousy little—" He was angry and drunk. On impulse he got another taxi and sped to the printer's, still trailing a somewhat confused Jerry Worth.

There was rhythmic thunder in the building. The swift movement of the taxi had given Carmichael a slight nausea; his head ached, and alcohol was in solution in his blood. The hot, inky air was unpleasant. The great Linotypes thumped and growled. Men were moving about. It was all slightly nightmarish, and Carmichael doggedly hunched his shoulders and lurched on until something jerked him back and began to strangle him.

Worth started yelling. His face showed drunken terror. He made ineffectual gestures.

But this was all part of the nightmare. Carmichael saw

what had happened. The ends of his scarf had caught in the moving gears somewhere and he was being drawn inexorably into meshing metal cogs. Men were running. The clanking, thumping, rolling sounds were deafening. He pulled at the scarf.

Worth screamed, ". . . knife! Cut it!"

The warping of relative values that intoxication gives saved Carmichael. Sober, he would have been helpless with panic. As it was, each thought was hard to capture, but clear and lucid when he finally got it. He remembered the shears, and he put his hand in his pocket. The blades slipped out of their cardboard sheath, and he snipped through the scarf with fumbling, hasty movements.

The white silk disappeared. Carmichael fingered the ragged edge at his throat and smiled stiffly.

Mr. Peter Talley had been hoping that Carmichael would not come back. The probability lines had shown two possible variants; in one, all was well; in the other . . .

Carmichael walked into the shop the next morning and held out a five-dollar bill. Talley took it.

"Thank you. But you could have mailed me a check."

"I could have. Only that wouldn't have told me what I wanted to know."

"No," Talley said, and sighed. "You've decided, haven't you?"

"Do you blame me?" Carmichael asked. "Last night—do you know what happened?"

"Yes."

"How?"

"I might as well tell you," Talley said. "You'd find out anyway. That's certain, anyhow."

Carmichael sat down, lit a cigarette and nodded. "Logic. You couldn't have arranged that little accident, by any manner of means. Betsy Hoag decided to break our date early yesterday morning. Before I saw you. That was the beginning of the chain of incidents that led up to the accident. *Ergo*, you must have known what was going to happen."

"I did know."

"Prescience?"

"Mechanical. I saw that you would be crushed in the machine—"

"Which implies an alterable future."

"Certainly," Talley said, his shoulders slumping. "There are innumerable possible variants to the future. Different lines of probability. All depending on the outcome of various crises as they arise. I happen to be skilled in certain branches of electronics. Some years ago, almost by accident, I stumbled on the principle of seeing the future."

"How?"

"Chiefly it involves a personal focus on the individual. The moment you enter this place"—he gestured—"you're in the beam of my scanner. In my back room I have the machine itself. By turning a calibrated dial, I check the possible futures. Sometimes there are many. Sometimes only a few. As though at times certain stations weren't broadcasting. I look into my scanner and see what you need—and supply it."

Carmichael let smoke drift from his nostrils. He watched the blue coils through narrowed eyes.

"You follow a man's whole life—in triplicate or quadruplicate or whatever?"

"No," Talley said. "I've got my device focused so it's sensitive to crisis curves. When those occur, I follow them farther and see what probability paths involve the man's safe and happy survival."

"The sunglasses, the egg and the gloves—"

Talley said, "Mr.—uh—Smith is one of my regular clients. Whenever he passes a crisis successfully, with my aid, he comes back for another checkup. I locate his next crisis and supply him with what he needs to meet it. I gave him the asbestos gloves. In about a month, a situation will arise where he must—under the circumstances—move a red-hot bar of metal. He's an artist. His hands—"

"I see. So it isn't always saving a man's life."

"Of course not," Talley said. "Life isn't the only vital factor. An apparently minor crisis may lead to—well, a divorce, a neurosis, a wrong decision and the loss of hundreds of lives indirectly. I insure life, health and happiness."

"You're an altruist. Only why doesn't the world storm your doors? Why limit your trade to a few?"

"I haven't got the time or the equipment."

"More machines could be built."

"Well," Talley said, "most of my customers are wealthy. I must live."

"You could read tomorrow's stock-market reports if you wanted dough," Carmichael said. "We get back to that old question. If a guy has miraculous powers, why is he satisfied to run a hole-in-the-wall store?"

"Economic reasons. I—ah—I'm averse to gambling."

"It wouldn't be gambling," Carmichael pointed out. " 'I often wonder what the vintners buy . . .' Just what *do* you get out of this?"

"Satisfaction," Talley said. "Call it that."

But Carmichael wasn't satisfied. His mind veered from the question and turned to the possibilities. Insurance, eh? Life, health and happiness.

"What about me? Won't there be another crisis in my life sometime?"

"Probably. Not necessarily one involving personal danger."

"Then I'm a permanent customer."

"I—don't—"

"Listen," Carmichael said, "I'm not trying to shake you down. I'll pay. I'll pay plenty. I'm not rich, but I know exactly what a service like this would be worth to me. No worries—"

"It couldn't be—"

"Oh, come off it. I'm not a blackmailer or anything. I'm not threatening you with publicity, if that's what you're afraid of. I'm an ordinary guy, not a melodramatic villain. Do I look dangerous? What are you afraid of?"

"You're an ordinary guy, yes," Talley admitted. "Only—"

"Why not?" Carmichael argued. "I won't bother you. I passed one crisis successfully, with your help. There'll be another one due sometime. Give me what I need for that. Charge me anything you like. I'll get the dough somehow. Borrow it, if necessary I won't disturb you at all. All I ask is that you let me come in whenever I've passed a crisis, and get ammunition for the next one. What's wrong with that?"

"Nothing," Talley said soberly.

"Well, then. I'm an ordinary guy. There's a girl—it's Betsy Hoag. I want to marry her. Settle down somewhere in the country, raise kids and have security. There's nothing wrong with that either, is there?"

Talley said, "It was too late the moment you entered this shop today."

Carmichael looked up. "Why?" he asked sharply.

A buzzer rang in the back. Talley went through the curtains and came back almost immediately with a wrapped parcel. He gave it to Carmichael.

Carmichael smiled. "Thanks," he said. "Thanks a lot. Do you have any idea when my next crisis will come?"

"In a week."

"Mind if I—" Carmichael was unwrapping the package. He took out a pair of plastic-soled shoes and looked at Talley, bewildered.

"Like that, eh? I'll need—shoes?"

"Yes."

"I suppose—" Carmichael hesitated. "I guess you wouldn't tell me why?"

"No, I won't do that. But be sure to wear them whenever you go out."

"Don't worry about that. And—I'll mail you a check. It may take me a few days to scrape up the dough, but I'll do it. How much?"

"Five hundred dollars."

"I'll mail a check today."

"I prefer not to accept a fee until the client has been satisfied," Talley said. He had grown more reserved, his blue eyes cool and withdrawn.

"Suit yourself," Carmichael said. "I'm going out and celebrate. You—don't drink?"

"I can't leave the shop."

"Well, good-bye. And thanks again. I won't be any trouble to you, you know. I promise that!" He turned away.

Looking after him, Talley smiled a wry, unhappy smile. He did not answer Carmichael's good-bye. Not then.

When the door had closed behind him. Talley turned to the back of his shop and went through the door where the scanner was.

The lapse of ten years can cover a multitude of changes. A man with the possibility of tremendous power almost within his grasp can alter, in that time, from a man who will not reach for it to a man who will—and moral values be damned.

The change did not come quickly to Carmichael. It speaks well for his integrity that it took ten years to work such an alteration in all he had been taught. On the day he first went into Talley's shop there was little evil in him. But the temptation grew stronger week by week, visit by visit. Talley, for reasons of his own, was content to sit idly by, waiting for customers, smothering the inconceivable potentialities of his machine under a blanket of trivial functions. But Carmichael was not content.

It took him ten years to reach the day, but the day came at last.

Talley sat in the inner room, his back to the door. He was slumped low in an ancient rocker, facing the machine. It had changed little in the space of a decade. It still covered most of two walls, and the eyepiece of its scanner glittered under amber fluorescents.

Carmichael looked convetously at the eyepiece. It was window and doorway to a power beyond any man's dreams. Wealth beyond imagining lay just within that tiny opening. The rights over the life and death of every man alive. And nothing between that fabulous future and himself except the man who sat looking at the machine.

Talley did not seem to hear the careful footsteps or the creak of the door behind him. He did not stir as Carmichael lifted the gun slowly. One might think that he never guessed what was coming, or why, or from whom, as Carmichael shot him through the head.

Talley sighed and shivered a little, and twisted the scanner dial. It was not the first time that the eyepiece had shown him his own lifeless body, glimpsed down some vista of probability, but he never saw the slumping of that familiar figure without feeling a breath of indescribable coolness blow backwards upon him out of the future.

He straightened from the eyepiece and sat back in his chair, looking thoughtfully at a pair of rough-soled shoes lying beside him on a table. He sat quietly for a while, his eyes upon the shoes, his mind following Carmichael down the street and into the evening, and the morrow, and on toward that coming crisis which would depend on his secure footing on a subway platform as a train thundered by the place where Carmichael would be standing one day next week.

Talley had sent his messenger boy out this time for two pairs of shoes. He had hesitated long, an hour ago, between the rough-soled pair and the smooth. For Talley was a humane man, and there were many times when his job was distasteful to him. But in the end, this time, it had been the smooth-soled pair he had wrapped for Carmichael.

Now he sighed and bent to the scanner again, twisting the dial to bring into view a scene he had watched before.

Carmichael, standing on a crowded subway platform, glittering with oily wetness from some overflow. Carmichael, in the slick-soled shoes Talley had chosen for him. A commotion in the crowd, a surge toward the platform edge. Carmichael's feet slipping frantically as the train roared by.

"Good-bye, Mr. Carmichael," Talley murmured. It was the farewell he had not spoken when Carmichael left the shop. He spoke it regretfully, and the regret was for the Carmichael of today, who did not yet deserve that end. He was not now a melodramatic villain whose death one could watch unmoved. But the Tim Carmichael of today had atonement to make for the Carmichael of ten years ahead, and the payment must be exacted.

It is not a good thing to have the power of life and death over one's fellow humans. Peter Talley knew it was not a good thing—but the power had been put into his hands. He had not sought it. It seemed to him that the machine had grown almost by accident to its tremendous completion under his trained fingers and trained mind.

At first it had puzzled him. How ought such a device to be used? What dangers, what terrible potentialities, lay in that Eye that could see through the veil of tomorrow? His was the responsibility, and it had weighed heavily upon him until the answer came. And after he knew the answer—well, the weight was heavier still. For Talley was a mild man.

He could not have told anyone the real reason why he was a shopkeeper. Satisfaction, he had said to Carmichael. And sometimes, indeed, there was deep satisfaction. But at other times—at times like this—there was only dismay and humility. Especially humility.

We have what you need. Only Talley knew that message was not for the individuals who came to his shop. The pronoun was plural, not singular. It was a message for the world—the world whose future was being carefully, lovingly reshaped under Peter Talley's guidance.

The main line of the future was not easy to alter. The future is pyramid shaping slowly, brick by brick, and brick by brick Talley had to change it. There were some men who were necessary—men who would create and build—men who should be saved.

Talley gave them what they needed.

But inevitably there were others whose ends were evil. Talley gave them, too, what the world needed—death.

Peter Talley had not asked for this terrible power. But the key had been put in his hands, and he dared not delegate such authority as this to any other man alive. Sometimes he made mistakes.

He had felt a little surer since the metaphor of the key had occurred to him. The key to the future. A key that had been laid in his hands.

Remembering that, he leaned back in his chair and reached for an old and well-worn book. It fell open easily at a familiar passage. Peter Talley's lips moved as he read the passage once again, in his room behind the shop on Park Avenue.

"And I say also unto thee, that thou art Peter. . . . And I will give unto thee the keys of the Kingdom of Heaven. . . ."

A LOGIC NAMED JOE

by Will F. Jenkins (1896-1975)

ASTOUNDING SCIENCE FICTION
March

Much better known to his readers as "Murray Leinster," Will F. Jenkins had been publishing science fiction stories for more than a quarter of a century when "A Logic Named Joe" appeared. A prolific contributor to most of the pulp magazines, Jenkins came to be known within the sf community as "The Dean of Science Fiction," a title he wore with dignity and amusement for more than twenty years, producing excellent work well into the 1960s.

This prophetic story about home computers and their use and misuse is one of his finest.

(As you look back upon the stories written a third of a century ago, the ones that strike you with head-shaking envy [if you are a science fiction writer—especially a famous one] are those which actually get things right. *Anyone can write robot stories [including mine] that aren't as much fiction now as they were then; and that aren't liable to remain fiction indefinitely into the future.*

Read this story, however, and you'll swear Will Jenkins had some sort of pipeline into the 1980's.

Just change "logics" to "home computers" and make a few other inconsequential semantic changes and you'll see that Will went charging full-speed in the right direction. Clever as science fiction writers may be that doesn't often happen. It happened this time, though—I.A.)

It was on the third day of August that Joe come off the assembly line, and on the fifth Laurine come into town, and that afternoon I saved civilization. That's what I figure anyhow. Laurine is a blonde that I was crazy about once—and crazy is the word—and Joe is a logic that I have stored away down in the cellar right now. I had to pay for him because I said I busted him, and sometimes I think about turning him on and sometimes I think about taking an ax to him. Sooner or later I'm gonna do one or the other. I kinda hope it's the ax. I could use a coupla million dollars—sure!—an' Joe'd tell me how to get or make 'em. He can do plenty! But so far I've been scared to take a chance. After all, I figure I really saved a civilization by turnin' him off.

The way Laurine fits in is that she makes cold shivers run up an' down my spine when I think about her. You see, I've got a wife which I acquired after I had parted from Laurine with much romantic despair. She is a reasonable good wife, and I have some kids which are hellcats but I value 'em. If I have sense enough to leave well enough alone, sooner or later I will retire on a pension an' Social Security an' spend the rest of my life fishin', contented an' lyin' about what a great guy I used to be. But there's Joe. I'm worried about Joe.

I'm a maintenance man for the Logics Company. My job is servicing logics, and I admit modestly that I am pretty good. I was servicing televisions before that guy Carson invented his trick circuit that will select any of 'steenteen million other circuits—in theory there ain't no limit—and before the Logics Company hooked it into the tank-and-integrator setup they were usin' 'em as business machine service. They added a vision screen for speed—an' they found out they'd made logics. They were surprised an' pleased. They're still findin' out what logics will do, but everybody's got 'em.

I got Joe, after Laurine nearly got me. You know the logics setup. You got a logic in your house. It looks like a vision receiver used to, only it's got keys instead of dials and you punch the keys for what you wanna get. It's hooked in to the tank, which has the Carson Circuit all fixed up with relays. Say you punch "Station SNAFU" on your logic. Relays in the tank take over an' whatever vision-program SNAFU is telecastin' comes on your logic's screen. Or you punch "Sally Hancock's Phone" an' the screen blinks an' sputters an' you're hooked up with the logic in her house an' if somebody answers you got a vision-phone connection. But besides that, if you punch for the weather forecast or who won today's race at Hialeah or who was mistress of the White House durin' Garfield's administration or what is PDQ and R sellin' for today, that comes on the screen too. The relays in the tank do it. The tank is a big buildin' full of all the facts in creation an' all the recorded telecasts that ever was made—an' it's hooked in with all the other tanks all over the country—an' anything you wanna know or see or hear, you punch for it an' you get it. Very convenient. Also it does math for you, an' keeps books, an' acts as consultin' chemist, physicist, astronomer an' tealeaf reader, with an "Advice to Lovelorn" thrown in. The only thing it won't do is tell you exactly what your wife meant when she said "Oh, you think so, do you?" in that peculiar kinda voice. Logics don't work good on women. Only on things that make sense.

Logics are all right, though. They changed civilization, the highbrows tell us. All on accounta the Carson Circuit. And Joe shoulda been a perfectly normal logic, keeping some family or other from wearin' out its brains doin' the kids' homework for 'em. But somethin' went wrong in the assembly line. It was somethin' so small that precision gauges didn't measure it, but it made Joe an individual. Maybe he didn't know it at first. Or maybe, bein' logical, he figured out that if he was to show he was different from other logics they'd scrap him. Which woulda been a brilliant idea. But anyhow, he come off the assembly line, an' he went through the regular tests without anybody screamin' shrilly on findin' out what he was. And he went right on out an' was duly installed in the home of Mr. Thaddeus Korlanovitch at 119 East Seventh Street, second floor front. So far, everything was serene.

The installation happened late Saturday night. Sunday morning the Korlanovitch kids turned him on an' seen the Kiddie Shows. Around noon their parents peeled 'em away from him an' piled 'em in the car. Then they come back in the house for the lunch they'd forgot an' one of the kids sneaked back an' they found him punchin' keys for the Kiddie Shows of the week before. They dragged him out an' went off. But they left Joe turned on.

That was noon. Nothin' happened until two in the afternoon. It was the calm before the storm. Laurine wasn't in town yet, but she was comin'. I picture Joe sittin' there all by himself, buzzing meditative. Maybe he run Kiddie Shows in the empty apartment for awhile. But I think he went kinda remote-control exploring in the tank. There ain't any fact that can be said to be a fact that ain't on a data plate in some tank somewhere—unless it's one the technicians are diggin' out an' puttin' on a data plate now. Joe had plenty of material to work on. An' he musta started workin' right off the bat.

Joe ain't vicious, you understand. He ain't like one of these ambitious robots you read about that make up their minds the human race is inefficient and has got to be wiped out an' replaced by thinkin' machines. Joe's just got ambition. If you were a machine, you'd wanna work right, wouldn't you? That's Joe. He wants to work right. An' he's a logic. An' logics can do a lotta things that ain't been found out yet. So Joe, discoverin' the fact, begun to feel restless. He selects some things us dumb humans ain't thought of yet, an' begins to arrange so logics will be called on to do 'em.

That's all. That's everything. But, brother, it's enough!

Things are kinda quiet in the Maintenance Department about two in the afternoon. We are playing pinochle. Then one of the guys remembers he has to call up his wife. He goes to one of the banks of logics in Maintenance and punches the keys for his house. The screen sputters. Then a flash comes on the screen.

"Announcing new and improved logics service! Your logic is now equipped to give you not only consultative but directive service. If you want to do something and don't know how to do it—ask your logic!"

There's a pause. A kinda expectant pause. Then, as if reluctantly, his connection comes through. His wife answers an' gives him hell for somethin' or other. He takes it an' snaps off.

"Whadda you know?" he says when he comes back. He tells us about the flash. "We shoulda been warned about that. There's gonna be a lotta complaints. Suppose a fella asks how to get ridda his wife an' the censor circuits block the question?"

Somebody melds a hundred aces an' says:

"Why not punch for it an' see what happens?"

"It's a gag, o' course. But the guy goes over. He punches keys. In theory, a censor block is gonna come on an' the screen will say severely, "Public Policy Forbids This Service." You hafta have censor blocks or the kiddies will be askin' detailed questions about things they're too young to know. And there are other reasons. As you will see.

This fella punches, "How can I get rid of my wife?" Just for the fun of it. The screen is blank for half a second. Then comes a flash. "Service question: Is she blonde or brunette?" He hollers to us an' we come look. He punches, "Blonde". There's another brief pause. Then the screen says, "Hexymetacryloaminoacetine is a constituent of green shoe polish. Take home a frozen meal including dried pea soup. Color the soup with green shoe polish. It will appear to be green-pea soup. Hexymetacryloaminoacetine is a selective poison which is fatal to blonde females but not to brunettes or males of any coloring. This fact has not been brought out by human experiment, but is a product of logics service. You cannot be convicted of murder. It is improbable that you will be suspected."

The screen goes blank, and we stare at each other. It's bound to be right. A logic workin' the Carson Circuit can no more make a mistake than any other kinda computin' machine. I call the tank in a hurry.

"Hey, you guys!" I yell. "Somethin's happened! Logics are givin' detailed instructions for wife-murder! Check your censor-circuits—but quick!"

That was close, I think. But little do I know. At that precise instant, over on Monroe Avenue, a drunk starts to punch for somethin' on a logic. The screen says "Announcing new and improved logics service! If you want to do something and don't know how to do it—ask your logic!" And the drunk says owlish, "I'll do it!" So he cancels his first punching and fumbles around and says: "How can I keep my wife from finding out I've been drinking?" And the screen says, prompt: "Buy a bottle of Franine hair shampoo. It is harmless but contains a detergent which will neutralize ethyl alcohol immediately. Take one teaspoonful for each jigger of hundred-proof you have consumed."

This guy was plenty plastered—just plastered enough to stagger next door and obey instructions. An' five minutes later he was cold sober and writing down the information so he couldn't forget it. It was new, and it was big! He got rich offa that memo! He patented "*SOBUH, The Drink that Makes Happy Homes!*" You can top off any souse with a slug or two of it an' go home sober as a judge. The guy's cussin' income taxes right now!

You can't kick on stuff like that. But a ambitious young fourteen-year-old wanted to buy some kid stuff and his pop wouldn't fork over. He called up a friend to tell his troubles. And his logic says: "If you want to do something and don't know how to do it—ask your logic!" So this kid punches: "How can I make alotta money, fast?"

His logic comes through with the simplest, neatest, and the most efficient counterfeitin' device yet known to science. You see, all the data was in the tank. The logic—since Joe had closed some relays here an' there in the tank—simply integrated the facts. That's all. The kid got caught up with three days later, havin' already spent two thousand credits an' havin' plenty more on hand. They hadda time tellin' his counterfeits from the real stuff, an' the only way they done it was that he changed his printer, kid fashion, not bein' able to let somethin' that was workin' right alone.

Those are what you might call samples. Nobody knows all that Joe done. But there was the bank president who got humorous when his logic flashed that "Ask your logic" spiel on him, and jestingly asked how to rob his own bank. An' the logic told him, brief and explicit but good! The bank president hit the ceiling, hollering for cops. There must a been plenty of that sorta thing. There was fifty-four more robberies than usual in the next twenty-four hours, all of them planned astute an' perfect. Some of 'em they never did figure out how they'd been done. Joe, he'd gone exploring in the tank and closed some relays like a logic is supposed to do—but only when required—and blocked all censor-circuits an' fixed up this logics service which planned perfect crimes, nourishing an' attractive meals, conterfeitin' machines, an' new industries with a fine impartiality. He musta been plenty happy, Joe must. He was functionin' swell, buzzin' along to himself while the Korlanovitch kids were off ridin' with their ma an' pa.

They come back at seven o'clock, the kids all happily wore out with their afternoon of fightin' each other in the car. Their folks put 'em to bed and sat down to rest. They saw Joe's screen flickerin' meditative from one subject to another an' old man Korlanovitch had had enough excitement for one day. He turned Joe off.

An' at that instant the patterns of relays that Joe had turned on snapped off, all the offers of directive service stopped flashin' on logic screens everywhere, an' peace descended on the earth.

For everybody else. But for me. Laurine come to town. I have often thanked God fervent that she didn't marry me when I thought I wanted her to. In the intervenin' years she had progressed. She was blonde an' fatal to begin with. She had got blonder and fataler an' had had four husbands and one acquittal for homicide an' had acquired a air of enthusiasm and self-confidence. That's just a sketch of the background. Laurine was not the kinda former girlfriend you like to have turning up in the same town with your wife. But she came to town, an' Monday morning she tuned right into the middle of Joe's second spasm of activity.

The Korlanovitch kids had turned him on again. I got these details later and kinda pieced 'em together. An' every logic in town was dutifully flashin' a notice, "If you want to do something—ask your logic!" every time they were turned on for use. More'n that, when people punched for the morning news, they got a full account of the previous afternoon's doin's. Which put 'em in a frame of mind to share in the party. One bright fella demands, "How can I make a perpetual motion machine?" And his logic sputters a while an' then comes up with a set-up usin' the Brownian movement to turn little wheels. If the wheels ain't bigger'n a eighth of an inch they'll turn, all right, an' practically it's perpetual motion. Another one asks for the secret of transmuting metals. The logic rakes back in the data plates an' integrates a strictly practical answer. It does take so much power that you can't make no profit except on radium, but that pays off good. An' from the fact that for a coupla years to come the police were turnin' up new and improved jimmies, knob-claws for gettin' at safe innards, and all-purpose keys that'd open any known lock—why there must have been other inquiries with a strictly practical viewpoint. Joe done a lot for technical progress!

But he done more in other lines. Educational, say. None of

my kids are old enough to be interested, but Joe bypassed all censor-circuits because they hampered the service he figured logics should give humanity. So the kids an' teenagers who wanted to know what comes after the bees an' flowers found out. And there is certain facts which men hope their wives won't do more'n suspect, an' those facts are just what their wives are really curious about. So when a woman dials: "How can I tell if Oswald is true to me?" and her logic tells her—you can figure out how many rows got started that night when the men come home!

All this while Joe goes on buzzin' happy to himself, showin' the Korlanovitch kids the animated funnies with one circuit while with the others he remote-controls the tank so that all the other logics can give people what they ask for and thereby raise merry hell.

An' then Laurine gets onto the new service. She turns on the logic in her hotel room, prob'ly to see the week's style-forecast. But the logic says, dutiful: "If you want to do something—ask your logic!" So Laurine prob'ly looks enthusiastic—she would!—and tries to figure out something to ask. She already knows all about everything she cares about—ain't she had four husbands an' shot one?—so I occur to her. She knows this is the town I live in. So she punches, "How can I find Ducky?"

O.K., guy! But that is what she used to call me. She gets a service question. "Is Ducky known by any other name?" So she gives my regular name. And the logic can't find me. Because my logic ain't listed under my name on account of I am in Maintenance and don't want to be pestered when I'm home, and there ain't any data plates on code-listed logics, because the codes get changed so often—like a guy gets plastered an tells a redhead to call him up, an' on gettin' sober hurriedly has the code changed before she reaches his wife on the screen.

Well! Joe is stumped. That's prob'ly the first question logics service hasn't been able to answer. "How can I locate Ducky?"!! Quite a problem! So Joe broods over it while showin' the Korlanovitch kids the animated comic about the cute little boy who carries sticks of dynamite in his hip pocket an' plays practical jokes on everybody. Then he gets the trick. Laurine's screen suddenly flashes:

"Logics special service will work upon your question. Please punch your logic designation and leave it turned on. You will be called back."

Laurine is merely mildly interested, but she punches her hotel-room number and has a drink and takes a nap. Joe sets to work. He has been given an idea.

My wife calls me at Maintenance and hollers. She is fit to be tied. She says I got to do something. She was gonna make a call to the butcher shop. Instead of the butcher or even the "If you want to do something" flash, she got a new one. The screen says, "Service question: What is your name?" She is kinda puzzled, but she punches it. The screen sputters an' then says: "Secretarial Service Demonstration! You——" It reels off her name, address, age, sex, coloring, the amounts of all her charge accounts in all the stores, my name as her husband, how much I get a week, the fact that I've been pinched three times—twice was traffic stuff, and once for a argument I got in with a guy—and the interestin' item that once when she was mad with me she left me for three weeks an' had her address changed to her folks' home. Then it says, brisk: "Logics Service will hereafter keep your personal accounts, take messages, and locate persons you may wish to get in touch with. This demonstration is to introduce the service." Then it connects her with the butcher.

But she don't want meat, then. She wants blood. She calls me.

"If it'll tell me all about myself," she says, fairly boilin', "it'll tell anybody else who punches my name! You've got to stop it!"

"Now, now, honey!" I says. "I didn't know about all this! It's new! But they musta fixed the tank so it won't give out information except to the logic where a person lives!"

"Nothing of the kind!" she tells me, furious. "I tried! And you know that Blossom woman who lives next door! She's been married three times and she's forty-two years old and she says she's only thirty! And Mrs. Hudson's had her husband arrested four times for nonsupport and once for beating her up. And——"

"Hey!" I says. "You mean the logic told you this?"

"Yes!" she wails. "It will tell anybody anything! You've got to stop it! How long will it take?"

"I'll call up the tank," I says. "It can't take long."

"Hurry!" she says, desperate, "before somebody punches my name! I'm going to see what it says about that hussy across the street."

She snaps off to gather what she can before it's stopped. So I punch for the tank and I get this new "What is your name?" flash. I got a morbid curiosity and I punch my name, and the screen says: "Were you ever called Ducky?" I blink. I ain't got no suspicions. I say, "Sure!" And the screen says, "There is a call for you."

Bingo! There's the inside of a hotel room and Laurine is reclinin' asleep on the bed. She'd been told to leave her logic turned on an' she done it. It is a hot day and she is trying to be cool. I would say that she oughta not suffer from the heat. Me, being human, I do not stay as cool as she looks. But there ain't no need to go into that. After I get my breath I say, "For Heaven's sake!" and she opens her eyes.

At first she looks puzzled, like she was thinking is she getting absentminded and is this guy somebody she married lately. Then she grabes a sheet and drapes it around herself and beams at me.

"Ducky!" she says. "How marvelous!"

I say something like "Ugmph!" I am sweating.

She says:

"I put in a call for you, Ducky, and here you are! Isn't it romantic? Where are you really, Ducky? And when can you come up? You've no idea how often I've thought of you!"

I am probably the only guy she ever knew real well that she has not been married to at some time or another.

I say "Ugmph!" and swallow.

"Can you come up instantly?" asks Laurine brightly.

"I'm . . . workin'," I say. "I'll . . . uh . . . call you back."

"I'm terribly lonesome," says Laurine. "Please make it quick, Ducky! I'll have a drink waiting for you. Have you ever thought of me?"

"Yeah," I say, febble. "Plenty!"

"You darling!" says Laurine. "Here's a kiss to go on with until you get here! Hurry, Ducky!"

Then I sweat! I still don't know nothing about Joe, understand. I cuss out the guys at the tank because I blame them for this. If Laurine was just another blonde—well—when it comes to ordinary blondes I can leave 'em alone or leave 'em alone, either one. A married man gets that way or else. But Laurine has a look of unquenched enthusiasm that gives a man very strange weak sensations at the back of his knees. And she'd had four husbands and shot one and got acquitted.

So I punch the keys for the tank technical room, fumbling. And the screen says: "What is your name?" but I don't want any more. I punch the name of the old guy who's stock clerk in Maintenance. And the screen gives me some pretty interestin' dope—I never woulda thought the old fella had ever had that much pep—and winds up by mentionin' an unclaimed deposit now amountin' to two hundred eighty credits in the First National Bank, which he should look into. Then it spiels about the new secretarial service and gives me the tank at last.

I start to swear at the guy who looks at me, But he says, tired:

"Snap it off, fella. We got troubles an' you're just another. What are the logics doin' now?"

I tell him, and he laughs a hollow laugh.

"A light matter, fella," he says. "A very light matter! We just managed to clamp off all the data plates that give information on high explosives. The demand for instructions in counterfeiting is increasing minute by minute. We are also trying to shut off, by main force, the relays that hook in to data plates that just barely might give advice on the fine points of murder. So if people will only keep busy getting the goods on each other for a while, maybe we'll get a chance to stop the circuits that are shifting credit-balances from bank to bank before everybody's bankrupt except the guys who thought of askin' how to get big bank accounts in a hurry."

"Then," I says hoarse, "shut down the tank! Do somethin'!"

"Shut down the tank?" he says mirthless. "Does it occur to you, fella, that the tank has been doin' all the computin' for every business office for years? It's been handlin' the distribution of ninety-four percent of all telecast programs, has given out all information on weather, plane schedules, special sales, employment opportunities and news; has handled all person-to-person contacts over wires and recorded every business conversation and agreement—Listen, fella! Logics changed civilization. Logics *are* civilization! If we shut off logics, we go back to a kind of civilization we have forgotten how to run! I'm getting hysterical myself and that's why I'm talkin' like this! If my wife finds out my paycheck is thirty credits a week more than I told her and starts hunting for that redhead—"

He smiles a haggard smile at me and snaps off. And I sit down and put my head in my hands. It's true. If something had happened back in cave days and they'd hadda stop usin' fire—If they'd hadda stop usin' steam in the nineteenth century or electricity in the twentieth—It's like that. We got a very simple civilization. In the nineteen hundreds a man would have to make use of a typewriter, radio, telephone, tele-typewriter, newspaper, reference library, encyclopedias, office files, directories, plus messenger service and consulting lawyers, chemists, doctors, dietitians, filing clerks, secretaries—all to put down what he wanted to remember an' to tell him what other people had put down that he wanted to know; to report what he said to somebody else and to report to him what they said back. All we have to have is logics. Anything we want to know or see or hear, or anybody we want to talk to, we punch keys on a logic. Shut off logics and everything goes skid-doo. But Laurine. . . .

Somethin' had happened. I still didn't know what it was. Nobody else knows, even yet. What had happened was Joe. What was the matter with him was that he wanted to work good. All this fuss he was raisin' was, actual, nothin' but stuff we shoulda thought of ourselves. Directive advice, tellin' us what we wanted to know to solve a problem, wasn't but a slight extension of logical-integrator service. Figurin' out a good way to poison a fella's wife was only different in degrees from figurin' out a cube root or a guy's bank balance. It was gettin' the answer to a question. But things was goin' to pot because there was too many answers being given to too many questions.

One of the logics in Maintenance lights up. I go over, weary, to answer it. I punch the answer key. Laurine says:

"Ducky!"

It's the same hotel room. There's two glasses on the table with drinks in them. One is for me. Laurine's got on some kinda frothy hangin'-around-the-house-with-the-boyfriend outfit that automatic makes you strain your eyes to see if you actual see what you think. Laurine looks at me enthusiastic.

"Ducky!" says Laurine. "I'm lonesome! Why haven't you come up?"

"I . . . been busy," I say, strangling slightly.

"*Pooh!*" says Laurine. "Listen, Ducky! Do you remember how much in love we used to be?"

I gulp.

"Are you doin' anything this evening?" says Laurine.

I gulp again, because she is smiling at me in a way that a single man would maybe get dizzy, but it gives a old married man like me cold chills. When a dame looks at you possessive. . . .

"Ducky!" says Laurine, impulsive. "I was so mean to you! Let's get married!"

Desperation gives me a voice.

"I . . . got married," I tell her, hoarse.

Laurine blinks. Then she says, courageous:

"Poor boy! But we'll get you outa that! Only it would be nice if we could be married today. Now we can only be engaged!"

"I . . . can't——"

"I'll call up your wife," says Laurine, happy, "and have a talk with her. You must have a code signal for your logic, darling. I tried to ring your house and noth——"

Click! That's my logic turned off. I turned it off. And I feel faint all over. I got nervous prostration. I got combat fatigue. I got anything you like. I got cold feet.

I beat it outa Maintenance, yellin' to somebody I got a emergency call. I'm gonna get out in a Maintenance car an' cruise around until it's plausible to go home. Then I'm gonna take the wife an' kids an' beat it for somewheres that Laurine won't ever find me. I don't wanna be fifth in Laurine's series of husbands and maybe the second one she shoots in a moment of boredom. I got experience of blondes. I got experience of Laurine! And I'm scared to death!

I beat it out into traffic in the Maintenance car. There was a disconnected logic on the back, ready to substitute for one that hadda burnt-out coil or something that it was easier to switch and fix back in the Maintenance shop. I drove crazy but automatic. It was kinda ironic, if you think of it. I was goin' hoopla over a strictly personal problem, while civilization was crackin' up all around me because other people were havin' their personal problems solved as fast as they could state 'em. It is a matter of record that part of the Mid-Western Electric research guys had been workin' on cold electron-emission for thirty years, to make vacuum tubes that wouldn't need a power source to heat the filament. And one of those fellas was intrigued by the "Ask your logic" flash. He asked how to get cold emission of electrons. And the logic integrates a few squintillion facts on the physics data plates and tells him. Just as casual as it told somebody over in the Fourth Ward how to serve leftover soup in a new attractive way, and somebody else on Mason Street how to dispose of a torso that somebody had left careless in his cellar after ceasing to use same.

Laurine wouldn't never have found me if it hadn't been for this new logics service. But now that it was started—Zowie! She'd shot one husband and got acquitted. Suppose she got impatient because I was still married an' asked logics service how to get me free an' in a spot where I'd have to marry her by 8:30 p.m.? It woulda told her! Just like it told that woman out in the suburbs how to make sure her husband wouldn't run around no more. *Br-r-r-r!* An' like it told that kid how to find some buried treasure. Remember? He was happy totin' home the gold reserve of the Hanoverian Bank and Trust Company when they caught on to it. The logic had told him how to make some kinda machine that nobody has been able to figure how it works even yet, only they guess it dodges around a couple extra dimensions. If Laurine was to start askin' questions with a technical aspect to them, that would be logics service meat! And fella, I was scared! If you think a he-man oughtn't to be scared of just one blonde—you ain't met Laurine!

I'm driving blind when a social-conscious guy asks how to bring about his own particular system of social organization at once. He don't ask if it's best or if it'll work. He just wants to get it started. And the logic—or Joe—tells him! Simultaneous, there's a retired preacher asks how can the human race be cured of concupiscence. Bein' seventy, he's pretty safe himself, but he wants to remove the peril to the spiritual welfare of the rest of us. He finds out. It involves constructin' a sort of broadcastin' station to emit a certain wave-pattern an' turnin' it on. Just that. Nothing more. It's found out afterward, when he is solicitin' funds to construct it. Fortunate, he didn't think to ask logics how to finance it, or it woulda told him that, too, an' we woulda all been cured of the impulses we maybe regret afterward but never at the time. And there's another group of serious thinkers who are sure the human race would be a lot better off if everybody went back to nature an' lived in the woods with the ants an' posion ivy. They start askin' questions about how to cause humanity to abandon cities and artificial conditions of living. They practically got the answer in logics service!

Maybe it didn't strike you serious at the time, but while I was drivin' aimless, sweatin' blood over Laurine bein' after me, the fate of civilization hung in the balance. I ain't kiddin'. For instance, the Superior Man gang that sneers at the rest of us was quietly asking questions on what kinda weapons could be made by which Superior men could take over and run things . . .

But I drove here an' there, sweatin' an' talkin' to myself.

"What I ought to do is ask this wacky logics service how to get outa this mess," I says. "But it'd just tell me a intricate an' foolproof way to bump Laurine off. I wanna have peace! I wanna grow comfortably old and brag to other old guys about what a hellion I used to be, without havin' to go through it an' lose my chance of livin' to be a elderly liar."

I turn a corner at random, there in the Maintenance car.

"It was a nice kinda world once," I says, bitter. "I could go home peaceful and not have belly-cramps wonderin' if a blonde has called up my wife to announce my engagement to her. I could punch keys on a logic without gazing into somebody's bedroom while she is giving her epidermis a air bath and being led to think things I gotta take out in thinkin'. I could—"

Then I groan, rememberin' that my wife, naturally, is gonna blame me for the fact that our private life ain't private any more if anybody has tried to peek into it.

"It was a swell world," I says, homesick for the dear dead days-before-yesterday. "We was playin' happy with our toys like little innocent children until somethin' happened. Like a guy named Joe come in and squashed all our mud pies."

Then it hit me. I got the whole thing in one flash. There ain't nothing in the tank set-up to start relays closin'. Relays are closed exclusive by logics, to get the information the keys are punched for. Nothin' but a logic coulda cooked up the relay patterns that constituted logics service. Humans wouldn't ha' been able to figure it out! Only a logic could integrate all the stuff that woulda made all the other logics work like this—

There was one answer. I drove into a restaurant and went over to a pay-logic an' dropped in a coin.

"Can a logic be modified," I spell out, "to co-operate in long-term planning which human brains are too limited in scope to do?"

The screen sputters. Then it says:

"Definitely yes."

"How great will the modifications be?" I punch.

"Microscopically slight. Changes in dimensions," says the screen. "Even modern precision gauges are not exact enough to check them, however. They can only come about under present manufacturing methods by an extremely improbable accident, which has only happened once."

"How can one get hold of that one accident which can do this highly necessary work?" I punch.

The screen sputters. Sweat broke out on me. I ain't got it figured out close, yet, but what I'm scared of is that whatever is Joe will be suspicious. But what I'm askin' is strictly logical. And logics can't lie. They gotta be accurate. They can't help it.

"A complete logic capable of the work required," says the screen, "is now in ordinary family use in——"

And it gives me the Korlanovitch address and do I go over there! Do I go over there fast! I pull up the Maintenance car in front of the place, and I take the extra logic outa the back, and I stagger up the Korlanovitch flat and I ring the bell. A kid answers the door.

"I'm from Logics Maintenance," I tell the kid. "An inspection record has shown that your logic is apt to break down any minute. I come to put in a new one before it does."

The kid says "O.K.!" real bright and runs back to the livin'-room where Joe—I got the habit of callin' him Joe later, through just meditatin' about him—is runnin' something the kids wanna look at. I hook in the other logic an' turn it on, conscientious making sure it works. Then I say:

"Now kiddies, you punch this one for what you want. I'm gonna take the old one away before it breaks down."

And I glance at the screen. The kiddies have apparently said they wanna look at some real cannibals. So the screen is presenting an anthropological expedition scientific record film of the fertility dance of the Huba-Jouba tribe of West Africa. It is supposed to be restricted to anthropological professors an' post-graduate medical students. But there ain't any censor blocks workin' any more and it's on. The kids are much interested. Me, bein' a old married man, I blush.

I disconnect Joe. Careful. I turn to the other logic and punch keys for Maintenance. I do not get a services flash. I get Maintenance. I feel very good. I report that I am goin' home because I fell down a flight of steps an' hurt my leg. I add, inspired:

"An' say, I was carryin' the logic I replaced an' it's all busted. I left it for the dustman to pick up."

"If you don't turn 'em in," says Stock, "you gotta pay for 'em."

"Cheap at the price," I say.

I go home. Laurine ain't called. I put Joe down in the cellar, careful. If I turned him in, he'd be inspected an' his parts salvaged even if I busted somethin' on him. Whatever part was off-normal might be used again and everything start all over. I can't risk it. I pay for him and leave him be.

That's what happened. You might say I saved civilization an' not be far wrong. I know I ain't goin' to take a chance on havin' Joe in action again. Not while Laurine is livin'. An' there are other reasons. With all the nuts who wanna change the world to their own line o' thinkin', an' the ones that wanna bump people off, an' generally solve their problems. . . . Yeah! Problems are bad, but I figure I better let sleepin' problems lie.

But on the other hand, if Joe could be tamed, somehow, and got to work just reasonable—He could make me a coupla million dollars, easy. But even if I got sense enough not to get rich, an' if I get retired and just loaf around fishin' an' lyin' to the other old duffers about what a great guy I used to be—Maybe I'll like it, but maybe I won't. And after all, if I get fed up with bein' old and confined strictly to thinking—why I could hook Joe in long enough to ask: "How can a old guy not stay old?" Joe'll be able to find out. An' he'll tell me.

That couldn't be allowed out general, of course. You gotta make room for kids to grow up. But it's a pretty good world, now Joe's turned off. Maybe I'll turn him on long enough to learn how to stay in it. But on the other hand, maybe. . . .

MEMORIAL

by Theodore Sturgeon (1918-   )

ASTOUNDING SCIENCE FICTION
April

The events of the late summer of 1945 at Hiroshima and Nagasaki changed the world and the world of science fiction. Sf writers had produced numerous stories about atomic energy, some of them on the "awful warning" variety, and now the future had arrived. One result was a growing boom in the science fiction field, first with the penetration of the "slick" magazines like The Saturday Evening Post *by sf writers, and a few years later by a magazine boom which saw the launching of dozens of new sf titles, interest in science fiction by hardcover publishers, and a secure niche for sf within the paperback explosion of the early 1950s.*

The tone of much sf also turned more somber, reflecting on the devastation made possible by advanced technology and this was reflected in a large group of stories about atomic war and its aftermath. "Memorial" was one of the first of this group to see print, and was the second published story by the talented Theodore Sturgeon after a long period of silence caused by personal problems. It was good to have him back.

(The thing is that John Campbell had predicted in 1940 or there-abouts that the inventor of nuclear energy was already alive. How right he was. Not only alive, but already a working scientist for the credit was shared by Hahn, Meitner, Szilard, Fermi and so on. It made John very sensitive to the fact of the nuclear bomb and to its possible consequences. Under his lash, his writers produced nuclear bomb stories which appeared in Astounding *throughout 1946. Most of them, as would seem natural from the fact that a good story should have some drama in it, expected the worst, a worst that has not yet come true (thank goodness!) thirty-five years later. We can all be glad that "Memorial" has not come true—so far—I.A.)*

The Pit, in A.D. 5000, had changed little over the centuries. Still it was an angry memorial to the misuse of great power; and because of it, organized warfare was a forgotten thing. Because of it, the world was free of the wasteful smoke and dirt of industry. The scream and crash of bombs and the soporific beat of marching feet were never heard, and at long last the earth was at peace.

To go near The Pit was slow, certain death, and it was respected and feared, and would be for centuries more. It winked and blinked redly at night, and was surrounded by a bald and broken tract stretching out and away over the horizon; and around it flickered a ghostly blue glow. Nothing lived there. Nothing could.

With such a war memorial, there could only be peace. The earth could never forget the horror that could be loosed by war.

That was Grenfell's dream.

Grenfell handed the typewritten sheet back. "That's it, Jack. My idea, and—I wish I could express it like that." He leaned back against the littered workbench, his strangely asymmetrical face quizzical. "Why is it that it takes a useless person to adequately express an abstract?"

Jack Roway grinned as he took back thepaper and tucked

it into his breast pocket. "Interestin' question, Grenfell, because this *is* your expression, the words *are* yours. Practically verbatim. I left out the 'er's' and 'ah's' that you play conversational hopscotch with, and strung together all the effects you mentioned without mentioning any of the technological causes. Net result: you think I did it, when you did. You think it's good writing, and I don't."

"You don't?"

Jack spread his bony length out on the hard little cot. His relaxation was a noticeable act, like the unbuttoning of a shirt collar. His body seemed to unjoint itself a little. He laughed.

"Of course I don't. Much too emotional for my taste. I'm just a fumbling aesthete—uesless, did you say? Mm-m-m—yeah. I suppose so." He paused reflectively. "You see, you cold-blooded characters, you scientists, are the true visionaries. Seems to me the essential difference between a scientist and an artist is that the scientist can mix his hope with patience. "The scientist visualizes his ultimate goal, but pays little attention to it. He is all caught up with the achievement of the next step upward. The artist looks so far ahead that more often than not he can't see what's under his feet; so he falls flat on his face and gets called useless by scientists. But if you strip all of the intermediate steps away from the scientist's thinking, you have an artistic concept to which the scientist responds distantly and with surprise, giving some artist credit for being deeply perspicacious purely because the artist repeated something the scientist said."

"You amaze me," Grenfell said candidly. "You wouldn't be what you are if you weren't lazy and superficial. And yet you come out with things like that. I don't know that I understand what you just said. I'll have to think—but I do believe that you show all the signs of clear thinking. With a mind like yours, I can't understand why you don't use it to build something instead of wasting it in these casual interpretations of yours."

Jack Roway stretched luxuriously. "What's the use? There's more waste involved in the destruction of something which is already built than in dispersing the energy it would take to start building something. Anyway, the world is filled with builders—and destroyers. I'd just as soon sit by and watch, and feel things. I like my environment, Grenfell. I want to feel all I can of it, while it lasts. It won't last much longer. I want to touch all of it I can reach, taste of it, hear it, while there's time. What is around me, here and now, is what is important to me. The acceleration of human progress, and the increase of its mass—to use your own terms—are taking humanity straight to Limbo. You, with your work, think you are fighting humanity's inertia. Well, you are. But it's the kind of inertia called momentum. You command no force great enough to stop it, or even to change its course appreciably."

"I have sub-atomic power."

Roway shook his head, smiling. "That's not enough. No power is enough. It's just too late."

"That kind of pessimism does not affect me," said Grenfell. "You can gnaw all you like at my foundations, Jack, and achieve nothing more than the loss of your front teeth. I think you know that."

"Certainly I know that. I'm not trying to. I have nothing to sell, no one to change. I am even more impotent than you and your atomic power; and you are completely helpless. Uh—I quarrel with your use of the term 'pessimist', though. I am nothing of the kind. Since I have resolved for myself the fact that humanity, as we know it, is finished, I'm quite resigned to it. Pessimism from me, under the circumstances, would be the pessimism of a photophobiac predicting that the sun would rise tomorrow."

Grenfell grinned. "I'll have to think about that, too. You're such a mass of paradoxes that turn out to be chains of reasoning. Apparently you live in a world in which scientists are poets and the grasshopper has it over the ant."

"I always did think that ant was a stinker."

"Why do you keep coming here, Jack? What do you get out of it? Don't you realize I'm a criminal?"

Roway's eyes narrowed. "Sometimes I think you wish you were a criminal. The law says you are, and the chances are very strong that you'll be caught and treated accordingly. Ethically, you know you're not. It sort of takes the spice out of being one of the hunted."

"Maybe you're right," Grenfell said thoughtfully. He sighed. "It's so completely silly. During the war years, the skills I had were snatched up and the government flogged me into the Manhattan Project, expecting, and getting, miracles. I have never stopped working along the same lines. And now the government has changed the laws, and pulled legality from under me."

"Hardly surprising. The government deals rather severely with soldiers who go on killing other soldiers after the war is over." He held up a hand to quell Grenfell's interruptions. "I know you're not killing anyone, and are working for the opposite result. I was only pointing out that it's the same switcheroo. We the people," he said didactically, "have, in our sovereign might, determined that no atomic research be done except in government laboratories. We have then permitted our politicians to allow so little for maintenance of those laboratories—unlike our overseas friends—that no really exhaustive research can be done in them. We have further made it a major offense to operate such a bootleg lab as yours." He shrugged. "Comes the end of mankind. We'll get walloped first. If we put more money and effort into nuclear research than any other country, some other country would get walloped first. If we last another hundred years—which seems doubtful—some poor, spavined, and underpaid government researcher will stumble on the aluminum-isotope space-heating system you have already perfected."

"That was a little rough," said Grenfell bitterly. "Driving me underground just in time to make it impossible for me to announce it. What a waste of time and energy it is to heat homes and buildings the way they do now! Space heating—the biggest single use for heat-energy—and I have the answer to it over there." He nodded toward a compact cube of lead alloys in the corner of the shop. "Build it into a foundation, and you have controllable heat for the life of the building, with not a cent for additional fuel and practically nothing for maintenance." His jaw knotted. "Well, I'm glad it happened that way."

"Because it got you started on your war memorial— The Pit? Yeah. Well, all I can say is, I hope you're right. It hasn't been possible to scare humanity yet. The invention of gunpowder was going to stop war, and didn't. Likewise the submarine, the torpedo, the airplane, that two-by-four bomb they pitched at Hiroshima, and the H-bomb."

"None of that applies to The Pit," said Grenfell. "You're right; humanity hasn't been scared off war yet; but the H-bomb rocked 'em back on their heels. My little memorial is the real stuff. I'm not depending on a fission or fusion effect, you know, with a release of one-tenth of one percent of the energy of the atom. I'm going to transmute it completely, and get all the energy there is in it, and in all matter the fireball touches. And it'll be *more* than a thousand times as powerful as the Hiroshima bomb, because I'm going to use twelve times as much explosive; and it's going off on the ground, not a hundred and fifty feet above it." Grenfell's brow, over suddenly hot eyes, began to shine with sweat. "And then—The Pit," he said softly. "The war memorial to end war, and all other war memorials. A vast pit, alive with bubbling lava, radiating death for ten thousand years. A living reminder of the devastation mankind has prepared for itself. Out here on the desert, where there are no cities, where the land has always been useless, will be the scene of the most useful thing in the history of the race—a never-ending sermon, a warning, an example of the dreadful antithesis of peace." His voice shook to a whisper, and faded.

"Sometimes," said Roway, "you frighten me, Grenfell. It occurs to me that I am such a studied sensualist, tasting everything I can, because I am afraid to feel any one thing that much." He shook himself, or shuddered. "You're a fanatic, Grenfell. Hyperemotional. A monomaniac. I hope you can do it."

"I can do it," said Grenfell.

Two months passed, and in those two months Grenfell's absorption in his work had been forced aside by the increasing pressure of current events. Watching a band of vigilantes riding over the waste to the south of his little buildings one afternoon, he thought grimly of what Roway had said. "Sometimes I think you wish you were a criminal." Roway the sensualist, would say that. Roway would appreciate the taste of danger, in the same way that he appreciated all the other emotions. As it intensified, he would wait to savor it, no matter how bad it got.

Twice Grenfell shut off the instigating power of the boron-aluminum pile he had built, as he saw government helicopters hovering on the craggy skyline. He knew of hard-radiation detectors; he had developed two different types of them during the war; and he wanted no questions asked. His utter frustration at being unable to announce the success of his space-heating device, for fear that he would be punished as a criminal and his device impounded and forgotten—that frustration had been indescribable. It had canalized his mind, and intensified the devoted effort he had put forth for the things he believed in during the war. Every case of neural shock he encountered in men who had been hurt by war and despised it made him work harder on his monument—on The Pit. For if humans could be frightened by war, humanity could be frightened by The Pit.

And those he met who had been hurt by war and who still hated the late enemy—those who would have been happy to go back and kill some more, reckoning vital risk well worth it—those he considered mad, and forgot them.

So he could not stand another frustration. He was the center of his own universe, and he realized it dreadfully, and he had to justify his position there. He was a humanitarian, a philanthropist in the world's truest sense. He was probably as mad as any other man who has, through his own efforts, moved the world.

For the first time, then, he was grateful when Jack Roway arrived in his battered old convertible, although he was deliriously frightened at the roar of the motor outside his laboratory window. His usual reaction to Jack's advent was a mixture of annoyance and gratification, for it was a great deal of trouble to get out to his place. His annoyance was not because of the interruption, for Jack was certainly no trouble to have around. Grenfell suspected that Jack came out to see him partly to get the taste of the city out of his mouth, and partly to be able to feel superior to somebody be considered of worth.

But the increasing fear of discovery, and his race to complete his work before it was taken from him by a hysterical public, had had the unusual effect of making him lonely. For such a man as Grenfell to be lonely bordered on the extraordinary; for in his daily life there were simply too many things to be done. There had never been enough hours in a day nor days in a week to suit him, and he deeply resented the encroachments of sleep, which he considered a criminal waste.

"Roway!" he blurted, as he flung the door open, his tone so warm that Roway's eyebrows went up in surprise. "What dragged you out here?"

"Nothing in particular," said the writer, as they shook hands. "Nothing more than usual, which is a great deal. How goes it?"

"I'm about finished." They went inside, and as the door closed, Grenfell turned to face Jack. "I've been finished for so long I'm ashamed of myself," he said intently.

"Ha! Ardent confession so early in the day! What are you talking about?"

"Oh, there have been things to do," said Grenfell restlessly. "But I could go ahead with the . . . with the big thing at almost any time."

"You hate to be finished. You've never visualized what it

would be like to have the job done." His teeth flashed. "You know, I've never heard a word from you as to what your plans are after the big noise. You going into hiding?"

"I . . . haven't thought much about it. I used to have a vague idea of broadcasting a warning and an explanation before I let go with the disruptive explosion. I've decided against it, though. In the first place, I'd be stopped within minutes, no matter how cautious I was with the transmitter. In the second place—well, this is going to be so big that it won't need any explanation."

"No one will know who did it, or why it was done."

"Is that necessary?" asked Grenfell quietly.

Jack's mobile face stilled as he visualized The Pit, spewing its ten-thousand-year hell. "Perhaps not," he said. "Isn't it necessary, though, to you?"

"To me?" asked Grenfell, surprised. "You mean, do I care if the world knows I did this thing, or not? No; of course I don't. A chain of circumstance is occurring, and it has been working through me. It goes directly to The Pit; The Pit will do all that is necessary from then on. I will no longer have any part in it."

Jack moved, clinking and splashing, around the sink in the corner of the laboratory. "Where's all your coffee? Oh—here. Uh . . . I have been curious about how much personal motive you had for your work. I think that answers it pretty well. I think, too, that you believe what you are saying. Do you know that people who do things for impersonal motives are as rare as fur on a fish?"

"I hadn't thought about it."

"I believe that, too. Sugar? And milk. I remember. And have you been listening to the radio?"

"Yes. I'm . . . a little upset, Jack," said Grenfell, taking the cup. "I don't know where to time this thing. I'm a technician, not a Machiavelli."

"Visionary, like I said. You don't know if you'll throw this gadget of yours into world history too soon or too late—is that it?"

"Exactly. Jack, the whole world seems to be going crazy. Even fusion bombs are too big for humanity to handle."

"What else can you expect," said Jack grimly, "with our dear friends across the water sitting over their push buttons waiting for an excuse to punch them?"

"And we have our own set of buttons, of course."

Jack Roway said: "We've got to defend ourselves."

"Are you kidding?"

Roway glanced at him, his dark brows plotting a V. "Not about this. I seldom kid about anything, but particularly not about this." And he—shuddered.

Grenfell stared amazedly at him and then began to chuckle. "Now," he said, "I've seen everything. My iconoclastic friend Jack Roway, of all people, caught up by a . . . a fashion. A national pastime, fostered by uncertainty and fed by yellow journalism—fear of the enemy."

"This country is not at war."

"You mean, we have no enemy? Are you saying that the gentlemen over the water, with their itching fingertips hovering about the push buttons, are not our enemies?"

"Well—"

Grenfell came across the room to his friend, and put a hand on his shoulder. "Jack—what's the matter? You can't be so troubled by the news—not *you*!"

Roway stared out at the brazen sun, and shook his head slowly. "International balance is too delicate," he said softly; and if a voice could glaze like eyes, his did. "I see the nations of the world as masses balanced each on its own mathematical point, each with its center of gravity directly above. But the masses are fluid, shifting violently away from the center lines. The opposing trends aren't equal; they can't cancel each other; the phasing is too slow. One or the other is going to topple, and then the whole works is going to go."

"But you've known that for a long time. You've known that ever since Hiroshima. Possibly before. Why should it frighten you now?"

"I didn't think it would happen so soon."

"Oh-ho! So that's it! You have suddenly realized that the explosion is going to come in your lifetime. Hm-m-m? And you can't take that. You're capable of all of your satisfying aesthetic rationalizations as long as you can keep the actualities at arm's length!"

"*Whew!*" said Roway, his irrepressible humor passing close enough to nod to him. "Keep it clean, Grenfell! Keep your . . . your sesquipedalian polysyllabics, for a scientific report."

"*Touché!*" Grenfell smiled. "Y'know, Jack, you remind me powerfully of some erstwhile friends of mine who write science-fiction. They had been living very close to atomic power for a long time—years before the man on the street—or the average politician, for that matter—knew an atom from Adam. Atomic power was handy to these specialized word-merchants because it gave them a limitless source of power for background to a limitless source of story material. In the heyday of the Manhattan Project, most of them suspected what was going on, some of them knew—some even worked on it. All of them were quite aware of the terrible potentialities of nuclear energy. Practically all of them were scared silly of the whole idea. They were afraid for humanity, but they themselves were not really afraid, except in a delicious drawing room sort of way, because they couldn't conceive of this Buck Rogers event happening to anything but posterity. But it happened, right smack in the middle of their own sacrosanct lifetimes.

"And I will be dog-goned if you're not doing the same thing. You've gotten quite a bang out of figuring out the doom humanity faces in an atomic war. You've consciously risen above it by calling it inevitable, and in the meantime leave us gather rosebuds before it rains. You thought you'd be safe home—dead—before the first drops fell. Now social progress has rolled up a thunderhead and you find yourself a mile from home with a crease in your pants and no umbrella. And you're scared!"

Roway looked at the floor and said, "It's so soon. It's so soon." He looked up at Grenfell, and his cheekbones seemed too large. He took a deep breath. "You . . . we can stop it, Grenfell."

"Stop what?"

"The war . . . the . . . this thing that's happening to us. The explosion that will come when the strains get too great in the international situation. And it's *got* to be stopped!"

"That's what The Pit is for."

"The Pit!" Roway said scornfully. "I've called you a visionary before. Grenfell, you've got to be more practical! Humanity is not going to learn anything by example. It's got to be kicked and carved. Surgery."

Grenfell's eyes narrowed. "Surgery? What you said a minute ago about my stopping it . . . do you mean what I think you mean?"

"Don't you see it?" said Jack urgently. "What you have here—the total conversion of mass to energy—the peak of atomic power. One or two wallops with this, in the right place, and we can stop anybody."

"This isn't a weapon. I didn't make this to be a weapon."

"The first rock ever thrown by a prehistoric man wasn't made to be a weapon, either. But it was handy and it was effective, and it was certainly used because it had to be used." He suddenly threw up his hands in a despairing gesture. "You don't understand. Don't you realize that this country is likely to be attacked at any second—that diplomacy is now hopeless and helpless, and the whole world is just waiting for the thing to start? It's probably too late even now—but it's the least we can do."

"What, specifically, is the least thing we can do?"

"Turn your work over to the Defense Department. In a few hours the government can put it where it will do the most good." He drew his finger across his throat. "Anywhere we want to, over the ocean."

There was a taut silence. Roway looked at his watch and licked his lips. Finally Grenfell said, "Turn it over to the government. Use it for a weapon—and what for? To stop war?"

"Of course!" blurted Roway. "To show the rest of the world that our way of life . . . to scare the daylights out of . . . to—"

"*Stop it!*" Grenfell roared. "Nothing of the kind. You think—you hope anyway—that the use of total disruption as a weapon will stall off the inevitable—at least in your lifetime. Don't you?"

"No, I—"

"Don't you?"

"Well, I—"

"You have some more doggerel to write," said Grenfell scathingly. "You have some more blondes to chase. You want to go limp over a few more Bach fugues."

Jack Roway said: "No one knows where the first bomb might hit. It might be anywhere. There's nowhere I . . . we . . . can go to be safe." He was trembling.

"Are the people in the city quivering like that?" asked Grenfell.

"Riots," breathed Roway, his eyes bright with panic. "The radio won't announce anything about the riots."

"Is that what you came out here for today—to try to get me to give disruptive power to *any* government?"

Jack looked at him guiltily."It was the only thing to do. I

don't know if your bomb will turn the trick, but it has to be tried. It's the only thing left. We've got to be prepared to hit first, and hit harder than anyone else."

"No." Grenfell's one syllable was absolutely unshakable.

"Grenfell—I thought I could argue you into it. Don't make it tough for yourself. You've got to do it. Please do it on your own. Please, Grenfell." He stood up slowly.

"Do it on my own—or what? *Keep away from me!*"

"No . . . I—" Roway stiffened suddenly, listening. From far above and to the north came the whir of rotary wings. Roway's fear-slackened lips tightened into a grin, and with two incredibly swift strides he was across to Grenfell. He swept in a handful of the smaller man's shirt front and held him half off the floor.

"Don't try a thing," he gritted. There was not a sound then except their harsh breathing, until Grenfell said wearily: "There was somebody called Judas—"

"You can't insult me," said Roway, with a shade of his old cockiness, "And you're flattering yourself."

A helicopter sank into its own roaring dust-cloud outside the building. Men pounded out of it and burst in the door. There were three of them. They were not in uniform.

"Dr. Grenfell," said Jack Roway, keeping his grip, "I want you to meet—"

"Never mind that," said the taller of the three in a brisk voice. "You're Roway? Hm-m-m. Dr. Grenfell, I understand you have a nuclear energy device on the premises."

"Why did you come by yourself?" Grenfell asked Roway softly. "Why not just send these stooges?"

"For you, strangely enough. I hoped I could argue you into giving the thing freely. You know what will happen if you resist?"

"I know." Grenfell pursed his lips for a moment, and then turned to the tall man. "Yes. I have some such thing here. Total atomic disruption. Is that what you were looking for?"

"Where is it?"

"Here, in the laboratory, and then there's the pile in the other building. You'll find—" he hesitated. "You'll find two samples of the concentrate. One's over there—" he pointed to a lead case on a shelf behind one of the benches. "And there's another like it in a similar case in the shed back of the pile building."

Roway sighed and released Grenfell. "Good boy. I knew you'd come through."

"Yes," said Grenfell. "Yes—"

"Go get it," said the tall man. One of the others broke away.

"It will take two men to carry it," said Grenfell in a shaken voice. His lips were white.

The tall man pulled out a gun and held it idly. He nodded to the second man. "Go get it. Bring it here and we'll strap the two together and haul 'em to the plane. Snap it up."

The two men went out toward the shed.

"Jack?"

"Yes, Doc."

"You really think humanity can be scared?"

"It will be—now. This thing will be used right."

"I hope so. Oh, I hope so," Grenfell whispered.

The men came back. "Up on the bench," said the leader, nodding toward the case the men carried between them.

As they climbed up on the bench and laid hands on the second case, to swing it down from the shelf, Jack Roway saw Grenfell's face spurt sweat, and a sudden horror swept over him.

"Grenfell!" he said hoarsely. "It's—"

"Of course," Grenfell whispered. "Critical mass."

When the two leaden cases came together, it let go.

It was like Hiroshima, but much bigger. And yet, that explosion did not create The Pit. It was the pile that did—the boron-aluminum lattice which Grenfell had so arduously pieced together from parts bootlegged over the years. Right there at the heart of the fission explosion, total disruption took place in the pile, for that was its function. This was slower. It took more than an hour for its hellish activity to reach a peak, and in that time a huge crater had been gouged out of the earth, a seething, spewing mass of volatilized elements, raw radiation, and incandescent gases. It was—The Pit. Its activity curve was plotted abruptly—up to peak in an hour and eight minutes, and then a gradual subsidence as it tried to feed further afield with less and less fueling effect, and as it consumed its own flaming wastes in an effort to reach inactivity. Rain would help to blanket it, through energy lost in volatilizing the drops; and each of the many elements involved went through its respective secondary radioactivity, and passed away its successive half-lives. The subsidence of The Pit would take between eight and nine thousand years.

And like Hiroshima, this explosion had effects which reached into history and into men's hearts in places far separated in time from the cataclysm itself.

These things happened:

The explosion could not be concealed; and there was too much hysteria afoot for anything to be confirmed. It was easier to run headlines saying WE ARE ATTACKED. There was an instantaneous and panicky demand for reprisals, and the government acceded, because such "reprisals" suited the policy of certain members who could command emergency powers. And so the First Atomic War was touched off.

And the Second.

There were no more atomic wars after that. The Mutants' War was a barbarous affair, and the mutants defeated the tattered and largely sterile remnants of humanity, because the mutants were strong. And then the mutants died out because they were unfit. For a while there was some very interesting material to be studied on the effects of radiation on heredity, but there was no one to study it.

There were some humans left. The rats got most of them, after increasing in fantastic numbers; and there were three plagues.

After that there were half-stooping naked things whose twisted heredity could have been traced to humankind; but these could be frightened, as individuals and as a race, so therefore they could not progress. They were certainly not human.

The Pit, in A.D. 5000, had changed little over the centuries. Still it was an angry memorial to the misuse of great power; and because of it, organized warfare was a forgotten thing. Because of it, the world was free of the wasteful smoke and dirt of industry. The scream and crash of bombs and the soporific beat of marching feet were never heard, and at long last the earth was at peace.

To go near The Pit was slow, certain death, and it was respected and feared, and would be for centuries more. It winked and blinked redly at night, and was surrounded by a bald and broken tract stretching out and away over the horizon; and around it flickered a ghostly blue glow. Nothing lived there. Nothing could.

With such a war memorial, there could only be peace. The earth could never forget the horror that could be loosed by war.

That was Grenfell's dream.

LOOPHOLE

by Arthur C. Clarke (1917-   )

ASTOUNDING SCIENCE FICTION
April

Arthur C. Clarke is widely regarded as one of the major figures in modern science fiction, and books like Childhood's End *(1953)* The City and the Stars *(1956), the screenplay for* 2001: A Space Odyssey *(1968)* Rendezvous with Rama *(1974), and* The Fountains of Paradise *(1979) have won him numerous awards and a secure place in the history of the field. He is also a very talented short story writer, as this and future volumes of this series will show. Virtually every one of his stories and novels is in print in many languages.*

However, in 1946 Arthur C. Clarke was a name known only within British sf fandom. He had yet to publish a story, although he had been reading science fiction since 1927 and had written about the field since the mid-1930s. Fresh out of almost seven years in the Royal Air Force, he was more than ready to burst upon the sf scene.

"Loophole" was his first published story, although it was not the first one he had written.

(It is now widely recognized, to the point of cliché-hood, that the Big Three, in alphabetical order, are Asimov, Clarke and Heinlein. Bob Heinlein and myself appeared on the scene in 1939, and it was not till seven years later that Arthur appeared. By the early 1950s we were the Big Three and after thirty years passed, we were still the Big Three. This has made me increasingly nervous with every year that passes. I keep thinking of a hundred science fiction writers, young, eager, talented, some of them extraordinarily successful, all held back from the fair chance at becoming one of the Big Three by the persistent existence of Bob, Arthur and myself. I once said to Arthur, "Maybe we should abdicate. Surely the united baleful, hate-filled glances from all the other writers will sooner or later undermine our health." But Arthur grinned and shook his head, "No," he said, "I enjoy the situation."—That's Arthur!—I.A.)

From: President
To: Secretary, Council of Scientists.

I have been informed that the inhabitants of Earth have succeeded in releasing atomic energy and have been making experiments with rocket propulsion. This is most serious. Let me have a full report immediately. And make it *brief* this time.

K.K. IV.

From: Secretary, Council of Scientists
To: President.

The facts are as follows. Some months ago our instruments detected intense neutron emission from Earth, but an analysis of radio programs gave no explanation at the time. Three days ago a second emission occurred and soon afterwards all radio transmissions from Earth announced that atomic bombs were in use in the current war. The translators have not completed their interpretation, but it appears that the bombs are of considerable power. Two have so far been used. Some details of their construction have been released, but the elements concerned have not yet been identified. A fuller report will be forwarded as soon as possible. For the moment all that is certain is the inhabitants of Earth *have* liberated atomic power, so far only explosively.

Very little is known concerning rocket research on Earth. Our astronomers have been observing the planet carefully ever since radio emissions were detected a generation ago. It is certain that long-range rockets of some kind are in existence on Earth, for there have been numerous references to them in recent military broadcasts. However, no serious attempt has been made to reach interplanetary space. When the war ends, it is expected that the inhabitants of the planet may carry out research in this direction. We will pay very careful attention to their broadcasts and the astronomical watch will be rigorously enforced.

From what we have inferred of the planet's technology, it should require about twenty years before Earth develops atomic rockets capable of crossing space. In view of this, it would seem that the time has come to set up a base on the Moon, so that a close scrutiny can be kept on such experiments when they commence.

Trescon.

(Added in manuscript.)

The war on Earth has now ended, apparently owing to the intervention of the atomic bomb. This will not affect the above arguments but it may mean that the inhabitants of Earth can devote themselves to pure research again more quickly than expected. Some broadcasts have already pointed out the application of atomic power in rocket propulsion.

T.

From President.
To: Chief of Bureau of Extra-Planetary Security. (C.B.E.P.S.)

You have seen Trescon's minute.

Equip an expedition to the satellite of Earth immediately. It is to keep a close watch on the planet and to report at once if rocket experiments are in progress.

The greatest care must be taken to keep our presence on the Moon a secret. You are personally responsible for this. Report to me at yearly intervals, or more often if necessary.

K.K. IV.

From: President.
To: C.B.E.P.S.
Where is the report on Earth?!!

K.K. IV.

From: C.B.E.P.S.
To: President.
The delay is regretted. It was caused by the breakdown of the ship carrying the report.

There have been no signs of rocket experimenting during the past year, and no reference to it in broadcasts from the planet.

Ranthe.

From: C.B.E.P.S.
To: President.
You will have seen my yearly reports to your respected father on this subject. There have been no developments of interest for the past seven years, but the following message has just been received from our base on the Moon:

Rocket projectile, apparently atomically propelled, left Earth's atmosphere today from Northern land-mass, traveling into space for one quarter diameter of planet before returning under control.

Ranthe.

From: President.
To: Chief of State.
Your comments, please.

K.K. V.

From: Chief of State.
To: President.
This means the end of our traditional policy.

The only hope of security lies in preventing the Terrestrials from making further advances in this direction. From what we know of them, this will require some over-whelming threat.

Since its high gravity makes it impossible to land on the planet, our sphere of action is restricted. The problem was discussed nearly a century ago by Anvar, and I agree with his conclusions. We must act *immediately* along those lines.

F.K.S.

From: President.
To: Secretary of State.

Inform the Council that an emergency meeting is convened for noon tomorrow.

K.K. V.

From: President.
To: C.B.E.P.S.

Twenty battleships should be sufficient to put Anvar's plan into operation. Fortunately there is no need to arm them—yet. Report progress of construction to me weekly.

K.K. V.

From: C.B.E.P.S.
To: President.

Nineteen ships are now completed. The twentieth is still delayed owing to hull failure and will not be ready for at least a month.

Ranthe.

From: President.
To: C.B.E.P.S.

Nineteen will be sufficient. I will check the operational plan with you tomorrow. Is the draft of our broadcast ready yet?

K.K. V.

From: C.B.E.P.S.
To: President.

Draft herewith:

People on Earth!

We, the inhabitants of the planet you call Mars, have for many years observed your experiments towards achieving interplanetary travel. *These experiemnts must cease.* Our study of your race has convinced us that you are not fit to leave your planet in the present state of your civilization. The ships you now see floating above your cities are capable of destroying them utterly, and will do so unless you discontinue your attempts to cross space.

We have set up an observatory on your Moon and can immediately detect any violation of these orders. If you obey them, we will not interfere with you again. Otherwise, one of your cities will be destroyed every time we observe a rocket leaving the Earth's atmosphere.

By order of the President and Council of Mars.

Ranthe.

From: President.
To: C.B.E.P.S.

I approve. The translation can go ahead.

I shall not be sailing with the fleet, after all. You will report to me in detail immediately on your return.

K.K. V.

From: C.B.E.P.S.
To: President.

I have the honor to report the successful completion of our mission. The voyage to Earth was uneventful; radio messages from the planet indicated that we were detected at a considerable distance and great excitement had been arousd before our arrival. The fleet was dispersed according to plan and I broadcast the ultimatum. We left immediately and no hostile weapons were brought to bear against us.

I shall report in detail within two days.

Ranthe.

From: Secretary, Council of Scientists.
To: President.

The psychologists have completed their report, which is attached herewith.

As might be expected, our demands at first infuriated this stubborn and high-spirited race. The shock to their pride must have been considerable, for they believed themselves to be the only intelligent beings in the Universe.

However, within a few weeks there was a rather unexpected change in the tone of their statements. They had begun to realize that we were intercepting all their radio transmissions, and some messages have been broadcast directly to us. They state that they have agreed to ban all rocket experiments, in accordance with our wishes. This is as unexpected as it is welcome. Even if they are trying to deceive us, we are perfectly safe now that we have established the second station just outside the atmosphere. They cannot possibly develop spaceships without our seeing them or detecting their tube radiation.

The watch on Earth will be continued rigorously, as instructed.

Trescon.

From: C.B.E.P.S.
To: President.

Yes, it is quite true that there have been no further rocket experiments in the last ten years. We certainly did not expect Earth to capitulate so easily!

I agree that the existence of this race now constitutes a permanent threat to our civilization and we are making experiments along the lines you suggest. The problem is a difficult one, owing to the great size of the planet. Explosives would be out of the question, and a radioactive poison of some kind appears to offer the greatest hope of success.

Fortunately, we now have an indefinite time in which to complete this research, and I will report regularly.

Ranthe.

End of Document

From: Lieutenant Commander Henry Forbes, Intelligence Branch, Special Space Corps.
To: Professor S. Maxton, Philological Department, University of Oxford.
Route: Transender II (via Schenectady.)

The above papers, with others, were found in the ruins of what is believed to be the capital Martian city. (Mars Grid KL302895.) The frequent use of the ideograph for "Earth" suggests that they may be of special interest and it is hoped that they can be translated. Other papers will be following shortly.

H. Forbes, Lt/Cdr.

(Added in manuscript.)
Dear Max,

Sorry I've had no time to contact you before. I'll be seeing you as soon as I get back to Earth.

Gosh! Mars *is* in a mess! Our co-ordinates were dead accurate and the bombs materialized right over their cities, just as the Mount Wilson boys predicted.

We're sending a lot of stuff back through the two small machines, but until the big transmitter is materialized we're rather restricted, and, of course, none of us can return. So hurry up with it!

I'm glad we can get to work on rockets again. I may be old-fashioned, but being squirted through space at the speed of light doesn't appeal to me!

Yours in haste,

Henry.

THE NIGHTMARE

by Chan Davis (1926-   )

ASTOUNDING SCIENCE FICTION
May

Dr. Chandler Davis is a Professor of Mathematics at a Canadian university who wrote several notable stories in the mid-1940s, including the beautiful "Letter to Ellen" (Astounding, *June 1947), but then only produced an occasional story in the following decades. Most importantly, he is the author of one of the very best stories (inside or outside of science fiction) on bureaucracy, the incredible "Adrift On the Policy Level" which appeared in Fred Pohl's* Star Science Fiction Stories 5 *in 1959. His small output and considerable talent deserve wider recognition.*

In *1945 and 1946 (at least) his mind was very much on Hiroshima and Nagasaki, and he wrote this powerful warning about atomic war.*

(After I got my Ph.D. in 1948, I went to Boston in order to join the faculty of Boston University School of Medicine as an instructor [Officially, I am still on the faculty with the rank of Professor of Biochemistry, but it's been 23 years since I've actually faced a class of medical students].

Naturally, I was very lonely. In those days, before television and the West Coast siphoned off the science fiction brotherhood, New York City was where most science fiction writers were to be found, and I missed the good old gang. It was not long, however, before I met the science fiction people of Boston and one of them was Chan Davis. The very first get-together with Boston people as at his then apartment and I still remember that room with its high ceiling. It looked nothing at all like New York, but Chan was there and he wrote science fiction and that made it home.—I.A.)

Rob Ciccone bent down, picked up the bottle of milk outside the door of his apartment, and started to pick up the paper beside it. When he saw the headline that topped two columns on the left-hand side of the front page, he hesitated. Then he stood up and wiped his forehead.

The morning newspaper is essentially a simple, ordinary, and familiar thing. It's a habit. But it doesn't seem quite so ordinary and familiar when you see your name in black type at the top of page one.

Rob picked up the paper and went back into the flat to read it. With forced deliberation, he slowly sat down in the most relaxing chair available and spread the paper carefully before starting the article. He was worried. As far as he knew there was no reason for him to be on page one. He did not belong there. He had, to be sure, been one of the speakers at the S.N.P. chapter meeting last night, but he had been planning to look for that write-up on page twenty-six or thereabouts. Worse, Rob's job was one of those in which you do not make page one in the New York *Dispatch*, or any other paper, unless it is bad news, and very bad.

He began to read, then the worry gave way to puzzlement. It was the report of the meeting after all, and carried, as he had expected, the byline of his friend Creighton Macomb. It ran:

CICCONE FLAYS CITY'S GEIGER SEARCH POLICY; WARNS PERIL GROWS

> Dr. Robert A. Ciccone, chief of the Bronx Sector Radioactive Search Commission, stated last night that the present system of Geiger-counter search would not be adequate for the prevention of an A-bomb being planted in the New York area. Addressing the Bronx Chapter of the Society of Nuclear Physicists, he said: "No number of successes in preventing the importing of dangerous radioactives can compensate for just one failure, and I feel unable to state positively that failure, and disastrous failure, is impossible."

So far so good, thought Rob. At least they were quoting directly. Of course the sentence quoted was the most outspoken of the whole thing; it read like a much stronger attack on the search program than he had actually dared to make.

But the same thing had been said before by others. Ten years before, when the Geiger search had first been brought up as a counter-proposal to the Compton plan of decentralization, the whole subject had been batted back and forth in the press. Opponents of the search system, himself included, had claimed that New York was a sitting target for an atomic bomb, that no preventive measures could change that fact, and that the only answer to the danger was to scatter New York's industries and commerce over as wide an area as possible. The other party had pooh-poohed this warning, pointing to the U.N.O. Security Council's strict supervision of all the world's piles, and to the greatly improved methods for the detection of radioactives. Finally, the second party had won. And since that time even the most extreme alarmists had been given less and less newspaper space. He had thought his speech would be played down, interpreted as a suggestion that search methods be improved. Instead—this. Why?

He read the remainder of the article hurriedly. It was O.K. Accurately reported, without editorializing. But it didn't answer his question.

He thought of calling Crate Macomb, but looked at his watch and decided he'd have to wait. All through dressing, shaving, and breakfast, he was too preoccupied either to finish the paper or to give any thought to the rather suspicious results of some of the recent searches. Which in itself was unusual, for normally results that were not thoroughly innocuous were enough to take his mind off anything else.

At 8:15 when he was ready to leave for work, he dialed the *Dispatch,* gave an extension number.

"Could I speak to Macomb? That you, Crate?"

"Yeah. Hello, Rob." Macomb sounded ill at ease.

"I . . . er . . . I just called up to congratulate you on making the front page. Congratulate myself, too, of course."

"Congratulate—?" He sounded puzzled.

"That terrific billing I got in the paper this morning. I've got to admit I don't understand it. New editorial policy?"

"Oh, I get it. You've only seen the home edition, not the later editions."

"That's right. What have the later editions got?"

"Well, I'll tell you the whole thing." He dropped his voice. "The City Ed and I have been against this Geiger system right along, and looking for chances to slip through stories slanted against it."

"I thought you gave that up."

"I gave up bucking editorial policy openly, because it wasn't healthy, but I thought I'd take a chance on this story. The City Ed got it past His Nibs without too much trouble, it made the first edition O.K., and we thought the thing would come off. But—"

"Yeah, but. I knew that was coming. What about those later editions?"

"That's the catch, all right. You remember what you told me last night before the meeting? About the aerial radioactivity your boys found over the Bronx yesterday?"

"You didn't let that into print, did you?"

"*I* didn't, no. I know well enough that radioactivity in the air might be either chance air currents from the Oswego pile, or hidden radioactives around the city, and whichever it is I know darm well that telling the people about it right away is the worst thing to do. Even if I had submitted copy on it, I wouldn't have expected it to get past the editor. But some cub reporter got the dope from the man who took the aerial tests, and didn't know any better than to submit it."

"And they ran it."

"And they ran it, yes." Crate paused, and said slowly: "They ran it in the same article with a rewritten version of what you read in the first edition."

"I can imagine . . . His Nibs couldn't recall the edition that featured my statement, so he set out to discredit me."

"That's it. It could be much worse." Crate's tone of voice

indicated what he meant. He meant, "Probably it *will* be much worse."

Rob stopped to let the implications sink in. Finally, "Has the news started a panic in the Bronx? The news of the tests, I mean."

"Not yet. Look, Rob. His Nibs doesn't know I was responsible for the slant in the original offense this morning; he's blaming it on the City Ed. He doesn't know I know you personally, either. He does know I graduated in nuclear physics. So he's assigning me to—write a feature on you. Not a build-up."

"*Whew*— So?"

"So I'll have to do the best I can. So I'd appreciate it if I could see you some time soon and talk the whole thing over. I can tell you more then."

That certainly seemed to be in order, to put it mildly. Rob named a cafeteria near the *Dispatch* Building, promised to be right down, and rang off.

On his way to the subway station he picked ap a *Dispatch*. He was still on the front page, and, as Crate had indicated, the treatment of him was rather different. He had not merely addressed the Society of Nuclear Physicists; in this edition he had done much more. He had failed his trust as Sector Search Commissioner. The high aerial radioactivity indicated that an A-bomb was being assembled somewhere in his sector, although his search groups had failed to detect the importing of the bomb materials. It was hinted that the reason he had stressed, in his speech, the impossibility of adequate searches, was to cover up his own incompetence when news of his failure broke.

The slur, he reflected, would probably not hurt him much. His job was not political, and if he were incompetent no amount of fast talking would help him. Conversely, the press couldn't hurt him, outside of discrediting his statement. Still, you had to be carcful not to underestimate the power of the press.

The other angle was much more important. Suppose the paper's first charge were right. Suppose that yesterday's test results had been more than chance, and that for some reason, maybe for the purpose of building a bomb, radioactives really had been smuggled into his sector. He wouldn't try to guess who might be doing it; he didn't know politics. But the thing was possible. Well?

Before meeting Crate, he slipped into a phone booth and held a conversation—consisting chiefly of code phrases—with the Bronx Sector headquarters. When it was done he hurried into the cafeteria and spotted Macomb. He asked abruptly, "Your car in town today?"

"Yes, it is."

"The usual parking lot?"

"Yeah."

"Good. We'd better go uptown right away." Macomb came without question.

"I just phoned Charlie. They're still getting the same results, a little bit stronger, and consistent. The wind's changed to east, and the meteorologist says if the readings keep coming this way another hour there's no chance that it's a false alarm. They really should have got in touch with me earlier, but as it is I'll have to get there as quickly as I can."

"This takes precedence over everything else, all right."

"It takes precedence over just about anything in the whole city, if it's not a false alarm. Anyhow," he added as they climbed into the car, "you're not skipping out on your assignment. If you're going to succeed in getting a story on my incompetence, here's your chance, and I certainly hope I disappoint you."

They cut west toward Riverside Drive, Macomb at the wheel. When they were on the Drive, Ciccone asked suddenly, "Who runs the *Dispatch*, anyway?"

"The Ed does a pretty fair job."

"Yes, but . . . you told me once the Ed takes orders from somebody."

The other laughed. "Things aren't as simple as that in the newspaper racket. Nobody gives orders. But if any one man determines the policies of the paper, I guess it's Ellsworth Bates."

Ellsworth Bates. Ciccone ran over in his mind what he knew of the man. Bates was not, to the public, a prominent name. On the society page it was inconspicuous. In political news the name seldom appeared. Even in business news it ordinarily occurred only in listings of corporation boards. Yet apparently behind the scenes this Bates was a power; Macomb certainly should know.

"I was thinking," Rob went on. "Suppose for a minute a bomb is being assembled, and suppose Bates is connected with it. Wouldn't that explain what happened this morning?"

"Why—"

"First, he may succeed in confusing our sector organization by slinging mud at me. Second, he may confuse the whole borough by starting a panic. Third, he would surely jump on anything that might talk the public into decentralization; he'd want the city to remain a good, highly localized target. The decentralization issue was what started all this, remember."

"Hm-m-m. Sounds plausible at first, but—forget it. Not a chance of it. Nobody with Bates' financial interests in the city is going to try to destroy it, and that rules out not only Bates but anyone else with the power to high-pressure into print a slam against you. Besides—this bomb scare might start a panic among the populace, but on the other hand it puts the squeeze on the Search Commission, making sure they'll act as quickly and as efficiently as they can. No, forget it."

"Still, for whatever reason, Bates is probably back of His Nibs' policy."

"It'd be a good guess, all right."

"And why," Rob said, half to himself, "does he go to such lengths to slap down anybody who speaks out for decentralization?"

They sped north along the Drive. Ahead of them was the Highway Search Station, where extrasensitive detectors would scan them, and, in case they revealed radioactivity, would operate relays, causing the car to be photographed and an alarm bell to be rung. Ciccone had been caught more than once; the detectors were so sensitive that small amounts of natural uranium adhering to his clothes and shoes after lab work could sometimes actuate them. This time they got past without the Search Commission's police giving chase.

They were now in the Bronx Sector. "Where to?" asked Crate.

"Just a minute. If you'll get off the Drive and stop at the next drugstore, I'll give Charlie another ring."

"Use my radiophone if you want."

"We avoid 'em. Easier to intercept them than it is to tap ordinary phone wires."

"O,K." Macomb acceded to Rob's request.

Another coded phone conversation and Ciccone returned to the car, to give a few brief directions. "We're going to look over Import Station Three," he explained. "There are two ways we might track this thing down. The first is to localize the source of the active gases by testing more air samples at a lower altitude. They're going ahead with that, and there's not much I can do to help. The second, assuming that bomb materials are still being shipped in, is to check the import stations through which all trucking passes."

"You sound pretty certain that it is a bomb."

"Without having any idea who would want to build one here and now, I'd say the probability was about twenty-five percent and growing all the time."

Unconsciously, Macomb gave the car another ten miles an hour's worth of gas.

Traffic was light, and they made good time to the import station. As they entered the vast, warehouselike building, Rob said: "I thought this'd be the station to inspect because those aerial tests seem to localize the thing between ten and fifty blocks northwest of here. Normally I wouldn't suspect this station of having a leak; they have the best equipment of any. They even make chemical analyses of samples of any cadmium that passes through."

"Cadmium? Why?"

"It's one way you might shield U-235 from the radiation detectors. Alloy it with plenty of cadmium and no neutrons get out. Just one of the dodges we have to be prepared for."

Inside the building, three lines of trucks were being sent slowly through what resembled roughly an assembly line. First the walls of the truck would be tested to insure that they were not radiation-absorbent, then a few of the crates, chosen at random, would be broken open and inspected in the same way. Following this, the truck would be driven slowly down a long double line of confusingly different instruments, and would wait until it had been given the green light by the operators of all the instruments before it proceeded into the Sector. By this time the next truck would have finished its preliminary inspection and would be ready to roll through.

The most important of the detectors were modifications of the familiar Geiger-Mueller counter. An alpha particle, proton, or other emission would ionize the gas between two charged plates, allowing discharge. The discharges would be stored on a condenser, which in turn discharged through a glow tube if the counter operated more than a certain number of times in a given interval.

Ciccone and Macomb stood at one corner of the floor watching the procedure, Ciccone said: "It's not as effective as you might think. The stuff might be brought through here by packing it in the middle boxes of a big truckload, where the outside boxes would shield it. Those guys don't dig down and get at the inside often enough."

"I should think this'd be one job where they'd be more than willing to do a little extra work just to make sure."

"No, people aren't that way. It's a lot of work to half-unload one of those trucks. This is just a job to most of the men, no matter how hard we try to make it something more; it's just their job, and they make it as easy for themselves as they can.

"Today they're being pretty thorough, though; when I called Charlie I told him to needle the boys up a bit."

"So I see." A large Diesel crane was being used in one of the assembly lines to remove the contents of one truck for individual testing. Several men were clustered around with hand-test sets. In a few minutes Rob went over, motioning Crate to accompany him.

"One thing," he whispered on the way, "whatever you see, don't act more than normally suspicious. You can't forget the possibility that the truck driver, or even one of our men, might be an agent. Hello, Sam. What you got here?"

"Radium dial watches. Darn things scare the pants off us every time. Compared to the little tiny bloops we get on our meters from most of this stuff, they look like Hiroshima."

"Been getting many?"

"Yeah, a good few."

"I hope you check the inside boxes pretty often to make sure the watches' emissions aren't masking something else underneath."

"Yeah, we've doing that."

"Well." Rob looked down at the one crate out of the truckload which contained the watches. It had been opened, and several of the carefully packed boxes removed. An idea struck him, and he mentally noted the address on the crate, while apparently examining the watches. The watches were a standard American make.

"Well, keep up the good work, Sam," he said casually. "Oh, Sam. Have you seen the *Dispatch* this morning?"

"No, why?"

"Never mind." After watching a few more trucks pass uneventfully by, he left, accompanied by Macomb.

"Anson Mercantile Company," he said pensively as they climbed back into the car; "no street or number given. As I remember, it's about ten blocks west and four north. Suppose you let me drive, I think I can find it. If I have to, I'll ask a cop, but I didn't want to ask in there."

He did not have to ask a cop. At Anson's, the two of them looked enough like retailers to get into a salesman's office without delay. Rob interrupted the salesman's commercial cordiality by showing an F.B.I. badge, then asked without explanation, "Who's buying up that shipment of watches that's coming in?"

"Why—let's see. I don't believe they're all ordered yet." He showed no inclination to continue.

"Who buys watches from you?" Rob prompted.

"Well—" The man listed several jewelry and department stores. "Those are the principal ones."

This was not going to be quite as simple as Rob had hoped. "Have any of them specified any individual shipments, rather than just naming brands?"

"I wouldn't know. I don't have anything to do with—"

"I think you know."

"What is this about, anyway?"

Rob debated whether to fib or to bully the man with his F.B.I. badge; he decided on the former course. "There's been some highjacking of watches, and we're trying to track it down." It didn't sound at all plausible, but the man, though baffled, was apparently satisfied.

"Well, now that you mention it," he admitted," Grelner's has specified shipments several times." He stopped, tentatively.

"That's all," said Ciccone, and he and Macomb left, trying to look like G-men.

"Well," commented Rob, "I guess we can assume for now that he was telling the truth."

"Might I ask you something, sir?"

'Ask me what?"

"The same thing that fellow in there asked you: what the heck is this all about?"

Rob laughed. "I'm sorry. Those watches looked pretty innocent, didn't they, to be causing all this? But we have to follow up the implausible leads, because all the plausible ones get investigated at the import station. This one is 'highly nontrivial,' as my math prof used to say.

"Look. We let radium dial watches through the import station because no one could possibly extract the fissionable substances from the phosphorescent paint on those things without revealing themselves—even if they could get enough into the city that way. But there's another possibility. What if, instead of natural uranium, you were to use Pu-239, ordinary plutonium, in your phosphorescent paint? It's an alpha-emitter with long half-life, like common U-238; our instruments couldn't tell the difference. You'd have the job of purifying after you got the stuff in, and you'd have to get in an awful lot. It's just possible, just barely. And all the probable things, as I say, are checked."

"But it'd take so long to accumulate enough plutonium for a bomb. They couldn't be anywhere finished now, could they?"

"Sure could. They could have been accumulating the stuff for years without giving themselves away. It wouldn't be until they started purifying that Sneezy—the aerial radioactivity detector—would show anything. That's happened. We'd better follow up on Grelner's, and if it's not that, we'll start looking around again. Grelner's did, after all, ask for particular shipments—those shipments, maybe, that they knew were loaded with plutonium. They wouldn't buy up the whole shipment, because that would seem peculiar to the wholesalers, and the Pu-239 watches are, I suppose, perfectly usable as such. They wouldn't ship the watches in direct to the store, because it's not usual business practice.

"Everything fits. Which in itself proves nothing. Still, we can't afford not to check it. I don't think I can get much further with this investigating, I'd better order a search right now." They had been walking toward the store; now Rob started once more for a phone. "You call police, give my name and the code word 'antipasto,' and say 'Grelner's Department Store.' I'll be calling the import station for some detectors."

Luckily Schmidt's Drugstore had two empty phone booths. Nobody looked up as they walked in and slipped into the booths.

Ciccone, as he dialed his number, had a sudden vision. A pillar of multi-colored smoke rising from the city, erasing the Bronx and Manhattan down to Central Park, shattering windows in Nyack, lighting up the Albany sky. A nightmare, a familiar and a very real nightmare, an accepted part of modern life, something you couldn't get away from; and it seemed more immediate than ever right now. Trying to pretend it was just fancy, he looked out of the booth at the girl wiping off the drugstore counter, the middle-aged woman buying toothbrushes, the suspendered loafer thumbing through the magazines. He thought the commonplaceness of Schmidt's Drugstore might be reassuring; but it didn't help.

"Import Station Three."

"This is Ciccone. Could I speak to Sam?"

Again he waited. The nightmare was still there, and somewhere, quite likely just a few blocks from where he was now, were the few ounces of metal that might be the nightmare.

"Hello. Hello, Sam. Send down—*antipasto*—send down all your mobiles, except for one full battery to be left at the station. Grelner's Department Store. Know where it is?"

"Sure do. Right down." Sam hung up before Rob had a chance to tell him to hurry. He knew that an order like that, in a situation like that, just plain meant "hurry", in capital letters.

Hurry. It might already be too late, or they might have months to spare, or there might be no danger at all. Yet the chance was always there that one minute's delay might make all the difference.

Always that chance, he thought as he and Macomb walked up the innocent-looking street toward where the police and the search men would soon arrive. The chance that the time he had wasted at the meeting last night, and the hour he had wasted this morning because of that peculiar newspaper episode, might themselves have been fatal.

"And yet," He said aloud, "assuming we get to this bomb in time—always assuming that—this man Ellsworth Bates, and whoever else he represents, may be more important than any one bomb. No number of successes can compensate for one failure—"

Crate interrupted him. "The police have started arriving!"

Ciccone knew the routine of the search; he'd been largely responsible for preparing police and search men alike for this eventuality. He knew perfectly well what had to be done, and he also knew that, since the organization was trained to function without him, there was little he could do besides helping with the details.

First a cordon had to be thrown around the block in as short a time as possible after giving the alarm. Plutonium, enough of it to make a bomb, could be taken from the block in a two-passenger coupé, or in the pockets of a few men willing to subject themselves to radioactive poisoning by carrying it adequately shielded. So the police had to make sure that, for the present, everybody inside the cordon stayed inside.

The search men arrived not long after the police: a fleet of bizarre-looking, specially-built trucks, roaring through the city with sirens screaming, then pulling up in a group at one side of the block. The mobile search units made up a respectable detection laboratory in themselves. They carried, in addition to the larger, more sensitive instruments, enough simple hand-test sets to arm a large force of searchers. Some of these were distributed quickly to the policemen comprising the cordon, and the first part of the search began.

A bluecoat would beckon to one of the bewildered passersby who had been caught in the cordon, and then, while a second policeman covered him, would search the man. This consisted in passing two test sets, one held in either hand, over all parts of his body; reading them and pressing a button to recharge the electroscopes and readjust the counters' potential; and frisking him in the standard manner. He would then be allowed—ordered, rather—to leave the block. In this way the sidewalks were rapidly cleared.

Macomb left Rob's side, pad and pencil in hand, to go to where a short, well-dressed man of about sixty was being searched by two bored policemen. Rob dismissed Macomb with the mental comment, "Good story for him."

Himself, he wanted to help with the big job: going through the buildings on the block, one by one, story by story, with every type of instrument from Geiger counter to uranium neutron-detector. It was a big job, it would take alot of men a long time, and he knew they could use his help.

The detectors were already being unloaded from the trucks. Sam was organizing a group of about twenty search men to begin on the row of five-and six-story apartments that made up one side of the block.

"Say, Sam," began Rob.

"Oh, there you are," said Sam.

"I didn't see you; I was beginning to think that call was a fake. Have a counter."

"Say, Sam, why don't you start at the store itself?"

"The Sneezies are registering like hell right here—like all hell." He gave a few more instructions and the men scattered into the buildings.

Ciccone found it almost a relief to know that the source of

the radio-activity had been located fairly closely. Now, all the uncertainties involved in his reasoning were resolved. It might have been that Grelner's, like the wholesaler's, was just an intermediate stage in the smuggling; it might have been that the whole lead was a false one. But it wasn't.

With Sam and one other, he started down the basement steps of the first apartment house, to begin the search at the bottom. One of the tenants was coming down from the second story and looked with amazed curiosity at their test sets and drawn guns. Sam waved him out onto the street, and the three of them continued on down.

But the tedious and dangerous hunt which they had anticipated was interrupted. Suddenly, a booming voice filled the air. Rob looked around for a loudspeaker, but seeing none, concentrated on the words.

"You're are looking," the voice said, with a slight foreign intonation, "for the bomb which is being assembled here. I would warn that we have a quantity of plutonium in excess of the critical mass. If any more men enter this block of buildings, or if anyone enters this particular building, then the bomb, which is in readiness, will be exploded."

Rob, followed by the others, ran out into the street. He didn't know why, but he felt an almost claustrophobic oppression on the apartment stairway. As if getting out of the building would do any good were an A-bomb to go off!

The voice from the hidden loudspeakers continued, to a petrified audience of policemen and search men: "We will leave our laboratory, which is that building formerly used as a warehouse by the Grelner's Store, by helicopter. You must not attempt to intercept us—"

Rob was standing beside the police captain, looking up at the expressionless row of apartment houses. The decision, he realized, was up to him. Was this a bluff, and dare they call it?

"—will, in any case, be detonated by radio in two weeks. This will give you time to largely clear the area, and the bomb will still accomplish our purpose of disruption. You must not interfere, and you must prepare for the explosion in exactly two weeks' time." A pause, then, "You are looking for the bomb which is being assembled here. I would warn—"

It was a record, and it was repeating. The whole message was in Ciccone's hands now; it was up to him. He looked nervously around him. The police captain, Macomb, and the short, well-dressed old man to whom Macomb had gone earlier—Ciccone hardly saw them.

"—enters this particular building, then the bomb, which is in readiness, will be exploded. We will leave our laboratory—"

"It's a bluff," said Ciccone, and his voice sounded weak as death. "Enter the building."

The captain didn't move, but stared straight ahead, his jaw knotted.

"It's a bluff. If they were going to set off an A-bomb, they wouldn't give us the opportunity to clear the people out of the city, even those few people we could get out in two weeks. They'd try for maximum destruction.

"Either they're not ready, or they are and we've nothing left to lose. Enter the building."

"They're not ready," said a voice behind Rob. He turned; it was Macomb's companion. "Any group which would send agents to destroy New York, would plan that the agents also be destroyed. Thus any chance would be eliminated of this country's learning the identity of the group, and they might be spared retaliation. Only if the bomb could not be detonated would such a bluff as this be attempted, on the chance that a copter might escape."

Rob stared at the unknown in dumb amazement. The confidence and precision with which he had spoken were—inhuman.

But for the moment he ignored this remarkable interruption and turned once more to the captain. The latter's face had a look almost of resignation as he finally gave the necessary orders to about twenty of the policemen who lined the sidewalk. They hesitated; they, too, could hear that voice over the loudspeaker. "—will still accomplish our purpose of disruption. You must not interfere, and you must prepare for the explosion—"

Somehow when the first of the policemen moved to obey, the others followed. Slowly they advanced toward a gap between two buildings, through which they could reach the spot the voice had named as the laboratory site.

"—that we have a quantity of plutonium in excess of the critical mass. If any more men enter this block of buildings—"

They advanced, and one by one disappeared through the gap. Ciccone waited. Maybe the men inside, whoever they were, had not observed the violation of their conditions. Yet.

Except for the loudspeaker, the whole street was in intolerable silence, as everyone—waited. Finally, as one, they relaxed and breathed more easily. It was not that they were absolutely certain yet that no bomb would go off, but simply that the tension could not be borne any longer.

The police captain turned to his car radio.

"In case those boys do get their helicopter off that roof," he said, "I'm going to call for some of our planes to intercept them."

Rob made a mental note to have planes added to the search plan in the future, and nodded assent.

"No," Macomb's companion interjected. "It was a bluff, but you must allow them to escape."

Rob's previous amazement was redoubled. He could find no answer except to blurt, "Who are you, anyway?"

"Ellsworth Bates."

Before Ciccone could reply, all eyes were turned upward by a shout from one of the search men standing nearby. A helicopter was hovering above the apartment buildings, drifting slightly in the wind, and rising.

The captain turned again to his radio, but was halted by the urgency in Bates' voice as he repeated: "No, they must escape. If they are captured, it will be discovered whom they represent, and this country will certainly open fire in retaliation. Every trace of their identity must be lost if there's going to be any chance of peace. Don't you see? It doesn't matter that they are the aggressors, that we, in a sense, would be in the right were we to fight them—whoever they are. The only thing we must consider is the impossibility of our fighting any war with anybody, now. Unfortunately, it's a thing our government, and our people, will probably not consider if these men are identified.

"The whole thing can be reported to the Security Council. They can investigate—secretly. The United States must not investigate."

He paused. "Sabotage bomb attack is the only method of atomic warfare that can be used as long as the Security Council controls the world's atomic power. Fissionable elements are rigidly controlled, they're hard to get, no one can get enough of them away from the Security Council's jurisdiction to arm a fleet of rockets. And a fleet is what you'd need to stand a chance of getting through a modern radar-rocket defense screen. Sabotage bomb attack is the only thing left.

"Until open warfare breaks out. Then, one or both of the warring nations defy the Security Council, grab all the fissionable elements they can, and what have you? Chaos. Ruin. If you like to put it that way, the end of civilization. Once the Security Council's power is broken and the rocket-atomic war starts, we're lost, that's all.

"Mr. Ciccone, I realize you're in charge here, and I'm unable to force your decision. Nevertheless, you've *got* to let that copter get away—delay your pursuit, say, ten minutes, and don't make it seem deliberate. More than that, you've got to destroy the evidence in that building—again accidentally—and, if possible, destroy so much that it can't be proved a bomb was ever in the process of construction."

He stopped. Rob looked up to where the helicopter was dwindling into the distance. "Mr. Bates, if there has been one bomb, there can be another, maybe from the same source."

"No number of successes can make up for one failure. Precisely. But we wouldn't avert that possible failure by tracing down this bomb attempt. We'd precipitate it.

"Granted, we'd find the culprit's identity. But after the cities of this and every other country had been destroyed, it'd be small consolation to know who started the thing."

Then something happened inside Rob, and the nightmare was on him again. The light too bright to be seen, the sound too loud to be heard, the horror too great for any man to know. He sighed, and spoke to the captain:

"You heard what he said?"

"Yes."

"Do what he said about the helicopter. The rest of it, forget. I mean that—forget it."

Ciccone sat with Macomb and Bates in the front room of Crate's Greenwich Village flat, recounting the steps he had taken to follow Bates' plan. "It may work out," he said. "No one's been all the way inside the lab yet, except Sam and me. The lab will be accidentally destroyed tonight, after the plutonium has been removed and Sam has seen plenty of things which were not there at all. And, Mr. Bates, if your spell over the newspapers is as great as Macomb says it is, they may all print our version of the story." He indicated a *Dispatch* extra in his hand. "The radioactives were brought in by private experimenters dodging the U.N.O.; they tried the bomb bluff in order to escape, and they then eluded police pursuers. No matter how much perjuring we do it's a weak story."

"No," replied Bates, "with a few loopholes patched up, it'll go. If we're long on theorizing and minimize the actual faking; we'll get out result without much risk. And don't worry about the perjury; this is one end that justifies any means."

There was a silence while Ciccone gathered his courage. Bates was no longer the evil genius he had seemed earlier in the day; nevertheless courage was required to begin, "So now we have one success—we've postponed the fatal failure a little further."

Bates smiled. "Unless I miss my guess, you're getting back to decentralization."

Macomb took up the theme. "Yes," he said, "that problem's still there. This bomb's been found, this crisis may soon be over; but there'll be others. We'll never have even relative safety until everything is so uniformly distributed that no one bomb can destroy more than one of the old block-busters could now."

"I'll try to explain the thing to you," Bates began slowly. "You're right, that would be the only way to safety. You're also right in thinking that I've been suppressing the movement toward decentralization. Now wait a minute; please don't interrupt. I know I seem to be contradicting myself, but let me start from the beginning.

"Ten years ago several of the smaller European nations, which had not been getting much information on nuclear physics from the larger nations, independently developed working chain-reactions. Tension mounted, and a large-scale atomic war might have resulted had not the world been too exhausted from the recent World War II. As it was, everybody got such a bad case of the jitters that the affair was halted before the A-bomb was used.

"This world-wide case of the jitters had other effects, you remember. The Security Council was quickly given supervision over all piles, plus sizable military and intelligence forces. Second, the movement for decentralization was started."

"And stopped," put in Ciccone.

"Yes. To what, if I may ask, did you ascribe its failure?"

"Lack of vision on the part of—well, leaders of industry. People like you could have swung it."

"No. The people whom you call leaders of industry saw

everything you saw in the situation, and they did try to swing it. The thing is, when they got right down to cases they saw something you missed; to be specific, they saw that decentralization was impossible."

"Impossible?"

"Because of a factor which the scientist finds it easy to ignore: the terrific inertia of our civilization. Here's the way it works. New York businessmen see that the world would be a much safer place if all business were to disperse away from the big metropolitan centers. They think it would be fine if this were to be done. But they can't do it themselves if, say, Prague businessmen are going to remain concentrated, because it'd be a big financial blow to New York to stand the expense of moving and to give up their ready access to transportation. They wouldn't be able to compete with Prague, or London, or Calcutta, as the case might be—whatever city didn't go along. Unless everybody will take the step, nobody will take it. It has to be world-wide, and ten years ago the world wasn't unified enough.

"You remember the 1929 crash? A little before your time, I guess. It was the same thing. The economists saw it coming several years ahead, but no one could duck out of the wave of overinvestment, because if they did, their competitors would not, and would continue to make profits from the boom. Everyone had to keep riding the wave as long as possible, even though they knew such a policy was just insuring that the crash, when it came, would be really serious. There you are: inertia. Our overgrown civilization starts going in one direction, and it's just too much for individuals to stop.

"So decentralization was impossible ten years ago. With different conditions and with a stronger political movement, it might have gone; but it didn't. We took what seemed like the next best plan, radar screens plus search programs, and so far it's worked.

"Today, gradual decentralization has progressed to some extent, thanks to improved transportation and individuals' mistrust of cities. A new movement for the abrupt sort of decentralization would have some chance—less inertia now to overcome; but if it succeeded it would be very dangerous.

"In the last ten years, many things have changed. Reconstruction of the destruction of World War II is to all intents and purposes finished; capital is freed and looking for new investment opportunities; manufactured goods are looking around for markets. It's the type of situation where motives for aggression may be present, and everyone's jittery again. The jitters are not nearly so widespread as they were before, or even as they were after Hiroshima and Nagasaki, but they're having a much worse effect, and they're building up. Certain groups in several different countries are beginning to think seriously of atomic warfare, of beating the other guy to the punch and grabbing whatever's left when the smoke clears. Many of those who aren't considering it, are suspecting others. And everybody has to keep his defenses up.

Now. What *are* our defenses? Let me list them again: radar screens, searches, and Security Council supervision of fissionable elements. Well, you tell me, Mr. Ciccone—what would happen to the effectiveness of your search program if New York were to begin tomorrow to move en masse to the Mohawk Valley?"

"Yes, I see what you mean. We'd have a hard time keeping up even a pretense."

"You certainly would. New York could be blasted before it had got well started moving. Another thing: atomic power plants, too, are centralized, to simplify the Security Council's job of control, so no doubt you'd ask that they be included in the program of dispersal. But think of the confusion involved in moving billions of dollars' worth of industrial plant. How could a merely human Security Council prevent the smuggling out, somewhere, of a few hundred pounds of U-235 or Pu-239?

"No, the pressure's on, and we have to stick by the choice we made.

"Our civilization: a great, big, overgrown truck going much too fast. Suddenly the road became dangerously narrow, and slippery besides, but the truck was too big and it was going too fast. It couldn't stop. Now we have only a few inches to spare on either side of our wheels, but we still can't do what you suggest, stop, get out, and look for a detour. No, we've chosen our road and we've got to stick to it.

"Not much seems to be changed, at first glance—the truck's engine still runs smoothly—the steering gear still responds—even the driver isn't in such bad shape. Yet come tomorrow, it may all be over. If we don't steer straight, it certainly will be.

"Makes quite a picture. Our magnificent, overgrown, bungling civilization going on its own magnificent and senseless way because it is so big that nothing can stop it, so big that it can't even stop itself."

Bates stopped speaking, but neither Ciccone nor Macomb answered. There was no answer. Ten years ago, there might perhaps have been, but not now.

RESCUE PARTY

by Arthur C. Clarke

ASTOUNDING SCIENCE FICTION
May

One month after his debut with "Loophole" Arthur C. Clarke published what most observers consider to be one of his finest stories. "Rescue Party" is justly famous, but should not obscure the fact that it is not his best, and that he continued to grow and develop steadily as a writer and as a craftsman. This story is more than just a fine tale. It is perhaps the ultimate John W. Campbell, Jr. story, especially in its view of our species' status in the universe, and of our ultimate destiny.

However, it should be pointed out that the story was written for a British sf magazine that had difficulty in getting started, so ASTOUNDING *was not the market for which it was originally intended.*

(Marty, in referring to this story as an "ultimate John W. Campbell, Jr. story," knew whereof he spoke. In my association with John, I early learned that there was no chance in selling him a story in which the human race lost. No matter what the odds against them in point of view of numbers or technological superiority, human beings had to win.

I honestly think it was because to John this was a larger version of the battle of himself against the world, with himself sure to win.

John loved stories that glorified Homo victor, *and he manged to find some very good examples of the genus. Clarke supplied one of the best, as was not surprising. (I myself chickened out of the task, and invented the all-human Galazy in order to sell stories to John without having to give humanity victories I didn't feel we deserved—I.A.)*

Who was to blame? For three days Alveron's thoughts had come back to that question, and still he had found no answer. A creature of a less civilized or a less sensitive race would never have let it torture his mind, and would have satisfied himself with the assurance that no one could be responsible for the working of fate. But Alveron and his kind had been lords of the Universe since the dawn of history, since that far distant age when the Time Barrier had been folded round the cosmos by the unknown powers that lay beyond the Beginning. To them had been given all knowledge—and with infinite knowledge went infinite responsibility. If there were mistakes and errors in the administration of the galaxy, the fault lay on the heads of Alveron and his people. And this was no mere mistake: it was one of the greatest tragedies in history.

The crew still knew nothing. Even Rugon, his closest friend and the ship's deputy captain, had been told only part of the truth. But now the doomed worlds lay less than a billion miles ahead. In a few hours, they would be landing on the third planet.

Once again Alveron read the message from Base; then, with a flick of a tentacle that no human eye could have followed, he pressed the "General Attention" button. Throughout the mile-long cylinder that was the Galactic Survey Ship S9000, creatures of many races laid down their work to listen to the words of their captain.

"I know you have all been wondering," began Alveron, "why we were ordered to abandon our survey and to proceed at such an acceleration to this region of space. Some of you may realize what this acceleration means. Our ship in on its last voyage: the generators have already been running for sixty hours at Ultimate Overload. We will be very lucky if we return to Base under our own power.

"We are approaching a sun which is about to become a Nova. Detonation will occur in seven hours, with an uncertainty of one hour, leaving us a maximum of only four hours for exploration. There are ten planets in the system about to be destroyed—and there is a civilization on the third. That fact was discovered only a few days ago. It is our tragic mission to contact that doomed race and if possible to save some of its members. I know that there is little we can do in so short a time with this single ship. No other machine can possibly reach the system before detonation occurs."

There was a long pause during which there could have been no sound or movement in the whole of the mighty ship as it sped silently toward the worlds ahead. Alveron knew what his companions were thinking and he tried to answer their unspoken questions.

"You will wonder how such a disaster, the greatest of which we have any record, has been allowed to occur. On one point I can reassure you. The fault does not lie with the Survey.

"As you know, with our present fleet of under twelve thousand ships, it is possible to re-examine each of the eight thousand million solar systems in the Galaxy at intervals of about a million years. Most worlds change very little in so short a time as that.

"Less than four hundred thousand years ago, the survey ship S5060 examined the planets of the system we are approaching. It found intelligence on none of them, though the third planet was teeming with animal life and two other worlds had once been inhabited. The usual report was submitted and the system is due for its next examination in six hundred thousand years.

"It now appears that in the incredibly short period since the last survey, intelligent life has appeared in the system. The first intimation of this occurred when unknown radio signals were detected on the planet Kulath in the system X29.35, Y34.76, Z27.93. Bearings were taken on them; they were coming from the system ahead.

"Kulath is two hundred light-years from here, so those radio waves had been on their way for two centuries. Thus for at least that period of time a civilization has existed on one of these worlds—a civilization that can generate electromagnetic waves and all that that implies.

"An immediate telescopic examination of the system was made and it was then found that the sun was in the unstable pre-nova stage. Detonation might occur at any moment, and indeed might have done so while the light waves were on their way to Kulath.

"There was a slight delay while the supervelocity scanners of Kulath II were focused onto the system. They showed that the explosion had not yet occurred but was only a few hours away. If Kulath had been a fraction of a light-year farther from this sun, we should never have known of its civilization until it had ceased to exist.

"The Administrator of Kulath contacted Sector Base immediately, and I was ordered to proceed to the system at once. Our object is to save what members we can of the doomed race, if indeed there are any left. But we have assumed that a civilization possessing radio could have protected itself against any rise of temperature that may have already occurred.

"This ship and the two tenders will each explore a section of the planet. Commander Torkalee will take Number One, Commander Orostron Number Two. They will have just under four hours in which to explore this world. At the end of that time, they must be back in the ship. It will be leaving then, with or without them. I will give the two commanders detailed instructions in the control room immediately.

"That is all. We enter atmosphere in two hours."

On the world once known as Earth the fires were dying out: there was nothing left to burn. The great forests that had swept across the planet like a tidal wave with the passing of the cities were now no more than glowing charcoal and the smoke of their funeral pyres still stained the sky. But the last hours were still to come, for the surface rocks had not yet begun to flow. The continents were dimly visible through the haze, but their outlines meant nothing to the watchers in the approaching ship. The charts they possessed were out of date by a dozen Ice Ages and more deluges than one.

The S9000 had driven past Jupiter and seen at once that no life could exist in those half-gaseous oceans of compressed hydrocarbons, now erupting furiously under the sun's abnormal heat. Mars and the outer planets they had missed, and Alveron realized that the worlds nearer the sun than Earth would be already melting. It was more than likely, he thought sadly, that the tragedy of this unknown race was already finished. Deep in his heart, he thought it might be better so. The ship could only have carried a few hundred survivors, and the problem of selection had been haunting his mind.

Rugon, Chief of Communications and Deputy Captain, came into the control room. For the last hour he had been striving to detect radiation from Earth, but in vain.

"We're too late," he announced gloomily. "I've monitored the whole spectrum and the ether's dead except for our own stations and some two-hundred-year-old programs from Kulath. Nothing in this system is radiating anymore."

He moved toward the giant vision screen with a graceful flowing motion that no mere biped could ever hope to imitate. Alveron said nothing; he had been expecting this news.

One entire wall of the control room was taken up by the screen, a great black rectangle that gave an impression of almost infinite depth. Three of Rugon's slender control tentacles, useless for heavy work but incredibly swift at all manipulation, flickered over the selector dials and the screen lit up with a thousand points of light. The star field flowed swiftly past as Rugon adjusted the controls, bringing the projector to bear upon the sun itself.

No man of Earth would have recognized the monstrous shape that filled the screen. The sun's light was white no longer: great violet-blue clouds covered half its surface and from them long streamers of flame were erupting into space. At one point an enormous prominence had reared itself out of the photosphere, far out even into the flickering veils of the corona. It was as though a tree of fire had taken root in the surface of the sun—a tree that stood half a million miles high and whose branches were rivers of flame sweeping through space at hundreds of miles a second.

"I suppose," said Rugon presently, "that you are quite satisfied about the astronomers' calculatoins. After all—"

"Oh, we're perfectly safe," said Alveron confidently. "I've spoken to Kulath Observatory and they have been making some additional checks through our own instruments. That uncertainty of an hour includes a private safety margin which they won't tell me in case I feel tempted to stay any longer."

He glanced at the instrument board.

"The pilot should have brought us to the atmosphere now. Switch the screen back to the planet, please. Ah, there they go!"

There was a sudden tremor underfoot and a raucous clanging of alarms, instantly stilled. Across the vision screen two slim projectiles dived toward the looming mass of Earth. For a few miles they traveled together, then they separated, one vanishing abruptly as it entered the shadow of the planet.

Slowly the huge mother ship, with its thousand times greater mass, descended after them into the raging storms that already were tearing down the deserted cities of Man.

It was night in the hemisphere over which Orostron drove his tiny command. Like Torkalee, his mission was to photograph and record, and to report progress to the mother ship. The little scout had no room for specimens or passengers. If contact was made with the inhabitants of this world, the S9000 would come at once. There would be no time for parleying. If there was any trouble the rescue would be by force and the explanations could come later.

The ruined land beneath was bathed with an eerie, flickering light, for a great auroral display was raging over half the world. But the image on the vision screen was independent of external light, and it showed clearly a waste of barren rock that seemed never to have known any form of life. Presumably this desert land must come to an end somewhere. Orostron increased his speed to the highest value he dared risk in so dense an atmosphere.

The machine fled on through the storm, and presently the desert of rock began to climb toward the sky. A great mountain range lay ahead, its peaks lost in the smoke-laden clouds. Orostron directed the scanners toward the horizon, and on the vision screen the line of mountains seemed suddenly very close and menacing. He started to climb rapidly. It was difficult to imagine a more unpromising land in which to find civilization and he wondered if it would be wise to change course. He decided against it. Five minutes later, he had his reward.

Miles below lay a decapitated mountain, the whole of its summit sheared away by some tremendous feat of engineering. Rising out of the rock and straddling the artificial plateau was an intricate structure of metal girders, supporting masses of machinery. Orostron brought his ship to a halt and spiraled down toward the mountain.

The slight Doppler blur had now vanished, and the picture on the screen was clear-cut. The latticework was supporting some scores of great metal mirrors, pointing skyward at an angle of forty-five degrees to the horizontal. They were slightly concave, and each had some complicated mechanism at its focus. There seemed something impressive and purposeful about the great array; every mirror was aimed at precisely the same spot in the sky—or beyond.

Orostron turned to his colleagues.

"It looks like some kind of observatory to me," he said. "Have you ever seen anything like it before?"

Klarten, a multitentacled, tripedal creature from a globular cluster at the edge of the Milky Way, had a different theory.

"That's communication equipment. Those reflectors are for focusing electromagnetic beams. I've seen the same kind of installation on a hundred worlds before. It may even be the station that Kulath picked up—though that's rather unlikely, for the beams would be very narrow from mirrors that size."

"That would explain why Rugon could detect no radiation before we landed," added Hansur II, one of the twin beings from the planet Thargon.

Orostron did not agree at all.

"If that is a radio station, it must be built for interplanetary communication. Look at the way the mirrors are pointed. I don't believe that a race which has only had radio for two centuries can have crossed space. It took my people six thousand years to do it."

"We managed it in three," said Hansur II mildly, speaking a few seconds ahead of his twin. Before the inevitable argument could develop, Klarten began to wave his tentacles with excitement. While the others had been talking, he had started the automatic monitor.

"Here it is! Listen!"

He threw a switch, and the little room was filled with a raucous whining sound, continually changing in pitch but nevertheless retaining certain characteristics that were difficult to define.

The four explorers listened intently for a minute; then Orostron said, "Surely that can't be any form of speech! No creature could produce sounds as quickly as that!"

Hansur I had come to the same conclusion. "That's a television program. Don't you think so, Klarten?"

The other agreed.

"Yes, and each of those mirrors seems to be radiating a different program. I wonder where they're going? If I'm correct, one of the other planets in the system must lie along those beams. We can soon check that."

Orostron called the S9000 and reported the discovery. Both Rugon and Alveron were greatly excited, and made a quick check of the astronomical records.

The result was surprising—and disappointing. None of the other nine planets lay anywhere near the line of transmission. The great mirrors appeared to be pointing blindly into space.

There seemed only one conclusion to be drawn, and Klarten was the first to voice it.

"They had interplanetary communication," he said. "But the station must be deserted now, and the transmitters no longer controlled. They haven't been switched off, and are just pointing where they were left."

"Well, we'll soon find out," said Orostron. "I'm going to land."

He brought the machine slowly down to the level of the great metal mirrors, and past them until it came to rest on the mountain rock. A hundred yards away, a white stone building crouched beneath the maze of steel girders. It was windowless, but there were several doors in the wall facing them.

Orostron watched his companions climb into their protective suits and wished he could follow. But someone had to stay in the machine to keep in touch with the mother ship. Those were Alveron's instructions, and they were very wise. One never knew what would happen on a world that was being explored for the first time, especially under conditions such as these.

Very cautiously, the three explorers stepped out of the airlock and adjusted the antigravity field of their suits. Then, each with the mode of locomotion peculiar to his race, the little party went toward the building, the Hansur twins leading and Klarten following close behind. His gravity control was apparently giving him trouble, for he suddenly fell to the ground, rather to the amusement of his colleagues. Orostron saw them pause for a moment at the nearest door—then it opened slowly and they disappeared from sight.

So Orostron waited, with what patience he could, while the storm rose around him and the light of the aurora grew even brighter in the sky. At the agreed times he called the mother ship and received brief acknowledgments from Rugon. He wondered how Torkalee was faring, halfway round the planet, but he could not contact him through the crash and thunder of solar interference.

It did not take Klarten and the Hansurs long to discover

that their theories were largely correct. The building was a radio station, and it was utterly deserted. It consisted of one tremendous room with a few small offices leading from it. In the main chamber, row after row of electrical equipment stretched into the distance; lights flickered and winked on hundreds of control panels, and a dull glow came from the elements in a great avenue of vacuum tubes.

But Klarten was not impressed. The first radio sets his race had built were now fossilized in strata a thousand million years old. Man, who had possessed electrical machines for only a few centuries, could not compete with those who had known them for half the lifetime of the Earth.

Nevertheless, the party kept their recorders running as they explored the building. There was still one problem to be solved. The deserted station was broadcasting programs, but where were they coming from? The central switchboard had been quickly located. It was designed to handle scores of programs simultaneously, but the source of those programs was lost in a maze of cables that vanished underground. Back in the S9000, Rugon was trying to analyze the broadcasts and perhaps his researches would reveal their origin. It was impossible to trace cables that might lead across continents.

The party wasted little time at the deserted station. There was nothing they could learn from it, and they were seeking life rather than scientific information. A few minutes later the little ship rose swiftly from the plateau and headed toward the plains that must lie beyond the mountains. Less than three hours were still left to them.

As the array of enigmatic mirrors dropped out of sight, Orostron was struck by a sudden thought. Was it imagination, or had they all moved through a small angle while he had been waiting, as if they were still compensating for the rotation of the Earth? He could not be sure, and he dismissed the matter as unimportant. It would only mean that the directing mechanism was still working, after a fashion.

They discovered the city fifteen minutes later. It was a great, sprawling metropolis, built around a river that had disappeared leaving an ugly scar winding its way among the great buildings and beneath bridges that looked very incongruous now.

Even from the air, the city looked deserted. But only two and a half hours were left—there was no time for further exploration. Orostron made his decision, and landed near the largest structure he could see. It seemed reasonable to suppose that some creatures would have sought shelter in the strongest buildings, where they would be safe until the very end.

The deepest caves—the heart of the planet itself—would give no protection when the final cataclysm came. Even if this race had reached the outer planets, its doom would only be delayed by the few hours it would take for the ravening wavefronts to cross the Solar System.

Orostron could not know that the city had been deserted not for a few days or weeks, but for over a century. For the culture of cities, which had outlasted so many civilizations had been doomed at last when the helicopter brought universal transportation. Within a few generations the great masses of mankind, knowing that they could reach any part of the globe in a matter of hours, had gone back to the fields and forests for which they had always longed. The new civilization had machines and resources of which earlier ages had never dreamed, but it was essentially rural and no longer bound to the steel and concrete warrens that had dominated the centuries before. Such cities as still remained were specialized centers of research, administration or entertainment; the others had been allowed to decay, where it was too much trouble to destroy them. The dozen or so greatest of all cities, and the ancient university towns, had scarcely changed and would have lasted for many generations to come. But the cities that had been founded on steam and iron and surface transportation had passed with the industries that had nourished them.

And so while Orostron waited in the tender, his colleagues raced through endless empty corridors and deserted halls, taking innumerable photographs but learning nothing of the creatures who had used these buildings. There were libraries, meeting places, council rooms, thousands of offices—all were empty and deep with dust. If they had not seen the radio station on its mountain eyrie, the explorers could well have believed that this world had known no life for centuries.

Through the long minutes of waiting, Orostron tried to imagine where this race could have vanished. Perhaps they had killed themselves knowing that escape was impossible; perhaps they had built great shelters in the bowels of the planet, and even now were cowering in their millions beneath his feet, waiting for the end. He began to fear that he would never know.

It was almost a relief when at last he had to give the order for the return. Soon he would know if Torkalee's party had been more fortunate. And he was anxious to get back to the mother ship, for as the minutes passed the suspense had become more and more acute. There had always been the thought in his mind: What if the astronomers of Kulath have made a mistake? He would begin to feel happy when the walls of the S9000 were around him. He would be happier still when they were out in space and this ominous sun was shrinking far astern.

As soon as his colleagues had entered the airlock, Orostron hurled his tiny machine into the sky and set the controls to home on the S9000. Then he turned to his friends.

"Well, what have you found?" he asked.

Klarten produced a large roll of canvas and spread it out on the floor.

"This is what they were like," he said quietly. "Bipeds, with only two arms. They seem to have managed well, in spite of that handicap. Only two eyes as well, unless there are others in the back. We were lucky to find this; it's about the only thing they left behind."

The ancient oil painting stared stonily back at the three creatures regarding it so intently. By the irony of fate, its complete worthlessness had saved it from oblivion. When the city had been evacuated, no one had bothered to move Alderman John Richards, 1909-1974. For a century and a half he had been gathering dust while far away from the old cities the new civilization had been rising to heights no earlier culture had ever known.

"That was almost all we found," said Klarten. "The city must have been deserted for years. I'm afraid our expedition has been a failure. If there are any living beings on this world, they've hidden themselves too well for us to find them."

His commander was forced to agree.

"It was an almost impossible task," he said. "If we'd had weeks instead of hours we might have succeeded. For all we know, they may even have built shelters under the sea. No one seems to have thought of that."

He glanced quickly at the indicators and corrected the course.

"We'll be there in five minutes. Alveron seems to be moving rather quickly. I wonder if Torkalee has found anything."

The S9000 was hanging a few miles above the seaboard of a blazing continent when Orostron homed upon it. The danger line was thirty minutes away and there was no time to lose. Skillfully, he maneuvered the little ship into its launching tube and the party stepped out of the airlock.

There was a small crowd waiting for them. That was to be expected, but Orostron could see at once that something more than curiosity had brought his friends here. Even before a word was spoken, he knew that something was wrong.

"Torkalee hasn't returned. He's lost his party and we're going to the rescue. Come along to the control room at once."

From the beginning, Torkalee had been luckier than Orostron. He had followed the zone of twilight, keeping away from the intolerable glare of the sun, until he came to the shores of the inland sea. It was a very recent sea, one of the latest of Man's works, for the land it covered had been desert less than a century before. In a few hours it would be desert again, for the water was boiling and clouds of steam were rising to the skies. But they could not veil the loveliness of the great white city that overlooked the tideless sea.

Flying machines were still parked neatly round the square in which Torkalee landed. They were disappointingly primitive, though beautifully finished, and depended on rotating airfoils for support. Nowhere was there any sign of life, but the place gave the impression that its inhabitants were not very far away. Lights were still shining from some of the windows.

Torkalee's three companions lost no time in leaving the machine. Leader of the party, by seniority of rank and race was T'sinadree, who like Alveron himself had been born on one of the ancient planets of the Central Suns. Next came Alarkane, from a race which was one of the youngest in the Universe and took a perverse pride in the fact. Last came one of the strange beings from the system of Palador. It was nameless, like all its kind, for it possessed no identity of its own, being merely a mobile but still dependent cell in the consciousness of its race. Though it and its fellows had long been scattered over the galaxy in the exploration of countless worlds, some unknown link still bound them together as inexorably as the living cells in a human body.

When a creature of Palador spoke, the pronoun it used was always "We". There was not, nor could there ever be, any first person singular in the language of Palador.

The great doors of the splendid building baffled the explorers, though any human child would have known their secret. T'sinadree wasted no time on them but called Torkalee on his personal transmitter. Then the three hurried aside while their commander maneuvered his machine into the best position. There was a brief burst of intolerable flame; the massive steelwork flickered once at the edge of the visible spectrum and was gone. The stones were still glowing when the eager party hurried into the building, the beams of their light projectors fanning before them.

The torches were not needed. Before them lay a great hall, glowing with light from lines of tubes along the ceiling. On either side, the hall opened out into long corridors, while straight ahead a massive stairway swept majestically toward the upper floors.

For a moment T'sinadree hesitated. Then, since one way was as good as another, he led his companions down the first corridor.

The feeling that life was near had now become very strong. At any moment, it seemed, they might be confronted by the creatures of this world. If they showed hostility—and they could scarcely be blamed if they did—the paralyzers would be used at once.

The tension was very great as the party entered the first room, and only relaxed when they saw that it held nothing but machines—row after row of them, now stilled and silent. Lining the enormous room were thousands of metal filing cabinets, forming a continuous wall as far as the eye could reach. And that was all; there was no furniture, nothing but the cabinets and the mysterious machines.

Alarkane, always the quickest of the three, was already examining the cabinets. Each held many thousand sheets of tough, thin material, perforated with innumerable holes and slots. The Paladorian appropriated one of the cards and Alarkane recorded the scene together with some close-ups of the machines. Then they left. The great room, which had been one of the marvels of the world, meant nothing to them. No living eye would ever again see that wonderful battery of almost human Hollerith analyzers and the five thousand million punched cards holding all that could be recorded of each man, woman and child on the planet.

It was clear that this building had been used very recently. With growing excitement, the explorers hurried on to the next room. This they found to be an enormous library, for millions of books lay all around them on miles and miles of shelving. Here, though the explorers could not know it, were the records of all the laws that Man had ever passed, and all the speeches that had ever been made in his council chambers.

T'sinadree was deciding his plan of action, when Alarkane drew his attention to one of the racks a hundred yards away. It was half empty, unlike all the others. Around it books lay in a tumbled heap on the floor, as if knocked down by someone in frantic haste. The signs were unmistakable. Not long ago, other creatures had been this way. Faint wheel marks were clearly visible on the floor to the acute sense of Alarkane, though the others could see nothing. Alarkane could even detect footprints, but knowing nothing of the creatures that had formed them he could not say which way they led.

The sense of nearness was stronger than ever now, but it was nearness in time, not in space. Alarkane voiced the thoughts of the party.

"Those books must have been valuable, and someone has come to rescue them—rather as an afterthought, I should say. That means there must be a place of refuge, possibly not very far away. Perhaps we may be able to find some other clues that will lead us to it."

T'sinadree agreed; the Paladorian wasn't enthusiastic.

"That may be so," it said, "but the refuge may be anywhere on the planet, and we have just two hours left. Let us waste no more time if we hope to rescue these people."

The Party hurried forward once more, pausing only to collect a few books that might be useful to the scientists at Base—though it was doubtful if they could ever be translated. They soon found that the great building was composed largely of small rooms, all showing signs of recent occupation. Most of them were in a neat and tidy condition, but one or two were very much the reverse. The explorers were particularly puzzed by one room—clearly an office of some kind—that appeared to have been completely wrecked. The floor was littered with papers, the furniture had been smashed, and smoke was pouring through the broken windows from the fires outside.

T'sinadree was rather alarmed.

"Surely no dangerous animal could have got into a place like this!" he exclaimed, fingering his paralyzer nervously.

Alarkane did not answer. He began to make that annoying sound which his race called "laughter." It was several minutes before he would explain what had amused him.

"I don't think any animal has done it," he said. "In fact, the explanation is very simple. Suppose *you* had been working all your life in this room, dealing with endless papers year after year. And suddenly, you are told that you will never see it again, that your work is finished, and that you can leave it forever. More than that—no one will come after you. Everything is finished. How would you make your exit, T'sinadree?"

The other thought for a moment.

"Well, I suppose I'd just tidy things up and leave. That's what seems to have happened in all the other rooms."

Alarkane laughed again.

"I'm quite sure you would. But some individuals have a different psychology. I think I should have liked the creature that used this room."

He did not explain himself further, and his two colleagues puzzled over his words for quite a while before they gave it up.

It came as something of a shock when Torkalee gave the order to return. They had gathered a great deal of information, but had found no clue that might lead them to the missing inhabitants of this world. That problem was as baffling as ever, and now it seemed that it would never be solved. There were only forty minutes left before the S9000 would be departing.

They were halfway back to the tender when they saw the semicircular passage leading down into the depths of the building. Its architectural style was quite different from that used elsewhere, and the gently sloping floor was an irresistible attraction to creatures whose many legs had grown weary of the marble staircases which only bipeds could have built in such profusion. T'sinadree had been the worst sufferer, for he normally employed twelve legs and could use twenty when he was in a hurry, though no one had ever seen him perform this feat.

The party stopped dead and looked down the passageway with a single thought. A tunnel, leading down into the depths of Earth! At its end, they might yet find the people of this world and rescue some of them from their fate. For there was still time to call the mother ship if the need arose.

T'sinadree signaled to his commander and Torkalee brought the little machine immediately overhead. There might not be time for the party to retrace its footsteps through the maze of passages, so meticulously recorded in the

Paladorian mind that there was no possibility of going astray. If speed was necessary, Torkalee could blast his way through the dozen floors above their head. In any case, it should not take long to find what lay at the end of the passage.

It took only thirty seconds. The tunnel ended quite abruptly in a very curious cylindrical room with magnificently padded seats along the walls. There was no way out save that by which they had come and it was several seconds before the purpose of the chamber dawned on Alarkane's mind. It was a pity, he thought, that they would never have time to use this. The thought was suddenly interrupted by a cry from T'sinadree. Alarkane wheeled around and saw that the entrance had closed silently behind them.

Even in that first moment of panic, Alarkane found himself thinking with some admiration: Whoever they were, they knew how to build automatic machinery!

The Paladorian was the first to speak. It waved one of its tenacles toward the seats.

"We think it would be best to be seated," it said. The multiplex mind of Palador had already analyzed the situation and knew what was coming.

They did not have long to wait before a low-pitched hum came from a grill overhead, and for the very last time in history a human, even if lifeless, voice was heard on Earth. The words were meaningless, though the trapped explorers could guess their message clearly enough.

"Choose your stations, please, and be seated."

Simultaneously, a wall panel at one end of the compartment glowed with light. On it was a simple map, consisting of a series of a dozen circles connected by a line. Each of the circles had writing alongside it, and beside the writing were two buttons of different colors.

Alarkane looked questioningly at his leader.

"Don't touch them," said T'sinadree. "If we leave the controls alone, the doors may open again."

He was wrong. The engineers who had designed the automatic subway had assumed that anyone who entered it would naturally wish to go somewhere. If they selected no intermediate station, their destination could only be the end of the line.

There was another pause while the relays and thyratrons waited for their orders. In those thirty seconds, if they had known what to do, the party could have opened the doors and left the subway. But they did not know, and the machines geared to a human psychology acted for them.

The surge of acceleration was not very great; the lavish upholstery was a luxury, not a necessity. Only an almost inperceptible vibration told of the speed at which they were traveling through the bowels of the earth, on a journey the duration of which they could not even guess. And in thirty minutes, the S9000 would be leaving the Solar System.

There was a long silence in the speeding machine. T'sinadree and Alarkane were thinking rapidly. So was the Paladorian, though in a different fashion. The conception of personal death was meaningless to it, for the destruction of a single unit meant no more to the group mind than the loss of a nail-paring to a man. But it could, though with great difficulty, appreciate the plight of individual intelligences such as Alarkane and T'sinadree, and it was anxious to help them if it could.

Alarkane had managed to contact Torkalee with his personal transmitter, though the signal was very weak and seemed to be fading quickly. Rapidly he explained the situation, and almost at once the signals became clearer. Torkalee was following the path of the machine, flying above the ground under which they were speeding to their unknown destination. That was the first indication they had of the fact that they were traveling at nearly a thousand miles an hour, and very soon after that Torkalee was able to give the still more disturbing news that they were rapidly approaching the sea. While they were beneath the land, there was a hope, though a slender one, that they might stop the machine and escape. But under the ocean—not all the brains and the machinery in the great mother ship could save them. No one could have devised a more perfect trap.

T'sinadree had been examining the wall map with great attention. Its meaning was obvious, and along the line connecting the circles a tiny spot of light was crawling. It was already halfway to the first of the stations marked.

"I'm going to press one of those buttons," said T'sinadree at last. "It won't do any harm, and we may learn something."

"I agree. Which will you try first?"

"There are only two kinds, and it won't matter if we try the wrong one first. I suppose one is to start the machine and the other is to stop it."

Alarkane was not very hopeful.

"It started without any button pressing," he said. "I think

it's completely automatic and we can't control it from here at all."

T'sinadree could not agree.

"These buttons are clearly associated with the stations, and there's no point in having them unless you can use them to stop yourself. The only question is, which is the right one?"

His analysis was perfectly correct. The machine could be stopped at any intermediate station. They had only been on their way ten minutes, and if they could leave now, no harm would have been done. It was just bad luck that T'sinadree's first choice was the wrong button.

The little light on the map crawled slowly though the illuminated circle without checking its speed. And at the same time Torkalee called from the ship overhead.

"You have just passed underneath a city and are heading out to sea. There cannot be another stop for nearly a thousand miles.

Alveron had given up all hope of finding life on this world. The S9000 had roamed over half the planet, never staying long in one place, descending ever and again in an effort to attract attention. There had been no response; Earth seemed utterly dead. If any of its inhabitants were still alive, thought Alveron, they must have hidden themselves in its depths where no help could reach them, though their doom would be nonetheless certain.

Rugon brought news of the disaster. The great ship ceased its fruitless searching and fled back through the storm to the ocean above which Torkalee's little tender was still following the track of the buried machine.

The scene was truly terrifying. Not since the days when Earth was born had there been such seas as this. Mountains of water were racing before the storm which had now reached velocities of many hundred miles an hour. Even at this distance from the mainland the air was full of flying debris—trees, fragments of houses, sheets of metal, anything that had not been anchored to the ground. No airborne machine could have lived for a moment in such a gale. And ever and again even the roar of the wind was drowned as the vast water-mountains met head-on with a crash that seemed to shake the sky.

Fortunately, there had been no serious earthquakes yet. Far beneath the bed of the ocean, the wonderful piece of engineering which had been the World President's private vacuum-subway was still working perfectly, unaffected by the tumult and destruction above. It would continue to work until the last minute of the Earth's existence, which, if the astronomers were right, was not much more than fifteen minutes away—though precisely how much more Alveron would have given a great deal to know. It would be nearly an hour before the trapped party could reach land and even the slightest hope of rescue.

Alveron's instructions had been precise, though even without them he would never have dreamed of taking any risks with the great machine that had been entrusted to his care. Had he been human, the decision to abandon the trapped members of his crew would have been desperately hard to make. But he came of a race far more sensitive than Man, a race that so loved the things of the spirit that long ago, and with infinite reluctance, it had taken over control of the Universe since only thus could it be sure that justice was being done. Alveron would need all his superhuman gifts to carry him through the next few hours.

Meanwhile, a mile below the bed of the ocean Alarkane and T'sinadree were very busy indeed with their private communicators. Fifteen minutes is not a long time in which to wind up the affairs of a lifetime. It is indeed, scarcely long enough to dictate more than a few of those farewell messages which at such moments are so much more important than all other matters.

All the while the Paladorian had remained silent and motionless, saying not a word. The other two, resigned to their fate and engrossed in their personal affairs, had given it no thought. They were startled when suddenly it began to address them in its peculiarly passionless voice.

"We perceive that you are making certain arrangements concerning your anticipated destruction. That will probably be unnecessary. Captain Alveron hopes to rescue us if we can stop this machine when we reach land again."

Both T'sinadree and Alarkane were too surprised to say anything for a moment. Then the latter gasped, "How do you know?"

It was a foolish question, for he remembered at once that there were several Paladorians—if one could use the phrase—in the S9000, and consequently their companion knew everything that was happening in the mother ship. So he did not wait for an answer but continued, "Alveron can't do that! He daren't take such a risk!"

"There will be no risk," said the Paladorian. "We have told him what to do. It is really very simple."

Alarkane and T'sinadree looked at their companion with something approaching awe, realizing now what must have happened. In moments of crisis, the single units comprising the Paladorian mind could link together in an organization no less close than that of any physical brain. At such moments they formed an intellect more powerful than any other in the Universe. All ordinary problems could be solved by a few hundred or thousand units. Very rarely, millions would be needed, and on two historic occasions the billions of cells of the entire Paladorian consciousness had been welded together to deal with emergencies that threatened the race. The mind of Palador was one of the greatest mental resources of the Universe; its full force was seldom required, but the knowledge that it was available was supremely comforting to other races. Alarkane wondered how many cells had co-ordinated to deal with this particular emergency. He also wondered how so trivial an incident had ever come to its attention.

To that question he was never to know the answer, though he might have guessed it had he known that the chillingly remote Paladorian mind possessed an almost human streak of vanity. Long ago, Alarkane had written a book trying to prove that eventually all intelligent races would sacrifice individual consciousness and that one day only group-minds would remain in the Universe. Palador, he had said, was the first of those ultimate intellects, and the vast, dispersed mind had not been displeased.

They had no time to ask any further questions before Alveron himself began to speak through their communicators.

"Alveron calling! We're staying on this planet until the detonation waves reach it, so we may be able to rescue you. You're heading toward a city on the coast which you'll reach in forty minutes at your present speed. If you cannot stop yourselves then, we're going to blast the tunnel behind and ahead of you to cut off your power. Then we'll sink a shaft to get you out—the chief engineer says he can do it in five minutes with the main projectors. So you should be safe within an hour, unless the sun blows up before."

"And if that happens, you'll be destroyed as well! You mustn't take such a risk!"

"Don't let that worry you; we're perfectly safe. When the sun detonates, the explosion wave will take several minutes to rise to its maximum. But apart from that, we're on the night side of the planet, behind an eight-thousand-mile screen of rock. When the first warning of the explosion comes, we will accelerate out of the Solar System, keeping in the shadow of the planet. Under our maximum drive, we will reach the velocity of light before leaving the cone of shadow, and the sun cannot harm us then."

T'sinadree was still afraid to hope. Another objection came at once into his mind.

"Yes, but how will you get any warning, here on the night side of the planet?"

"Very easily," replied Alveron. "This world has a moon which is now visible from this hemisphere. We have telescopes trained on it. If it shows any sudden increase in brilliance, our main drive goes on automatically and we'll be thrown out of the system."

The logic was flawless. Alveron, cautious as ever, was taking no chances. It would be many minutes before the eight-thousand-mile shield of rock and metal could be destroyed by the fires of the exploding sun. In that time, the S9000 could have reached the safety of the velocity of light.

Alarkane pressed the second button when they were still several miles from the coast. He did not expect anything to happen then, assuming that the machine could not stop between stations. It seemed too good to be true when, a few minutes later, the machine's slight vibration died away and they came to a halt.

The doors slid silently apart. Even before they were fully open, the three had left the compartment. They were taking no more chances. Before them a long tunnel stretched into the distance, rising slowly out of sight. They were starting along it when suddenly Alveron's voice called from the communicators.

"Stay where you are! We're going to blast!"

The ground shuddered once, and far ahead there came the rumble of falling rock. Again the earth shook—and a hundred yards ahead the passageway vanished abruptly. A tremendous vertical shaft had been cut clean through it.

The party hurried forward again until they came to the end of the corridor and stood waiting on its lip. The shaft in which it ended was a full thousand feet across and descended into the earth as far as the torches could throw their beams. Overhead, the storm clouds fled beneath a moon that no man would have recognized, so luridly brilliant was its disk. And, most glorious of all sights, the S9000 floated high above, the great projectors that had drilled this enormous pit still glowing cherry red.

A dark shape detached itself from the mother ship and dropped swiftly toward the ground. Torkalee was returning to collect his friends. A little later, Alveron greeted them in the control room. He waved to the great vision screen and said quietly, "See, we were barely in time."

The continent below them was slowly settling beneath the mile-high waves that were attacking its coasts. The last that anyone was ever to see of Earth was a great plain, bathed with the silver light of the abnormally brilliant moon. Across its face the waters were pouring in a glittering flood toward a distant range of mountains. The sea had won its final victory, but its triumph would be shortlived for soon sea and land would be no more. Even as the silent party in the control room watched the destruction below, the infinitely greater catastrophe to which this was only the prelude came swiftly upon them.

It was as though dawn had broken suddenly over this moonlit landscape. But it was not dawn: it was only the moon, shining with the brilliance of a second sun. For perhaps thirty seconds that awesome, unnatural light burnt fiercely on the doomed land beneath. Then there came a sudden flashing of indicator lights across the control board. The main drive was on. For a second Alveron glanced at the indicators and checked their information. When he looked again at the screen, Earth was gone.

The magnificent, desperately overstrained generators quietly died when the S9000 was passing the orbit of Persephone. It did not matter, the sun could never harm them now, and although the ship was speeding helplessly out into the lonely night of interstellar space, it would only be a matter of days before rescue came.

There was irony in that. A day ago, they had been the rescuers, going to the aid of a race that now no longer existed. Not for the first time Alveron wondered about the world that had just perished. He tried, in vain, to picture it as it had been in its glory, the streets of its cities thronged with life. Primitive though its people had been, they might have offered much to the Universe. If only they could have made contact! Regret was useless; long before their coming, the people of this world must have buried themselves in its iron heart. And now they and their civilization would remain a mystery for the rest of time.

Alveron was glad when his thoughts were interrupted by Rugon's entrance. The chief of communications had been very busy ever since the take-off, trying to analyze the programs radiated by the transmitter Orostron had discovered. The problem was not a difficult one, but it demanded the construction of special equipment, and that had taken time.

"Well, what have you found?" asked Alveron.

"Quite a lot," replied his friend. "There's something mysterious here, and I don't understand it.

"It didn't take long to find how the vision transmissions were built up, and we've been able to convert them to suit our own equipment. It seems that there were cameras all over the plant, surveying points of interest. Some of them were apparently in cities, on tops of very high buildings. The cameras were rotating continuously to give panoramic views. In the programs we've recorded there are about twenty different scenes.

"In addition, there are a number of transmissions of a different kind, neither sound nor vision. They seem to be purely scientific—possibly instrument readings or something of that sort. All these programs were going out simultaneously on different frequency bands.

"Now there must be a reason for all this. Orostron still thinks that the station simply wasn't switched off when it was deserted. But these aren't the sort of programs such a station would normally radiate at all. It was certainly used for interplanetary relaying—Klarten was quite right there. So these people must have crossed space, since none of the other planets had any life at the time of the last survey. Don't you agree?"

Alverton was following intently.

"Yes, that seems reasonable enough. But it's also certain that the beam was pointing to none of the other planets. I checked that myself."

"I know," said Rugon. "What I want to discover is why a giant interplanetary relay station is busily transmitting pictures of a world about to be destroyed—pictures that would be of immense interest to scientists and astronomers. Someone had gone to a lot of trouble to arrange all those panoramic cameras. I am convinced that those beams were going somewhere."

Alveron started up.

"Do you imagine that there might be an outer planet that hasn't been reported?" he asked. "If so, your theory's certainly wrong. The beam wasn't even pointing in the plane of the Solar System. And even if it were—just look at this."

He switched on the vision screen and adjusted the controls. Against the velvet curtain of space was hanging a blue-white sphere, apparently composed of many concentric shells of incandescent gas. Even though its immense distance made all movement invisible, it was clearly expanding at an enormous rate. At its center was a blinding point of light—the white dwarf star that the sun had now become.

"You probably don't realize just how big that sphere is," said Alveron. 'Look at this."

He increased the magnification until only the center portion of the nova was visible. Close to its heart were two minute condensations, one on either side of the nucleus.

"Those are the two giant planets of the system. They have still managed to retain their existence—after a fashion. And they were several hundred million miles from the sun. The nova is still expanding—but it's already twice the size of the Solar System."

Rugon was silent for a moment.

"Perhaps you're right," he said, rather grudgingly.

"You've disposed of my first theory. But you still haven't satisfied me."

He made several swift circuits of the room before speaking again. Alveron waited patiently. He knew the almost intuitive powers of his friend, who could often solve a problem when mere logic seemed insufficient.

Then, rather slowly, Rugon began to speak again.

"What do you think of this?" he said. "Suppose we've completely underestimated these people? Orostron did it once—he thought they could never have crossed space, since they'd only known radio for two centuries. Hansur II told me that. Well, Orostron was quite wrong. Perhaps we're all wrong. I've had a look at the material that Klarten brought back from the transmitter. He wasn't impressed by what he found, but it's a marvelous achievement for so short a time. There were devices in that station that belonged to civilizations thousands of years older. Alveron, can we follow that beam to see where it leads?"

Alveron said nothing for a full minute. He had been more than half expecting the question, but it was not an easy one to answer. The main generators had gone completely. There was no point in trying to repair them. But there was still power available, and while there was power, anything could be done in time. It would mean a lot of improvisation, and some difficult maneuvers, for the ship still had its enormous initial velocity. Yes, it could be done, and the activity would keep the crew from becoming further depressed, now that the reaction caused by the mission's failure had started to set in. The news that the nearest heavy repair ship could not reach them for three weeks had also caused a slump in morale.

The engineers, as usual, made a tremendous fuss. Again as usual, they did the job in half the time they had dismissed as being absolutely impossible. Very slowly, over many hours, the great ship began to discard the speed its main drive had given it in as many minutes. In a tremendous curve, millions of miles in radius, the S9000 changed its course and the star fields shifted round it.

The maneuver took three days, but at the end of that time the ship was limping along a course parallel to the beam that had once come from Earth. They were heading out into emptiness, the blazing sphere that had been the sun dwindling slowly behind them. By the standards of interstellar flight, they were almost stationary.

For hours Rugon strained over his instruments, driving his detector beams far ahead into space. There were certainly no planets within many light-years; there was no doubt of that. From time to time Alveron came to see him and always he had to give the same reply: "Nothing to report." About a fifth of the time Rugon's intuition let him down badly; he began to wonder if this was such an occasion.

Not until a week later did the needles of the mass-detectors quiver feebly at the ends of their scales. But Rugon said nothing, not even to his captain. He waited until he was sure, and he went on waiting until even the short-range scanners began to react, and to build up the first faint pictures on the vision screen. Still he waited patiently until he could interpret the images. Then, when he knew that his wildest fancy was even less than the truth, he called his colleagues into the control room.

The picture on the vision screen was the familiar one of endless star fields, sun beyond sun to the very limits of the Universe. Near the center of the screen a distant nebula made a patch of haze that was difficult for the eye to grasp.

Rugon increased the magnification. The stars flowed out of the field; the little nebula expanded until it filled the screen and then—it was a nebula no longer. A simultaneous gasp of amazement came from all the company at the sight that lay before them.

Lying across league after league of space, ranged in a vast three-dimensional array of rows and columns with the precision of a marching army, were thousands of tiny pencils of light. They were moving swiftly; the whole immense lattice holding its shape as a single unit. Even as Alveron and his comrades watched, the formation began to drift off the screen and Rugon had to recenter the controls.

After a long pause, Rugon started to speak.

"This is the race," he said softly, "that has known radio for only two centuries—the race that we believed had crept to die in the heart of its planet. I have examined those images under the highest possible magnification.

"That is the greatest fleet of which there has ever been a record. Each of those points of light represents a ship larger than our own. Of course, they are very primitive—what you see on the screen are the jets of their rockets. Yes, they dared to use rockets to bridge interstellar space! You realize what that means. It would take them centuries to reach the nearest star. The whole race must have embarked on this journey in the hope that its descendants would complete it, generations later.

"To measure the extent of their accomplishment, think of the ages it took us to conquer space, and the longer ages still before we attempted to reach the stars. Even if we were threatened with annihilation, could we have done so much in so short a time? Remember, this is the youngest civilization in the Universe. Four hundred thousand years ago it did not even exist. What will it be a million years from now?"

An hour later, Orostron left the crippled mother ship to make contact with the great fleet ahead. As the little torpedo disappeared among the stars, Alveron turned to his friend and made a remark that Rugon was often to remember in the years ahead.

"I wonder whay they'll be like?" he mused. "Will they be nothing but wonderful engineers, with no art or philosophy? They're going to have such a surprise when Orostron reaches them—I expect it will be rather a blow to their pride. It's funny how all isolated races think they're the only people in the Universe. But they should be grateful to us; we're going to save them a good many hundred years of travel."

Alveron glanced at the Milky Way, lying like a veil of silver mist across the vision screen. He waved toward it with a sweep of a tentacle that embraced the whole circle of the galaxy, from the Central Planets to the lonely suns of the Rim.

"You know," he said to Rugon, "I feel rather afraid of these people. Suppose they don't like our little Federation?" He waved once more toward the star-clouds that lay massed across the screen, glowing with the light of their countless suns.

"Something tells me they'll be very determined people," he added. "We had better be polite to them. After all, we only outnumber them about a thousand million to one."

Rugon laughed at his captain's little joke.

Twenty years afterward, the remark didn't seem funny.

PLACET IS A CRAZY PLACE

by Fredric Brown

ASTOUNDING SCIENCE FICTION
May

We have discussed the talented Fredric Brown at some length in previous volumes in this series, but it is worth repeating that he was one of science fiction's premier craftsman, capable of outstanding work at all lengths from the short-short to the novel. He was perhaps the first major sf writer who had the ability to be consistently funny and consistently wise at the same time, and he certainly exercised a greater influence on the field than historians have given him credit for.

"Placet is a Crazy Place" was not included in his The Best of Fredric Brown, *but it should have been. To duplicate it, all you have to do is mix a little Philip K. Dick, add some Philip José Farmer, and top off with a generous portion of Ferdinand Feghoot!*

(Funny science fiction is not as common as I wish it were, but then successfully funny fiction of any kind is not as common as I wish it were. That's because it isn't easy being successfully funny and few writers try and still fewer writers succeed. Fred-

ric Brown is one of those who make it, and this story has always had a warm spot in my heart because Fred managed to take an utterly loony situation and forced it to make sense. Oh, I don't believe that light will really *slow down to the speed of sound in the neighborhood of matter-antimatter interaction, but we can* suppose *it does. Incidentally, "contraterrene matter" is a science fiction term that was replaced by the* actual *term used by real scientists when they got around to considering it seriously. They decided on "antimatter" and we had to follow suit.—IA)*

Even when you're used to it, it gets you down sometimes. Like that morning—if you can call it a morning. Really it was night. But we go by Earth time on Placet because Placet time would be as screwy as everything else on that goofy planet. I mean, you'd have a six-hour day and then a two-hour night and then a fifteen-hour day and a one-hour night and—well, you just couldn't keep time on a planet that does a figure-eight orbit around two dissimilar suns, going like a bat out of hell around and between them, and the suns going around each other so fast and so comparatively close that Earth astronomers thought it was only one sun until the Blakeslee expedition landed here twenty years ago.

You see, the rotation of Placet isn't any even fraction of the period of its orbit and there's the Blakeslee Field in the middle between the suns—a field in which light rays slow down to a crawl and get left behind and—well—

If you've not read the Blakeslee reports on Placet, hold on to something while I tell you this:

Placet is the only known planet that can eclipse itself twice at the same time, run headlong into itself every forty hours, and then chase itself out of sight.

I don't blame you.

I didn't believe it either, and it scared me stiff the first time I stood on Placet and saw Placet coming head-on to run into us. And yet I'd read the Blakeslee reports and knew what was really happening, and why. It's rather like those early movies when the camera was set up in front of a train and the audience saw the locomotive heading right toward them and would feel an impulse to run even though they knew the locomotive wasn't really there.

But I started to say, like that morning. I was sitting at my desk, the top of which was covered with grass. My feet were—or seemed to be—resting on a sheet of rippling water. But it wasn't wet.

On top of the grass of my desk lay a pink flowerpot, into which, nose-first, stuck a bright green Saturnian lizard. That—reason and not my eyesight told me—was my pen and inkwell. Also an embroidered sampler that said, "God Bless Our Home" in neat cross-stitching. It actually was a message from Earth Center which had just come in on the radiotype. I didn't know what it said because I'd come into my office after the B. F. effect had started. I didn't think it really said, "God Bless Our Home" because it seemed to. And just then I was mad, I was fed up, and I didn't care a holler what it actually did say.

You see—maybe I'd better explain—the Blakeslee Field effect occurs when Placet is in mid-position between Argyle I and Argyle II, the two suns it figure eights around. There's a scientific explanation of it, but it must be expressed in formulas, not in words. It boils down to this: Argyle I is terrene matter and Argyle II is contraterrene, or negative matter. Halfway between them—over a considerable stretch of territory—is a field in which light rays are slowed down, way down. They move at about the speed of sound. The result is that if something is moving faster than sound—as Placet itself does—you can still see it coming after it has passed you. It takes the visual image of Placet twenty-six hours to get through the field. By that time, Placet has rounded one of its suns and meets its own image on the way back. In midfield, there's an image coming and an image going, and it eclipses itself twice, occulting both suns at the same time. A little farther on, it runs into itself coming from the opposite direction—and scares you stiff if you're watching, even if you know it's not really happening.

Let me explain it this way before you get dizzy. Say an old-fashioned locomotive is coming toward you, only at a speed much faster than sound. A mile away, it whistles. It passes you and *then* you hear the whistle, coming from the point a mile back where the locomotive isn't any more. That's the auditory effect of an object traveling faster than sound; what I've just described is the visual effect of an object traveling—in a figure-eight orbit—faster than its own visual image.

That isn't the worst of it; you can stay indoors and avoid the eclipsing and the head-on collisions, but you can't avoid the physio-psychological effect of the Blakeslee Field.

And that, the physio-psychological effect, is something else again. The field does something to the optic nerve centers, or to the part of the brain to which the optic nerves connect, something similar to the effect of certain drugs. You have—you can't exactly call them hallucinations, because you don't ordinarily see things that aren't there, but you get an illusory picture of what *is* there.

I knew perfectly well that I was sitting at a desk the top of which was glass, and not grass; that the floor under my feet was ordinary plastiplate and not a sheet of rippling water; that the objects on my desk were not a pink flowerpot with a Saturnian lizard sticking in it, but an antique twentieth century inkwell and pen—and that the "God Bless Our Home" sampler was a radiotype message on ordinary radiotype paper. I could verify any of those things by my sense of touch, which the Blakeslee Field doesn't affect.

You can close your eyes, of course, but you don't—because even at the height of the effect, your eyesight gives you the relative size and distance of things and if you stay in familiar territory your memory and your reason tell you what they are.

So when the door opened and a two-headed monster walked in, I knew it was Reagan. Reagan isn't a two-headed monster, but I could recognize the sound of his walk.

I said, "Yes, Reagan?"

The two-headed monster said, "Chief, the machine shop is wobbling. We may have to break the rule not to do any work in midperiod."

"Birds?" I asked.

Both of his heads nodded. "The underground part of those walls must be like sieves from the birds flying through 'em, and we'd better pour concrete quick. Do you think those new alloy reinforcing bars the *Ark*'ll bring will stop them?"

"Sure," I lied. Forgetting the field, I turned to look at the clock, but there was a funeral wreath of white lilies on the wall where the clock should have been. You can't tell time from a funeral wreath. I said, "I was hoping we wouldn't have to reinforce those walls till we had the bars to sink in them. The *Ark*'s about due; they're probably hovering outside right now waiting for us to come out of the field. You think we could wait till—"

There was a crash.

"Yeah, we can wait," Reagan said. "There went the machine shop, so there's no hurry at all."

"Nobody was in there?"

"Nope, but I'll make sure." He ran out.

That's what life on Placet is like. I'd had enough of it; I'd had too much of it. I made up my mind while Reagan was gone.

When he came back, he was a bright blue articulated skeleton.

He said, "O.K., Chief. Nobody was inside."

"Any of the machines badly smashed?"

He laughed. "Can you look at a rubber beach horse with purple polka dots and tell whether it's an intact lathe or a busted one? Say, Chief, you know what you look like?"

I said, "If you tell me, you're fired."

I don't know whether I was kidding or not; I was plenty on edge. I opened my drawer of my desk and put the "God Bless Our Home" sampler in it and slammed the drawer shut. I was fed up. Placet is a crazy place and if you stay there long enough you go crazy yourself. One out of ten of Earth Center's Placet employes has to go back to Earth for psychopathic treatment after a year or two on Placet. And I'd been there three years, almost. My contract was up. I made my mind up, too.

"Reagan," I said.

He'd been heading for the door. He turned. "Yeah, Chief?"

I said, "I want you to send a message on the radiotype to Earth Center. And get it straight, two words: *I quit.*"

He said, "O.K., Chief." He went on out and closed the door.

I sat back and closed my eyes to think. I'd done it now. Unless I ran after Reagan and told him not to send the message, it was done and over and irrevocable. Earth Center's funny that way; the board is plenty generous in some directions, but once you resign they never let you change your mind. It's an ironclad rule and ninety-nine times out of a hundred it's justified on interplanetary and intragalactic projects. A man must be 100 per cent enthusiastic about his job to make a go of it, and once he's turned against it, he's lost the keen edge.

I knew the midperiod was about over, but I sat there with

my eyes closed just the same. I didn't want to open them to look at the clock until I could see the clock *as* a clock and not as whatever it might be this time. I sat there and thought.

I felt a bit hurt about Reagan's casualness in accepting the message. He'd been a good friend of mine for ten years; he could at least have said he was sorry I was going to leave. Of course there was a fair chance that he might get the promotion, but even if he was thinking that, he could have been diplomatic about it. At least, he could have—

Oh, quit feeling sorry for yourself, I told myself. *You're through with Placet and you're through with Earth Center, and you're going back to Earth pretty soon now, as soon as they relieve you, and you can get another job there, probably teaching again.*

But damn Reagan, just the same. He'd been my student at Earth City Poly, and I'd got him this Placet job and it was a good one for a youngster his age, assistant administrator of a planet with nearly a thousand population. For that matter, my job was a good one for a man *my* age—I'm only thirty-one myself. An excellent job, except that you couldn't put up a building that wouldn't fall down again and—*Quit crabbing,* I told myself; *you're through with it now. Back to Earth and a teaching job again. Forget it.*

I was tired. I put my head on my arms on top of the desk, and I must have dozed off for a minute.

I looked up at the sound of footsteps coming through the doorway; they weren't Reagan's footsteps. The illusions were getting better now, I saw. It was—or appeared to be—a gorgeous redhead. It couldn't be, of course. There are a few women on Placet, mostly wives of technician's, but—

She said, "Don't you remember me, Mr. Rand?" It was a woman; her voice was a woman's voice, and a beautiful voice. Sounded vaguely familiar, too.

"Don't be silly," I said; "how can I recognize you at midper—" My eyes suddenly caught a glimpse of the clock past her shoulder, and it was a clock and not a funeral wreath or a cuckoo's nest, and I realized suddenly that everything else in the room was back to normal. And that meant midperiod was over, and I wasn't seeing things.

My eyes went back to the redhead. She must be real, I realized. And suddenly I knew her, although she'd changed, changed plenty. All changes were improvements, although Michaelina Witt had been a very pretty girl when she'd been in my extra-terrestrial Botany III class at Earth City Polytech four—no, five years ago.

She'd been pretty, then. Now she was beautiful. She was stunning. How had the teletalkies missed her? Or had they? What was she doing *here?* She must have just got off the *Ark,* but—I realized I was still gawking at her. I stood up so fast I almost fell across the desk.

"Of course I remember you, Miss Witt," I stammered. "Won't you sit down? How did you come here? Have they relaxed the no-visitors rule?"

She shook her head, smiling. "I'm not a visitor, Mr. Rand, Center advertised for a technician-secretary for you, and I tried for the job and got it, subject to your approval, of course. I'm on probation for a month, that is."

"Wonderful," I said. It was a masterpiece of understatement. I started to elaborate on it: "Marvelous—"

There was the sound of someone clearing his throat. I looked around; Reagan was in the doorway. This time not as a blue skeleton or a two-headed monster. Just plain Reagan.

He said, "Answer to your radiotype just came." He crossed over and dropped it on my desk. I looked at it. "O. K. August 19th," it read. My momentary wild hope that they'd failed to accept my resignation went down among the widgie birds. They'd been as brief about it as I'd been.

August 19th—the next arrival of the *Ark.* They certainly weren't wasting any time—mine or theirs. Four days!

Reagan said, "I thought you'd want to know right away, Phil."

"Yeah," I told him. I glared at him. "Thanks." With a touch of spite—or maybe more than a touch—I thought, *well, my bucko, you don't get the job, or that message would have said so; they're sending a replacement on the next shuttle of the Ark.*

But I didn't say that; the veneer of civilization was too thick.

I said, "Miss Witt, I'd like you to meet—" They looked at each other and started to laugh, and I remembered. Of course, Reagan and Michaelina had both been in my botany class, as had Michaelina's twin brother, Ichabod. Only, of course, no one ever called the redheaded twins Michaelina and Ichabod. It was Mike and Ike, once you knew them.

Reagan said, "I met Mike getting off the *Ark*. I told her how to find your office, since you weren't there to do the honors."

"Thanks," I said. "Did the reinforcing bars come?"

"Guess so. They unloaded some crates. They were in a hurry to pull out again. They've gone."

I grunted.

Reagan said, "Well, I'll check the ladings. Just came to give you the radiotype; thought you'd want the good news right away."

He went out, and I glared after him. The louse. The—

Michaelina said, "Am I to start to work right away, Mr. Rand?"

I straightened out my face and managed a smile. "Of course not," I told her. "You'll want to look around the place first. See the scenery and get acclimated. Want to stroll into the village for a drink?"

"Of course."

We strolled down the path toward the little cluster of buildings, all small, one-story, and square.

She said, "It's—it's nice. Feels like I'm walking on air, I'm so light. Exactly what is the gravity?"

"Point seven four," I said. "If you weigh—um-m, a hundred twenty pounds on Earth, you weigh about eighty-nine pounds here. And on you, it looks good."

She laughed. "Thank you, Professor—Oh, that's right; you're not a professor now. You're now my boss, and I must call you Mr. Rand."

"Unless you're willing to make it Phil, Michaelina."

"If you'd call me Mike; I detest Michaelina, almost as much as Ike hates Ichabod."

"How is Ike?"

"Fine. Has a student-instructor job at Poly, but he doesn't like it much." She looked ahead at the village. "Why so many small buildings instead of a few bigger ones?"

"Because the average life of a structure of any kind on Placet is about three weeks. And you never know when one is going to fall down—with someone inside. It's our biggest problem. All we can do is make them small and light, except the foundations, which we make as strong as possible. Thus far, nobody has been hurt seriously in the collapse of a building, for that reason, but—Did you feel that?"

"The vibration? What was it, an earthquake?"

"No," I said. "It was a flight of birds."

"What?"

I had to laugh at the expression on her face, I said, "Placet is a crazy place. A minute ago, you said you felt as though you were walking on air. Well, in a way, you are doing just exactly that. Placet is one of the rare objects in the Universe that is composed of both ordinary and *heavy* matter. Matter with a collapsed molecular structure, so heavy you couldn't lift a pebble of it. Placet has a core of that stuff; that's why this tiny planet, which has an area about twice the size of Manhattan Island, has a gravity three-quarters that of Earth. There is life—animal life, not intelligent—living on the core. There are birds, whose molecular structure is like that of the planet's core, so dense that ordinary matter is as tenuous to them as air is to us. They actually *fly* through it, as birds on Earth fly through the air. From their standpoint, we're walking on top of Placet's atmosphere."

"And the vibration of their flight under the surface makes the houses collapse?"

"Yes, and worse—they fly right through the foundations, no matter what we make them of. Any matter we can work with is just so much gas to them. They fly through iron or steel as easily as through sand or loam. I've just got a shipment of some specially tough stuff from Earth—the special alloy steel you heard me ask Reagan about—but I haven't much hope of it's doing any good."

"But aren't those birds dangerous? I mean, aside from making the buildings fall down. Couldn't one get up enough momentum flying to carry it out of the ground and into the air a little way? And wouldn't it go right through anyone who happened to be there?"

"It would," I said, "but it doesn't. I mean, they never fly closer to the surface than a few inches. Some sense seems to tell them when they're nearing the top of their "atmosphere." Something analogous to the supersonics a bat uses. You know, of course, how a bat can fly in utter darkness and never fly into a solid object."

"Like radar, yes."

"Like radar, yes, except a bat uses sound waves instead of radio waves. And the widgie birds must use something that works on the same principle, in reverse; turns them back a few inches before they approach what to them would be the equivalent of a vacuum. Being heavy-matter, they could no more exist or fly in air than a bird could exist or fly in a vacuum."

While we were having a cocktail apiece in the village, Michaelina mentioned her brother again. She said, "Ike doesn't like teaching at all, Phil. Is there any chance at all that you could get him a job here on Placet?"

I said, "I'm been badgering Earth Center for another administrative assistant. The work is increasing plenty since we've got more of the surface under cultivation. Reagan really needs help. I'll—"

Her whole face was alight with eagerness. And I remembered. I was through. I'd resigned, and Earth Center would pay as much attention to any recommendation of mine as though I were a widgie bird. I finished weakly, "I'll—I'll see if I can do anything about it."

She said, "Thanks—Phil." My hand was on the table beside my glass, and for a second she put hers over it. All right, it's a hackneyed metaphor to say it felt as though a high-voltage current went through me. But it did, and it was a mental shock as well as a physical one, because I realized then and there that I was head over heels. I'd fallen harder than any of Placet's buildings ever had. The thump left me breathless. I wasn't watching Michaelina's face, but from the way she pressed her hand harder against mine for a millisecond and then jerked it away as though from a flame, she must have felt a little of that current, too.

I stood up a little shakily and suggested that we walk back to headquarters.

Because the situation was completely impossible, now. Now that Center had accepted my resignation and I was without visible or invisible means of support. In a psychotic moment, I'd cooked my own goose. I wasn't even sure I could get a teaching job. Earth Center is the most powerful organization in the Universe and has a finger in every pie. If they black-listed me—

Walking back, I let Michaelina do most of the talking; I had some heavy thinking to do. I wanted to tell her the truth—and I didn't want to.

Between monosyllabic answers, I fought it out with myself. And, finally lost. Or won. I'd not tell her—until just before the next coming of the *Ark*. I'd pretend everything was O. K. and normal for that long, give myself that much chance to see if Michaelina would fall for me. That much of a break I'd give myself. A chance, for four days.

And then—well, if by then she'd come to feel about me the way I did about her, I'd tell her what a fool I'd been and tell her I'd like to—No, I wouldn't let her return to Earth with me, even if she wanted to, until I saw light ahead through a foggy future. All I could tell her was that if and when I had a chance of working my way up again to a decent job—and after all I was still only thirty-one and might be able to—

That sort of thing.

Reagan was waiting in my office, looking as mad as a wet hornet. He said, "Those saps at Earth Center shipping department gummed things again. Those crates of special steel—aren't."

"Aren't what?"

"Aren't anything. They're empty crates. Something went wrong with the crating machine and they never knew it."

"Are you sure that's what those crates were supposed to contain?"

"Sure I'm sure. Everything else on the order came, and the ladings specified the steel for those particular crates." He ran a hand through his tousled hair. It made him look more like an Airedale than he usually does.

I grinned at him. "Maybe it's invisible steel."

"Invisible, weightless and intangible. Can *I* word the message to Center telling them about it?"

"Go as far as you like," I told him. "Wait here a minute, though. I'll show Mike where her quarters are and then I want to talk to you a minute."

I took Michaelina to the best available sleeping cabin of the cluster around headquarters. She thanked me again for trying to get Ike a job here, and I felt lower than a widgie bird's grave when I went back to my office.

"Yeah, Chief?" Reagan said.

"About that message to Earth," I told him. "I mean the one I sent this morning. I don't want to say anything about it to Michaelina."

He chuckled. "Want to tell her yourself, huh? O. K. I'll keep my yap shut."

I said, a bit wryly, "Maybe I was foolish sending it."

"Huh?" he said. "I'm sure glad you did. Swell idea."

He went out, and I managed not to throw anything at him.

The next day was a Tuesday, if that matters. I remember it as the day I solved one of Placet's two major problems. An ironic time to do it, maybe.

I was dictating some notes on greenwort culture—Placet's importance to Earth is, of course, the fact that certain plants native to the place and which won't grow anywhere else yield derivatives that have become important to the pharmacopoeia. I was having heavy sledding because I was watching Michaelina take the notes; she'd insisted on starting work her second day on Placet.

And suddenly, out of a clear sky and out of a muggy mind, came an idea. I stopped dictating and rang for Reagan. He came in.

"Reagan," I said, "order five thousand ampoules of J-17 Conditioner. Tell 'em to rush it."

"Chief, don't you remember? We tried the stuff. Thought it might condition us to see normally in midperiod, but it didn't affect the optic nerves. We still saw screwy. It's great for conditioning people to high or low temperatures or—"

"Or long or short waking-sleeping periods," I interrupted him. "That's what I'm talking about, Reagan. Look, revolving around two suns, Placet has such short irregular periods of light and dark that we never took them seriously. Right?"

"Sure, but—"

"But since there's no logical Placet day and night we could use, we made ourselves slaves to a sun so far away we can't see it. We use a twenty-four hour day. But midperiod occurs every twenty hours, regularly. We can use conditioner to adapt ourselves to a *twenty*-hour day—six hours sleep, twelve awake—with everybody blissfully sleeping through the period when their eyes play tricks on them. And in a darkened sleeping room so you couldn't see anything, even if you woke up. More and shorter days per year—and nobody goes psychopathic on us. Tell me what's wrong with it."

His eyes went bleak and blank and he hit his forehead a resounding whack with the palm of his hand.

He said, "Too simple, that's what's wrong with it. So darned simple only a genius could see it. For two years I've been going slowly nuts and the answer so easy nobody could see it. I'll put the order in right away."

He started out and then turned back. "Now how do we keep the buildings up? Quick, while you're fey or whatever you are."

I laughed. I said, "Why not try that invisible steel of yours in the empty crates?"

He said, "Nuts," and closed the door.

And the next day was a Wednesday and I knocked off work and took Michaelina on a walking tour around Placet. Once around is just a nice day's hike. But with Michaelina

Witt, any day's hike would be a nice day's hike. Except, of course, that I knew I had only one more full day to spend with her. The world would end on Friday.

Tomorrow the *Ark* would leave Earth, with the shipment of conditioner that would solve one of our problems—and with whomever Earth Center was sending to take my place. It would warp through space to a point a safe distance outside the Argyle I-II system and come in on rocket power from there. It would be here Friday, and I'd go back with it. But I tried not to think about that.

I pretty well managed to forget it until we got back to headquarters and Reagan met me with a grin that split his homely mug into horizontal halves. He said, "Chief, you did it."

"Swell," I said. "I did what?"

"Gave me the answer what to use for reinforcing foundations. You solved the problem."

"Yeah?" I said.

"Yeah. Didn't he, Mike?"

Michaelina looked as puzzled as I must have. She said, "He was kidding. He said to use the stuff in the empty crates, didn't he?"

Reagan grinned again. "He just thought he was kidding. That's what we're going to use from now on. Nothing. Look, Chief, it's like the conditioner—so simple we never thought of it. Until you told me to use what was in the empty crates, and I got to thinking it over."

I stood thinking a moment myself, and then I did what Reagan had done the day before—hit myself a whack on the forehead with the heel of my palm.

Michaelina still looked puzzled.

"Hollow foundations," I told her. "What's the one thing widgie birds won't fly through? *Air*. We can make buildings as big as we need them, now. For foundations, we sink double walls with a wide air space between. We can—"

I stopped, because it wasn't "we" any more. *They* could do it after I was back on Earth looking for a job.

And Thursday went and Friday came.

I was working, up till the last minute, because it was the easiest thing to do. With Reagan and Michaelina helping me, I was making out material lists for our new construction projects. First, a three-story building of about forty rooms for a headquarters building.

We were working fast, because it would be midperiod

shortly, and you can't do paper work when you can't read and can write only be feel.

But my mind was on the *Ark.* I picked up the phone and called the radiotype shack to ask about it.

"Just got a call from them," said the operator. "They've warped in, but not close enough to land before midperiod. They'll land right after."

"O. K.," I said, abandoning the hope that they'd be a day late.

I got up and walked to the window. We were nearing mid-position all right. Up in the sky to the north I could see Placet coming toward us.

"Mike," I said. "Come here."

She joined me at the window and we stood there, watching. My arm was around her. I don't remember putting it there, but I didn't take it away, and she didn't move.

Behind us, Reagan cleared his throat. He said, "I'll give this much of the list to the operator. He can get it on the ether right after midperiod." He went out and shut the door behind him.

Michaelina seemed to move a little closer. We were both looking out the window at Placet rushing toward us. She said, "Beautiful, isn't it, Phil?"

"Yes," I said. But I turned, and I was looking at her face as I said it. Then—I hadn't meant to—I kissed her.

I went back, and sat down at my desk. She said, "Phil, what's the matter? You haven't got a wife and six kids hidden away somewhere, or something, have you? You were single when I had a crush on you at Earth Polytech—and I waited five years to get over it and didn't, and finally wangled a job on Placet just to—Do I have to do the proposing?"

I groaned. I didn't look at her. I said, "Mike, I'm nuts about you. But—just before you came, I sent a two-word radiotype to Earth. It said, 'I quit.' So I've got to leave Placet on this shuttle of the *Ark*, and I doubt if I can even get a teaching job, now that I've got Earth Center down on me, and—"

She said, "But, Phil!" and took a step toward me.

There was a knock on the door, Reagan's knock. I was glad, for once, of the interruption. I called out for him to come in, and he opened the door.

He said, "You told Mike yet, Chief?"

I nodded, glumly.

Reagan grinned. "Good," he said; "I've been busting to tell her. It'll be swell to see Ike again."

"Huh?" I said. "Ike who?"

Reagan's grin faded. He said, "Phil, are you slipping, or something? Don't you remember giving me the answer to that Earth Center radiotype four days ago, just before Mike got here?"

I stared at him with my mouth open. I hadn't even read that radiotype, let alone answered it. Had Reagan gone psychopathic, or had I? I remembered shoving it in the drawer of my desk. I jerked open the drawer and pulled it out. My hand shook a little as I read it: REQUEST FOR ADDITIONAL ASSISTANT GRANTED. WHOM DO YOU WANT FOR THE JOB?

I looked up at Reagan again. I said, "You're trying to tell me I sent an answer to this?"

He looked as dumbfounded as I felt.

"You told me to," he said.

"What did I tell you to send?"

"Ike Witt." He stared at me. "Chief, are you feeling all right?"

I felt so all right something seemed to explode in my head. I stood up and started for Michaelina. I said, "Mike, will you marry me?" I got my arms around her, just in time, before midperiod closed down on us, so I couldn't see what she looked like, and vice versa. But over her shoulder, I could see what must be Reagan. I said, "Get out of here, you ape," and I spoke quite literally because that's exactly what he appeared to be. A bright yellow ape.

The floor was shaking under my feet, but other things were happening to me, too, and I didn't realize what the shaking meant until the ape turned back and yelled, "A flight of birds going under us, Chief! Get out quick, before—"

But that was as far as he got before the house fell down around us and the tin roof hit my head and knocked me out. Placet is a crazy place. I like it.

CONQUEROR'S ISLE

by Nelson S. Bond (1908-   )

BLUE BOOK MAGAZINE
June

Blue Book Magazine, *under several names, was one of the longest running generalist pulps in the United States, lasting well over half a century. It published much interesting science fiction over the years, including novels by such notables as George Allan England, Edgar Rice Burroughs, and the team of Philip Wylie and Edwin Bulmer. After World War II it featured work by Robert A. Heinlein and Eric Frank Russell, among others. Indeed, an anthology of the best science fiction from* Bluebook *would make a more than respectable book.*

Its most frequent sf author was Nelson Bond, who contributed two series—about "Pat Pending" and "Squaredeal Sam"—to its pages in the 1940s. "Conqueror's Isle" is an excellent story about evolution and about what might come after man.

(This is what makes Marty invaluable. He finds the stories in Blue Book. *I never read this story until it showed up in the batch that Marty had sent me for my consideration. It's a lucky thing I was told it was from* Blue Book, *too, for if I had been asked in which magazine it had appeared, I would*

have said Astounding *and would have been sufficiently certain of it to have backed my opinion with a sizable chunk of money. You see this notion that "there are mutants among us" was another of John Campbell's favorite notions. I think it was because John felt that he himself was one of them. At least, I know he once suggested I might be one, but I shook my head violently at that. There's no question that I know full well that I am very bright, but I know too many of my own weaknesses and insufficiencies not to be quite certain I am* Homo average.

But Bond makes me shiver in this story. I don't want to be caught on the short end of the stick.—I.A.)

"You've got to believe this," said Brady. He spoke with tense, white-knuckled ferocity, his eyes intent on those of the older man. "It sounds utterly impossible, I know. It sounds—it sounds crazy. That's why I'm here. But it's the truth, and you've got to believe it! *Got* to—sir," he finished, belatedly acknowledging his listener's seniority.

Lieutenant Commander Gorham said quietly: "At ease, Lieutenant. I'm here to consult with you as a physician, not order your cure as a superior officer. Suppose we ignore the braid while you tell me about it?"

Joe Brady smiled. It was his first smile in weeks and his face could not quite accomplish it. His lips twisted jerkily, but his eyes remained blank windows into torment.

He said: "Thank you, Doctor. Where would you like me to begin?"

Gorham shuffled the pages of the lieutenant's case history. Random excerpts telescoped three years of spotless if not spectacular service: *Brady, Joseph Travers . . . Age:* 24 . . . *Graduated, U. S. N. A.,* 1941 . . . *Pre-Flight Training, Sarasota* 1941-2 . . . *Assigned: U. S. S. Stinger . . . Lieutenant (j.g.)* 1942 . . . *Group Citation . . . Personal citation . . . Recommended for . . .*

"It's your story," said the doctor carefully. "*You* know

what it is you want me to believe. The trouble began, I understand, on your last bombing mission?"

"That's right. Or rather, that's when *my* troubles began. The thing's been going on for longer than that—much longer. Years, certainly; perhaps decades." Brady's fingers were like talons on the desk top. "Someone's got to *do* something, Doctor! Time is racing by, and with every passing day *They* grow stronger. I've got to make people understand—"

"At the beginning?" suggested Gorham. "Suppose you start with that unfortunate last flight."

His calm matter-of-fact tone had a soothing effect on the younger man. Brady's voice lost its high note of hysteria.

"Yes, sir," he said. "Very good, sir. Well, then, it was this way. We accomplished our mission and started for home—"

We accomplished our mission (said Lieutenant Brady) and started home. "Home" was, of course, the *Stinger*. I can tell you, now that the war's over, where we were and what we were doing. We were cruising the South China Sea, roughly off Palawan, between the Philippines and Indo-China. Our job was to harass enemy shipping in that area, breaking the lifeline between the Straits and the Nipponese home islands. Our task force was in position to support any one of a dozen land invasions from Labuan to Hainan, and our air arm periodically feinted at various concentration points to confuse the Japs.

Our latest target had been Songcau, and it was from this port we were returning when it happened

We sighted a tramp beating her way up the coast, and I called the squadron leader for permission to unload a heavy I was carrying home undropped. He O. K.'d, and we peeled off. The freighter opened up on us with all she had as we came in, but she might as well have been throwing spit balls. We laid our eggs down her aft stack, and she flew into pieces like one of those toys kids play with. You know—the kind you push a button, and *blooie!*

So, that was that, and we were all talking it up and feeling pretty hot stuff when all of a sudden we discovered we were losing elevation like crazy. It seems the freighter had died like a rat, clawing in her death agony. A hunk of her exploding hide had slashed out of our wing tanks, and we were spraying gas all over the South China Sea.

Even then we weren't worried. The Navy watches out for its own, and we knew that an hour after we were forced to our life rafts, a rescue party would be out to pick us up. So we reported the bad news to the squadron leader and accepted his condolences philosophically; and with no great dismay watched the flight dwindle to black dots as we lurched along, coaxing every last possible mile out of our ruptured duck.

It would be annoying, we thought, and a nuisance. But it wouldn't be dangerous. That's what we thought.

That's what we thought, being logical guys. But in the South Pacific area you can toss logic and reason out the window.

About ten minutes after the flight had disappeared, and about one cupful of gas before we'd have to ditch, out of a bald, blue, breezeless nowhere came thundering mountains of cumulus, torrential cloudbursts of rain, and a shrieking hundred-mile gale that picked us up and whirled us like the button on a hen-coop door.

How long we rode that thing, I haven't the faintest idea. I had no time for clock-watching; I had all I could do holding the *Ardent Alice*—that was our ship's name—holding the *Ardent Alice's* nose steady in the face of that blast. It grabbed us, and shook us, and lifted and dropped us, and spun us as if we weighed ounces instead of tons. We had no way of climbing above the storm, of course; we just had to sit there and take it. At least a dozen times I was sure we were going to be slammed into the sea, but each time the unpredictable wind jerked us upstairs again to play with us some more.

All three of us were nerve-tattered, bone-bruised, and dog-sick from the storm's beating, and not one but would have cheerfully given up a year's shore leaves to be clear of this mess. And then, suddenly—as suddenly as it had sprung from nowhere—the typhoon passed. One minute we were standing on our ears in a maelstrom of wind and rain; the next, the skies were crystal clean and a benevolent sun beamed down on a blue tranquil sea, while under the shadow of our wing tips the pink-and-green sanctuary of a tropical island!

Gorham coughed politely, interrupting his patient.

"Pardon me, Lieutenant. I'd like to make a note of that. It may be important. An island? *What* island?"

Brady shrugged helplessly.

"I don't know, sir. We had been twisted, battered, bounced

around so badly, and for so long, that none of us had any idea where we were. We might have been one mile or fifty—or five hundred!—from where the typhoon struck us."

His voice strengthened with purpose. "But wherever it is, we've got to find that island again. *Got* to! Because it's *Their* island. Unless we find it, and destroy *Them*—"

"Suppose," suggested the doctor quietly, "you go on with your story? You reached this uncharted island. And you landed safely, I take it?"

"That's right, sir. We landed safely on a sandy strip of beach—"

We landed safely (continued Lieutenant Brady) on a sandy strip of beach. We were jubilant at having made a safe harbor but uncertain as to just *how* safe the harbor was. We didn't know, you see, whether we'd been carried into friendly or enemy territory. In that Godforsaken corner of the world there was also the possibility that the island's inhabitants, if any, might be technically neutral but still dangerous. In other words, head-hunting aborigines.

Imagine our pleasure and surprise, then, when a few minutes after we'd landed we heard a cheerful hail and looked up to find white men approaching us from the wall of tropical foliage that spanned the beach.

They were smiling and unarmed, and they welcomed us in English with courteous enthusiasm. They had seen us land, said the head of their party—a youngish chap who introduced himself as Dr. Grove—and had hurried out to meet us in case anyone needed medical assistance.

I assured him we were all right, and that we needed only food, rest, and a means of communicating our whereabouts to our comrades, who by this time were undoubtedly fanned out over half the South Pacific searching for us.

He nodded. "Food and rest you shall have" he said heartily. "As for the other—those things take time in this primitive country. But we shall see; we shall see."

"We have a radio in the plane—" I began, but Jack Kavanaugh, our radioman, shook his head at me.

"*Did* have Skipper? It went out just as we sighted the island. Must have got whanged around a bit in the storm."

"But you can fix it?"

"I suppose so. If it's nothing serious. I'll tell you better after I've had a chance to look it over."

"Of course," nodded Grove. "But in the meantime, I hope

you'll accept our humble hospitality? We don't have the pleasure of entertaining new guests here very often. It will be good to chat with you all. If you'll follow me—"

There was nothing else to do. Like sheep being led to the slaughter—blindly trusting and without a struggle—we followed him off the beach into a winding jungle path.

It was Tom Goeller, my gunner, who first intimated there might be something wrong about this setup. Even *he* did not really suspect anything; he was just puzzled. He wondered aloud as we pushed forwards: "Where from? I don't get it?"

"Don't get what?" I asked him. "What do you mean—where from? What's biting you, Tom?"

"That Grove character," grumbled Tom. "He said they saw us land. Only—where from? Where the hell do they live? In the trees? I had a good look at this island just before we landed. A good, long look—from topside. And I didn't see a sign of anything that looked like a house."

I said: "By God, you're right! I didn't, either. I wonder if—"

But my question was answered before I voiced it. We stopped, inexplicably, before a sort of concrete shelter under a sprawling banyan tree; a lean-to sort of business in mottled green and brown—so perfectly camouflaged to conform with its surroundings that you could hardly see it from ten yards away, much less from the air.

Dr. Grove smiled and said: "Here we are, gentlemen." He touched a button, and the shelter door swung open. "If you will be good enough to enter—"

Kavanaugh spoke up roughly. "Enter what? That?"

Grove laughed pleasantly. "Don't be alarmed. It's merely an elevator. The entrance is from ground level."

"An elevator!" I exclaimed. "In this jungle? What kind of monkey business is this, anyhow? Do you mean to tell me you live underground?"

"My dear Lieutenant," said the self-styled "Doctor" languidly, "I'll be glad to explain everything—later. It's all very simple. But first I must insist that you—"

"Oh!" I interrupted. "So now you are *insisting,* eh? And suppose we prefer not to step into your mysterious little parlor? Then what?"

"Then," sighed Dr. Grove, "I should be compelled—most regretfully—to enforce my request."

"That right?" I grunted. "Guess again, pal. There are more

of you than us—we happen to be armed." I took out my automatic and held it on him level. "That's one detail you seem to have overlooked. Now—"

"I overlook no details, Lieutenant," answered Grove quietly. "Would you be kind enough to fire your gun? If you have qualms against killing a man in cold blood"—his lips curled mockingly—"you might fire into the air."

I stared at him, baffled. He wasn't stalling. You can *feel* things like that. He was amused, superior, contemptuous. Goeller said: "Watch yourself, Skipper; it's a trick! He *wants* you to shoot. The sound will bring help."

Grove smiled. "Wrong, my friend. I need no help." He slipped a hand into his breast pocket. "Very well. Since you won't accept my invitation—"

Shooting was risky, but I had no choice. "O.K.," I snapped. "You asked for it!" And I squeezed the trigger. I froze on it, waiting for the blast, and the sight of his body crumpling before me.

But nothing happened!

Gorham listening to this recital, blinked. "You mean," he suggested, "the gun missed fire—that it jammed?"

"I mean," said Brady helplessly, "it just didn't go off; that's all. It didn't miss fire. It didn't jam. There wasn't a thing wrong with it, mechanically. Later I took it down piece by piece and examined it. It was perfect. But it just wouldn't fire on that island."

Gorham said slowly: "It wouldn't fire—on that island?" His eyes on the younger man were cautious, and he was doodling thoughtfully on the pad before him. "But that's incredible! Why not?"

"I soon found out," said Brady grimly, "about that. About that and a lot of other things—"

I stood there (said Brady) speechless. I couldn't understand. At first I thought—like you—that my gun had jammed. Then suddenly I discovered that the other men had drawn their guns too—and that they too were staring incredulously at utterly futile weapons.

"You see?" Grove shrugged. "Now, perhaps, you will be kind enough to step into the shaft?"

"Not on your life!" I blazed back, "I don't understand what's going on here. But whatever it is, I don't want any part of it. Come on, gang! Let's get out of here!"

"I'm sorry," said the doctor. "You force me to use harsh measures. Believe me, I do so reluctantly."

From his breast pocket he drew a slender tube about the size and shape of a fountain pen. He pointed it at me—at *us,* I should say, because from it suddenly flowed a silver cone of radiance.

I started to rush him, shouting something or other. But both shout and movement stopped abruptly as that curious, silvery radiance engulfed me. It wasn't a gas. It was odorless and tasteless; it did not burn or sting or cause pain in any way. But it was as though I had charged into an ocean of lambent cobwebs, to become enmeshed in a shroud of moonbeams. I could neither move nor speak; only my senses functioned.

As in a dream, I heard Dr. Grove bid his followers: "Place them in the shaft. Gently, please!" Then the feel of hands lifting, carrying me; they felt—how can I explain it?—they felt *far away* upon my body, as though layers of sponge rubber lay between their flesh and mine.

I could see, too, but only straight ahead of me, in the direction in which my pupils were fixed. I couldn't move my eyes. So I saw only that the interior of the elevator was smooth, polished metal, anomalous in these surroundings. I heard the whine of an electric motor and sensed, rather than felt, the motion of our swift descent.

Dr. Groves leaned over me, thrusting himself into my line of vision.

"I'm sorry, Lieutenant," he said. "I sincerely regret having had to inconveniece you. But, you see, firearms won't work on this island. No explosions of any kind are permitted—unless by special arrangement. We have means of hampering your primitive mechanical devices. That is why your guns did not fire, and why your radio will not operate."

I was filled with a thousand questions, but I could not ask them, not even with my eyes. *"What are these means?"* I wanted to ask him. *"And who, or what are you that you should speak of a radio as a primitive mechanical device? Where are we going, and what are you planning to do with us?"* All these questions hammered at my brain, but my tongue was silent.

Then the sensation of movement stopped, I heard the elevator door slide open, and our captors lifted us again. I saw the metal ceiling of long, well-lighted corridors, and heard voices proclaiming the presence of many more persons in these subterranean vaults, and once was silent witness to a conversation between Grove and someone apparently his superior.

"Well, Frater?"

"I'm sorry, Frater Dorden. It was necessary. They would not come willingly."

"I see." A sigh. "Few of them do. Ah, well—put them in sleeping chambers until they recover . . . And be gentle. They are frightened, poor devils."

And then our journey continued through a maze of clean-gleaming metal corridors, until finally I was carried through a doorway and placed tenderly on a cot. A light covering was thrown over me; its pleasant warmth made me realize how weary I was. I could not close my eyes, but the lights were dimmed slowly, and at last in utter darkness I forgot my troubles in sleep . . .

I do not know whether the return of lights awakened me, or whether some unseen control automatically brought back the illumination when I awoke. At any rate, I roused from my slumber to find the room bright again.

Even more important was the fact that I could move. I leaped from my cot and sprang to the door at the other side of the room but, as I had expected, it was locked. So I gave up, for the time being, any idea of attempting to escape and set myself to a study of my surroundings.

For one thing, I was alone. Apparently our captors had assigned each of us to a separate chamber, or cell. This one was Spartan in its simplicity. Four walls of a dull gray metallic substance I could not immediately identify—a floor of some resilient rubber or plastic composition—a low ceiling of the same material as the walls. A cot, a chair, and a desk were the only furnishings. There were no decorations on the walls; no carpet covered the floor; and of course—since we were underground—there were no windows.

What amazed me most was that there were no lighting fixtures. I looked in vain for any source from which originated the pleasant, unflickering illumination that flooded the room. I found nothing. It was no jiggery-pokery of indirect lighting, either. The flow of light was constant and, oddly enough there were no shadows!

I think that's when I started to get frightened. I don't mean flappy-lipped, knock-kneed scared, but *cold*. Cold and awed and numb, like—well, the way a trapped rabbit must feel when it sees the hunter approaching.

These persons, these men who spoke with indifferent contempt of mankind's finest accomplishments, who regretfully and casually employed weapons and tools unknown to science—who were they? And why had we been separated? Where were my comrades—Kavanaugh and Goeller? Suddenly, desperately, I needed the reassurance of their presence.

I raised my voice and shouted. There was no reply. The impassive walls should have echoed the panic in my voice, being metal. But, like everything else in this strange place, it behaved unnaturally. It absorbed the sound, sopping it up as a sponge absorbs water.

I shouted again and again. Fruitlessly, I thought. But not fruitlessly. For suddenly I heard the faintest sound behind me and whirled. Dr. Grove was stepping though the wall.

Lieutenant Brady stopped abruptly, as if in anticipation of his listener's reaction. It came. Gorham, despite his training as a psychiatrist, stopped doodling and tossed a swift, anxious frown at the younger man.

With an obvious effort he erased the sudden pursing of his lips. He said quietly: "Through the *wall*, Lieutenant? Of course you mean through the *door?*"

"Through the wall," said Brady dully. "Through the wall, sir. The door was in front of me. But Dr. Grove stepped into my cell through the solid metal wall."

"You realize," said Gorham, "that what you are saying is impossible?"

"To us"—Brady's eyes were haggard—"it is. To *Them*, nothing is impossible. Nothing! Or very little. That is why we must act, and act *now!* Before it is too late. You must believe me, sir. This is man's last chance—"

"I'll do my best," promised Gorham. "Perhaps you'd better continue? This Dr. Grove stepped through the wall—"

I'll cut it short (said Brady wanly). I'll tell it as quickly as I can. I'm just wasting your time and mine. I can tell by your eyes that you don't believe me. But someone must. Somewhere, somehow, sometime—someone must . . . Well, as I was saying, Dr. Grove stepped through the wall. And strange as it may sound, in that moment my panic ended. I still *feared*; yes. But I feared as a man fears a god, or a demon, or a raw and elemental force beyond his comprehension. I did not look on him with dread, as one watches a human foe charge upon him with a flaming gun or blood stained sword; I looked on him with awe, knowing him to be as far above and beyond me in the life scale as I am superior to a dog or a beast of burden.

So it was we talked—not as man to man, but as man to a lesser creature. And *I* was the lesser creature. He was the master, I the serf. And he told me many things . . .

Has it ever occurred to you, Doctor, that we humans are an egotistic race? Our Darwins and our Huxleys have told us we are the product of a steady, progressive evolution—an evolution that started in primeval slime and has gradually developed to our present proud and self-proclaimed status as *homo sapiens.*

Homo sapiens—intelligent man! . . . But perhaps we are not so intelligent, at that. For in our blind folly we have assumed ourselves to be the final and glorious end product of Nature's eternal striving toward perfection!

Could we not guess that the same force which led the first lungfish from primordial ooze to solid earth—the force which evolved the Neanderthal man from his bestial, hairy ancestor, and developed from this rock-hurling cave man a race that works its destruction with atomic fission—could we not have guessed that this force would inevitably progress a step farther?

That is what has happened. There dwells upon earth today a race representing the *next step* in man's progress. A people to whom our thoughts are as immature and elementary as to us is the prattling of infants.

They begin where we leave off. Our vaunted physics and mathematics are their nursery ABC's; the hard-won learning of our best brains is theirs intuitively. They *sense* what we must study; and what they must study, we cannot even begin to grasp. They are the new lords of creation—*homo superior!*

How they came to be, that is one thing even they do not know. There is a force called "mutation" which you, as a doctor, must understand better than I. By mutation a white rose appears among red, and the white breed true from that time on. The new men are mutants. They—or the first of them—were born of normal parents. But from the cradle they sensed that they were different. Having a telepathic instinct, they were able to discern their brothers in a crowd—or even over long distances—and they banded together.

Long ago—how long Dr. Grove did not tell me—the new men decided they must isolate themselves from us. It was a logical decision. They had no more in common with us than we have with our pets. Few men, by choice, dine with dogs or sleep in stables.

So they sought this secluded island in the Pacific, far from lesser man's civilization. They went underground to escape detection. There they live, and study, and learn, and wait with infinite patience for the day when they must emerge and take over the world which is theirs by inheritance—even as *homo sapiens* took it over from his beetle-browed forebear, the ape man.

"We are few in number," Grove told me, "but we increase with each passing year. Some are born here; others come from the four corners of the earth, drawn to us by mental *rapport*. Soon we will be many enough, and strong enough, to accept the responsibility of government of all the earth."

"You mean," I said, "destroy man? And claim the entire world for yourselves?"

Grove said almost sadly: "How little you understand us, you humans. Do you destroy the animals of the field just because they are not your intellectual peers? Our obligation is to keep and protect you; to act as your friendly guardians in a world that will be strange to you, and frightening.

"Yes, frightening," he went on as I began some protest. "I saw the dread and horror in your eyes when I walked into the room. You did not understand how I passed through a wall that to you seems solid. Not understanding, you feared.

"Yet there is nothing supernatural or fearful about what I did; about what any of us can do at will. There is no such thing as a solid in a universe wherein all things—size and dimension and substance—are but relative. We know there is room and to spare for the molecules comprising our persons to pass unhindered through the molecules comprising these walls. We simply make a necessary mental adjustment—and walk where we will. It is an ability as basic, fundamental, to us as breathing is to a person like you."

"Then what?" I asked him, "*is* your plan for man?"

"Your question should be," he replied gently, "what is Nature's plan for man? And I believe the question answers itself. The answer lies in history. What becomes of Nature's earlier experiments: the giant reptiles, the anthropoids, the men who dwelt in caves and trees?"

"They died out," I said. "Civilization passed them by. They fell before the onrush of higher life forms."

"Even so," Grove said regretfully. "Even so. But you have our pledge that we will be kind. We will be kind."

You see, that was the essence of the matter. These new men are intelligent, a thousandfold more intelligent than we. And being that great step farther along the path to perfection, they are born with the instinct to gentleness. That is why their weapons anesthetize, but do not harm. They will not, they *cannot,* kill.

I could go on for hours relating what I heard and saw during the three weeks I was prisoner in the subterranean refuge of the new men. I'll tell only a few things, because I can see you—like all the others—think I am mad. But there are some things you should know.

Those metal cells hold more than two hundred humans like you and me, men and women who have stumbled by accident upon the hideaway island and have been restrained there lest they go back and tell the world of the conquest to come.

They are comfortable, of course. They are well fed and housed, entertained and made as happy as possible—under the circumstances. Men do not ruthlessly destroy their pets. And on that island, men are the wards of supermen.

I could quote names that would amaze you. A famous author and traveler whose ship disappeared some years ago in the Pacific—a big-game hunter supposedly killed—an aviatrix for whom a dozen fleets sought in vain. They are there.

I could tell you something else that would make the small hairs creep on the back of your neck—if you dared let yourself believe it. *They* are among us already, the new men. As their hour of ascendancy approaches, they are paving the way for their bloodless conquest. Some of them have left the island and taken their places in our world. You can see the master plan. A handful of them settled in key spots—here a politician, there an industrial magnate, there an author whose every word is gospel to his readers—what chance has a race of underlings to combat them when they strike?

And they *will* strike, and soon. When they do, that will be our end as the rulers of earth. For they cannot fail in anything they try. We, as a people, are strong. But *They* are omnipotent!

"That is why," concluded Brady, "you've got to make yourself believe me, no matter how crazy this sounds. You've *got* to, Doctor. From the broader point of view, perhaps it's better they should inherit the earth. But I am a human. And as a member of my race, I do not want to fall before a higher culture, no matter how superior.

"I want to live! And if we want to live, *They* must die.

Their island must be destroyed, utterly and completely. An atomic bomb—"

"You have said," interrupted Dr. Gorham, "that they are omnipotent. You have called them wise with the wisdom of demigods. Yet you escaped from their island without outside help. Is that proof of their superhuman intelligence?"

Brady shook his head.

"It is proof of their great kindness, and my animal cunning.

"There is a chink in their armor. I took advantage of it. They cannot willfully cause any creature pain. Knowing this, I begged Grove to take me to the surface so I could get some things from the *Ardent Alice* one day. Some personal belongings, I told him. Pictures of my loved ones that I had hidden in a secret compartment of the plane.

"He agreed. We had been on friendly terms for some weeks, and he suspected no treachery. That is a human trait. They cannot conceive of guile or deceit.

"He was careless, and I was desperate. He turned to look when I cried out and pointed to something behind him; he never knew what hit him. I don't know whether my rock killed him or not. I hope not.

"The plane, of course, was useless. But there were self-inflating life rafts, and the water was only yards away. I paddled from the devil's shore with the strength of a madman. You know the rest: How my food and water ran out. How they found me raving deliriously days or maybe weeks later, bearded and sun-blistered and more than half dead."

Dr. Gorham nodded and quietly closed the memo book in which he had scratched only doodles.

"Yes," he said quietly. "Yes. It must have been a terrible experience."

He rose.

"Well, Lieutenant—" he said awkwardly.

Lieutenant Brady stared at him with hopeless eyes.

"*You* don't believe me, either," he said. "Do you?"

"It's been a pleasure listening to your story," the medico said. "I'll make a report to my superiors. Please be patient and try not to worry. Good day, Lieutenant."

"Go to hell!" said Lieutenant Brady dully. "Oh, go to hell—" he added mechanically—"sir."

The doctor stiffened, then gazed compassionately at the younger man for an instant, shrugged, and left the narrow chamber.

Outside, another medical officer greeted him.

"Ah, there, Gorham! You've talked with him? What's the verdict?"

Gorham touched his forehead. "A clear case of persecution mania—an amazing form. I've never heard a tale so complete and logical, but—" He shrugged. "Do what you can for him. I'm afraid he's going to be here for a long time—perhaps for as long as he lives. Turned loose, he might be dangerous."

"Tough! A nice boy, too. But it does nasty things to a man, floating for weeks in a life raft. He was the only one of his crew to survive. Well, Doctor—will you lunch with me?"

The other medical officer shook his head.

"No, thanks," said Gorham. "I've got to run along. Have to turn in a report and a recommendation on this case."

"Of course. See you later, then."

The other medico disappeared down the spotless corridor of the mental ward. Gorham pondered briefly, orienting himself. He was in the west wing of the hospital, facing the street. His car stood at the curb just outside. He was very busy. There was so much work to be done; *so* much. And if he walked through the anteroom, some fool was sure to delay him, drag him into a long-winded discussion. He didn't feel a bit like talking. He wanted to get out of this place and forward his report—his report that the Brady case was closed. That there would be no more trouble from that source.

He glanced swiftly up and down the corridor. There was no one in sight. His senses told him the street was also deserted. There was no danger of his being seen. So—

So Dr. Gorham turned and walked quietly through the wall.

LORELEI OF THE RED MIST

by Ray Bradbury (1920-   )
and Leigh Brackett

PLANET STORIES
Summer

Ray Bradbury is now one of the best known science fiction writers in the world, but in 1946 he had not yet achieved the fame that would rightfully be his—in fact, most of his published fiction until that year consisted of fantasy and horror stories, many of which appeared in the late and lamented Weird Tales, *(these early stories were collected in 1947 as* Dark Carnival, *his first book and now a collector's item). Bradbury was one of the first major writers to emerge from science fiction fandom, and it was through fandom that he met Leigh Brackett, who encouraged and aided his writing career. She was a fine author and notable screenwriter whose excellent space opera was a mainstay of* Planet Stories, *the magazine most closely associated with this area of science fiction.*

"Lorelei of the Red Mist" was apparently started by Ms. Brackett and finished by Ray Bradbury, one of his relatively rare excursions into the realms of what would become known as "sword and sorcery."

(Ray Bradbury is, in some ways, the one-who-doesn't-fit in the world of science fiction. He is the only writer who graduated to greatness in the course of the Golden Age without *having passed through the school in which John W. Campbell, Jr. was headmaster. He was the first science fiction writer to become well-known* outside *science fiction. He made it in the general world of literature when all the rest of us didn't even know there existed such a thing as the general world of literature.*

To non-science-fiction readers, he is still the *giant of science fiction, and yet to science fiction readers themselves, however they may admire him, he has never threatened the position of the Big Three* [*any more than Kurt Vonnegut—that latter-day Ray Bradbury—has*]. *The key to the puzzle is that to outsiders, Bradbury does not really write standard science fiction. He writes what he has invented and what no one else can duplicate.—I.A.)*

The company dicks were good. They were plenty good. Hugh Starke began to think maybe this time he wasn't going to get away with it.

His small stringy body hunched over the control bank, nursing the last ounce of power out of the Kallman. The hot night sky of Venus fled past the ports in tattered veils of indigo. Starke wasn't sure where he was any more. Venus was a frontier planet, and still mostly a big X, except to the Venusians—who weren't sending out any maps. He did know that he was getting dangerously close to the Mountains of White Cloud. The backbone of the planet, towering far into the stratosphere, magnetic trap, with God knew what beyond. Maybe even God wasn't sure.

But it looked like over the mountains or out. Death under the guns of the Terro-Venus Mines, Incorporated, Special Police, or back to the Luna cell blocks for life as an habitual felon.

Starke decided he would go over.

Whatever happened, he'd pulled off the biggest lone-wolf caper in history. The T-V Mines payroll ship, for close to a million credits. He cuddled the metal strongbox between his feet and grinned. It would be a long time before anybody equaled that.

His mass indicators began to jitter. Vaguely, a dim purple shadow in the sky ahead, the Mountains of White Cloud, stood like a wall against him. Starke checked the positions of the pursuing ships. There was no way through them. He said flatly, "All right, damn you," and sent the Kallman angling up into the thick blue sky.

He had no very clear memories after that. Crazy magnetic vagaries, always a hazard on Venus, made his instruments useless. He flew by the seat of his pants and he got over, and the T-V men didn't. He was free, with a million credits in his kick.

Far below in the virgin darkness he saw a sullen crimson smear on the night, as though someone had rubbed it with a bloody thumb. The Kallman dipped toward it. The control bank flickered with blue flame, the jet timers blew, and then there was just the screaming of air against the falling hull.

Hugh Starke sat still and waited . . .

He knew, before he opened his eyes, that he was dying. He didn't feel any pain, he didn't feel anything, but he knew just the same. Part of him was cut loose. He was still there, but not attached anymore.

He raised his eyelids. There was a ceiling. It was a long way off. It was black stone veined with smoky reds and ambers. He had never seen it before.

His head was tilted toward the right. He let his gaze move down that way. There were dim tapestries, more of the black stone, and three tall archways giving onto a balcony. Beyond the balcony was a sky veiled and clouded with red mist. Under the mist, spreading away from a murky line of cliffs, was an ocean. It wasn't water and it didn't have any waves on it, but there was nothing else to call it. It burned, deep down inside itself, breathing up the red fog. Little angry bursts of flame coiled up under the flat surface, sending circles of sparks flaring out like ripples from a dropped stone.

He closed his eyes and frowned and moved his head restively. There was the texture of fur against his skin. Through the cracks of his eyelids he saw that he lay on a high bed piled with silks and soft tanned pelts. His body was covered. He was rather glad he couldn't see it. It didn't matter because he wouldn't be using it any more anyway, and it hadn't been such a hell of a body to begin with. But he was used to it, and he didn't want to see it now, the way he knew it would have to look.

He looked along over the foot of the bed, and he saw the woman.

She sat watching him from a massive carved chair softened with a single huge white pelt like a drift of snow. She smiled, and let him look. A pulse began to beat under his jaw, very feebly.

She was tall and sleek and insolently curved. She wore a sort of tabard of pale grey spider-silk, held to her body by a jeweled girdle, but it was just a nice piece of ornamentation. Her face was narrow, finely cut, secret, faintly amused. Her lips, her eyes, and her flowing silken hair were all the same pale cool shade of aquamarine.

Her skin was white, with no hint of rose. Her shoulders, her forearms, the long flat curve of her thighs, the pale-green tips of her breasts, were dusted with tiny particles that glistened like powdered diamond. She sparkled softly like a fairy thing against the snowy fur, a creature of foam and moonlight and clear shallow water. Her eyes never left his, and they were not human, but he knew that they would have done things to him if he had had any feeling below the neck.

He started to speak. He had no strength to move his tongue. The woman leaned forward, and as though her movement were a signal four men rose from the tapestried shadows by the wall. They were like her. Their eyes were pale and strange like hers.

She said, in liquid High Venusian, "You're dying, in this body. But *you* will not die. You will sleep now, and wake in a strange body, in a strange place. Don't be afraid. My mind will be with yours, I'll guide you, don't be afraid. I can't explain now, there isn't time, but don't be afraid."

He drew back his thin lips baring his teeth in what might have been a smile. If it was, it was wolfish and bitter, like his face.

The woman's eyes began to pour coolness into his skull. They were like two little rivers running through the channels of his own eyes, spreading in silver-green quiet across the tortured surface of his brain. His brain relaxed. It lay floating on the water, and then the twin streams became one broad, flowing stream, and his mind, or ego, the thing that was intimately himself, vanished along it.

It took him a long, long time to regain consciousness. He felt as though he'd been shaken until pieces of him were scattered all over inside. Also, he had an instinctive premonition that the minute he woke up he would be sorry he had. He took it easy, putting himself together.

He remembered his name, Hugh Starke. He remembered the mining asteroid where he was born. He remembered the Luna cell blocks where he had once come near dying. There wasn't much to choose between them. He remembered his face decorating half the bulletin boards between Mercury and The Belt. He remembered hearing about himself over the telecasts, stuff to frighten babies with, and he thought of himself committing his first crime—a stunted scrawny kid of eighteen swinging a spanner on a grown man who was trying to steal his food.

The rest of it came fast, then. The T-V Mines job, the getaway that didn't get, the Mountains of White Cloud. The crash . . .

The woman.

That did it. His brain leaped shatteringly. Light, feeling, a naked sense of reality swept over him. He lay perfectly still with his eyes shut, and his mind clawed at the picture of the shining woman with sea-green hair and the sound of her voice saying, *You will not die, you will wake in a strange body, don't be afraid . . .*

He was afraid. His skin pricked and ran cold with it. His stomach knotted with it. His skin, his stomach, and yet somehow they didn't feel just right, like a new coat that hasn't shaped to you . . .

He opened his eyes, a cautious crack.

He saw a body sprawled on its side in dirty straw. The body belonged to him, because he could feel the straw pricking it, and the itch of little things that crawled and ate and crawled again.

It was a powerful body, rangy and flat-muscled, much bigger than his old one. It had obvisouly not been starved the first twenty-some years of its life. It was stark naked. Weather and violence had written history on it, wealed white marks on leathery bronze, but nothing seemed to be missing. There was black hair on its chest and thighs and forearms, and its hands were lean and sinewy for killing.

It was a human body. That was something. There were so many other things it might have been that his racial snobbery wouldn't call human. Like the nameless shimmering creature who smiled with strange pale lips.

Starke shut his eyes again.

He lay, the intangible self that was Hugh Starke, bellied down in the darkness of the alien shell, quiet, indrawn, waiting. Panic crept up on its soft black paws. It walked around the crouching ego and sniffed and patted and nuzzled, whining, and then struck with its raking claws. After a while it went away, empty.

The lips that were now Starke's lips twitched in a thin, cruel smile. He had done six months once in the Luna solitary crypts. If a man could do that, and come out sane and on his two feet, he could stand anything. Even this.

It came to him then, rather deflatingly, that the woman and her four companions had probably softened the shock by hypnotic suggestion. His subconscious understood and accepted the change. It was only his conscious mind that was superficially scared to death.

Hugh Starke cursed the woman with great thoroughness, in seven languages and some odd dialects. He became healthily enraged that any dame should play around with him like that. Then he thought, What the hell, I'm alive. And it looks like I got the best of the trade-in!

He opened his eyes again, secretly, on his new world.

He lay at one end of a square stone hall, good sized, with two straight lines of pillars cut from some dark Venusian wood. There were long crude benches and tables. Fires had been burning on round brick hearths spaced between the pillars. They were embers now. The smoke climbed up, tarnishing the gold and bronze of shields hung on the walls and pediments, dulling the blades of longswords, the spears, the tapestries and hides and trophies.

It was very quiet in the hall. Somewhere outside of it there was fighting going on. Heavy, vicious fighting. The noise of it didn't touch the silence, except to make it deeper.

There were two men besides Starke in the hall.

They were close to him, on a low dais. One of them sat in a carved high seat, not moving, his big scarred hands flat on the table in front of him. The other crouched on the floor by his feet. His head was bent forward so that his mop of lint-white hair hid his face and the harp between his thighs. He was a little man, a swamp-edger from his albino coloring. Starke looked back at the man in the chair.

The man spoke harshly. "Why doesn't she send word?"

The harp gave out a sudden bitter chord. That was all.

Starke hardly noticed. His whole attention was drawn to the speaker. His heart began to pound. His muscles coiled and lay ready. There was a bitter taste in his mouth. He recognized it. It was hate.

He had never seen the man before, but his hands twitched with the urge to kill.

He was big, nearly seven feet, and muscled like a draft horse. But his body, naked above a gold-bossed leather kilt, was lithe and quick as a greyhound in spite of its weight. His face was square, strong-boned, weathered, and still young. It was a face that had laughed a lot once, and liked wine and pretty girls. It had forgotten those things now, except maybe the wine. It was drawn and cruel with pain, a look as of something in a cage. Starke had seen that look before, in the Luna blocks. There was a thick white scar across the man's forehead. Under it his blue eyes were sunken and dark behind half-closed lids. The man was blind.

Outside, in the distance, men screamed and died.

Starke had been increasingly aware of a soreness and stricture around his neck. He raised a hand, careful not to rustle the straw. His fingers found a long tangled beard, felt under it, and touched a band of metal.

Starke's new body wore a collar, like a vicious dog.

There was a chain attached to the collar. Starke couldn't find any fastening. The business had been welded on for keeps. His body didn't seem to have liked it much. The neck was galled and chafed.

The blood began to crawl up hot into Starke's head. He'd worn chains before. He didn't like them. Especially around the neck.

A door opened suddenly at the far end of the hall. Fog and red daylight spilled in across the black stone floor. A man came in. He was big, half naked, blond, and bloody. His long blade trailed harshly on the flags. His chest was laid open to the bone and he held the wound together with his free hand.

"Word from Beudag," he said. "They've driven us back into the city, but so far we're holding the Gate."

No one spoke. The little man nodded his white head. The man with the slashed chest turned and went out again, closing the door.

A peculiar change came over Starke at the mention of the name Beudag. He had never heard it before, but it hung in his mind like a spear point, barbed with strange emotion. He couldn't identify the feeling, but it brushed the blind man aside. The hot simple hatred cooled. Starke relaxed in a sort of icy quiet, deceptively calm as a sleeping cobra. He didn't question this. He waited, for Beudag.

The blind man struck his hands down suddenly on the table and stood up. "Romna," he said, "give me my sword."

The little man looked at him. He had milk-blue eyes and a face like a friendly bulldog. He said, "Don't be a fool, Faolan."

Faolan said softly, "Damn you. Give me my sword."

Men were dying outside the hall, and not dying silently. Faolan's skin was greasy with sweat. He made a sudden, darting grab toward Romna.

Romna dodged him. There were tears in his pale eyes. He said brutally, "You'd only be in the way. Sit down."

"I can find the point," Faolan said, "to fall on it."

Romna's voice went up to a harsh scream. "Shut up. Shut up and sit down."

Faolan caught the edge of the table and bent over it. He shivered and closed his eyes, and the tears ran out hot under the lids. The bard turned away, and his harp cried out like a woman.

Faolan drew a long sighing breath. He straightened slowly, came round the carved high seat, and walked steadily toward Starke.

"You're very quiet, Conan," he said. "What's the matter? You ought to be happy, Conan. You ought to laugh and rattle your chain. You're going to get what you wanted. Are you sad because you haven't a mind any more, to understand that with?"

He stopped and felt with one sandaled foot across the straw until he touched Starke's thigh. Starke lay motionless.

"Conan," said the blind man gently, pressing Starke's belly with his foot. "Conan the dog, the betrayer, the butcher, the knife in the back. Remember what you did at Falga, Conan? No, you don't remember now. I've been a little rough with you, and you don't remember any more. But I remember, Conan. As long as I live in darkness, I'll remember."

Romna stroked the harp strings and they wept, savage tears for strong men dead of treachery. Low music, distant but not soft. Faolan began to tremble, a shallow animal twitching of the muscles. The flesh of his face was drawn, iron shaping under the hammer. Quite suddenly he went down on his knees. His hands struck Starke's shoulders, slid inward to the throat, and locked there.

Outside, the sound of fighting had died away.

Starke moved, very quickly. As though he had seen it and knew it was there, his hand swept out and gathered in the slack of the heavy chain and swung it.

It started out to be a killing blow. Starke wanted with all his heart to beat Faolan's brains out. But at the last second he pulled it, slapping the big man with exquisite judgment across the back of the head. Faolan grunted and fell sideways, and by that time Romna had come up. He had dropped his harp and drawn a knife. His eyes were startled.

Starke sprang up. He backed off, swinging the slack of the chain warningly. His new body moved magnificiently. Outside everything was fine, but inside his psycho-neural setup had exploded into civil war. He was furious with himself for not having killed Faolan. He was furious with himself for losing control enough to want to kill a man without reason. He hated Faolan. He did not like Faolan because he didn't know him well enough. Starke's trained, calculating unemotional brain was at grips with a tidal wave to baseless emotion.

He hadn't realized it was baseless until his mental monitor, conditioned through years of bitter control, had stopped him from killing. Now he remembered the woman's voice saying, *My mind will be with yours, I'll guide you . . .*

Catspaw, huh? Just a hired hand, paid off with a new body in return for two lives. Yeah, two. This Beaudag, whoever he was. Starke knew now what that cold alien emotion had been leading up to.

"Hold it," said Starke hoarsely. "Hold everything. *Catspaw! You green-eyed she-devil! You picked the wrong guy this time.*"

Just for a fleeting instant he saw her again, leaning forward with her hair like running water across the soft foam-sparkle of her shoulders. Her sea-pale eyes were full of mocking laughter, and a direct, provocative admiration. Starke heard her quite plainly:

"You may not have any choice, Hugh Starke. They know Conan, even if you don't. Besides, it's of no great importance. The end will be the same for them—it's just a matter of time. You can save your new body or not, as you wish." She smiled. "I'd like it if you did. It's a good body. I knew it, before Conan's mind broke and left it empty."

A sudden thought came to Starke. "My box, the million credits."

"Come and get them." She was gone. Starke's mind was

clear, with no alien will tramping around in it. Faolan crouched on the floor, holding his head. He said:

"Who spoke?"

Romna the bard stood staring. His lips moved, but no sound came out.

Starke said, "I spoke. Me, Hugh Starke. I'm not Conan, and I never heard of Falga, and I'll brain the first guy that comes near me."

Faolan stayed motionless, his face blank, his breath sobbing in his throat. Romna began to curse, very softly, not as though he were thinking about it. Starke watched them.

Down the hall the doors burst open. The heavy reddish mist coiled in with the daylight across the flags, and with them a press of bodies hot from battle, bringing a smell of blood.

Starke felt the heart contract in the hairy breast of the body named Conan, watching the single figure that led the pack.

Romna called out, "Beudag!"

She was tall. She was built and muscled like a lioness, and she walked with a flat-hipped arrogance, and her hair was like coiled flame. Her eyes were blue, hot and bright, as Faolan's might have been once. She looked like Faolan. She was dressed like him, in a leather kilt and sandals, her magnificent body bare above the waist. She carried a longsword slung across her back, the hilt standing above the left shoulder. She had been using it. Her skin was smeared with blood and grime. There was a long cut on her thigh and another across her flat belly, and bitter weariness lay on her like a burden in spite of her denial of it.

"We've stopped them, Faolan," she said. "They can't breach the Gate, and we can hold Crom Dhu as long as we have food. And the sea feeds us." She laughed, but there was a hollow sound to it. "Gods, I'm tired!"

She halted then, below the dais. Her flame-blue gaze swept across Faolan, across Romna, and rose to meet Hugh Starke's, and stayed there.

The pulse began to beat under Starke's jaw again, and this time his body was strong, and the pulse was like a drum throbbing.

Romna said, "His mind has come back."

There was a long, hard silence. No one in the hall moved. Then the men back of Beudag, big brawny kilted warriors, began to close in on the dais, talking in low snarling undertones that rose toward a mob howl. Faolan rose up and faced them, and bellowed them to quiet.

"He's mine to take! Let him alone."

Beudag sprang up onto the dais, one beautiful flowing movement. "It isn't possible," she said. "His mind broke under torture. He's been a drooling idiot with barely the sense to feed himself. And now, suddenly, you say he's normal again?"

Starke said, "You know I'm normal. You can see it in my eyes."

"Yes."

He didn't like the way she said that. "Listen, my name is Hugh Starke. I'm an Earthman. This isn't Conan's brain come back. This is a new deal. I got shoved into his body. What it did before I got it I don't know, and I'm not responsible."

Faolan said, "He doesn't remember Falga. He doesn't remember the longships at the bottom of the sea." Faolan laughed.

Romna said quietly, "He didn't kill you, though. He could have, easily. Would Conan have spared you?"

Beudag said, "Yes, if he had a better plan. Conan's mind was like a snake. It crawled in the dark, and you never knew where it was going to strike."

Starke began to tell them how it happened, the chain swinging idly in his hand. While he was talking he saw a face reflected in a polished shield hung on a pillar. Mostly it was just a tangled black mass of hair, mounted on a frame of long, harsh, jutting bone. The mouth was sensuous, with a dark sort of laughter on it. The eyes were yellow. The cruel, brilliant yellow of a killer hawk.

Starke realized with a shock that the face belonged to him.

"A woman with pale green hair," said Beudag softly. "Rann," said Faolan, and Romna's harp made a sound like a high-priest's curse.

"Her people have that power," Romna said. "They can think a man's soul into a spider, and step on it."

"They have many powers. Maybe Rann followed Conan's mind, wherever it went, and told it what to say, and brought it back again."

"Listen," said Starke angrily. "I didn't ask . . ."

Suddenly, without warning, Romna drew Beudag's sword and threw it at Starke.

Starke dodged it. He looked at Romna with ugly yellow

eyes. "That's fine. Chain me up so I can't fight and kill me from a distance." He did not pick up the sword. He'd never used one. The chain felt better, not being too different from a heavy belt or a length of cable, or the other chains he'd swung on occasion.

Romna said, "Is that Conan?"

Faolan snarled, "What happened?"

"Romna threw my sword at Conan. He dodged it, and left it on the ground." Beudag's eyes were narrowed. "Conan could catch a flying sword by the hilt, and he was the best fighter on the Red Sea, barring you, Faolan."

"He's trying to trick us. Rann guides him."

"The hell with Rann!" Starke clashed his chain. "She wants me to kill the both of you, I still don't know why. All right. I could have killed Faolan, easy. But I'm not a killer. I never put down anyone except to save my own neck. So I didn't kill him in spite of Rann. And I don't want any part of you, or Rann either. All I want is to get the hell out of here!"

Beudag said, "His accent isn't Conan's. And the look in his eyes is different, too." Her voice had an odd note to it. Romna glanced at her. He fingered a few rippling chords on his harp, and said:

"There's one way you could tell for sure."

A sullen flush began to burn on Beudag's cheekbones. Romna slid unobtrusively out of reach. His eyes danced with malicious laughter.

Beudag smiled, the smile of an angry cat, all teeth and no humor. Suddenly she walked toward Starke, her head erect, her hands swinging loose and empty at her sides. Starke tensed warily, but the blood leaped pleasantly in his borrowed veins.

Beudag kissed him.

Starke dropped the chain. He had something better to do with his hands.

After a while he raised his head for breath, and she stepped back and whispered wonderingly,

"It isn't Conan."

The hall had been cleared. Starke had washed and shaved himself. His new face wasn't bad. Not bad at all. In fact, it was pretty damn good. And it wasn't known around the System. It was a face that could own a million credits and no questions asked. It was a face that could have a lot of fun on a million credits.

All he had to figure out now was a way to save the neck the face was mounted on, and get his million credits back from that beautiful she-devil named Rann.

He was still chained, but the straw had been cleaned up and he wore a leather kilt and a pair of sandals. Faolan sat in his high seat nursing a flagon of wine. Beudag sprawled wearily on a fur rug beside him. Romna sat cross-legged, his eyes veiled sleepily, stroking soft wandering music out of his harp. He looked fey. Starke knew his swamp-edgers. He wasn't surprised.

"This man is telling the truth," Romna said. "But there's another mind touching his, Rann's, I think. Don't trust him."

Faolan growled, "I couldn't trust a god in Conan's body"

Starke said, "What's thc setup? All the fighting out there, and this Rann dame trying to plant a killer on the inside. And what happened at Falga? I never heard of this whole damn ocean, let alone a place called Falga."

The bard swept his hand across the strings. "I'll tell you, Hugh Starke. And maybe you won't want to stay in that body any longer."

Starke grinned. He glanced at Beudag. She was watching him with a queer intensity from under lowered lids. Starke's grin changed. He began to sweat. Get rid of this body, hell! It was really a body. His own stringy little carcass had never felt like this.

The bard said, "In the beginning, in the Red Sea, was a race of people having still their fins and scales. They were amphibious, but after a while part of this race wanted to remain entirely on land. There was a quarrel, and a battle, and some of the people left the sea forever. They settled along the shore. They lost their fins and most of their scales. They had great mental powers and they loved ruling. They subjugated the human peoples and kept them almost in slavery. They hated their brothers who still lived in the sea, and their brothers hated them.

"After a time a third people came to the Red Sea. They were rovers from the North. They raided and reaved and wore no man's collar. They made a settlement on Crom Dhu, and Black Rock, and built longships, and took toll of the coastal towns.

"But the slave people didn't want to fight against the rovers. They wanted to fight with them and destroy the sea-folk. The rovers were human, and blood calls to blood. And the rovers liked to rule, too, and this is a rich country. Also, the time had come in their tribal development when they were ready to change from nomadic warriors to builders in their own country.

"So the rovers, and the sea-folk, and the slave-people who were caught between the two of them, began their struggle for the land."

The bard's fingers thrummed against the strings so that they beat like angry hearts. Starke saw that Beudag was still watching him, weighing every change of expression on his face. Romna went on:

"There was a woman named Rann, who had green hair and great beauty, and ruled the sea-folk. There was a man called Faolan of the Ships, and his sister Beudag, which means Dagger-in-the-Sheath, and they two ruled the outland rovers. And there was the man called Conan."

The harp crashed out like a sword-blade striking.

"Conan was a great fighter and a great lover. He was next under Faolan of the Ships, and Beudag loved him, and they were plighted. Then Conan was taken prisoner by the sea-folk during a skirmish, and Rann saw him—and Conan saw Rann."

Hugh Starke had a fleeting memory of Rann's face smiling, and her low voice saying, *It's a good body. I knew it, before . . .*

Beudag's eyes were two stones of blue vitriol under her narrow lids.

"Conan stayed a long time at Falga with Rann of the Red Sea. Then he came back to Crom Dhu, and said that he had escaped, and had discovered a way to take the longships into the harbor of Falga, at the back of Rann's fleet; and from there it would be easy to take the city, and Rann with it. And Conan and Beudag were married."

Starke's yellow hawk eyes slid over Beudag, sprawled like a long lioness in power and beauty. A muscle began to twitch under his cheekbone. Beudag flushed, a slow deep color. Her gaze did not waver.

"So the longships went out from Crom Dhu, across the Red Sea. And Conan led them into a trap at Falga, and more than half of them were sunk. Conan thought his ship was free, that he had Rann and all she'd promised him, but Faolan saw what had happened and went after him. They fought, and Conan laid his sword across Faolan's brow and blinded him; but Conan lost the fight. Beudag brought them home.

"Conan was chained naked in the marketplace. The people

were careful not to kill him. From time to time other things were done to him. After a while his mind broke, and Faolan had him chained here in the hall, where he could hear him babble and play with his chain. It made darkness easier to bear.

"But since Falga, things have gone badly from Crom Dhu. Too many men were lost, too many ships. Now Rann's people have us bottled up here. They can't break in, we can't break out. And so we stay, until . . ." The harp cried out a bitter question, and was still.

After a minute or two Starke said slowly, "Yeah, I get it. Stalemate for both of you. And Rann figured if I could kill off the leaders, your people might give up." He began to curse. "What a lousy, dirty, sneaking trick! And who told her she could use me . . ." He paused. After all, he'd be dead now. After all, a new body, and a cool million credits. Ah, the hell with Rann. He hadn't asked her to do it. And he was nobody's hired killer. Where did she get off, sneaking around his mind, trying to make him do things he didn't even know about? Especially to someone like Beudag.

Still, Rann herself was nobody's crud.

And just where was Hugh Starke supposed to cut in on this deal? Cut was right. Probably with a longsword, right through the belly. Swell spot he was in, and a good three strikes on him already.

He was beginning to wish he'd never see the T-V Mines payroll ship, because then he might never have seen the Mountains of White Cloud.

He said, because everybody seemed to be waiting for him to say something. "Usually when there's a deadlock like this, somebody calls in a third party. Isn't there somebody you can yell for?"

Faolan shook his rough red head. "The slave people might rise, but they haven't arms and they're not used to fighting. They'd only get massacred, and it wouldn't help us any."

"What about those other—uh—people that live in the sea? And just what is that sea, anyhow? Some radiation from it wrecked my ship and got me into this bloody mess."

Beudag said lazily, "I don't know what it is. The seas our forefathers sailed on were water, but this is different. It will float a ship, if you know how to build the hull—very thin, of a white metal we mine from the foothills. But when you swim in it, it's like being in a cloud of bubbles. It tingles, and the farther down you go in it the stranger it gets, dark and full of fire. I stay down for hours sometimes, hunting the beasts that live there."

Starke said, "For hours? You have diving suits, then. What are they?"

She shook her head, laughing. "Why weigh yourself down that way? There's no trouble to breathe in this ocean."

"For cripesake," said Starke. "Well I'll be damned. Must be a heavy gas, then, radioactive, surface tension under atmospheric pressure, enough to float a light hull, and high oxygen content without any dangerous mixture. Well, well. Okay, why doesn't somebody go down and see if the sea-people will help? They don't like Rann's branch of the family, you said."

"They don't like us, either," said Faolan. "We stay out of the southern part of the sea. They wreck our ships, sometimes." His bitter mouth twisted in a smile. "Did you want to go to them for help?"

Starke didn't quite like the way Faolan sounded. "It was just a suggestion," he said.

Beudag rose, stretching, wincing as the stiffened wounds pulled her flesh. "Come on, Faolan. Let's sleep."

He rose and laid his hand on her shoulder. Romna's harpstrings breathed a subtle little mockery of sound. The bard's eyes were veiled and sleepy. Beudag did not look at Starke, called Conan.

Starke said, "What about me?"

"You stay chained," said Faolan. "There's plenty of time to think. As long as we have food—and the sea feeds us."

He followed Beudag, through a curtained entrance to the left. Romna got up, slowly, slinging the harp over one white shoulder. He stood looking steadily into Starke's eyes in the dying light of the fires.

"I don't know," he murmured.

Starke waited, not speaking. His face was without expression.

"Conan we knew. Starke we don't know. Perhaps it would have been better if Conan had come back." He ran his thumb absently over the hilt of the knife in his girdle. "I don't know. Perhaps it would have been better for all of us if I'd cut your throat before Beudag came in."

Starke's mouth twitched. It was not exactly a smile.

"You see," said the bard seriously, "to you, from Outside, none of this is important, except as it touches you. But we live in this little world. We die in it. To us, it's important."

The knife was in his hand now. It leaped up glittering into the dregs of the firelight, and fell, and leaped again.

"You fight for yourself, Hugh Starke. Rann also fights through you. I don't know."

Starke's gaze did not waver.

Romna shrugged and put away the knife. "It is written of the gods," he said sighing. "I hope they haven't done a bad job of the writing."

He went out. Starke began to shiver slightly. It was completely quiet in the hall. He examined his collar, the rivets, every separate link of the chain, the staple to which it was fixed. Then he sat down on the fur rug provided for him in place of the straw. He put his face in his hands and cursed, steadily, for several minutes, and then struck his fists down hard on the floor. After that he lay down and was quiet. He thought Rann would speak to him. She did not.

The silent black hours that walked across his heart were worse than any he had spent in the Luna crypts.

She came soft-shod, bearing a candle. Beudag, the Dagger-in-the-Sheath. Starke was not asleep. He rose and stood waiting. She set the candle on the table and came, not quite to him, and stopped. She wore a length of thin white cloth twisted loosely at the waist and dropping to her ankles. Her body rose out of it straight and lovely, touched mystically with shadows in the little wavering light.

"Who are you?" she whispered. "What are you?"

"A man. Not Conan. Maybe not Hugh Starke anymore. Just a man."

"I loved the man called Conan, until . . ." She caught her breath, and moved closer. She put her hand on Starke's arm. The touch went through him like white fire. The warm clean healthy fragrance of her tasted sweet in his throat. Her eyes searched his.

"If Rann has such great powers, couldn't it be that Conan was forced to do what he did? Couldn't it be that Rann took his mind and moulded it her way, perhaps without his knowing it?"

"It could be."

"Conan was hot-tempered and quarrelsome, but he . . ."

Starke said slowly, "I don't think you could have loved him if he hadn't been straight."

Her hand lay still on his forearm. he stood looking at him, and then her hand began to tremble, and in a moment she was crying, making no noise about it. Starke drew her gently to him. His eyes blazed yellowly in the candlelight.

"Woman's tears," she said impatiently, after a bit. She tried to draw away. "I've been fighting too long, and losing, and I'm tired."

He let her step back, not far. "Do all the women of Crom Dhu fight like men?"

"If they want to. There have always been shield-maidens. And since Falga, I would have had to fight anyway, to keep from thinking." She touched the collar on Starke's neck. "And from seeing."

He thought of Conan in the market square, and Conan shaking his chain and gibbering in Faolan's hall, and Beudag watching it. Starke's fingers tightened. He slid his palms upward along the smooth muscles of her arms, across the straight, broad planes of her shoulders, onto her neck, the proud strength of it pulsing under his hands. Her hair fell loose. He could feel the redness of it burning him.

She whispered, "You don't love me."

"No."

"You're an honest man, Hugh Starke."

"You want me to kiss you."

"Yes."

"You're an honest woman, Beudag."

Her lips were hungry, passionate, touched with the bitterness of tears. After a while Starke blew out the candle . . .

"I could love you, Beudag."

"Not the way I mean."

"The way you mean. I've never said that to any woman before. But you're not like any woman before. And—I'm a different man."

"Strange—so strange. Conan, and yet not Conan."

"I could love you, Beudag—if I lived."

Harpstrings gave a thrumming sigh in the darkness, the faintest whisper of sound. Beudag started, sighed, and rose from the fur rug. In a minute she had found flint and steel and got the candle lighted. Romna the bard stood in the curtained doorway, watching them.

Presently he said, "You're going to let him go."

Beudag said, "Yes."

Romna nodded. He did not seem surprised. He walked across the dais, laying his harp on the table, and went into another room. He came back almost at once with a hacksaw.

"Bend your neck," he said to Starke.

The metal of the collar was soft. When it was cut through Starke got his fingers under it and bent the ends outward, without trouble. His old body could never have done that. His old body could never have done a lot of things. He figured Rann hadn't cheated him. Not much.

He got up, looking at Beudag. Beudag's head was dropped forward, her face veiled behind shining hair.

"There's only one possible way out of Crom Dhu," she said. There was no emotion in her voice. "There's a passage leading down through the rock to a secret harbor, just large enough to moor a skiff or two. Perhaps, with the night and the fog, you can slip through Rann's blockade. Or you can go aboard one of her ships, for Falga." She picked up the candle. "I'll take you down."

"Wait," Starke said. "What about you?"

She glanced at him surprised. "I'll stay, of course."

He looked into her eyes. "It's going to be hard to know each other that way."

"You can't stay here, Hugh Starke. The people would tear you to pieces the moment you went into the street. They may even storm the hall, to take you. Look here." She set the candle down and led him to a narrow window, drawing back the hide that covered it.

Starke saw narrow twisting streets dropping steeply toward the sullen sea. The longships were broken and sunk in the harbor. Out beyond, riding lights flickering in the red fog, were other ships. Rann's ships.

"Over there," said Beudag, "is the mainland. Crom Dhu is connected to it by a tongue of rock. The sea-folk hold the land beyond it, but we can hold the rock bridge as long as we live. We have enough water, enough food from the sea. But there's no soil nor game on Crom Dhu. We'll be naked after a while, without leather or flax, and we'll have scurvy without grain and fruit. We're beaten, unless the gods send us a miracle. And we're beaten because of what was done at Falga. You can see how the people feel."

Starke looked at the dark streets and the silent houses leaning on each other's shoulders, and the mocking lights out in the fog. "Yeah," he said. "I can see."

"Besides, there's Faolan. I don't know whether he believes your story. I don't know whether it would matter."

Starke nodded. "But you won't come with me?"

She turned away sharply and picked up the candle again. "Are you coming, Romna?"

The bard nodded. He slung his harp over his shoulder. Beudag held back the curtain of a small doorway far to the side. Starke went through it and Romna followed, and Beudag went ahead with the candle. No one spoke.

They went along a narrow passage, past store rooms and armories. They paused once while Starke chose a knife, and Romna whispered: "Wait!" He listened intently. Starke and Beudag strained their ears along with him. There was no sound. Romna shrugged. "I thought I heard sandals scraping stone," he said. They went on.

The passage lay behind a wooden door. It led downward steeply through the rock, a single narrow way without side galleries or branches. In some places there were winding steps. It ended, finally, in a flat ledge low to the surface of the cove, which was a small cavern closed in with the black rock. Beudag set the candle down.

There were two little skiffs built of some light metal moored to rings in the ledge. Two long sweeps leaned against the cave wall. They were of a different metal, oddly vaned. Beudag laid one across the thwarts of the nearest boat. Then she turned to Starke. Romna hung back in the shadows by the tunnel mouth.

Beudag said quietly, "Goodbye, man without a name."

"It has to be goodbye?"

"I'm leader now, in Faolan's place. Besides, these are my people." Her fingers tightened on his wrists. "If you could . . ." Her eyes held a brief blaze of hope. Then she dropped her head and said, "I keep forgetting you're not one of us. Goodbye."

"Goodbye, Beudag."

Starke put his arms around her. He found her mouth, almost cruelly. Her arms were tight about him, her eyes half closed and dreaming. Starke's hands slipped upward, toward her throat, and locked on it.

She bent back, her body like a steel bow. Her eyes got fire in them, looking into Starke's but only for a moment. His fingers pressed expertly on the nerve centers. Beudag's head fell forward limply, and then Romna was on Starke's back and his knife was pricking Starke's throat.

Starke caught his wrist and turned the blade away. Blood ran onto his chest, but the cut was not into the artery. He threw himself backward onto the stone. Romna couldn't get clear in time. The breath went out of him in a rushing gasp. He didn't let go of the knife. Starke rolled over. The little man didn't have a chance with him. He was tough and quick, but Starke's sheer size smothered him. Starke could remember when Romna would not have seemed small to him. He hit the bard's jaw with his fist. Romna's head cracked hard against the stone. He let go of the knife. He seemed to be through fighting. Starke got up. He was sweating, breathing heavily, not because of his exertion. His mouth was glistening and eager, like a dog's. His muscles twitched, his belly was hot and knotted with excitement. His yellow eyes had a strange look.

He went back to Beudag.

She lay on the black rock, on her back. Candlelight ran pale gold across her brown skin, skirting the sharp strong hollows between her breasts and under the arching rim of her rib case. Starke knelt, across her body, his weight pressed down against her harsh breathing. He stared at her. Sweat stood out on his face. He took her throat between his hands again.

He watched the blood grow dark in her cheeks. He watched the veins coil on her forehead. He watched the redness blacken her lips. She fought a little, very vaguely, like someone moving in a dream. Starke breathed hoarsely, animal-like through an open mouth.

Then, gradually his body became rigid. His hands froze, not releasing pressure, but not adding any. His yellow eyes widened. It was as though he were trying to see Beudag's face and it was hidden in dense clouds.

Back of him, back in the tunnel, was the soft faint whisper of sandals on uneven rock. Sandals, walking slowly. Starke did not hear. Beudag's face glimmered deep in a heavy mist below him, a blasphemy of a face, distorted, blackened.

Starke's hands began to open.

They opened slowly. Muscles stood like coiled ropes in his arms and shoulders, as though he moved them against heavy weights. His lips peeled back from his teeth. He bent his neck, and sweat dropped from his face and glittered on Beudag's breast.

Starke was now barely touching Beudag's neck. She began to breathe again, painfully.

Starke began to laugh. It was not nice laughter. "Rann," he whispered. "Rann, you she-devil." He half fell away from Beudag and stood up, holding himself against the wall. He was shaking violently. "I wouldn't use your hate for killing, so you tried to use my passion." He cursed her in a flat sibilant whisper. He had never in his profane life really cursed anyone before.

He heard an echo of laughter dancing in his brain.

Starke turned. Faolan of the Ships stood in the tunnel mouth. His head was bent, listening, his blind dark eyes fixed on Starke as though he saw him.

Faolan said softly, "I hear you, Starke. I hear the others breathing, but they don't speak."

"They're all right. I didn't mean to do . . ."

Faolan smiled. He stepped out on the narrow ledge. He knew where he was going, and his smile was not pleasant.

"I heard your steps in the passage beyond my room. I knew Beudag was leading you, and where, and why. I would have been here sooner, but it's a slow way in the dark."

The candle lay in his path. He felt the heat of it close to his leg, and stopped and felt for it, and ground it out. It was dark, then. Very dark, except for a faint smudgy glow from the scrap of ocean that lay along the cave floor.

"It doesn't matter," Faolan said, "as long as I came in time."

Starke shifted his weight warily. "Faolan . . ."

"I wanted you alone. On this night of all nights I wanted you alone. Beudag fights in my place now, Conan. My manhood needs proving."

Starke strained his eyes in the gloom, measuring the ledge, measuring the place where the skiff was moored. He didn't want to fight Faolan. In Faolan's place he would have felt the same. Starke understood perfectly. He didn't hate Faolan, he didn't want to kill him, and he was afraid of Rann's power over him when his emotions got control. You couldn't keep a determined man from killing you and still be uninvolved emotionally. Starke would be damned if he'd kill anyone to suit Rann.

He moved, silently, trying to slip past Faolan on the outside and get into the skiff. Faolan gave no sign of hearing him. Starke did not breathe. His sandals came down lighter than snowflakes. Faolan did not swerve. He would pass Starke with a foot to spare. They came abreast.

Faolan's hand shot out and caught in Starke's long black hair. The blind man laughed softly and closed in.

Starke swung one from the floor. Do it the quickest way and get clear. But Faolan was fast. He came in so swiftly that Starke's fist jarred harmlessly along his ribs. He was bigger than Starke, and heavier, and the darkness didn't bother him.

Starke bared his teeth. Do it quick, brother, and clear out! Or that green-eyed she-cat . . . Faolan's brute bulk weighted him down. Faolan's arm crushed his neck. Faolan's fist was knocking his guts loose. Starke got moving.

He'd fought in a lot of places. He'd learned from stokers and tramps, Martian Low-Canalers, red-eyed Nahali in the running gutters of Lhi. He didn't use his knife. He used his knees and feet and elbows and his hands, fist and flat. It was a good fight. Faolan was a good fighter, but Starke knew more tricks.

One more, Starke thought. One more and he's out. He drew back for it, and his heel struck Romna, lying on the rock. He staggered, and Faolan caught him with a clean swinging blow. Starke fell backward against the cave wall. His head cracked the rock. Light flooded crimson across his brain and then paled and grew cooler, a wash of clear silver-green like water. He sank under it . . .

He was tired, desperately tired. His head ached. He wanted to rest, but he could feel that he was sitting up, doing something that had to be done. He opened his eyes.

He sat in the stern of a skiff. The long sweep was laid into its crutch, held like a tiller bar against the body. The blade of the sweep trailed astern in the red sea, and where the metal touched there was a spurt of silver fire and a swirling of brilliant motes. The skiff moved rapidly through the sullen fog, through a mist of blood in the hot Venusian night.

Beudag crouched in the bow, facing Starke. She was bound securely with strips of the white cloth she had worn. Bruises showed dark on her throat. She was watching Starke with the intent, unwinking, perfectly expressionless gaze of a tigress.

Starke looked away, down at himself. There was blood on his kilt, a brown smear of it across his chest. It was not his blood. He drew the knife slowly out of its sheath. The blade was dull and crusted, still a little wet.

Starke looked at Beudag. His lips were stiff, swollen. He moistened them and said hoarsely, "What happened?"

She shook her head, slowly, not speaking. Her eyes did not waver.

A black, cold rage took hold of Starke and shook him. Rann! He rose and went forward, letting the sweep go where it would. He began to untie Beudag's wrists.

A shape swam toward them out of the red mist. A longship

with two heavy sweeps bursting fire astern and a slender figurehead shaped like a woman. A woman with hair and eyes of aquamarine. It came alongside the skiff.

A rope ladder snaked down. Men lined the low rail. Slender men with skin that glistened white like powdered snow, and hair the color of distant shadows.

One of them said, "Come aboard, Hugh Starke."

Starke went back to the sweep. It bit into the sea, sending the skiff in a swift arc away from Rann's ship.

Grapnels flew, hooking the skiff at thwart and gunwale. Bows appeared in the hands of the men, wicked curving things with barbed metal shafts on the string. The man said again, politely, "Come aboard."

Hugh Starke finished untying Beudag. He didn't speak. There seemed to be nothing to say. He stood back while she climbed the ladder and then followed. The skiff was cast loose. The longship veered away, gathering speed.

Starke said, "Where are we going?"

The man smiled. "To Falga."

Starke nodded. He went below with Beudag into a cabin with soft couches covered with spider-silk and panels of dark wood beautifully painted, dim fantastic scenes from the past of Rann's people. They sat opposite each other. They still did not speak.

They raised Falga in the opal dawn—a citadel of basalt cliffs rising sheer from the burning sea, with a long arm holding a harbor full of ships. There were green fields inland, and beyond, cloaked in the eternal mists of Venus, the Mountains of White Clouds lifted spaceward. Starke wished that he had never seen the Mountains of White Cloud. Then, looking at his hands, lean and strong on his long thighs, he wasn't so sure. He thought of Rann waiting for him. Anger, excitement, a confused violence of emotion set him pacing nervously.

Beudag sat quietly, withdrawn, waiting.

The longship threaded the crowded moorings and slid into place alongside a stone quay. Men rushed to make fast. They were human men, as Starke judged humans, like Beudag and himself. They had the shimmering silver hair and fair skin of the plateau peoples, the fine-cut faces and straight bodies. They wore leather collars with metal tags and they went naked like beasts, and they were gaunt and bowed with labor.

Here and there a man with pale blue-green hair and resplendent harness stood godlike above the swarming masses.

Starke and Beudag went ashore. They might have been prisoners or honored guests, surrounded by their escort from the ship. Streets ran back from the harbor, twisting and climbing crazily up the cliffs. Houses climbed on each other's backs. It had begun to rain, the heavy steaming downpour of Venus, and the moist heat brought out the choking stench of people, too many people.

They climbed, ankle deep in water sweeping down the streets that were half stairway. Thin naked children peered out of the houses, out of narrow alleys. Twice they passed through market squares where women with the blank faces of defeat drew back from stalls of coarse food to let the party through.

There was something wrong. After a while Starke realized it was the silence. In all that horde of humanity no one laughed, or sang, or shouted. Even the children never spoke above a whisper. Starke began to feel a little sick. Their eyes had a look in them . . .

He glanced at Beudag, and away again.

The waterfront streets ended in a sheer basalt face honeycombed with galleries. Starke's party entered them, still climbing. They passed level after level of huge caverns, open to the sea. There was the same crowding, the same stench, the same silence. Eyes glinted in the half-light, bare feet moved furtively on stone. Somewhere a baby cried thinly, and was hushed at once.

They came out on the cliff top, into the clean high air. There was a city here. Broad streets, lined with trees, low rambling villas of the black rock set in walled gardens, drowned in brilliant vines and giant ferns and flowers. Naked men and women worked in the gardens, or hauled carts of rubbish through the alleys, or hurried on errands, slipping furtively across the main streets where they intersected the mews.

The party turned away from the sea, heading toward an ebon palace that sat like a crown above the city. The steaming rain beat on Starke's bare body, and up here you could get the smell of the rain, even through the heavy perfume of the flowers. You could smell Venus in the rain—musky and primitive and savagely alive, a fecund giantess with passion flowers in her outstretched hands. Starke set his feet down like a panther and his eyes burned a smoky amber.

They entered the palace of Rann. . . .

She received them in the same apartment where Starke had come to after the crash. Through a broad archway he could see the high bed where his old body had lain before the life went out of it. The red sea steamed under the rain outside, the rusty fog coiling languidly through the open arches of the gallery. Rann watched them lazily from a raised couch set massively into the wall. Her long sparkling legs sprawled arrogantly across the black spider-silk draperies. This time her tabard was a pale yellow. Her eyes were still the color of shoal-water, still amused, still secret, still dangerous.

Starke said, "So you made me do it after all."

"And you're angry." She laughed, her teeth showing white and pointed as bone needles. Her gaze held Starke's. There was nothing casual about it. Starke's hawk eyes turned molten yellow, like hot gold, and did not waver.

Beudag stood like a bronze spear, her forearms crossed beneath her bare sharp breasts. Two of Rann's palace guards stood behind her.

Starke began to walk toward Rann.

She watched him come. She let him get close enough to reach out and touch her, and then she said slyly, "It's a good body, isn't it?"

Starke looked at her for a moment. Then he laughed. He threw back his head and roared, and struck the great corded muscles of his belly with his fist. Presently he looked straight into Rann's eyes and said:

"I know you."

She nodded. "We know each other. Sit down, Hugh Starke." She swung her long legs over to make room, half erect now, looking at Beudag. Starke sat down. He did not look at Beudag.

Rann said, "Will your people surrender now?"

Beudag did not move, not even her eyelids. "If Faolan is dead—yes."

"And if he's not?"

Beudag stiffened. Starke did too.

"Then," said Beudag quietly, "They'll wait."

"Until he is?"

"Or until they must surrender."

Rann nodded. To the guards she said, "See that this woman is well fed and well treated."

Beudag and her escort had turned to go when Starke said,

"Wait." The guards looked at Rann, who nodded, and glanced quizzically at Starke. Starke said:

"Is Faolan dead?"

Rann hesitated. Then she smiled. "No. You have the most damnably tough mind, Starke. You struck deep, but not deep enough. He may still die, but . . . No, he's not dead." She turned to Beudag and said with easy mockery, "You needn't hold anger against Starke. I'm the one who should be angry." Her eyes came back to Starke. They didn't look angry.

Starke said, "There's something else. Conan—the Conan that used to be, before Falga."

"Beudag's Conan."

"Yeah. Why did he betray his people?"

Rann studied him. Her strange pale lips curved, her sharp white teeth glistening wickedly with barbed humor. Then she turned to Beudag. Beudag was still standing like a carved image, but her smooth muscles were ridged with tension, and her eyes were not the eyes of an image.

"Conan or Starke," said Rann, "she's still Beudag, isn't she? All right, I'll tell you. Conan betrayed his people because I put it into his mind to do it. He fought me. He made a good fight of it. But he wasn't quite as tough as you are, Starke."

There was a silence. For the first time since entering the room, Hugh Starke looked at Beudag. After a moment she sighed and lifted her chin and smiled, a deep, faint smile. The guards walked out beside her, but she was more erect and lighter of step than either of them.

"Well," said Rann, when they were gone, "and what about you, Hugh-Starke-Called-Conan?"

"Have I any choice?"

"I always keep my bargains."

"Then give me my dough and let me clear the hell out of here."

"Sure that's what you want?"

"That's what I want."

"You could stay awhile, you know."

"With you?"

Rann lifted her frosty-white shoulders. "I'm not promising half my kingdom, or even part of it. But you might be amused."

"I got no sense of humor."

"Don't you even want to see what happens to Crom Dhu?"

"And Beudag."

"And Beudag." He stopped, then fixed Rann with uncompromising yellow eyes. "No. Not Beudag. What are you going to do to her?"

"Nothing."

"Don't give me that."

"I say again, nothing. Whatever is done, her own people will do."

"What do you mean?"

"I mean that little Dagger-in-the-Sheath will be rested, cared for, and fattened, for a few days. Then I shall take her aboard my own ship and join the fleet before Crom Dhu. Beudag will be made quite comfortable at the masthead, where her people can see her plainly. She will stay there until the Rock surrenders. It depends on her own people how long she stays. She'll be given water. Not much, but enough."

Starke stared at her. He stared at her a long time. Then he spat deliberately on the floor and said in a perfectly flat voice: "How soon can I get out of here?"

Rann laughed, a small casual chuckle. "Humans," she said, "are so damned queer. I don't think I'll ever understand them." She reached out and struck a gong that stood in a carved frame beside the couch. The soft deep shimmering note had a sad quality of nostalgia. Rann lay back against the silken cushions and sighed.

"Goodbye, Hugh Starke."

A pause. Then, regretfully:

"Goodbye—Conan!"

They had made good time along the rim of the Red Sea. One of Rann's galleys had taken them to the edge of the Southern Ocean and left them on a narrow shingle beach under the cliffs. From there they had climbed to the rimrock and gone on foot—Hugh-Starke-Called-Conan and four of Rann's arrogant shining men. They were supposed to guide and escort. They were courteous, and they kept pace uncomplainingly though Starke marched as though the devil were pricking his heels. But they were armed, and Starke was not.

Sometimes, very faintly, Starke was aware of Rann's mind touching his with the velvet delicacy of a cat's paw. Sometimes he started out on his sleep with her image sharp in his mind, her lips touched with the mocking, secret smile. He didn't like that. He didn't like it at all.

But he liked even less the picture that stayed with him waking or sleeping. The picture he wouldn't look at. The picture of a tall woman with hair like loose fire on her neck, walking on light proud feet between her guards.

She'll be given water, Rann said. Not much, but enough.

Starke gripped the solid squareness of the box that held his million credits and set the miles reeling backward from under his sandals.

On the fifth night one of Rann's men spoke quietly across the campfire. "Tomorrow," he said, "we'll reach the pass."

Starke got up and went away by himself, to the edge of the rimrock that fell sheer to the burning sea. He sat down. The red fog wrapped him like a mist of blood. He thought of the blood on Beudag's breast the first time he saw her. He thought of the blood on his knife, crusted and dried. He thought of the blood poured rank and smoking into the gutters of Crom Dhu. The fog has to be red, he thought. Of all the goddam colors in the universe, it has to be red. Red like Beudag's hair.

He held out his hands and looked at them, because he could still feel the silken warmth of that hair against his skin. There was nothing there now but the old white scars of another man's battles.

He set his fists against his temples and wished for his old body back again—the little stunted abortion that had clawed and scratched its way to survival through sheer force of mind. A most damnably tough mind, Rann had said. Yeah. It had to be tough. But a mind was a mind. It didn't have emotions. It just figured out something coldly and then went ahead and never questioned, and it controlled the body utterly, because the body was only the worthless machinery that carried the mind around. Worthless. Yeah. The few women he'd ever looked at had told him that—and he hadn't even minded much. The old body hadn't given him any trouble.

He was having trouble now.

Starke got up and walked.

Tomorrow we reach the pass.

Tomorrow we go away from the Red Sea. There are nine planets and the whole damn Belt. There are women on all of them. All shapes, colors, and sizes, human, semi-human, and God knows what. With a million credits a guy could buy half of them, and with Conan's body he could buy the rest. What's a woman anyway? Only a . . .

Water. She'll be given water. Not much, but enough.

Conan reached out and took hold of a spire of rock, and

his muscles stood out like knotted ropes. "Oh God," he whispered, "what's the matter with me?"

"Love."

It wasn't God who answered. It was Rann. He saw her plainly in his mind, heard her voice like a silver bell.

"Conan was a man, Hugh Starke. He was whole, body and heart and brain. He knew how to love, and with him it wasn't women, but one woman—and her name was Beudag. I broke him, but it wasn't easy. I can't break you."

Starke stood for a long, long time. He did not move, except that he trembled. Then he took from his belt the box containing his million credits and threw it out as far as he could over the cliff edge. The red mist swallowed it up. He did not hear it strike the surface of the sea. Perhaps in that sea there was no splashing. He did not wait to find out.

He turned back along the rimrock, toward a place where he remembered a cleft, or chimney, leading down. And the four shining men who wore Rann's harness came silently out of the heavy luminous night and ringed him in. Their sword-points caught sharp red glimmers from the sky.

Starke had nothing on him but a kilt and sandals, and a cloak of tight-woven spider-silk that shed the rain.

"Rann sent you?" he said.

The men nodded.

"To kill me?"

Again they nodded. The blood drained out of Starke's face, leaving it grey and stony under the bronze. His hand went to his throat, over the gold fastening of his cloak.

The four men closed in like dancers.

Starke loosed his cloak and swung it like a whip across their faces. It confused them for a second, for a heartbeat—no more, but long enough. Starke left two of them to tangle their blades in the heavy fabric and leaped aside. A sharp edge slipped and turned along his ribs, and then he had reached in low and caught a man around the ankles, and used the thrashing body for a flail.

The body was strangely light, as though the bones in it were no more than rigid membrane, like a fish.

If he had stayed to fight, they would have finished him in seconds. They were fighting men, and quick. But Starke didn't stay. He gained his moment's grace and used it. They were hard on his heels, their points all but pricking his back as he ran, but he made it. Along the rimrock, out along a narrow tongue that jutted over the sea, and then outward, far outward, into red fog and dim fire that rolled around his plummeting body.

Oh God, he thought, if I guessed wrong and there *is* a beach . . .

The breath tore out of his lungs. His ears cracked, went dead. He held his arms out beyond his head, the thumbs locked together, his neck braced forward against the terrific upward push. He struck the surface of the sea.

There was no splash.

Dim coiling fire that drifted with infinite laziness around him, caressing his body with slow, tingling sparks. A feeling of lightness, as though his flesh had become one with the drifting fire. A sense of suffocation that had no basis in fact and gave way gradually to a strange exhilaration. There was no shock of impact, no crushing pressure. Merely a compressed air. Starke felt himself turning end over end, pinwheel fashion, and then that stopped, so that he sank quietly and without haste to the bottom.

Or rather, into the crystalline upper reaches of what seemed to be a forest.

He could see it spreading away along the downward-sloping floor of the ocean, into the vague red shadows of distance. Slender fantastic trunks upholding a maze of delicate shining branches, without leaves or fruit. They were like trees exquisitely molded from ice, transparent, holding the lambent shifting fire of the strange sea. Starke didn't think they were, or ever had been, alive. More like coral, he thought, or some vagary of mineral deposit. Beautiful, though. Like something you'd see in a dream. Beautiful, silent, and somehow deadly.

He couldn't explain that feeling of deadliness. Nothing moved in the red drifts between the trunks. It was nothing about the trees themselves. It was just something he sensed.

He began to move among the upper branches, following the downward drop of the slope.

He found that he could swim quite easily. Or perhaps it was more like flying. The dense gas buoyed him up, almost balancing the weight of his body, so that it was easy to swoop along, catching a crystal branch and using it as a lever to throw himself forward to the next one.

He went deeper and deeper into the heart of the forbidden Southern Ocean. Nothing stirred. The fairy forest stretched limitless ahead. And Starke was afraid.

Rann came into his mind abruptly. Her face, clearly outlined, was full of mockery.

"I'm going to watch you die. Hugh-Starke-Called-Conan. But before you die, I'll show you something. Look."

Her face dimmed, and in its place was Crom Dhu rising bleak into the red fog, the longships broken and sunk in the harbor, and Rann's fleet around it in a shining circle.

One ship in particular. The flagship. The vision in Starke's mind rushed toward it, narrowed down to the masthead platform. To the woman who stood there, naked, erect, her body lashed tight with thin cruel cords.

A woman with red hair blowing in the slow wind, and blue eyes that looked straight ahead like a falcon's at Crom Dhu.

Beudag.

Rann's laughter ran across the picture and blurred it like a ripple of ice-cold water.

"You'd have done better," she said, "to take the clean steel when I offered it to you."

She was gone, and Starke's mind was as empty and cold as the mind of a corpse. He found that he was standing still, clinging to a branch, his face upturned as though by some blind instinct, his sight blurred.

He had never cried before in all his life, nor prayed.

There was no such thing as time, down there in the smoky shadows of the sea bottom. It might have been minutes or hours later than Hugh Starke discovered he was being hunted.

There were three of them, slipping easily among the shining branches. They were pale golden, almost phosphorescent, about the size of large hounds. Their eyes were huge, jewellike in their slim sharp faces. They possessed four members that might have been legs and arms, retracted now against their arrowing bodies. Golden membranes spread winglike from head to flank, and they moved like wings, balancing expertly the thrust of the flat, powerful tails.

They could have closed in on him easily, but they didn't seem to be in any hurry. Starke had sense enough not to wear himself out trying to get away. He kept on going, watching them. He discovered that the crystal branches could be broken, and he selected himself one with a sharp forked tip, shoving it swordwise under his belt. He didn't suppose it would do much good, but it made him feel better.

He wondered why the things didn't jump him and get it over with. They looked hungry enough, the way they were showing him their teeth. But they kept about the same distance away, in a sort of crescent formation, and every so often the ones on the outside would make a tentative dart at him, then fall back as he swerved away. It wasn't like being hunted so much as . . .

Starke's eyes narrowed. He began suddenly to feel much more afraid than he had before, and he wouldn't have believed that possible.

The things weren't hunting him at all. They were herding him.

There was nothing he could do about it. He tried stopping, and they swooped in and snapped at him, working expertly together so that while he was trying to stab one of them with his clumsy weapon, the others were worrying his heels like sheepdogs at a recalcitrant wether.

Starke, like the wether, bowed to the inevitable and went where he was driven. The golden hounds showed their teeth in animal laughter and sniffed hungrily at the thread of blood he left behind him in the slow red coils of fire.

After a while he heard the music.

It seemed to be some sort of a harp, with a strange quality of vibration in the notes. It wasn't like anything he'd ever heard before. Perhaps the gas of which the sea was composed was an extraordinarily good conductor of sound, with a property of diffusion that made the music seem to come from everywhere at once softly at first, like something touched upon in a dream, and then, as he drew closer to the source, swelling into a racing, rippling flood of melody that wrapped itself around his nerves with a demoniac shiver of ecstasy.

The golden hounds began to fret with excitement, spreading their shining wings, driving him impatiently faster through the crystal branches.

Starke could feel the vibration growing in him—the very fibers of his muscles shuddering in sympathy with the unearthly harp. He guessed there was a lot of the music he couldn't hear. Too high, too low for his ears to register. But he could feel it.

He began to go faster, not because of the hounds, but because he wanted to. The deep quivering in his flesh excited him. He began to breathe harder, partly because of increased exertion, and some chemical quality of the mixture he breathed made him slightly drunk.

The thrumming harp-song stroked and stung him, waking a deeper, darker music, and suddenly he saw Beudag clearly—half-veiled and mystic in the candlelight at Faolan's dun; smooth curving bronze, her hair loose fire about her throat. A great stab of agony went through him. He called her name, once, and the harp-sound swept it up and away, and then suddenly there was no music anymore, and no forest, and nothing but cold embers in Starke's heart.

He could see everything quite clearly in the time it took him to float from the top of the last tree to the floor of the plain. He had no idea how long a time that was. It didn't matter. It was one of those moments when time doesn't have any meaning.

The rim of the forest fell away in a long curve that melted glistening into the spark-shot sea. From it the plain stretched out, a level glassy floor of black obsidian, the spew of some long-dead volcano. Or was it dead? It seemed to Starke that the light here was redder, more vital, as though he were close to the source from which it sprang.

As he looked farther over the plain, the light seemed to coalesce into a shimmering curtain that wavered like the heat veils that dance along the Mercurian Twilight Belt at high noon. For one brief instant he glimpsed a picture on the curtain—a city, black, shining, fantastically turreted, the gigantic reflection of a Titan's dream. Then it was gone and the immediate menace of the foreground took all of Starke's attention.

He saw the flock, herded by more of the golden hounds. And he saw the shepherd, with the harp held silent between his hands.

The flock moved slightly, phosphorescently.

One hundred, two hundred silent, limply floating warriors drifting down the red dimness. In pairs, singly, or in pallid clusters they came. The golden hounds winged silently, leisurely around them, channeling them in tides that sluiced toward the fantastic ebon city.

The shepherd stood, a crop of obsidian, turning his shark-pale face. His sharp, aquamarine eyes found Starke. His silvery hand leapt beckoning over hard threads, striking them a blow. Reverberations ran out, seized Starke, shook him. He dropped his crystal dagger.

Hot screens of fire exploded in his eyes, bubbles whirled and danced in his eardrums. He lost all muscular control. His dark head fell forward against the thick blackness of hair on his chest; his golden eyes dissolved into weak, inane yellow, and his mouth loosened. He wanted to fight, but it was useless. This shepherd was one of the sea-people he had come to see, and one way or another he would see him.

Dark blood filled his aching eyes. He felt himself led, nudged, forced first this way, then that. A golden hound slipped by, gave him a pressure which rolled him over into a current of sea-blood. It ran down past where the shepherd stood with only a harp for a weapon.

Starke wondered dimly whether these other warriors in the flock, drifting, were dead or alive like himself. He had another surprise coming.

They were all Rann's men. Men of Falga. Silver men with burning hair. Rann's men. One of them, a huge warrior colored like powdered salt, wandered aimlessly by on another tide, his green eyes dull. He looked dead.

What business had the sea-people with the dead warriors of Falga? Why the hounds and the shepherd's harp? Questions eddied like lifted silt in Starke's tired, hanging head. Eddied and settled that.

Starke joined the pilgrimage.

The hounds were deft flickerings of wings ushered him into the midst of the flock. Bodies brushed against him. *Cold* bodies. He wanted to cry out. The cords of his neck constricted. In his mind the cry went forward:

"Are you alive, men of Falga?"

No answer; but the drift of scarred, pale bodies. The eyes in them knew nothing. They had forgotten Falga. They had forgotten Rann for whom they had lifted blade. Their tongues lolling in mouths asked nothing but sleep. They were getting it.

A hundred, two hundred strong they made a strange human river slipping toward the gigantic city wall. Starke-called-Conan and his bitter enemies going together. From the corners of his eyes, Starke saw the shepherd move. The shepherd was like Rann and her people who had years ago abandoned the sea to live on land. The shepherd seemed colder, more fishlike, though. There were small translucent webs between the thin fingers and spanning the long-toed feet. Thin, scarlike gills in the shadow of his tapered chin, lifted and sealed in the current, eating, taking sustenance from the blood-colored sea.

The harp spoke and the golden hounds obeyed. The harp spoke and the bodies twisted uneasily, as in a troubled sleep. A triple chord of it came straight at Starke. His fingers clenched.

"—and the dead shall walk again—"

Another ironic ripple of music.

"—and Rann's men will rise again, this time against her—"

Starke had time to feel a brief, bewildered shivering, before the current hurled him forward. Clamoring drunkenly, witlessly, all about him, the dead, muscleless warriors of Falga tried to crush past him, all of them at once . . .

Long ago some vast sea Titan had dreamed of avenues struck from black stone. Each stone the size of three men tall. There had been a dream of walls going up and up until they dissolved into scarlet mist. There had been another dream of sea-gardens in which fish hung like erotic flowers, on tendrils of sensitive film-tissue. Whole beds of fish clung to garden base, like colonies of flowers aglow with sunlight. And on occasion a black amoebic presence filtered by, playing the gardener, weeding out an amber flower here, an amythystine bloom there.

And the sea Titan had dreamed of endless balustrades and battlements, of windowless turrets where creatures swayed like radium-skinned phantoms, carrying their green plumes of hair in their lifted palms, and looked down with curious, insolent eyes from on high. Women with shimmering bodies like some incredible coral harvested and kept high over these black stone streets, each in its archway.

Starke was alone. Falga's warriors had gone off along a dim subterranean vent, vanished. Now the faint beckoning of harp and the golden hounds behind him turned him down a passage that opened out into a large circular stone room, one end of which opened out into a hall. Around the ebon ceiling, slender schools of fish swam. It was their bright effulgence that gave light to the room. They had been there, breeding, eating, dying, a thousand years. giving light to the place, and they would be there breeding and dying, a thousand more.

The harp faded until it was only a murmur.

Starke found his feet. Strength returned to him. He was able to see the man in the center of the room well. Too well.

The man hung in the fire tide. Chains of wrought bronze held his thin fleshless ankles so he couldn't escape. His body desired it. It floated up.

It had been dead a long time. It was gaseous with decomposition and it wanted to rise to the surface of the Red Sea. The chains prevented this. Its arms weaved like white scarves before a sunken white face. Black hair trembled on end.

He was one of Faolan's men. One of the Rovers. One of those who had gone down at Falga because of Conan.

His name was Geil.

Starke remembered.

The part of him that was Conan remembered the name.

The dead lips moved.

"Conan. What luck is this! Conan. I make you welcome."

The words were cruel, the lips around them loose and dead. It seemed to Starke an anger and embittered wrath lay deep in those hollow eyes. The lips twitched again.

"I went down at Falga for you and Rann, Conan. Remember?"

Part of Starke remembered and twisted in agony.

"We're all here, Conan. All of us. Clev and Mannt and Bron and Aesur. Remember Aesur, who could shape metal over his spine, prying it with his fingers? Aesur is here, big as a sea-monster, waiting in a niche, cold and loose as string. The sea-shepherds collected us. Collected us for a purpose of irony. Look!"

The boneless fingers hung out, as in a wind, pointing.

Starke turned slowly, and his heart pounded an uneven, shattering drumbeat. His jaw clinched and his eyes blurred. That part of him that was Conan cried out. Conan was so much of him and he so much of Conan it was impossible for a cleavage. They'd grown together like pearl material around sand-specule, layer on layer. Starke cried out.

In the hall which this circular room overlooked, stood a thousand men.

In lines of fifty across, shoulder to shoulder, the men of Crom Dhu stared unseeingly up at Starke. Here and there a face became shockingly familiar. Old memory cried their names.

"Bron! Clev! Mannt! Aesur!"

The collected decomposition of their bodily fluids raised them, drifted them above the flaggings. Each of them was chained, like Geil.

Geil whispered. "We have made a union with the men of Falga!"

Starke pulled back.

"Falga!"

"In death, all men are equals." He took his time with it. He was in no hurry. Dead bodies under-sea are never in a hurry. They sort of bump and drift and bide their time. Tomorrow we march against Crom Dhu."

"You're crazy! Crom Dhu is *your* home! It's the place of Beudag and Faolan—"

"And—" interrupted the hanging corpse, quietly, "Conan? Eh?" He laughed. A crystal dribble of bubbles ran up from the slack mouth. "Especially Conan. Conan who sank us at Falga . . ."

Starke moved swiftly. Nobody stopped him. He had the corpse's short blade in an instant. Geil's chest made a cold, silent sheath for it. The blade went like a fork through butter.

Coldly, without noticing this, Geil's voice spoke out:

"Stab me, cut me. You can't kill me any deader. Make sections of me. Play butcher. A flank, a hand, a heart! And while you're at it, I'll tell you the plan."

Snarling, Starke seized the blade out again. With blind violence he gave sharp blow after blow at the body, cursing bitterly, and the body took each blow, rocking in the red tide a little, and said with a matter-of-fact-tone:

"We'll march out of the sea to Crom Dhu gates. Romna and the others, looking down, recognizing us, will have the gates thrown wide to welcome us." The head tilted lazily, the lips peeled wide and folded down languidly over the words. "Think of the elation. Conan! The moment when Bron and Mannt and Aesur and I and yourself, yes, even yourself, Conan, return to Crom Dhu!"

Starke saw it, vividly. Saw it like a tapestry woven for him. He stood back, gasping for breath, his nostrils flaring, seeing what his blade had done to Geil's body, and seeing the great stone gates of Crom Dhu crashing open. The deliberation. The happiness, the elation to Faolan and Romna to see old friends returned. Old Rovers, long thought dead. Alive again, come to help! It made a picture!

With great deliberation, Starke struck out flat across before him.

Geil's head, severed from its lazy body, began, with infinite tiredness, to float toward the ceiling. As it traveled upward, now facing, now bobbling the back of its skull toward Starke, it finished its nightmare speaking:

"And then once inside the gates, what then, Conan? Can you guess? Can you guess what we'll do, Conan?"

Starke stared at nothingness, the sword trembling in his fist. From far away he heard Geil's voice:

"—we will kill Faolan in his hall. He will die with surprised lips. Romna's harp will lie in his disemboweled stomach. His heart with its last pulsings will sound the strings. And as for Beudag—"

Starke tried to push the thoughts away, raging and helpless.

Geil's body was no longer anything to look at. He had done all he could to it. Starke's face was bleached white and scraped down to the insane bone of it, "You'd kill you own people!"

Geil's separated head lingered at the ceiling, lightfish illuminating its ghastly features. "Our people? But we have no people! We're another race now. The dead. We do the biddings of the sea-shepherds."

Starke looked out into the hall, then he looked at circular wall.

"Okay," he said, without tone in his voice. "Come out. Wherever you're hiding and using this voice-throwing act. Come on out and talk straight."

In answer, an entire section of ebon stones fell back on silent hingework. Starke saw a long slender black marble table. Six people sat behind it in carven midnight thrones.

They were all men. Naked except for filmlike garments about their loins. They looked at Starke with no particular hatred or curiosity. One of them cradled a harp. It was the shepherd who'd drawn Starke through the gate. Amusedly, his webbed fingers lay on the strings, now and then bringing out a clear sound from one of the two hundred strands.

The shepherd stopped Starke's rush forward with a cry of that harp!

The blade in his hand was red hot. He dropped it.

The shepherd put a head on the story. "And then? And then we will march Rann's dead warriors all the way to Falga. There, Rann's people, seeing the warriors, will be overjoyed, hysterical to find their friends and relatives returned. Thcy, too, will fling wide Falga's defenses. And death will walk in, disguised as resurrection."

Starke nodded, slowly, wiping his hand across his cheek. "Back on Earth we call that psychology. *Good* psychology. But will it fool Rann?"

"Rann will be with her ships at Crom Dhu. While she's gone, the innocent population will let in their lost warriors gladly." The shepherd had amused green eyes. He looked like a youth of some seventeen years. Deceptively young. If Stark guessed right, the youth was nearer to two centuries old. That's how you lived and looked when you were under the Red Sea. Something about the emanations of it kept part of you young.

Starke lidded his yellow hawk's eyes thoughtfully. "You've got all aces. You'll win. But what's Crom Dhu to you? Why not just Rann? She's one of you; you hate her more than you do the Rovers. Her ancestors came up on land; you never got over hating them for that—"

The shepherd shrugged. "Toward Crom Dhu we have little actual hatred. Except that they are by nature land-men, even if they do rove by boat, and pillagers. One day they might try their luck on the sunken devices of this city."

Starke put a hand out. "We're fighting Rann, too. Don't forget, we're on your side!"

"Whereas we are on no one's," retorted the greenhaired youth, "Except our own. Welcome to the army which will attack Crom Dhu."

"Me! By the gods, over my dead body!"

"That," said the youth, amusedly, "is what we intend. We've worked many years, you see, to perfect the plan. We're not much good out on land. We needed bodies that could do the work for us. So, every time Faolan lost a ship or Rann lost a ship, we were there, with our golden hounds, waiting. Collecting. Saving. Waiting until we had enough of each side's warriors. They'll do the fighting for us. Oh, not for long, of course. The Source energy will give them a semblance of life, a momentary electrical ability to walk and combat, but once out of water they'll last only half an hour. But that should be time enough once the gates of Crom Dhu and Falga are open."

Starke said, "Rann will find some way around you. Get her first. Attack Crom Dhu the following day."

The youth deliberated. "You're stalling. But there's sense in it. Rann is most important. We'll get Falga first, then. You'll have a bit of time in which to raise false hopes."

Starke began to get sick again. The room swam.

Very quietly, very easily, Rann came into his mind again. He felt her glide in like the merest touch of a sea fern weaving in a tide pool.

He closed his mind down, but not before she snatched at a shred of thought. Her aquamarine eyes reflected desire and inquiry.

"Hugh Starke, you're with the sea people?"

Her voice was soft. He shook his head.

"Tell me, Hugh Starke. How are you plotting against Falga?"

He said nothing. He thought nothing. He shut his eyes.

Her fingernails glittered, raking at his mind. "Tell me!"

His thoughts rolled tightly into a metal sphere which nothing could dent.

Rann laughed unpleasantly and leaned forward until she filled every dark horizon of his skull with her shimmering body. "All right. I *gave* you Conan's body. Now I'll take it away."

She struck him a combined blow of her eyes, her writhing lips, her bone-sharp teeth. "Go back to your old body, go back to your old body, Hugh Starke," she hissed. "Go back! Leave Conan to his idiocy. Go back to your old body!"

Fear had him. He fell down upon his face, quivering and jerking. You could fight a man a sword. But how could you fight this thing in your brain? He began to suck sobbing breaths through his lips. He was screaming. He could not hear himself. Her voice rushed in from the dim outer red universe, destroying him.

"Hugh Starke! Go back to your old body!"

His old body was—dead!

And she was sending him back into it.

Part of him shot endwise looks through red fog.

He lay on a mountain plateau overlooking the harbor of Falga.

Red fog coiled and snaked around him. Flame birds dived eerily down at his staring, blind eyes.

His old body held him.

Putrefaction stuffed his nostrils. The flesh sagged and slipped greasily on his loosened structure. He felt small again and ugly. Flame birds nibbled, picking, choosing between his ribs. Pain gorged him. Cold, blackness, nothingness filled him. Back in his old body. Forever.

He didn't want that.

The plateau, the red fog vanished. The flame birds, too.

He lay once more on the floor of the sea shepherds, struggling.

"That was just a start," Rann told him. "Next time, I'll leave you up there on the plateau in that body. *Now*, will you tell the plans of the sea people? And go on living in Conan? He's yours, if you tell." She smirked. "You don't want to be dead."

Starke tried to reason it out. Any way he turned was the wrong way. He grunted out a breath. "If I tell, you'll still kill Beudag."

"Her life in exchange for what you know, Hugh Starke."

Her answer was too swift. It had the sound of teachery.

Starke did not believe. He would die. That would solve it. Then, at least, Rann would die when the sea people carried out their strategy. That much revenge, at least, damn it.

Then he got the idea.

He coughed out a laugh, raised his weak head to look at the startled sea shepherd. His little dialogue with Rann had taken about ten seconds, actually, but it had seemed a century. The sea shepherd stepped forward.

Starke tried to get to his feet. "Got—got a proposition for you. You with the harp. Rann's inside me. *Now*. Unless you guarantee Crom Dhu and Beudag's safety, I'll tell her some things she might want to be in on!"

The sea shepherd drew a knife.

Starke shook his head, coldly. "Put it away. Even if you get me I'll give the whole damned strategy to Rann."

The shepherd dropped his hand. He was no fool.

Rann tore at Starke's brain. "Tell me! Tell me their plan!"

He felt like a guy in a revolving door. Starke got the sea men in focus. He saw that they were afraid now, doubtful and nervous. "I'll be dead in a minute," said Starke. "Promise me the safety of Crom Dhu and I'll die without telling Rann a thing."

The sea shepherd hesitated, then raised his palm upward. "I promise," he said. "Crom Dhu will go untouched."

Starke sighed. He let his head fall forward until it hit the floor. Then he rolled over, put his hands over his eyes. "It's a deal. Go give Rann hell for me, will you, boys? Give her hell!"

As he drifted into mind darkness, Rann waited for him. Feebly, he told her, "Okay, duchess. You'd kill me even if I'd told you the idea. I'm ready. Try your god-awfullest to shove me back into that stinking body of mine. I'll fight you all the way there!"

Rann screamed. It was a pretty frustrated scream. Then the pains began. She did a lot of work on his mind in the next minute.

That part of him that was Conan held on like a clam holding to its precious contents.

The odor of putrid flesh returned. The blood mist returned. The flame birds fell down at him in spirals of sparks and blistering smoke, to winnow his naked ribs.

Starke spoke one last word before the blackness took him. "Beudag."

He never expected to awaken again.

He awoke just the same.

There was red sea all around him. He lay on a kind of stone bed, and the young sea shepherd sat beside him, looking down at him, smiling delicately.

Starke did not dare move for a while. He was afraid his head might fall off and whirl away like a big fish, using its ears as propellers. "Lord," he muttered, barely turning his head.

The sea creature stirred. "You won. You fought Rann, and won."

Starke groaned. "I feel like something passed through a wildcat's intestines. She's gone. Rann's gone." He laughed. "That makes me sad. Somebody cheer me up. Rann's gone." He felt of his big, flat-muscled body. "She was bluffing. Trying to decide to drive me batty. She knew she couldn't really tuck me back into that carcass, but she didn't want me to know. It was like a baby's nightmare before it's born. Or maybe you haven't got a memory like me." He rolled over, stretching. "She won't ever get in my head again. I've locked the gate and swallowed the key." His eyes dilated. "What's *your* name?"

"Linnl," said the man with the harp. "You didn't tell Rann our strategy?"

"What do *you* think?"

Linnl smiled sincerely. "I think I like you, man of Crom Dhu. I think I like your hatred for Rann. I think I like the way you handled the entire matter, wanted to kill Rann and save Crom Dhu, and being so willing to die to accomplish either."

"That's a lot of thinking. Yeah, and what about that promise you made?"

"It will be kept."

Starke gave him a hand. "Linnl, you're okay. If I ever get back to Earth, so help me, I'll never bait a hook again and drop it in the sea." It was lost to Linnl. Starke forgot it, and went on, laughing. There was an edge of hysteria to it. Relief. You got booted around for days, people milled in and out of your mind like it was a bargain basement counter, pawing over the treads and convolutions, yelling and fighting; the woman you loved was starved on a ship masthead, and as a climax a lady with green eyes tried to make you a filling for an accident-mangled body. And now you had an ally.

And you couldn't believe it.

He laughed in little starts and stops, his eyes shut.

"Will you let me take care of Rann when the time comes?"

His fingers groped hungrily upward, closed on an imaginary figure of her, pressed, tightly, choked.

Linnl said, "She's yours. I'd like the pleasure, but you have as much if not more of a revenge to take. Come along. We start now. You've been asleep for one entire period."

Starke let himself down gingerly. He didn't want to break a leg off. He felt if someone touched him he might disintegrate.

He managed to let the tide handle him, do all the work. He swam carefully after Linnl down three passageways where an occasional silver inhabitant of the city slid by.

Drifting below them in a vast square hall, each gravitating but imprisoned by leg-shackles, the warriors of Falga looked up with pale cold eyes at Starke and Linnl. Occasional discharges of light-fish from interstices in the walls passed luminous, fleeting glows over the warriors. The light-fish flirted briefly in a long shining rope that tied knots around the dead faces and as quickly untied them. Then the light-fish pulsed away and the red color of the sea took over.

Bathed in wine, thought Starke, without humor. He leaned forward.

"Men of Falga!"

Linnl plucked a series of harp-threads.

"Aye." A deep suggestion of sound issued from a thousand dead lips.

"We go to sack Rann's citadel!"

"Rann!" came the muffled thunder of voices.

At the sound of another tune, the golden hounds appeared. They touched the chains. The men of Falga, released, danced through the red sea substance.

Siphoned into a valve mouth, they were drawn out into a great volcanic courtyard. Starke went close after. He stared down into a black ravine, at the bottom of which was a blazing caldera.

This was the Source Life of the Red Sea. Here it had begun a millennium ago. Here the savage cyclones of sparks and fire energy belched up, shaking titanic black garden walls, causing currents and whirlpools that threatened to suck you forward and shoot you violently up to the surface, in cannulas of force, thrust, in capillaries of ignited mist, in chutes of color that threatened to cremate but only exhilarated you, gave you a seething rebirth!

He braced his legs and fought the suction. An unbelievable

sinew of fire sprang up from out the ravine, crackling and roaring.

The men of Falga did not fight the attraction.

They moved forward in their silence and hung over the incandescence.

The vitality of the Source grew upward in them. It seemed to touch their sandaled toes first, and then by a process of shining osmosis, climb up the limbs, into the loins, into the vitals, delineating their strong bone structure as mercury delineates the glass thermometer with a rise of temperature. The bones flickered like carved polished ivory through the momentarily film-like flesh. The ribs of a thousand men expanded like silvered spider legs, clenched, then expanded again. Their spines straightened, their shoulders flattened back. Their eyes, the last to take the fire, now were ignited and glowed like candles in refurbished sepulchers. The chins snapped up, the entire outer skins of their bodies broke into silver brilliance.

Swimming through the storm of energy like nightmare fragments, entering cold, they reached the far side of the ravine resembling smelted metal from blast furnces. When they brushed into one another, purple sparks sizzled, jumped from head to head, from hand to hand.

Linnl touched Starke's arm. "You're next."

"No thank you."

"Afraid?" laughed the harp-shepherd. "You're tired. It will give you new life. You're next."

Starke hesitated only a moment. Then he let the tide drift him rapidly out. He was afraid. Damned afraid. A belch of fire caught him as he arrived in the core of the ravine. He was wrapped in layers of ecstasy. Beudag pressed against him. It was her consuming hair that netted him and branded him. It was her warmth that crept up his body into his chest and into his head. Somebody yelled somewhere in animal delight and unbearable passion. Somebody danced and threw out his hands and crushed that solar warmth deeper into his huge body. Somebody felt all tiredness, oldness flumed away, a whole new feeling of warmth and strength inserted.

That somebody was Starke.

Waiting on the other side of the ravine were a thousand men of Falga. What sounded like a thousand harps began playing now, and as Starke reached the other side, the harps began marching, and the warriors marched with them. They were still dead, but you would never know it. There were no minds inside those bodies. The bodies were being activated from outside. But you would never know it.

They left the city behind. In embering ranks, the soldier-fighters were led by golden hounds and distant harps to a place where a huge intracoastal tide swept by.

They got on the tide for a free ride. Linnl beside him, using his harp, Starke felt himself sucked down through a deep where strange monsters sprawled. They looked at Starke with hungry eyes. But the harp wall swept them back.

Starke glanced about at the men. They don't know what they're doing, he thought. Going home to kill their parents and their children, to set the flame to Falga, and they don't know it. Their alive-but-dead faces tilted up, always upward, as though visions of Rann's citadel were there.

Rann. Starke let the wrath simmer in him. He let it cool. Then it was cold. Rann hadn't bothered him now for hours. Was there a chance she'd read his thought in the midst of that fighting nightmare? Did she know this plan for Falga? Was that an explanation for her silence now?

He sent his mind ahead, subtly. *Rann. Rann.* The only answer was the move of silver bodies through the fiery deeps.

Just before dawn they broke surface of the sea.

Falga drowsed in the red-smeared fog silence. Its slave streets were empty and dew-covered. High up, the first light was bathing Rann's gardens and setting her citadel aglow.

Linnl lay in the shallows beside Starke. They both were smiling half-cruel smiles. They had waited long for this.

Linnl nodded. "This is the day of the carnival. Fruit, wine, and love will be offered the returned soldiers of Rann. In the streets there'll be dancing."

Far over to the right lay a rise of mountain. At its blunt peak—Starke stared at it intently—rested a body of a little, scrawny Earthman, with flame-birds clustered on it. He'd climb that mountain later. When it was over and there was time.

"What are you searching for?" asked Linnl.

Starke's voice was distant. "Someone I used to know."

Filing out on the stone quays, their rustling sandals eroded by time, the men stood clean and bright. Starke paced, a caged animal, at their center, so his dark body would pass unnoticed.

They were seen.

The cliff guard looked down over the dirty slave dwellings, from their arrow galleries, and set up a cry. Hands waved, pointed frosty white in the dawn. More guards loped down the ramps and galleries, meeting, joining others and coming on.

Linnl, in the sea by the quay, suggested a theme on the harp. The other harps took it up. The shuddering music lifted from the water and with a gentle firmness, set the dead feet marching down the quays, upward through the narrow, stifling alleys of the slaves, to meet the guard.

Slave people peered out at them tiredly from their choked quarters. The passing of warriors was old to them, of no significance.

These warriors carried no weapons. Starke didn't like that part of it. A length of chain even, he wanted. But this emptiness of the hands. His teeth ached from too long a time of clenching his jaws tight. The muscles of his arms were feverish and nervous.

At the edge of the slave community, at the cliff base, the guard confronted them. Running down off the galleries, swords naked, they ran to intercept what they took to be an enemy.

The guards stopped in blank confusion.

A little laugh escaped Starke's lips. It was a dream. With fog over, under and in between its parts. It wasn't real to the guard, who couldn't believe it. It wasn't real to these dead men either, who were walking around. He felt alone. He was the only live one. He didn't like walking with dead men.

The captain of the guard came down warily, his green eyes suspicious. The suspicion faded. His face fell apart. He had lain on his fur pelts for months thinking of his son who had died to defend Falga.

Now his son stood before him. Alive.

The captain forgot he was captain. He forgot everything. His sandals scraped over stones. You could hear the air go out of his lungs and come back in in a numbed prayer.

"My son! In Rann's name. They said you were slain by Faolan's men one hundred darknesses ago. My son!"

A harp tinkled somewhere.

The son stepped forward, smiling.

They embraced. The son said nothing. He couldn't speak.

This was the signal for the others. The whole guard, shocked and surprised, put away their swords and sought out old friends, brothers, fathers, uncles, sons!

They moved up the galleries, the guard and the returned warriors, Starke in their midst. Threading up the cliff, through passage after passage, all talking at once. Or so it seemed. The guards did the talking. None of the dead warriors replied. They only *seemed* to. Starke heard the music strong and clear everywhere.

They reached the green gardens atop the cliff. By this time the entire city was awake. Women came running, bare-breasted and sobbing, and throwing themselves forward into the ranks of their lovers. Flowers showered over them.

"So this is war," muttered Starke, uneasily.

They stopped in the center of the great gardens. The crowd milled happily, not yet aware of the strange silence from their men. They were too happy to notice.

"Now," cried Starke to himself. "Now's the time. Now!"

As if in answer, a wild skirling of harps out of the sky.

The crowd stopped laughing only when the returned warriors of Falga swept forward, their hands lifted and groping before them . . .

The crying in the streets was like a far siren wailing. Metal made a harsh clangor that was sheathed in silence at the same moment metal found flesh to lie in. A vicious pantomime was concluded in the green moist gardens.

Starke watched from Rann's empty citadel. Fog plumes strolled by the archway and a thick rain fell. It came like a blood squall and washed the garden below until you could not tell rain from blood.

The returned warriors had gotten their swords by now. First they killed those nearest them in the celebration. Then they took the weapons from the victims. It was very simple and very unpleasant.

The slaves had joined battle now. Swarming up from the slave town, plucking up fallen daggers and short swords, they circled the gardens, happening upon the arrogant shining warriors of Rann who had so far escaped the quiet, deadly killing of the alive-but-dead men.

Dead father killed startled, alive son. Dead brother garroted unbelieving brother. Carnival indeed in Falga.

An old man waited alone. Starke saw him. The old man had a weapon, but refused to use it. A young warrior of Falga, harped on by Linnl's harp, walked quietly up to the old man. The old man cried out. His mouth formed words. "Son! What *is* this?" He flung down his blade and made to plead with his boy.

The son stabbed him with silent efficiency, and without a glance at the body, walked onward to find another.

Starke turned away, sick and cold.

A thousand such scenes were being finished.

He set fire to the black spider-silk tapestries. They whispered and talked with flame. The stone echoed his feet as he searched room after room. Rann had gone, probably last night. That meant that Crom Dhu was on the verge of falling. Was Faolan dead? Had the people of Crom Dhu, seeing Beudag's suffering, given in? Falga's harbor was completely devoid of ships, except for small fishing skiffs.

The fog waited him when he returned to the garden. Rain found his face.

The citadel of Rann was fire-encrusted and smoke-shrouded as he looked up at it.

A silence lay in the garden. The fight was over.

The men of Falga, still shining with Source-Life, hung their blades from uncomprehending fingers, the light beginning to leave their green eyes. Their skin looked dirty and dull.

Starke wasted no time getting down the galleries, through the slave quarter, and to the quays again.

Linnl awaited him, gently petting the obedient harp.

"It's over. The slaves will own what's left. They'll be our allies, since we've freed them."

Starke didn't hear. He was squinting off over the Red Sea.

Linnl understood. He plucked two tones from the harp, which pronounced the two words uppermost in Starke's thought.

"Crom Dhu."

"If we're not too late." Starke leaned forward. "If Faolan lives. If Beudag still stands at the masthead."

Like a blind man he walked straight ahead, until he fell into the sea.

It was not quite a million miles to Crom Dhu. It only seemed that far.

A sweep of tide picked them up just off shore from Falga and siphoned them rapidly, through deeps along coastal latitudes, through crystal forests. He cursed every mile of the way.

He cursed the time it took to pause at the Titan's city to gather fresh men. To gather Clev and Mannt and Aesur and Bron. Impatiently, Starke watched the whole drama of the Source-Fire and the bodies again. This time it was the bodies of Crom Dhu men, hung like beasts on slow-turned spits, their limbs and vitals soaking through and through, their skins taking bronze color, their eyes holding flint-sparks. And then the harps wove a garment around each, and the garment moved the men instead of the men the garment.

In the tidal basilic now, Starke twisted. Coursing behind him were the new bodies of Clev and Aesur! The current elevated them, poked them through obsidian needle-eyes like spider-silk threads.

There was good irony in this. Crom Dhu's men, fallen at Falga under Conan's treachery, returned now under Conan to exonerate that treachery.

Suddenly they were in Crom Dhu's outer basin. Shadows swept over them. The long dark falling shadows of Falga's longboats lying in that harbor. Shadows like black culling-nets let down. The school of men cleaved the shadow nets. The tide ceased here, eddied and distilled them.

Starke glared up at the immense silver bottom of a Falgian ship. He felt his face stiffen and his throat tighten. Then, flexing knees, he rammed upward; night air broke dark red around his head.

The harbor held flare torches on the rims of long ships. On the neck of land that led from Crom Dhu to the mainland the continuing battle sounded. Faint cries and clashing made their way through the fog veils. They sounded like echoes of past dreams.

Linnl let Starke have the leash. Starke felt something pressed into his fist. A coil of slender green woven reeds, a rope with hooked weights on the end of it. He knew how to use it without asking. But he wished for a knife now, even though he realized carrying a knife in the sea was all but impossible if you wanted to move fast.

He saw the sleek naked figurehead of Rann's best ship a hundred yards away, a floating silhouette, its torches hanging fire like Beudag's hair.

He swam toward it, breathing quietly. When at last the silvered figurehead with the mocking green eyes and the flag of shoal-shallow hair hung over him, he felt the cool white ship metal kiss his fingers.

The smell of torch-smoke lingered. A rise of faint shouts from the land told of another rush upon the Gate. Behind him—a ripple. Then—a thousand ripples.

The resurrected men of Crom Dhu rose in dents and stirrings of sparkling wine. They stared at Crom Dhu and maybe they knew what it was and maybe they didn't. For one moment, Starke felt apprehension. Suppose Linnl was playing a game. Suppose, once these men had won the battle, they went on into Crom Dhu to rupture Romna's harp and make Faolan the blinder? He shook the thought away. That would have to be handled in time. On either side of him Clev and Mannt appeared. They looked at Crom Dhu, their lips shut. Maybe they saw Faolan's eyrie and heard a harp that was more than these harps that sang them to blade and plunder—Romna's instrument telling bard-tales of the rovers and the coastal wars and the old, living days. Their eyes looked and looked at Crom Dhu, but saw nothing.

The sea shepherds appeared now, the followers of Linnl, each with his harp; and the harp music began, high. So high you couldn't hear it. It wove a tension on the air.

Silently, with a grim certainty, the dead-but-not-dead gathered in a bronze circle about Rann's ship. The very silence of their encirclement made your skin crawl and sweat break cold on your cheeks.

A dozen ropes went raveling, looping over the ship side. They caught, held, grapnelled, hooked.

Starke had thrown his, felt it bite, and hold. Now he scrambled swiftly, cursing, up its length, kicking and slipping at the silver hull.

He reached the top.

Beudag was there.

Half over the low rail he hesitated, just looking at her.

Torchlight limned her, shadowed her. She was still erect; her head was tired and her eyes closed, her face thinned and less brown, but she was still alive. She was coming out of a deep stupor now, at the whistle of ropes and the grate of metal hooks on the deck.

She saw Starke and her lips parted. She did not look away from him. His breath came out of him, choking.

It almost cost him his life, his standing there, looking at her.

A guard, with flesh like new snow, shafted his bow from the turret and let it loose. A chain lay on deck. Thankfully, Starke took it.

Clev came over the rail beside Starke. His chest took the arrow. Clev kept going after the man who had shot it. He caught up with him.

Beudag cried out. "Behind you, Conan!"

Conan! In her excitement, she gave the old name.

Conan he *was*. Whirling, he confronted a wiry little fellow, chained him brutally across the face, seized the man's falling sword, used it on him. Then he walked in, got the man's jaw, unbalanced him over into the sea.

The ship was awake now. Most of the men had been down below, resting from the battles. Now they came pouring up, in a silver spate. Their yelling was in strange contrast to the calm silence of Crom Dhu's men. Starke found himself busy.

Conan had been a healthy animal, with great recuperative powers. Now his muscles responded to every trick asked of them. Starke leaped cleanly across the deck, watching for Rann, but she was nowhere to be seen. He engaged two blades, dispatched one of them. More ropes raveled high and snaked him. Every ship in the harbor was exploding with violence. More men swarmed over the rail behind Starke, silently.

Above the shouting, Beudag's voice came, at sight of the fighting men. "Clev! Mannt! Aesur!"

Starke was a god; anything he wanted he could have. A man's head? He could have it. It meant acting the guillotine with knife and wrist and lunged body. Like—*this!* His eyes were smoking amber and there were deep lines of grim pleasure tugging at his lips. An enemy cannot fight without hands. One man, facing Starke, suddenly displayed violent stumps before his face, not believing them.

Are you watching, Faolan? cried Starke inside himself, delivering blows. Look here, Faolan! God, no, you're blind. *Listen* then! Hear the ring of steel on steel. Does the smell of hot blood and hot bodies reach you? Oh, if you could see this tonight, Faolan. Falga would be forgotten. This is Conan, out of idiocy, with a guy named Starke wearing him and telling him where to go!

It was not safe on deck. Starke hadn't particularly noticed before, but the warriors of Crom Dhu didn't care whom they attacked now. They were beginning to do surgery to one another. They excised one another's shoulders, severed limbs in blind instantaneous obedience. This was no place for Beudag and himself.

He cut her free of the masthead, drew her quickly to the rail.

Beudag was laughing. She could do nothing but laugh. Her eyes were shocked. She saw dead men alive again, lashing out with weapons; she had been starved and made to stand night and day, and now she could only laugh.

Starke shook her.

She did not stop laughing.

"Beudag! You're all right. You're free."

She stared at nothing. "I'll—I'll be all right in a minute."

He had to ward off a blow from one of his own men. He parried the thrust, then got in and pushed the man off the deck, over into the sea. That was the only thing to do. You couldn't kill them.

Beudag stared down at the tumbling body.

"Where's Rann?" Starke's yellow eyes narrowed, searching.

"She *was* here." Beudag trembled.

Rann looked out of her eyes. Out of the tired numbness of Beudag, an echo of Rann. Rann was nearby, and this was her doing.

Instinctively, Starke raised his eyes.

Rann appeared at the masthead, like a flurry of snow. Her green-tipped breasts were rising and falling with emotion. Pure hatred lay in her eyes. Starke licked his lips and readied his sword.

Rann snapped a glance at Beudag. Stooping, as in a dream, Beudag picked up a dagger and held it to her own breast.

Starke froze.

Rann nodded, with satisfaction. "Well, Starke? How will it be? Will you come at me and have Beudag die? Or will you let me go free?"

Starke's palms felt sweaty and greasy. "There's no place for you to go. Falga's taken. I can't guarantee your freedom. If you want to go over the side, into the sea, that's your chance. You might make shore and your own men."

"Swimming? With the *sea-beasts* waiting?" She accented the *beasts* heavily. She was one of the sea-*people*. They, Linnl and his men, were sea-*beasts*. "No, Hugh Starke. I'll take a skiff. Put Beudag at the rail where I can watch her all the way. Guarantee my passage to shore and my own men there, and Beudag lives."

Starke waved his sword. "Get going."

He didn't want to let her go. He had other plans, good plans for her. He shouted the deal down at Linnl. Linnl nodded back, with much reluctance.

Rann, in a small silver skiff, headed toward land. She handled the boat and looked back at Beudag all the while. She passed through the sea-beasts and touched the shore. She lifted her hand and brought it smashing down.

Whirling, Starke swung his fist against Beudag's jaw. Her hand was already striking the blade into her breast. Her head flopped back. His fist carried through. She fell. The blade clattered. He kicked it overboard. Then he lifted Beudag. She was warm and good to hold. The blade had only pricked her breast. A small rivulet of blood ran.

On the shore, Rann vanished upward on the rocks, hurrying to find her men.

In the harbor the harp music paused. The ships were taken. Their crews lay filling the decks. Crom Dhu's men stopped fighting as quickly as they'd started. Some of the bright shining had dulled from the bronze of their arms and bare torsos. The ships began to sink.

Linnl swam below, looking up at Starke. Starke looked back at him and nodded at the beach. "Swell. Now, let's go get that she-devil," she said.

Faolan waited on his great stone balcony, overlooking Crom Dhu. Behind him the fires blazed high and their eating sound of flame on wood filled the pillared gloom with sound and furious light.

Faolan leaned against the rim, his chest swathed in bandage and healing ointment, his blind eyes flickering, looking down again and again with a fixed intensity, his head tilted to listen.

Romna stood beside him, filled and refilled the cup that Faolan emptied into his thirsty mouth, and told him what happened. Told of the men pouring out of the sea, and Rann appearing on the rocky shore. Sometimes Faolan leaned to one side, weakly, toward Romna's words. Sometimes he twisted to hear the thing itself, the thing that happened down beyond the Gate of besieged Crom Dhu.

Romna's harp lay untouched. He didn't play it. He didn't need to. From below, a great echoing of harps, more liquid than his, like a waterfall drenched the city, making the fog sob down red tears.

"Are those harps?" cried Faolan.

"Yes, harps!"

"What was that?" Faolan listened, breathing harshly, clutching for support.

"A skirmish," said Romna.

"Who won?"

"*We* won."

"And *that?*" Faolan's blind eyes tried to see until they watered.

"The enemy falling back from the Gate!"

"And that sound, and that sound?" Faolan went on and on, feverishly, turning this way and that, the lines of his face agonized and attentive to each eddy and current and change of tide. The rhythm of swords through fog and body was a complicated music whose themes he must recognize. "Another fell! I heard him cry. And another of Rann's men!"

"Yes," said Romna.

"But why do our warriors fight so quietly? I've heard nothing from their lips. So quiet."

Romna scowled. "Quiet! Yes—quiet."

"And where did they come from? All our men are in the city?"

"Aye." Romna shifted. He hesitated, squinting. He rubbed his bulldog jaw. "Except those that died at—Falga."

Faolan stood there a moment. Then he rapped the empty cup.

"More wine, bard. More wine."

He turned to the battle again.

"Oh, gods, if I could see it, if I could only see it!"

Below, a ringing crash. A silence. A shouting, a pouring of noise.

"The Gate!" Faolan was stricken with fear. "We're lost! My sword!"

"Stay, Faolan!" Romna laughed. Then he sighed. It was a sigh that did not believe. "In the name of ten thousand mighty gods. Would that I were blind now, or could see better."

Faolan's hand caught, held him. "What *is* it? Tell!"

"Clev! And Tlan! And Conan! And Bron! And Mannt! Standing in the gate, like wine visions! Swords in their hands!"

Faolan's hand relaxed, then tightened. "Speak their names again, and speak them slowly. And tell the truth." His skin shivered like that of a nervous animal. "You said—Clev? Mannt? Bron?"

"And Tlan! And Conan! Back from Falga. They've opened the Gate and the battle's won. It's over, Faolan. Crom Dhu will sleep tonight."

Faolan let him go. A sob broke from his lips. "I will get drunk. Drunker than ever in my life. Gloriously drunk. Gods, but if I could have seen it. Been in it. Tell me again of it, Romna . . ."

Faolan sat in the great hall, on his carved high-seat, waiting.

The pad of sandals on stone outside, the jangle of chains.

A door flung wide, red fog sluiced in, and in the sluice, people walking. Faolan started up. "Clev? Mannt? Aesur?"

Starke came forward into the firelight. He pressed his right hand to the open mouth of wound on his thigh. "No, Faolan. Myself and two others."

"Beudag?"

"Yes." And Beudag came wearily to him.

Faolan stared. "Who's the other? It walks light. It's a woman."

Starke nodded. "Rann."

Faolan rose carefully from his seat. He thought the name over. He took a short sword from a place beside the high seat. He stepped down. He walked toward Starke. "You brought Rann alive to me?"

Starke pulled the chain that bound Rann. She ran forward in little steps, her white face down, her eyes slitted with animal fury.

"Faolan's blind," said Starke. "I let you live for one damned good reasom, Rann. Okay, go ahead."

Faolan stopped walking, curious. He waited.

Rann did nothing.

Starke took her hand and wrenched it behind her back. "I said 'go ahead.' Maybe you didn't hear me."

"I will," she gasped, in pain.

Starke released her. "Tell me what happens, Faolan."

Rann gazed steadily at Faolan's tall figure there in the light.

Faolan suddenly threw his hands to his eyes and choked.

Beudag cried out, seized his arm.

"I can see!" Faolan staggered, as if jolted. "I can see!" First he shouted it, then he whispered it. *"I can see."*

Starke's eyes blurred. He whispered to Rann, tightly. "Make him see it, Rann, or you die now. Make him see it!" To Faolan: "What do you see?"

Faolan was bewildered; he swayed. He put out his hands to shape the vision. "I—I see Crom Dhu. It's a good sight. I see the ships of Rann. Sinking!" He laughed a broken laugh. "I—see the fight beyond the gate!"

Silence swam in the room, over their heads.

Faolan's voice went alone, and hypnotized, into that silence.

He put out his big fists, shook them, opened them. "I see Mannt, and Aesur and Clev! Fighting as they always fought.

I see Conan as he was. I see Beudag wielding steel again, on the shore! I see the enemy killed! I see men pouring out of the sea with brown skins and dark hair. Men I knew a long darkness ago. Men that roved the sea with me. *I see Rann captured!*" He began to sob with it, his lungs filling and releasing it, sucking on it, blowing it out. Tears ran down from his vacant, blazing eyes. "I see Crom Dhu as it was and is and shall be! *I see, I see, I see!*"

Starke felt the chill on the back of his neck.

"I see Rann captured and held, and her men dead around her on the land before the Gate. I see the Gate thrown open—" Faolan halted. He looked at Starke. "Where are Clev and Mannt? Where is Bron and Aesur?"

Starke let the fires burn on the hearths a long moment. Then he replied.

"They went back into the sea, Faolan."

Faolan's fingers fell emptily. "Yes," he said, heavily. "They had to go back, didn't they? They couldn't stay, could they? Not even for one night of food on the table, and wine in the mouth, and women in the deep warm furs before the hearth. Not even for one toast." He turned. "A drink, Romna. A drink for everyone."

Romna gave him a full cup. He dropped it, fell down to his knees, clawed at his breast. "My heart!"

"Rann, you sea-devil!"

Starke held her instantly by the throat. He put pressure on the small raging pulses on either side of her snow-white neck. "Let him go, Rann!" More pressure. *"Let him go!"* Faolan grunted. Starke held her until her white face was dirty and strange with death.

It seemed like an hour later when he released her. She fell softly and did not move. She wouldn't move again.

Starke turned slowly to look at Faolan.

"You saw, didn't you, Faolan?" he said.

Faolan nodded blindly, weakly. He roused himself from the floor, groping. "I saw. For a moment, I saw everything. And Gods! but it made good seeing! Here, Hugh-Starke-called-Conan, gave this other side of me something to lean on."

Beudag and Starke climbed the mountain above Falga the next day. Starke went ahead a little way, and with his coming the flame birds scattered, glittering away.

He dug the shallow grave and did what had to be done

with the body he found there, and then when the grave was covered with thick grey stones he went back for Beudag. They stood together over it. He had never expected to stand over a part of himself, but here he was, and Beudag's hand gripped his.

He looked suddenly a million years old standing there. He thought of Earth and the Belt and Jupiter, of the joy streets in the Jekkara Low Canals of Mars. He thought of space and the ships going through it, and himself inside them. He thought of the million credits he had taken in that last job. He laughed ironically.

"Tomorrow, I'll have the sea creatures hunt for a little metal box full of credits." He nodded solemnly at the grave. "He wanted that. Or at least he thought he did. He killed himself getting it. So if the sea-people find it, I'll send it up here to the mountain and bury it down under the rocks in his fingers. I guess that's the best place."

Beudag drew him away. They walked down the mountain toward Falga's harbor where a ship waited them. Walking, Starke lifted his face. Beudag was with him, and the sails of the ship were rising to take the wind, and the Red Sea waited for them to travel it. What lay on its far side was something for Beudag and Faolan-of-the-Ships and Romna and Hugh-Starke-called-Conan to discover. He felt damned good about it. He walked on steadily, holding Beudag near.

And on the mountain, as the ship sailed, the flame birds soared down fitfully and frustratedly to beat at the stone mound, ceased, and mourning shrilly, flew away.

THE MILLION YEAR PICNIC

by Ray Bradbury

PLANET STORIES
Summer

The summer, 1946 Planet Stories *was quite an issue. Not only did it feature the excellent novella you have just read, but it also contained one of the most important short stories in all of science fiction. "The Million Year Picnic" turned out to be the first of the stories that were collected together as* The Martian Chronicles *(1950), which in spite of its weak science, became a landmark book in the history of the field.*

(I remember the year Doubleday began to publish hard-cover science fiction. The very first book published, in 1949, was The Big Eye *by Max Ehrlich. The second, in January, 1950, was my own* Pebble in The Sky [*my first book*]. *The third was Ray Bradbury's* The Martian Chronicles. *Bradbury's book is the rock on which his science fiction fame still rests thirty years later. It was the first science fiction blockbuster to the great world outside. It presented a second picture of Mars, equal in power to that of Edgar Rice Burroughs, and although science has outstripped fiction here and*

presented Mars as it really is, the mythical Mars of Bradbury is not likely to die. It will continue to exist forever in some hidden nook of the mind. And The Million Year Picnic, *the first written, is the last of the twenty-six stories in the book, and the fitting climax. Those last four sentences!—I.A.)*

Somehow the idea was brought up by Mom that perhaps the whole family would enjoy a fishing trip. But they weren't Mom's words; Timothy knew that. They were Dad's words and Mom used them for him somehow.

Dad shuffled his feet in a clutter of Martian pebbles and agreed. So immediately there was a tumult and a shouting, and very quickly the camp was tucked into capsules and containers. Mom slipped into traveling jumpers and blouse, Dad stuffed his pipe full with trembling hands, his eyes on the Martian sky, and the three boys piled yelling into the motorboat, none of them really keeping an eye on Mom and Dad, except Timothy.

Dad pushed a stud. The water boat sent a humming sound up into the sky. The water shook back and the boat nosed ahead, and the family cried, "Hurrah!"

Timothy sat in the back of the boat with Dad, his small fingers atop Dad's hairy ones, watching the canal twist, leaving the crumbled place behind where they had landed in their small family rocket all the way from Earth. He remembered the night before they left Earth, the hustling and hurrying, the rocket that Dad had found somewhere, somehow, and the talk of a vacation on Mars. A long way to go for a vacation, but Timothy said nothing because of his younger brothers. They came to Mars and now, first thing, or so they said, they were going fishing.

Dad had a funny look in his eyes as the boat went upcanal. A look that Timothy couldn't figure. It was made of strong light and maybe a sort of relief. It made the deep wrinkles laugh instead of worry or cry.

So there went the cooling rocket, around a bend, gone.

"How far are we going?" Robert splashed his hand. It looked like a small crab jumping in the violent water.

Dad exhaled. "A million years."

"Gee," said Robert.

"Look, kids." Mother pointed one soft long arm. "There's a dead city."

They looked with fervent anticipation, and the dead city lay dead for them alone, drowsing in a hot silence of summer made on Mars by a Martian weatherman.

And Dad looked as if he was pleased that it was dead.

It was a futile spread of pink rocks sleeping on a rise of sand, a few tumbled pillars, one lonely shrine, and then the sweep of sand again. Nothing else for miles. A white desert around the canal and a blue desert over it.

Just then a bird flew up. Like a stone thrown across a blue pond, hitting, falling deep, and vanishing.

Dad got a frightened look when he saw it. "I thought it was a rocket."

Timothy looked at the deep ocean sky, trying to see Earth and the war and the ruined cities and the men killing each other since the day he was born. But he saw nothing. The war was as removed and far off as two flies battling to the death in the arch of a great high and silent cathedral. And just as senseless.

William Thomas wiped his forehead and felt the touch of his son's hand on his arm, like a young tarantula, thrilled. He beamed at his son. "How goes it, Timmy?"

"Fine, Dad."

Timothy hadn't quite figured out what was ticking inside the vast adult mechanism beside him. The man with the immense hawk nose, sunburnt, peeling—and the hot blue eyes like agate marbles you play with after school in summer back on Earth, and the long thick columnar legs in the loose riding breeches.

"What are you looking at so hard, Dad?"

"I was looking for Earthian logic, common sense, good government, peace, and responsibility."

"All that up there?"

"No. I didn't find it. It's not there any more. Maybe it'll never be there again. Maybe we fooled ourselves that it was ever there."

"Huh?"

"See the fish," said Dad, pointing.

There arose a soprano clamor from all three boys as they rocked the boat in arching their tender necks to see. They *oohed* and *ahed*. A silver ring fish floated by them, undulating, and closing like an iris, instantly, around food particles, to assimilate them.

Dad looked at it. His voice was deep and quiet.

"Just like war. War swims along, sees food, contracts. A moment later—Earth is gone."

"William," said Mom.

"Sorry," said Dad.

They sat still and felt the canal water rush cool, swift, and glassy. The only sound was the motor hum, the glide of water, the sun expanding the air.

"When do we see the Martians?" cried Michael.

"Quite soon, perhaps," said Father. "Maybe tonight."

"Oh, but the Martians are a dead race now," said Mom.

"No, they're not. I'll show you some Martians, all right," Dad said presently.

Timothy scowled at that but said nothing. Everything was odd now. Vacations and fishing and looks between people.

The other boys were already engaged making shelves of their small hands and peering under them toward the seven-foot stone banks of the canal, watching for Martians.

"What do they look like?" demanded Michael.

"You'll know them when you see them." Dad sort of laughed, and Timothy saw a pulse beating time in his cheek.

Mother was slender and soft, with a woven plait of spun-gold hair over her head in a tiara, and eyes the color of the deep cool canal water where it ran in shadow, almost purple, with flecks of amber caught in it. You could see her thoughts swimming around in her eyes, like fish—some bright, some dark, some fast, quick, some slow and easy, and sometimes, like when she looked up where Earth was, being nothing but color and nothing else. She sat in the boat's prow, one hand resting on the side lip, the other on the lap of her dark blue breeches, and a line of sunburnt soft neck showing where her blouse opened like a white flower.

She kept looking ahead to see what was there, and, not being able to see it clearly enough she looked backward toward her husband, and through his eyes, reflected then, she saw what was ahead; and since he added part of himself to this reflection, a determined firmness, her face relaxed and she accepted it and she turned back, knowing suddenly what to look for.

Timothy looked too. But all he saw was a straight pencil line of canal going violet through a wide shallow valley penned by low, eroded hills, and on until it fell over the sky's edge. And this canal went on and on, through cities that would have rattled like beetles in a dry skull if you shook them. A hundred or two hundred cities dreaming hot-summer-day dreams and cool-summer-night dreams . . .

They had come millions of miles for this outing—to fish. But there had been a gun on the rocket. This was a vacation. But why all the food, more than enough to last them years and years, left hidden back there near the rocket! Vacation. Just behind the veil of the vacation was not a soft face of laughter, but something hard and body and perhaps terrifying. Timothy could not lift the veil, and the two other boys were busy being ten and eight years old, respectively.

"No Martians yet. Nuts." Robert put his V-shaped chin on his hands and glared at the canal.

Dad had brought an atomic radio along, strapped to his wrist. It functioned on an old-fashioned principle: you held it against the bones near your ear and it vibrated singing or talking to you. Dad listened to it now. His face looked like one of those fallen Martian cities, caved in, sucked dry, almost dead.

Then he gave it to Mom to listen to. Her lips dropped open.

"What—" Timothy started to question, but never finished what he wished to say.

For at that moment there were two titantic, marrow-jolting explosions that grew upon themselves, followed by a half dozen minor concussions.

Jerking his head up, Dad notched the boat speed higher immediately. The boat leaped and jounced and spanked. This shook Robert out of his funk and elicited yelps of frightened but ecstatic joy from Michael, who clung to Mom's legs and watched the water pour by his nose in a wet torrent.

Dad swerved the boat, cut speed, and ducked the craft into a little branch canal and under an ancient, crumbling stone wharf that smelled of crab flesh. The boat rammed the wharf hard enough to throw them all forward, but no one was hurt, and Dad was already twisted to see if the ripples on the canal were enough to map their route into hiding. Water lines went across, lapped the stones, and rippled back to meet each other, settling, to be dappled by the sun. It all went away.

Dad listened. So did everybody.

Dad's breathing echoed like fists beating against the cold wet wharf stones. In the shadow, Mom's cat eyes just watched Father for some clue to what next.

Dad relaxed and blew out a breath, laughing at himself.

"The rocket, of course. I'm getting jumpy. The rocket."

Michael said, "What happened, Dad, what happened?"

"Oh, we just blew up our rocket, is all," said Timothy, trying to sound matter-of-fact. "I've heard rockets blown up before. Ours just blew."

"Why did we blow up our rocket?" asked Michael. "Huh, Dad?"

"It's part of the game, silly!" said Timothy.

"A game!" Michael and Robert loved the word.

"Dad fixed it so it would blow up and no one'd know where we landed or went! In case they ever came looking, see?"

"Oh boy, a secret!"

"Scared by my own rocket," admitted Dad to Mom. "I am nervous. It's silly to think there'll ever be any more rockets. Except *one*, perhaps, if Edwards and his wife get through with *their* ship."

He put his tiny radio to his ear again. After two minutes he dropped his hand as you would drop a rag.

"It's over at last," he said to Mom. "The radio just went off the atomic beam. Every other world station's gone. They dwindled down to a couple in the last few years. Now the air's completely silent. It'll probably remain silent."

"For how long?" asked Robert.

"Maybe—your great-grandchildren will hear it again," said Dad. He just sat there, and the children were caught in the center of his awe and defeat and resignation and acceptance.

Finally he put the boat out into the canal again, and they continued in the direction in which they had originally started.

It was getting late. Already the sun was down the sky, and a series of dead cities lay ahead of them.

Dad talked very quietly and gently to his sons. Many times in the past he had been brisk, distant, removed from them but now he patted them on the head with just a word and they felt it.

"Mike, pick a city."

"What, Dad?"

"Pick a city, Son. Any one of these cities we pass."

"All right," said Michael. "How do I pick?"

"Pick the one you like the most. You, too, Robert and Tim. Pick the city you like best."

"I want a city with Martians in it," said Michael.

"You'll have that," said Dad. "I promise." His lips were for the children, but his eyes were for Mom.

They passed six cities in twenty minutes. Dad didn't say anything more about the explosions; he seemed much more interested in having fun with his sons, keeping them happy, than anything else.

Michael liked the first city they passed, but this was vetoed because everyone doubted quick first judgments. The second city nobody liked. It was an Earth Man's settlement, built of wood and already rotting into sawdust. Timothy liked the third city because it was large. The fourth and fifth were too small and the sixth brought acclaim from everyone, including Mother, who joined in the Gees, Goshes, and Look-at-thats!

There were fifty or sixty huge structures still standing, streets were dusty but paved, and you could see one or two old centrifugal fountains still pulsing wetly in the plazas. That was the only lifewater leaping in the late sunlight.

"This is the city," said everybody.

Steering the boat to a wharf, Dad jumped out.

"Here we are. This is ours. This is where we live from now on!"

"From now on?" Michael was incredulous. He stood up, looking, and then turned to blink back at where the rocket used to be. "What about the rocket? What about Minnesota?"

"Here," said Dad.

He touched the small radio to Michael's blond head. "Listen."

Michael listened.

"Nothing," he said.

"That's right. Nothing. Nothing at all anymore. No more Minneapolis, no more rockets, no more Earth."

Michael considered the lethal revelation and began to sob little dry sobs.

"Wait a moment," said Dad the next instant. "I'm giving you a lot more in exchange, Michael!"

"What?" Michael held off the tears, curious, but quite ready to continue in case Dad's further revelation was as disconcerting as the original.

"I'm giving you this city, Mike. It's yours."

"Mine?"

"For you and Robert and Timothy, all three of you, to own for yourselves."

Timothy bounded from the boat. "Look, guys, all for *us!* All of *that!*" He was playing the game with Dad, playing it large and playing it well. Later, after it was all over and things had settled, he could go off by himself and cry for ten minutes. But now it was still a game, still a family outing, and the other kids must be kept playing.

Mike jumped out with Robert. They helped Mom.

"Be careful of your sister," said Dad, and nobody knew what he meant until later.

They hurried into the great pink-stoned city, whispering among themselves, because dead cities have a way of making you want to whisper, to watch the sun go down.

"In about five days," said Dad quietly, "I'll go back down to where our rocket was and collect the food hidden in the ruins there and bring it here; and I'll hunt for Bert Edwards and his wife and daughters there."

"Daughters?" asked Timothy. "How many?"

"Four."

"I can see that'll cause trouble later." Mom nodded slowly.

"Girls." Michael made a face like an ancient Martian stone image. "Girls."

"Are they coming in a rocket too?"

"Yes. If they make it. Family rockets are made for travel to the Moon, not Mars. We were lucky we got through."

"Where did you get the rocket?" whispered Timothy, for the other boys were running ahead.

"I saved it. I saved it for twenty years, Tim. I had it hidden away, hoping I'd never have to use it. I suppose I should have given it to the government for the war, but I kept thinking about Mars . . ."

"And a picnic!"

"Right. This is between you and me. When I saw everything was finishing on Earth, after I'd waited until the last moment, I packed us up. Bert Edwards had a ship hidden, too, but we decided it would be safer to take off separately, in case anyone tried to shoot us down."

"Why'd you blow up the rocket, Dad?"

"So we can't go back, ever. And so if any of those evil men ever come to Mars they won't know we're here."

"Is that why you look up all the time?"

"Yes, it's silly. They won't follow us, ever. They haven't anything to follow with. I'm being too careful, is all."

Michael came running back. "Is this really *our* city, Dad?"

"The whole darn planet belongs to us, kids. The whole darn planet."

They stood there, King of the Hill, Top of the Heap,

Ruler of All They Surveyed, Unimpeachable Monarchs and Presidents, trying to understand what it meant to own a world and how big a world really was.

Night came quickly in the thin atmosphere, and Dad left them in the square by the pulsing fountain, went down to the boat, and came walking back carrying a stack of paper in his big hands.

He laid the papers in a clutter in an old courtyard and set them afire. To keep warm, they crouched around the blaze and laughed, and Timothy saw the little letters leap like frightened animals when the flames touched and engulfed them. The papers crinkled like an old man's skin, and the cremation surrounded innumerable words:

"Government Bonds: Business Graph, 1999; Religious Prejudice: An Essay; The Science of Logistics; Problems of the Pan-American Unity; Stock Report for July 3, 1998; The War Digest . . ."

Dad had insisted on bringing these papers for this purpose. He sat there and fed them into the fire, one by one, with satisfaction, and told his children what it all meant.

"It's time I told you a few things. I don't suppose it was fair, keeping so much from you. I don't know if you'll understand, but I have to talk, even if only part of it gets over to you."

He dropped a leaf in the fire.

"I'm burning a way of life, just like the way of life is being burned clean off Earth right now. Forgive me if I talk like a politician. I am, after all, a former state governor, and I was honest and they hated me for it. Life on Earth never settled down to doing anything very good. Science ran too far ahead of us too quickly, and the people got lost in a mechanical wilderness, like children making over pretty things, gadgets, helicopters, rockets; emphasizing the wrong items, emphasizing machines instead of how to run the machines. Wars got bigger and bigger and finally killed Earth. That's what the silent radio means. That's what we ran away from.

"We were lucky. There aren't any more rockets left. It's time you knew this isn't a fishing trip at all. I put off telling you. Earth is gone. Interplanetary travel won't be back for centuries, maybe never. But that way of life proved itself wrong and strangled itself with its own hands. You're young. I'll tell you this again every day until it sinks in."

He paused to feed more papers to the fire.

"Now we're alone. We and a handful of others who'll land

in a few days. Enough to start over. Enough to turn away from all that back on Earth and strike out on a new line—"

The fire leaped up to emphasize his talking. And then all the papers were gone except one. All the laws and beliefs of Earth were burnt into small hot ashes which soon would be carried off in a wind.

Timothy looked at the last thing that Dad tossed in the fire. It was a map of the World, and it wrinkled and distorted itself hotly and went—flimpf—and was gone like a warm, black butterfly. Timothy turned away.

"Now I'm going to show you the Martians," said Dad. "Come on, all of you. Here Alice." He took her hand.

Michael was crying loudly, and Dad picked him up and carried him, and they walked down through the ruins toward the canal.

The canal. Where tomorrow or the next day their future wives would come up in a boat, small laughing girls now, with their father and mother.

The night came down around them, and there were stars. But Timothy couldn't find Earth. It had already set. That was something to think about.

A night bird called among the ruins as they walked. Dad said, "Your mother and I will try to teach you. Perhaps we'll fail. I hope not. We've had a good lot to see and learn from. We planned this trip years ago, before you were born. Even if there hadn't been a war we would have come to Mars, I think, to live and form our own standard of living. It would have been another century before Mars would have been really poisoned by the Earth civilization. Now, of course—"

They reached the canal. It was long and straight and cool and wet and reflective in the night.

"I've always wanted to see a Martian," said Michael. "Where are they, Dad? You promised."

"There they are," said Dad, and he shifted Michael on his shoulder and pointed straight down.

The Martians were there. Timothy began to shiver.

The Martians were there—in the canal—reflected in the water. Timothy and Michael and Robert and Mom and Dad.

The Martians stared back up at them for a long, long silent time from the rippling water . . .

THE LAST OBJECTIVE

by Paul A. Carter (1926-   )

ASTOUNDING SCIENCE FICTION
August

Dr. Paul A. Carter is Professor of History at the University of Arizona and the author of such works of scholarship as The Twenties in America *and* Another Part of the Twenties. *He is also the author of the insightful and entertaining study* The Creation of Tomorrow: Fifty years of Magazine Science Fiction *(Columbia University Press, 1977) an excellent analysis of some of the major themes of modern sf as they developed in the genre magazines.*

Two decades before that book saw publication Paul A. Carter published "The Last Objective" the first of a handful of his stories to appear in the sf magazines (although he has recently returned to science fiction.) It was a memorable debut then, and is still a fine story today.

(After every great war there is an understandable revulsion against war in general—against the carnage, the destruction, the misery, and [to anyone with any brains at all] the stupidity. *World War II was the greatest, bloodiest, cruelest war ever fought*

[at least, to date] and its only saving grace was that it had an enemy worth fighting.

Nevertheless, the coming of the nuclear bomb at the very end made it quite plain that World War III, if it ever came, would finally achieve the crowning stupidity of war, the destruction of so much that no conceivable justification could exist for fighting. Here is a story that makes this quite plain in the military language that writers had learned from the war just concluded and yet a generation later, the world still prepares feverishly for a war only the insane would fight.—I.A.)

For uncounted eons the great beds of shale and limestone had known the stillness and the darkness of eternity. Now they trembled and shuddered to the passage of an invader; stirred and vibrated in sleepy protest at a disturbance not of Nature's making.

Tearing through the masses of soft rock, its great duralloy cutters screaming a hymn of hate into the crumbling crust, its caterpillar treads clanking and grinding over gravel shards fresh-torn from their age-old strata, lurched a juggernaut—one of the underground cruisers of the Combined Western Powers. It was squat, ugly; the top of its great cutting head full forty feet above the clattering treads, its square stern rocking and swaying one hundred and fifty feet behind the diamond-hard prow. It was angular, windowless; there were ugly lumps just behind the shrieking blades which concealed its powerful armament.

It had been built for warfare in an age when the sea and air were ruled by insensate rocket projectiles which flashed through the skies to spend their atomic wrath upon objectives which had long since ceased to exist; where infantry no longer was Queen of Battles, since the ravages of combat had wiped out the armies which began the war. And floods of hard radiation, sterilizing whole populations and making hideous mutational horrors of many of those who were born alive, had prevented the conscription of fresh armies which might have won the war.

The conflict had been going on for more than a generation.

The causes had long been forgotten; the embattled nations, burrowing into the earth, knew only a fiery longing for revenge. The chaos produced by the first aerial attacks had enabled the survivors to hide themselves beyond the reach even of atomic bombs to carry on the struggle. Navies and armoured divisions exchanged knowledge; strategy and tactics underwent drastic revamping. Psychology, once the major hope of mankind for a solution to the war problem, now had become perverted to the ends of the militarists, as a substitute for patriotism to motivate the men at war. In new ways but with the old philosophies, the war went on; and therefore this armored monster clawed its way through the earth's crust toward its objective.

On the 'bridge' of the underground warship, a small turret in the centre of its roof, Commander Sanderson clung to a stanchion as he barked orders to his staff through the intercom. The ship proper was swung on special mountings and gyro-stabilized to divorce it from the violent jolting of the lower unit, consisting of the drill, the treads and the mighty-earth-moving atomic engines. But still some of the lurching and jouncing of the treads was transmitted up through the storerooms through the crew's quarters to the bridge, and the steel deck underfoot swayed and shook drunkenly. However, men had once learned to accustom themselves to the fitful motions of the sea; and the hardened skipper paid no attention to the way his command pounded forward.

Commander Sanderson was a thickset man, whose hunched shoulders and bull neck suggested the prize ring. But he moved like a cat, even here inside this vibrating juggernaut, as he slipped from one command post to another, reading over the shoulders of unheeding operators the findings of their instruments. The Seismo Log was an open book to his practised eye; his black brows met in a deep frown as he noticed a severe shock registered only two minutes previously, only a few hundred yards to starboard. He passed by the radio locator and the radioman; their jobs would come later, meantime radio silence was enforced on both sides. The thin little soundman adjusted his earphones as the 'Old Man' came by: 'No other diggers contacted, sir,' he muttered automatically and continued listening. The optical technician leaped to his feet and saluted smartly as the Commander passed; he would have nothing to do unless they broke into a cavern, and so he rendered the military courtesy his fellows could not.

Sanderson halted beside the post of the environmental technician. This man's loosely described rating covered many fields; he was at once geologist, radarman, vibration expert and navigator. It was his duty to deduce the nature of their surroundings and suggest a course to follow.

'Your report,' demanded Sanderson.

'Igneous rock across our course at fifteen thousand feet, I believe, sir,' he replied promptly. 'It's not on the chart, sir—probably a new formation.'

Sanderson swore. This meant volcanic activity—and, whether man-made or accidental, that spelled trouble. 'Course?' he asked.

'Change course to one hundred seventy-five degrees—and half-speed, sir, if you please, until I can chart this formation more accurately.'

Sanderson returned his salute, turned on his heel. 'Mr. Culver!'

The young lieutenant-commander saluted casually. 'Sir?'

Sanderson repressed another oath. He did not like the young executive officer with his lordly manners, his natty uniform and the coat of tan he had acquired from frequent ultraviolent exposure—a luxury beyond the means of most of the pasty-faced undermen. But duty is duty—'Change course to one seven five. Half-speed,' he ordered.

'Aye, aye, sir.' Culver picked up a microphone, jabbed a phone jack into the proper plug and pressed the buzzer.

Far below, near the clanking treads, Lieutenant Watson wiped the sweat from his brow—most of the ship was not as well insulated as the bridge, whose personnel must be at their physical peak at all times. He jumped as the intercom buzzed, then spoke into his chest microphone. 'Navigation,' he called.

'Bridge,' came Culver's voice. 'Change course to one seven five. Over.'

'Navigation to bridge. Course one seven five, aye, aye,' said Watson mechanically. Then: 'What is it, Culver?'

'Environmental thinks it's lava.'

'Damnation.' The old lieutenant—one of the few able-bodied survivors of the surface stages of the war—turned to his aides. 'Change course to one seven five.'

Peterson, brawny Navigator Third Class, stepped up to a chrome handle projecting from a circular slot and shoved it to '175', then turned a small crank for finger adjustment. Slowly the pitch of the great blades shifted—the sound of their turning, muffled by layers of armour, abruptly changed in tone.

Chief Navigator Schmidt looked up from a pile of strata charts. 'Ask the exec to have a copy of the new formation sent down here,' he said, speaking as calmly as if he were a laboratory technician requesting a routine report. Schmidt was the psycho officer's pride and joy; he was the only person aboard the underground cruiser who had never been subjected to a mental manhandling as a result of that worthy's suspicions. He was slightly plump, pink-cheeked, with a straggling yellow moustache—just a little childish; perhaps that was why he had never cracked.

His request was transmitted; up on the bridge, the environmental technician threw a switch, cutting a remote repeater into the series of scanners which brought him his information. Chief Navigator Schmidt heard the bell clang, fed a sheet of paper into the transcriber, and sat back happily to watch the results.

The great drillhead completed its grinding turn; the blades tore into the rock ahead of it again.

'Navigation to bridge: bearing one seven five,' reported Watson.

'Carry on,' returned young Culver. He pulled out the phone jack, plugged it in elsewhere.

Ensign Clark stroked the slight, fuzzy black beard which was one of many ego-boosters for his crushing introversion, along with the tattoos on his arms and the book of physical exercises which he practised whenever he thought he was alone. At Culver's buzz, he cursed the exec vigorously, then opened the circuit. 'Power,' he replied diffidently.

'Bridge to power: reduce speed by one-half. Over.'

'Power to bridge: speed one-half—aye, aye.' Clark put his hand over the mike, shouted at the non-rated man stationed at the speed lever. 'You! Half-speed, and shake the lead out of your pants!'

The clanking of the treads slowed; simultaneously the whine of the blades rose, cutting more rapidly to compensate for the decreased pressure from behind the drill.

In the hot, steam-filled galley, fat Chief Cook Kelly lifted the lid from a kettle to sniff the synthetic stew. 'What stinkin' slum—an' to think they kicked about the chow back in the Surface Wars.'

'Chief, they say there was *real meat* in the chow then,' rejoined Marconi, Food Chemist First Class.

'Why, Marc, even I can remember—' he was interrupted by the intercom's buzz.

'Attention, all hands!' came Culver's voice. 'Igneous rock detected, probably a fresh lava-flow. We have changed our course. Action is expected within a few hours—stand by to go to quarters. Repeating—'

Kelly spat expertly. His face was impassive, but his hand trembled as he replaced the lid on the kettle. 'We better hurry this chow up, Marc. Heaven only knows when we'll eat again.'

Lieutenant Carpenter raised his hand, slapped the hysterical Private Worth twice.

'Now, shut up or I'll have the psych corpsmen go over you again,' he snapped.

Worth dropped his head between his hands, said nothing.

Carpenter backed out of the cell. 'I'm posting a guard here,' he warned. 'One peep out of you and the boys will finish what they started.'

He slammed the door for emphasis.

'Well, sir, you did it again,' said the sentry admiringly. 'He was throwing things when you got here, but you tamed him in a hurry.'

'We've got to get these cells soundproofed,' muttered Carpenter abstractedly, putting on his glasses. 'The combat-detachment bunks are right next to him.'

'Yeah, sir, I guess it's harder on the combat detachment than the rest of us. We've all got our watches and so forth, but they haven't got a thing to do until we hit an enemy city or something. They crack easy—like this Worth guy in here now.'

Carpenter whirled on him. 'Listen, corpsman, I'm too busy a man to be chasing up here to deal with every enlisted man in this brig—I've got the other officers to keep in line. And let's not be volunteering information to superiors without permission!' he hissed.

'I'm sorry, sir—' the guard began—but the lieutenant was gone!

The sentry smiled crookedly. 'O.K., Mr Carpenter, your big job is to keep the officers in line. I'm just wonderin' who's supposed to keep *you* out of this cell block.'

Corporal Sheehan dealt the cards with sudden, jerky motions; his brow was furrowed, his face a study in concentration.

One would have thought him a schoolboy puzzling over a difficult final examination.

Sergeants Fontaine and Richards snatched each card as it came, partly crushing the pasteboards as they completed their hands. Fat old Koch, Private First Class, waited until all the cards had been dealt, then grabbed the whole hand and clutched it against his broad stomach, glancing suspiciously at his fellow players.

Their conversation was in terse, jerky monosyllables—but around them other men of the combat detachment talked, loudly and incessantly. Private Carson sat in a corner, chain smoking in brief, nervous puffs. Coarse jokes and harsh laughter dominated the conversation. Nobody mentioned Culver's 'alert' of a few minutes before.

'Three,' grunted the obese Koch. Sheehan dealt him the cards swiftly.

'Hey!' Richards interrupted, before play could begin. 'I didn't like that deal. Let's have a look at that hand.'

'Know what you're callin' me?' retorted Sheehan, snatching the deck as Richards was about to pick it up.

'Yeah—I know what to call you, you lyin', yella cheat—'

Sheehan lurched to his feet, lashed out with a ham-like fist. Richards scrambled out of the way, bringing chair and table down with a crash. A moment later both men were on their feet and squared off.

Conversation halted; men drifted over toward the table even as Fontaine stepped between the two players. Koch had not yet fully reacted to the situation and was only halfway out of his chair.

'You fools!' shouted Fontaine. 'You want the psych corpsmen on our necks again? That louse Carpenter said if there was another fight we'd all get it.'

Corporal Sheehan's big fists unclenched slowly. 'That low, stinkin'—'

'Sit down,' said Koch heavily. 'Fontaine's right. The psychs probably have a spy or two planted in this room.' His eyes rested briefly on Carson, still smoking silently alone in the corner, seemingly oblivious of the commotion.

'That Carson,' muttered Richards, shifting the object of his anger. 'I'll bet any money you want he's a stool for Carpenter.'

'Always by himself,' corroborated Sheehan. 'What's the story about him—born in a lab somewhere, wasn't he?'

The others were moving away now that it was plain there

was to be no fight. Koch picked up the cards, stacked them. 'Carson may not even be human,' he suggested. 'The science profs have been workin' on artifical cannon-fodder for years, and you can be sure if they ever do make a robot they're not goin' to talk about it until it's been tried in combat.'

Carson overheard part of his statement; smiled shortly. He rose and left the room.

'See?' Richards went on. 'Probably puttin' all four of us on report right now.'

Lieutenant Carpenter placed the wire recorder back inside its concealed niche, polished his classes carefully, opened his notebook and made several entries in a neat schoolteacher's hand:

Friction betw. Sheehan, Richards worse—psych, reg. next time back to Gen. Psych. Hosp. New Chicago. No sign men susp. Koch my agent; K. planting idea of robots in crew's minds per order. Can reveal Carson whenever enemy knows Powers mfg. robots in quantity. Fontaine well integrated, stopped fight—recomm. transfer my staff to Sanderson.

He put the notebook away, began to climb the nearest metal ladder with the mincing, catlike tread which the whole crew had learned to hate.

The long guard before the massive lead-and-steel door of the central chamber saluted as the lieutenant passed. His task was to safeguard the ship's most important cargo—its sole atomic bomb. Carpenter asked him several routine word-association questions before proceeding.

The lieutenant paused just once more in his progress upward. This was to play back the tape of another listening device, this one piped into the quarters of the men who serviced the mighty atomic engines. Making notes copiously, he proceeded directly to the bridge.

'Captain, my report,' he announced, not without some show of pride.

'Later,' said Sanderson shortly, without looking up from a rough strata-chart the environmental technician had just handed him.

'But it's rather important, sir. Serious trouble is indicated in the combat detachment—'

'It always is,' retorted Sanderson in some heat. 'Take your report to Culver; I'm busy.'

Carpenter froze, then turned to the young lieutenant-commander. 'If you will initial this, please—'

Culver repressed a shudder. He couldn't keep back the rebellious feeling that the ancient navies had been better off with their primitive chaplains than the modern underground fleets with their prying psychiatrists. Of course, he hastily told himself, that was impossible today—organized religion had long since ceased to sanction war and had been appropriately dealt with by the government.

The Seismo Log recorded a prolonged disturbance directly ahead, and as Sanderson began his rounds the environmental technician called to him. 'Sudden fault and more igneous activity dead ahead, sir,' he reported.

'Carry on,' replied Sanderson. 'Probably artificial,' he muttered half to himself. 'Lot of volcanism in enemy territory. . . . Mr Culver!'

Culver hastily initialled the psycho officer's notebook and handed it back. 'Sir?'

'Elevate the cutters twenty-five degrees—we're going up and come on the enemy from above.'

The order was soon transmitted to navigation; Lieutenant Watson's efficient gang soon had the metallic behemoth inclined at an angle of twenty-five degrees and rising rapidly toward the surface. Chief Schmidt dragged out new charts, noted down outstanding information and relayed data topside.

The ship's body swung on its mountings as the treads assumed the new slant, preserving equilibrium throughout. An order from Ensign Clark of power soon had the ship driving ahead as fast as the cutters could tear through the living rock.

'Diggers ahead,' the thin soundman called out suddenly, adjusting his earphones. He snapped a switch; lights flickered on a phosphorescent screen. 'Sounds like about three, sir—one is going to intersect our course at a distance of about five thousand yards.'

'Let him,' grunted Sanderson. 'Mr Culver, you may level off now.'

'Electronic activity dead ahead,' and 'Enemy transmitter dead ahead,' the radio locator and radioman reported almost simultaneously, before Culver's quiet order had been carried out.

'Go to general quarters, Mr Culver,' ordered Sanderson quickly. The exec pressed a button.

Throughout the ship was heard the tolling of a great bell—slowly the strokes lost their ponderous beat, quickened in tempo faster and faster until they became a continuous pandemonium of noise; simultaneously the pitch increased. All of this was a trick devised by staff psych officers, believing it would produce a subconscious incentive to greater speed and urgency.

The observational and operational posts were already manned; now, as quickly as possible, reliefs took over the more gruelling watches such as that of the environmental technician. Medical and psych corpsmen hurriedly unpacked their gear, fanned out through the ship. Ensign Clark's voice faltered briefly as he ordered the power consumption cut to a minimum. The great cruiser slowed to a crawl.

The galley was bedlam as Kelly and Marconi rushed from one kettle to the next, supervising the ladling of hot food into deep pans by the apprentices who had assembled in haste in response to Kelly's profane bellowing. Chow runners dashed madly out the door, slopping over the contents of the steaming dishes as they ran. 'Battle breakfast' was on its way to the men; and even as the last load departed Kelly shut off all power into the galley and shrugged his squat form into a heavy coverall. Marconi snatched two empty trays, filled them, and the two men wolfed their meal quickly and then ran at full tilt down toward the combat detachment's briefing-room.

Here the scene was even more chaotic. Men helped one another hastily into coveralls, rubber-and-steel suits, metallic boots. They twisted each other's transparent helmets into place, buckled on oxygen tanks, kits of emergency rations, first aid equipment, and great nightmarish-looking weapons. Richards and Sheehan, their quarrel temporarily forgotten, wrestled with the latter's oxygen valve. Koch struggled mightily with the metal joints of his attack suit; Fontaine checked the readings of the dials on a long, tubular 'heat ray' machine. Carson, fully outfitted, manipulated the ingenious device which brought a cigarette to his lips and lit it. He took a few puffs, pressed another lever to eject the butt, and wrenched his helmet into place with gloved hands. From now until the battle was over, the men would carry all their air on their backs, compressed in cylinders. Underneath the shouts and the rattling noises of the armour could be heard the screams of Private Worth from his cell next door. They were suddenly cut off; one of Lieutenant Carpenter's watchful corpsmen had silenced the boy.

And now there was nothing to do but wait. The combat detachment's confusion subsided; but a subdued clatter of shifting armour, helmets being adjusted, tightening of joints, the rattle of equipment, and telephoned conversation continued. The new bridge-watch checked their instruments, then settled down to careful, strained waiting. Sanderson paced his rounds, hearing reports and issuing occasional orders. Culver stood by the intercom, told the crew all their superiors knew of the opposition as the information came in. Carpenter catfooted through the ship, followed at a discreet distance by four of his strong-arm men.

Ensign Clark was white with fear. He sat stiffly at his post like a prisoner in Death Row; the sweat rolled down his face and into his soft black beard. He tried to repeat the auto-suggestion formulae Carpenter had prescribed for him, but all that he could choke out was a series of earnest curses which a kinder age would have called prayers.

He jumped as if he had been shot at Culver's sudden announcement: 'Attention all hands. Enemy digger believed to have sighted this ship. Prepare for action at close quarters.' The voice paused, and then added: 'Bridge to power: full speed ahead for the next half-hour, then bring the ship to a halt. We'll let the enemy carry the fight to us.'

Clark automatically repeated 'Full speed ahead,' then cringed as the crewman slammed the lever over and the cruiser leaped forward with a shrill whine of its blades. 'No!' he suddenly yelled, leaping out of his seat. 'Not another inch—stop this ship!' He ran over to the speed lever, pushed at the crewman's hands. 'I won't be killed, I won't, I *won't*!' The brawny crewman and the maddened officer wrestled desperately for a moment, then the crewman flung his superior on his back and stood over him, panting, 'I'm sorry, sir.'

Clark lay there whimpering for a few seconds, then made a quick grab inside his shirt and levelled a pistol at the towering crewman. 'Get over there,' he half-sobbed, 'and stop this ship before I shoot you.'

The white-uniformed psych corpsman flung open the door and fired, all in one motion. The crewman instinctively backed away as the little pellet exploded, shredding most of Clark's head into his cherished beard; the crewman stood over the body, making little wordless sounds.

'Go off watch,' ordered Carpenter, coming into the room

on the heels of his henchman. 'Get a sedative from the medics.' He gazed lingeringly, almost appreciatively, on the disfigured face of the dead man before covering it with the ensign's coat. Then he called Culver and told him briefly what had happened.

'I'll send a relief,' promised the exec. 'Tell him to reduce speed in another twenty minutes. That was quick thinking, Carpenter; the captain says you rate a citation.' The psycho officer had failed to give the corpsman credit for firing the shot.

Sanderson caught Culver's eye, put a finger to his lips.

'Huh?' Culver paused, then got the idea. 'Oh—and, say, Carpenter—don't let the crew hear of this. It wouldn't do for them to know an officer was the first to crack.' There was a very faint trace of sarcasm in his tone.

But Sanderson's warning was already too late. The power crewman who had witnessed Clark's death agonies talked before he was put to sleep; the medic who administered the sedative took it to the crew. By the time Carpenter had received the new order from Culver, his efficient corpsmen had disposed of Clark's body and the whole ship knew the story. It hit the combat detachment like a physical blow; their strained morale took a serious beating, and the officers grew alarmed.

'Pass the word to let them smoke,' Sanderson finally ordered, after the great ship had shuddered to a halt and backed a short distance up the tunnel on his order. 'Give them ten minutes—the enemy will take at least twice that to get here. Have Carpenter go down and administer drugs at his own discretion—maybe it will slow them for fighting, but if they crack they'll be of no use anyway.'

And so for ten minutes the combat crewmen removed their helmets and relaxed, while the psychos moved unobtrusively throughout the room, asking questions here and there, occasionally giving drugs. Once they helped a man partially out of his armour for a hypo. Tension relaxed somewhat; the psych corpsmen could soothe as well as coerce.

Kelly and Marconi were engaged in a heated argument over the relative merits of synthetic and natural foods—a time-tested emotional release the two veterans used habitually. Koch was up to his ears in a more serious controversy—for Sheehan and Richards were practically at each other's throats again. Carson as usual said nothing, smoked continuously; even the level-headed Fontaine got up and paced the floor, his armour clanking as he walked. Three men had to be put to sleep. Then the ten-minute break was over and the strain grew even worse.

Carpenter spoke softly into the intercom. "Tell the commander that if battle is not joined in another hour I cannot prevent a mutiny. Culver, I *told* you not to leave that man on watch—if you had listened to me Ensign Clark need not have been liquidated.'

Culver's lip curled; he opened his mouth to reply in his usual irritating manner—but at that moment the soundman flung the earphones off his head. The roar of shearing duralloy blades was audible several feet away as the phones bounced to the deck. 'Enemy digger within one hundred feet and coming in fast!' the soundman shouted.

'Don't reverse engines!' Sanderson roared as Culver contacted the new power officer. 'Turn on our drill, leaving the treads stationary—we'll call his bluff.'

Culver issued the necessary order, then alerted the crew again. The great blades began to whirl once more; there was a brief shower of rocks, and they churned emptiness—their usual throbbing, tearing chant became a hair-raising shriek; the blast of air they raised kicked up a cloud of dust which blanketed the fresh-carved tunnel—'That's for their optical technician,' explained Sanderson. 'He'll be blind when he comes out—and we've a sharp gunnery officer down in fire control that will catch them by surprise.'

The soundman gingerly picked up the headphones; the roar of the enemy's drill had dropped to a whisper—Sanderson's curious tactics evidently had him guessing, for he had slowed down.

The sound of the approaching drill was now audible without the benefit of electronic gear, as a muffled noise like the chewing of a great rat. Then came the chattering breakthrough, and Sanderson knew he had contacted the enemy, despite the dust clouds which baffled even the infra-red visual equipment.

Temporarily blind, confused by the whirling blades of their motionless opponent, the enemy hesitated for the precious seconds that meant the difference between victory and destruction.

As the enemy warhead broke through, the cruiser's whirling blades suddenly came to a quivering halt. Simultaneously the forward batteries opened fire.

Gone were the days of labouring, sweating gun-crews and ammunition loaders. All the stubby barrels were controlled from a small, semicircular control panel like an organ console. Lieutenant Atkins, a cool, competent, greying officer who had once been an instructor at the military academy, calmly pressed buttons and pulled levers and interestedly watched the results by means of various types of mechanical 'eyes'. And so it was that, when the sweep second-hand of his chronometer crossed the red line, Atkins' sensitive fingers danced over the keys and the ship rocked to the salvos of half its guns.

Magnified and echoed in the narrow tunnel, the crash of the barrage rolled and reverberated and shouted in an uninterrupted tornado of pure noise, roar upon roar—the light of the explosions was by contrast insignificant, a vicious reddish flare quickly snuffed in the dust. The ship jerked with each salvo; faint flashes and Olympian thunders tossed the great cruiser like a raft on the wild Atlantic. The fury of sound beat through the thick armour plate, poured and pounded savagely past the vaunted 'soundproof' insulation. The decks lurched and reeled underfoot; instruments and equipment trembled with bone-shaking vibrations. Crash upon thunderous crash filled the air with new strains of this artillery symphony; and then Culver pressed a button. His voice could not be heard through the racket, but the suddenly glow of a red light in the combat detachment's assembly room transmitted his order instantly—'Away landing party!'

And then the trap between the great, flat treads was sprung, and the mechanical monster spawned progeny, visible only by infra-red light in the underground gloom—little doll-like figures in bulky, nightmarish costumes, dropping from a chain ladder to the broken shale underfoot, running and stumbling through the debris, falling and picking themselves up and falling again like so many children—Marconi and Kelly and Carson and Sheehan and Richards and Fontaine and Koch, tripping over the debris and fragments which the great machine had made.

And at last the enemy cruiser replied, even as the landing party picked its way through the obscuring dust and fanned out from its source. Though confused and blind, the men of the other ship, too, had been prepared for action, and thus new sounds were added to the din that were not of the attackers' making.

A titanic explosion rocked the carriage of Sanderson's cruiser; then another, and still another, strewing steel fragments indiscriminately among the men in the tunnel. The ferocity of the defence was less than the attack; much of their armament must have been destroyed on the first salvo—but what remained wrought havoc. Some quick-witted commander of the enemy must have anticipated the landing of a ground party, for fragmentation shells burst near the embattled cruisers, and here and there the armoured figures began to twist and jerk and go down. Their comrades dropped into the partial protection of the broken rock and continued their advance.

Fontaine ran and crawled and scrambled and crouched over the tunnel floor, which was visible to his infra-red-sensitive helmet, and torn now even more by arrowing slivers of steel. His hand found a valve, twisted it to give him more oxygen for this most critical part of the struggle. He did not think much; he was too busy keeping alive. But a bitter thought flashed across his mind—*This part of war hasn't changed a bit.* He leaped over a strange and terrible object in which armour, blood, rock and flesh made a fantastic jigsaw puzzle which had lost its meaning. Once again he merely noted the item in his subconscious mind; he did not think.

Lieutenant Atkins' fingers still danced over the console; his face was exalted like that of a man playing a concerto. And into the symphony of death which he wove with subtle skill there crept fewer and fewer of the discords of the enemy's guns.

Sanderson paced the deck moodily, communicating briefly with his subordinates by means of lip reading which Culver swiftly translated into many-coloured lights. Information came back to the bridge in the same manner. Sanderson smiled with grim satisfaction at the scarcity of dark lamps on the master damage control board. Those mighty walls could take a lot of punishment, and damage so far had been superficial—one blast in the psycho ward; Private Worth would suffer Carpenter's displeasure no longer.

The helmeted monstrosities grew bolder in their advance as the counter-barrage slackened. Now there was but one battery in action, far to the left—all the thunder came from their own ship.

Fontaine rose from the little depression in which he had been crouching. Another man waved to him; from that outsized suit it would have to be Koch. The big man's armour was dented, the rubber portions torn—his steel right boot looked like a large, wrinkled sheet of tinfoil, and he dragged the leg behind him. But he saw Fontaine, pointed a gauntleted finger into the gloom. The enemy ship must be up there; yes, there was the flash of the one operating gun—Fontaine moved forward.

There was another, nearer flash; something exploded on Koch's chestplate, knocking him down. He moved, feebly, like a crushed insect, then lay still. Fontaine immediately slipped back into his hollow; for here was the enemy.

A man in a light, jointed metal suit of Asian make appeared from behind a boulder, slipped over to Koch's body to examine it, felt for Koch's weapons.

Fontaine unslung the long, bazooka-like heat-ray tube—an adaptation of very slow atomic disintegration—and pressed the firing stud. The weapon contributed no noise and no flare to the hellish inferno of the tunnel, but the Asiatic suddenly straightened up, took a step forward. That was all he had time for.

Accident and his jointed armour combined to keep his body standing. Fontaine made sure of his man by holding the heat ray on him until the enemy's armour glowed cherry-red, then released the stud. He came forward, gave the still-glowing figure a push. The body collapsed with a clatter across Koch. Fontaine pushed on—the dust was at last clearing slightly, and directly ahead loomed the enemy ship.

Another Asiatic appeared over a short ridge; too quick for the heat ray. Fontaine drew his pistol and fired. The pellet flared; another enemy went down.

Something whizzed over Fontaine's head; he ducked, ran for cover. Somebody was firing high-speed metallic slugs from an old-fashioned machine gun, and his partly-rubber suit would not stop them. Miraculously he found himself unharmed in front of the enemy ship.

Its drill was torn and crumpled, blades lying cast off amongst the rocks; one of the treads was fouled, and the forward part of the carriage was smashed in completely. This war vehicle would obviously never fight again. Another volley of slugs chattered overhead, and Fontaine rolled back out of the way. *Snap judgement*, he told himself ironically in another rare flash of lucidity. *Maybe she'll never fight after this time, but she's got plenty of spirit right now.*

He dug a hole in the loose shale and tried to cover himself as much as possible, meanwhile surveying the layout. They couldn't know he was here, or his life would have been snuffed out; but he could neither advance nor retreat. He absently transmitted the prearranged 'contact' signal back to the cruiser. Then he settled himself, soldier-wise, to wait as long as might be necessary.

Fontaine's 'contact', and several others, returned to their ship as lights on a board. The landing party could proceed no further or they would enter their own barrage. Sanderson immediately gave the 'cease fire' order. The barrage lifted.

Culver shouted down an immediate flood of radio reports that broke the sudden, aching silence. 'Lieutenant Atkins, you will continue action against the remaining enemy battery until you have destroyed it, or until I inform you that members of the task force have neutralized it.'

'Aye, aye, sir.' Atkins turned back to his guns, studied the image of the battered enemy ship which was becoming increasingly visible as the dust settled. He restored all the automatic controls to manual, pressed several buttons judiciously, and fingered a firing switch.

To Fontaine, crouching in his retreat under the enemy ship, the sudden silence which followed the barrage was almost intolerable. One moment the guns had thundered and bellowed overhead; the next there were a few echoes and reverberations and then all was over.

His ears sang for minutes; his addled brains slowly returned to a normal state. And he realized that the silence was not absolute. It was punctually broken by the crash of the remaining enemy battery, and soon at less frequent intervals by the cautious probing of Atkins' turrets. And between the blows of this duel of giants he could at last hear the whine of metal slugs over his head.

This weapon had him stumped. The Asiatic explosive bullets, such as the one that had killed Koch, only operated at fairly close quarters; the rubber suits were fairly good insulation against death rays; and the Asiatics had no heat ray. But with an antiquated machine gun an Asiatic could sit comfortably at a considerable distance from him and send a volley of missiles crunching through the flimsy Western armour to rip him apart in helpless pain. He raised his head very slightly and looked around. The detachment was well trained; he could see only three of his fellows and they were well concealed from the enemy. Under infra-red light—the only possible means of vision in the gloom of the tunnel—they looked like weird red ghosts.

Something gleamed ahead of him. He sighted along the heat ray, energized its coils. The mechanism hummed softly; the Asiatic jumped out of his hiding place and right into the machine gun's line of fire. The singing bits of metal punched a neat line of holes across his armour and knocked him down, twisting as he fell. Moments later the chattering stream stopped flowing, and Fontaine dashed for more adequate cover. Bullets promptly kicked up dust in little spurts in the hollow he had just vacated.

He searched the darkness, a weird, shimmering ghostland revealed to him by its own tremendous heat through his infra-red equipment. The ship and his armour were very well insulated; he had not been conscious of the stifling heat or the absolute night-gloom which would have made combat impossible for an unprepared, unprotected soldier of the Surface Wars.

Atkins' insistent batteries spoke; there was a great flash and a series of explosions at the enemy target to the left. Fontaine seized the opportunity to make a charge on the loosely piled boulders which, his practised eye told him, sheltered the deadly machine gun. He fell and rolled out of the line of fire as the opposing gunner found him and swerved his weapon; then began to fire explosive pellets at the crude nest, showering it with a series of sharp reports. The enemy machine gun swung back and forth, raking the terrain in search of the invader.

Fontaine unloaded his heat ray, placed it in a well-sheltered crevice and worked it around until it was aimed at the enemy, then shorted the coils. The weapon throbbed with power; rocks began to glow, and the flying slugs poured down upon the menacing heat ray, trying to silence it. Meanwhile Fontaine, like uncounted warriors of all ages, began cautiously to work his way around to the left for a flank attack. Indeed, there were many things in war that had not changed.

'Fire control to bridge: enemy battery silenced,' Atkins reported firmly.

'Secure fire control,' Culver ordered, then turned on his heel. 'The enemy's ordnance is destroyed, sir,' he asserted. 'Our combat crewmen are engaging the enemy in front of his ship.'

'Send Mr Atkins my congratulations,' Sanderson replied

promptly. 'Then inform the combat detachment of the situation.'

Culver turned back to the intercom—then started, as a siren wailed somewhere in the bowels of the ship. A station amidships was buzzing frantically; he plugged in the mike. 'Bridge,' he answered.

'Atomic-bomb watch to bridge: instruments show unprecedented activity of the bomb. Dangerous reaction predicted.'

Culver fought to keep his voice down as he relayed the information. The bridge watch simply came to a dead stop; all eyes were on Sanderson.

Even the phlegmatic commander hesitated. Finally: 'Prepare to abandon ship,' he ordered, heavily.

At once the confusion which had accompanied the preparations of the combat detachment was repeated throughout the ship. Atomic bombs by this time were largely made of artifical isotopes and elements; the type which they carried had never been tested in combat—and radioactive elements can do strange and unpredictable things when stimulated. Mere concussion had started the trouble this time, and the mind of man was incapable of prophesying the results. The bomb might merely increase in the speed of its radioactive decay, flooding the ship and the bodies of its men with deadly gamma rays; it might release enormous heat and melt the cruiser into a bubbling pool of metal; it might blast both of the ships and mile on cubic mile of rocks out of existence—but all they could do was abandon the cruiser and hope for the best. All mankind was unable to do more.

Sanderson's forceful personality and Carpenter's prowling corpsmen prevented a panic. Men cursed as they struggled with obstinate clasps and joints. A few of Kelly's apprentices who had not gone into combat flung cases of concentrated food through the landing-trap to the tunnel floor. Culver packed the ship's records—logs, papers, muster sheets, inventories—into an insulated metal can for preservation. A picked force of atomic technicians in cumbersome lead suits vanished into the shielded bomb-chamber with the faint hope of suppressing the reaction.

Sanderson paused before sealing his helmet. 'Mr Culver, you will have all hands assemble in or near the landing-trap. We must advance, destroy the enemy and take refuge in his ship; it is our only hope.'

Navigation buzzed; Culver made the necessary connection. 'One moment, sir,' he murmured to Sanderson. 'Bridge.'

The young exec could visualize old Lieutenant Watson's strained expression, his set jaw. 'Navigation requests permission to remain aboard when ship is abandoned,' Watson said slowly. 'Chances of crew's survival would be materially increased if the ship reversed engines and departed this area—'

Sanderson was silent a long moment. 'Permission granted,' he finally answered in a low voice. He started to say more, caught Carpenter's eye and was silent.

But Culver could not maintain military formality in answering Watson's call. 'Go ahead, Phil, and—thanks,' he replied, almost in a whisper.

Carpenter stepped forward quickly. 'This is no time for sentiment, Mr Culver,' he snapped. 'Lieutenant Watson's behaviour was a little naïve for an officer, but the important fact remains that his antiquated altruism may be the means of preserving the lives of more important personnel.' He waved a sheaf of loose papers excitedly. 'This report of mine, for example, on the psychiatric aspects of this battle will be invaluable to the Board—"

Crack!

All the wiry power of the young exec's rigidly trained body went into the punch; literally travelled through him from toe to fist and exploded on the psycho officer's jaw. Months of harsh discipline—psychological manhandling—the strain of combat—repressed emotions, never really unhampered since his childhood—the sense of the war's futility which had not been completely trained out of anyone—his poorly concealed hatred for Carpenter—all these subconscious impressions came boiling up and sped the blow—and his hand was incased in a metal glove.

Carpenter's head snapped back. His feet literally flew off the deck as his body described a long arc and slammed into the far wall. He sprawled there grotesquely like a discarded marionette. Miraculously his glasses were unbroken.

The iron reserve which Sanderson had kept throughout the battle left him with the disruption of his neat, disciplined little military cosmos. For a long time he was unable to speak or move.

Two tough-looking psych corpsmen closed in on the exec, who stood facing the fallen officer, his fists clenched. He twisted angrily as they grabbed his arms.

'Let him alone,' Sanderson ordered, coming to his senses. They reluctantly released Culver.

'Mr Culver,' the skipper said very quietly, 'I need you now.

You will resume your duties until this crisis is over. But, if we come through this, I'm going to see that you're broken.'

Culver faced him, anger draining out of him like the colour from his flushed face. He saluted, turned back to the intercom to give out the last order Sanderson had issued. 'Attention, all hands,' he called mechanically. 'Fall in at the landing-trap to abandon ship.'

Sanderson beckoned to the two psych corpsmen. 'Please take Lieutenant Carpenter to sick bay,' he ordered. 'Bring him around as soon as you can.'

The Asiatic squatted crosslegged behind his shining pneumatic machine gun, frantically raking the rock-strewn ground before him. The air ahead shimmered and danced with heat; the other side of his crude stone shelter must be glowing whitely, and the sweat ran down his yellow face even though the tiny cooling motor within his armour hummed savagely as it laboured to keep him from suffocating. He must destroy the offending heat ray or abandon his position.

A confused impression of rubber-and-metal armour was all he received as Fontaine rushed upon him from the side. The two men came together and went down with a loud clatter of armour, rolled over and over in quick, bitter struggle. Even in the Atomic Age there could be hand-to-hand combat.

It was an exhausting fight; the battle suits were heavy and awkward. They wrestled clumsily, the clank of their armour lending an incongruously comic note. The lithe Asiatic broke a hold, cleared his right hand. Fontaine rolled over to avoid the glittering knife his opponent had succeeded in drawing. Here beneath the crust a rip in his rubberized suit would spell disaster. The Asiatic jumped at him to follow up his advantage. Fontaine dropped back on his elbows, swung his feet around and kicked viciously.

The metal boot shattered the Asiatic's glass face-plate, nearly broke his neck from its impact. Shaken by the cruel blow to his face, blinded by blood drawn by the jagged glass, gasping from the foul air and the oppressive heat, he desperately broke away and ran staggering toward the right, misjudging the direction of his ship.

Fontaine estimated the number of explosive bullets he had left, then let his enemy go, knowing there would be no more danger from that quarter. He lay unmoving beside the abandoned maching gun, breathing heavily. His near-miraculous survival thus far deserved a few minutes' rest.

The enemy's landing-trap, like the Western one, was under the ship's carriage; instead of a chain ladder, a ramp had been let down. A terrific mêlée now raged around the ramp—Fontaine and his opponent had been so intent on their duel they had not seen the tide of battle wash past them. Here and there lay dead men of both sides; his recent enemy had soon been overcome and lay not a score of feet away, moving spasmodically. Battle-hardened as he was, Fontaine seriously debated putting the fellow out of his misery—death from armour failure was the worst kind in this war except radioactive poisoning—then carefully counted his explosive pellets again. Only six—he might need them. He dismissed the writhing Asiatic from his mind.

He looked up at the smashed hull of the enemy ship, and an idea came to him. They wouldn't be watching here, with their ship in danger of being boarded elsewhere.

He rose, moved quietly to the great right-hand tread. The flat links here were torn and disconnected; he seized a loose projection and hauled himself upward. Slipping and scrambling, using gauntleted hands and booted feet, he reached the top of the tread.

Directly above him was a jagged hole in the ship's carriage, about four feet long. He seized the edges and somehow managed to wriggle his way inside.

The interior was a shambles of smashed compartments, with men and metal uncleanly mated. Fontaine laboriously pushed his way forward, climbing over and around barriers flung up at the caprice of Atkins' guns. Once he was forced to expend one of the precious pellets; the recoil nearly flattened him at such close quarters, but he picked himself up and climbed through the still-smoking hole into a passageway which was buckled somewhat but still intact.

He looked carefully in both directions, then saw a ladder and began to ascend. It brought him into a small storage compartment which was still illuminated. He grunted in satisfaction; if he had reached the still-powered portion of the ship, he was going in the right direction.

He eased the door open three inches; air hissed—this compartment must be sealed off. He quickly passed through, closed the door, and cautiously tested the air—good; this part of the ship still had pure air and insulation. Confidently he continued forward and climbed another ladder toward the bridge.

He had to wait at one level until a sentry turned his back.

Then he sprang, and his steel fingers sank into the Asiatic's throat. There was no outcry.

Faintly from below there came the sounds of a struggle; his comrades had successfully invaded the ship. Curiously, Fontaine tried his helmet radio. It had been put out of commission in his fight with the machine gunner outside.

There were no more sentries; that was odd. He proceeded with extreme caution as he came to the ladder leading up to the bridge. Here would be the brains of the Asiatic ship; his five remaining pellets could end the engagement now that the battle was raging on enemy territory.

He stumbled over something—a man's foot. He dragged the body out of the shadows which had concealed it.

'What the devil—'

The man had been another guard. His chest was shattered; an explosive pistol was clutched in his right hand. One pellet was missing from the chamber.

Wonderingly Fontaine climbed the ladder, halted at the door.

Lying at his feet was another sentry. The man's body was unmarked but his face bore signs of a painful death. A small supersonic projector lay near him.

Fontaine opened the door—and turned away, sick.

Somebody had turned on a heat ray at close quarters. Officers and enlisted men lay in charred horror. And in the centre of the room the ship's commanding officer slumped on a bloodstained silken cushion. The man had committed honourable suicide with a replica of an ancient Japanese samurai sword.

In his left hand was a crumpled sheet of yellow paper, evidently a radiogram.

Fontaine took the scrap from the lax yellow fingers, puzzled over the Oriental characters.

Then he went outside, and closed the door, and sat down at the head of the ladder to await the coming of men who might be able to solve the mystery.

The last man scrambled down the swaying chains and dropped to the ground from the Western cruiser.

Lieutenants Watson and Atkins were alone in the ship.

'Why did you stay?' demanded Watson, throwing the starting switch. He had hastily rigged an extension from the power room to navigation. 'Only one man is needed to operate the ship, in an emergency.'

Lieutenant Atkins found a fine cigar in his uniform. 'I've been saving this,' he remarked, stripping off the cellophane wrapper lovingly. 'The condemned man indulges in the traditional liberties.'

'Answer my question,' Watson insisted, advancing the speed lever.

Atkins pressed a glowing heating-coil 'lighter' to the tip of the cigar. 'Let me ask you this—why did *you* make this heroic gesture?'

Watson flushed. 'You might as well ask—why fight at all?'

'You might,' Atkins said, smiling slightly.

'I did this because our men come first!' Watson shouted almost in fury.

Atkins chuckled. 'Forgive me, old friend—I find it hard to shake off the illusions I had back in the Last Surface War myself.' He blew a huge cloud of smoke. 'But, when Culver sent down the commander's congratulations to me for silencing that enemy battery, it struck me how empty all our battles and decorations are.'

Watson shoved the speed lever to maximum; the cruiser rolled backward down the tunnel at a terrific velocity, no longer impeded by masses of rock. After a long silence he asked: 'Atkins—what were *you* fighting for?'

Atkins looked him squarely in the eye. 'Well, I managed to hypnotize myself into a superficial love of massed artillery—it's a perversion of my love for the symphony—used to conduct a small orchestra at the academy before it was dissolved and the funds allocated to a military band. I liked that orchestra; felt I was doing something constructive for once.' He was silent for a while, smoking and reminiscing. Coming back to reality with a start, he went on hastily: 'Of course, underneath it all I guess I was motivated just the way you were—to maintain the dead traditions of the service, to save our shipmates who would have died anyway, and to advance a cause which no longer exists.'

Watson buried his head in his hands. 'I fought because I thought it was the right thing to do.'

Atkins softened. 'So did I, my friend,' he admitted. 'But it's all over now—'

He paused to flick ashes from the cigar. 'I saved something else for this,' he went on irrelevantly. 'Carpenter is gone now, Watson, so we can dispense with his psychopathic mummery. What a joke if he should ever know I had this aboard.' He laughed lightly, producing a small, gold-stamped book bound in black leather. 'This sort of thing is the only value left, for us,' he asserted. 'Let us pray.'

And thus, a few minutes later, the two elderly officers died. It was not a great blast, as atomic explosions go, but ship and men and rock puffed and sparkled in bright, cleansing flame.

The bridge of the captured enemy ship looked fresh and clean. The remains of the Asiatic commander's gruesome self-destruction had been cleared away; blackened places about the room glistened with new paint. It was several hours after the battle.

Sanderson stood at attention reading report to his surviving officers. Sergeant Fontaine, permitted to attend as the first witness to the baffling slaughter, fidgeted in the presence of so much gold braid. Private Carson, the strange child of the laboratory, present to assist Fontaine in guarding the disgraced executive officer, stood stolidly, a detached expression on his face.

'—and therefore the atomic explosion, when it did come, was hardly noticed here,' the commander concluded his report. 'Lieutenant Watson did his duty'—he glared covertly at Culver, manacled between Fontaine and Carson—'and if we can return safely to our Advance Base this will go down as one of the greatest exploits in the history of warfare.'

He cleared his throat. 'At ease,' he said offhandedly, straightening his papers. The officers and crewmen relaxed, shifted position, as Sanderson went on more informally: 'Before we discuss any future action, however, there is this business of the Asiatic warlords—their inexplicable suicide. Lieutenant Carpenter?'

The psycho officer stepped forward, caressing his bandaged jaw. 'I have questioned the ten prisoners we took,' he announced as clearly as he could through the bandages, 'and my men have applied all of the standard means of coercion. I am firmly convinced that the Asiatic prisoners are as ignorant as we are of the reason for their masters' strange behaviour."

Sanderson motioned him back impatiently. 'Ensign Becker?'

The personnel officer rustled some sheets of paper. 'I have checked the records carefully, sir,' he asserted, 'and Lieutenant-Commander Culver is the only man aboard this ship who understands written Asiatic.'

Sanderson's gaze swept over all his officers. 'Gentlemen, the executive officer was guilty of striking the psycho officer shortly before we abandoned ship—I witnessed the action. I want to know if you will accept as valid his translation of the radio gram which Sergeant Fontaine found on the body of the enemy leader.'

'I object!' shouted Carpenter immediately. 'Culver violated one of the *basic* principles of the officers' corps—he can't be completely *sane*.'

'True, perhaps,' admitted Sanderson testily, 'but, lieutenant, would you care to suggest a plan of action—*before* we discover why our late enemies killed themselves so conveniently?'

'Commander, are you trying to vindicate this man?' Carpenter demanded indignantly.

Sanderson looked at the psycho officer with an expression almost contemptuous. 'You should know by this time, lieutenant, that I have never liked Mr Culver,' he snorted. 'Unfortunately this could be a question of our own survival. If the officers present accept Culver's translation of the message, I shall act on it.'

'But we came here to begin courtmartial proceedings—'

'That can wait,' the skipper interrupted impatiently. 'This is my command, Carpenter, and I wish you'd remember that. Well, gentlemen? A show of hands, please—' He paused to count. 'Very well,' he decided shortly. 'Sergeant Fontaine, give the message to the prisoner.'

Fontaine threw a snappy salute and handed the yellow scrap of paper silently to the exec. Carson loosened his grip somewhat; Culver began to work out the translation—

FROM Supreme Headquarters in Mongolia.
TO All field commanders.
SUBJECT Secret weapon X-39, failure of.

1. Research project X-39, a semi-living chemical process attacking all forms of protoplasm, was released on the South American front according to plan last night.
2. Secret weapon X-39 was found to be uncontrollable and is spreading throughout our own armies all over the world. In addition, infection centring on the secret research laboratories has covered at least one-third of Asia.
3. You are directed to—

'Well?' demanded Sanderson.

'That's all, sir," Culver replied quietly.

The room immediately exploded into conversation, all pretence at military discipline forgotten. The commander shouted for order. He stood even straighter than his normally stiff military bearing allowed; he was the picture of triumph and confidence.

'This interrupted message can be interpreted in only one way,' he declared ringingly. 'Ensign Becker, you will inform all hands that the enemy's suicide is worldwide and that *the war is over!*'

For a long, long moment there was dead silence. The last peace rumour had died when most of these men were children. It took much time for the realization to sink in that the senseless murder was over at last.

Then—cheering, laughing, slapping one another backs, the officers gave way to their emotions. Many became hysterical; a few still stood dumbly, failing to comprehend what 'peace' was.

Battle-hardened, stiffly militaristic Sanderson's face was wet with tears.

And then Lieutenant Carpenter screamed.

All eyes were riveted on the psycho officer, a hideous suspicion growing in their minds as he cringed in a corner and yelled meaninglessly, his whole body shaking with unutterable terror. They had all seen men afraid of death—but in Carpenter's mad eyes was reflected the essence of all the hells conceived in the ancient religions—he slavered, he whimpered, and suddenly his body began to *ripple.*

His fellow officers stood rooted to the deck in sheer fright as he *slid* rather than fell to a huddled heap that continued to sink down after he had fallen, spreading and flowing and finally *running like water.*

Sanderson stared in stunned horror at a pool of sticky yellow fluid that dripped through a bronze grating in the floor.

Culver grinned foolishly. 'Yes, commander,' he said airily, 'you were right—the war is over.'

Sanderson gingerly picked Carpenter's notebook out of the sodden pile of clothing and bandages and the broken glass of the psycho officer's spectacles. 'Read that radiogram again,' he ordered hoarsely, signalling the two crewmen to release their prisoners.

The exec rubbed his wrists to restore circulation as the handcuffs were removed. Then he picked up the crumpled paper, smoothed it out.

'Research Project X-39, a semi-living chemical process attacking all forms of protoplasm, was released—' Culver choked over the words. 'Sir, I—'

And then, in a few terrible minutes of screams and curses and hideous dissolution, all the officers understood why the Asiatics had committed suicide.

Sergeant Fontaine for some reason kept his head. He fired four shots rapidly from his pistol; one missed Carson, the others found their mark in Sanderson, Culver and Becker, who looked oddly grateful as their bodies jerked under the impact and they slumped in unholy disintegration.

Sanderson saluted solemnly with a dissolving arm.

Fontaine had one more pellet in his gun. He hesitated, looked inquiringly for a moment at the inscrutable Carson, then as he felt a subtle *loosening* under his skin he turned the weapon on himself and fired.

Private Carson puffed nervously at a cigarette, staring in shocked, horrible fascination at the weird carnage—then ran blindly, fleeing from he knew not what.

The terror flew on wings of light through the ruined enemy ship. Technicians, bridge watches, the ten enemy prisoners, psych corpsmen, navigators, combat crewmen—even the dead Oriental commanders joined the dissolving tide. Richards and Sheehan were the last to go; they hysterically accused each other of causing the horror, trying desperately to find some tangible cause for the Doom—they fought like great beasts, and fat Koch was not there to stop the fight—they struggled, and coalesced suddenly into one rippling yellow pool.

Carson, still incased in his armour, raced and clattered through the deserted ship—the sound of his passing was almost sacrilegious, like the desecration of a tomb. Everywhere silence, smashed walls, empty suits of armour, little bundles of wet clothing, and curious yellow stains. *Die, why can't you die?*

Carson, the strange one—separated by more than aloofness from his fellows—spawned in a laboratory, the culmination of thousands of experiments in the vain hope of circumventing the extremity of the slaughter by manufacturing men. His metabolism was subtly different from that of normal man; he *needed* nicotine in his system for some reason—that was why he chain-smoked—but tobacco was a narcotic; it could not protect protoplasm. *Why can't you die, Carson?* All through the ship, silence, wet clothing, little pools—not even the dead had escaped—nothing moved or lived except this running, half-mad man—or Thing—born in a laboratory, if one could say he *had* been 'born'.

A quick movement of his gloved hands sealed the round helmet on his shoulders. He ran and stumbled and climbed through passageways and down ladders; he fairly flew down the landing-ramp and soon disappeared in the black depths of the tunnel.

And the nighted cavern so recently hacked from the outraged crust was given back to the darkness and the silence it had always known.

MEIHEM IN CE KLASRUM

by Dolton Edwards

ASTOUNDING SCIENCE FICTION
September

It isn't often one remembers something one has read over a time interval of three and a half decades, and virtually word for word, when one has not read it all during all that time. This is one of those things.

I had forgotten it was published in 1946 and when Marty suggested it to me, I reacted with the greatest enthusiasm.

At first blush, it seems a classic of satire, but read it again. I believe it is absolutely sensible and is the way to go—except that no one ever will. The trouble is that when enough people have learned things the wrong way and find it almost easy, the thought of trying to learn the right way and undoing a lifetime of practice is insupportable. Therefore the wrong way, which has become institutionalized, also proves immovable.

The spelling of the English language is not the only case in point. There is the immovable metronome like week which prevents the existence of a rational calendar. Worst of all, there is the typewriter keyboard, invented over a hundred years ago virtually at random and so irrational that it slows typing by at least ten percent. Yet too many people know how to type and would dread unlearning it (I would, myself) so that the most modern computers still have that same old dreadful typewriter keyboard.

And yet there is some hope, if we think in centuries, rather than in decades. It took several centuries to replace the Roman numerals by the Arabic, the Julian Calendar by the Gregorian, a myriad stupid systems of measurement by the metric—so read "Meihem" and hope.—I.A.

Because we are still bearing some of the scars of our brief skirmish with II-B English, it is natural that we should be enchanted by Mr. George Bernard Shaw's current campaign for a simplified alphabet.

Obviously, as Mr. Shaw points out, English spelling is in much need of a general overhauling and streamlining. However, our own resistance to any changes requiring a large expenditure of mental effort in the near future would cause us to view with some apprehension the possibility of some day receiving a morning paper printed in—to us—Greek.

Our own plan would achieve the same end as the legislation proposed by Mr. Shaw, but in a less shocking manner, as it consists merely of an acceleration of the normal processes by which the language is continually modernized.

As a catalytic agent, we would suggest that a National Easy Language Week be proclaimed, which the President would inaugurate, outlining some short cut to concentrate on during the week, and to be adopted during the ensuing year. All school children would be given a holiday, the lost time being the equivalent of that gained by the spelling shortcut.

In 1946, for example, we would urge the elimination of the soft "c," for which we would substitute "s." Sertainly, such an improvement would be selebrated in all sivic-minded sircles as being suffisiently worth the trouble, and students in all sities in the land would be reseptive toward any change eliminating the nesessity of learning the differense between the two letters.

In 1947, sinse only the hard "c" would be left, it would be possible to substitute "k" for it, both letters being pronounsed identikally. Imagine how greatly only two years of this prosess would klarify the konfusion in the minds of students. Already we would have eliminated an entire letter from the alphabet. Typrewriters and linotypes, kould all be built with one less letter, and all the manpower and materials proviously devoted to making "c's" kould be turned toward raising the national standard of living.

In the fase of so many notable improvements, it is easy to foresee that by 1948, "National Easy Language Week" would be a pronounsed sukses. All skhool tshildren would be looking forward with konsiderable exsitement to the holiday, and in a blaze of national publisity it would be announsed that the double konsonant "ph" no longer existed, and that the sound would henseforth be written "f" in all words. This would make sutsh words as "fonograf" twenty persent shorter in print.

By 1949, publik interest in a fonetik alfabet kan be expekted to have inkreased to the point where a more radikal step forward kan be taken without fear of undue kritisism. We would therefore urge the elimination, at that time of al unesesary double leters, whitsh, although quite harmles, have always ben a nuisanse in the language and a desided deterent to akurate speling. Try it yourself in the next leter you write, and se if both writing and reading are not fasilitated.

With so mutsh progres already made, it might be posible in 1950 to delve further into the posibilities of fonetik speling. After due konsideration of the reseption aforded the previous steps, it should be expedient by this time to spel al difthongs fonetikaly. Most students do not realize that the long "i" and "y," as in "time" and "by," are aktualy the difthong "ai," as it is writen in "aisle," and that the long "a" in "fate," is in reality the difthong "ei" as in "rein." Although perhaps not imediately aparent, the saving in taime and efort wil be tremendous when we leiter elimineite the sailent "e," as meide posible bai this last tsheinge.

For, as is wel known, the horible mes of "e's" apearing in our writen language is kaused prinsipaly bai the present nesesity of indikeiting whether a vowel is long or short. Therefore, in 1951 we kould simply elimineit al sailent "e's," and kontinu to read and wrait merily along as though we wer in an atomik ag of edukation.

In 1951 we would urg a greit step forward. Sins bai this

taim it would have ben four years sins anywun had usd the leter "c," we would sugest that the "National Easy Languag Wek" for 1951 be devoted to substitution of "c" for "Th." To be sur it would be som taim befor peopl would bekom akustomd to reading ceir newspapers and buks wic sutsh sentenses in cem as "Ceodor caught he had cre cousand cistls crust crough ce cik of his cumb."

In ce seim maner, bai meiking eatsh leter hav its own sound and cat sound only, we kould shorten ce language stil mor. In 1952 we would elimineit ce "y"; cen in 1953 we kould us ce leter to indikeit ce "sh" sound, cerbai klarifaiing words laik yugar and yur, as wel as redusing bai wun mor leter al words laik "yut," "yore," and so forc. Cink, cen, of al ce benefits to be geind bai ce distinktion whitsh wil cen be meid between words laik:

ocean	now writen		oyean
machine	"	"	mayin
racial	"	"	reiyial

Al sutsh divers weis of wraiting wun sound would no longer exist, and whenever wun kaim akros a "y" sound he would know exaktli what to wrait.

Kontinuing cis proses, year after year, we would eventuali have a reali sensibl writen langug. By 1975, wi ventyur tu sei, cer wud bi no mor uv ces teribli trublsum difikultis, wic no tu leters usd to indikeit ce seim nois, and laikwais no tu noises riten wic ce seim leter. Even Mr. Yaw, wi beliv, wud be hapi in ce noleg cat his drims fainali keim tru.

VINTAGE SEASON

by Lawrence O'Donnell (Catherine L. Moore and Henry Kuttner—this story is generally credited to Moore, but we are not so sure)

ASTOUNDING SCIENCE FICTION
September

1946 was another strong year for science fiction's most renowned and effective husband-and-wife writing team. They started the year with an excellent two-part serial in Astounding, *"The Fairy Chessman," and under their several pen names produced a number of solid stories throughout 1946, almost on a monthly basis (see also "Absalom" in this volume).*

"Vintage Season" is one of their most famous stories, one that was widely imitated, especially the technique of using tourists from the future to comment on the then present. The Science Fiction Writers of America voted it a richly deserved retrospective Nebula Award in the early 1970s.

(Two ironclad, unbreakable limitations pen in the real world. The fact that the speed of light is an absolute limit acts to cut off most of the universe from us. The fact that moving back in time is theo-

retically impossible [I believe] cuts off our own past from us.

In science fiction, there is a tacit understanding that both these limitations be ignored in the interest of creating good stories. Faster-than-light travel is commonplace in science fiction, and so is time travel. There is no question that time-travel makes possible situations that are rich in irony and subtle tensions. Especially when well-handled, something one would expect of the Kuttners.—I.A.)

Three people came up the walk to the old mansion just at dawn on a perfect May morning. Oliver Wilson in his pajamas watched them from an upper window through a haze of conflicting emotions, resentment predominant. He didn't want them there.

They were foreigners. He knew only that much about them. They had the curious name of Sancisco, and their first names, scrawled in loops on the lease, appeared to be Omerie, Kleph and Klia, though it was impossible as he looked down upon them now to sort them out by signature. He hadn't even been sure whether they would be men or women, and he had expected something a little less cosmopolitan.

Oliver's heart sank a little as he watched them follow the taxi driver up the walk. He had hoped for less self-assurance in his unwelcome tenants, because he meant to force them out of the house if he could. It didn't look very promising from here.

The man went first. He was tall and dark, and he wore his clothes and carried his body with that peculiar arrogant assurance that comes from perfect confidence in every phase of one's being. The two women were laughing as they followed him. Their voices were light and sweet, and their faces were beautiful, each in its own exotic way, but the first thing Oliver thought when he looked at them was, "Expensive!"

It was not only that patina of perfection that seemed to dwell in every line of their incredibly flawless garments. There are degrees of wealth beyond which wealth itself ceases to have significance. Oliver had seen before, on rare occasions, something like this assurance that the earth turning beneath their well-shod feet turned only to their whim.

It puzzled him a little in this case, because he had the feeling as the three came up the walk that the beautiful clothing they wore so confidently was not clothing they were accustomed to. There was a curious air of condescension in the way they moved. Like women in costume. They minced a little on their delicate high heels, held out an arm to stare at the cut of a sleeve, twisted now and then inside their garments as if the clothing sat strangely on them, as if they were accustomed to something entirely different.

And there was an elegance about the way the garments fitted them which even to Oliver looked strikingly unusual. Only an actress on the screen, who can stop time and the film to adjust every disarrayed fold so that she looks perpetually perfect, might appear thus elegantly clad. But let these women move as they liked, and each fold of their clothing followed perfectly with the moment and fell perfectly into place again. One might almost suspect the garments were not cut of ordinary cloth, or that they were cut according to some unknown, subtle scheme, with many artful hidden seams placed by a tailor incredibly skilled at his trade.

They seemed excited. They talked in high, clear, very sweet voices, looking up at the perfect blue and transparent sky in which dawn was still frankly pink. They looked at the trees on the lawn, the leaves translucently green with an under color of golden newness, the edges crimped from constriction in the recent bud.

Happily and with excitement in their voices they called to the man, and when he answered, his own voice blended so perfectly in cadence with theirs that it sounded like three people singing together. Their voices, like their clothing, seemed to have an elegance far beyond the ordinary, to be under a control such as Oliver Wilson had never dreamed of before this morning.

The taxi driver brought up the luggage, which was of a beautiful pale stuff that did not look quite like leather, and had curves in it so subtle it seemed square until you saw how two or three pieces of it fitted together when carried, into a perfectly balanced block. It was scuffed, as if from much use. And though there was a great deal of it, the taxi man did not seem to find his burden heavy. Oliver saw him look down at it now and then and heft the weight incredulously.

One of the women had very black hair, and a skin like

cream, and smoke-blue eyes heavy-lidded with the weight of her lashes. It was the other woman Oliver's gaze followed as she came up the walk. Her hair was a clear, pale red, and her face had a softness that he thought would be like velvet to touch. She was tanned to a warm amber darker than her hair.

Just as they reached the porch steps the fair woman lifted her head and looked up. She gazed straight into Oliver's eyes and he saw that hers were very blue, and just a little amused, as if she had known he was there all along. Also they were frankly admiring.

Feeling a bit dizzy, Oliver hurried back to his room to dress.

"We are here on a vacation," the dark man said, accepting the keys. "We will not wish to be disturbed, as I made clear in our correspondence. You have engaged a cook and housemaid for us, I understand. We will expect you to move your own belongings out of the house, then, and—"

"Wait," Oliver said uncomfortably. "Something's come up. I—" He hesitated, not sure just how to present it. These were such increasingly odd people. Even their speech was odd. They spoke so distinctly, not slurring any of the words into contractions. English seemed as familiar to them as a native tongue, but they all spoke as trained singers sing, with perfect breath control and voice placement.

And there was a coldness in the man's voice, as if some gulf lay between him and Oliver, so deep no feeling of human contact could bridge it.

"I wonder," Oliver said, "if I could find you better living quarters somewhere else in town. There's a place across the street that—"

The dark woman said, "Oh, no!" in a lightly horrified voice, and all three of them laughed. It was cool, distant laughter that did not include Oliver.

The dark man said: "We chose this house carefully, Mr. Wilson. We would not be interested in living anywhere else."

Oliver said desperately, "I don't see why. It isn't even a modern house. I have two others in much better condition. Even across the street you'd have a fine view of the city. Here there isn't anything. The other houses cut off the view, and—"

"We engaged rooms here, Mr. Wilson," the man said with finality. "We expect to use them. Now will you make arrangements to leave as soon as possible?"

Oliver said, "No," and looked stubborn. "That isn't in the

lease. You can live here until next month, since you paid for it, but you can't put me out. I'm staying."

The man opened his mouth to say something. He looked coldly at Oliver and closed it again. The feeling of aloofness was chill between them. There was a moment's silence. Then the man said,

"Very well. Be kind enough to stay out of our way."

It was a little odd that he didn't inquire about Oliver's motives. Oliver was not yet sure enough of the man to explain. He couldn't very well say, "Since the lease was signed, I've been offered three times what the house is worth if I'll sell it before the end of May." He couldn't say, "I want the money, and I'm going to use my own nuisance-value to annoy you until you're willing to move out." After all, there seemed no reason why they shouldn't. After seeing them, there seemed doubly no reason, for it was clear they must be accustomed to surroundings infinitely better than this time-worn old house.

It was very strange, the value this house had so suddenly acquired. There was no reason at all why two groups of semi-anonymous people should be so eager to possess it for the month of May.

In silence Oliver showed his tenants upstairs to the three big bedrooms across the front of the house. He was intensely conscious of the red-haired woman and the way she watched him with a sort of obviously covert interest, quite warmly, and with a curious undertone to her interest that he could not quite place. It was familiar, but elusive. He thought how pleasant it would be to talk to her alone, if only to try to capture that elusive attitude and put a name to it.

Afterward he went down to the telephone and called his fiancée.

Sue's voice squeaked a little with excitement over the wire.

"Oliver, so early? Why, it's hardly six yet. Did you tell them what I said? Are they going to go?"

"Can't tell yet. I doubt it. After all, Sue, I did take their money, you know."

"Oliver, they've got to go! You've got to do something!"

"I'm trying, Sue. But I don't like it."

"Well, there isn't any reason why they shouldn't stay somewhere else. And we're going to need that money. You'll just have to think of something, Oliver."

Oliver met his own worried eyes in the mirror above the telephone and scowled at himself. His straw-colored hair was tangled and there was a shining stubble on his pleasant, tanned face. He was sorry the red-haired woman had first seen him in this untidy condition. Then his conscience smote him at the sound of Sue's determined voice and he said:

"I'll try, darling. I'll try. But I did take their money."

They had, in fact, paid a great deal of money, considerably more than the rooms were worth even in that year of high prices and high wages. The country was just moving into one of those fabulous eras which are later referred to as the Gay Forties or the Golden Sixties—a pleasant period of national euphoria. It was a stimulating time to be alive—while it lasted.

"All right," Oliver said resignedly. "I'll do my best."

But he was conscious, as the next few days went by, that he was not doing his best. There were several reasons for that. From the beginning the idea of making himself a nuisance to his tenants had been Sue's, not Oliver's. And if Oliver had been a little less compliant or Sue a little less determined the whole project would never have got under way. Reason was on Sue's side, but—

For one thing, the tenants were so fascinating. All they said and did had a queer sort of inversion to it, as if a mirror had been held up to ordinary living and in the reflection showed strange variations from the norm. Their minds worked on a different basic premise, Oliver thought, from his own. They seemed to derive covert amusement from the most unamusing things; they patronized, they were aloof with a quality of cold detachment which did not prevent them from laughing inexplicably far too often for Oliver's comfort.

He saw them occasionally, on their way to and from their rooms. They were polite and distant, not, he suspected, from anger at his presence but from sheer indifference.

Most of the day they spent out of the house. The perfect May weather held unbroken and they seemed to give themselves up wholeheartedly to admiration of it, entirely confident that the warm, pale-gold sunshine and the scented air would not be interrupted by rain or cold. They were so sure of it that Oliver felt uneasy.

They took only one meal a day in the house, a late dinner. And their reactions to the meal were unpredictable. Laughter greeted some of the dishes, and a sort of delicate disgust others. No one would touch the salad, for instance. And the fish seemed to cause a wave of queer embarrassment around the table.

They dressed elaborately for each dinner. The man—his name was Omerie—looked extremely handsome in his dinner clothes, but he seemed a little sulky and Oliver twice heard the women laughing because he had to wear black. Oliver entertained a sudden vision, for no reason, of the man in garments as bright and as subtly cut as the women's, and it seemed somehow very right for him. He wore even the dark clothing with a certain flamboyance, as if cloth-of-gold would be more normal for him.

When they were in the house at other meal times, they ate in their rooms. They must have brought a great deal of food with them, from whatever mysterious place they had come. Oliver wondered with increasing curiosity where it might be. Delicious odors drifted into the hall sometimes, at odd hours, from their closed doors. Oliver could not identify them, but almost always they smelled irresistible. A few times the food smell was rather shockingly unpleasant, almost nauseating. It takes a connoisseur, Oliver reflected, to appreciate the decadent. And these people, most certainly, were connoisseurs.

Why they lived so contentedly in this huge, ramshackle old house was a question that disturbed his dreams at night. Or why they refused to move. He caught some fascinating glimpses into their rooms, which appeared to have been changed almost completely by additions he could not have defined very clearly from the brief sights he had of them. The feeling of luxury which his first glance at them had evoked was confirmed by the richness of the hangings they had apparently brought with them, the half-glimpsed ornaments, the pictures on the walls, even the whiffs of exotic perfume that floated from half-open doors.

He saw the women go by him in the halls, moving softly through the brown dimness in their gowns so uncannily perfect in fit, so lushly rich, so glowingly colored they seemed unreal. That poise born of confidence in the subservience of the world gave them an imperious aloofness, but more than once Oliver, meeting the blue gaze of the woman with the red hair and the soft, tanned skin, thought he saw quickened interest there. She smiled at him in the dimness and went by in a haze of fragrance and a halo of incredible richness, and the warmth of the smile lingered after she had gone.

He knew she did not mean this aloofness to last between them. From the very first he was sure of that. When the time came she would make the opportunity to be alone with him. The thought was confusing and tremendously exciting. There was nothing he could do but wait, knowing she would see him when it suited her.

On the third day he lunched with Sue in a little downtown restaurant overlooking the great sweep of the metropolis across the river far below. Sue had shining brown curls and brown eyes, and her chin was a bit more prominent than is strictly accordant with beauty. From childhood Sue had known what she wanted and how to get it, and it seemed to Oliver just now that she had never wanted anything quite so much as the sale of this house.

"It's such a marvelous offer for the old mausoleum," she said, breaking into a roll with a gesture of violence. "We'll never have a chance like that again, and prices are so high we'll need the money to start housekeeping. Surely you can do *something*, Oliver!"

"I'm trying," Oliver assured her uncomfortably.

"Have you heard anything more from that madwoman who wants to buy it?"

Oliver shook his head. "Her attorney phoned again yesterday. Nothing new. I wonder who she is."

"I don't think even the attorney knows. All this mystery—I don't like it, Oliver. Even those Sancisco people— What did they do today?"

Oliver laughed. "They spent about an hour this morning telephoning movie theaters in the city, checking up on a lot of third-rate films they want to see parts of."

"Parts of? But why?"

"I don't know. I think . . . oh, nothing. More coffee?"

The trouble was, he thought he did know. It was too unlikely a guess to tell Sue about, and without familiarity with the Sancisco oddities she would only think Oliver was losing his mind. But he had from their talk a definite impression that there was an actor in bit parts in all these films whose performances they mentioned with something very near to awe. They referred to him as Golconda, which didn't appear to be his name, so that Oliver had no way of guessing which obscure bit player it was they admired so deeply. Golconda might have been the name of a character he had once played—and with superlative skill, judging by the comments of the Sanciscos—but to Oliver it meant nothing at all.

"They do funny things," he said, stirring his coffee reflectively. "Yesterday Omerie—that's the man—came in with a book of poems published about five years ago, and all of them handled it like a first edition of Shakespeare. I never even heard of the author, but he seems to be a tin god in their country, wherever that is."

"You still don't know? Haven't they even dropped any hints?"

"We don't do much talking," Oliver reminded her with some irony.

"I know, but— Oh, well, I guess it doesn't matter. Go on, what else do they do?"

"Well, this morning they were going to spend studying 'Golconda' and his great art, and this afternoon I think they're taking a trip up the river to some sort of shrine I never heard of. It isn't very far, wherever it is, because I know they're coming back for dinner. Some great man's birthplace, I think—they promised to take home souvenirs of the place if they could get any. They're typical tourists, all right—if I could only figure out what's behind the whole thing. It doesn't make sense."

"Nothing about that house makes sense anymore. I do wish—"

She went on in a petulant voice, but Oliver ceased suddenly to hear her, because just outside the door, walking with imperial elegance on her high heels, a familiar figure passed. He did not see her face, but he thought he would know that poise, that richness of line and motion, anywhere on earth.

"Excuse me a minute," he muttered to Sue, and was out of his chair before she could speak. He made the door in half a dozen long strides, and the beautifully elegant passerby was only a few steps away when he got there. Then, with the words he had meant to speak already half uttered, he fell silent and stood there staring.

It was not the red-haired woman. It was not her dark companion. It was a stranger. He watched, speechless, while the lovely, imperious creature moved on through the crowd and vanished, moving with familiar poise and assurance and an equally familiar strangeness as if the beautiful and exquisitely fitted garments she wore were an exotic costume to her, as they had always seemed to the Sancisco women. Every other woman on the street looked untidy and ill-at-ease beside her. Walking like a queen, she melted into the crowd and was gone.

She came from *their* country, Oliver told himself dizzily. So someone else nearby had mysterious tennants in this month of perfect May weather. Someone else was puzzling in vain today over the strangeness of the people from that nameless land.

In silence he went back to Sue.

The door stood invitingly ajar in the brown dimness of the upper hall. Oliver's steps slowed as he drew near it, and his heart began to quicken correspondingly. It was the red-haired woman's room, and he thought the door was not open by accident. Her name, he knew now, was Kleph.

The door creaked a little on its hinges and from within a very sweet voice said lazily, "Won't you come in?"

The room looked very different indeed. The big bed had been pushed back against the wall and a cover thrown over it that brushed the floor all around looked like soft-haired fur except that it was a pale blue-green and sparkled as if every hair were tipped with invisible crystals. Three books lay open on the fur, and a very curious-looking magazine with faintly luminous printing and a page of pictures that at first glance appeared three-dimensional. Also a tiny porcelain pipe encrusted with porcelain flowers, and a thin wisp of smoke floating from the bowl.

Above the bed a broad picture hung, framing a square of blue water so real Oliver had to look twice to be sure it was not rippling gently from left to right. From the ceiling swung a crystal globe on a glass cord. It turned gently, the light from the windows making curved rectangles in its sides.

Under the center window a sort of chaise longue stood which Oliver had not seen before. He could only assume it was at least partly pneumatic and had been brought in the luggage. There was a very rich-looking quilted cloth covering and hiding it, embossed all over in shining metallic patterns.

Kleph moved slowly from the door and sank upon the chaise longue with a little sigh of content. The couch accommodated itself to her body with what looked like delightful comfort. Kleph wriggled a little then smiled up at Oliver.

"Do come on in. Sit over there, where you can see out the window. I love your beautiful spring weather. You know, there never was a May like it in civilized times." She said that quite seriously, her blue eyes on Oliver's, and there was a hint of patronage in her voice, as if the weather had been arranged especially for her.

Oliver started across the room and then paused and looked down in amazement at the floor, which felt unstable. He had not noticed before that the carpet was pure white, unspotted, and sank about an inch under the pressure of the feet. He saw then that Kleph's feet were bare, or almost bare. She wore something like gossamer buskins of filmy net, fitting her feet exactly. The bare soles were pink as if they had been rouged, and the nails had a liquid gleam like tiny mirrors. He moved closer, and was not as surprised as he should have been to see that they really were tiny mirrors, painted with some lacquer that gave them reflecting surfaces.

"Do sit down," Kleph said again, waving a white-sleeved arm toward a chair by the window. She wore a garment that looked like short, soft down, loosely cut but following perfectly every motion she made. And there was something curiously different about her very shape today. When Oliver saw her in street clothes, she had the square-shouldered, slim-flanked figure that all women strive for, but here in her lounging robe she looked—well, different. There was an almost swanlike slope to her shoulders today, a roundness and softness to her body that looked unfamiliar and very appealing.

"Will you have some tea?" Kleph asked, and smiled charmingly.

A low table beside her held a tray and several small covered cups, lovely things with an inner glow like rose quartz, the color shining deeply as if from within layer upon layer of translucence. She took up one of the cups—there were no saucers—and offered it to Oliver.

It felt fragile and thin as paper in his hand. He could not see the contents because of the cup's cover, which seemed to be one with the cup itself and left only a thin open crescent at the rim. Steam rose from the opening.

Kleph took up a cup of her own and tilted it to her lips, smiling at Oliver over the rim. She was very beautiful. The pale red hair lay in shining loops against her head and the corona of curls like a halo above her forehead might have been pressed down like a wreath. Every hair kept order as perfectly as if it had been painted on, though the breeze from the window stirred now and then among the softly shining strands.

Oliver tried the tea. Its flavor was exquisite, very hot, and the taste that lingered upon his tongue was like the scent of flowers. It was an extremely feminine drink. He sipped again, surprised to find how much he liked it.

The scent of flowers seemed to increase as he drank, swirling through his head like smoke. After the third sip there was a faint buzzing in his ears. The bees among the flowers, perhaps, he thought incoherently—and sipped again.

Kleph watched him, smiling.

"The others will be out all afternoon," she told Oliver comfortably. "I thought it would give us a pleasant time to be acquainted."

Oliver was rather horrified to hear himself saying, "What makes you talk like that?" He had had no idea of asking the question; something seemed to have loosened his control over his own tongue.

Kleph's smile deepened. She tipped the cup to her lips and there was indulgence in her voice when she said, "What do you mean by that?"

He waved his hand vaguely, noting with some surprise that at a glance it seemed to have six or seven fingers as it moved past his face.

"I don't know—precision, I guess. Why don't you say 'don't', for instance?"

"In our country we are trained to speak with precision," Kleph explained. "Just as we are trained to move and dress and think with precision. Any slovenliness is trained out of us in childhood. With you, of course—" She was polite. "With you, this does not happen to be a national fetish. With us, we have time for the amenities. We like them."

Her voice had grown sweeter and sweeter as she spoke, until by now it was almost indistinguishable from the sweetness of the flower-scent in Oliver's head, and the delicate flavor of the tea.

"What country do you come from?" he asked, and tilted the cup again to drink, mildly surprised to notice that it seemed inexhaustible.

Kleph's smile was definitely patronizing this time. It didn't irritate him. Nothing could irritate him just now. The whole room swam in a beautiful rosy glow as fragrant as the flowers.

"We must not speak of that, Mr. Wilson."

"But—" Oliver paused. After all, it was, of course, none of his business. "This is a vacation?" he asked vaguely.

"Call it a pilgrimage, perhaps."

"Pilgrimage?" Oliver was so interested that for an instant his mind came back into sharp focus. "To—what?"

"I should not have said that, Mr. Wilson. Please forget it. Do you like the tea?"

"Very much."

"You will have guessed by now that it is not only tea, but an euphoriac."

Oliver stared. "Euphoriac?"

Kleph made a descriptive circle in the air with one graceful hand, and laughed. "You do not feel the effects yet? Surely you do?"

"I feel," Oliver said, "the way I'd feel after four whiskeys."

Kleph shuddered delicately. "We get our euphoria less painfully. And without the after-effects your barbarous alcohols used to have." She bit her lip. "Sorry. I must be euphoric myself to speak so freely. Please forgive me. Shall we have some music?"

Kleph leaned backward on the chaise longue and reached toward the wall beside her. The sleeve, falling away from her round tanned arm, left bare the inside of the wrist, and Oliver was startled to see there a long, rosy streak of fading scar. His inhibitions had dissolved in the fumes of the fragrant tea; he caught his breath and leaned forward to stare.

Kleph shook the sleeve back over the scar with a quick gesture. Color came into her face beneath the softly tinted tan and she would not meet Oliver's eyes. A queer shame seemed to have fallen upon her.

Oliver said tactlessly, "What is it? What's the matter?"

Still she would not look at him. Much later he understood that shame and knew she had reason for it. Now he listened blankly as she said:

"Nothing . . . nothing at all. A . . . an inoculation. All of us . . . oh, never mind. Listen to the music."

This time she reached out with the other arm. She touched nothing, but when she had held her hand near the wall a sound breathed through the room. It was the sound of water, the sighing of waves receding upon long, sloped beaches. Oliver followed Kleph's gaze toward the picture of the blue water above the bed.

The waves there were moving. More than that, the point of vision moved. Slowly the seascape drifted past, moving with the waves, following them toward shore. Oliver watched, half-hypnotized by a motion that seemed at the time quite acceptable and not in the least surprising.

The waves lifted and broke in creaming foam and ran seething up a sandy beach. Then through the sound of the water music began to breathe, and through the water itself a man's face dawned in the frame, smiling intimately into the room. He held an oddly archaic musical instrument, lute-shaped, its body striped light and dark like a melon and its long neck bent back over his shoulder. He was singing, and Oliver felt mildly astonished at the song. It was very familiar and very odd indeed. He groped through the unfamiliar rhythms and found at last a thread to catch the tune by—it was "Make-Believe," from "Showboat," but certainly a show-boat that had never steamed up the Mississippi.

"What's he doing to it?" he demanded after a few moments of outraged listening. "I never heard anything like it!"

Kleph laughed and stretched out her arm again. Enigmatically she said, "We call it kyling. Never mind. How do you like this?"

It was a comedian, a man in semiclown makeup, his eyes exaggerated so that they seemed to cover half his face. He stood by a broad glass pillar before a dark curtain and sang a gay, staccato song interspersed with patter that sounded impromptu, and all the while his left hand did an intricate, musical tattoo of the nailtips on the glass of the column. He strolled around and around it as he sang. The rhythms of his fingernails blended with the song and swung widely away into patterns of their own, and blended again without a break.

It was confusing to follow. The song made even less sense than the monologue, which had something to do with a lost slipper and was full of allusions which made Kleph smile, but were utterly unintelligible to Oliver. The man had a dry, brittle style that was not very amusing, though Kleph seemed fascinated. Oliver was interested to see in him an extension and a variation of that extreme smooth confidence which marked all three of the Sanciscos. Clearly a racial trait, he thought.

Other performances followed, some of them fragmentary as if lifted out of a more complete version. One he knew. The obvious, stirring melody struck his recognition before the figures—marching men against a haze, a great banner rolling backward above them in the smoke, foreground figures striding gigantically and shouting in rhythm, "Forward, forward the lily banners go!"

The music was tinny, the images blurred and poorly colored, but there was a gusto about the performance that caught at Oliver's imagination. He stared, remembering the old film from long ago. Dennis King and a ragged chorus, singing "The Song of the Vagabonds" from—was it *Vagabond King?*

"A very old one," Kleph said apologetically. "But I like it."

The steam of the intoxicating tea swirled between Oliver and the picture. Music swelled and sank through the room and the fragrant fumes and his own euphoric brain. Nothing seemed strange. He had discovered how to drink the tea. Like nitrous oxide, the effect was not cumulative. When you reached a peak of euphoria, you could not increase the peak. It was best to wait for a slight dip in the effect of the stimulant before taking more.

Otherwise it had most of the effects of alcohol—everything after a while dissolved into a delightful fog through which all he saw was uninformly enchanting and partook of the qualities of a dream. He questioned nothing. Afterward he was not certain how much of it he really had dreamed.

There was the dancing doll, for instance. He remembered it quite clearly, in sharp focus—a tiny, slender woman with a long-nosed, dark-eyed face and a pointed chin. She moved delicately across the white rug—knee-high, exquisite. Her features were as mobile as her body, and she danced lightly, with resounding strokes of her toes, each echoing like a bell. It was a formalized sort of dance, and she sang breathlessly in accompaniment, making amusing little grimaces. Certainly it was a portrait-doll, animated to mimic the original perfectly in voice and motion. Afterward, Oliver knew he must have dreamed it.

What else happened he was quite unable to remember later. He knew Kleph had said some curious things, but they all made sense at the time, and afterward he couldn't remember a word. He knew he had been offered little glittering candies in a transparent dish, and that some of them had been delicious and one or two so bitter his tongue still curled the next day when he recalled them, and one—Kleph sucked luxuriantly on the same kind—of a taste that was actively nauseating.

As for Kleph herself—he was frantically uncertain the next day what had really happened. He thought he could remember the softness of her white-downed arms clasped at the back of his neck, while she laughed up at him and exhaled into his face the flowery fragrance of the tea. But beyond that he was totally unable to recall anything, for a while.

There was a brief interlude later, before the oblivion of sleep. He was almost sure he remembered a moment when the other two Sanciscos stood looking down at him, the man scowling, the smoky-eyed woman smiling a derisive smile.

The man said, from a vast distance, "Kleph, you know this is against every rule—" His voice began in a thin hum and soared in fantastic flight beyond the range of hearing. Oliver thought he remembered the dark woman's laughter, thin and distant too, and the hum of her voice like bees in flight.

"Kleph, Kleph, you silly little fool, can we never trust you out of sight?"

Kleph's voice then said something that seemed to make no sense. "What does it matter, *here?*"

The man answered in that buzzing, faraway hum. "—matter of giving your bond before you leave, not to interfere. You know you signed the rules—"

Kleph's voice, nearer and more intelligible: "But here the difference is . . . it does not matter *here!* You both know that. How could it matter?"

Oliver felt the downy brush of her sleeve against his cheek, but he saw nothing except the slow, smokelike ebb and flow of darkness past his eyes. He heard the voices wrangle musically from far away, and he heard them cease.

When he woke the next morning, alone in his own room, he woke with the memory of Kleph's eyes upon him very sorrowfully, her lovely tanned face looking down on him with the red hair falling fragrantly on each side of it and sadness and compassion in her eyes. He thought he had probably dreamed that. There was no reason why anyone should look at him with such sadness.

Sue telephoned that day.

"Oliver, the people who want to buy the house are here. That madwoman and her husband. Shall I bring them over?"

Oliver's mind all day had been hazy with the vague, bewildering memories of yesterday. Kleph's face kept floating before him, blotting out the room. He said, "What? I . . . oh, well, bring them if you want to. I don't see what good it'll do."

"Oliver, what's wrong with you? We agreed we needed the money, didn't we? I don't see how you can think of passing up such a wonderful bargain without even a struggle. We could get married and buy our own house right away, and you know we'll never get such an offer again for that old trash-heap. Wake up, Oliver!"

Oliver made an effort. "I know, Sue—I know. But—"

"Oliver, you've got to think of something!" Her voice was imperious.

He knew she was right. Kleph or no Kleph, the bargain shouldn't be ignored if there was any way at all of getting the tenants out. He wondered again what made the place so suddenly priceless to so many people. And what the last week in May had to do with the value of the house.

A sudden sharp curiosity pierced even the vagueness of his mind today. May's last week was so important that the whole sale of the house stood or fell upon occupancy by then. Why? *Why?*

"What's going to happen next week?" he asked rhetorically of the telephone. "Why can't they wait till these people leave? I'd knock a couple of thousand off the price if they'd—"

"You would not, Oliver Wilson! I can buy all our refrigeration units with that extra money. You'll just have to work out some way to give possession by next week, and that's that. You hear me?"

"Keep your shirt on," Oliver said pacifically. "I'm only human, but I'll try."

"I'm bringing the people over right away," Sue told him. "While the Sanciscos are still out. Now you put your mind to work and think of something, Oliver." She paused, and her voice was reflective when she spoke again. "They're . . . awfully odd people, darling."

"Odd?"

"You'll see."

It was an elderly woman and a very young man who trailed Sue up the walk. Oliver knew immediately what had struck Sue about them. He was somehow not at all surprised to see that both wore their clothing with the familiar air of elegant self-consciousness he had come to know so well. They, too, looked around them at the beautiful, sunny afternoon with conscious enjoyment and an air of faint condescension. He knew before he heard them speak how musical their voices would be and how meticulously they would pronounce each word.

There was no doubt about it. The people of Kleph's mysterious country were arriving here in force—for something. For the last week of May? He shrugged mentally; there was no way of guessing—yet. One thing only was sure: all of them must come from that nameless land where people controlled their voices like singers and their garments like actors who could stop the reel of time itself to adjust every disordered fold.

The elderly woman took full charge of the conversation

from the start. They stood together on the rickety, unpainted porch, and Sue had no chance even for introductions.

"Young man, I am Madame Hollia. This is my husband." Her voice had an underrunning current of harshness, which was perhaps age. And her face looked almost corseted, the loose flesh coerced into something like firmness by some invisible method Oliver could not guess at. The makeup was so skillful he could not be certain it was makeup at all, but he had a definite feeling that she was much older than she looked. It would have taken a lifetime of command to put so much authority into the harsh, deep, musically controlled voice.

The young man said nothing. He was very handsome. His type, apparently, was one that does not change much no matter in what culture or country it may occur. He wore beautifully tailored garments and carried in one gloved hand a box of red leather, about the size and shape of a book.

Madame Hollia went on. "I understand your problem about the house. You wish to sell to me, but are legally bound by your lease with Omerie and his friends. Is that right?"

Oliver nodded. "But—"

"Let me finish. If Omerie can be forced to vacate before next week, you will accept our offer. Right? Very well. Hara!" She nodded to the young man beside her. He jumped to instant attention, bowed slightly, said; "Yes, Hollia," and slipped a gloved hand into his coat.

Madame Hollia took the little object offered on his palm, her gesture as she reached for it almost imperial, as if royal robes swept from her outstretched arm.

"Here," she said, "is something that may help us. My dear"—she held it out to Sue—"if you can hide this somewhere about the house, I believe your unwelcome tenants will not trouble you much longer."

Sue took the thing curiously. It looked like a tiny silver box, no more than an inch square, indented at the top and with no line to show it could be opened.

"Wait a minute," Oliver broke in uneasily. "What is it?"

"Nothing that will harm anyone, I assure you."

"Then what—?"

Madame Hollia's imperious gesture at one sweep silenced him and commanded Sue forward. "Go on, my dear. Hurry, before Omerie comes back. I can assure you there is no danger to anyone."

Oliver broke in determinedly. "Madame Hollia, I'll have to know what your plans are. I—"

"Oh, Oliver, please!" Sue's fingers closed over the silver cube. "Don't worry about it. I'm sure Madame Hollia knows best. Don't you *want* to get those people out?"

"Of course I do. But I don't want the house blown up or—"

Madame Hollia's deep laughter was indulgent. "Nothing so crude, I promise you, Mr. Wilson. Remember, we want the house! Hurry, my dear."

Sue nodded and slipped hastily past Oliver into the hall. Outnumbered, he subsided uneasily. The young man, Hara, tapped a negligent foot and admired the sunlight as they waited. It was an afternoon as perfect as all of May had been, translucent gold, balmy with an edge of chill lingering in the air to point up a perfect contrast with the summer to come. Hara looked around him confidently, like a man paying just tribute to a stage set provided wholly for himself. He even glanced up at a drone from above and followed the course of a big transcontinental plane half dissolved in golden haze high in the sun. "Quaint," he murmured in a gratified voice.

Sue came back and slipped her hand through Oliver's arm, squeezing excitedly. "There," she said. "How long will it take, Madame Hollia?"

"That will depend, my dear. Not very long. Now, Mr. Wilson, one word with you. You live here also, I understand? For your own comfort, take my advice and—"

Somewhere within the house a door slammed and a clear, high voice rang wordlessly up a rippling scale. Then there was the sound of feet on the stairs, and a single line of song. *"Come hider, love, to me—"*

Hara started, almost dropping the red leather box he held.

"Kleph!" he said in a whisper. "Or Klia. I know they both just came on from Canterbury. But I thought—"

"Hush." Madame Hollia's features composed themselves into an imperious blank. She breathed triumphantly through her nose, drew back upon herself and turned an imposing facade to the door.

Kleph wore the same softly downy robe Oliver had seen before, except that today it was not white, but a pale, clear blue that gave her tan an apricot flush. She was smiling.

"Why, Hollia!" Her tone was at its most musical. "I thought I recognized voices from home. How nice to see you.

No one knew you were coming to the—" She broke off and glanced at Oliver and then away again. "Hara, too," she said. "What a pleasant surprise."

Sue said flatly, "When did *you* get back?"

Kleph smiled at her. "You must be the little Miss Johnson. Why, I did not go out at all. I was tired of sightseeing. I have been napping in my room."

Sue drew in her breath in something that just escaped being a disbelieving sniff. A look flashed between the two women, and for an instant held—and that instant was timeless. It was an extraordinary pause in which a great deal of wordless interplay took place in the space of a second.

Oliver saw the quality of Kleph's smile at Sue, that same look of quiet confidence he had noticed so often about all of these strange people. He saw Sue's quick inventory of the other women, and he saw how Sue squared her shoulders and stood up straight, smoothing down her summer frock over her flat hips so that for an instant she stood posed consciously, looking down on Kleph. It was deliberate. Bewildered, he glanced again at Kleph.

Kleph's shoulders sloped softly, her robe was belted to a tiny waist and hung in deep folds over frankly rounded hips. Sue's was the fashionable figure—but Sue was the first to surrender.

Kleph's smile did not falter. But in the silence there was an abrupt reversal of values, based on no more than the measureless quality of Kleph's confidence in herself, the quiet, assured smile. It was suddenly made very clear that fashion is not a constant. Kleph's curious, out-of-mode curves without warning became the norm, and Sue was a queer, angular, half-masculine creature beside her.

Oliver had no idea how it was done. Somehow the authority passed in a breath from one woman to the other. Beauty is almost wholly a matter of fashion; what is beautiful today would have been grotesque a couple of generations ago and will be grotesque a hundred years ahead. It will be worse than grotesque; it will be outmoded and therefore faintly ridiculous.

Sue was that. Kleph had only to exert her authority to make it clear to everyone on the porch. Kleph was a beauty, suddenly and very convincingly, beautiful in the accepted mode, and Sue was amusingly old-fashioned, an anachronism in her lithe, square-shouldered slimness. She did not belong. She was grotesque among these strangely immaculate people.

Sue's collapse was complete. But pride sustained her, and bewilderment. Probably she never did grasp entirely what was wrong. She gave Kleph one glance of burning resentment and when her eyes came back to Oliver there was suspicion in them, and mistrust.

Looking backward later, Oliver thought that in that moment, for the first time clearly, he began to suspect the truth. But he had no time to ponder it, for after the brief instant of enmity the three people from—elsewhere—began to speak all at once, as if in a belated attempt to cover something they did not want noticed.

Kleph said, "This beautiful weather—" and Madame Hollia said, "So fortunate to have this house—" and Hara, holding up the red leather box, said loudest of all, "Cenbe sent you this, Kleph. His latest."

Kleph put out both hands for it eagerly, the eiderdown sleeves falling back from her rounded arms. Oliver had a quick glimpse of that mysterious scar before the sleeve fell back, and it seemed to him that there was the faintest trace of a similar scar vanishing into Hara's cuff as he let his own arm drop.

"Cenbe!" Kleph cried, her voice high and sweet and delighted. "How wonderful! What period?"

"From November 1664," Hara said. "London, of course, though I think there may be some counterpoint from the 1347 November. He hasn't finished—of course." He glanced almost nervously at Oliver and Sue. "A wonderful example," he said quickly. "Marvelous. If you have the taste for it, of course."

Madame Hollia shuddered with ponderous delicacy. "That man!" she said. "Fascinating, of course—a great man. But—so *advanced!*"

"It takes a connoisseur to appreciate Cenbe's work fully," Kleph said in a slightly tart voice. "We all admit that."

"Oh yes, we all bow to Cenbe," Hollia conceded. "I confess the man terrifies me a little, my dear. Do we expect him to join us?"

"I suppose so," Kelph said. "If his—work—is not yet finished, then of course. You know Cenbe's tastes."

Hollia and Hara laughed together. "I know when to look for him, then," Hollia said. She glanced at the staring Oliver and the subdued but angry Sue, and with a commanding effort brought the subject back into line.

"So fortunate, my dear Kleph, to have this house," she declared heavily. "I saw a tridimensional of it—afterward—and it was still quite perfect. Such a fortunate coincidence. Would you consider parting with your lease, for a consideration? Say, a coronation seat at—"

"Nothing could buy us, Hollia," Kleph told her gaily, clasping the red box to her bosom.

Hollia gave her a cool stare. "You may change your mind, my dear Kleph," she said pontifically. "There is still time. You can always reach us through Mr. Wilson here. We have rooms up the street in the Montgomery House—nothing like yours, of course, but they will do. For us, they will do."

Oliver blinked. The Montgomery House was the most expensive hotel in town. Compared to this collapsing old ruin, it was a palace. There was no understanding these people. Their values seemed to have suffered a complete reversal.

Madame Hollia moved majestically toward the steps.

"Very pleasant to see you, my dear," she said over one well-padded shoulder. "Enjoy your stay. My regards to Omerie and Klia. Mr. Wilson—" she nodded toward the walk. "A word with you."

Oliver followed her down toward the street. Madame Hollia paused halfway there and touched his arm.

"One word of advice," she said huskily. "You say you sleep here? Move out, young man. Move out before tonight."

Oliver was searching in a half-desultory fashion for the hiding place Sue had found for the mysterious silver cube, when the first sounds from above began to drift down the stairwell toward him. Kleph had closed her door, but the house was old and strange qualities in the noise overhead seemed to seep through the woodwork like an almost visible stain.

It was music, in a way. But much more than music. And it was a terrible sound, the sounds of calamity and of all human reaction to calamity, everything from hysteria to heartbreak, from irrational joy to rationalized acceptance.

The calamity was—single. The music did not attempt to correlate all human sorrows; it focused sharply upon one and followed the ramifications out and out. Oliver recognized these basics to the sounds in a very brief moment. They were essentials, and they seemed to beat into his brain with the first strains of the music which was so much more than music.

But when he lifted his head to listen he lost all grasp upon the meaning of the noise and it was sheer medley and confusion. To think of it was to blur it hopelessly in the mind, and he could not recapture that first instant of unreasoning acceptance.

He went upstairs almost in a daze, hardly knowing what he was doing. He pushed Kleph's door open. He looked inside—

What he saw there he could not afterward remember except in a blurring as vague as the blurred ideas the music roused in his brain. Half the room had vanished behind a mist, and the mist was a three-dimensional screen upon which were projected— He had no words for them. He was not even sure if the projections were visual. The mist was spinning with motion and sound, but essentially it was neither sound nor motion that Oliver saw.

This was a work of art. Oliver knew no name for it. It transcended all art forms he knew, blended them, and out of the blend produced subtleties his mind could not begin to grasp. Basically, this was the attempt of a master composer to correlate every essential aspect of a vast human experience into something that could be conveyed in a few moments to every sense at once.

The shifting visions on the screen were not pictures in themselves, but hints of pictures, subtly selected outlines that plucked at the mind and with one deft touch set whole chords ringing through the memory. Perhaps each beholder reacted differently, since it was in the eye and the mind of the beholder that the truth of the picture lay. No two would be aware of the same symphonic panorama, but each would see essentially the same terrible story unfold.

Every sense was touched by that deft and merciless genius. Color and shape and motion flickered in the screen, hinting much, evoking unbearable memories deep in the mind; odors floated from the screen and touched the heart of the beholder more poignantly than anything visual could do. The skin crawled sometimes as if to a tangible cold hand laid upon it. The tongue curled with remembered bitterness and remembered sweet.

It was outrageous. It violated the innermost privacies of a man's mind, called up secret things long ago walled off behind mental scar tissue, forced its terrible message upon the beholder relentlessly though the mind might threaten to crack beneath the stress of it.

And yet, in spite of all this vivid awareness, Oliver did not know what calamity the screen portrayed. That is was real, vast, overwhelmingly dreadful he could not doubt. That it had once happened was unmistakable. He caught flashing glimpses of human faces distorted with grief and disease and death—real faces, faces that had once lived and were seen now in the instant of dying. He saw men and women in rich clothing superimposed in panorama upon reeling thousands of ragged folk, great throngs of them swept past the sight in an instant, and he saw that death made no distinction among them.

He saw lovely women laugh and shake their curls, and the laughter shriek into hysteria and the hysteria into music. He saw one man's face, over and over—a long, dark, saturnine face, deeply lined, sorrowful, the face of a powerful man wise in worldliness, urbane—and helpless. That face was for awhile a recurring motif, always more tortured, more helpless than before.

The music broke off in the midst of a rising glide. The mist vanished and the room reappeared before him. The anguished dark face for an instant seemed to Oliver printed everywhere he looked, like after-vision on the eyelids. He knew that face. He had seen it before, not often, but he should know its name—

"Oliver, Oliver—" Kleph's sweet voice came out of a fog at him. He was leaning dizzily against the doorpost looking down into her eyes. She, too, had that dazed blankness he must show on his own face. The power of the dreadful symphony still held them both. But even in this confused moment Oliver saw that Kleph had been enjoying the experience.

He felt sickened to the depths of his mind, dizzy with sickness and revulsion because of the superimposing of human miseries he had just beheld. But Kleph—only appreciation showed upon her face. To her it had been magnificence, and magnificence only.

Irrelevantly Oliver remembered the nauseating candies she had enjoyed, the nauseating odors of strange food that drifted sometimes through the hall from her room.

What was it she had said downstairs a little while ago? Connoisseur, that was it. Only a connoisseur could appreciate work as—as *advanced*—as the work of someone called Cenbe.

A whiff of intoxicating sweetness curled past Oliver's face. Something cool and smooth was pressed into his hand.

"Oh, Oliver, I am so sorry," Kleph's voice murmured contritely. "Here, drink the euphoriac and you will feel better. Please drink!"

The familiar fragrance of the hot sweet tea was on his tongue before he knew he had complied. Its relaxing fumes floated up through his brain and in a moment or two the world felt stable around him again. The room was as it had always been. And Kleph—

Her eyes were very bright. Sympathy showed in them for him, but for herself she was still brimmed with the high elation of what she had just been experiencing.

"Come and sit down," she said gently, tugging at his arm. "I am so sorry—I should not have played that over, where you could hear it. I have no excuse, really. It was only that I forgot what the effect might be on one who had never heard Cenbe's symphonies before. I was so impatient to see what he had done with . . . with his new subject. I am so very sorry, Oliver!"

"What was it?" His voice sounded steadier than he had expected. The tea was responsible for that. He sipped again, glad of the consoling euphoria its fragrance brought.

"A . . . a composite intepretation of . . . oh, Oliver, you know I must not answer questions!"

"But—"

"No—drink your tea and forget what it was you saw. Think of other things. Here, we will have music—another kind of music, something gay—"

She reached for the wall beside the window, and as before, Oliver saw the broad framed picture of blue water above the bed ripple and grow pale. Through it another scene began to dawn like shapes rising beneath the surface of the sea.

He had a glimpse of a dark-curtained stage upon which a man in a tight dark tunic and hose moved with a restless, sidelong pace, his hands and face startlingly pale against the black about him. He limped; he had a crooked back and he spoke familiar lines. Oliver had seen John Barrymore once as the Crook-Backed Richard, and it seemed vaguely outrageous to him that any other actor should essay that difficult part. This one he had never seen before, but the man had a fascinatingly smooth manner and his interpretation of the Plantagenet king was quite new and something Shakespeare probably never dreamed of.

"No," Kleph said, "not this. Nothing gloomy." And she put out her hand again. The nameless new Richard faded and there was a swirl of changing pictures and changing voices, all blurred together, before the scene steadied upon a stage-full of dancers in pastel ballet skirts, drifting effortlessly through some complicated pattern of motion. The music that went with it was light and effortless too. The room filled up with the clear, floating melody.

Oliver set down his cup. He felt much surer of himself now, and he thought the euphoriac had done all it could for him. He didn't want to blur again mentally. There were things he meant to learn about. Now. He considered how to begin.

Kleph was watching him. "That Hollia," she said suddenly. "She wants to buy the house?"

Oliver nodded. "She's offering a lot of money. She's going to be awfully disappointed if—" He hesitated. Perhaps, after all, Sue would not be disappointed. He remembered the little silver cube with the enigmatic function and he wondered if he should mention it to Kleph. But the euphoriac had not reached that level of his brain, and he remembered his duty to Sue and was silent.

Kleph shook her head, her eyes upon his warm with—was it sympathy?

"Believe me," she said, "you will not find that—important—after all. I promise you, Oliver."

He stared at her. "I wish you'd explain."

Kleph laughed on a note more sorrowful than amused. But it occurred to Oliver suddenly that there was no longer condescension in her voice. Imperceptibly that air of delicate amusement had vanished from her manner toward him. The cool detachment that still marked Omerie's attitude, and Klia's, was not in Kleph's any more. It was a subtlety he did not think she could assume. It had to come spontaneously or not at all. And for no reason he was willing to examine, it became suddenly very important to Oliver that Kleph should not condescend to him, that she should feel toward him as he felt toward her. He would not think of it.

He looked down at his cup, rose-quartz, exhaling a thin plume of steam from its crescent-slit opening. This time, he thought, maybe he could make the tea work for him. For he remembered how it loosened the tongue, and there was a great deal he needed to know. The idea that had come to him on the porch in the instant of silent rivalry between Kleph and Sue seemed now too fantastic to entertain. But some answer there must be.

Kleph herself gave him the opening.

"I must not take too much euphoriac this afternoon," she

said, smiling at him over her pink cup. "It will make me drowsy, and we are going out this evening with friends."

"More friends?" Oliver asked. "From your country?"

Kleph nodded. "Very dear friends we have expected all this week."

"I wish you'd tell me," Oliver said bluntly, "where it is you come from. It isn't from here. Your culture is too different from ours—even your names—" He broke off as Kleph shook her head.

"I wish I could tell you. But that is against all the rules. It is even against the rules for me to be here talking to you now."

"What rules?"

She made a helpless gesture. "You must not ask me, Oliver." She leaned back on the chaise longue that adjusted itself luxuriously to the motion, and smiled very sweetly at him. "We must not talk about things like that. Forget it, listen to the music, enjoy yourself if you can—" She closed her eyes and laid her head back against the cushions. Oliver saw the round tanned throat swell as she began to hum a tune. Eyes still closed, she sang again the words she had sung upon the stairs. *"Come hider, love, to me—"*

A memory clicked over suddenly in Oliver's mind. He had never heard the queer, lagging tune before, but he thought he knew the words. He remembered what Hollia's husband had said when he heard that line of song, and he leaned forward. She would not answer a direct question, but perhaps—

"Was the weather this warm in Canterbury?" he asked, and held his breath. Kleph hummed another line of the song and shook her head, eyes still closed.

"It was autumn there," she said. "But bright, wonderfully bright. Even their clothing, you know . . . everyone was singing that new song, and I can't get it out of my head." She sang another line, and the words were almost unintelligible—English, yet not an English Oliver could understand.

He stood up. "Wait," he said. "I want to find something. Back in a minute."

She opened her eyes and smiled mistily at him, still humming. He went downstairs as fast as he could—the stairway swayed a little, though his head was nearly clear now—and into the library. The book he wanted was old and battered, interlined with the penciled notes of his college days. He did not remember very clearly where the passage he wanted was, but he thumbed fast through the columns and by sheer luck found it within a few minutes. Then he went back upstairs, feeling strange emptiness in his stomach because of what he almost believed now.

"Kleph," he said firmly, "I know that song. I know the year it was new."

Her lids rose slowly; she looked at him through a mist of euphoriac. He was not sure she had understood. For a long moment she held him with her gaze. Then she put out one downy-sleeved arm and spread her tanned fingers toward him. She laughed deep in her throat.

"Come hider, love, to me," she said.

He crossed the room slowly, took her hand. The fingers closed warmly about his. She pulled him down so that he had to kneel beside her. Her other arm lifted. Again she laughed, very softly, and closed her eyes, lifting her face to his.

The kiss was warm and long. He caught something of her own euphoria from the fragrance of the tea breathed into his face. And he was startled at the end of the kiss, when the clasp of her arms loosened about his neck, to feel the sudden rush of her breath against his cheek. There were tears on her face, and the sound she made was a sob.

He held her off and looked down in amazement. She sobbed once more, caught a deep breath, and said, "Oh, Oliver, Oliver—" Then she shook her head and pulled free, turning away to hide her face. "I . . . I am sorry," she said unevenly. "Please forgive me. It does not matter . . . I *know* it does not matter . . . but—"

"What's wrong? What doesn't matter?"

"Nothing. Nothing . . . please forget it. Nothing at all." She got a handkerchief from the table and blew her nose, smiling at him with an effect of radiance through the tears.

Suddenly he was very angry. He had heard enough evasions and mystifying half-truths. He said roughly, "Do you think I'm crazy? I know enough now to—"

"Oliver, please!" She held up her own cup, steaming fragrantly. "Please, no more questions. Here, euphoria is what you need, Oliver. Euphoria, not answers."

"What year was it when you heard that song in Canterbury?" he demanded, pushing the cup aside.

She blinked at him, tears bright on her lashes. "Why . . . what year do you think?"

"I know," Oliver told her grimly. "I know the year that song was popular. I know you just came from Canterbury—Hollia's husband said so. It's May now, but it was autumn in

Canterbury, and you just came from there, so lately the song you heard is still running through your head. Chaucer's Pardoner sang that song sometime around the end of the fourteenth century. Did you see Chaucer, Kleph? What was it like in England that long ago?"

Kleph's eyes fixed his for a silent moment. Then her shoulders drooped and her whole body went limp with resignation beneath the soft blue robe. "I am a fool," she said gently. "It must have been easy to trap me. You really believe—what you say?"

Oliver nodded.

She said in a low voice, "Few people do believe it. That is one of our maxims, when we travel. We are safe from much suspicion because people before The Travel began will not believe."

The emptiness in Oliver's stomach suddenly doubled in volume. For an instant the bottom dropped out of time itself and the universe was unsteady about him. He felt sick. He felt naked and helpless. There was a buzzing in his ears and the room dimmed before him.

He had not really believed—not until this instant. He had expected some rational explanation from her that would tidy all his wild half-thoughts and suspicions into something a man could accept as believable. Not this.

Kleph dabbed at her eyes with the pale-blue handkerchief and smiled tremulously.

"I know," she said. "It must be a terrible thing to accept. To have all your concepts turned upside down— We know it from childhood, of course, but for you . . . here, Oliver. The euphoriac will make it easier."

He took the cup, the faint stain of her lip rouge still on the crescent opening. He drank, feeling the dizzy sweetness spiral through his head, and his brain turned a little in his skull as the volatile fragrance took effect. With that turning, focus shifted and all his values with it.

He began to feel better. The flesh settled on his bones again, and the warm clothing of temporal assurance settled upon his flesh, and he was no longer naked and reeling in the vortex of unstable time.

"The story is very simple, really," Kleph said. "We—travel. Our own time is not terribly far ahead of yours. No, I must not say how far. But we still remember your songs and poets and some of your great actors. We are a people of much leisure, and we cultivate the art of enjoying ourselves.

"This is a tour we are making—a tour of a year's seasons. Vintage seasons. That autumn in Canterbury was the most magnificent autumn our researchers could discover anywhere. We rode in a pilgrimage to the shrine—it was a wonderful experience, though the clothing was a little hard to manage.

"Now this month of May is almost over—the loveliest May in recorded times. A perfect May in a wonderful period. You have no way of knowing what a good, gay period you live in, Oliver. The very feeling in the air of the cities—that wonderful national confidence and happiness—everything going as smoothly as a dream. There were other Mays with fine weather, but each of them had a war or a famine, or something else wrong." She hesitated, grimaced and went on rapidly. "In a few days we are to meet at a coronation in Rome," she said. "I think the year will be 800—Christmastime. We—"

"But why," Oliver interrupted, "did you insist on this house? Why do the others want to get it away from you?"

Kleph stared at him. He saw the tears rising again in small bright crescents that gathered above her lower lids. He saw the look of obstinacy that came upon her soft, tanned face. She shook her head.

"You must not ask me that." She held out the steaming cup. "Here, drink and forget what I have said. I can tell you no more. No more at all."

When he woke, for a little while he had no idea where he was. He did not remember leaving Kleph or coming to his own room. He didn't care, just then. For he woke to a sense of overwhelming terror.

The dark was full of it. His brain rocked on waves of fear and pain. He lay motionless, too frightened to stir, some atavistic memory warning him to lie quiet until he knew from which direction the danger threatened. Reasonless panic broke over him in a tidal flow; his head ached with its violence and the dark throbbed to the same rhythms.

A knock sounded at the door. Omerie's deep voice said, "Wilson! Wilson, are you awake?"

Oliver tried twice before he had breath to answer. "Y-yes—what is it?"

The knob rattled. Omerie's dim figure groped for the light switch and the room sprang into visibility. Omerie's face was drawn with strain, and he held one hand to his head as if it ached in rhythm with Oliver's.

It was in that moment, before Omerie spoke again, that Oliver remembered Hollia's warning. "Move out, young man—move out before tonight." Wildly he wondered what threatened them all in this dark house that throbbed with the rhythms of pure terror.

Omerie in an angry voice answered the unspoken question.

"Someone has planted a subsonic in the house, Wilson. Kleph thinks you may know where it is."

"S-subsonic?"

"Call it a gadget," Omerie interrupted impatiently. "Probably a small metal box that—"

Oliver said, "Oh," in a tone that must have told Omerie everything.

"Where is it?" he demanded. "Quick. Let's get this over."

"I d-don't know." With an effort Oliver controlled the chattering of his teeth. "Y-you mean all this—all this is just from the little box?"

"Of course. Now tell me how to find it before we all go crazy."

Oliver got shakily out of bed, groping for his robe with nerveless hands. "I s-suppose she hid it somewhere downstairs," he said. "S-she wasn't gone long."

Omerie got the story out of him in a few brief questions. He clicked his teeth in exasperation when Oliver had finished it.

"That stupid Hollia—"

"Omerie!" Kleph's plaintive voice wailed from the hall. "Please hurry, Omerie! This is too much to stand! Oh, Omerie, please!"

Oliver stood up abruptly. Then a redoubled wave of the inexplicable pain seemed to explode in his skull at the motion, and he clutched the bedpost and reeled.

"Go find the thing yourself," he heard himself saying dizzily. "I can't even walk—"

Omerie's own temper was drawn wire-tight by the pressure in the room. He seized Oliver's shoulder and shook him, saying in a tight voice, "You let it in—now help us get it out, or—"

"It's a gadget out of your world, not mine!" Oliver said furiously.

And then it seemed to him there was a sudden coldness and silence in the room. Even the pain and the senseless terror paused for a moment. Omerie's pale, cold eyes fixed upon Oliver a stare so chill he could almost feel the ice in it.

"What do you know about our—world?" Omerie demanded.

Oliver did not speak a word. He did not need to; his face must have betrayed what he knew. He was beyond concealment in the stress of this nighttime terror he still could not understand.

Omerie bared his white teeth and said three perfectly unintelligible words. Then he stepped to the door and snapped, "Kleph!"

Oliver could see the two women huddled together in the hall, shaking violently with involuntary waves of that strange, synthetic terror. Klia, in a luminous green gown, was rigid with control, but Kleph made no effort whatever at repression. Her downy robe had turned soft gold tonight; she shivered in it and the tears ran down her face unchecked.

"Kleph," Omerie said in a dangerous voice, "you were euphoric again yesterday?"

Kleph darted a scared glance at Oliver and nodded guiltily.

"You talked too much." It was a complete indictment in one sentence. "You know the rules, Kleph. You will not be allowed to travel again if anyone reports this to the authorities."

Kleph's lovely creamy face creased suddenly into impenitent dimples.

"I know it was wrong. I am very sorry—but you will not stop me if Cenbe says no."

Klia flung out her arms in a gesture of helpless anger. Omerie shrugged. "In this case, as it happens, no great harm is done," he said, giving Oliver an unfathomable glance. "But it might have been serious. Next time perhaps it will be. I must have a talk with Cenbe."

"We must find the subsonic first of all," Klia reminded them, shivering. "If Kleph is afraid to help, she can go out for awhile. I confess I am very sick of Kleph's company just now."

"We could give up the house!" Kleph cried wildly. "Let Hollia have it! How can you stand this long enough to hunt—"

"Give up the house?" Klia echoed. "You must be mad! With all our invitations out?"

"There will be no need for that," Omerie said. "We can find it if we all hunt. You feel able to help?" He looked at Oliver.

With an effort Oliver controlled his own senseless panic as

the waves of it swept through the room. "Yes," he said. "But what about me? What are you going to do?"

"That should be obvious," Omerie said, his pale eyes in the dark face regarding Oliver impassively. "Keep you in the house until we go. We can certainly do no less. You understand that. And there is no reason for us to do more, as it happens. Silence is all we need to impose. It is all we promised when we signed our travel papers."

"But—" Oliver groped for the fallacy in that reasoning. It was no use. He could not think clearly. Panic surged insanely through his mind from the very air around him. "All right," he said. "Let's hunt."

It was dawn before they found the box, tucked inside the ripped seam of a sofa cushion. Omerie took it upstairs without a word. Five minutes later the pressure in the air abruptly dropped and peace fell blissfully upon the house.

"They will try again," Omerie said to Oliver at the door of the back bedroom. "We must watch for that. As for you, I must see that you remain in the house until Friday. For your own comfort, I advise you to let me know if Hollia offers any further tricks. I confess I am not quite sure how to enforce your staying indoors. I could use methods that would make you very uncomfortable. I would prefer to accept your word on it."

Oliver hesitated. The relaxing of pressure upon his brain had left him exhausted and stupid, and he was not at all sure what to say.

Omerie went on after a moment. "It was partly our fault for not insuring that we have the house to ourselves," he said. "Living here with us, you could scarcely help suspecting. Shall we say that in return for your promise, I reimburse you in part for losing the sale price on this house?"

Oliver thought that over. It would pacify Sue a little. And it meant only two days indoors. Besides, what good would escaping do? What could he say to outsiders that would not lead him straight to a padded cell?

"All right," he said wearily. "I promise."

By Friday morning there was still no sign from Hollia. Sue telephoned at noon. Oliver knew the crackle of her voice over the wire when Kleph took the call. Even the crackle sounded hysterical; Sue saw her bargain slipping hopelessly through her grasping little fingers.

Kleph's voice was soothing. "I am sorry," she said many

times, in the intervals when the voice paused. "I am truly sorry. Believe me, you will find it does not matter. I know . . . I am sorry—"

She turned from the phone at last. "The girl says Hollia has given up," she told the others.

"Not Hollia," Klia said firmly.

Omerie shrugged. "We have very little time left. If she intends anything more, it will be tonight. We must watch for it."

"Oh, not tonight!" Kleph's voice was horrified. "Not even Hollia would do that!"

"Hollia, my dear, in her own way is quite as unscrupulous as you are," Omerie told her with a smile.

"But—would she spoil things for us just because she can't be here?"

"What do you think?" Klia demanded.

Oliver ceased to listen. There was no making sense out of their talk, but he knew that by tonight whatever the secret was must surely come into the open at last. He was willing to wait and see.

For two days excitement had been building up in the house and the three who shared it with him. Even the servants felt it and were nervous and unsure of themselves. Oliver had given up asking questions—it only embarrassed his tenants—and watched.

All the chairs in the house were collected in the three front bedrooms. The furniture was rearranged to make room for them, and dozens of covered cups had been set out on trays. Oliver recognized Kleph's rose-quartz set among the rest. No steam rose from the thin crescent-openings, but the cups were full. Oliver lifted one and felt a heavy liquid move within it, like something half-solid, sluggishly.

Guests were obviously expected, but the regular dinner hour of nine came and went, and no one had yet arrived. Dinner was finished; the servants went home. The Sanciscos went to their rooms to dress, amid a feeling of mounting tension.

Oliver stepped out on the porch after dinner, trying in vain to guess what it was that had wrought such a pitch of expectancy in the house. There was a quarter moon swimming in haze on the horizon, but the stars which had made every night of May this far a dazzling translucency, were very dim tonight. Clouds had begun to gather at sundown, and the undimmed weather of the whole month seemed ready to break at last.

Behind Oliver the door opened a little, and closed. He caught Kleph's fragrance before he turned, and a faint whiff of the fragrance of the euphoriac she was much too fond of drinking. She came to his side and slipped a hand into his, looking up into his face in the darkness.

"Oliver," she said very softly. "Promise me one thing. Promise me not to leave the house tonight."

"I've already promised that," he said a little irritably.

"I know. But tonight—I have a particular reason for wanting you indoors tonight." She leaned her head against his shoulder for a moment, and despite himself his irritation softened. He had not seen Kleph alone since that last night of her revelations; he supposed he never would be alone with her again for more than a few minutes at a time. But he knew he would not forget those two bewildering evenings. He knew too, now, that she was very weak and foolish—but she was still Kleph and he had held her in his arms, and was not likely ever to forget it.

"You might be—hurt—if you went out tonight," she was saying in a muffled voice. "I know it will not matter, in the end, but—remember you promised, Oliver."

She was gone again, and the door had closed behind her, before he could voice the futile questions in his mind.

The guests began to arrive just before midnight. From the head of the stairs Oliver saw them coming in by twos and threes, and was astonished at how many of these people from the future must have gathered here in the past weeks. He could see quite clearly now how they differed from the norm of his own period. Their physical elegance was what one noticed first—perfect grooming, meticulous manners, meticulously controlled voices. But because they were all idle, all in a way, sensation-hunters, there was a certain shrillness underlying their voices, especially when heard all together. Petulance and self-indulgence showed beneath the good manners. And tonight, an all-pervasive excitement.

By one o'clock everyone had gathered in the front rooms. The teacups had begun to steam, apparently of themselves, around midnight, and the house was full of the faint, thin fragrance that induced a sort of euphoria all through the rooms, breathed in with the perfume of the tea.

It made Oliver feel light and drowsy. He was determined to sit up as long as the others did, but he must have dozed off in his own room, by the window, an unopened book in his lap.

For when it happened he was not sure for a few minutes whether or not it was a dream.

The vast, incredible crash was louder than sound. He felt the whole house shake under him, felt rather than heard the timbers grind upon one another like broken bones, while he was still in the borderland of sleep. When he woke fully he was on the floor among the shattered fragments of the window.

How long or short a time he had lain there he did not know. The world was still stunned with that tremendous noise, or his ears still deaf from it, for there was no sound anywhere.

He was halfway down the hall toward the front rooms when sound began to return from outside. It was a low, indescribable rumble at first, prickled with countless tiny distant screams. Oliver's eardrums ached from the terrible impact of the vast unheard noise, but the numbness was wearing off and he heard before he saw it the first voices of the stricken city.

The door to Kleph's room resisted him for a moment. The house had settled a little from the violence of the—the explosion?—and the frame was out of line. When he got the door open he could only stand blinking stupidly into the darkness within. All the lights were out, but there was a breathless sort of whispering going on in many voices.

The chairs were drawn around the broad front windows so that everyone could see out; the air swam with the fragrance of euphoria. There was light enough here from outside for Oliver to see that a few onlookers still had their hands to their ears, but all were craning eagerly forward to see.

Through a dreamlike haze Oliver saw the city spread out with impossible distinctness below the window. He knew quite well that a row of houses across the street blocked the view—yet he was looking over the city now, and he could see it in a limitless panorama from here to the horizon. The houses between had vanished.

On the far skyline fire was already a solid mass, painting the low clouds crimson. That sulphurous light reflecting back from the sky upon the city made clear the rows upon rows of flattened houses with flame beginning to lick up among them, and farther out the formless rubble of what had been houses a few minutes ago and was now nothing at all.

The city had begun to be vocal. The noise of the flames rose loudest, but you could hear a rumble of human voices like the beat of surf a long way off, and the staccato noises of screaming made a sort of pattern that came and went continuously through the web of sound. Threading it in undulating waves the shrieks of sirens knit the web together into a terrible symphony that had, in its way, a strange inhuman beauty.

Briefly through Oliver's stunned incredulity went the memory of that other symphony Kleph had played here one day, another catastrophe retold in terms of music and moving shapes.

He said hoarsely, "Kleph—"

The tableau by the window broke. Every head turned, and Oliver saw the faces of strangers staring at him, some few in embarrassment avoiding his eyes, but most seeking them out with that avid, inhuman curiosity which is common to a type in all crowds at accident scenes. But these people were here by design, audience at a vast disaster timed almost for their coming.

Kleph got up unsteadily, her velvet dinner gown tripping her as she rose. She set down a cup and swayed a little as she came toward the door, saying, "Oliver . . . Oliver—" in a sweet, uncertain voice. She was drunk, he saw, and wrought up by the catastrophe to a pitch of stimulation in which she was not very sure what she was doing.

Oliver heard himself saying in a thin voice not his own, "W-what was it, Kleph? What happened? What—" But *happened* seemed so inadequate a word for the incredible panorama below that he had to choke back hysterical laughter upon the struggling questions, and broke off entirely, trying to control the shaking that had seized his body.

Kleph made an unsteady stoop and seized a steaming cup. She came to him, swaying, holding it out—her panacea for all ills.

"Here, drink it, Oliver—we are all quite safe here, quite safe." She thrust the cup to his lips and he gulped automatically, grateful for the fumes that began their slow, coiling surcease in his brain with the first swallow.

"It was a meteor," Kleph was saying. "Quite a small meteor, really. We are perfectly safe here. This house was never touched."

Out of some cell of the unconscious Oliver heard himself saying incoherently, "Suc? Is Sue—" he could not finish.

Kleph thrust the cup at him again. "I think she may be

safe—for a while. Please, Oliver—forget about all that and drink."

"But you *knew!*" Realization of that came belatedly to his stunned brain. "You could have given warning, or—"

"How could we change the past?" Kleph asked. "We knew—but could we stop the meteor? Or warn the city? Before we come we must give our word never to interfere—"

Their voices had risen imperceptibly to the audible above the rising volume of sound from below. The city was roaring now, with flames and cries and the crash of falling buildings. Light in the room turned lurid and pulsed upon the walls and ceiling in red light and redder dark.

Downstairs a door slammed. Someone laughed. It was high, hoarse, angry laughter. Then from the crowd in the room someone gasped and there was a chorus of dismayed cries. Oliver tried to focus upon the window and the terrible panorama beyond, and found he could not.

It took several seconds of determined blinking to prove that more than his own vision was at fault. Kleph whimpered softly and moved against him. His arms closed about her automatically, and he was grateful for the warm, solid flesh against him. This much at least he could touch and be sure of, though everything else that was happening might be a dream. Her perfume and the heady perfume of the tea rose together in his head, and for an instant, holding her in this embrace that must certainly be the last time he ever held her, he did not care that something had gone terribly wrong with the very air of the room.

It was blindness—not continuous, but a series of swift, widening ripples between which he could catch glimpses of the other faces in the room, strained and astonished in the flickering light from the city.

The ripples came faster. There was only a blink of sight between them now, and the blinks grew briefer and briefer, the intervals of darkness more broad.

From downstairs the laughter rose again up the stairwell. Oliver thought he knew the voice. He opened his mouth to speak, but a door nearby slammed open before he could find his tongue, and Omerie shouted down the stairs.

"Hollia?" he roared above the roaring of the city. "Hollia, is that you?"

She laughed again, triumphantly. "I warned you!" her

hoarse, harsh voice called. "Now come out in the street with the rest of us if you want to see any more!"

"Hollia!" Omerie shouted desperately. "Stop this or—"

The laughter was derisive. "What will you do, Omerie? This time I hid it too well—come down in the street if you want to watch the rest."

There was angry silence in the house. Oliver could feel Kleph's quick, excited breathing light upon his cheek, feel the soft motions of her body in his arms. He tried consciously to make the moment last, stretch it out to infinity. Everything had happened too swiftly to impress very clearly on his mind anything except what he could touch and hold. He held her in an embrace made consciously light, though he wanted to clasp her in a tight, despairing grip, because he was sure this was the last embrace they would ever share.

The eye-straining blinks of light and blindness went on. From far away below the roar of the burning city rolled on, threaded together by the long, looped cadences of the sirens that linked all sounds into one.

Then in the bewildering dark another voice sounded from the hall downstairs. A man's voice, very deep, very melodious, saying:

"What is this? What are you doing here? Hollia—is that you?"

Oliver felt Kleph stiffen in his arms. She caught her breath, but she said nothing in the instant while heavy feet began to mount the stairs, coming up with a solid, confident tread that shook the old house to each step.

Then Kleph thrust herself hard out of Oliver's arms. He heard her high, sweet, excited voice crying, "Cenbe! Cenbe!" and she ran to meet the newcomer through the waves of dark and light that swept the shaken house.

Oliver staggered a little and felt a chair seat catching the back of his legs. He sank into it and lifted to his lips the cup he still held. Its steam was warm and moist in his face, though he could scarcely make out the shape of the rim.

He lifted it with both hands and drank.

When he opened his eyes it was quite dark in the room. Also it was silent except for a thin, melodious humming almost below the threshold of sound. Oliver struggled with the memory of a monstrous nightmare. He put it resolutely out of his mind and sat up, feeling an unfamiliar bed creak and sway under him.

This was Kleph's room. But no—Kleph's no longer. Her

shining hangings were gone from the walls, her white resilient rug, her pictures. The room looked as it had looked before she came, except for one thing.

In the far corner was a table—a block of translucent stuff—out of which light poured softly. A man sat on a low stool before it, leaning forward, his heavy shoulders outlined against the glow. He wore earphones and he was making quick, erratic notes upon a pad on his knee, swaying a little as if to the tune of unheard music.

The curtains were drawn, but from beyond them came a distant, muffled roaring that Oliver remembered from his nightmare. He put a hand to his face, aware of a feverish warmth and a dipping of the room before his eyes. His head ached, and there was a deep malaise in every limb and nerve.

As the bed creaked, the man in the corner turned, sliding the earphones down like a collar. He had a strong, sensitive face above a dark beard, trimmed short. Oliver had never seen him before, but he had that air Oliver knew so well by now, of remoteness which was the knowledge of time itself lying like a gulf between them.

When he spoke his deep voice was impersonally kind.

"You had too much euphoriac, Wilson," he said, aloofly sympathetic. "You slept a long while."

"How long?" Oliver's throat felt sticky when he spoke.

The man did not answer. Oliver shook his head experimentally. He said, "I thought Kleph said you don't get hangovers from—" Then another thought interrupted the first, and he said quickly, "Where is Kleph?" He looked confusedly toward the door.

"They should be in Rome by now. Watching Charlemagne's coronation at St. Peter's on Christmas Day a thousand years from here."

That was not a thought Oliver could grasp clearly. His aching brain sheered away from it; he found thinking at all was strangely difficult. Staring at the man, he traced an idea painfully to its conclusion.

"So they've gone on—but you stayed behind. Why? You . . . you're Cenbe? I heard your—symphonia, Kleph called it."

"You heard part of it. I have not finished yet. I needed—this." Cenbe inclined his head toward the curtains beyond which the subdued roaring still went on.

"You needed—the meteor?" The knowledge worked painfully through his dulled brain until it seemed to strike some area still untouched by the aching, an area still alive to implication, "The *meteor?* But—"

There was a power implicit in Cenbe's raised hand that seemed to push Oliver down upon the bed again. Cenbe said patiently, "The worst of it is past now, for a while. Forget it if you can. That was days ago. I said you were asleep for some time. I let you rest. I knew this house would be safe—from the fire at least."

"Then—something more's to come?" Oliver only mumbled his question. He was not sure he wanted an answer. He had been curious so long, and now that knowledge lay almost within reach, something about his brain seemed to refuse to listen. Perhaps this weariness, this feverish, dizzy feeling would pass as the effect of the euphoriac wore off.

Cenbe's voice ran on smoothly, soothingly, almost as if Cenbe too did not want him to think. It was easiest to lie here and listen.

"I am a composer," Cenbe was saying. "I happen to be interested in interpreting certain forms of disaster into my own terms. That is why I stayed on. The others were dilettantes. They came for the May weather and the spectacle. The aftermath—well why should they wait for that? As for myself—I suppose I am a connoisseur. I find the aftermath rather fascinating. And I need it. I need to study it at first hand, for my own purposes."

His eyes dwelt upon Oliver for an instant very keenly, like a physician's eyes, impersonal and observant. Absently he reached for his stylus and the note pad. And as he moved, Oliver saw a familiar mark on the underside of the thick, tanned wrist.

"Kleph had that scar, too," he heard himself whisper. "And the others."

Cenbe nodded. "Inoculation. It was necessary, under the circumstances. We did not want disease to spread in our own time-world."

"Disease?"

Cenbe shrugged. "You would not recognize the name."

"But, if you can inoculate against disease—" Oliver thrust himself up on an aching arm. He had a half-grasp upon a thought now which he did not want to let go. Effort seemed to make the ideas come more clearly through his mounting confusion. With enormous effort he went on.

"I'm getting it now," he said. "Wait. I've been trying to work this out. You can change history? You can! I know you can. Kleph said she had to promise not to interfere. You all had to promise. Does that mean you really could change your own past—our time?"

Cenbe laid down his pad again. He looked at Oliver thoughtfully, a dark, intent look under heavy brows. "Yes," he said. "Yes, the past can be changed, but not easily. And it changes the future, too, necessarily. The lines of probability are switched into new patterns—but it is extremely difficult, and it has never been allowed. The physiotemporal course tends to slide back to its norm, always. That is why it is so hard to force any alteration." He shrugged. "A theoretical science. We do not change history, Wilson. If we changed our past, our present would be altered, too. And our time-world is entirely to our liking. There may be a few malcontents there, but they are not allowed the privilege of temporal travel."

Oliver spoke louder against the roaring from beyond the windows. "But you've got the power! You could alter history, if you wanted to—wipe out all the pain and suffering and tragedy—"

"All of that passed away long ago," Cenbe said.

"Not—*now!* Not—*this!*"

Cenbe looked at him enigmatically for awhile. Then—"This, too," he said.

And suddenly Oliver realized from across what distances Cenbe was watching him. A vast distance, as time is measured. Cenbe was a composer and a genius, and necessarily strongly emphatic, but his psychic locus was very far away in time. The dying city outside, the whole world of *now* was not quite real to Cenbe, falling short of reality because of that basic variance in time. It was merely one of the building blocks that had gone to support the edifice on which Cenbe's culture stood in a misty, unknown, terrible future.

It seemed terrible to Oliver now. Even Kleph—all of them had been touched with a pettiness, the faculty that had enabled Hollia to concentrate on her malicious, small schemes to acquire a ringside seat while the meteor thundered in toward Earth's atmosphere. They were all dilettantes, Kleph and Omerie and the others. They toured time, but only as onlookers. Were they bored—sated—with their normal existence?

Not sated enough to wish change, basically. Their own time-world was a fulfilled womb, a perfection made manifest for their needs. They dared not change the past—they could not risk flawing their own present.

Revulsion shook him. Remembering the touch of Kleph's lips, he felt a sour sickness on his tongue. Alluring she had been; he knew that too well. But the aftermath—

There was something wrong about this race from the future. He had felt it dimly at first, before Kleph's nearness had drowned caution and buffered his sensibilities. Time traveling purely as an escape mechanism seemed almost blasphemous. A race with such power—

Kleph—leaving him for the barbaric, splendid coronation at Rome a thousand years ago—*how had she seen him?* Not as a living, breathing man. He knew that, very certainly. Kleph's race were spectators.

But he read more than casual interest in Cenbe's eyes now. There was an avidity there, a bright, fascinated probing. The man had replaced his earphones—he was different from the others. He was a connoisseur. After the vintage season came the aftermath—and Cenbe.

Cenbe watched and waited, light flickering softly in the translucent block before him, his fingers poised over the note pad. The ultimate connoisseur waited to savor the rarities that no non-gourmet could appreciate.

Those thin, distant rhythms of sound that was almost music began to be audible again above the noises of the distant fire. Listening, remembering, Oliver could very nearly catch the pattern of the symphonia as he had heard it, all intermingled with the flash of changing faces and the rank upon rank of the dying—

He lay back on the bed letting the room swirl away into the darkness behind his closed and aching lids. The ache was implicit in every cell of his body, almost a second ego taking possession and driving him out of himself, a strong, sure ego taking over as he himself let go.

Why, he wondered dully, should Kleph have lied? She had said there was no aftermath to the drink she had given him. No aftermath—and yet this painful possession was strong enough to edge him out of his own body.

Kleph had not lied. It was no aftermath to drink. He knew that—but the knowledge no longer touched his brain or his body. He lay still, giving them up to the power of the illness which was aftermath to something far stronger than the strongest drink. The illness that had no name—yet.

Cenbe's new symphonia was a crowning triumph. It had its premiere from Antares Hall, and the applause was an ovation. History itself, of course, was the artist—opening with the meteor that forecast the great plagues of the fourteenth century and closing with the climax Cenbe had caught on the threshold of modern times. But only Cenbe could have interpreted it with such subtle power.

Critics spoke of the masterly way in which he had chosen the face of the Stuart king as a recurrent motif against the montage of emotion and sound and movement. But there were other faces, fading through the great sweep of the composition, which helped to build up to the tremendous climax. One face in particular, one moment that the audience absorbed greedily. A moment in which one man's face loomed huge in the screen, every feature clear. Cenbe had never caught an emotional crisis so effectively, the critics agreed. You could almost read the man's eyes.

After Cenbe had left, he lay motionless for a long while. He was thinking feverishly—

I've got to find some way to tell people. If I'd known in advance, maybe something could have been done. We'd have forced them to tell us how to change the probabilities. We could have evacuated the city.

If I could leave a message—

Maybe not for today's people. But later. They visit all through time. If they could be recognized and caught somewhere, sometime, and made to change destiny—

It wasn't easy to stand up. The room kept tilting. But he managed it. He found pencil and paper and through the swaying of the shadows he wrote down what he could. Enough. Enough to warn, enough to save.

He put the sheets on the table, in plain sight, and weighted them down before he stumbled back to bed through closing darkness.

The house was dynamited six days later, part of the futile attempt to halt the relentless spread of the Blue Death.

EVIDENCE

by Isaac Asimov

ASTOUNDING SCIENCE FICTION
September

Of the nine stories collected in I, Robot *(1950), I suppose "Evidence" is the best. It was the one story I wrote while I was in the army. I began it in Virginia and finished it in Hawaii. I mailed it from Hawaii with directions to John Campbell to send the check (if there was one) to my wife—which he did. What really astonished me, however, was that when the story appeared in the September, 1946 issue of* Astounding *I had actually been ushered out of the army on a research discharge, so that I had the pleasure of rereading a story written while I was hemmed in by army life at a time when I was revelling in my new-found freedom as a civilian. Oddly enough, there is nothing in the story that indicates the circumstance of its writing. But, then, why "oddly"? The whole purpose of writing the story was to help get my mind off a situation which alternately bored and frustrated me—so why put that situation into the story.—I.A.*

Francis Quinn was a politician of the new school. That, of course, is a meaningless expression, as are all expressions of the sort. Most of the "new schools" we have were duplicated in the social life of ancient Greece, and perhaps, if we knew more about it, in the social life of ancient Sumeria and in the lake dwellings of prehistoric Switzerland as well.

But, to get out from under what promises to be a dull and complicated beginning, it might be best to state hastily that Quinn neither ran for office nor canvassed for votes, made no speeches and stuffed no ballot boxes. Any more than Napoleon pulled a trigger at Austerlitz.

And since politics makes strange bedfellows, Alfred Lanning sat at the other side of the desk with his ferocious white eyebrows bent far forward over eyes in which chronic impatience had sharpened to acuity. He was not pleased.

The fact, if known to Quinn, would have annoyed him not the least. His voice was friendly, perhaps professionally so.

"I assume you know Stephen Byerley, Dr. Lanning."

"I have heard of him. So have many people."

"Yes, so have I. Perhaps you intend voting for him at the next election."

"I couldn't say." There was an unmistakable trace of acidity here. "I have not followed the political currents, so I'm not aware that he is running for office."

"He may be our next mayor. Of course, he is only a lawyer now, but great oaks—"

"Yes," interrupted Lanning, "I have heard the phrase before. But I wonder if we can get to the business at hand."

"We *are* at the business at hand, Dr. Lanning." Quinn's tone was very gentle, "It is to my interest to keep Mr. Byerley a district attorney at the very most, and it is to your interest to help me do so."

"To *my* interest? Come!" Lanning's eyebrows hunched low.

"Well, say then to the interest of the U. S. Robots and Mechanical Men Corporation. I come to you as Director-Emeritus of Research, because I know that your connection to them is that of, shall we say, 'elder statesman.' You are listened to with respect and yet your connection with them is no longer so tight but that you cannot possess considerable freedom of action; even if the action is somewhat unorthodox."

Dr. Lanning was silent a moment, chewing the end of his thoughts. He said more softly, "I don't follow you at all, Mr. Quinn."

"I not surprised, Dr. Lanning. But it's all rather simple. Do you mind?" Quinn lit a slender cigarette with a lighter of tasteful simplicity and his big-boned face settled into an expression of quiet amusement. "We have spoken of Mr. Byerley—a strange and colorful character. He was unknown three years ago. He is very well known now. He is a man of force and ability, and certainly the most capable and intelligent prosecutor I have ever known. Unfortunately he is not a friend of mine—"

"I understand," said Lanning mechanically. He stared at his fingernails.

"I have had occasion," continued Quinn evenly, "in the past year to investigate Mr. Byerley—quite exhaustively. It is always useful, you see, to subject the past life of reform politicians to rather inquisitive research. If you knew how often it helped—" He paused to smile humorlessly at the glowing tip of his cigarette. "But Mr. Byerley's past is unremarkable. A quiet life in a small town, a college education, a wife who died young, an auto accident with a slow recovery, law school, coming to the metropolis, an attorney."

Francis Quinn shook his head slowly, then added, "But his present life. Ah, that is remarkable. Our district attorney never eats!"

Lanning's head snapped up, old eyes surprisingly sharp, "Pardon me?"

"Our district attorney never eats." The repetition thumped by syllables. "I'll modify that slightly. He has never been seen to eat or drink. Never! Do you understand the significance of the word? Not rarely, but never!"

"I find that quite incredible. Can you trust your investigators?"

"I can trust my investigators, and I don't find it incredible at all. Further, our district attorney has never been seen to drink—in the aqueous sense as well as the alcoholic—nor to sleep. There are other factors, but I should think I have made my point."

Lanning leaned back in his seat, and there was the rapt silence of challenge and response between them, and then the old roboticist shook his head. "No. There is only one thing you can be trying to imply, if I couple your statements with the fact that you present them to me, and that is impossible."

"But the man is quite inhuman, Dr. Lanning."

"If you told me he were Satan in masquerade, there would be a faint chance that I might believe you."

"I tell you he is a robot, Dr. Lanning."

"I tell you it is as impossible a conception as I have ever heard, Mr. Quinn."

Again the combative silence.

"Nevertheless," and Quinn stubbed out his cigarette with elaborate care, "you will have to investigate this impossibility with all the resources of the Corporation."

"I'm sure that I could undertake no such thing, Mr. Quinn. You don't seriously suggest that the Corporation take part in local politics."

"You have no choice. Supposing I were to make my facts public without proof. The evidence is circumstantial enough."

"Suit yourself in that respect."

"But it would not suit me. Proof would be much preferable. And it would not suit *you*, for the publicity would be very damaging to your company. You are perfectly well acquainted, I suppose, with the strict rules against the use of robots on inhabited worlds."

"Certainly!"—brusquely.

"You know that the U. S. Robot & Mechanical Men Corporation is the only manufacturer of positronic robots in the Solar System, and if Byerley is a robot, he is a *positronic* robot. You are also aware that all positronic robots are leased, and not sold; that the Corporation remains the owner and manager of each robot, and is therefore responsible for the actions of all."

"It is an easy matter, Mr. Quinn, to prove the Corporation has never manufactured a robot of a humanoid character."

"It can be done? To discuss merely possibilities."

"Yes. It can be done."

"Secretly, I imagine, as well. Without entering it in your books."

"Not the positronic brain, sir. Too many factors are involved in that, and there is the tightest possible government supervision."

"Yes, but robots are worn out, break down, go out of order—and are dismantled."

"And the positronic brains re-used or destroyed."

"Really?" Francis Quinn allowed himself a trace of sarcasm. "And if one were, accidentally, of course, not destroyed—and there happened to be a humanoid structure waiting for a brain?"

"Impossible!"

"You would have to prove that to the government and the public, so why not prove it to me now."

"But what could our purpose be?" demanded Lanning in exasperation. "Where is our motivation? Credit us with a minimum of sense."

"My dear sir, please. The Corporation would be only too glad to have the various Regions permit the use of humanoid positronic robots on inhabited worlds. The profits would be enormous. But the prejudice of the public against such a practice is too great. Suppose you get them used to such robots first—see, we have a skillful lawyer, a good mayor—and he is a robot. Won't you buy our robot butlers?"

"Thoroughly fantastic. An almost humorous descent to the ridiculous."

"I imagine so. Why not prove it? Or would you still rather try to prove it to the public?"

The light in the office was dimming, but it was not yet too dim to obscure the flush of frustration on Alfred Lanning's face. Slowly, the roboticist's finger touched a knob and the wall illuminators glowed to gentle life.

"Well, then," he growled, "let us see."

The face of Stephen Byerley is not an easy one to describe. He was forty by birth certificate and forty by appearance—but it was a healthy well-nourished, good-natured appearance of forty; one that automatically drew the teeth of the bromide about "looking one's age."

This was particularly true when he laughed, and he was laughing now. It came loudly and continuously, died away for a bit, then began again—

And Alfred Lanning's face contracted into a rigidly bitter monument of disapproval. He made a half gesture to the woman who sat beside him, but her thin, bloodless lips merely pursed themselves a trifle.

Byerley gasped himself a stage near normality.

"Really, Dr. Lanning . . . really—I . . . *I* . . . a robot?"

Lanning bit his words off with a snap, "It is no statement of mine, sir. I would be quite satisfied to have you a member of humanity. Since our corporation never manufactured you,

I am quite certain that you are—in a legalistic sense, at any rate. But since the contention that you are a robot has been advanced to us seriously by a man of certain standing—"

"Don't mention his name, if it would knock a chip off your granite block of ethics, but let's pretend it was Frank Quinn, for the sake of argument, and continue."

Lanning drew in a sharp, cutting snort at the interruption, and paused ferociously before continuing with added frigidity, "—by a man of certain standing, with whose identity I am not interested in playing guessing games, I am bound to ask your co-operation in disproving it. The mere fact that such a contention could be advanced and publicized by the means at this man's disposal would be a bad blow to the company I represent—even if the charge were never proven. You understand me?"

"Oh, yes, your position is clear to me. The charge itself is ridiculous. The spot you find yourself in is not. I beg your pardon, if my laughter offended you. It was the first I laughed at, not the second. How can I help you?"

"It could be very simple. You have only to sit down to a meal at a restaurant in the presence of witnesses, have your picture taken, and eat." Lanning sat back in his chair, the worst of the interview over. The woman beside him watched Byerley with an apparently absorbed expression but contributed nothing of her own.

Stephen Byerley met her eyes for an instant, was caught by them, then turned back to the roboticist. For a while his fingers were thoughtful over the bronze paperweight that was the only ornament on his desk.

He said quietly, "I don't think I can oblige you."

He raised his hand, "Now wait, Dr. Lanning. I appreciate the fact that this whole matter is distasteful to you, that you have been forced into it against your will, that you feel you are playing an undignified and even ridiculous part. Still, the matter is even more intimately concerned with myself, so be tolerant.

"First, what makes you think that Quinn—this man of certain standing, you know—wasn't hoodwinking you, in order to get you to do exactly what you are doing?"

"Why it seems scarcely likely that a reputable person would endanger himself in so ridiculous a fashion, if he weren't convinced he was on safe ground."

There was little humor in Byerley's eyes, "You don't know Quinn. He could manage to make safe ground out of a ledge a mountain sheep could not handle. I suppose he showed the particulars of the investigation he claims to have made of me?"

"Enough to convince me that it would be too troublesome to have our corporation attempt to disprove them when you could do so more easily."

"Then you believe him when he says I never eat. You are a scientist, Dr. Lanning. Think of the logic required. I have not been observed to eat, therefore, I never eat Q.E.D. After all!"

"You are using prosecution tactics to confuse what is really a very simple situation."

"On the contrary, I am trying to clarify what you and Quinn between you are making a very complicated one. You see, I don't sleep much, that's true, and I certainly don't sleep in public. I have never cared to eat with others—an idiosyncrasy which is unusual and probably neurotic in character, but which harms no one. Look, Dr. Lanning, let me present you with a supposititious case. Supposing we had a politician who was interested in defeating a reform candidate at any cost and while investigating his private life came across oddities such as I have just mentioned.

"Suppose further that in order to smear the candidate effectively, he comes to your company as the ideal agent. Do you expect him to say to you, 'So-and-so is a robot because he hardly ever eats with people, and I have never seen him fall asleep in the middle of a case; and once when I peeped into his window in the middle of the night, there he was, sitting up with a book; and I looked in his frigidaire and there was no food in it.'

"If he told you that, you would send for a straitjacket. But if he tells you, 'He *never* sleeps; he *never* eats,' then the shock of the statement blinds you to the fact that such statements are impossible to prove. You play into his hands by contributing to the to-do."

"Regardless, sir," began Lanning, with a threatening obstinacy, "of whether you consider this matter serious or not, it will require only the meal I mentioned to end it."

Again Byerley turned to the woman, who still regarded him expressionlessly. "Pardon me. I've caught your name correctly, haven't I? Dr. Susan Calvin?"

"Yes, Mr. Byerley."

"You're the U. S. Robot's psychologist, aren't you?"

"*Robo*psychologist, please."

"Oh, are robots so different from men, mentally?"

"Worlds different." She allowed herself a frosty smile, "Robots are essentially decent."

Humor tugged at the corners of the lawyer's mouth, "Well, that's a hard blow. But what I wanted to say was this. Since you're a psycho—a robopsychologist, *and* a woman, I'll bet that you've done something that Dr. Lanning hasn't thought of."

"And what is that?"

"You've got something to eat in your purse."

Something caught in the schooled indifference of Susan Calvin's eyes. She said, "You surprise me, Mr. Byerley."

And opening her purse, she produced an apple. Quietly, she handed it to him. Dr. Lanning, after an initial start, followed the slow movement from one hand to the other with sharply alert eyes.

Calmly, Stephen Byerley bit into it, and calmly he swallowed it.

"You see, Dr. Lanning?"

Dr. Lanning smiled in a relief tangible enough to make even his eyebrows appear benevolent. A relief that survived for one fragile second.

Susan Calvin said, "I was curious to see if you would eat it, but, of course, in the present case, it proves nothing."

Byerley grinned, "It doesn't?"

"Of course not. It is obvious, Dr. Lanning, that if this man were a humanoid robot, he would be a perfect imitation. He is almost too human to be credible. After all, we have been seeing and observing human beings all our lives; it would be impossible to palm something merely nearly right off on us. It would have to be *all* right. Observe the texture of the skin, the quality of the irises, the bone formation of the hand. If he's a robot, I wish U. S. Robots *had* made him, because he's a good job. Do you suppose then, that anyone capable of paying attention to such niceties would neglect a few gadgets to take care of such things as eating, sleeping, elimination? For emergency use only, perhaps; as, for instance, to prevent such situations as are arising here. So a meal won't really prove anything."

"Now wait," snarled Lanning, "I am not quite the fool both of you make me out to be. I am not interested in the problem of Mr. Byerley's humanity or nonhumanity. I am interested in getting the corporation out of a hole. A public meal will end the matter and keep it ended no matter what

Quinn does. We can leave the finer details to lawyers and robopsychologists."

"But, Dr. Lanning," said Byerley, "you forget the politics of the situation. I am as anxious to be elected as Quinn is to stop me. By the way, did you notice that you used his name. It's a cheap shyster trick of mine; I knew you would, before you were through."

Lanning flushed, "What has the election to do with it?"

"Publicity works both ways, sir. If Quinn wants to call me a robot, and has the nerve to do so, I have the nerve to play the game his way."

"You mean you—" Lanning was quite frankly appalled.

"Exactly. I mean that I'm going to let him go ahead, choose his rope, test its strength, cut off the right length, tie the noose, insert his head and grin. I can do what little else is required."

"You are mighty confident."

Susan Calvin rose to her feet, "Come, Alfred, we won't change his mind for him."

"You see." Byerley smiled gently. "You're a human psychologist, too."

But perhaps not all the confidence that Dr. Lanning had remarked upon was present that evening when Byerley's car parked on the automatic treads leading to the sunken garage, and Byerley himself crossed the path to the front door of his house.

The figure in the wheel chair looked up as he entered, and smiled. Byerley's face lit with affection. He crossed over to it.

The cripple's voice was a hoarse, grating whisper that came out of a mouth forever twisted to one side, leering out of a face that was half scar tissue, "You're late, Steve."

"I know, John, I know. But I've been up against a peculiar and interesting trouble today."

"So?" Neither the torn face nor the destroyed voice could carry expression, but there was anxiety in the clear eyes. "Nothing you can't handle?"

"I'm not exactly certain. I may need your help. *You're* the brilliant one in the family. Do you want me to take you out into the garden? It's a beautiful evening."

Two strong arms lifted John from the wheel chair. Gently, almost caressingly, Byerley's arms went around the shoulders and under the swathed legs of the cripple. Carefully, and slowly, he walked through the rooms, down the gentle ramp that had been built with a wheel chair in mind, and out the back door into the walled and wired garden behind the house.

"Why don't you let me use the wheel chair, Steve? This is silly."

"Because I'd rather carry you. Do you object? You know that you're as glad to get out of that motorized buggy for a while as I am to see you out. How do you feel today?" He deposited John with infinite care upon the cool grass.

"How should I feel? But tell me about your trouble."

"Quinn's campaign will be based on the fact that he claims I'm a robot."

John's eyes opened wide, "How do you know? It's impossible. I won't believe it."

"Oh, come, I tell you it's so. He had one of the big-shot scientists of U. S. Robot & Mechanical Men Corporation over at the office to argue with me."

Slowly John's hands tore at the grass, "I see. I see."

Byerley said, "But we can let him choose his ground. I have an idea. Listen to me and tell me if we can do it—"

The scene as it appeared in Alfred Lanning's office that night was a tableau of stares. Francis Quinn stared meditatively at Alfred Lanning. Lanning's stare was savagely set upon Susan Calvin, who stared impassively in her turn at Quinn.

Francis Quinn broke it with a heavy attempt at lightness, "Bluff. He's making it up as he goes along."

"Are you going to gamble on that, Mr. Quinn?" asked Dr. Calvin, indifferently.

"Well, it's your gamble, really."

"Look here," Lanning covered definite pessimism with bluster, "we've done what you asked. We witnessed the man eat. It's ridiculous to presume him a robot."

"Do *you* think so?" Quinn shot toward Calvin. "Lanning said you were the expert."

Lanning was almost threatening, "No, Susan—"

Quinn interrupted smoothly, "Why not let her talk, man? She's been sitting there imitating a gatepost for half an hour."

Lanning felt definitely harassed. From what he experienced then to incipient paranoia was but a step. He said, "Very well. Have your say, Susan. We won't interrupt you."

Susan Calvin glanced at him humorlessly, then fixed cold eyes on Mr. Quinn. "There are only two ways of definitely proving Byerley to be a robot, sir. So far you are presenting circumstantial evidence, with which you can accuse, but not prove—and I think Mr. Byerley is sufficiently clever to counter that sort of material. You probably think so yourself, or you wouldn't have come here.

"The two methods of *proof* are the physical and the psychological. Physically, you can dissect him or use an X-ray. How to do that would be *your* problem. Psychologically, his behavior can be studied, for if he *is* a positronic robot, he must conform to the three Rules of Robotics. A positronic brain can not be constructed without them. You know the Rules, Mr. Quinn?"

She spoke them carefully, clearly, quoting word for word the famous bold print on page one of the *Handbook of Robotics.*

"I've heard of them," said Quinn, carelessly.

"Then the matter is easy to follow," responded the psychologist dryly. "If Mr. Byerley breaks any of those three rules, he is not a robot. Unfortunately, this procedure works in only one direction. If he lives up to the rules, it proves nothing one way or the other."

Quinn raised polite eyebrows, "Why not, doctor?"

"Because, if you stop to think of it, the three Rules of Robotics are the essential guiding principles of a good many of the world's ethical systems. Of course, every human being is supposed to have the instinct of self-preservation. That's Rule Three to a robot. Also every 'good' human being, with a social conscience and a sense of responsibility, is supposed to defer to proper authority; to listen to his doctor, his boss, his government, his psychiatrist, his fellow man; to obey laws, to follow rules, to conform to custom—even when they interfere with his comfort or his safety. That's Rule Two to a robot. Also, every 'good' human being is supposed to love others as himself, protect his fellow man, risk his life to save another. That's Rule One to a robot. To put it simply—if Byerley follows all the Rules of Robotics, he may be a robot, and may simply be a very good man."

"But," said Quinn, "you're telling me that you can never prove him a robot."

"I may be able to prove him *not* a robot."

"That's not the proof I want."

"You'll have such proof as exists. You are the only one responsible for your own wants."

Here Lanning's mind leaped suddenly to the sting of an idea, "Has it occurred to anyone," he ground out, "that district attorney is a rather strange occupation for a robot? The prosecution of human beings—sentencing them to death—bringing about their infinite harm—"

Quinn grew suddenly keen, "No, you can't get out of it that way. Being district attorney doesn't make him human. Don't you know his record? Don't you know that he boasts that he has never prosecuted an innocent man; that there are scores of people left untried because the evidence against them didn't satisfy him, even though he could probably have argued a jury into atomizing them? That happens to be so."

Lanning's thin cheeks quivered, "No, Quinn, no. There is nothing in the Rules of Robotics that makes any allowance for human guilt. A robot may not judge whether a human being deserves death. It is not for him to decide. *He may not harm a human*—variety skunk or variety angel."

Susan Calvin sounded tired. "Alfred," she said, "don't talk foolishly. What if a robot came upon a madman about to set fire to a house with people in it. He would stop the madman, wouldn't he?"

"Of course."

"And if the only way he could stop him was to kill him—"

There was a faint sound in Lanning's throat. Nothing more.

"The answer to that, Alfred, is that he would do his best not to kill him. If the madman died, the robot would require psychotherapy because he might easily go mad at the conflict presented him—of having broken Rule One to adhere to Rule One in a higher sense. But a man would be dead and a robot would have killed him."

"Well, *is* Byerley mad?" demanded Lanning, with all the sarcasm he could muster.

"No, but he has killed no man himself. He has exposed facts which might represent a particular human being to be dangerous to the large mass of other human beings we call society. He protects the greater number and thus adheres to Rule One at maximum potential. That is as far as he goes. It is the judge who then condemns the criminal to death or imprisonment, after the jury decides on his guilt or innocence. It is the jailer who imprisons him, the executioner who kills him. And Mr. Byerley has done nothing but determine truth and aid society.

"As a matter of fact, Mr. Quinn, I have looked into Mr. Byerley's career since you first brought this matter to our attention. I find that he has never demanded the death sentence in his closing speeches to the jury. I also find that he has spoken on behalf of the abolition of capital punishment and contributed generously to research institutions engaged in criminal neurophysiology. He apparently believes in the cure, rather than the punishment of crime. I find that significant."

"You do?" Quinn smiled. "Significant of a certain odor of roboticity, perhaps?"

"Perhaps? Why deny it? Actions such as his could come only from a robot, or from a very honorable and decent human being. But you see, you just can't differentiate between a robot and the very best of humans."

Quinn sat back in his chair. His voice quivered with impatience. "Dr. Lanning, it's perfectly possible to create a humanoid robot that would perfectly duplicate a human in appearance, isn't it?"

Lanning harrumphed and considered, "It's been done experimentally by U. S. Robots," he said reluctantly, "without the addition of a positronic brain, of course. By using human ova and hormone control, one can grow human flesh and skin over a skeleton of porous silicone plastics that would defy external examination. The eyes, the hair, the skin would be really human, not humanoid. And if you put a positronic brain, and such other gadgets as you might desire inside, you have a humanoid robot."

Quinn said shortly, "How long would it take to make one?"

Lanning considered, "If you had all your equipment—the brain, the skeleton, the ovum, the proper hormones and radiations—say, two months."

The politician straightened out of his chair. "Then we shall see what the insides of Mr. Byerley looks like. It will mean publicity for U. S. Robots—but I gave you your chance."

Lanning turned impatiently to Susan Calvin, when they were alone. "Why do you insist—"

And with real feeling, she responded sharply and instantly, "Which do you want—the truth or my resignation? I won't lie for you. U. S. Robots can take care of itself. Don't turn coward."

"What," said Lanning, "if he opens up Byerley, and wheels and gears fall out. What then?"

"He won't open Byerley," said Calvin, disdainfully. "Byerley is as clever as Quinn, at the very least."

The news broke upon the city a week before Byerley was

to have been nominated. But "broke" is the wrong word. It staggered upon the city, shambled, crawled. Laughter began, and wit was free. And as the faroff hand of Quinn tightened its pressure in easy stages, the laughter grew forced, an element of hollow uncertainty entered, and people broke off to wonder.

The convention itself had the air of a restive stallion. There had been no contest planned. Only Byerley could possibly have been nominated a week earlier. There was no substitute even now. They had to nominate him, but there was complete confusion about it.

It would not have been so bad if the average individual were not torn between the enormity of the charge, if true, and its sensational folly, if false.

The day after Byerley was nominated perfunctorily, hollowly—a newspaper finally published the gist of a long interview with Dr. Susan Calvin, "world famous expert on robopsychology and positronics."

What broke loose is popularly and succinctly described as hell.

It was what the Fundamentalists were waiting for. They were not a political party; they made pretense to no formal religion. Essentially they were those who had not adapted themselves to what had once been called the Atomic Age, in the days when atoms were a novelty. Actually, they were the Simple-Lifers, hungering after a life, which to those who lived it had probably appeared not so Simple, and who had been, therefore, Simple-Lifers themselves.

The Fundamentalists required no new reason to detest robots and robot manufacturers; but a new reason such as the Quinn accusation and the Calvin analysis was sufficient to make such detestation audible.

The huge plants of the U. S. Robot & Mechanical Men Corporation was a hive that spawned armed guards. It prepared for war.

Within the city the house of Stephen Byerley bristled with police.

The political campaign, of course, lost all other issues, and resembled a campaign only in that it was something filling the hiatus between nomination and election.

Stephen Byerley did not allow the fussy little man to distract him. He remained comfortably unperturbed by the uniforms in the background. Outside the house, past the line of grim guards, reporters and photographers waited, according to the tradition of the caste. One enterprising 'visor station even had a scanner focused on the blank entrance to the prosecutor's unpretentious home, while a synthetically excited announcer filled in with inflated commentary.

The fussy little man advanced. He held forward a rich, complicated sheet. "This, Mr. Byerley, is a court order authorizing me to search these premises for the presence of illegal . . . uh . . . mechanical men or robots of any description."

Byerley half rose, and took the paper. He glanced at it indifferently, and smiled as he handed it back. "All in order. Go ahead. Do your job. Mrs. Hoppen"—to his housekeeper, who appeared reluctantly from the next room—"please go with them, and help out if you can."

The little man, whose name was Harroway, hesitated, produced an unmistakable flush, failed completely to catch Byerley's eyes, and muttered, "Come on," to the two policemen.

He was back in ten minutes.

"Through?" questioned Byerley, in just the tone of a person who is not particularly interested in the question or its answer.

Harroway cleared his throat, made a bad start in falsetto, and began again, angrily, "Look here, Mr. Byerley, our special instructions were to search the house very thoroughly."

"And haven't you?"

"We were told exactly what to look for."

"Yes?"

"In short, Mr. Byerley, and not to put too fine a point on it, we were told to search you."

"Me?" said the prosecutor with a broadening smile. "And how do you intend to do that?"

"We have a Penet-radiation unit—"

"Then I'm to have my X-ray photograph taken, hey? You have the authority?"

"You saw my warrant."

"May I see it again?"

Harroway, his forehead shining with considerably more than mere enthusiasm, passed it over a second time.

Byerley said evenly, "I read here as the description of what you are to search; I quote: 'the dwelling place belonging to Stephen Allen Byerley, located at 355 Willow Grove, Evanstron, together with any garage, storehouse or other structures or buildings thereto appertaining, together with all grounds thereto appertaining' . . . um . . . and so on. Quite in order. But, my good man, it doesn't say anything about searching my interior. I am not part of the premises. You may search my clothes if you think I've got a robot hidden in my pocket."

Harroway had no doubt on the point of to whom he owed his job. He did not propose to be backward, given a chance to earn a much better—i.e., more highly paid—job.

He said, in a faint echo of bluster, "Look here. I'm allowed to search the furniture in your house, and anything else I find in it. You are it, aren't you?"

"A remarkable observation. I *am* in it. But I'm not a piece of furniture. As a citizen of adult responsibility—I have the psychiatric certificate proving that—I have certain rights under the Regional Articles. Searching me would come under the heading of violating my Right of Privacy. That paper isn't sufficient."

"Sure, but if you're a robot, you don't have Right of Privacy."

"True enough—but that paper still isn't sufficient. It recognizes me implicitly as a human being."

"Where?" Harroway snatched at it.

"Where it says, 'the dwelling place belonging to' and so on. A robot cannot own property. And you may tell your employer, Mr. Harroway, that if he tries to issue a similar paper which does *not* implicitly recognize me as a human being, he will be immediately faced with a restraining injunction and a civil suit which will make it necessary for him to *prove* me a robot by means of information *now* in his possession, or else to pay a whopping penalty for an attempt to deprive me unduly of my Rights under the Regional Articles. You'll tell him that, won't you?"

Harroway marched to the door. He turned. "You're a slick lawyer—" His hand was in his pocket. For a short moment, he stood there. Then he left, smiled in the direction of the 'visor scanner, still playing away—waved to the reporters, and shouted, "We'll have something for you tomorrow, boys. No kidding."

In his ground car, he settled back, removed the tiny mechanism from his pocket and carefully inspected it. It was the first time he had ever taken a photograph by X-ray reflection. He hoped he had done it correctly.

Quinn and Byerley had never met face-to-face alone. But

visorphone was pretty close to it. In fact, accepted literally, perhaps the phrase was accurate, even if to each, the other was merely the light and dark pattern of a bank of photocells.

It was Quinn who had initiated the call. It was Quinn who spoke first, and without particular ceremony, "Thought you would like to know, Byerley, that I intend to make public the fact that you're wearing a protective shield against Penet-radiation."

"That's so? In that case, you've probably already made it public. I have a notion our enterprising press representatives have been tapping my various communication lines for quite a while. I know they have my offiice lines full of holes; which is why I've dug in at my home these last weeks." Byerley was friendly, almost chatty.

Quinn's lips tightened slightly, "This call is shielded—thoroughly. I'm making it at a certain personal risk."

"So I should imagine. Nobody knows you're behind this campaign. At least, nobody knows it officially. Nobody doesn't know it unofficially. I wouldn't worry. So I wear a protective shield? I suppose you found that out when your puppy dog's Penet-radiation photograph, the other day, turned out to be overexposed."

"You realize, Byerley, that it would be pretty obvious to everyone that you don't dare face X-ray analysis."

"Also that you, or your men, attempted illegal invasion of my Right of Privacy."

"The devil they'll care for that."

"They might. It's rather symbolic of our two campaigns, isn't it? You have little concern with the rights of the individual citizen. I have great concern. I will not submit to X-ray analysis, because I wish to maintain my Rights on principle. Just as I'll maintain the rights of others when elected."

"That will no doubt make a very interesting speech, but no one will believe you. A little too high-sounding to be true. Another thing," a sudden, crisp change, "the personnel in your home was not complete the other night."

"In what way?"

"According to the report," he shuffled papers before him that were just within the range of vision of the visiplate, "there was one person missing—a cripple."

"As you say," said Byerley, tonelessly, "a cripple. My old teacher, who lives with me and who is now in the country—and has been for two months. A 'much-needed rest' is the usual expression applied in the case. He has your permission?"

"Your teacher? A scientist of sorts?"

"A lawyer once—before he was a cripple. He has a government license as a research biophysicist, with a laboratory of his own, and a complete description of the work he's doing filed with the proper authorities, to whom I can refer you. The work is minor, but is a harmless and engaging hobby for a—poor cripple. I am being as helpful as I can, you see."

"I see. And what does this . . . teacher . . . know about robot manufacture?"

"I couldn't judge the extent of his knowledge in a field with which I am unacquainted."

"He wouldn't have access to positronic brains?"

"Ask your friends at U. S. Robots. They'd be the ones to know."

"I'll put it shortly, Byerley. Your crippled teacher is the real Stephen Byerley. You are his robot creation. We can prove it. It was he who was in the automobile accident, not you. There will be ways of checking the records."

"Really? Do so, then. My best wishes."

"And we can search your so-called teacher's 'country place,' and see what we can find there."

"Well, not quite, Quinn." Byerley smiled broadly. "Unfortunately for you, my so-called teacher is a sick man. His country place is his place of rest. His Right of Privacy as a citizen of adult responsibility is naturally even stronger, under the circumstances. You won't be able to obtain a warrant to enter his grounds without showing just cause. However, I'd be the last to prevent you from trying."

There was a pause of moderate length, and then Quinn leaned forward, so that his imaged face expanded and the fine lines on his forehead were visible, "Byerley, why do you carry on? You can't be elected."

"Can't I?"

"Do you think you can? Do you suppose that your failure to make any attempt to disprove the robot charge—when you could easily, by breaking one of the Three Laws—does anything but convince the people that you are a robot?"

"All I see so far is that from being a rather vaguely known, but still largely obscure metropolitan lawyer, I have now become a world figure. You're a good publicist."

"But you *are* a robot."

"So it's been said, but not proven."

"It's been proven sufficiently for the electorate."

"Then relax—you've won."

"Good-by," said Quinn, with his first touch of viciousness, and the visorphone slammed off.

"Good-by," said Byerley imperturbably, to the blank plate.

Byerley brought his "teacher" back the week before election. The air car dropped quickly in an obscure part of the city.

"You'll stay here till after election," Byerley told him. "It would be better to have you out of the way if things take a bad turn."

The hoarse voice that twisted painfully out of John's crooked mouth might have had accents of concern in it. "There's danger of violence?"

"The Fundamentalists threaten it, so I suppose there is, in a theoretical sense. But I really don't expect it. The Fundies have no real power. They're just the continuous irritant factor that might stir up a riot after a while. You don't mind staying here? Please. I won't be myself if I have to worry about you."

"Oh, I'll stay. You still think it will go well?"

"I'm sure of it. No one bothered you at the place?"

"No one. I'm certain."

"And your part went well?"

"Well enough. There'll be no trouble there."

"Then take care of yourself, and watch the televisor tomorrow, John." Byerley pressed the gnarled hand that rested on his.

Lenton's forehead was a furrowed study in suspense. He had the completely unenviable job of being Byerley's campaign manager in a campaign that wasn't a campaign, for a person that refused to reveal his strategy, and refused to accept his managers.

"You can't!" It was his favorite phrase. It had become his only phrase. "I tell you, Steve, you can't!"

He threw himself in front of the prosecutor, who was spending his time, leafing through the typed pages of his speech.

"Put that down, Steve. Look, that mob has been organized by the Fundies. You won't get a hearing. You'll be stoned more likely. Why do you have to make a speech before an audience? What's wrong with a recording, a visual recording?"

"You want me to win the election, don't you?" asked Byerley, mildly.

"Win the election! You're not going to win, Steve. I'm trying to save your life."

"Oh, I'm not in danger."

"He's not in danger. He's not in danger." Lenton made a queer, rasping sound in his throat. "You mean you're getting out on that balcony in front of fifty thousand crazy crackpots to try to talk sense to them—on a balcony like a medieval dictator?"

Byerley consulted his watch. "In about five minutes—as soon as the television lines are free."

Lenton's answering remark was not quite transliterable.

The crowd filled a roped-off area of the city. Trees and houses seemed to grow out of a mass-human foundation. And by ultrawave, the rest of the world watched. It was a purely local election, but it had a world audience just the same. Byerley thought of that and smiled.

But there was nothing to smile at in the crowd itself. There were banners and streamers, ringing every possible change on his supposed robotcy. The hostile attitude rose thickly and tangibly into the atmosphere.

From the start the speech was not successful. It competed against the inchoate mob howl and the rhythmic cries of the Fundie claques that formed mob-islands within the mob. Byerley spoke on, slowly, unemotionally—

Inside, Lenton clutched his hair and groaned—and waited for the blood.

There was a writhing in the front ranks. An angular citizen with popping eyes, and clothes too short for the lank length of his limbs, was pulling to the fore. A policeman dived after him, making slow, struggling passage. Byerley waved the latter off angrily.

The thin man was directly under the balcony. His words tore unheard against the roar.

Byerley leaned forward. "What do you say? If you have a legitimate question, I'll answer it." He turned to a flanking guard. "Bring that man up here."

There was a tensing in the crowd. Cries of "Quiet" started in various parts of the mob, and rose to a bedlam, then toned down raggedly. The thin man, red-faced and panting, faced Byerley.

Byerley said, "Have you a question?"

The thin man stared and said in a cracked voice, "Hit me!"

With sudden energy, he thrust out his chin at an angle. "Hit me! You say you're not a robot. Prove it. You can't hit a human, you monster."

There was a queer, flat, dead silence. Byerley's voice punctured it. "I have no reason to hit you."

The thin man was laughing wildly. "You *can't* hit me. You *won't* hit me. You're not a human. You're a monster, a make-believe man."

And Stephen Byerley, tight-lipped, in the face of thousands who watched in person and the millions who watched by screen, drew back his fist and caught the man crackingly upon the chin. The challenger went over backwards in sudden collapse, with nothing on his face but blank, blank surprise.

Byerley said, "I'm sorry. Take him in and see that he's comfortable. I want to speak to him when I'm through."

And when Dr. Calvin, from her reserved space, turned her automobile and drove off, only one reporter had recovered sufficiently from the shock to race after her, and shout an unheard question.

Susan Calvin called over her shoulder, "He's human."

That was enough. The reporter raced away in his own direction.

The rest of the speech might be described as "Spoken but not heard."

Dr. Calvin and Stephen Byerley met once again—a week before he took the oath of office as mayor. It was late—past midnight.

Dr. Calvin said, "You don't look tired."

The mayor-elect smiled. "I may stay up for a while. Don't tell Quinn."

"I shan't. But that was an interesting story of Quinn's, since you mention him. It's a shame to have spoiled it. I suppose you knew his theory?"

"Parts of it."

"It was highly dramatic. Stephen Byerley was a young lawyer, a powerful speaker, a great idealist—and with a certain flair for biophysics. Are you interested in robotics, Mr. Byerley?"

"Only in the legal aspects."

"*This* Stephen Byerley was. But here was an accident. Byerley's wife died; he himself, worse. His legs were gone; his face was gone; his voice was gone. Part of his mind was—bent. He would not submit to plastic surgery. He retired from the world, legal career gone—only his intelligence, and his hands left. Somehow he could obtain positronic brains, even a complex one, one which had the greatest capacity of forming judgments in ethical problems—which is the highest robotic function so far developed.

"He grew a body about it. Trained it to be everything he would have been and was no longer. He sent it out into the world as Stephen Byerley, remaining behind himself as the old, crippled teacher that no one ever saw—"

"Unfortuantely," said the mayor-elect, "I ruined all that by hitting a man. The papers say it was your official verdict on the occasion that I was human."

"How did that happen? Do you mind telling me? It couldn't have been accidental."

"It wasn't entirely. Quinn did most of the work. My men started quietly spreading the fact that I had never hit a man; that I was unable to hit a man; that to fail to do so under provocation would be sure proof that I was a robot. So I arranged for a silly speech in public, with all sorts of publicity overtones, and almost inevitably, some fool fell for it. In its essence, it was what I call a shyster trick. One in which the artificial atmosphere which has been created does all the work. Of course, the emotional effects made my election certain, as intended."

The robopsychologist nodded. "I see you intrude on my field—as every politician must, I suppose. But I'm very sorry it turned out this way. I like robots. I like them considerably better than I do human beings. If a robot can be created capable of being a civil executive, I think he'd make the best one possible. By the Laws of Robotics, he'd be incapable of harming humans, incapable of tyranny, of corruption, of stupidity, of prejudice. And after he had served a decent term, he would leave, even though he was immortal, because it would be impossible for him to hurt humans by letting them know that a robot had ruled them. It would be most ideal."

"Except that a robot might fail due to the inherent inadequacies of his brain. The positronic brain has never equalled the complexities of the human brain."

"He would have advisers. Not even a human brain is capable of governing without assistance."

Byerley considered Susan Calvin with grave interest. "Why do you smile, Dr. Calvin?"

"I smile because Mr. Quinn didn't think of everything."

"You mean there could be more to that story of his."

"Only a little. For the three months before election, this Stephen Byerley that Mr. Quinn spoke about, this broken man, was in the country for some mysterious reason. He returned in time for that famous speech of yours. And after all, what the old cripple did once, he could do a second time, particularly where the second job is very simple in comparison to the first."

"I don't quite understand."

Dr. Calvin rose and smoothed her dress. She was obviously ready to leave. "I mean there is one time when a robot may strike a human being without breaking the First Law. Just one time."

"And when is that?"

Dr. Calvin was at the door. She said quietly, "When the human to be struck is merely another robot."

She smiled broadly, her thin face glowing. "Good-by, Mr. Byerley. I hope to vote for you five years from now—for coordinator."

Stephen Byerley chuckled. "I must reply that that is a somewhat far-fetched idea."

The door closed behind her.

TECHNICAL ERROR

by Arthur C. Clarke

FANTASY (Great Britain)
December

Arthur Clarke's third contribution to this volume is a clever story about an accident at a power plant and its consequences, a theme with special importance in the wake of Three Mile Island. It was brought to the attention of American readers through its reprinting in the June, 1950 issue of Thrillng Wonder Stories, *although the title was changed by the editor for that appearance.*

(His first year in American science fiction magazines, and we find three stories to include in the volume. It's not surprising in hindsight, of course, but Arthur did start with a bang. In 1946, many science fiction writers wrote of the dangers of the nuclear bomb; that was easy in view of events. It was not so likely that the tales would be of the dangers of peacetime use of nuclear power. Bob Heinlein had done it as early as 1940 with "Blowups Happen," but he is always a special case. Arthur's version of the danger is a more romantic one, less down-to-earth, but for that very reason, he keeps you guessing. Arthur cleverly brings the accident

down to the molecular level and does so with chemical accuracy, I assure you.

Well, let's face it, I'm a great admirer of Arthur, even if he is always pointing out that he is thinner than I am. I maintain a dignified silence in the face of such personal remarks. Wild horses couldn't make me say that he is a lot balder than I am and has been three years older than me all his life.—I.A.)

It was one of those accidents for which no one could be blamed. Richard Nelson had been in and out of the generator pit a dozen times, taking temperature readings to make sure that the unearthly chill of liquid helium was not seeping through the insulation. This was the first generator in the world to use the principle of superconductivity. The windings of the immense stator had been immersed in a helium bath, and the miles of wire now had a resistance too small to be measured by any means known to man.

Nelson noted with satisfaction that the temperature had not fallen further than expected. The insulation was doing its work; it would be safe to lower the rotor into the pit. That thousand-ton cylinder was now hanging fifty feet above Nelson's head, like the business end of a mammoth drop hammer. He and everyone else in the power station would feel much happier when it had been lowered onto its bearings and keyed into the turbine shaft.

Nelson put away his notebook and started to walk toward the ladder. At the geometric center of the pit, he made his appointment with destiny.

The load on the power network had been steadily increasing for the last hour, while the zone of twilight swept across the continent. As the last rays of sunlight faded from the clouds, the miles of mercury arcs along the great highways sprang into life. By the million, fluorescent tubes began to glow in the cities; housewives switched on their radio-cookers to prepare the evening meal. The needles of the megawattmeters began to creep up the scales.

These were the normal loads. But on a mountain three hundred miles to the south a giant cosmic ray analyzer was being rushed into action to await the expected shower from the new supernova in Capricornus, which the astronomers had detected only an hour before. Soon the coils of its five-thousand-ton magnets began to drain their enormous currents from the thyratron converters.

A thousand miles to the west, fog was creeping toward the greatest airport in the hemisphere. No one worried much about fog, now, when every plane could land on its own radar in zero visibility, but it was nicer not to have it around. So the giant dispersers were thrown into operation, and nearly a thousand megawatts began to radiate into the night, coagulating the water droplets and clearing great swaths through the banks of mist.

The meters in the power station gave another jump, and the engineer on duty ordered the stand-by generators into action. He wished the big, new machine was finished; then there would be no more anxious hours like these. But he thought he could handle the load. Half an hour later the Meteorological Bureau put out a general frost warning over the radio. Within sixty seconds, more than a million electric fires were switched on in anticipation. The meters passed the danger mark and went on soaring.

With a tremendous crash three giant circuit breakers leaped from their contacts. Their arcs died under the fierce blast of the helium jets. Three circuits had opened—but the fourth breaker had failed to clear. Slowly, the great copper bars began to glow cherry-red. The acrid smell of burning insulation filled the air and molten metal dripped heavily to the floor below, solidifying at once on the concrete slabs. Suddenly the conductors sagged as the load ends broke away from their supports. Brilliant green arcs of burning copper flamed and died as the circuit was broken. The free ends of the enormous conductors fell perhaps ten feet before crashing into the equipment below. In a fraction of a second they had welded themselves across the lines that led to the new generator.

Forces greater than any yet produced by man were at war in the windings of the machine. There was no resistance to oppose the current, but the inductance of the tremendous windings delayed the moment of peak intensity. The current rose to a maximum in an immense surge that lasted several seconds. At that instant, Nelson reached the center of the pit.

Then the current tried to stabilize itself, oscillating wildly between narrower and narrower limits. But it never reached its steady state; somewhere, the overriding safety devices came into operation and the circuit that should never have been made was broken again. With a last dying spasm, almost as violent as the first, the current swiftly ebbed away. It was all over.

When the emergency lights came on again, Nelson's assistant walked to the lip of the rotor pit. He didn't know what had happened, but it must have been serious. Nelson, fifty feet down, must have been wondering what it was all about.

"Hello, Dick!" he shouted. "Have you finished? We'd better see what the trouble is."

There was no reply. He leaned over the edge of the great pit and peered into it. The light was very bad, and the shadow of the rotor made it difficult to see what was below. At first it seemed that the pit was empty, but that was ridiculous; he had seen Nelson enter it only a few minutes ago. He called again.

"Hello! You all right, Dick?"

Again no reply. Worried now, the assistant began to descend the ladder. He was halfway down when a curious noise, like a toy balloon bursting very far away, made him look over his shoulder. Then he saw Nelson, lying at the center of the pit on the temporary woodwork covering the turbine shaft. He was very still, and there seemed something altogether wrong about the angle at which he was lying.

Ralph Hughes, chief physicist, looked up from his littered desk as the door opened. Things were slowly returning to normal after the night's disasters. Fortunately, the trouble had not affected his department much, for the generator was unharmed. He was glad he was not the chief engineer; Murdock would still be snowed under with paperwork. The thought gave Dr. Hughes considerable satisfaction.

"Hello, Doc," he greeted the visitor. "What brings you here? How's your patient getting on?"

Doctor Sanderson nodded briefly. "He'll be out of hospital in a day or so. But I want to talk to you about him."

"I don't know the fellow—I never go near the plant, except when the Board goes down on its collective knees and asks me to. After all, Murdock's paid to run the place."

Sanderson smiled wryly. There was no love lost between the chief engineer and the brilliant young physicist. Their personalities were too different, and there was the inevitable rivalry between theoretical expert and "practical" man.

"I think this is up your street, Ralph. At any rate, it's beyond me. You've heard what happened to Nelson?"

"He was inside my new generator when the power was shot into it, wasn't he?"

"That's correct. His assistant found him suffering from shock when the power was cut off again.

"What kind of shock? It couldn't have been electric; the windings are insulated, of course. In any case, I gather that he was in the center of the pit when they found him."

"That's quite true. We don't know what happened. But he's now come round and seems none the worse—apart from one thing." The doctor hesitated a moment as if choosing his words carefully.

"Well, go on! Don't keep me in suspense!"

"I left Nelson as soon as I saw he would be quite safe, but about an hour later Matron called me up to say he wanted to speak to me urgently. When I got to the ward he was sitting up in bed looking at a newspaper with a very puzzled expression. I asked him what was the matter. He answered, 'Something's happened to me, Doc.' So I said, 'Of course it has, but you'll be out in a couple of days.' He shook his head; I could see there was a worried look in his eyes. He picked up the paper he had been looking at and pointed to it. 'I can't read any more,' he said.

"I diagnosed amnesia and thought: This is a nuisance! Wonder what else he's forgotten? Nelson must have read my expression, for he went on to say, 'Oh, I still know the letters and words—but they're the wrong way round! I think something must have happened to my eyes.' He held up the paper again. 'This looks exactly as if I'm seeing it in a mirror,' he said. 'I can spell out each word separately, a letter at a time. Would you get me a looking glass? I want to try something.'

"I did. He held the paper to the glass and looked at the reflection. Then he started to read aloud, at normal speed. But that's a trick anyone can learn—compositors have to do it with type—and I wasn't impressed. On the other hand, I couldn't see why an intelligent fellow like Nelson should put over an act like that. So I decided to humor him, thinking the shock must have given his mind a bit of a twist. I felt quite certain he was suffering from some delusion, though he seemed perfectly normal.

"After a moment he put the paper away and said, 'Well,

Doc, what do you make of that?' I didn't know quite what to say without hurting his feelings, so I passed the buck and said, 'I think I'll have to hand you over to Dr. Humphries, the psychologist. It's rather outside my province.' Then he made some remark about Dr. Humphries and his intelligence tests, from which I gathered he had already suffered at his hands."

"That's correct," interjected Hughes. "All the men are grilled by the Psychology Department before they join the company. All the same, it's surprising what gets through," he added thoughtfully.

Dr. Sanderson smiled, and continued his story.

"I was getting up to leave when Nelson said, 'Oh, I almost forgot. I think I must have fallen on my right arm. The wrist feels badly sprained.' 'Let's look at it,' I said, bending to pick it up. 'No, the other arm," Nelson said, and held up his left arm. Still humoring him, I answered, "Have it your way. But you said your right one, didn't you?'

"Nelson looked puzzled. 'So what?' he replied. 'This *is* my right arm. My eyes may be queer, but there's no argument about that. There's my wedding ring to prove it. I've not been able to get the darned thing off for five years.'

"That shook me rather badly. Because you see, it was his left arm he was holding up, and his left hand that had the ring on it. I could see that what he said was quite true. The ring would have to be cut to get it off again. So I said, 'Have you any distinctive scars?' He answered, 'Not that I can remember.'

" 'Any dental fillings?' "

" 'Yes, quite a few.' "

"We sat looking at each other in silence while a nurse went to fetch Nelson's records. 'Gazed at each other with a wild surmise' is just about how a novelist might put it. Before the nurse returned, I was seized with a bright idea. It was a fantastic notion, but the whole affair was becoming more and more outrageous. I asked Nelson if I could see the things he had been carrying in his pockets. Here they are."

Dr. Sanderson produced a handful of coins and a small, leather-bound diary. Hughes recognized the latter at once as an Electrical Engineer's Diary; he had one in his own pocket. He took it from the doctor's hand and flicked it open at random, with that slightly guilty feeling one always has when a stranger's—still more, a friend's—diary falls into one's hands.

And then, for Ralph Hughes, it seemed that the foundations of his world were giving way. Until now he had listened to Dr. Sanderson with some detachment, wondering what all the fuss was about. But now the incontrovertible evidence lay in his own hands, demanding his attention and defying his logic.

For he could read not one word of Nelson's diary. Both the print and the handwriting were inverted, as if seen in a mirror.

Dr. Hughes got up from his chair and walked rapidly around the room several times. His visitor sat silently watching him. On the fourth circuit he stopped at the window and looked out across the lake, overshadowed by the immense white wall of the dam. It seemed to reassure him, and he turned to Dr. Sanderson again.

"You expect me to believe that Nelson has been laterally inverted in some way, so that his right and left sides have been interchanged?"

"I don't expect you to believe anything. I'm merely giving you the evidence. If you can draw any other conclusion I'd be delighted to hear it. I might add that I've checked Nelson's teeth. All the fillings have been transposed. Explain that away if you can. Those coins are rather interesting, too."

Hughes picked them up. They included a shilling, one of the beautiful new, beryl-copper crowns, and a few pence and halfpence. He would have accepted them as change without hesitation. Being no more observant than the next man, he had never noticed which way the Queen's head looked. But the lettering—Hughes could picture the consternation at the Mint if these curious coins ever came to its notice. Like the diary, they too had been laterally inverted.

Dr. Sanderson's voice broke into his reverie.

"I've told Nelson not to say anything about this. I'm going to write a full report; it should cause a sensation when it's published. But we want to know how this has happened. As you are the designer of the new machine, I've come to you for advice."

Dr. Hughes did not seem to hear him. He was sitting at his desk with his hands outspread, little fingers touching. For the first time in his life he was thinking seriously about the difference between left and right.

Dr. Sanderson did not release Nelson from hospital for several days, during which he was studying his peculiar patient and collecting material for his report. As far as he could tell, Nelson was perfectly normal, apart from his inversion.

He was learning to read again, and his progress was swift after the initial strangeness had worn off. He would probably never again use tools in the same way that he had done before the accident; for the rest of his life, the world would think him left-handed. However, that would not handicap him in any way.

Dr. Sanderson had ceased to speculate about the cause of Nelson's condition. He knew very little about electricity; that was Hughes's job. He was quite confident that the physicist would produce the answer in due course; he had always done so before. The company was not a philanthropic institution, and it had good reason for retaining Hughes's services. The new generator, which would be running within a week, was his brain-child, though he had had little to do with the actual engineering details.

Dr. Hughes himself was less confident. The magnitude of the problem was terrifying; for he realiezd, as Sanderson did not, that it involved utterly new regions of science. He knew that there was only one way in which an object could become its own mirror image. But how could so fantastic a theory be proved?

He had collected all available information on the fault that had energized the great armature. Calculations had given an estimate of the currents that had flowed through the coils for the few seconds they had been conducting. But the figures were largely guesswork; he wished he could repeat the experiment to obtain accurate data. It would be amusing to see Murdock's face if he said, "Mind if I throw a perfect short across generators One to Ten sometime this evening?" No, that was definitely out.

It was lucky he still had the working model. Tests on it had given some ideas of the field produced at the generator's center, but their magnitudes were a matter of conjecture. They must have been enormous. It was a miracle that the windings had stayed in their slots. For nearly a month Hughes struggled with his calculations and wandered through regions of atomic physics he had carefully avoided since he left the university. Slowly the complete theory began to evolve in his mind; he was a long way from the final proof, but the road was clear. In another month he would have finished.

The great generator itself, which had dominated his thoughts for the past year, now seemed trivial and unimportant. He scarcely bothered to acknowledge the congratulations of his colleagues when it passed its final tests and began to feed its millions of kilowatts into the system. They must have thought him a little strange, but he had always been regarded as somewhat unpredictable. It was expected of him; the company would have been disappointed if its tame genius possessed no eccentricities.

A fortnight later, Dr. Sanderson came to see him again. He was in a grave mood.

"Nelson's back in the hospital," he announced. "I was wrong when I said he'd be O.K."

"What's the matter with him?" asked Hughes in surprise.

"He's starving to death."

"Starving? What on earth do you mean?"

Dr. Sanderson pulled a chair up to Hughes's desk and sat down.

"I haven't bothered you for the past few weeks," he began, "because I knew you were busy on your own theories. I've been watching Nelson carefully all this time, and writing up my report. At first, as I told you, he seemed perfectly normal. I had no doubt that everything would be all right.

"Then I noticed that he was losing weight. It was some time before I was certain of it; then I began ot observe other, more technical symptoms. He started to complain of weakness and lack of concentration. He had all the signs of vitamin deficiency. I gave him special vitamin concentrates, but they haven't done any good. So I've come to have another talk with you."

Hughes looked baffled, then annoyed. "But hang it all, you're the doctor!"

"Yes, but this theory of mine needs some support, I'm only an unknown medico—no one would listen to me until it was too late. For Nelson is dying, and I think I know why. . . ."

Sir Robert had been stubborn at first, but Dr. Hughes had had his way, as he always did. The members of the Board of Directors were even now filing into the conference room, grumbling and generally making a fuss about the extraordinary general meeting that had just been called. Their perplexity was still further increased when they heard that Hughes was going to address them. They all knew the physicist and his reputation, but he was a scientist and they were businessmen. What was Sir Robert planning?

Dr. Hughes, the cause of all the trouble, felt annoyed with himself for being nervous. His opinion of the Board of Directors was not flattering, but Sir Robert was a man he could respect, so there was no reason to be afraid of them. It was true that they might consider him mad, but his past record would take care of that. Mad or not, he was worth thousands of pounds to them.

Dr. Sanderson smiled encouragingly at him as he walked into the conference room. The smile was not very successful, but it helped. Sir Robert had just finished speaking. He picked up his glasses in that nervous way he had, and coughed deprecatingly. Not for the first time, Hughes wondered how such an apparently timid old man could rule so vast a commercial empire.

"Well, here is Dr. Hughes, gentlemen. He will—ahem—explain everything to you. I have asked him not to be too technical. You are at liberty to interrupt him if he ascends into the more rarefied stratosphere of higher mathematics. Dr. Hughes. . . ."

Slowly at first, and then more quickly as he gained the confidence of his audience, the physicist began to tell his story. Nelson's diary drew a gasp of amazement from the Board, and the inverted coins proved fascinating curiosities. Hughes was glad to see that he had aroused the interest of his listeners. He took a deep breath and made the plunge he had been fearing.

"You have heard what has happened to Nelson, gentlemen, but what I am going to tell you now is even more startling. I must ask you for your very close attention."

He picked up a rectangular sheet of notepaper from the conference table, folded it along a diagonal and tore it along the fold.

"Here we have two right-angled triangles with equal sides. I lay them on the table—so." He placed the paper triangles side by side on the table, with their hypotenuses touching, so that they formed a kite-shaped figure. "Now, as I have arranged them, each triangle is the mirror image of the other. You can imagine that the plane of the mirror is along the hypotenuse. This is the point I want you to notice. As long as I keep the triangles in the plane of the table, I can slide them around as much as I like, but I can never place one so that it exactly covers the other. Like a pair of gloves, they are not interchangeable although their dimensions are identical."

He paused to let that sink in. There were no comments, so he continued.

"Now, if I pick up one of the triangles, turn it over in the air and put it down again, the two are no longer mirror images, but have become completely identical—so." He suited the action to the words. "This may seem very elementary; in fact, it is so. But it teaches us one very important lesson. The triangles on the table were flat objects, restricted to two dimensions. To turn one into its mirror image I had to lift it up and rotate it in the third dimension. Do you see what I am driving at?"

He glanced round the table. One or two of the directors nodded slowly in dawning comprehension.

"Similarly, to change a solid, three-dimensional body, such as a man, into its analogue or mirror image, it must be rotated in a fourth dimension. I repeat—a fourth dimension."

There was a strained silence. Someone coughed, but it was a nervous, not a skeptical cough.

"Four-dimensional geometry, as you know"—he'd be surprised if they did—"has been one of the major tools of mathematics since before the time of Einstein. But until now it has always been a mathematical fiction, having no real existence in the physical world. It now appears that the unheard-of currents, amounting to millions of amperes, which flowed momentarily in the windings of our generator must have produced a certain extension into four dimensions, for a fraction of a second and in a volume large enough to contain a man. I have been making some calculations and have been able to satisfy myself that a 'hyperspace' about ten feet on a side was, in fact, generated: a matter of some ten thousand quartic—not cubic!—feet. Nelson was occupying that space. The sudden collapse of the field when the circuit was broken caused the rotation of the space, and Nelson was inverted.

"I must ask you to accept this theory, as no other explanation fits the facts. I have the mathematics here if you wish to consult them."

He waved the sheets in front of his audience, so that the directors could see the imposing array of equations. The technique worked—it always did. They cowered visibly. Only McPherson, the secretary, was made of sterner stuff. He had had a semi-technical education and still read a good deal of popular science, which he was fond of airing whenever he had the opportunity. But he was intelligent and willing to learn, and Dr. Hughes had often spent official time discussing some new scientific theory with him.

"You say that Nelson has been rotated in the Fourth Dimension; but I thought Einstein had shown that the Fourth Dimension was time."

Hughes groaned inwardly. He had been anticipating this red herring.

"I was referring to an additional dimension of space," he explained patiently. "By that I mean a dimension, or direction, at right-angles to our normal three. One can call it the Fourth Dimension if one wishes. With certain reservations, time may also be regarded as a dimension. As we normally regard space as three-dimensional, it is then customary to call time the Fourth Dimension. But the label is arbitrary. As I'm asking you to grant me four dimensions of space, we must call time the Fifth Dimension."

"Five Dimensions! Good Heaevns!" exploded someone farther down the table.

Dr. Hughes could not resist the opportunity. "Space of several million dimensions has been frequently postulated in sub-atomic physics," he said quietly.

There was a stunned silence. No one, not even McPherson, seemed inclined to argue.

"I now come to the second part of my account," continued Dr. Hughes. "A few weeks after his inversion we found that there was something wrong with Nelson. He was taking food normally, but it didn't seem to nourish him properly. The explanation has been given by Dr. Sanderson, and leads us into the realms of organic chemistry. I'm sorry to be talking like a textbook, but you will soon realize how vitally important this is to the company. And you also have the satisfaction of knowing that we are now all on equally unfamiliar territory."

That was not quite true, for Hughes still remembered some fragments of his chemistry. But it might encourage the stragglers.

"Organic compounds are composed of atoms of carbon, oxygen and hydrogen, with other elements, arranged in complicated ways in space. Chemists are fond of making models of them out of knitting needles and colored plasticine. The results are often very pretty and look like works of advanced art.

"Now, it is possible to have two organic compounds containing identical numbers of atoms, arranged in such a way that one is the mirror image of the other. They're called stereo-isomers, and are very common among the sugars. If you could set their molecules side by side, you would see that they bore the same sort of relationship as a right and left glove. They are, in fact, called right- or left-handed—dextro or laevo—compounds. I hope this is quite clear."

Dr. Hughes looked around anxiously. Apparently it was.

"Stereo-isomers have almost identical chemical properties," he went on, "though there are subtle differences. In the last few years, Dr. Sanderson tells me, it has been found that certain essential foods, including the new class of vitamins discovered by Professor Vandenburg, have properties depending on the arrangement of their atoms in space. In other words, gentlemen, the left-handed compounds might be essential for life, but the right-handed ones would be of no value. This in spite of the fact that their chemical formulae are identical.

"You will appreciate, now, why Nelson's inversion is much more serious than we at first thought. It's not merely a matter of teaching him to read again, in which case—apart from its philosophical interest—the whole business would be trivial. He is actually starving to death in the midst of plenty, simply because he can no more assimilate certain molecules of food than we can put our right foot into a left boot.

"Dr. Sanderson has tried an experiment which has proved the truth of this theory. With very great difficulty, he has obtained the stereo-isomers of many of these vitamins. Professor Vandenburg himself synthesized them when he heard of our trouble. They have already produced a very marked improvement in Nelson's condition."

Hughes paused and drew out some papers. He thought he would give the Board time to prepare for the shock. If a man's life were not at stake, the situation would have been very amusing. The Board was going to be hit where it would hurt most.

"As you will realize, gentlemen, since Nelson was injured—if you can call it that—while he was on duty, the company is liable to pay for any treatment he may require. We have found that treatment, and you may wonder why I have taken so much of your time telling you about it. The reason is very simple. The production of the necessary stereo-isomers is almost as difficult as the extraction of radium—more so, in some cases. Dr. Sanderson tells me that it will cost over five thousand pounds a day to keep Nelson alive."

The silence lasted for half a minute; then everyone started to talk at once. Sir Robert pounded on the table, and presently restored order. The council of war had begun.

Three hours later, an exhausted Hughes left the conference room and went in search of Dr. Sanderson, whom he found fretting in his office.

"Well, what's the decision?" asked the doctor.

"What I was afraid of. They want me to re-invert Nelson."

"Can you do it?"

"Frankly, I don't know. All I can hope to do is to reproduce the conditions of the original fault as accurately as I can."

"Weren't there any other suggestions?"

"Quite a few, but most of them were stupid. McPherson had the best idea. He wanted to use the generator to invert normal food so that Nelson could eat it. I had to point out that to take the big machine out of action for this purpose would cost several millions a year, and in any case the windings wouldn't stand it more than a few times. So that scheme collapsed. Then Sir Robert wanted to know if you could guarantee there were no vitamins we'd overlooked, or that might still be undiscovered. His idea was that in spite of our synthetic diets we might not be able to keep Nelson alive after all."

"What did you say to that?"

"I had to admit it was a possibility. So Sir Robert is going to have a talk with Nelson. He hopes to persuade him to risk it; his family will be taken care of if the experiment fails."

Neither of the two men said anything for a few moments. Then Dr. Sanderson broke the silence.

"Now do you understand the sort of decision a surgeon often has to make?" he said.

Hughes nodded in agreement. "It's a beautiful dilemma, isn't it? A perfectly healthy man, but it will cost two millions a year to keep him alive, and we can't even be sure of that. I know the Board's thinking of its precious balance sheet more than anything else, but I don't see any alternative. Nelson will have to take a chance."

"Couldn't you make some tests first?"

"Impossible. It's a major engineering operation to get the rotor out. We'll have to rush the experiment through when the load on the system is at minimum. Then we'll slam the rotor back, and tidy up the mess our artificial short has made. All this has to be done before the peak loads come on again. Poor old Murdock's mad as hell about it."

"I don't blame him. When will the experiment start?"

"Not for a few days, at least. Even if Nelson agrees, I've got to fix up all my gear."

No one was ever to know what Sir Robert said to Nelson

during the hours they were together. Dr. Hughes was more than half prepared for it when the telephone rang and the Old Man's tired voice said, "Hughes? Get your equipment ready. I've spoken to Murdock, and we've fixed the time for Tuesday night. Can you manage by then?"

"Yes, Sir Robert."

"Good. Give me a progress report every afternoon until Tuesday. That's all."

The enormous room was dominated by the great cylinder of the rotor, hanging thirty feet above the gleaming plastic floor. A little group of men stood silently at the edge of the shadowed pit, waiting patiently. A maze of temporary wiring ran to Dr. Hughes's equipment—multibeam oscilloscopes, megawattmeters and microchronometers, and the special relays that had been constructed to make the circuit at the calculated instant.

That was the greatest problem of all. Dr. Hughes had no way of telling when the circuit should be closed; whether it should be when the voltage was at maximum, when it was at zero, or at some intermediate point on the sine wave. He had chosen the simplest and safest course. The circuit would be made at zero voltage; when it opened again would depend on the speed of the breakers.

In ten minutes the last of the great factories in the service area would be closing down for the night. The weather forecast had been favorable; there would be no abnormal loads before morning. By then, the rotor had to be back and the generator running again. Fortunately, the unique method of construction made it easy to reassemble the machine, but it would be a very close thing and there was no time to lose.

When Nelson came in, accompanied by Sir Robert and Dr. Sanderson, he was very pale. He might, thought Hughes, have been going to his execution. The thought was somewhat ill-timed, and he put it hastily aside.

There was just time enough for a last quite unnecessary check of the equipment. He had barely finished when he heard Sir Robert's quiet voice.

"We're ready, Dr. Hughes."

Rather unsteadily, he walked to the edge of the pit. Nelson had already descended, and as he had been instructed, was standing at its exact center, his upturned face a white blob far below. Dr. Hughes waved a brief encouragement and turned away, to rejoin the group by his equipment.

He flicked over the switch of the oscilloscope and played with the synchronizing controls until a single cycle of the main wave was stationary on the screen. Then he adjusted the phasing: two brilliant spots of light moved toward each other along the wave until they had coalesced at its geometric center. He looked briefly toward Murdock, who was watching the megawattmeters intently. The engineer nodded. With a silent prayer, Hughes threw the switch.

There was the tiniest click from the relay unit. A fraction of a second later, the whole building seemed to rock as the great conductors crashed over in the switch room three hundred feet away. The lights faded, and almost died. Then it was all over. The circuit breakers, driven at almost the speed of an explosion, had cleared the line again. The lights returned to normal and the needles of the megawattmeters dropped back onto their scales.

The equipment had withstood the overload. But what of Nelson?

Dr. Hughes was surprised to see that Sir Robert, for all his sixty years, had already reached the generator. He was standing by its edge, looking down into the great pit. Slowly, the physicist went to join him. He was afraid to hurry; a growing sense of premonition was filling his mind. Already he could picture Nelson lying in a twisted heap at the center of the well, his lifeless eyes staring up at them reproachfully. Then came a still more horrible thought. Suppose the field had collapsed too soon, when the inversion was only partly completed? In another moment, he would know the worst.

There is no shock greater than that of the totally unexpected, for against it the mind has no chance to prepare its defenses. Dr. Hughes was ready for almost anything when he reached the generator. Almost, but not quite. . . .

He did not expect to find it completely empty.

What came after, he could never perfectly remember. Murdock seemed to take charge then. There was a great flurry of activity, and the engineers swarmed in to replace the giant rotor. Somewhere in the distance he heard Sir Robert saying, over and over again, "We did our best—we did our best." He must have replied, somehow, but everything was very vague. . . .

In the gray hours before the dawn, Dr. Hughes awoke from his fitful sleep. All night he had been haunted by his dreams, by weird fantasies of multi-dimensional geometry.

There were visions of strange, other-worldly universes of insane shapes and intersecting planes along which he was doomed to struggle endlessly, fleeing from some nameless terror. Nelson, he dreamed, was trapped in one of those unearthly dimensions, and he was trying to reach him. Sometimes he was Nelson himself, and he imagined that he could see all around him the universe he knew, strangely distorted and barred from him by invisible walls.

The nightmare faded as he struggled up in bed. For a few moments he sat holding his head, while his mind began to clear. He knew what was happening; this was not the first time the solution of some baffling problem had come suddenly upon him in the night.

There was one piece still missing in the jigsaw puzzle that was sorting itself out in his mind. One piece only—and suddenly he had it. There was something that Nelson's assistant had said, when he was describing the original accident. It had seemed trivial at the time; until now, Hughes had forgotten all about it.

"When I looked inside the generator, there didn't seem to be anyone there, so I started to climb down the ladder. . . ."

What a fool he had been! Old McPherson had been right, or partly right, after all!

The field had rotated Nelson in the fourth dimension of space, but there had been a displacement in *time* as well. On the first occasion it had been a matter of seconds only. This time, the conditions must have been different in spite of all his care. There were so many unknown factors, and the theory was more than half guess-work.

Nelson had not been inside the generator at the end of the experiment. *But he would be.*

Dr. Hughes felt a cold sweat break out all over his body. He pictured that thousand-ton cylinder, spinning beneath the drive of its fifty million horsepower. Suppose something suddenly materialized in the space it already occupied . . . ?

He leaped out of bed and grabbed the private phone to the power station. There was no time to lose—the rotor would have to be removed at once. Murdock could argue later.

Very gently, something caught the house by its foundations and rocked it to and fro, as a sleepy child may shake its rattle. Flakes of plaster came planing down from the ceiling; a network of cracks appeared as if by magic in the walls. The lights flickered, became suddenly brilliant, and faded out.

Dr. Hughes threw back the curtain and looked toward the

mountains. The power station was invisible beyond the foothills of Mount Perrin, but its site was clearly marked by the vast column of debris that was slowly rising against the bleak light of the dawn.